THE BEST OF Archie® COMICS

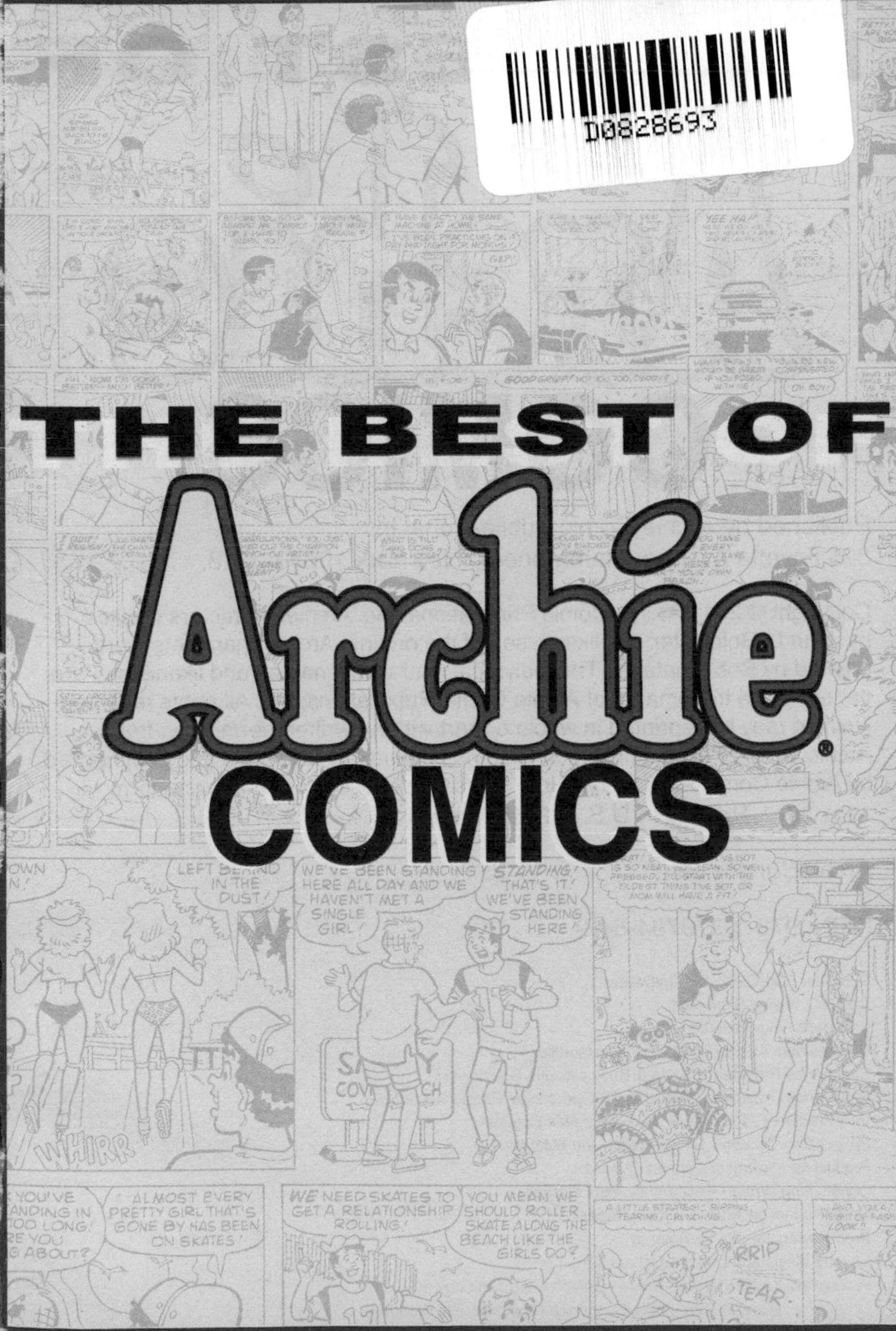
LEFT BEHIND IN THE DUST!
WE'VE BEEN STANDING HERE ALL DAY AND WE HAVEN'T MET A SINGLE GIRL!
STANDING! THAT'S IT! WE'VE BEEN STANDING HERE!
WHIRR
ALMOST EVERY PRETTY GIRL THAT'S GONE BY HAS BEEN ON SKATES!
WE NEED SKATES TO GET A RELATIONSHIP ROLLING!
YOU MEAN WE SHOULD ROLLER SKATE ALONG THE BEACH LIKE THE GIRLS DO?
RRIP
TEAR
GOOD GRIEF! NOT YOU TOO, REGGIE!

THE BEST OF

Archie
COMICS

Published by Archie Comic Publications, Inc.
325 Fayette Avenue, Mamaroneck, New York 10543-2318.

ArchieComics.com

ISBN: 978-1-879794-84-9

Publisher / Co-CEO: Jon Goldwater
Co-CEO: Nancy Silberkleit
President: Mike Pellerito
Co-President / Editor-In-Chief: Victor Gorelick
Senior Vice President - Sales & Business: Jim Sokolowski
Senior Vice President - Publishing & Operations: Harold Buchholz
Vice President - Publicity & Marketing: Alex Segura
Project Coordinator & Book Design: Joe Morciglio
Production Manager: Stephen Oswald
Contributing Writer / Researcher: Paul Castiglia
Lead Production Artist: Carlos Antunes
Proofreader: Jamie Lee Rotante
Editorial Assistant: Duncan McLachlan
Production: Kari Silbergleit, Steven Golebiewski, Jon Gray,
        Rosario "Tito" Peña, Suzannah Rowntree, Pat Woodruff

Stories written by:

Vic Bloom, Fra Doyle,
George Gladir, Bill lliher,
Dick Malmgren, Kathlee Webb,
Hy Eisman, Dan rent,
Al Hartley, Paul Ca glia,
Mike Gallagher, Fernando uiz,
Michael Uslan, J. Tres

Artwork by:

Bob Montana, Al Fagaly,
Harry Lucey, Dan DeCarlo,
George Frese, Bob Bolling,
Samm Schwartz, Stan Goldberg,
Rex Lindsey, Dan DeCarlo Jr.,
Fernando Ruiz, Mike Esposito,
Dave Manak, Jeff Shultz,
Rick Burchett, Joe Edwards,
Bill Woggon, Norm Breyfogle,
Rudy Lapick, Terry Austin,
Rod Ollerenshaw, Bob Smith,
Jon D'Agostino, Rich Koslowski,
Joe Rubinstein, Bill Yoshida,
Jack Morelli, John Workman,
Barry Grossman, Glenn Whitmore,
Joe Morciglio, Jason Jensen

Welcome to The Best of Archie Comics!

For 70 s, Archie Comics has entertained readers with stories featuring unforgettable cast of characters. When we began looking our 200,000-page library, we realized we had a real challenge before us! With so much great material, how would we decide what to include in a best-of book?

First, we decided to focus on Archie's humor titles, saving for future volumes characters ranging from The Fly to Sonic the Hedgehog.

Second, we requested story nominations from inside and outside the company to include a variety of viewpoints on what makes an Archie story "the best." Thanks to everyone who nominated their favorites!

Third, we turned to resident Archie expert, Co-President and Editor-in-Chief Victor Gorelick, who has worked with Archie Comics since 1958. Victor, with his valuable historical knowledge and strong editorial instincts, filled in gaps that other story nominations underrepresented to provide a balanced selection of quality Archie stories from throughout the years.

Next, so that we'd be able to include a wide sampling, we made the decision to focus on shorter stories. We received many excellent nominations for stories of 20 pages or more, but only one made the cut: a chapter from Archie Marries Veronica, part of the best-reviewed comic series in Archie's history, the all-new *Life with Archie Magazine*.

Finally, we did something we've never done before on such a scale: we asked dozens of people to reminisce and personally share what makes Archie special to them. The responses are varied and paint a rich picture of the impact our talented team of writers and artists have had on readers over the years (we estimate that Archie stories have had a total of 50 billion readings!).

We've worked from the best available materials to reproduce these classic stories. In most cases, scans of the artists' line art were combined with modern recoloring. For some stories, if line art wasn't available, scans from the comic books themselves were used. Many of these scanned stories are being reprinted for the very first time.

The end result is a book that broadly represents Archie's best work over the years. We hope you'll enjoy some new discoveries as well as old favorites. If we left out your favorite, we're sorry—please know you're not alone. There were so many more great stories we wanted to share.

Enjoy!

Archie®
The Mirth of a Nation

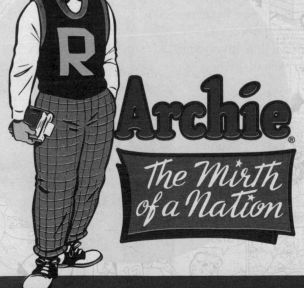

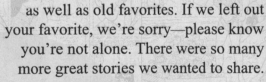

The 1940s

The 1940s are often remembered as "The Greatest Decade" in America. While it may not have seemed like the happiest of times, the progress and changes the 1940s introduced to American culture paved the way for years to come, with advancements in medicine, science, technology and even entertainment. The 1940s started on an uncertain note, as the country was still feeling the effects of the 1930s' Great Depression. All that changed on December 7, 1941 when Japanese forces bombed Pearl Harbor, a US naval base in Hawaii, thus involving America in World War II.

During these hard times, people looked to many forms of entertainment, especially if they could do so inexpensively. People, particularly children and teenagers, turned to sports, music, radio shows and movies as an "escape" of sorts. It was also around this time that these "teenagers" would separate themselves as a group independent from both children and adults.

In 1941, the term "teenager" first appeared in print in, of all places, an issuc of *Popular Science Monthly* magazine. The same year also marked the debut appearance of Archie Andrews, in issue #22 of *Pep Comics*, a popular publication previously filled with funny animals, monsters and superheroes from fledgling publisher MLJ Magazines, whose name derived from the initials of its three partners, Maurice Coyne, Louis Silberkleit and John L. Goldwater.

Having made their debut just a few years earlier, comic books had captured the hearts of youth across America. After all, here was a product they could buy with their own money at the local drugstore or newsstand. In the wake of Superman's huge success, colorful, costumed heroes dominated those early years. MLJ's publisher, John Goldwater, reasoned that if a "super man" could sell copies, how much more would an "every man" appeal to readers? Perhaps inspired by his own youth as an orphan in East Harlem, Goldwater envisioned an "every-teen" that young readers could aspire to be and teenagers could directly relate to.

Based on Goldwater's character outlines, talented young cartoonist Bob Montana created the original likenesses of Archie, Betty, Jughead, Veronica, Reggie and the rest of the Riverdale gang. While they would be expanded on in decades to come, the basic qualities readers associate with their favorite comic book teens prevail to this day: Archie's girl-crazy, klutzy yet kind-hearted ways; Betty's sweetness and true-blue loyalty; Veronica's sense of entitlement; Jughead's worldly-wise ways and overbearing appetite; and Reggie's drive to be number one with the ladies and to pull any prank necessary to put his rivals out of commission.

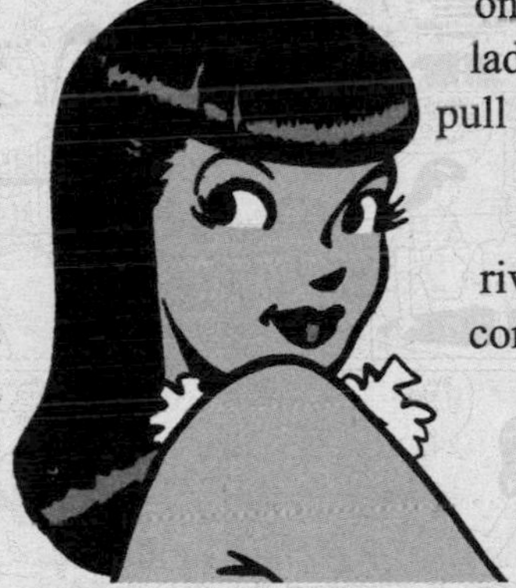

By 1943, Archie had his own national radio program that ran for over ten years, followed by a hugely successful newspaper comic strip in 1946. It was also in 1946 that MLJ changed its name to Archie Comics, rightfully admitting that Archie was its main success and here to stay.

For the first time, there were stories designed to speak to teens and pre-teens directly. They were able to see fresh reflections of themselves. In a very short time, Archie had made a permanent impression on the American public and would prove to be the most enduring teenage property in U.S. history, still going strong 70 years later.

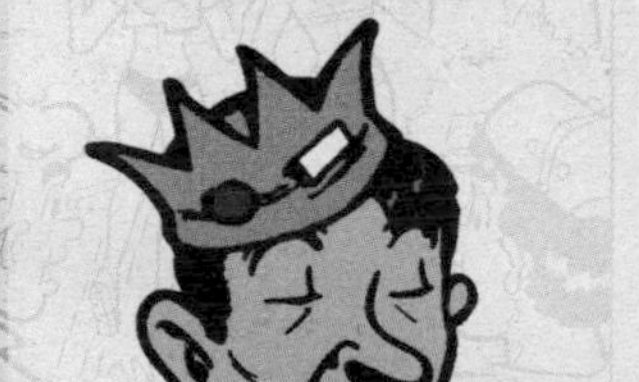

Archie
Pep #22, 1941
by Vic Bloom
and Bob Montana

The genesis, the beginning—the dawn of a new era in the comic book business. The day that Archie Andrews appears for the very first time when *Pep #22* hits the newsstands. Archie is everything that America wants and needs: a hero, not in the traditional sense, but a hero that Americans can both relate to and aspire to. He is everyman, yet he is unique. The story tells a wonderful and funny tale of Archie trying to impress Betty. He ultimately succeeds, and Archie and his pals—including the world famous Jughead—are instantly embraced by America. That was 70 years ago. Archie, Betty, Veronica, Jughead and Reggie are part of our culture, and we are so proud to publish their stories.

--Jonathan Goldwater
Co-CEO, Archie Comics

Prom Pranks/
Who's Who in Riverdale
Archie #1, 1942
by Bob Montana

"Prom Pranks" might well be considered the basic foundation for every story written over the past 70 years featuring Archie and the gang. In this story, Archie has been writing letters to debutante Veronica Lodge. However, he never sends them to the beautiful, rich socialite. Archie just fantasizes what it would be like to date her. Besides, he's going steady with Betty Cooper. The plot thickens when his fantasy letter is mailed and Veronica accepts his invitation. This was the beginning of the famous Archie/Betty/Veronica love triangle, the underlying theme of Archie's success.

--Victor Gorelick
Co-President/Editor-in-Chief,
Archie Comics

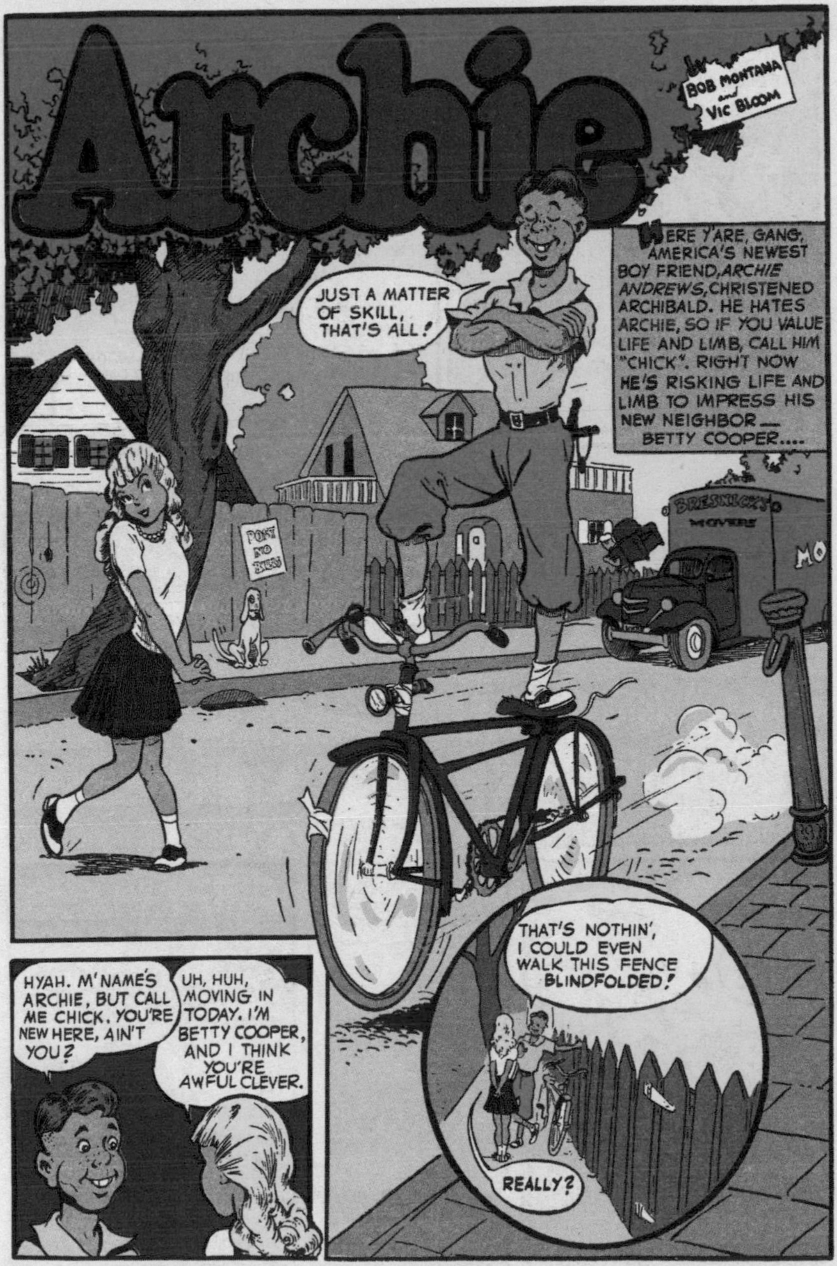
Archie
by BOB MONTANA and VIC BLOOM
HERE Y'ARE, GANG, AMERICA'S NEWEST BOY FRIEND, ARCHIE ANDREWS, CHRISTENED ARCHIBALD. HE HATES ARCHIE, SO IF YOU VALUE LIFE AND LIMB, CALL HIM "CHICK". RIGHT NOW HE'S RISKING LIFE AND LIMB TO IMPRESS HIS NEW NEIGHBOR — BETTY COOPER....
JUST A MATTER OF SKILL, THAT'S ALL!
POST NO BILLS
BRESNICK'S MOVERS
MO
HYAH. M'NAME'S ARCHIE, BUT CALL ME CHICK. YOU'RE NEW HERE, AIN'T YOU?
UH, HUH, MOVING IN TODAY. I'M BETTY COOPER, AND I THINK YOU'RE AWFUL CLEVER.
THAT'S NOTHIN', I COULD EVEN WALK THIS FENCE BLINDFOLDED!
REALLY?

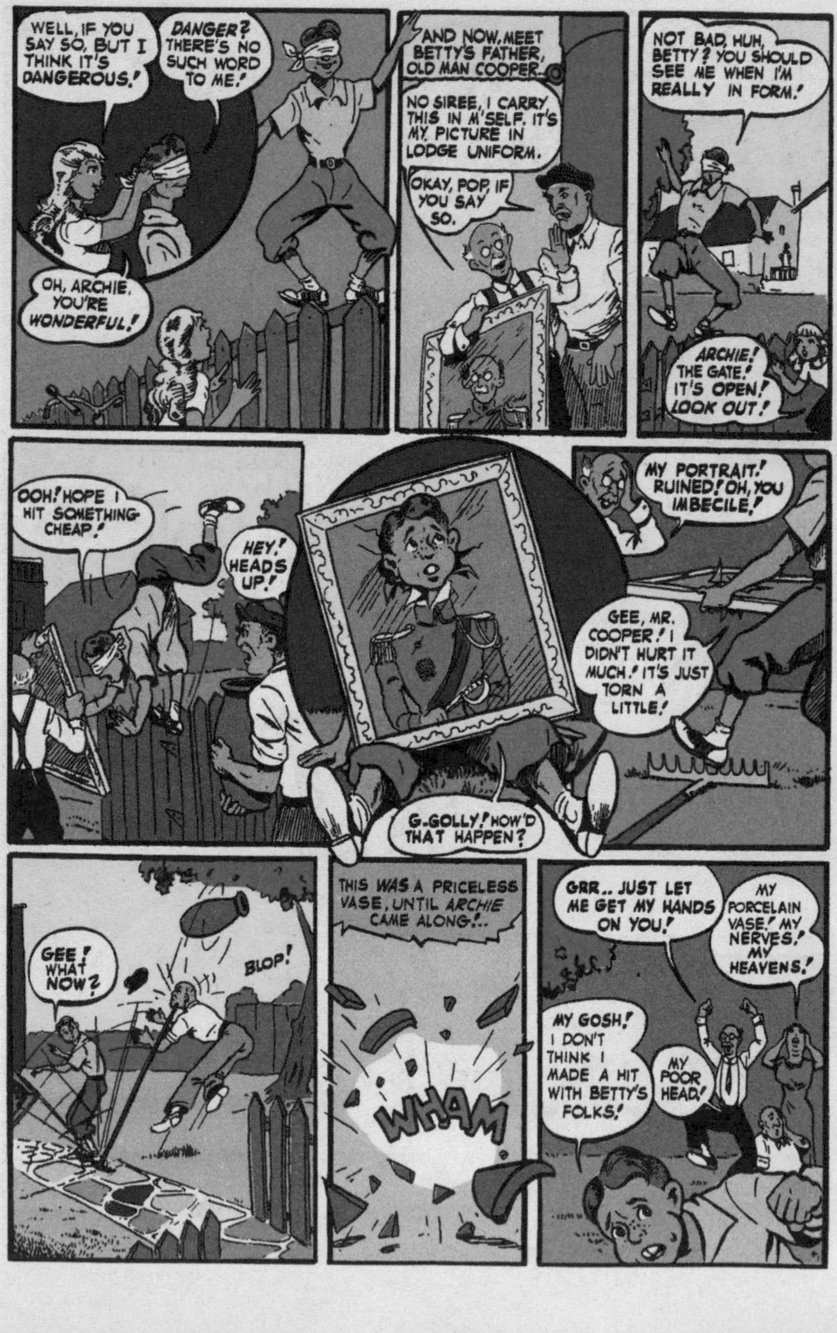
WELL, IF YOU SAY SO, BUT I THINK IT'S DANGEROUS!
DANGER? THERE'S NO SUCH WORD TO ME!
OH, ARCHIE, YOU'RE WONDERFUL!
AND NOW, MEET BETTY'S FATHER, OLD MAN COOPER
NO SIREE, I CARRY THIS IN M'SELF. IT'S MY PICTURE IN LODGE UNIFORM.
OKAY, POP, IF YOU SAY SO.
NOT BAD, HUH, BETTY? YOU SHOULD SEE ME WHEN I'M REALLY IN FORM!
ARCHIE! THE GATE! IT'S OPEN! LOOK OUT!
OOH! HOPE I HIT SOMETHING CHEAP!
HEY! HEADS UP!
MY PORTRAIT! RUINED! OH, YOU IMBECILE!
GEE, MR. COOPER! I DIDN'T HURT IT MUCH! IT'S JUST TORN A LITTLE!
G-GOLLY! HOW'D THAT HAPPEN?
GEE! WHAT NOW?
BLOP!
THIS WAS A PRICELESS VASE, UNTIL ARCHIE CAME ALONG!..
WHAM
GRR.. JUST LET ME GET MY HANDS ON YOU!
MY PORCELAIN VASE! MY NERVES! MY HEAVENS!
MY GOSH! I DON'T THINK I MADE A HIT WITH BETTY'S FOLKS!
MY POOR HEAD!

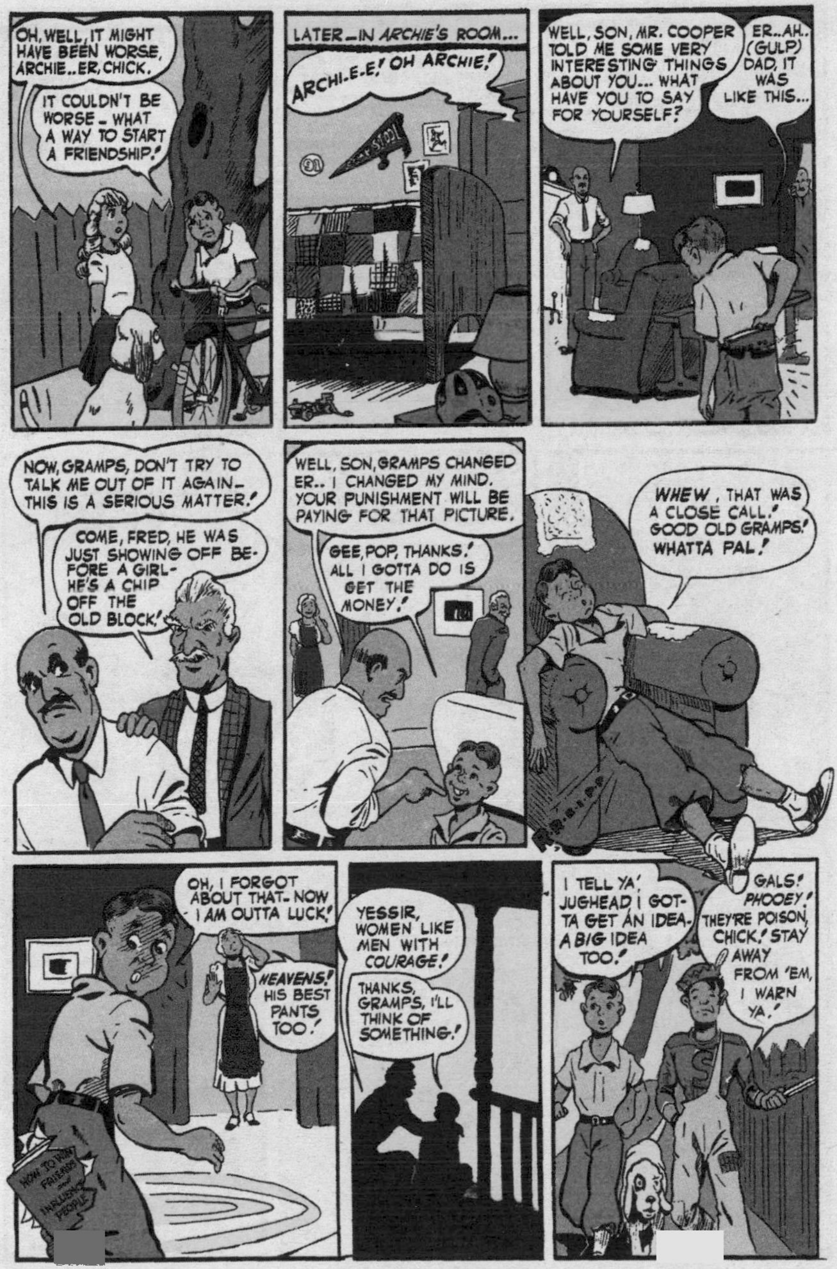
OH, WELL, IT MIGHT HAVE BEEN WORSE, ARCHIE.. ER, CHICK.
IT COULDN'T BE WORSE - WHAT A WAY TO START A FRIENDSHIP!
LATER - IN ARCHIE'S ROOM...
ARCHI-E-E! OH ARCHIE!
WELL, SON, MR. COOPER TOLD ME SOME VERY INTERESTING THINGS ABOUT YOU... WHAT HAVE YOU TO SAY FOR YOURSELF?
ER..AH.. (GULP) DAD, IT WAS LIKE THIS...
NOW, GRAMPS, DON'T TRY TO TALK ME OUT OF IT AGAIN - THIS IS A SERIOUS MATTER!
COME, FRED, HE WAS JUST SHOWING OFF BEFORE A GIRL - HE'S A CHIP OFF THE OLD BLOCK!
WELL, SON, GRAMPS CHANGED ER.. I CHANGED MY MIND. YOUR PUNISHMENT WILL BE PAYING FOR THAT PICTURE.
GEE, POP, THANKS! ALL I GOTTA DO IS GET THE MONEY!
WHEW, THAT WAS A CLOSE CALL! GOOD OLD GRAMPS! WHATTA PAL!
OH, I FORGOT ABOUT THAT - NOW I AM OUTTA LUCK!
HEAVENS! HIS BEST PANTS TOO!
HOW TO WIN FRIENDS and INFLUENCE PEOPLE
YESSIR, WOMEN LIKE MEN WITH COURAGE!
THANKS, GRAMPS, I'LL THINK OF SOMETHING!
I TELL YA' JUGHEAD I GOTTA GET AN IDEA - A BIG IDEA TOO!
GALS! PHOOEY! THEY'RE POISON, CHICK! STAY AWAY FROM 'EM, I WARN YA!

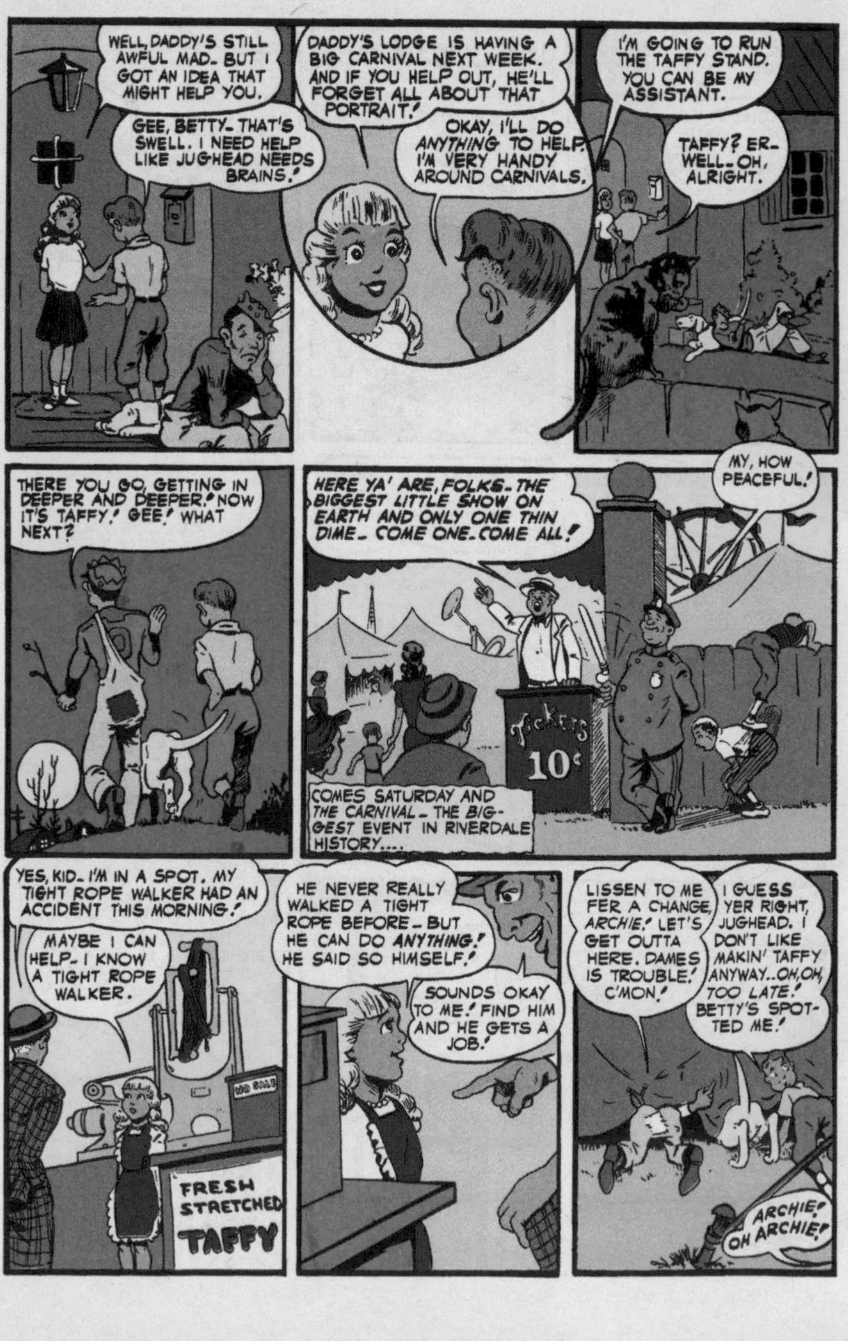
WELL, DADDY'S STILL AWFUL MAD- BUT I GOT AN IDEA THAT MIGHT HELP YOU.
GEE, BETTY- THAT'S SWELL. I NEED HELP LIKE JUGHEAD NEEDS BRAINS.!
DADDY'S LODGE IS HAVING A BIG CARNIVAL NEXT WEEK. AND IF YOU HELP OUT, HE'LL FORGET ALL ABOUT THAT PORTRAIT.!
OKAY, I'LL DO ANYTHING TO HELP. I'M VERY HANDY AROUND CARNIVALS.
I'M GOING TO RUN THE TAFFY STAND. YOU CAN BE MY ASSISTANT.
TAFFY? ER- WELL- OH, ALRIGHT.
THERE YOU GO, GETTING IN DEEPER AND DEEPER.! NOW IT'S TAFFY.! GEE.! WHAT NEXT?
HERE YA' ARE, FOLKS- THE BIGGEST LITTLE SHOW ON EARTH AND ONLY ONE THIN DIME- COME ONE- COME ALL.!
MY, HOW PEACEFUL.!
TICKETS 10¢
COMES SATURDAY AND THE CARNIVAL- THE BIGGEST EVENT IN RIVERDALE HISTORY....
YES, KID- I'M IN A SPOT. MY TIGHT ROPE WALKER HAD AN ACCIDENT THIS MORNING.!
MAYBE I CAN HELP- I KNOW A TIGHT ROPE WALKER.
FRESH STRETCHED TAFFY
HE NEVER REALLY WALKED A TIGHT ROPE BEFORE- BUT HE CAN DO ANYTHING.! HE SAID SO HIMSELF.!
SOUNDS OKAY TO ME.! FIND HIM AND HE GETS A JOB.!
LISSEN TO ME FER A CHANGE, ARCHIE.! LET'S GET OUTTA HERE. DAMES IS TROUBLE.! C'MON.!
I GUESS YER RIGHT, JUGHEAD. I DON'T LIKE MAKIN' TAFFY ANYWAY..OH, OH, TOO LATE.! BETTY'S SPOTTED ME.!
ARCHIE.! OH ARCHIE.!

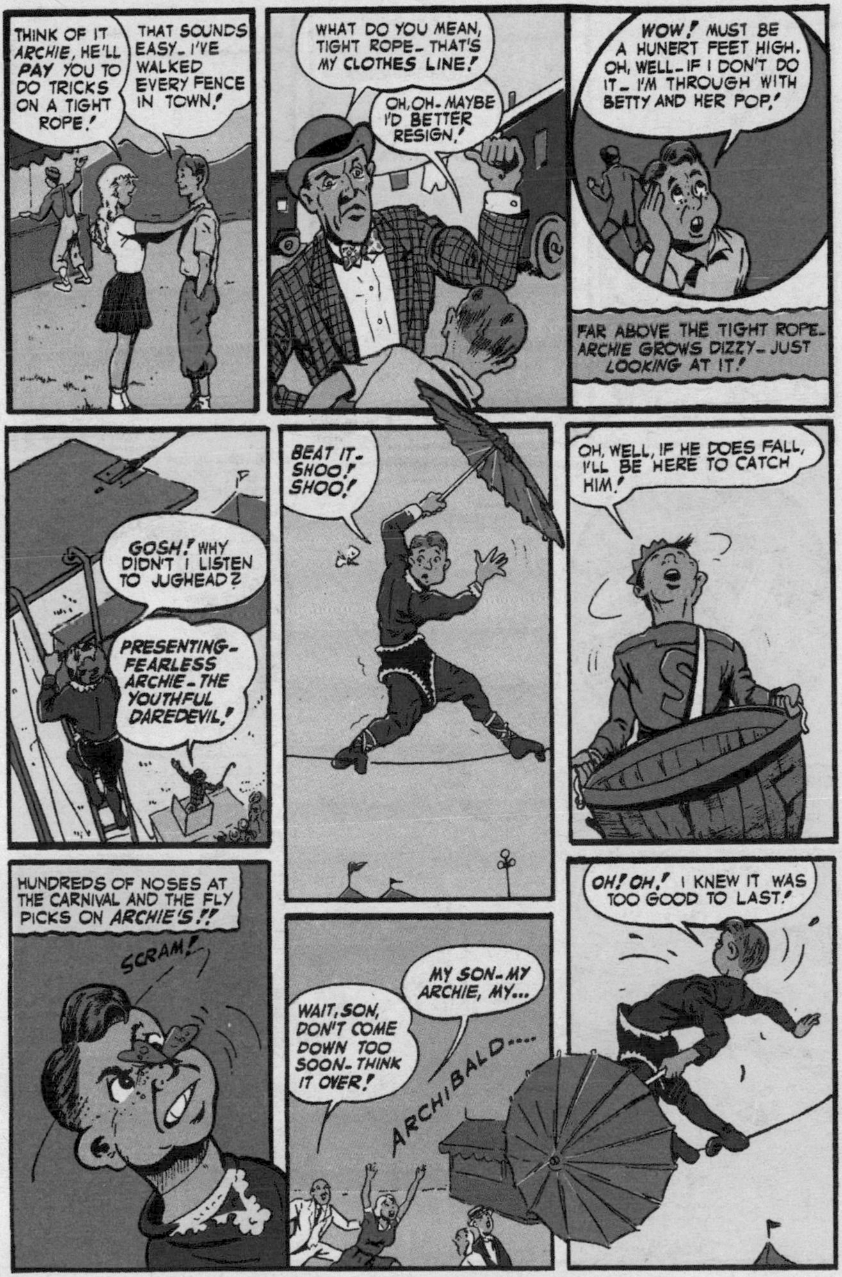
THINK OF IT ARCHIE, HE'LL PAY YOU TO DO TRICKS ON A TIGHT ROPE!
THAT SOUNDS EASY- I'VE WALKED EVERY FENCE IN TOWN!
WHAT DO YOU MEAN, TIGHT ROPE- THAT'S MY CLOTHES LINE!
OH, OH- MAYBE I'D BETTER RESIGN!
WOW! MUST BE A HUNERT FEET HIGH. OH, WELL- IF I DON'T DO IT- I'M THROUGH WITH BETTY AND HER POP!
FAR ABOVE THE TIGHT ROPE- ARCHIE GROWS DIZZY- JUST LOOKING AT IT!
GOSH! WHY DIDN'T I LISTEN TO JUGHEAD?
PRESENTING- FEARLESS ARCHIE- THE YOUTHFUL DAREDEVIL!
BEAT IT- SHOO! SHOO!
OH, WELL, IF HE DOES FALL, I'LL BE HERE TO CATCH HIM!
HUNDREDS OF NOSES AT THE CARNIVAL AND THE FLY PICKS ON ARCHIE'S!!
SCRAM!
MY SON- MY ARCHIE, MY...
WAIT, SON, DON'T COME DOWN TOO SOON- THINK IT OVER!
ARCHIBALD....
OH! OH! I KNEW IT WAS TOO GOOD TO LAST!

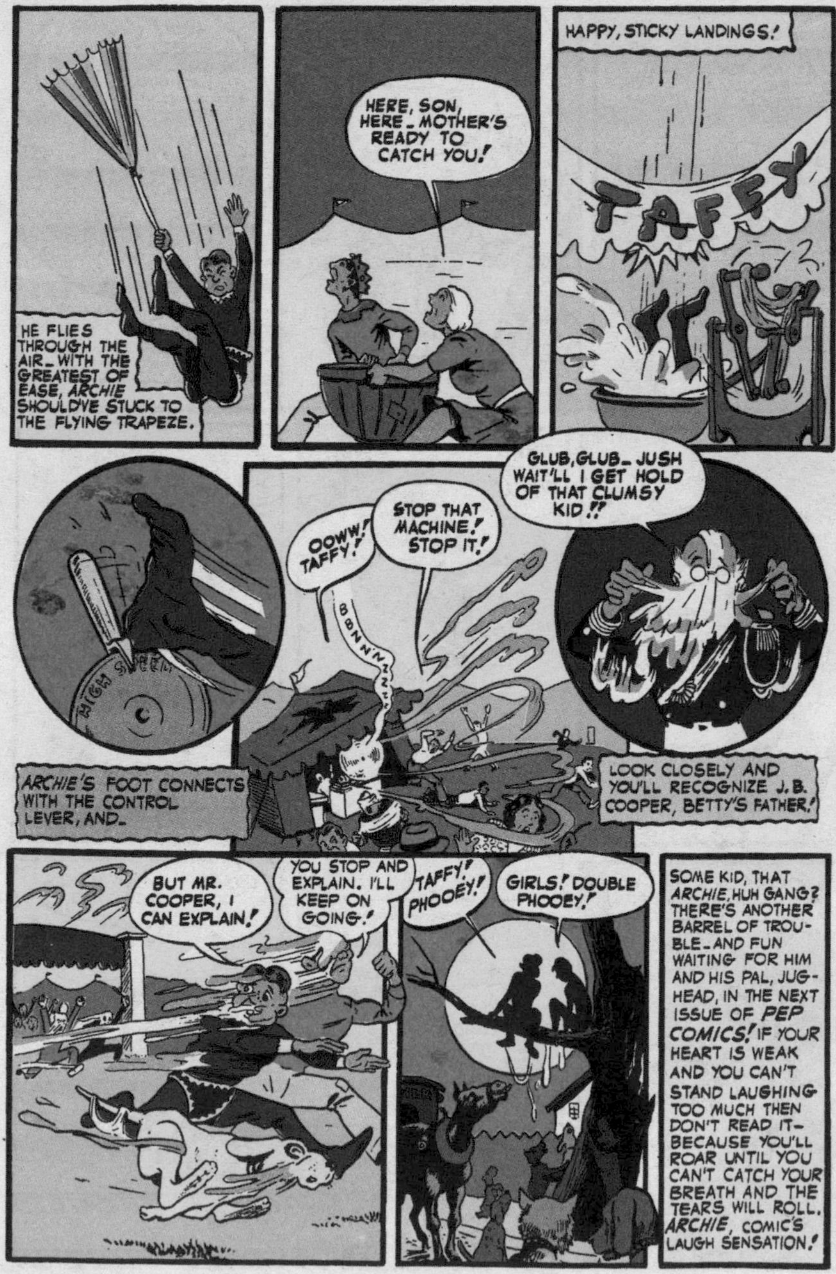
HE FLIES THROUGH THE AIR—WITH THE GREATEST OF EASE, ARCHIE SHOULD'VE STUCK TO THE FLYING TRAPEZE.
HERE, SON, HERE—MOTHER'S READY TO CATCH YOU!
HAPPY, STICKY LANDINGS!
TAFFY
HIGH SPEED
ARCHIE'S FOOT CONNECTS WITH THE CONTROL LEVER, AND—
OOWW! TAFFY!
STOP THAT MACHINE! STOP IT!
BBNNNZZZ
GLUB, GLUB—JUSH WAIT'LL I GET HOLD OF THAT CLUMSY KID!!
LOOK CLOSELY AND YOU'LL RECOGNIZE J. B. COOPER, BETTY'S FATHER!
BUT MR. COOPER, I CAN EXPLAIN!
YOU STOP AND EXPLAIN. I'LL KEEP ON GOING!
TAFFY! PHOOEY!
GIRLS! DOUBLE PHOOEY!
SOME KID, THAT ARCHIE, HUH GANG? THERE'S ANOTHER BARREL OF TROUBLE—AND FUN WAITING FOR HIM AND HIS PAL, JUGHEAD, IN THE NEXT ISSUE OF PEP COMICS! IF YOUR HEART IS WEAK AND YOU CAN'T STAND LAUGHING TOO MUCH THEN DON'T READ IT—BECAUSE YOU'LL ROAR UNTIL YOU CAN'T CATCH YOUR BREATH AND THE TEARS WILL ROLL. ARCHIE, COMIC'S LAUGH SENSATION!

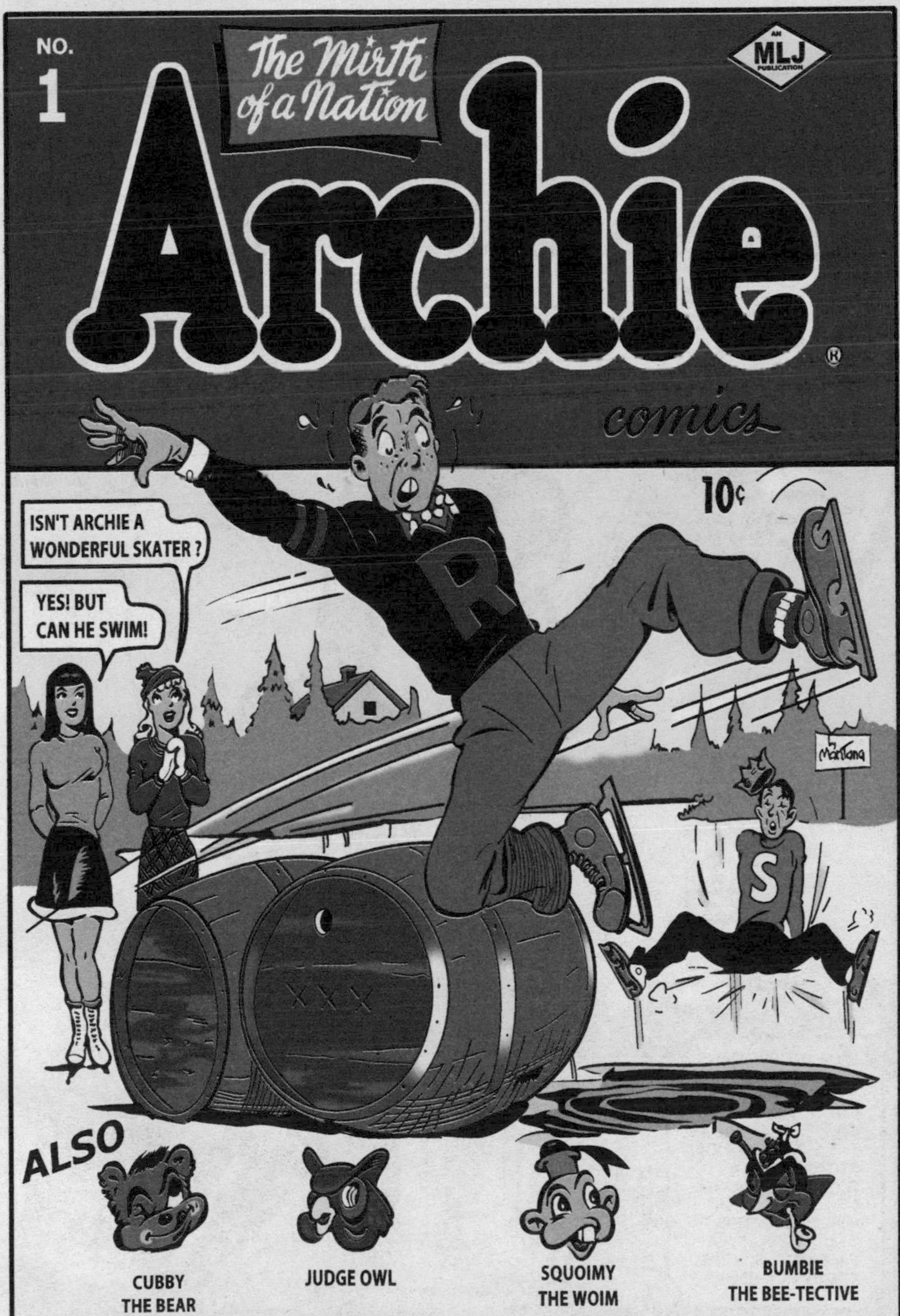
NO. 1
The Mirth of a Nation
AN MLJ PUBLICATION
Archie
comics
10¢
ISN'T ARCHIE A WONDERFUL SKATER ?
YES! BUT CAN HE SWIM!
ALSO
CUBBY THE BEAR
JUDGE OWL
SQUOIMY THE WOIM
BUMBIE THE BEE-TECTIVE

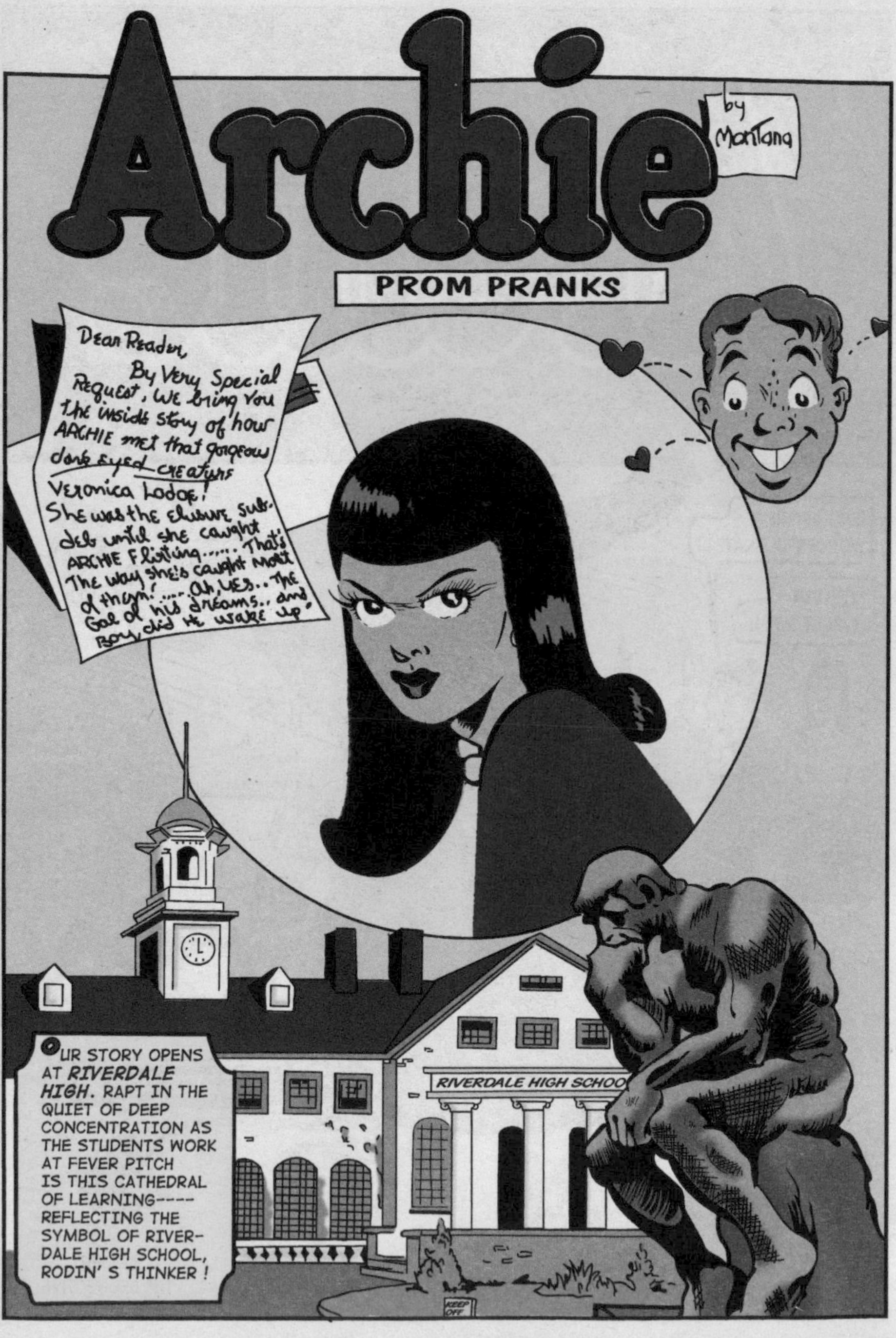
Archie
by MonTana
PROM PRANKS
Dear Reader,
By Very Special Request, We bring You the inside story of how ARCHIE met that gorgeous dark eyed creature Veronica Lodge!
She was the elusive sub-deb until she caught ARCHIE Flirting...... That's The way she's caught most of them! .....Oh, Yes.. The Gal of his dreams.. and Boy, did he wake up!
OUR STORY OPENS AT *RIVERDALE HIGH*. RAPT IN THE QUIET OF DEEP CONCENTRATION AS THE STUDENTS WORK AT FEVER PITCH IS THIS CATHEDRAL OF LEARNING---- REFLECTING THE SYMBOL OF RIVER-DALE HIGH SCHOOL, RODIN' S THINKER !
RIVERDALE HIGH SCHOO
KEEP OFF

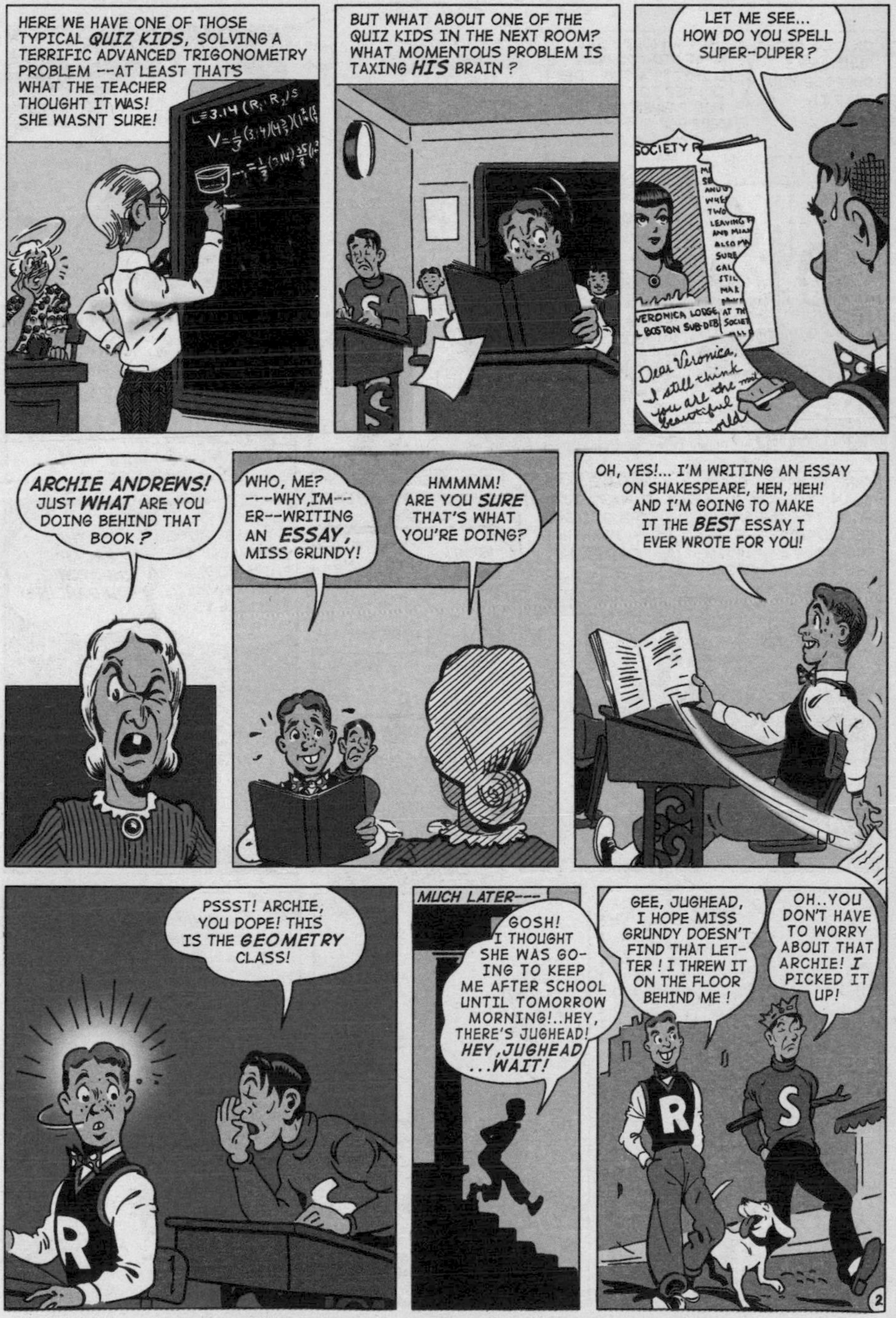
HERE WE HAVE ONE OF THOSE TYPICAL QUIZ KIDS, SOLVING A TERRIFIC ADVANCED TRIGONOMETRY PROBLEM --AT LEAST THAT'S WHAT THE TEACHER THOUGHT IT WAS! SHE WASNT SURE!
BUT WHAT ABOUT ONE OF THE QUIZ KIDS IN THE NEXT ROOM? WHAT MOMENTOUS PROBLEM IS TAXING HIS BRAIN ?
LET ME SEE... HOW DO YOU SPELL SUPER-DUPER?
SOCIETY
VERONICA LODGE BOSTON SUB-DEB
Dear Veronica, I still think you are the most beautiful
ARCHIE ANDREWS! JUST WHAT ARE YOU DOING BEHIND THAT BOOK ?
WHO, ME? ---WHY, I'M--- ER--WRITING AN ESSAY, MISS GRUNDY!
HMMMM! ARE YOU SURE THAT'S WHAT YOU'RE DOING?
OH, YES!... I'M WRITING AN ESSAY ON SHAKESPEARE, HEH, HEH! AND I'M GOING TO MAKE IT THE BEST ESSAY I EVER WROTE FOR YOU!
PSSST! ARCHIE, YOU DOPE! THIS IS THE GEOMETRY CLASS!
MUCH LATER---
GOSH! I THOUGHT SHE WAS GOING TO KEEP ME AFTER SCHOOL UNTIL TOMORROW MORNING!..HEY, THERE'S JUGHEAD! HEY, JUGHEAD ...WAIT!
GEE, JUGHEAD, I HOPE MISS GRUNDY DOESN'T FIND THAT LETTER ! I THREW IT ON THE FLOOR BEHIND ME !
OH..YOU DON'T HAVE TO WORRY ABOUT THAT ARCHIE! I PICKED IT UP!
2

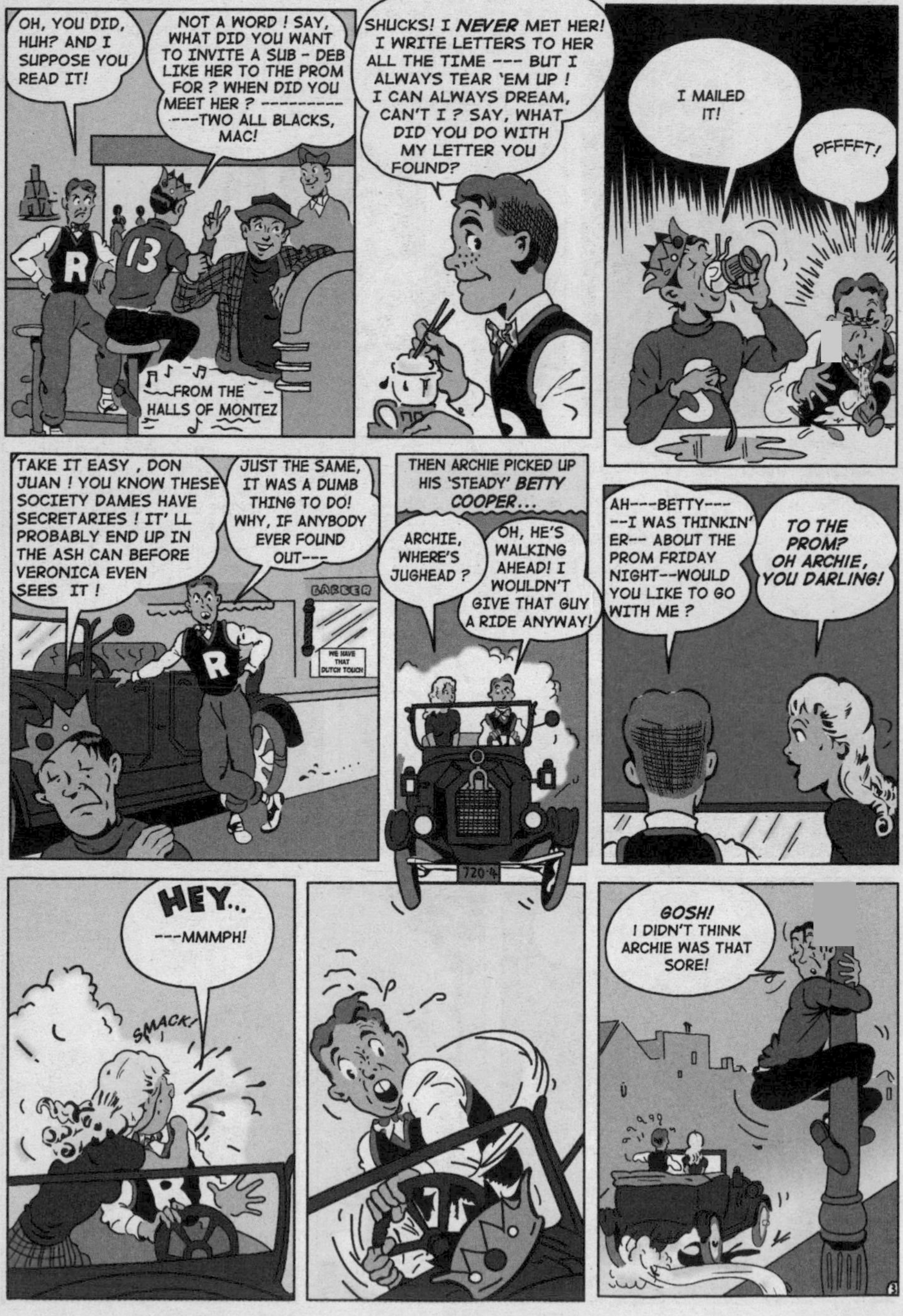
OH, YOU DID, HUH? AND I SUPPOSE YOU READ IT!
NOT A WORD ! SAY, WHAT DID YOU WANT TO INVITE A SUB - DEB LIKE HER TO THE PROM FOR ? WHEN DID YOU MEET HER ? ---------- ----TWO ALL BLACKS, MAC!
FROM THE HALLS OF MONTEZ
SHUCKS! I NEVER MET HER! I WRITE LETTERS TO HER ALL THE TIME --- BUT I ALWAYS TEAR 'EM UP ! I CAN ALWAYS DREAM, CAN'T I ? SAY, WHAT DID YOU DO WITH MY LETTER YOU FOUND?
I MAILED IT!
PFFFFT!
TAKE IT EASY , DON JUAN ! YOU KNOW THESE SOCIETY DAMES HAVE SECRETARIES ! IT' LL PROBABLY END UP IN THE ASH CAN BEFORE VERONICA EVEN SEES IT !
JUST THE SAME, IT WAS A DUMB THING TO DO! WHY, IF ANYBODY EVER FOUND OUT---
BARBER
WE HAVE THAT DUTCH TOUCH
THEN ARCHIE PICKED UP HIS 'STEADY' BETTY COOPER...
ARCHIE, WHERE'S JUGHEAD ?
OH, HE'S WALKING AHEAD! I WOULDN'T GIVE THAT GUY A RIDE ANYWAY!
720-4
AH---BETTY--- --I WAS THINKIN' ER-- ABOUT THE PROM FRIDAY NIGHT--WOULD YOU LIKE TO GO WITH ME ?
TO THE PROM? OH ARCHIE, YOU DARLING!
HEY... ---MMMPH!
SMACK!
GOSH! I DIDN'T THINK ARCHIE WAS THAT SORE!

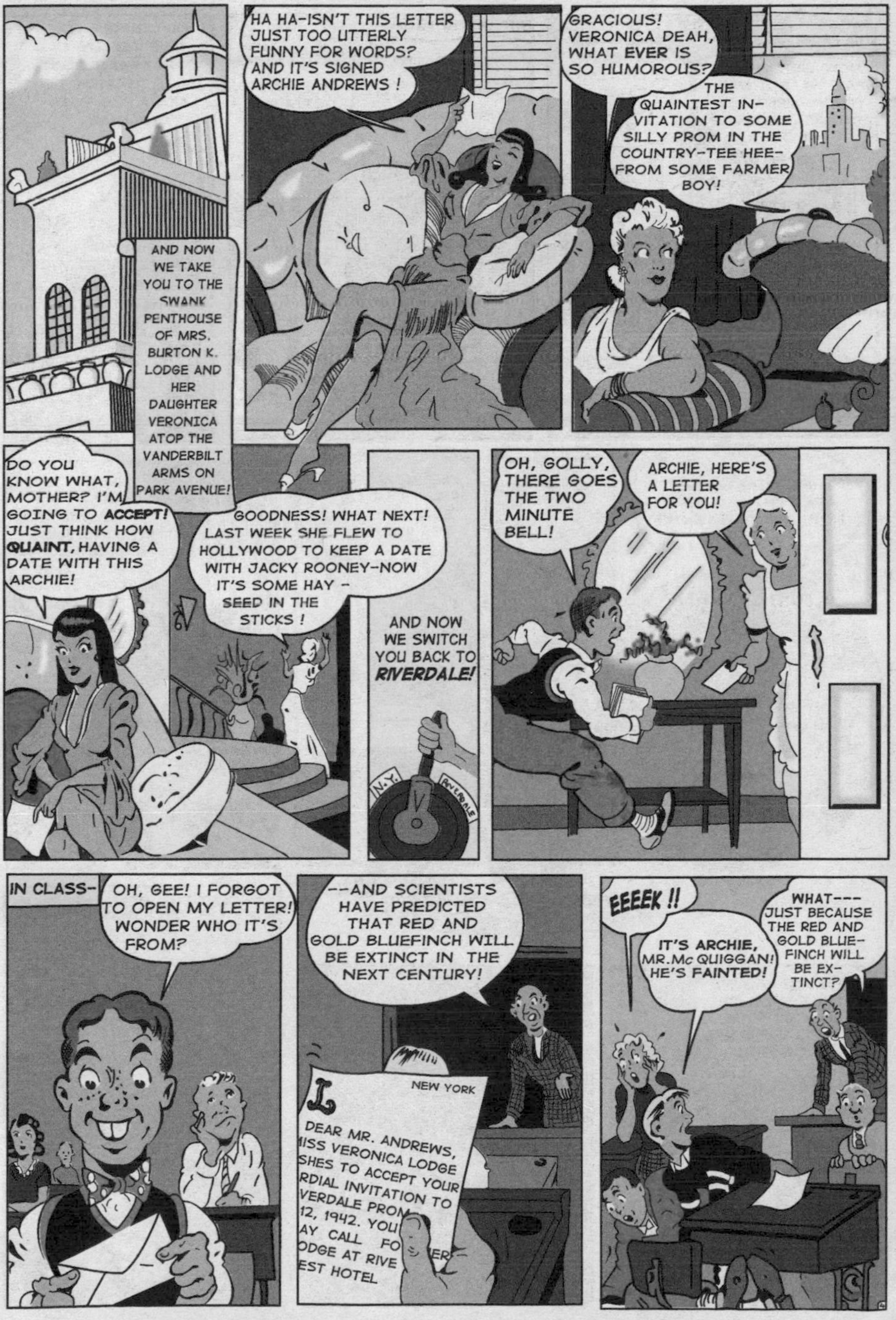
AND NOW WE TAKE YOU TO THE SWANK PENTHOUSE OF MRS. BURTON K. LODGE AND HER DAUGHTER VERONICA ATOP THE VANDERBILT ARMS ON PARK AVENUE!
HA HA-ISN'T THIS LETTER JUST TOO UTTERLY FUNNY FOR WORDS? AND IT'S SIGNED ARCHIE ANDREWS !
GRACIOUS! VERONICA DEAH, WHAT EVER IS SO HUMOROUS?
THE QUAINTEST IN-VITATION TO SOME SILLY PROM IN THE COUNTRY-TEE HEE-FROM SOME FARMER BOY!
DO YOU KNOW WHAT, MOTHER? I'M GOING TO ACCEPT! JUST THINK HOW QUAINT, HAVING A DATE WITH THIS ARCHIE!
GOODNESS! WHAT NEXT! LAST WEEK SHE FLEW TO HOLLYWOOD TO KEEP A DATE WITH JACKY ROONEY-NOW IT'S SOME HAY-SEED IN THE STICKS !
AND NOW WE SWITCH YOU BACK TO RIVERDALE!
N.Y.
RIVERDALE
OH, GOLLY, THERE GOES THE TWO MINUTE BELL!
ARCHIE, HERE'S A LETTER FOR YOU!
IN CLASS-
OH, GEE! I FORGOT TO OPEN MY LETTER! WONDER WHO IT'S FROM?
--AND SCIENTISTS HAVE PREDICTED THAT RED AND GOLD BLUEFINCH WILL BE EXTINCT IN THE NEXT CENTURY!
NEW YORK
DEAR MR. ANDREWS,
IISS VERONICA LODGE
SHES TO ACCEPT YOUR
RDIAL INVITATION TO
VERDALE PROM
12, 1942. YOU
AY CALL FO ER
ODGE AT RIVE
EST HOTEL
EEEEK !!
IT'S ARCHIE, MR. Mc QUIGGAN! HE'S FAINTED!
WHAT--- JUST BECAUSE THE RED AND GOLD BLUE-FINCH WILL BE EX-TINCT?

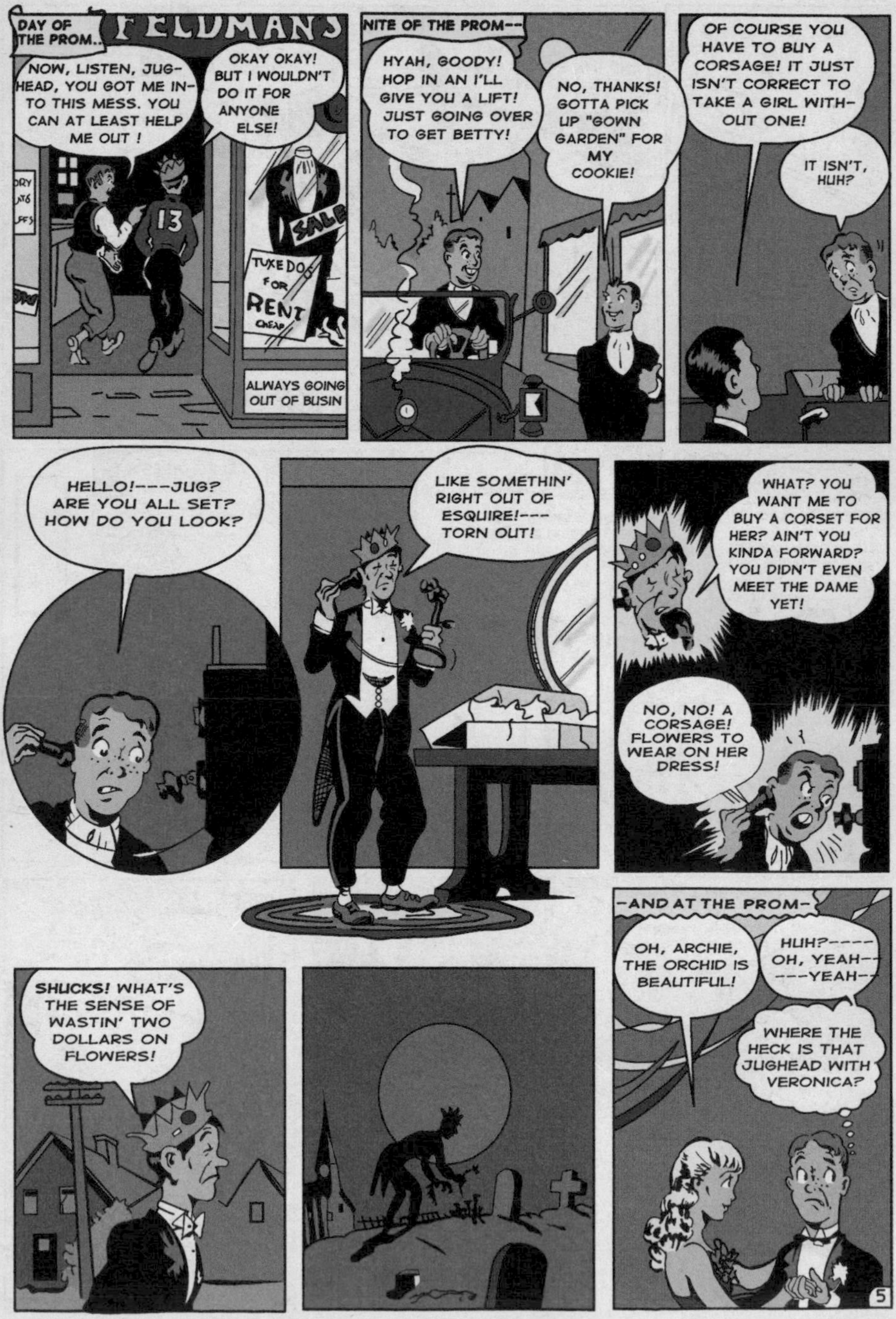
DAY OF THE PROM..
FELDMAN'S
NOW, LISTEN, JUGHEAD, YOU GOT ME INTO THIS MESS. YOU CAN AT LEAST HELP ME OUT !
OKAY OKAY! BUT I WOULDN'T DO IT FOR ANYONE ELSE!
SALE
TUXEDO FOR RENT CHEAP
ALWAYS GOING OUT OF BUSIN
NITE OF THE PROM--
HYAH, GOODY! HOP IN AN I'LL GIVE YOU A LIFT! JUST GOING OVER TO GET BETTY!
NO, THANKS! GOTTA PICK UP "GOWN GARDEN" FOR MY COOKIE!
OF COURSE YOU HAVE TO BUY A CORSAGE! IT JUST ISN'T CORRECT TO TAKE A GIRL WITHOUT ONE!
IT ISN'T, HUH?
HELLO!---JUG? ARE YOU ALL SET? HOW DO YOU LOOK?
LIKE SOMETHIN' RIGHT OUT OF ESQUIRE!--- TORN OUT!
WHAT? YOU WANT ME TO BUY A CORSET FOR HER? AIN'T YOU KINDA FORWARD? YOU DIDN'T EVEN MEET THE DAME YET!
NO, NO! A CORSAGE! FLOWERS TO WEAR ON HER DRESS!
SHUCKS! WHAT'S THE SENSE OF WASTIN' TWO DOLLARS ON FLOWERS!
-AND AT THE PROM-
OH, ARCHIE, THE ORCHID IS BEAUTIFUL!
HUH?---- OH, YEAH-- ---YEAH--
WHERE THE HECK IS THAT JUGHEAD WITH VERONICA?
5

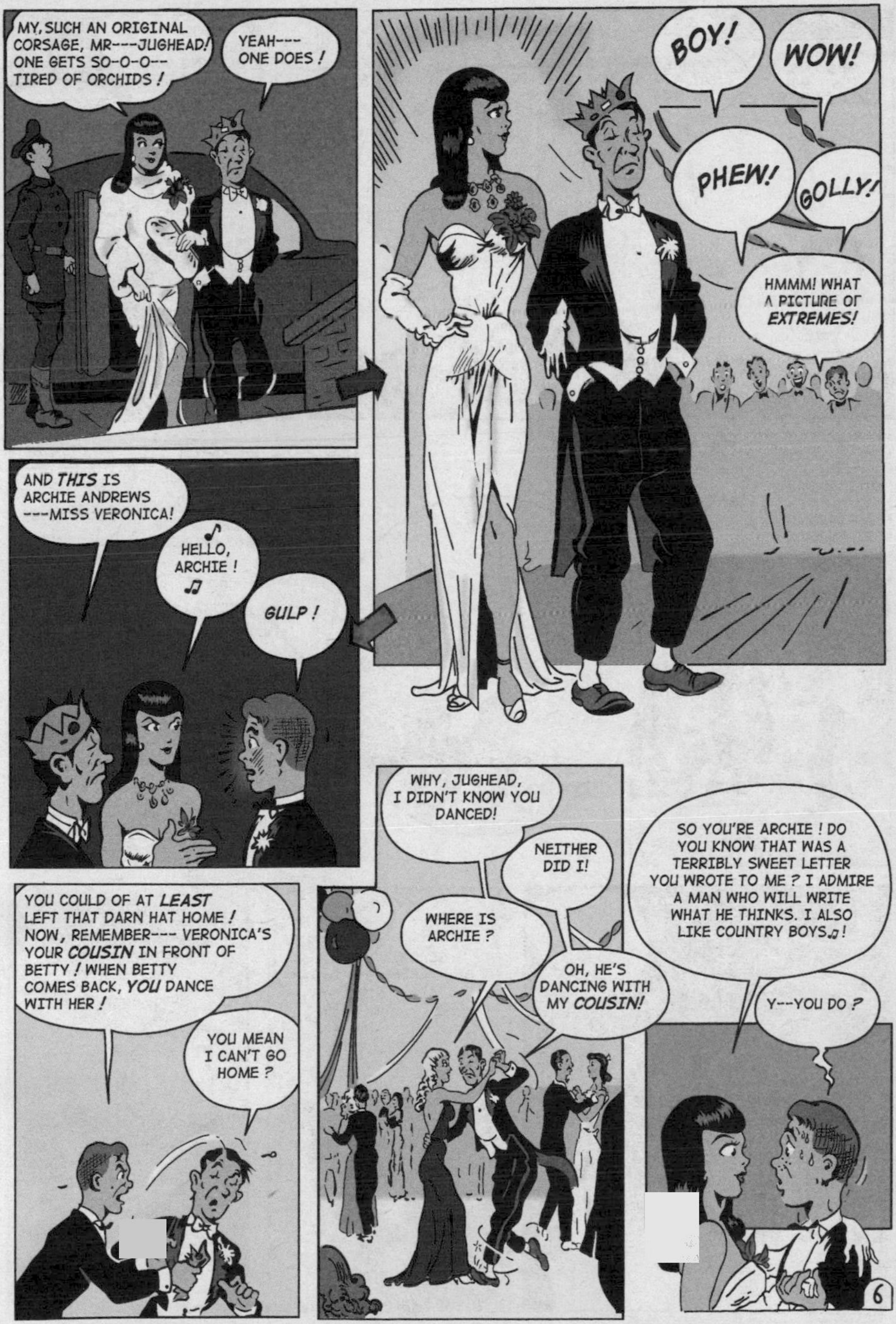
MY, SUCH AN ORIGINAL CORSAGE, MR---JUGHEAD! ONE GETS SO-O-O-- TIRED OF ORCHIDS !
YEAH--- ONE DOES !
BOY!
WOW!
PHEW!
GOLLY!
HMMM! WHAT A PICTURE OF EXTREMES!
AND THIS IS ARCHIE ANDREWS ---MISS VERONICA!
HELLO, ARCHIE !
GULP !
YOU COULD OF AT LEAST LEFT THAT DARN HAT HOME ! NOW, REMEMBER--- VERONICA'S YOUR COUSIN IN FRONT OF BETTY ! WHEN BETTY COMES BACK, YOU DANCE WITH HER !
YOU MEAN I CAN'T GO HOME ?
WHY, JUGHEAD, I DIDN'T KNOW YOU DANCED!
NEITHER DID I!
WHERE IS ARCHIE ?
OH, HE'S DANCING WITH MY COUSIN!
SO YOU'RE ARCHIE ! DO YOU KNOW THAT WAS A TERRIBLY SWEET LETTER YOU WROTE TO ME ? I ADMIRE A MAN WHO WILL WRITE WHAT HE THINKS. I ALSO LIKE COUNTRY BOYS !
Y--YOU DO ?
6

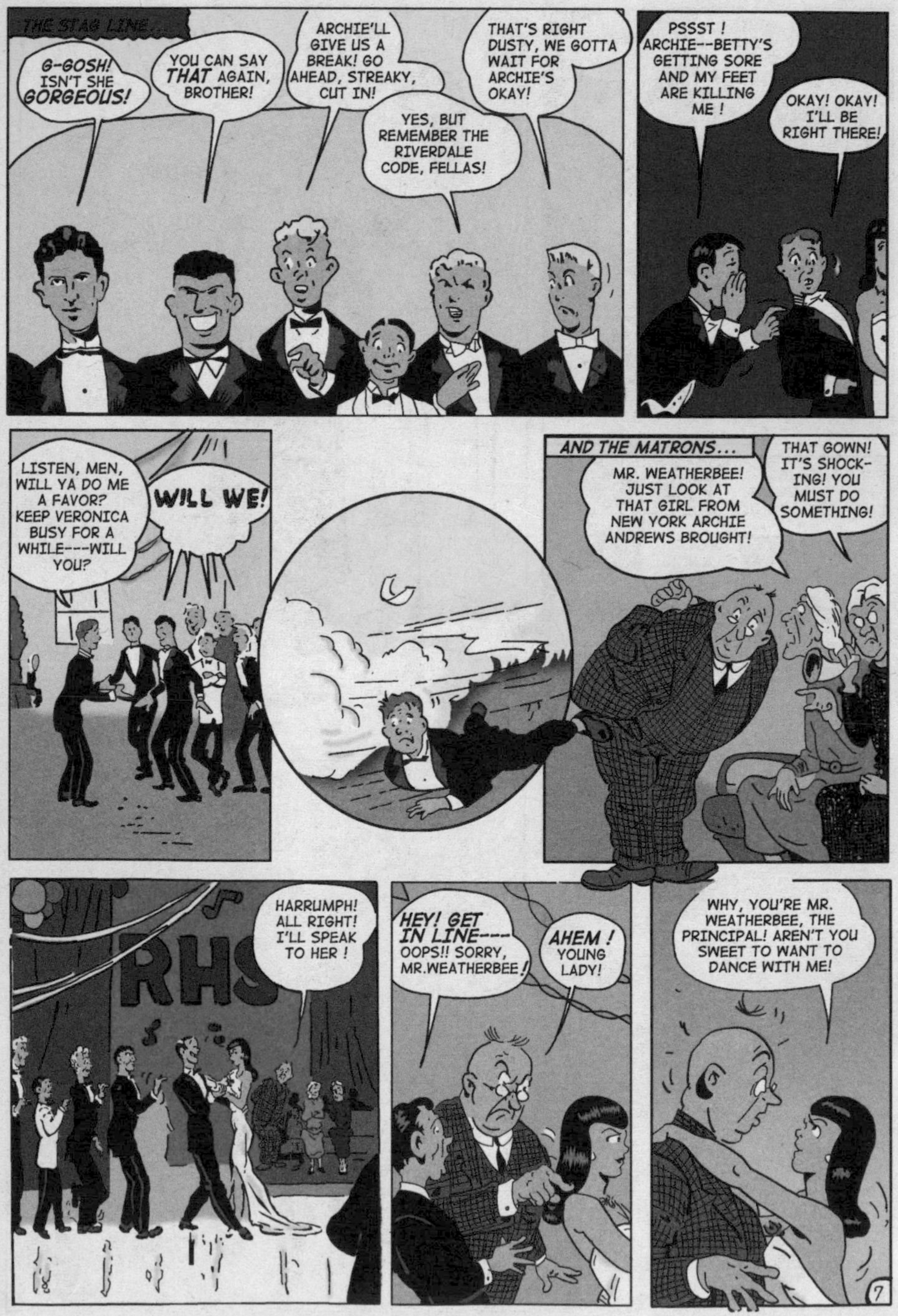
THE STAG LINE...
G-GOSH! ISN'T SHE GORGEOUS!
YOU CAN SAY THAT AGAIN, BROTHER!
ARCHIE'LL GIVE US A BREAK! GO AHEAD, STREAKY, CUT IN!
YES, BUT REMEMBER THE RIVERDALE CODE, FELLAS!
THAT'S RIGHT DUSTY, WE GOTTA WAIT FOR ARCHIE'S OKAY!
PSSST ! ARCHIE--BETTY'S GETTING SORE AND MY FEET ARE KILLING ME !
OKAY! OKAY! I'LL BE RIGHT THERE!
LISTEN, MEN, WILL YA DO ME A FAVOR? KEEP VERONICA BUSY FOR A WHILE---WILL YOU?
WILL WE!
AND THE MATRONS...
MR. WEATHERBEE! JUST LOOK AT THAT GIRL FROM NEW YORK ARCHIE ANDREWS BROUGHT!
THAT GOWN! IT'S SHOCKING! YOU MUST DO SOMETHING!
HARRUMPH! ALL RIGHT! I'LL SPEAK TO HER !
RHS
HEY! GET IN LINE--- OOPS!! SORRY, MR.WEATHERBEE!
AHEM ! YOUNG LADY!
WHY, YOU'RE MR. WEATHERBEE, THE PRINCIPAL! AREN'T YOU SWEET TO WANT TO DANCE WITH ME!
7

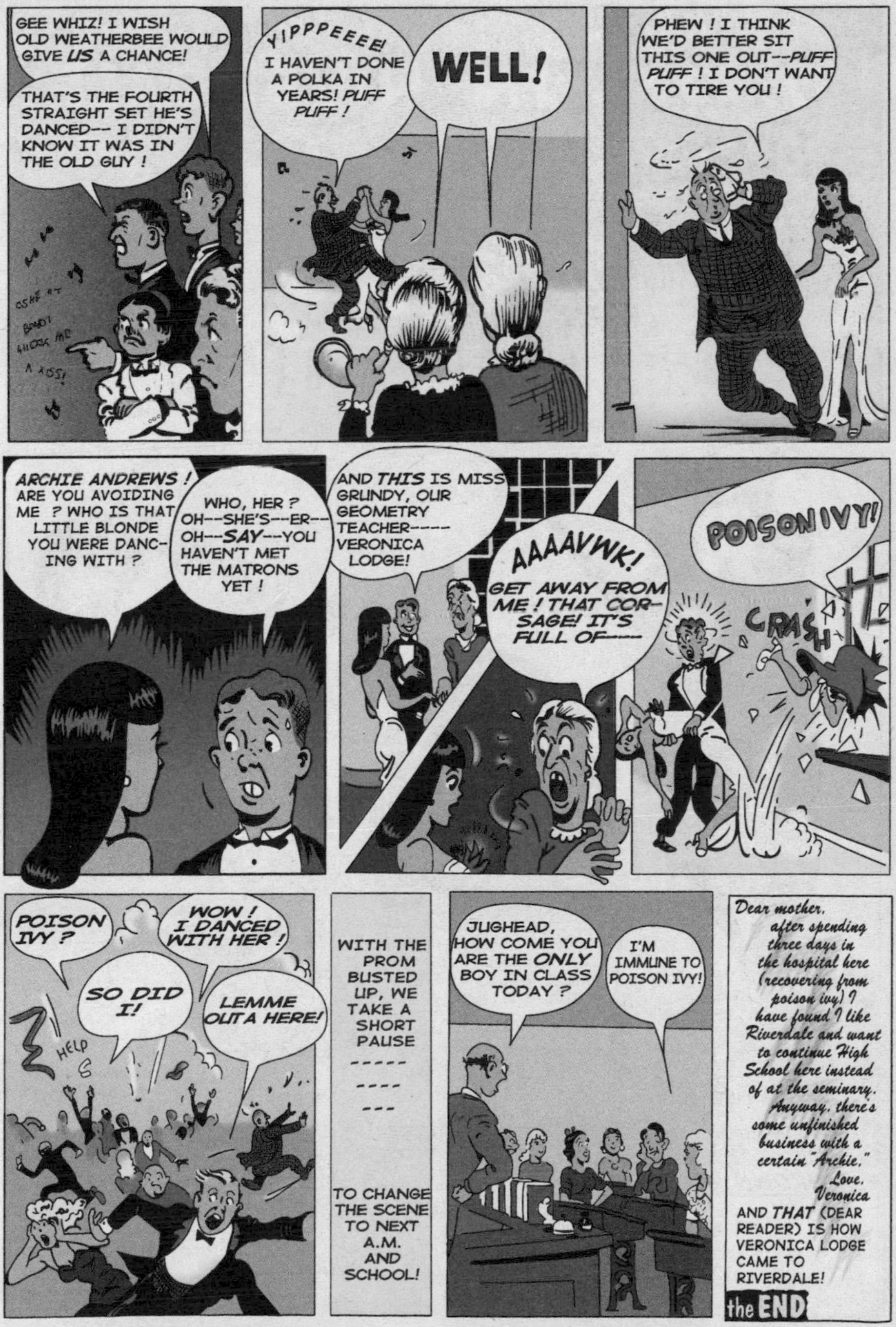
GEE WHIZ! I WISH OLD WEATHERBEE WOULD GIVE *US* A CHANCE!
THAT'S THE FOURTH STRAIGHT SET HE'S DANCED-- I DIDN'T KNOW IT WAS IN THE OLD GUY !
YIPPPEEEE! I HAVEN'T DONE A POLKA IN YEARS! *PUFF PUFF* !
WELL!
PHEW ! I THINK WE'D BETTER SIT THIS ONE OUT--*PUFF PUFF* ! I DON'T WANT TO TIRE YOU !
ARCHIE ANDREWS ! ARE YOU AVOIDING ME ? WHO IS THAT LITTLE BLONDE YOU WERE DANCING WITH ?
WHO, HER ? OH--SHE'S--ER--OH--*SAY*--YOU HAVEN'T MET THE MATRONS YET !
AND *THIS* IS MISS GRUNDY, OUR GEOMETRY TEACHER---- VERONICA LODGE!
AAAAVWK!
GET AWAY FROM ME ! THAT CORSAGE! IT'S FULL OF----
POISON IVY!
CRASH
POISON IVY ?
WOW ! I DANCED WITH HER !
SO DID I!
LEMME OUTA HERE!
HELP
WITH THE PROM BUSTED UP, WE TAKE A SHORT PAUSE
----- ---- ---
TO CHANGE THE SCENE TO NEXT A.M. AND SCHOOL!
JUGHEAD, HOW COME YOU ARE THE *ONLY* BOY IN CLASS TODAY ?
I'M IMMUNE TO POISON IVY!
Dear mother, after spending three days in the hospital here (recovering from poison ivy) I have found I like Riverdale and want to continue High School here instead of at the seminary. Anyway, there's some unfinished business with a certain "Archie." Love, Veronica
AND *THAT* (DEAR READER) IS HOW VERONICA LODGE CAME TO RIVERDALE!
the END

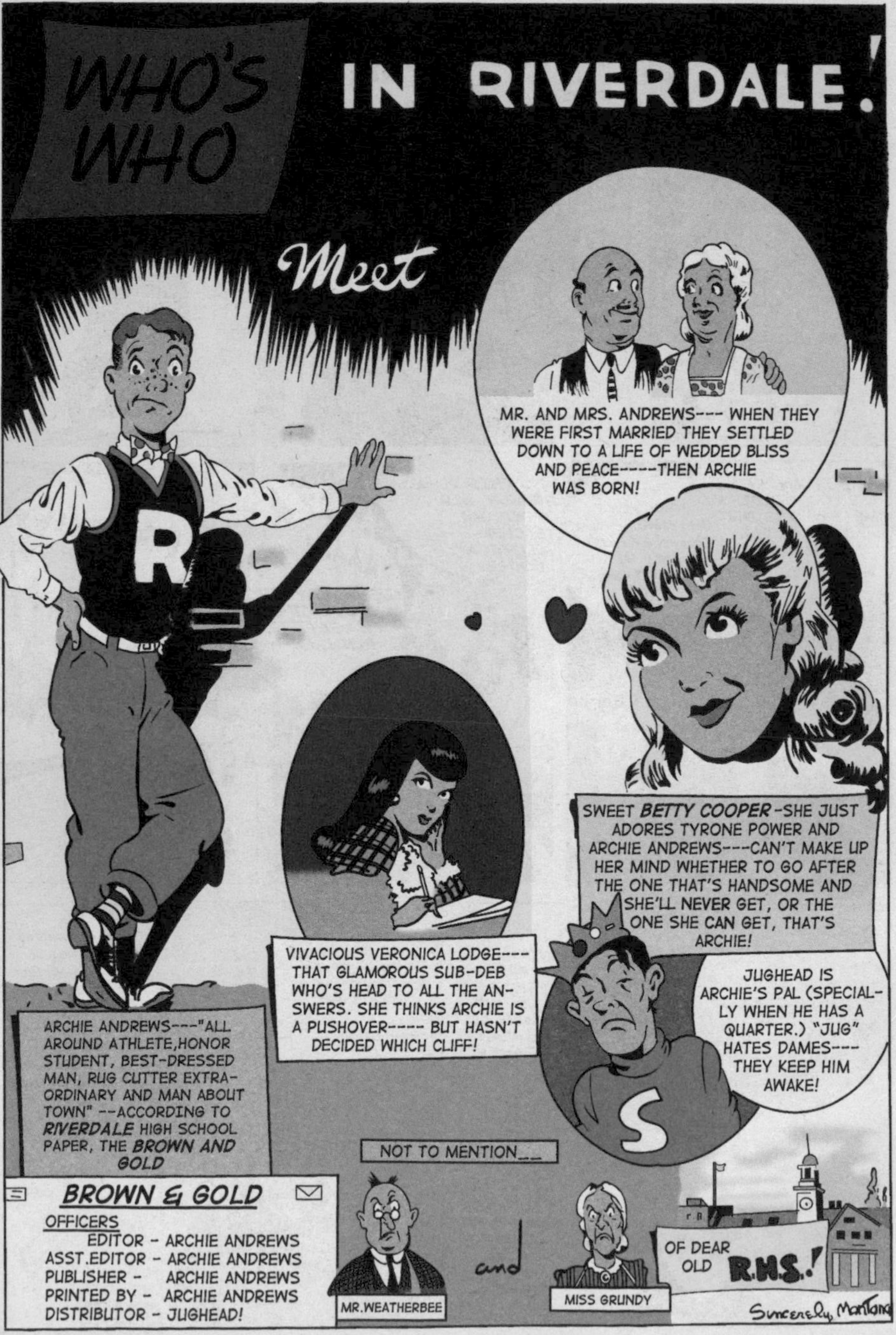
WHO'S WHO IN RIVERDALE!
Meet
MR. AND MRS. ANDREWS--- WHEN THEY WERE FIRST MARRIED THEY SETTLED DOWN TO A LIFE OF WEDDED BLISS AND PEACE----THEN ARCHIE WAS BORN!
SWEET BETTY COOPER -SHE JUST ADORES TYRONE POWER AND ARCHIE ANDREWS---CAN'T MAKE UP HER MIND WHETHER TO GO AFTER THE ONE THAT'S HANDSOME AND SHE'LL NEVER GET, OR THE ONE SHE CAN GET, THAT'S ARCHIE!
VIVACIOUS VERONICA LODGE--- THAT GLAMOROUS SUB-DEB WHO'S HEAD TO ALL THE AN-SWERS. SHE THINKS ARCHIE IS A PUSHOVER---- BUT HASN'T DECIDED WHICH CLIFF!
JUGHEAD IS ARCHIE'S PAL (SPECIAL-LY WHEN HE HAS A QUARTER.) "JUG" HATES DAMES--- THEY KEEP HIM AWAKE!
ARCHIE ANDREWS---"ALL AROUND ATHLETE,HONOR STUDENT, BEST-DRESSED MAN, RUG CUTTER EXTRA-ORDINARY AND MAN ABOUT TOWN" --ACCORDING TO RIVERDALE HIGH SCHOOL PAPER, THE BROWN AND GOLD
BROWN & GOLD
OFFICERS
EDITOR - ARCHIE ANDREWS
ASST.EDITOR - ARCHIE ANDREWS
PUBLISHER - ARCHIE ANDREWS
PRINTED BY - ARCHIE ANDREWS
DISTRIBUTOR - JUGHEAD!
NOT TO MENTION__
MR.WEATHERBEE
and
MISS GRUNDY
OF DEAR OLD R.H.S.!
Sincerely, Montana

Daily Newspaper Strips 1948
by Bob Montana

Just after World War II, artist Bob Montana began a 29-year stint as artist of the new Archie newspaper strip.

This set of six daily strips from 1948 are great examples of classic Montana—beautiful design and lush brushwork mixed with broad, high-spirited comedy.

It's also fun to see Montana's deft reworking of the same dance climax scene from "Prom Pranks" on page 23 six years later at the end of this sequence.

I was twelve years old when I went up to MLJ, the forerunner of Archie Comics. Bob Montana was just finishing the penciling of an Archie story. At his request, I inked the story Bob had penciled. That was over 70 years ago, and I'm as thrilled today about that occurrence as I was so many years ago.

--Joe Kubert
Legendary artist & writer/ founder, The Kubert School

Ants in the Plants
Laugh #27, 1948

Wilbur Wilkin debuted in *Zip Comics #18* in September, 1941, actually predating Archie Andrews by three months as Archie Comics' first successful teen character. Though not as well known as Archie is today, Wilbur had his own very popular comic book series that ran for 15 years. "Ants in the Plants" is irresistibly silly, a great example of Archie Comics' other boy-next-door.

--Harold Buchholz
Executive Director of Publishing & Operations, Archie Comics

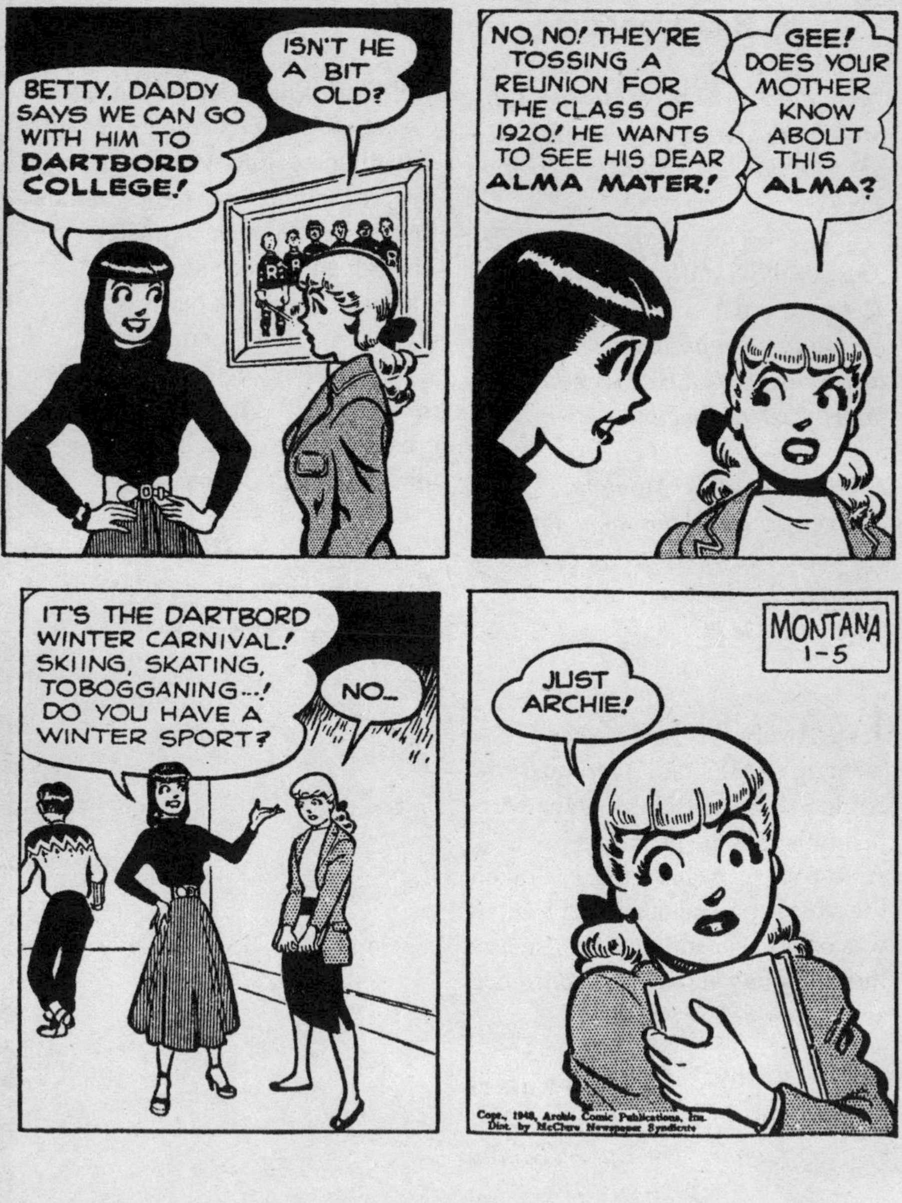
BETTY, DADDY SAYS WE CAN GO WITH HIM TO **DARTBORD COLLEGE!**
ISN'T HE A BIT OLD?
NO, NO! THEY'RE TOSSING A REUNION FOR THE CLASS OF 1920! HE WANTS TO SEE HIS DEAR **ALMA MATER!**
GEE! DOES YOUR MOTHER KNOW ABOUT THIS **ALMA?**
IT'S THE DARTBORD WINTER CARNIVAL! SKIING, SKATING, TOBOGGANING...! DO YOU HAVE A WINTER SPORT?
NO..
MONTANA 1-5
JUST ARCHIE!
Copr., 1948, Archie Comic Publications, Inc. Dist. by McClure Newspaper Syndicate

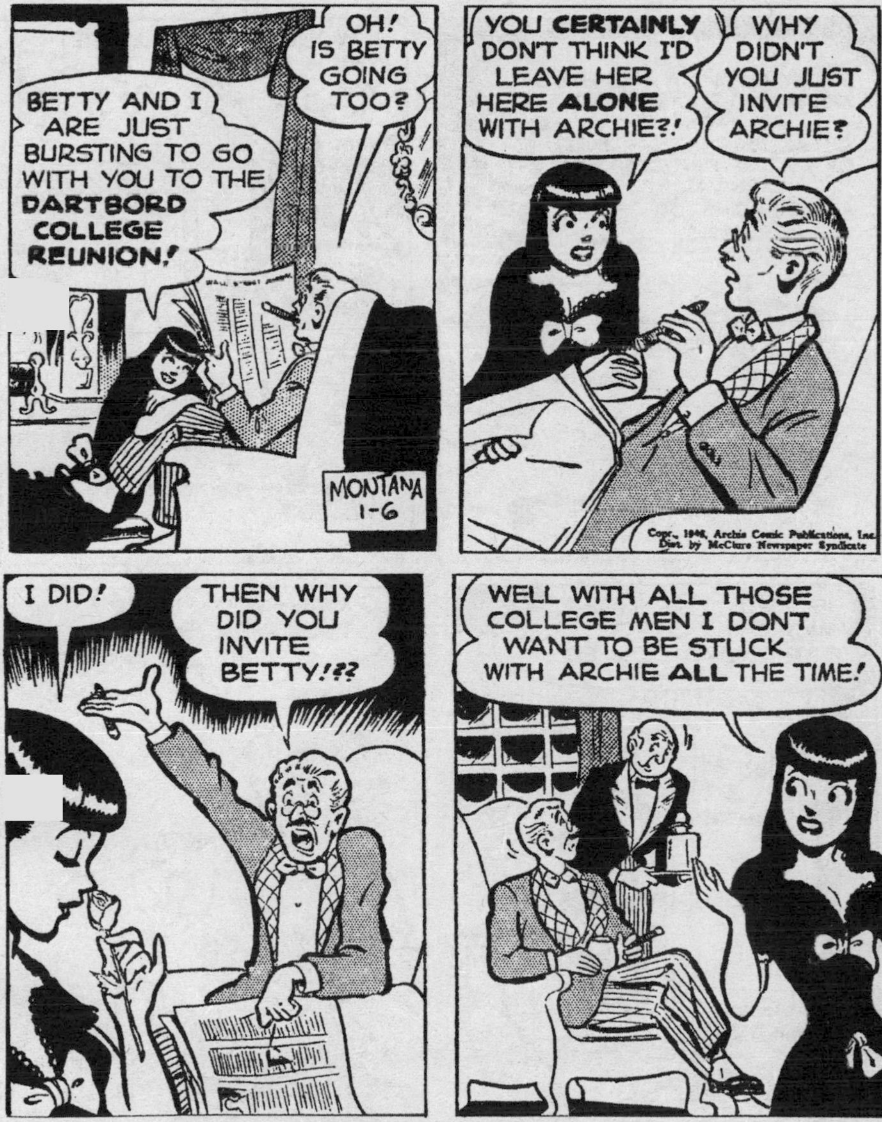
BETTY AND I ARE JUST BURSTING TO GO WITH YOU TO THE DARTBORD COLLEGE REUNION!
OH! IS BETTY GOING TOO?
MONTANA 1-6
YOU CERTAINLY DON'T THINK I'D LEAVE HER HERE ALONE WITH ARCHIE?!
WHY DIDN'T YOU JUST INVITE ARCHIE?
Copr., 1946, Archie Comic Publications, Inc.
Dist. by McClure Newspaper Syndicate
I DID!
THEN WHY DID YOU INVITE BETTY!??
WELL WITH ALL THOSE COLLEGE MEN I DON'T WANT TO BE STUCK WITH ARCHIE ALL THE TIME!

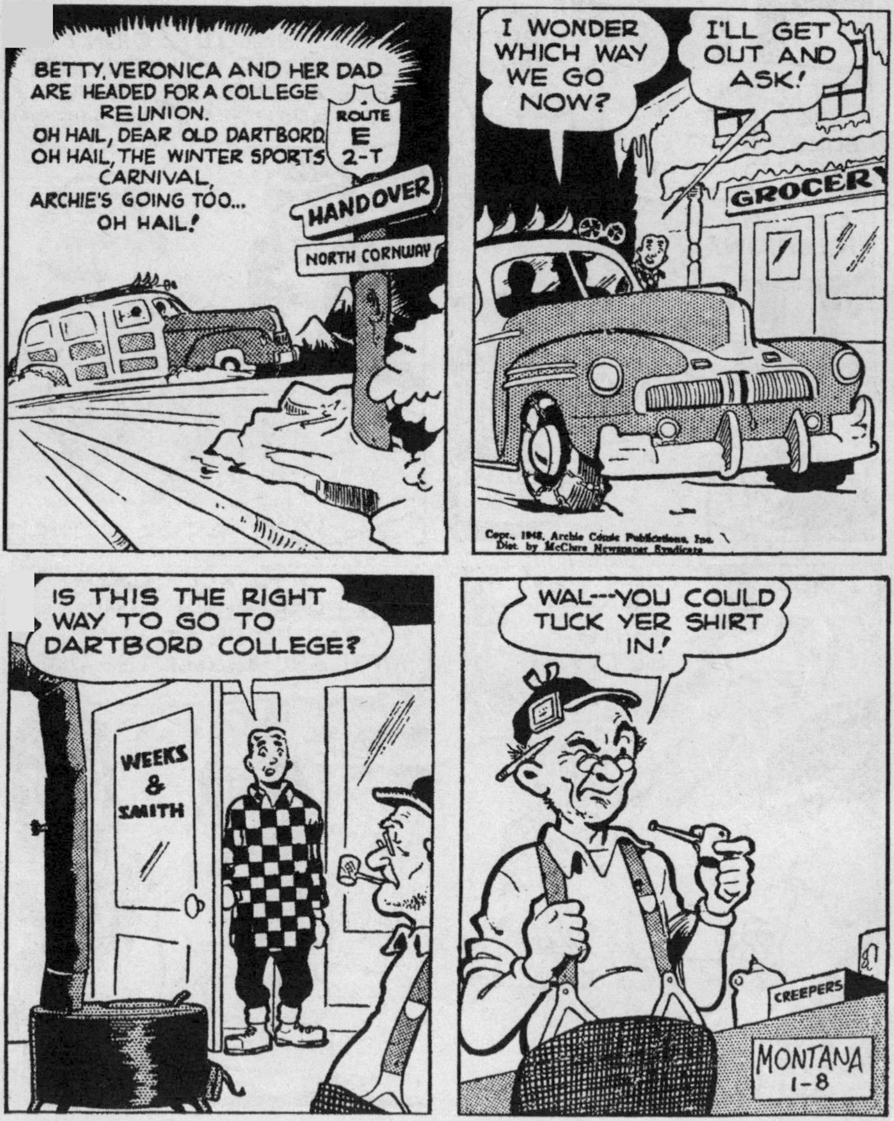
BETTY, VERONICA AND HER DAD ARE HEADED FOR A COLLEGE REUNION.
OH HAIL, DEAR OLD DARTBORD.
OH HAIL, THE WINTER SPORTS CARNIVAL,
ARCHIE'S GOING TOO...
OH HAIL!
ROUTE E 2-T
HANDOVER
NORTH CORNWAY
I WONDER WHICH WAY WE GO NOW?
I'LL GET OUT AND ASK!
GROCERY
Copr., 1948, Archie Comic Publications, Inc.
Dist. by McClure Newspaper Syndicate
IS THIS THE RIGHT WAY TO GO TO DARTBORD COLLEGE?
WEEKS & SMITH
WAL---YOU COULD TUCK YER SHIRT IN!
CREEPERS
MONTANA 1-8

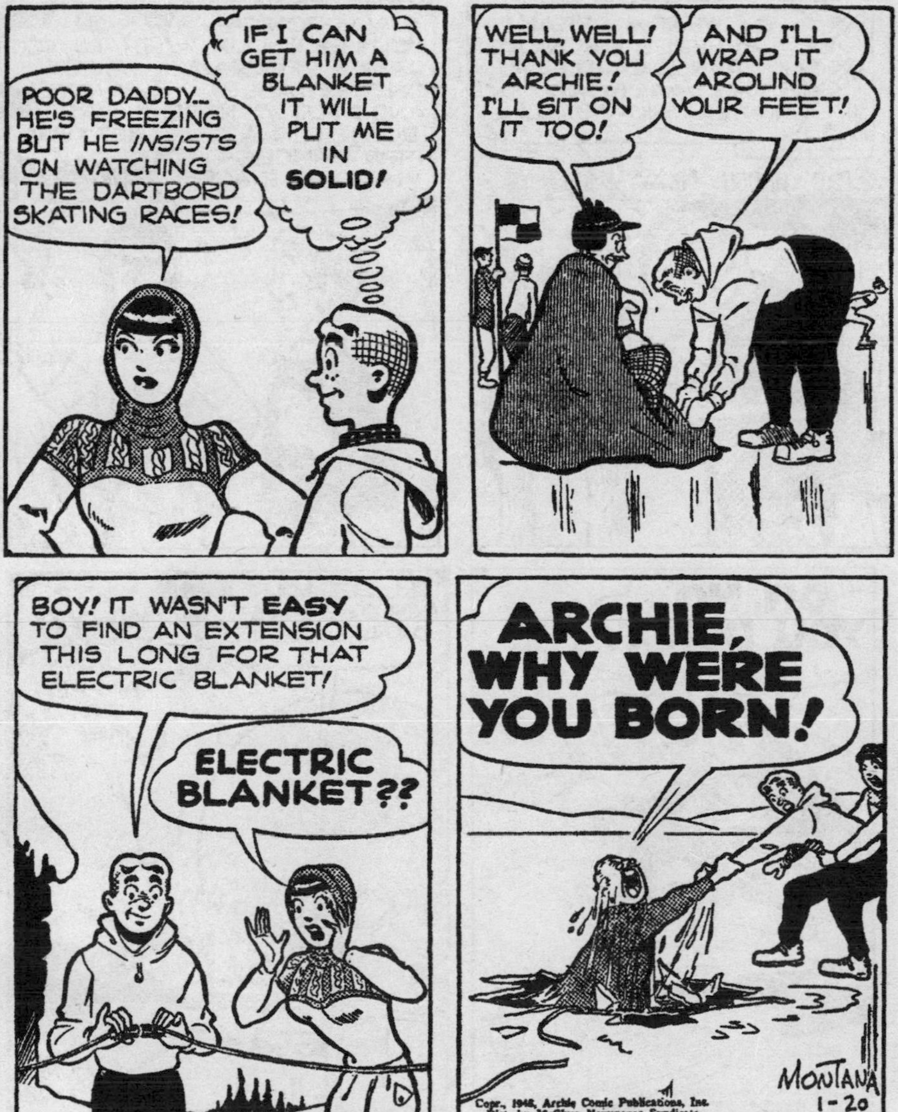
POOR DADDY... HE'S FREEZING BUT HE *INSISTS* ON WATCHING THE DARTBORD SKATING RACES!
IF I CAN GET HIM A BLANKET IT WILL PUT ME IN **SOLID!**
WELL, WELL! THANK YOU ARCHIE! I'LL SIT ON IT TOO!
AND I'LL WRAP IT AROUND YOUR FEET!
BOY! IT WASN'T **EASY** TO FIND AN EXTENSION THIS LONG FOR THAT ELECTRIC BLANKET!
ELECTRIC BLANKET??
ARCHIE, WHY WERE YOU BORN!
MONTANA
1-20
Copr., 1948, Archie Comic Publications, Inc.
Dist. by McClure Newspaper Syndicate

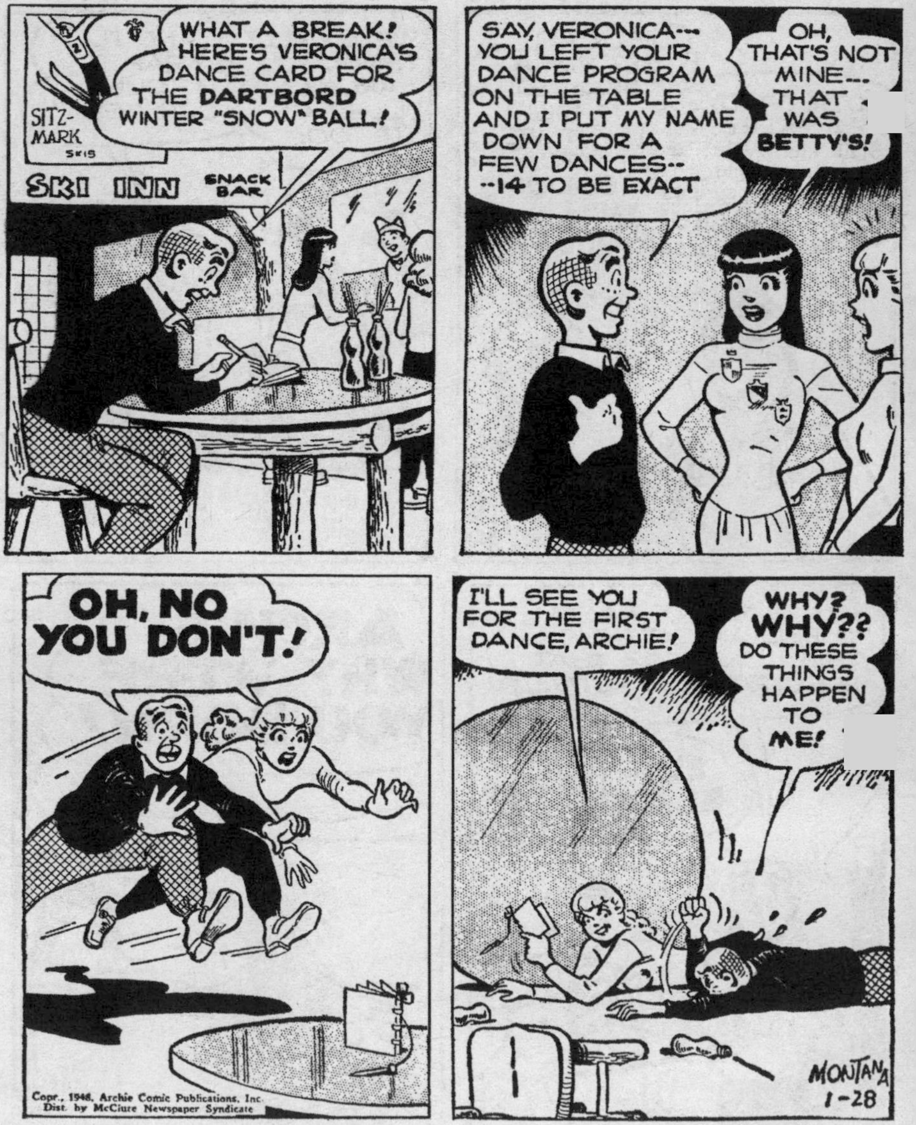
SITZ-MARK SKIS
WHAT A BREAK! HERE'S VERONICA'S DANCE CARD FOR THE DARTBORD WINTER "SNOW" BALL!
SKI INN
SNACK BAR
SAY, VERONICA--- YOU LEFT YOUR DANCE PROGRAM ON THE TABLE AND I PUT MY NAME DOWN FOR A FEW DANCES-- --14 TO BE EXACT
OH, THAT'S NOT MINE--- THAT WAS BETTY'S!
OH, NO YOU DON'T!
Copr., 1948, Archie Comic Publications, Inc. Dist. by McClure Newspaper Syndicate
I'LL SEE YOU FOR THE FIRST DANCE, ARCHIE!
WHY? WHY?? DO THESE THINGS HAPPEN TO ME!
MONTANA
1-28

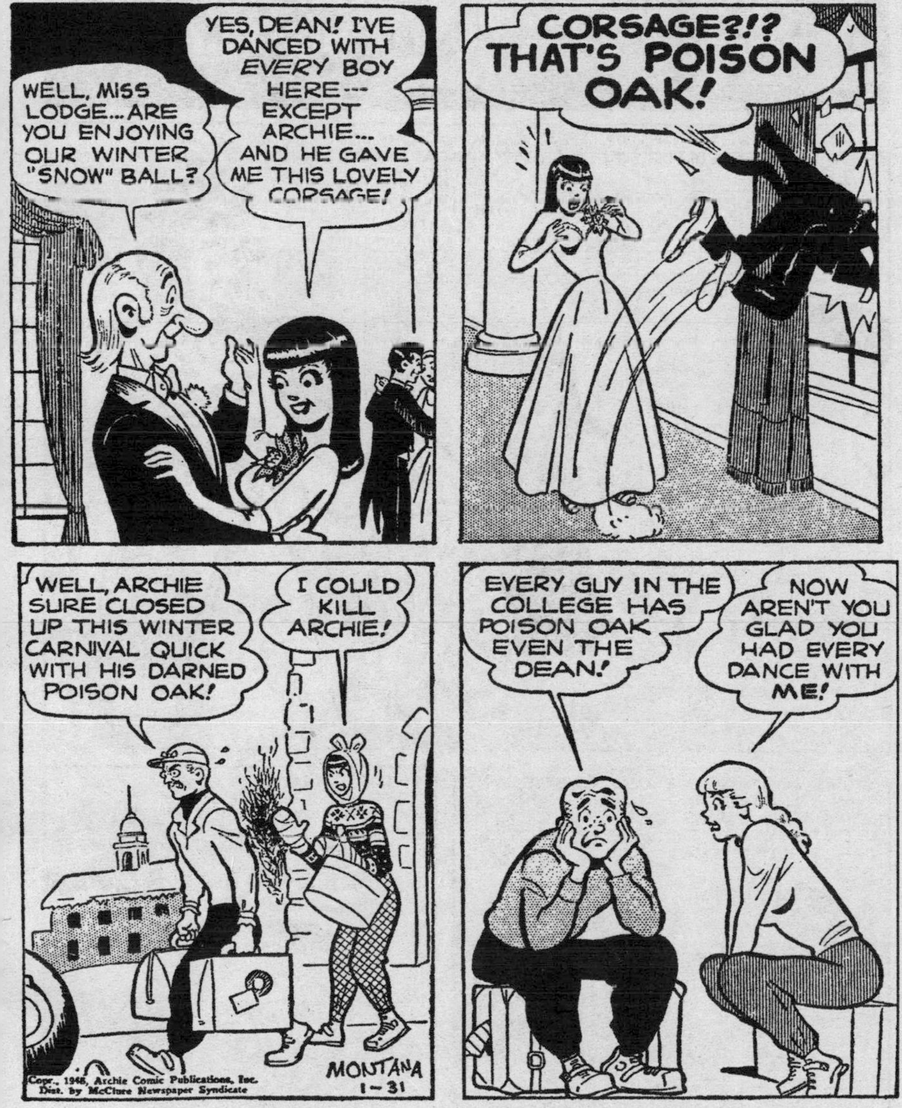
WELL, MISS LODGE...ARE YOU ENJOYING OUR WINTER "SNOW" BALL?
YES, DEAN! I'VE DANCED WITH EVERY BOY HERE--- EXCEPT ARCHIE... AND HE GAVE ME THIS LOVELY CORSAGE!
CORSAGE?!? THAT'S POISON OAK!
WELL, ARCHIE SURE CLOSED UP THIS WINTER CARNIVAL QUICK WITH HIS DARNED POISON OAK!
I COULD KILL ARCHIE!
MONTANA 1-31
Copr., 1946, Archie Comic Publications, Inc. Dist. by McClure Newspaper Syndicate
EVERY GUY IN THE COLLEGE HAS POISON OAK EVEN THE DEAN!
NOW AREN'T YOU GLAD YOU HAD EVERY DANCE WITH ME!

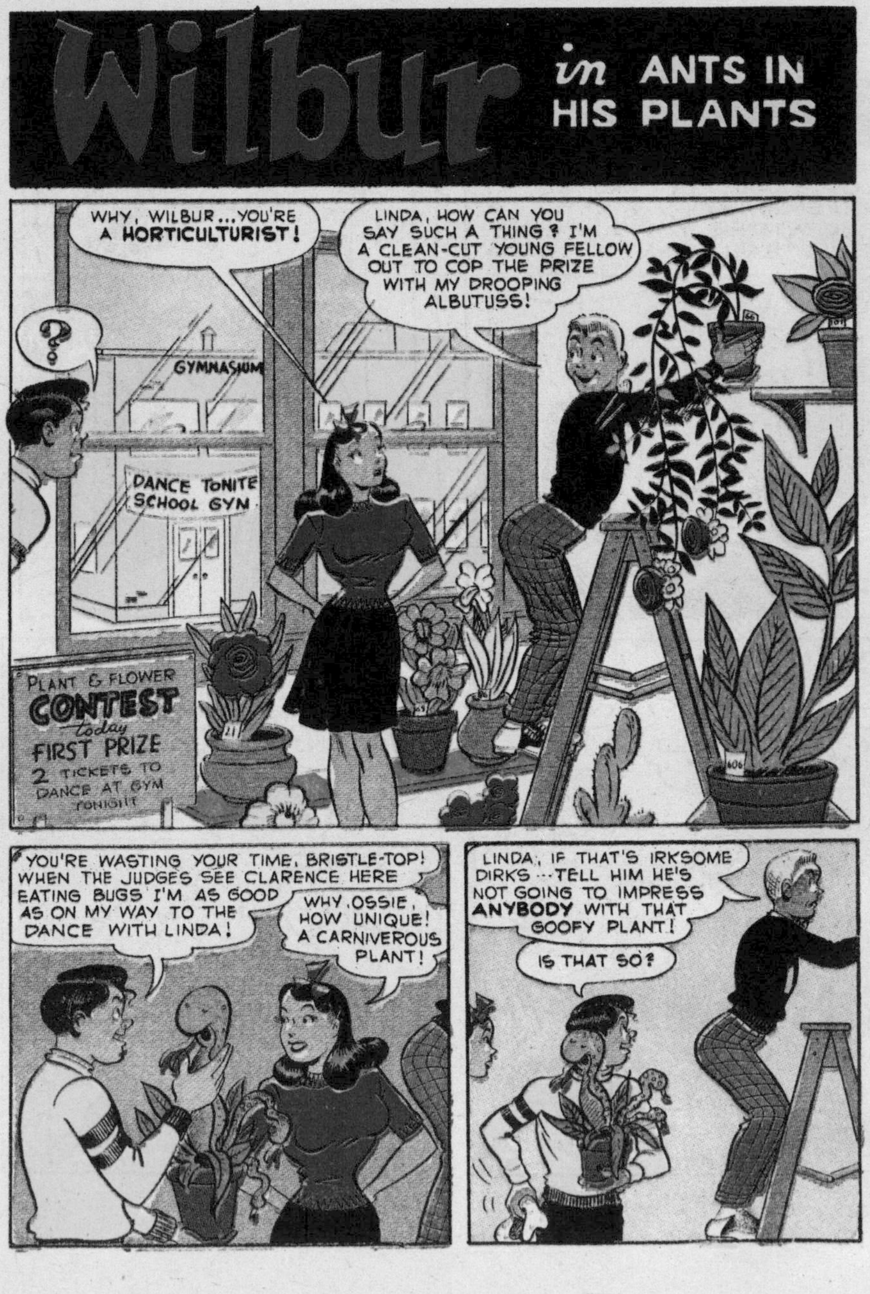
Wilbur in ANTS IN HIS PLANTS
WHY, WILBUR...YOU'RE A HORTICULTURIST!
LINDA, HOW CAN YOU SAY SUCH A THING? I'M A CLEAN-CUT YOUNG FELLOW OUT TO COP THE PRIZE WITH MY DROOPING ALBUTUSS!
?
GYMNASIUM
DANCE TONITE SCHOOL GYM
PLANT & FLOWER CONTEST today FIRST PRIZE 2 TICKETS TO DANCE AT GYM TONIGHT
YOU'RE WASTING YOUR TIME, BRISTLE-TOP! WHEN THE JUDGES SEE CLARENCE HERE EATING BUGS I'M AS GOOD AS ON MY WAY TO THE DANCE WITH LINDA!
WHY, OSSIE, HOW UNIQUE! A CARNIVEROUS PLANT!
LINDA, IF THAT'S IRKSOME DIRKS --- TELL HIM HE'S NOT GOING TO IMPRESS ANYBODY WITH THAT GOOFY PLANT!
IS THAT SO?

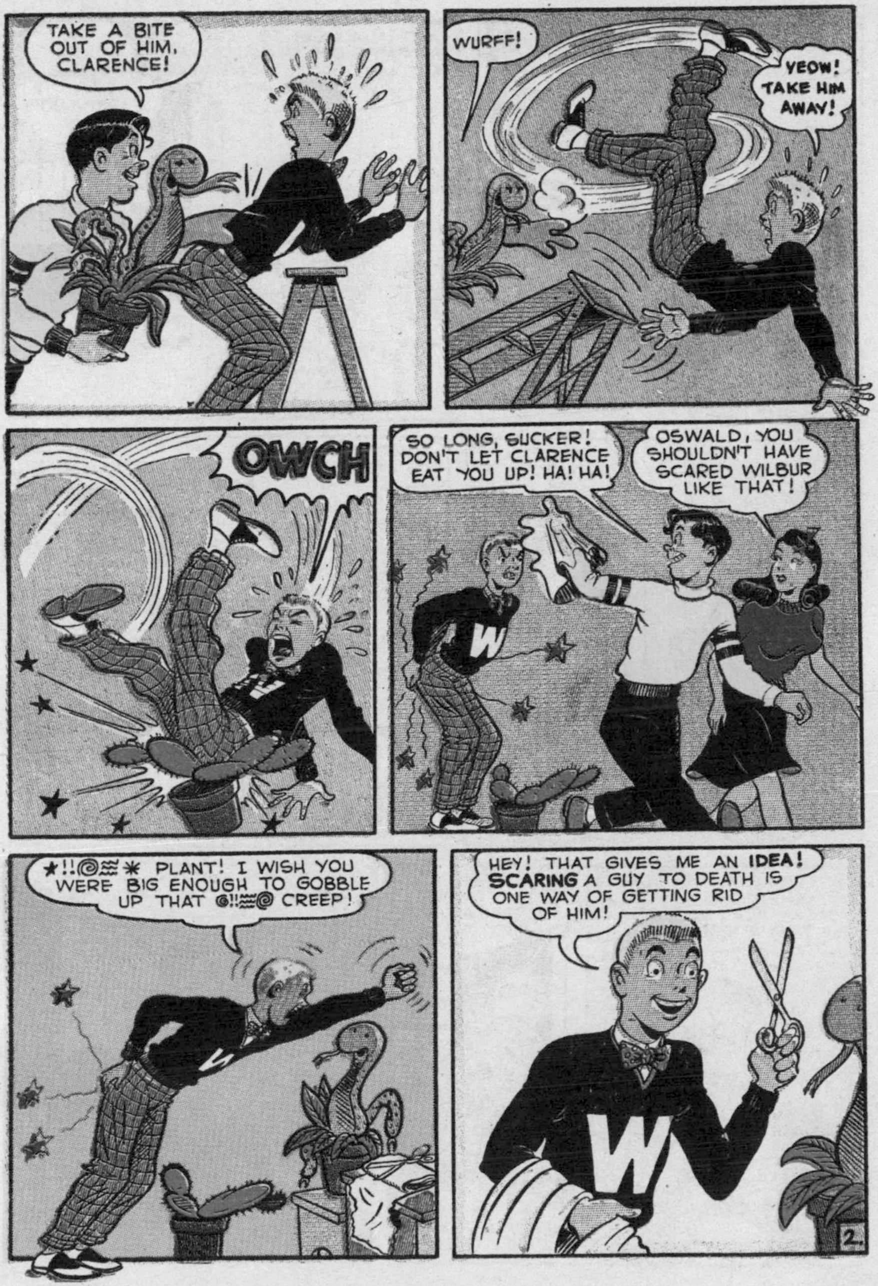
TAKE A BITE OUT OF HIM, CLARENCE!
WURFF!
YEOW! TAKE HIM AWAY!
OWCH
SO LONG, SUCKER! DON'T LET CLARENCE EAT YOU UP! HA! HA!
OSWALD, YOU SHOULDN'T HAVE SCARED WILBUR LIKE THAT!
★!!@≋✳ PLANT! I WISH YOU WERE BIG ENOUGH TO GOBBLE UP THAT @!!≋@ CREEP!
HEY! THAT GIVES ME AN IDEA! SCARING A GUY TO DEATH IS ONE WAY OF GETTING RID OF HIM!
2.

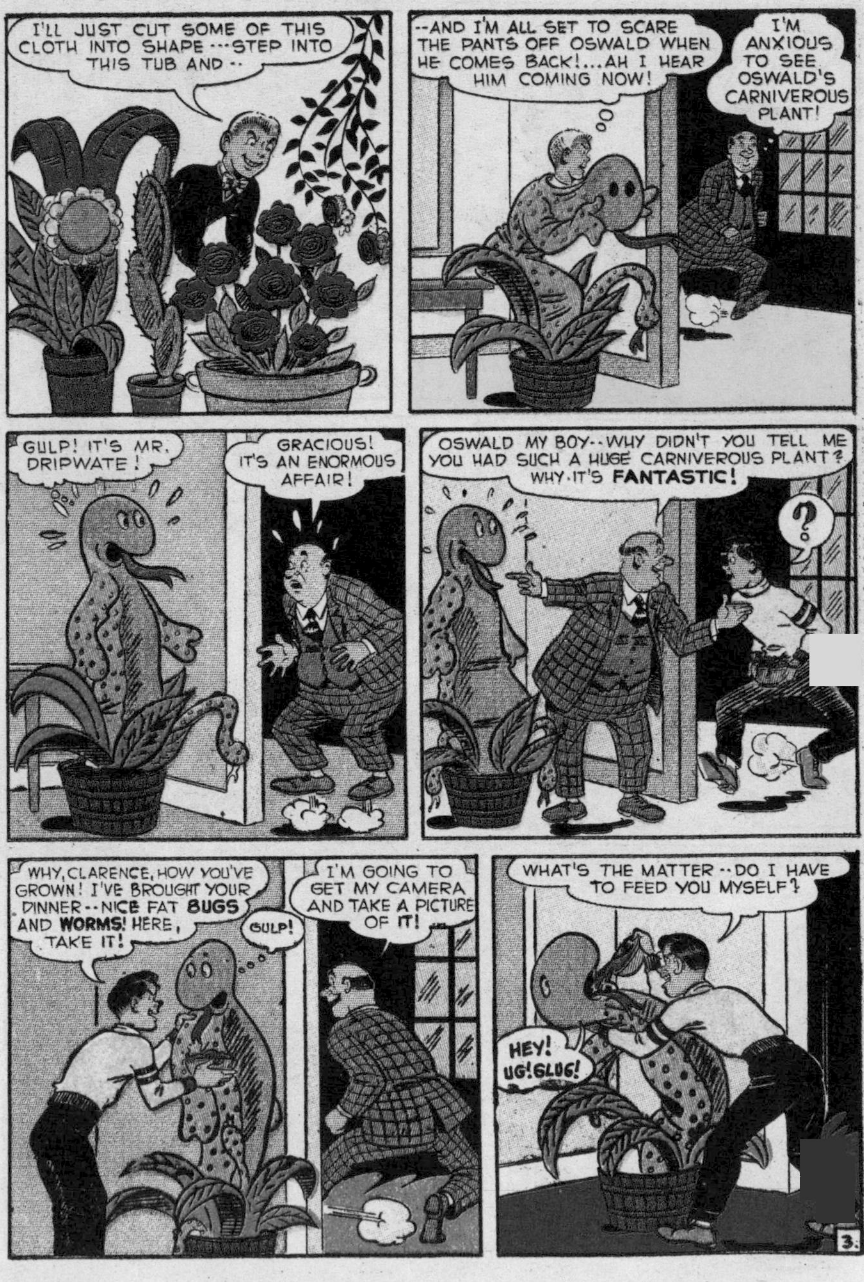
I'LL JUST CUT SOME OF THIS CLOTH INTO SHAPE ---STEP INTO THIS TUB AND --
--AND I'M ALL SET TO SCARE THE PANTS OFF OSWALD WHEN HE COMES BACK!...AH I HEAR HIM COMING NOW!
I'M ANXIOUS TO SEE OSWALD'S CARNIVEROUS PLANT!
GULP! IT'S MR. DRIPWATE!
GRACIOUS! IT'S AN ENORMOUS AFFAIR!
OSWALD MY BOY--WHY DIDN'T YOU TELL ME YOU HAD SUCH A HUGE CARNIVEROUS PLANT? WHY IT'S FANTASTIC!
?
WHY, CLARENCE, HOW YOU'VE GROWN! I'VE BROUGHT YOUR DINNER--NICE FAT BUGS AND WORMS! HERE, TAKE IT!
GULP!
I'M GOING TO GET MY CAMERA AND TAKE A PICTURE OF IT!
WHAT'S THE MATTER--DO I HAVE TO FEED YOU MYSELF?
HEY! UG! GLUG!
3.

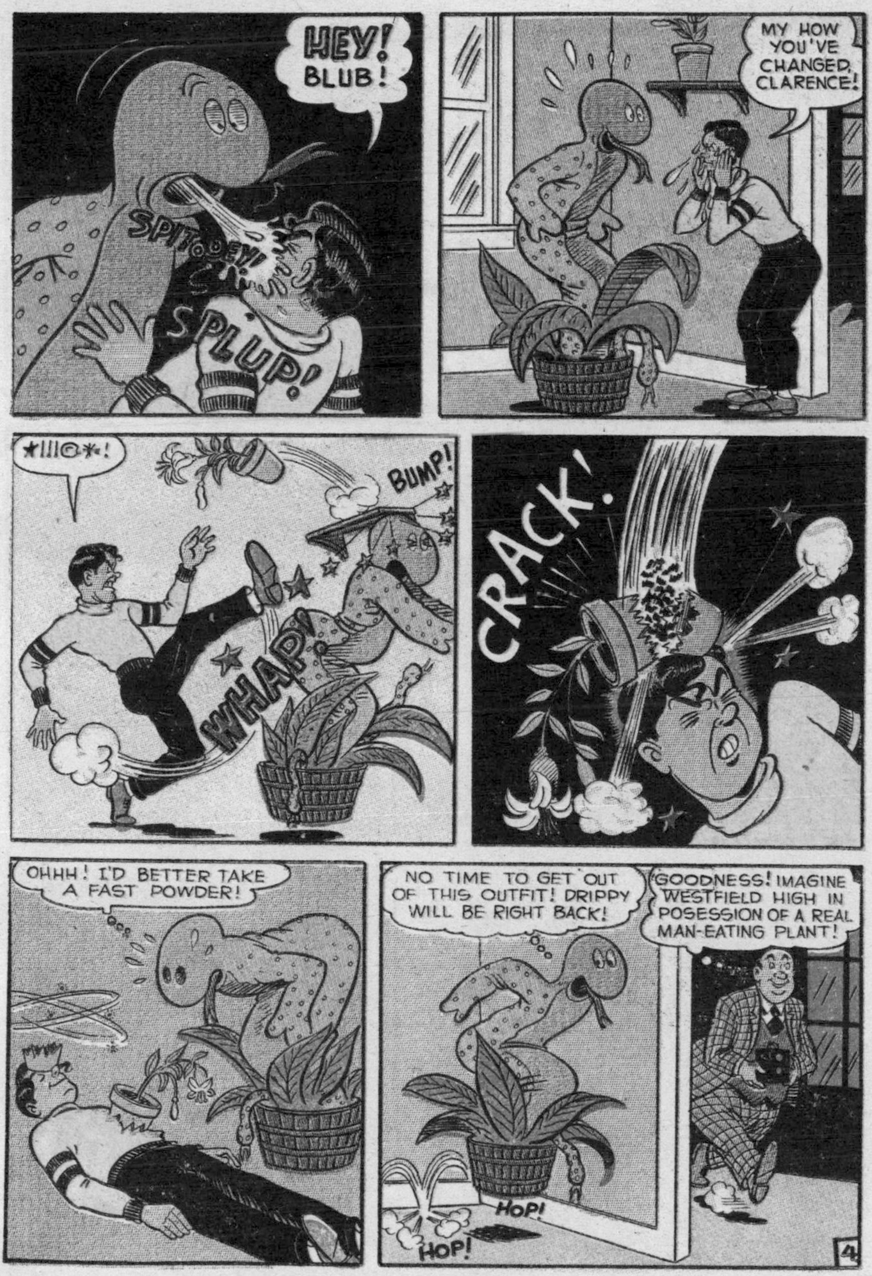
HEY! BLUB!
SPITOOEY!
SPLUP!
MY HOW YOU'VE CHANGED, CLARENCE!
BUMP!
WHAP!
CRACK!
OHHH! I'D BETTER TAKE A FAST POWDER!
NO TIME TO GET OUT OF THIS OUTFIT! DRIPPY WILL BE RIGHT BACK!
GOODNESS! IMAGINE WESTFIELD HIGH IN POSESSION OF A REAL MAN-EATING PLANT!
HOP!
HOP!
4

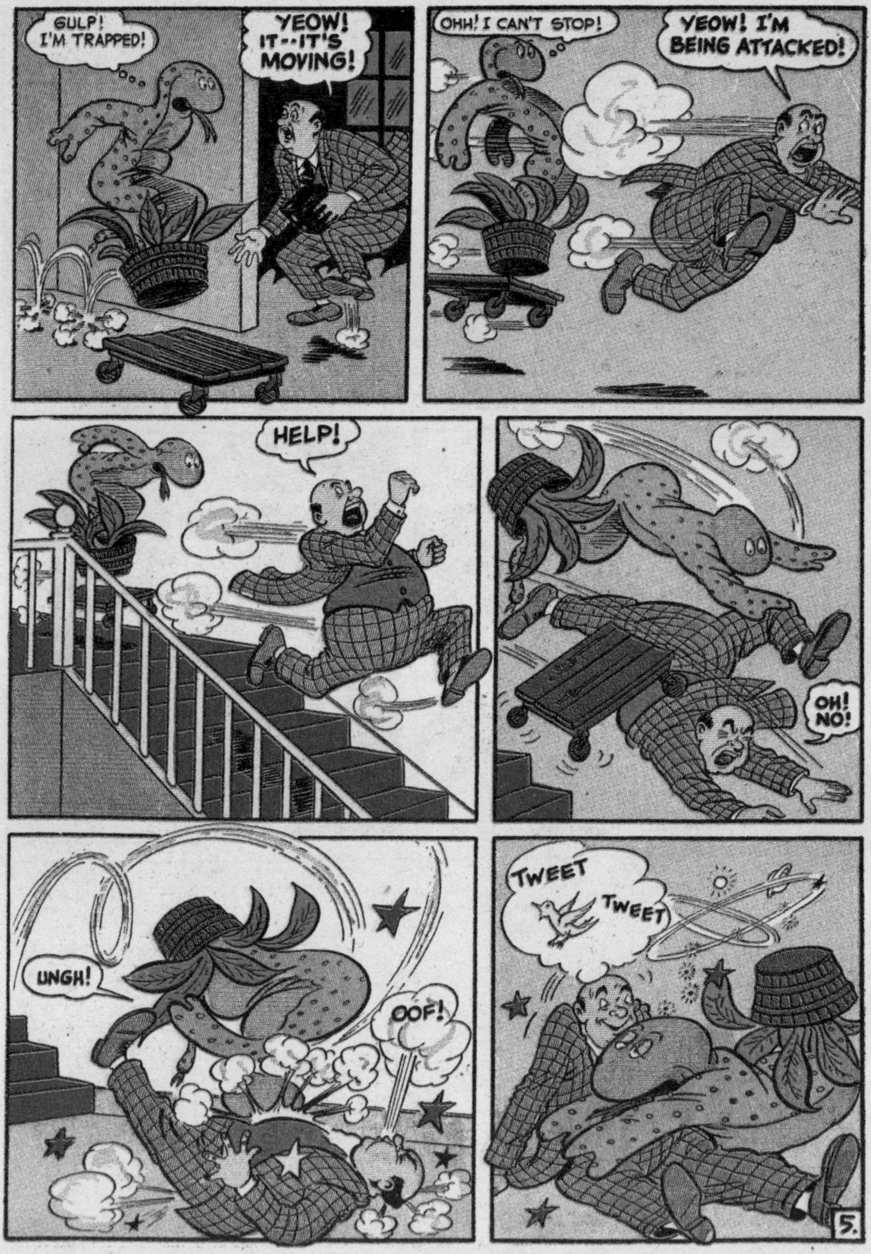
GULP! I'M TRAPPED!
YEOW! IT--IT'S MOVING!
OHH! I CAN'T STOP!
YEOW! I'M BEING ATTACKED!
HELP!
OH! NO!
UNGH!
OOF!
TWEET
TWEET
5.

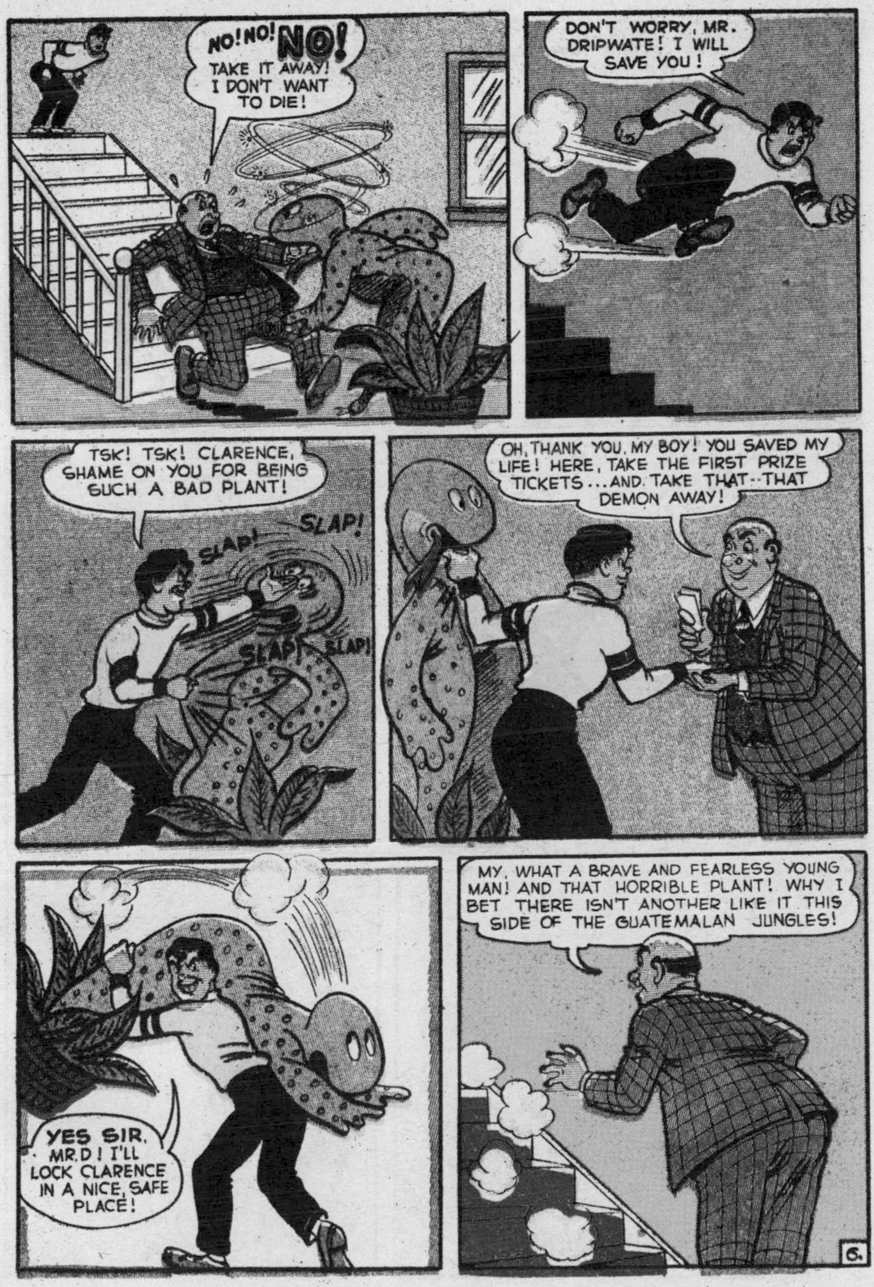
NO! NO! NO!
TAKE IT AWAY! I DON'T WANT TO DIE!
DON'T WORRY, MR. DRIPWATE! I WILL SAVE YOU!
TSK! TSK! CLARENCE, SHAME ON YOU FOR BEING SUCH A BAD PLANT!
SLAP! SLAP! SLAP! SLAP!
OH, THANK YOU, MY BOY! YOU SAVED MY LIFE! HERE, TAKE THE FIRST PRIZE TICKETS ... AND TAKE THAT--THAT DEMON AWAY!
YES SIR, MR. D! I'LL LOCK CLARENCE IN A NICE, SAFE PLACE!
MY, WHAT A BRAVE AND FEARLESS YOUNG MAN! AND THAT HORRIBLE PLANT! WHY I BET THERE ISN'T ANOTHER LIKE IT THIS SIDE OF THE GUATEMALAN JUNGLES!
6.

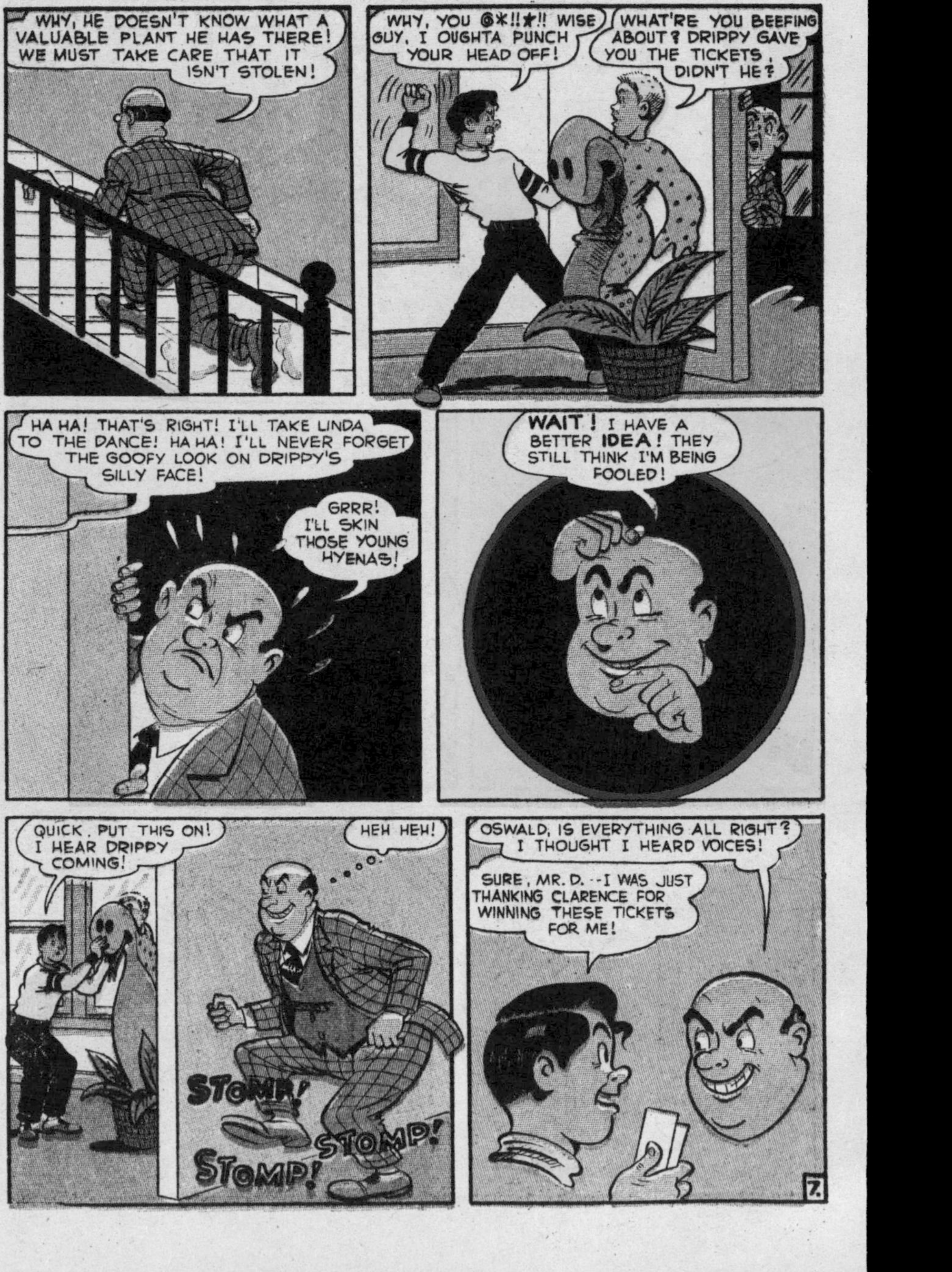
WHY, HE DOESN'T KNOW WHAT A VALUABLE PLANT HE HAS THERE! WE MUST TAKE CARE THAT IT ISN'T STOLEN!
WHY, YOU @*!!*!! WISE GUY, I OUGHTA PUNCH YOUR HEAD OFF!
WHAT'RE YOU BEEFING ABOUT? DRIPPY GAVE YOU THE TICKETS, DIDN'T HE?
HA HA! THAT'S RIGHT! I'LL TAKE LINDA TO THE DANCE! HA HA! I'LL NEVER FORGET THE GOOFY LOOK ON DRIPPY'S SILLY FACE!
GRRR! I'LL SKIN THOSE YOUNG HYENAS!
WAIT! I HAVE A BETTER IDEA! THEY STILL THINK I'M BEING FOOLED!
QUICK, PUT THIS ON! I HEAR DRIPPY COMING!
HEH HEH!
STOMP!
STOMP!
STOMP!
OSWALD, IS EVERYTHING ALL RIGHT? I THOUGHT I HEARD VOICES!
SURE, MR. D.--I WAS JUST THANKING CLARENCE FOR WINNING THESE TICKETS FOR ME!
7.

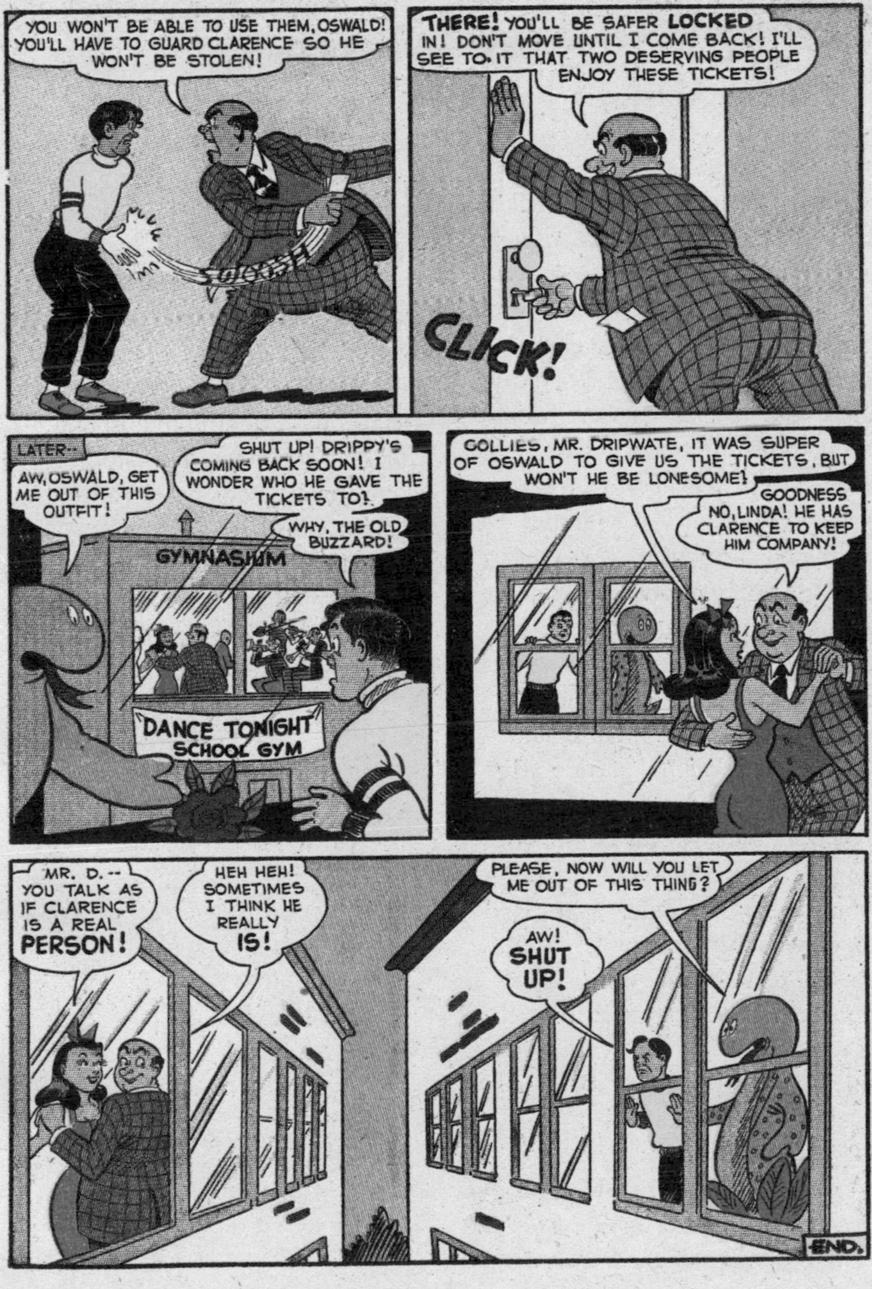
YOU WON'T BE ABLE TO USE THEM, OSWALD! YOU'LL HAVE TO GUARD CLARENCE SO HE WON'T BE STOLEN!
THERE! YOU'LL BE SAFER LOCKED IN! DON'T MOVE UNTIL I COME BACK! I'LL SEE TO IT THAT TWO DESERVING PEOPLE ENJOY THESE TICKETS!
CLICK!
LATER--
AW, OSWALD, GET ME OUT OF THIS OUTFIT!
SHUT UP! DRIPPY'S COMING BACK SOON! I WONDER WHO HE GAVE THE TICKETS TO?
WHY, THE OLD BUZZARD!
GYMNASIUM
DANCE TONIGHT SCHOOL GYM
GOLLIES, MR. DRIPWATE, IT WAS SUPER OF OSWALD TO GIVE US THE TICKETS, BUT WON'T HE BE LONESOME?
GOODNESS NO, LINDA! HE HAS CLARENCE TO KEEP HIM COMPANY!
MR. D.-- YOU TALK AS IF CLARENCE IS A REAL PERSON!
HEH HEH! SOMETIMES I THINK HE REALLY IS!
PLEASE, NOW WILL YOU LET ME OUT OF THIS THING?
AW! SHUT UP!
END.

The Egg
Super Duck #19, 1948
by Al Fagaly

In 1979 at the age of 13, I picked up a copy of *Little Archie Annual Digest #3*. A couple of reprinted stories by Al Fagaly featuring Super Duck, a feathered character crazier than Donald, grabbed my attention. The stories were rough around the edges and full of brash, reckless energy—perfect for a young kid enamored with the animated cartoons of Tex Avery. I later learned *Super Duck* ran an impressive 94 issues from 1945 to 1960. Although today few may know of him, in his heyday in the late Forties, Super Duck was hugely popular, particularly with teenage boys. It appears that *Donald Duck* was the comic your parents would buy you, but when you were a little older, *Super Duck* was the comic you bought for yourself. In this story, Supe attempts to use a rooster to coax a Tasmanian Flunkie hen to hurry up and lay him her annual egg. Mayhem ensues.

--Harold Buchholz
Executive Director of Publishing & Operations, Archie Comics

The Dangerous Sex
Jughead #1, 1949
by Samm Schwartz

The early look of Archie is so different from what most, myself included, think of as Archie. I admit, it didn't interest me because of the crude style. What a mistake! The early years of Archie are among some of the best and funniest in comics. This story is among my personal favorites in Archie history! It also shows why these are some of the best characters in comics, and why Jughead might be the greatest character ever!

--Mike Pellerito
President, Archie Comics

SUPER DUCK

THE COCKEYED WONDER

By AL Fagaly

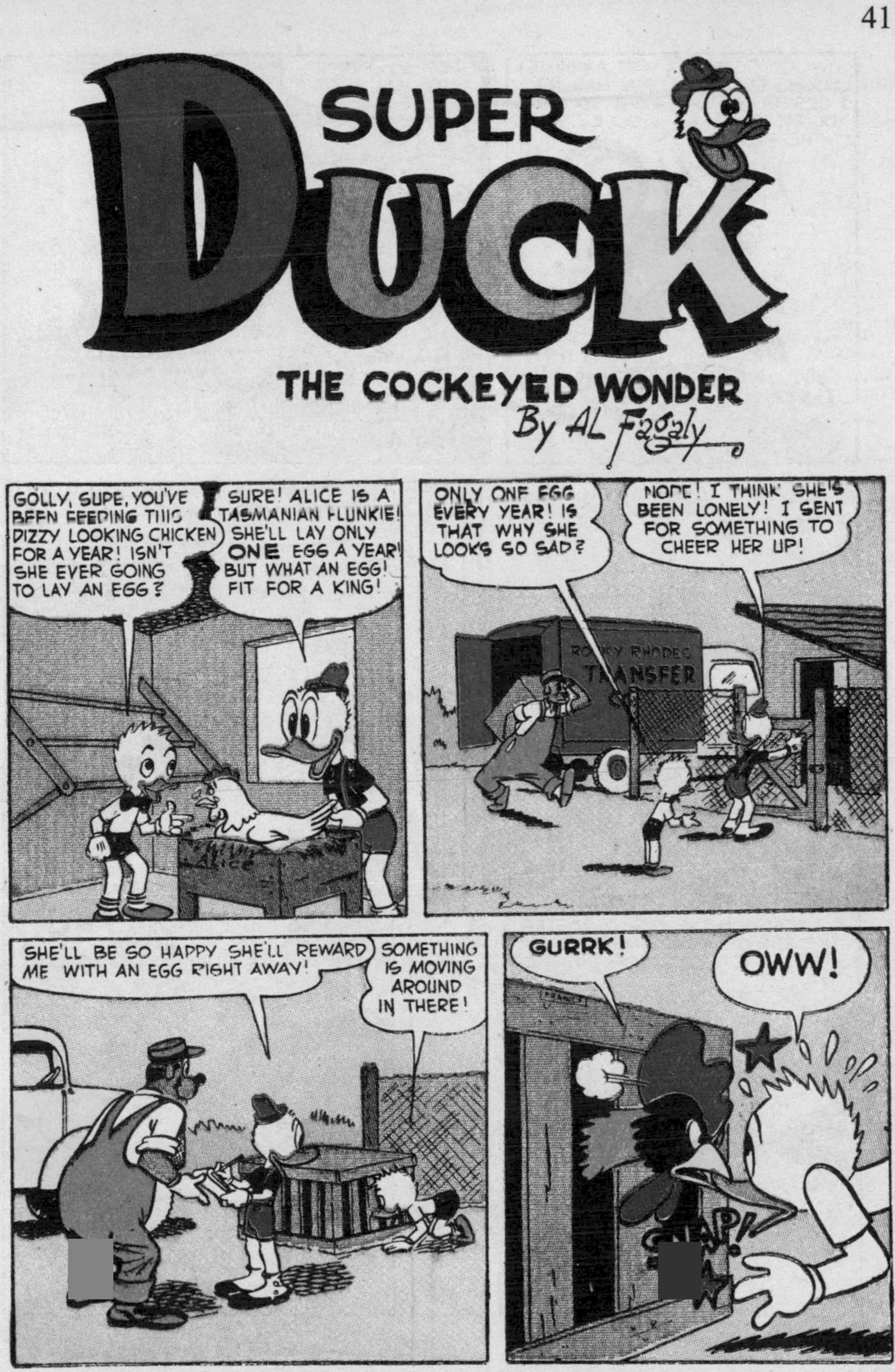
GOLLY, SUPE, YOU'VE BEEN FEEDING THIS DIZZY LOOKING CHICKEN FOR A YEAR! ISN'T SHE EVER GOING TO LAY AN EGG?
SURE! ALICE IS A TASMANIAN FLUNKIE! SHE'LL LAY ONLY ONE EGG A YEAR! BUT WHAT AN EGG! FIT FOR A KING!
ALICE
ONLY ONE EGG EVERY YEAR! IS THAT WHY SHE LOOKS SO SAD?
NOPE! I THINK SHE'S BEEN LONELY! I SENT FOR SOMETHING TO CHEER HER UP!
TRANSFER
SHE'LL BE SO HAPPY SHE'LL REWARD ME WITH AN EGG RIGHT AWAY!
SOMETHING IS MOVING AROUND IN THERE!
GURRK!
OWW!

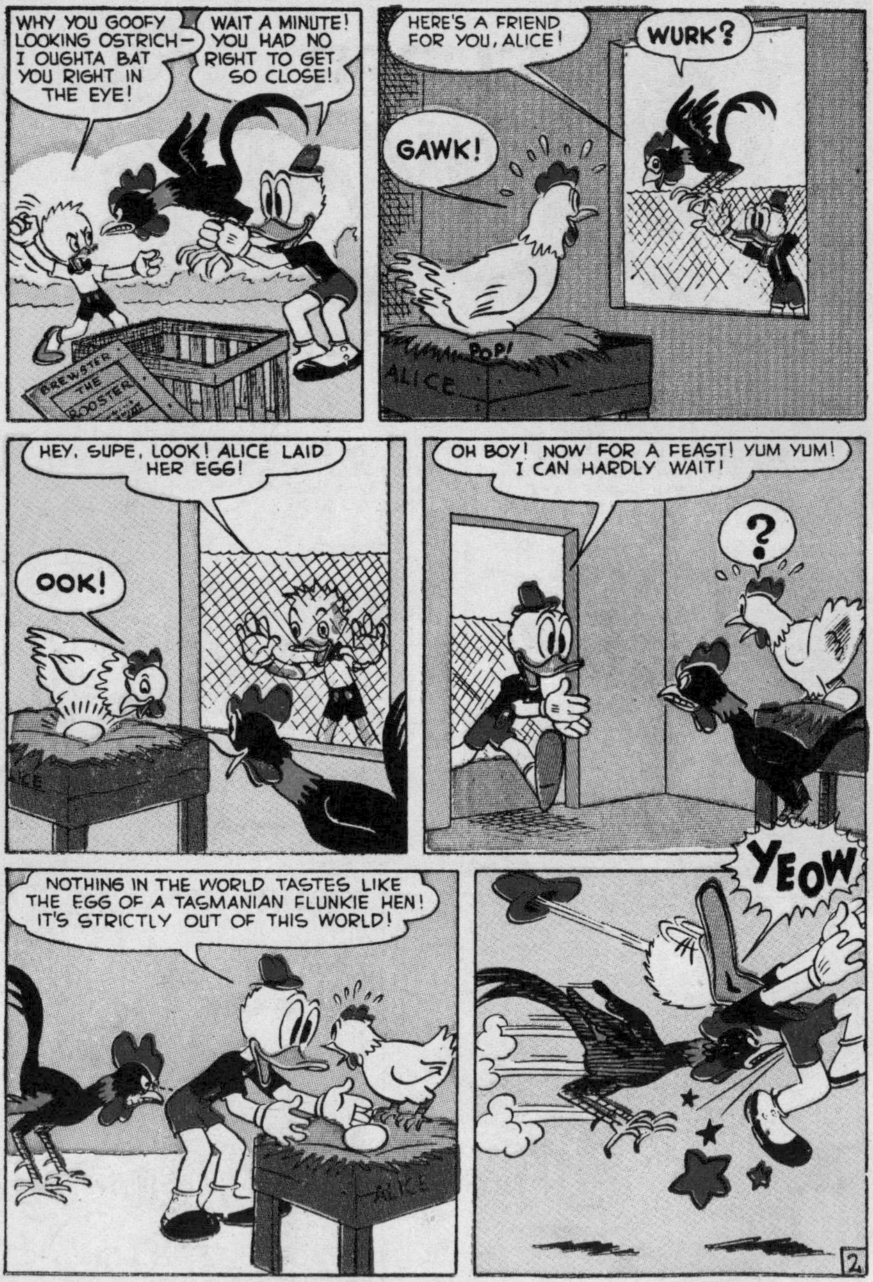
WHY YOU GOOFY LOOKING OSTRICH— I OUGHTA BAT YOU RIGHT IN THE EYE!
WAIT A MINUTE! YOU HAD NO RIGHT TO GET SO CLOSE!
BREWSTER THE ROOSTER
HERE'S A FRIEND FOR YOU, ALICE!
WURK?
GAWK!
POP!
ALICE
HEY, SUPE, LOOK! ALICE LAID HER EGG!
OOK!
OH BOY! NOW FOR A FEAST! YUM YUM! I CAN HARDLY WAIT!
?
NOTHING IN THE WORLD TASTES LIKE THE EGG OF A TASMANIAN FLUNKIE HEN! IT'S STRICTLY OUT OF THIS WORLD!
ALICE
YEOW
2

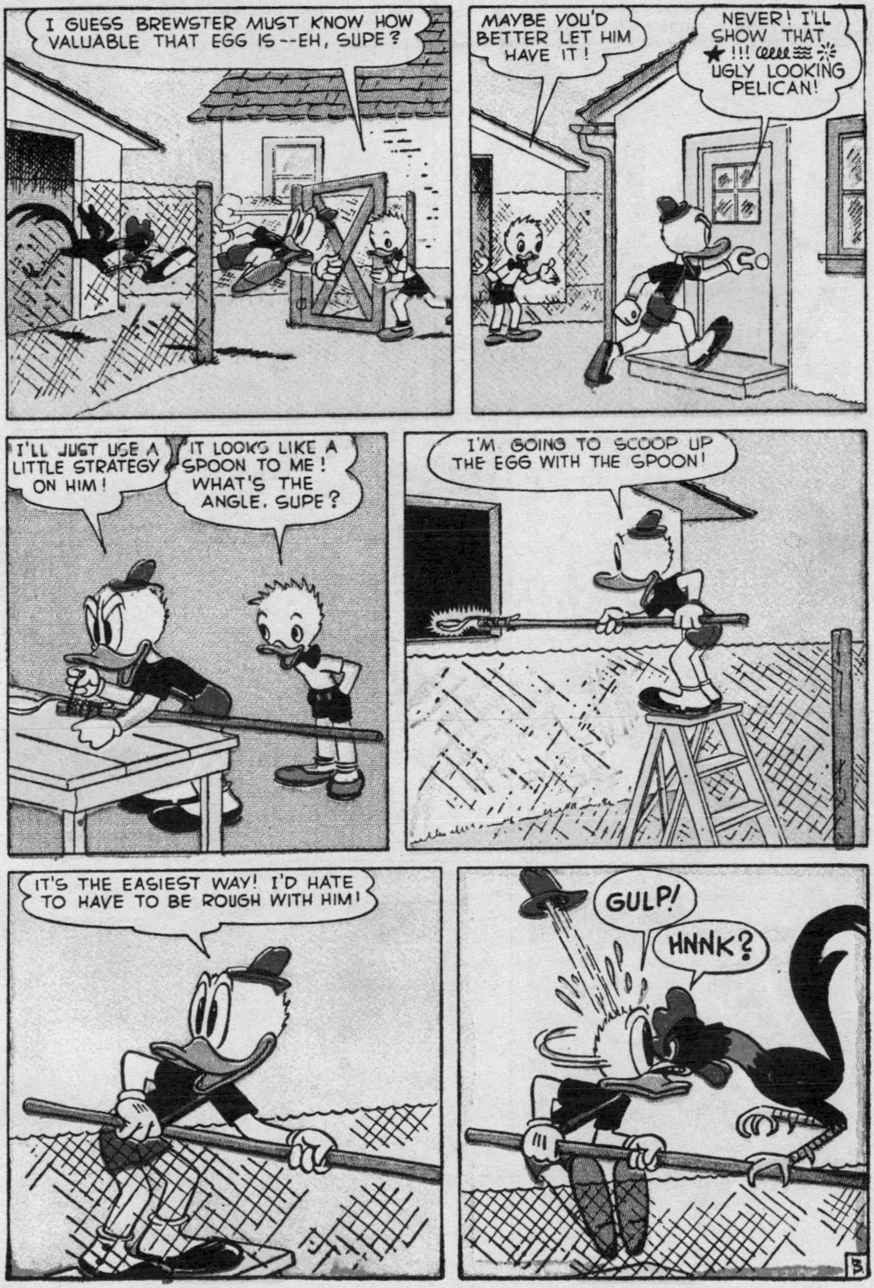
I GUESS BREWSTER MUST KNOW HOW VALUABLE THAT EGG IS--EH, SUPE?
MAYBE YOU'D BETTER LET HIM HAVE IT!
NEVER! I'LL SHOW THAT ★!!! ꞓℓℓℓ≋ ҉ UGLY LOOKING PELICAN!
I'LL JUST USE A LITTLE STRATEGY ON HIM!
IT LOOKS LIKE A SPOON TO ME! WHAT'S THE ANGLE, SUPE?
I'M GOING TO SCOOP UP THE EGG WITH THE SPOON!
IT'S THE EASIEST WAY! I'D HATE TO HAVE TO BE ROUGH WITH HIM!
GULP!
HNNK?

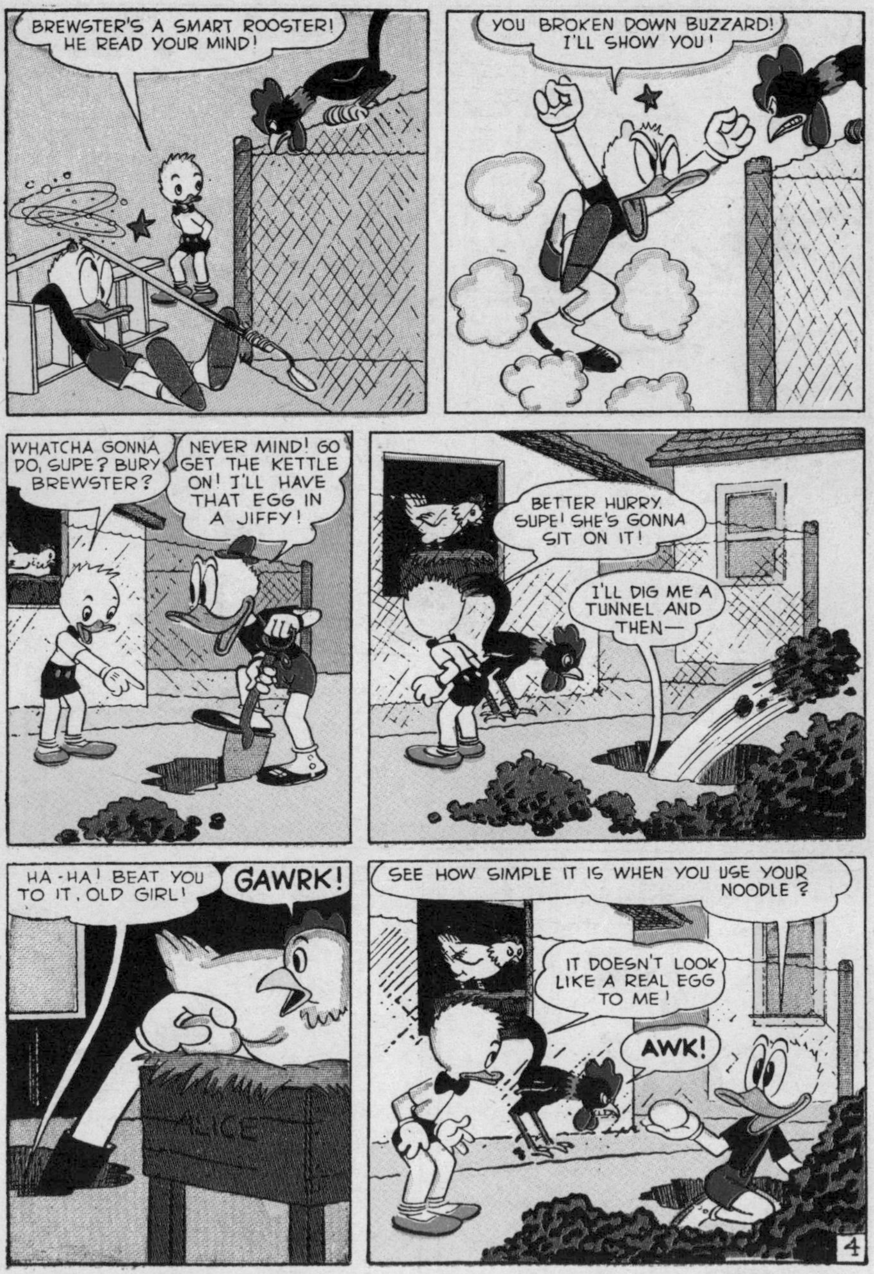
BREWSTER'S A SMART ROOSTER! HE READ YOUR MIND!
YOU BROKEN DOWN BUZZARD! I'LL SHOW YOU!
WHATCHA GONNA DO, SUPE? BURY BREWSTER?
NEVER MIND! GO GET THE KETTLE ON! I'LL HAVE THAT EGG IN A JIFFY!
BETTER HURRY, SUPE! SHE'S GONNA SIT ON IT!
I'LL DIG ME A TUNNEL AND THEN—
HA-HA! BEAT YOU TO IT, OLD GIRL!
GAWRK!
ALICE
SEE HOW SIMPLE IT IS WHEN YOU USE YOUR NOODLE?
IT DOESN'T LOOK LIKE A REAL EGG TO ME!
AWK!
4

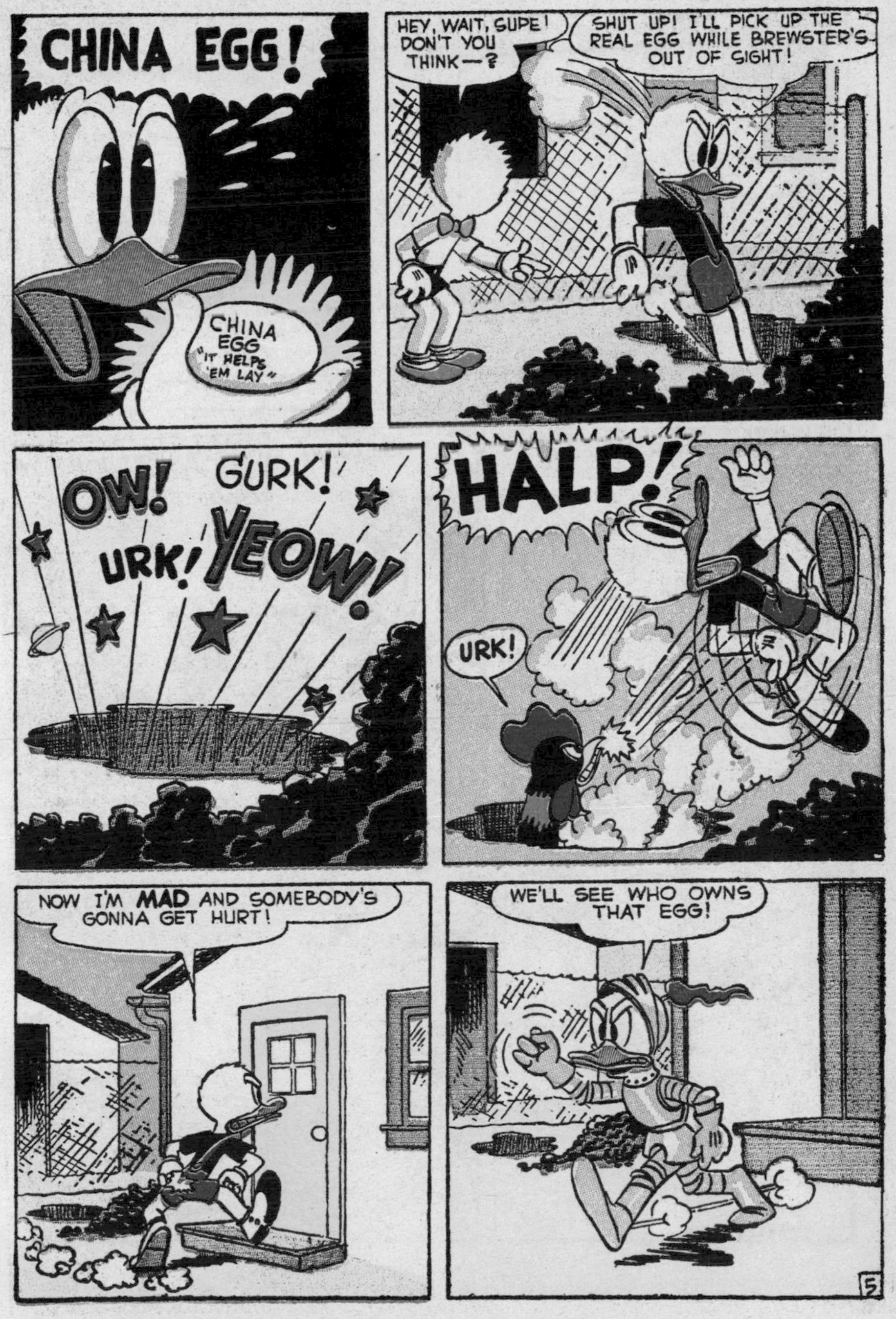
CHINA EGG!
CHINA EGG "IT HELPS 'EM LAY"
HEY, WAIT, SUPE! DON'T YOU THINK—?
SHUT UP! I'LL PICK UP THE REAL EGG WHILE BREWSTER'S OUT OF SIGHT!
OW!
GURK!
URK!
YEOW!
HALP!
URK!
NOW I'M MAD AND SOMEBODY'S GONNA GET HURT!
WE'LL SEE WHO OWNS THAT EGG!
5

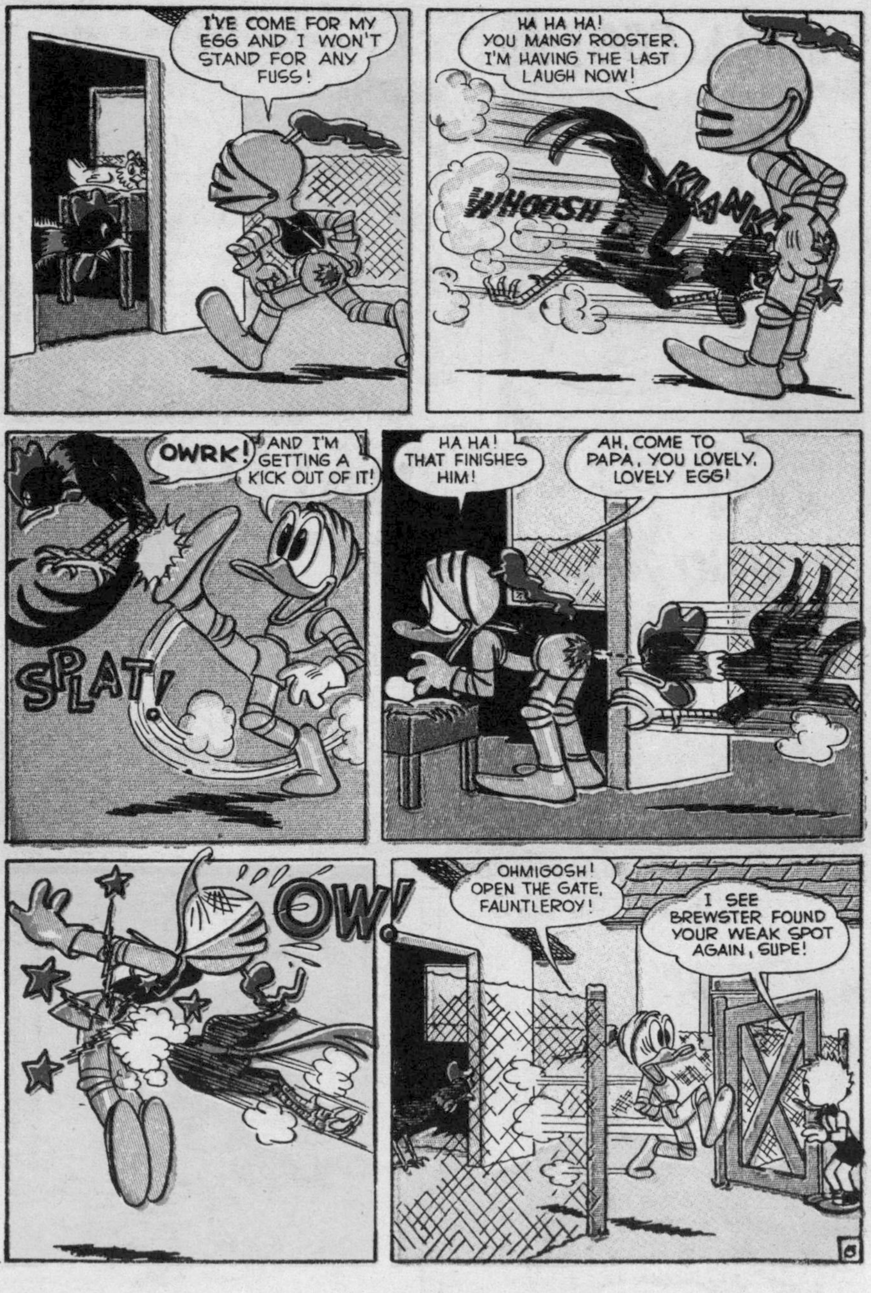
I'VE COME FOR MY EGG AND I WON'T STAND FOR ANY FUSS!
HA HA HA! YOU MANGY ROOSTER. I'M HAVING THE LAST LAUGH NOW!
WHOOSH
KLANK!
OWRK!
AND I'M GETTING A KICK OUT OF IT!
SPLAT!
HA HA! THAT FINISHES HIM!
AH, COME TO PAPA, YOU LOVELY, LOVELY EGG!
OW!
OHMIGOSH! OPEN THE GATE, FAUNTLEROY!
I SEE BREWSTER FOUND YOUR WEAK SPOT AGAIN, SUPE!

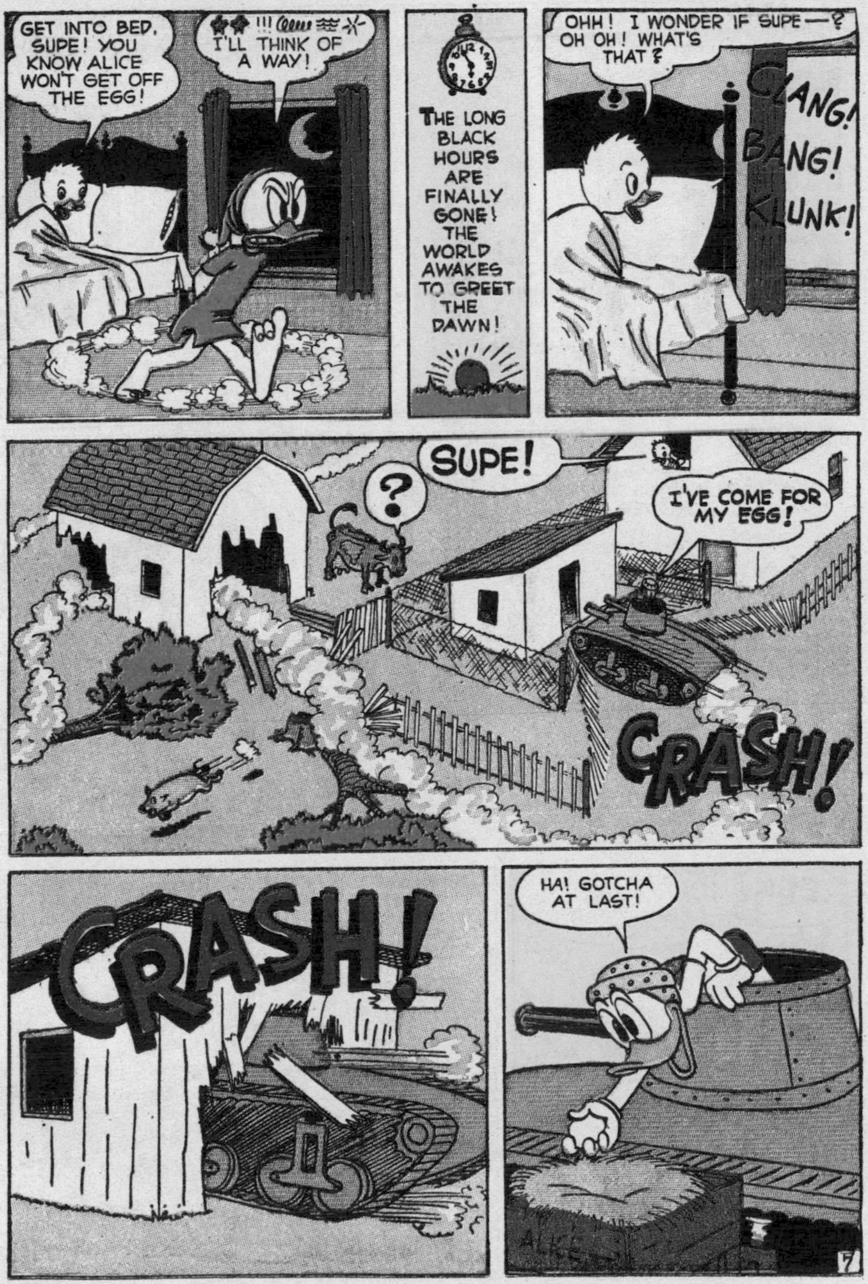
GET INTO BED, SUPE! YOU KNOW ALICE WON'T GET OFF THE EGG!
!!! I'LL THINK OF A WAY!
THE LONG BLACK HOURS ARE FINALLY GONE! THE WORLD AWAKES TO GREET THE DAWN!
OHH! I WONDER IF SUPE—? OH OH! WHAT'S THAT?
CLANG! BANG! KLUNK!
SUPE!
?
I'VE COME FOR MY EGG!
CRASH!
CRASH!
HA! GOTCHA AT LAST!
7

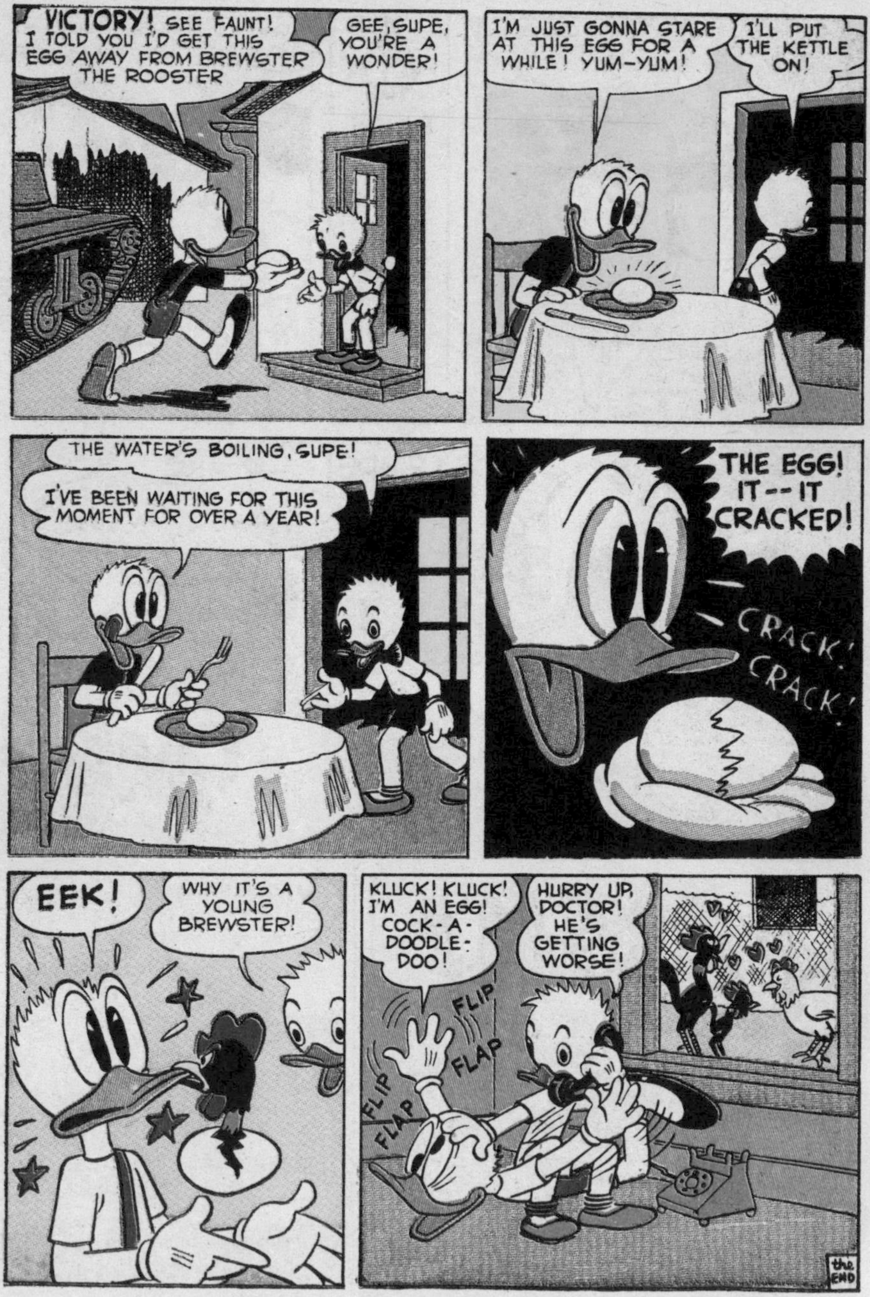
VICTORY! SEE FAUNT! I TOLD YOU I'D GET THIS EGG AWAY FROM BREWSTER THE ROOSTER
GEE, SUPE, YOU'RE A WONDER!
I'M JUST GONNA STARE AT THIS EGG FOR A WHILE! YUM-YUM!
I'LL PUT THE KETTLE ON!
THE WATER'S BOILING, SUPE!
I'VE BEEN WAITING FOR THIS MOMENT FOR OVER A YEAR!
THE EGG! IT--IT CRACKED!
CRACK! CRACK!
EEK!
WHY IT'S A YOUNG BREWSTER!
KLUCK! KLUCK! I'M AN EGG! COCK-A-DOODLE-DOO!
HURRY UP, DOCTOR! HE'S GETTING WORSE!
FLIP FLAP FLIP FLAP
the END

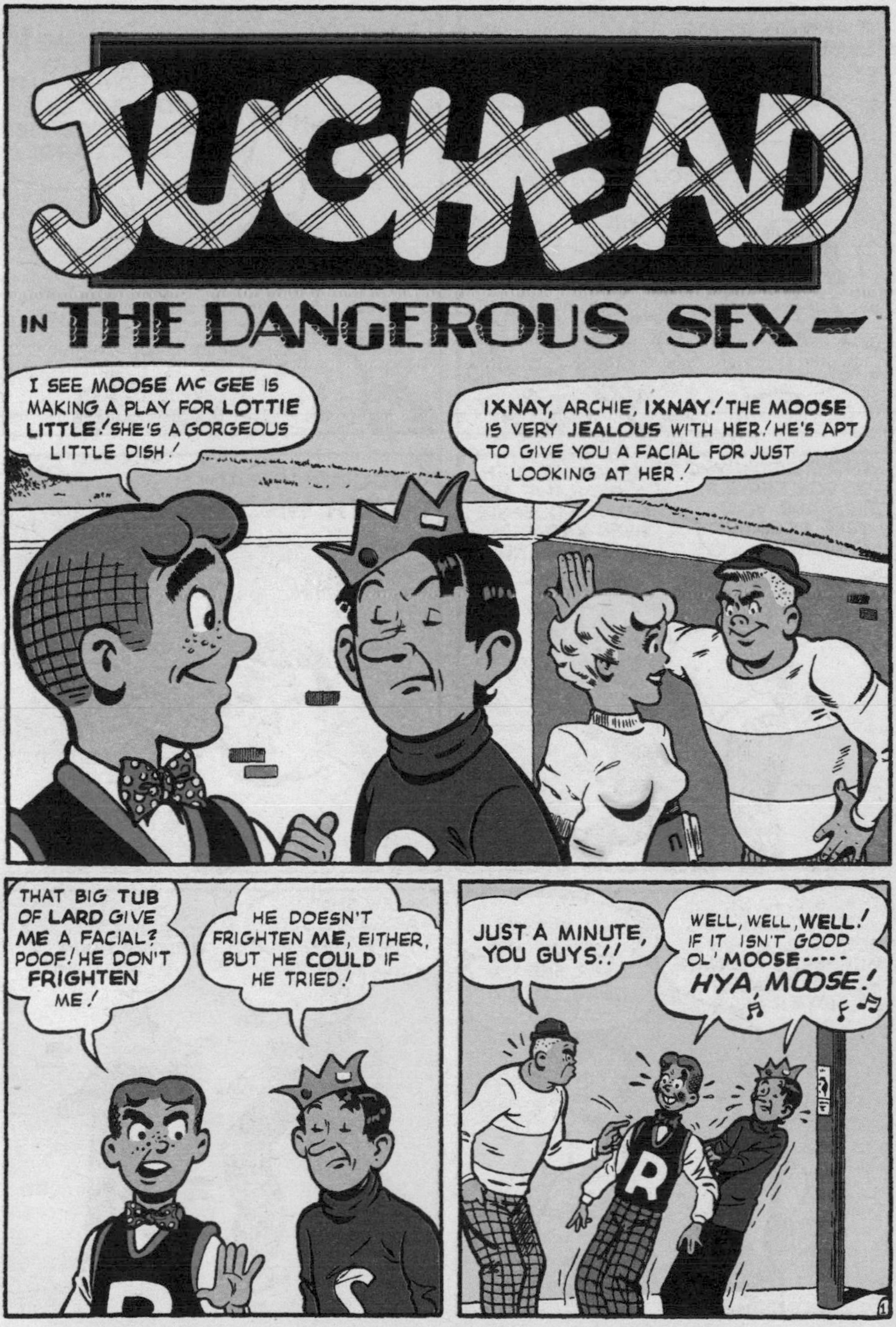
JUGHEAD
IN THE DANGEROUS SEX –
I SEE MOOSE Mc GEE IS MAKING A PLAY FOR LOTTIE LITTLE! SHE'S A GORGEOUS LITTLE DISH!
IXNAY, ARCHIE, IXNAY! THE MOOSE IS VERY JEALOUS WITH HER! HE'S APT TO GIVE YOU A FACIAL FOR JUST LOOKING AT HER!
THAT BIG TUB OF LARD GIVE ME A FACIAL? POOF! HE DON'T FRIGHTEN ME!
HE DOESN'T FRIGHTEN ME, EITHER, BUT HE COULD IF HE TRIED!
JUST A MINUTE, YOU GUYS!!
WELL, WELL, WELL! IF IT ISN'T GOOD OL' MOOSE----- HYA, MOOSE!

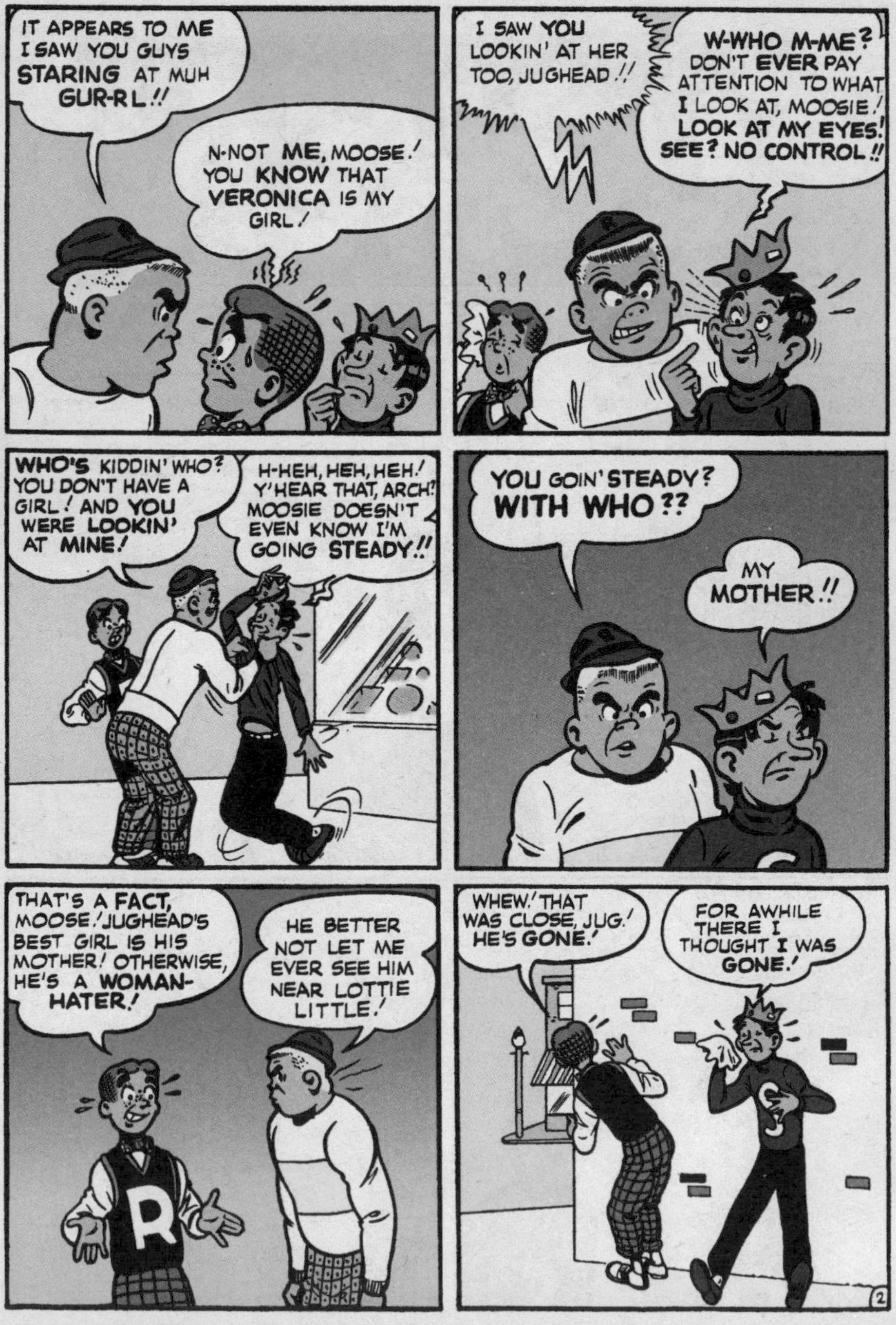
IT APPEARS TO ME I SAW YOU GUYS STARING AT MUH GUR-RL!!
N-NOT ME, MOOSE! YOU KNOW THAT VERONICA IS MY GIRL!
I SAW YOU LOOKIN' AT HER TOO, JUGHEAD!!
W-WHO M-ME? DON'T EVER PAY ATTENTION TO WHAT I LOOK AT, MOOSIE! LOOK AT MY EYES! SEE? NO CONTROL!!
WHO'S KIDDIN' WHO? YOU DON'T HAVE A GIRL! AND YOU WERE LOOKIN' AT MINE!
H-HEH, HEH, HEH! Y'HEAR THAT, ARCH? MOOSIE DOESN'T EVEN KNOW I'M GOING STEADY!!
YOU GOIN' STEADY? WITH WHO??
MY MOTHER!!
THAT'S A FACT, MOOSE! JUGHEAD'S BEST GIRL IS HIS MOTHER! OTHERWISE, HE'S A WOMAN-HATER!
HE BETTER NOT LET ME EVER SEE HIM NEAR LOTTIE LITTLE!
WHEW! THAT WAS CLOSE, JUG! HE'S GONE!
FOR AWHILE THERE I THOUGHT I WAS GONE!
2

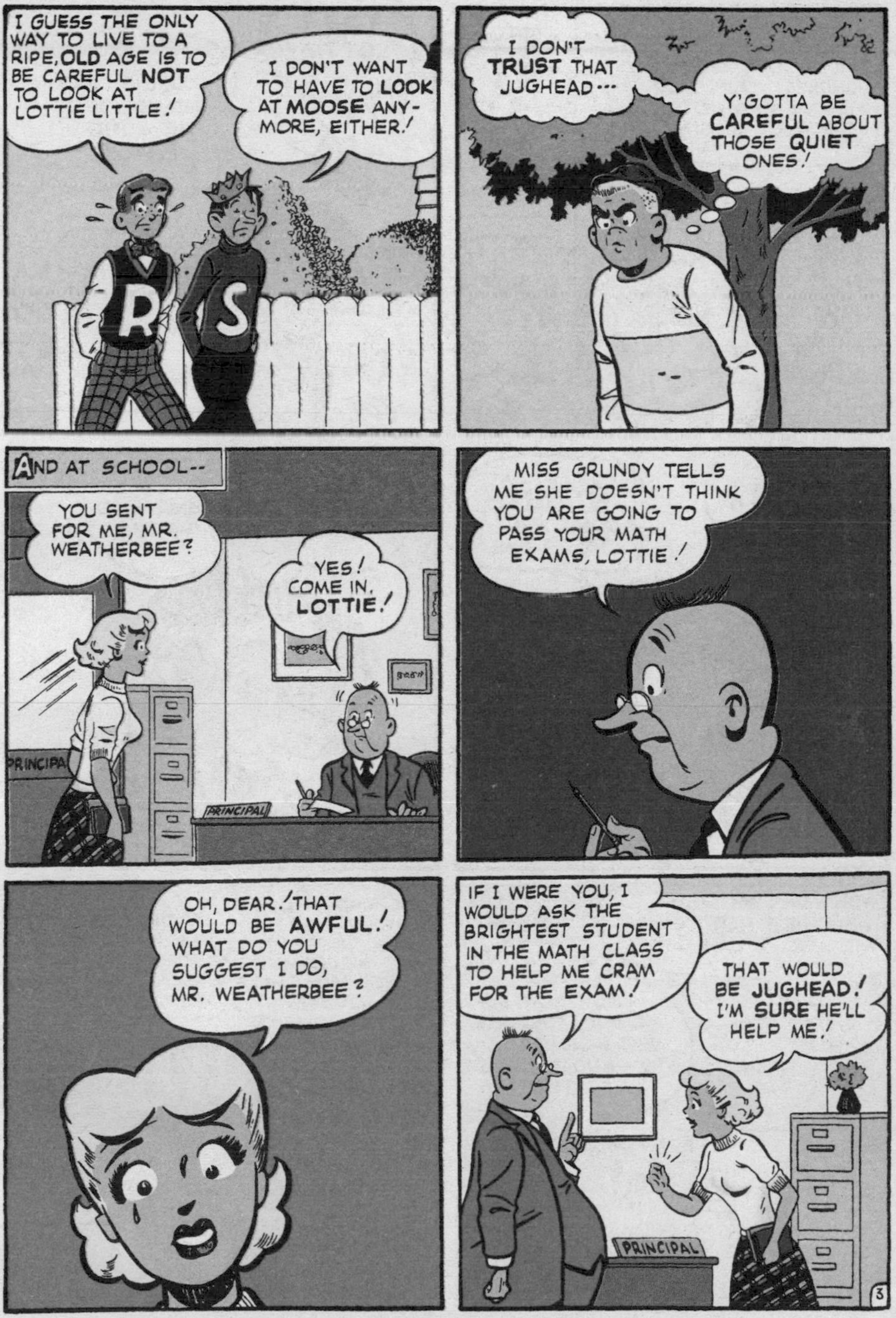
I GUESS THE ONLY WAY TO LIVE TO A RIPE, OLD AGE IS TO BE CAREFUL NOT TO LOOK AT LOTTIE LITTLE!
I DON'T WANT TO HAVE TO LOOK AT MOOSE ANY-MORE, EITHER!
R
S
I DON'T TRUST THAT JUGHEAD---
Y'GOTTA BE CAREFUL ABOUT THOSE QUIET ONES!
AND AT SCHOOL--
YOU SENT FOR ME, MR. WEATHERBEE?
YES! COME IN, LOTTIE!
PRINCIPA
PRINCIPAL
MISS GRUNDY TELLS ME SHE DOESN'T THINK YOU ARE GOING TO PASS YOUR MATH EXAMS, LOTTIE!
OH, DEAR! THAT WOULD BE AWFUL! WHAT DO YOU SUGGEST I DO, MR. WEATHERBEE?
IF I WERE YOU, I WOULD ASK THE BRIGHTEST STUDENT IN THE MATH CLASS TO HELP ME CRAM FOR THE EXAM!
THAT WOULD BE JUGHEAD! I'M SURE HE'LL HELP ME!
PRINCIPAL
3

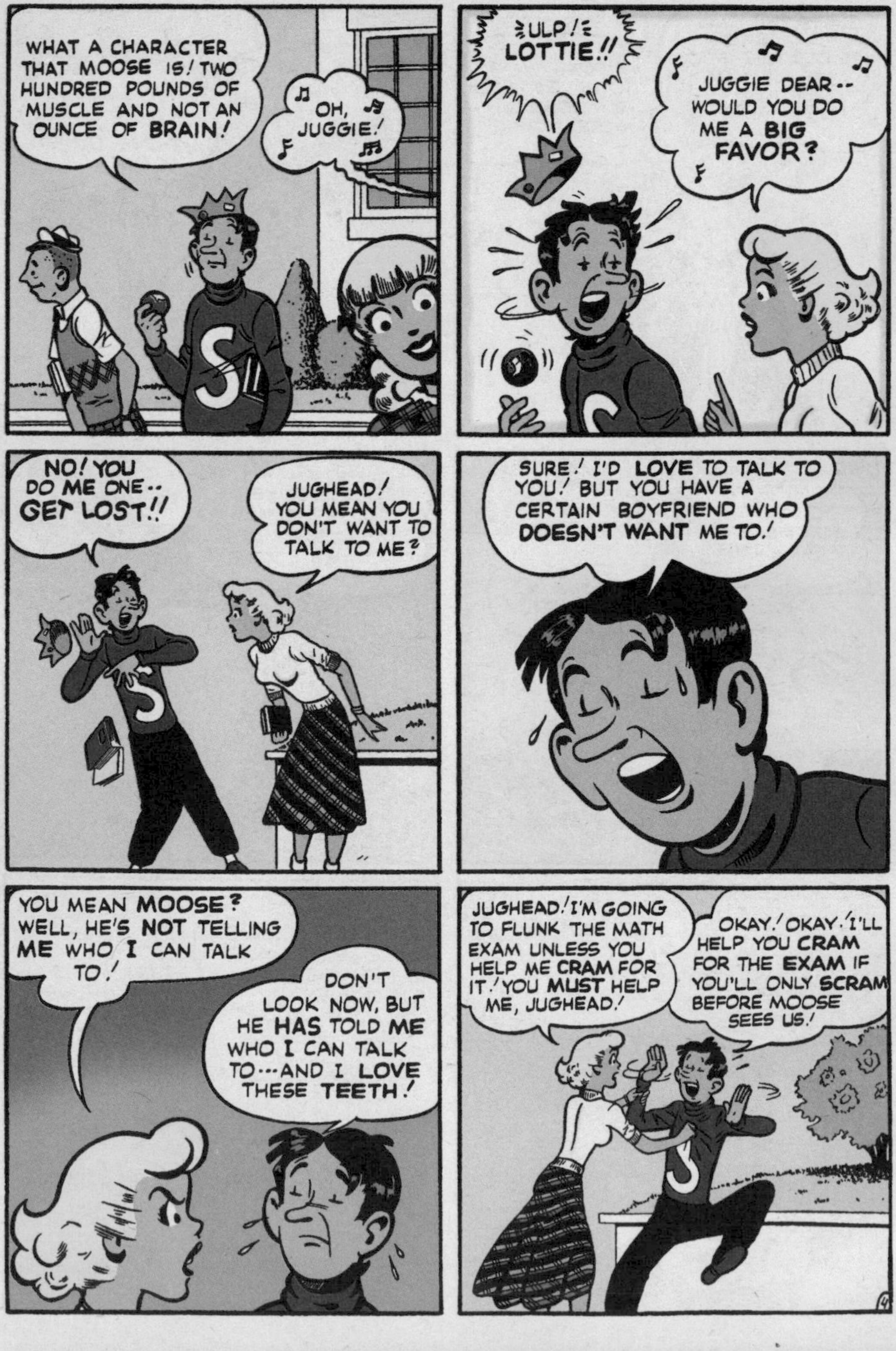
WHAT A CHARACTER THAT MOOSE IS! TWO HUNDRED POUNDS OF MUSCLE AND NOT AN OUNCE OF BRAIN!
OH, JUGGIE!
ULP! LOTTIE!!
JUGGIE DEAR -- WOULD YOU DO ME A BIG FAVOR?
NO! YOU DO ME ONE -- GET LOST!!
JUGHEAD! YOU MEAN YOU DON'T WANT TO TALK TO ME?
SURE! I'D LOVE TO TALK TO YOU! BUT YOU HAVE A CERTAIN BOYFRIEND WHO DOESN'T WANT ME TO!
YOU MEAN MOOSE? WELL, HE'S NOT TELLING ME WHO I CAN TALK TO!
DON'T LOOK NOW, BUT HE HAS TOLD ME WHO I CAN TALK TO --- AND I LOVE THESE TEETH!
JUGHEAD! I'M GOING TO FLUNK THE MATH EXAM UNLESS YOU HELP ME CRAM FOR IT! YOU MUST HELP ME, JUGHEAD!
OKAY! OKAY! I'LL HELP YOU CRAM FOR THE EXAM IF YOU'LL ONLY SCRAM BEFORE MOOSE SEES US!
4

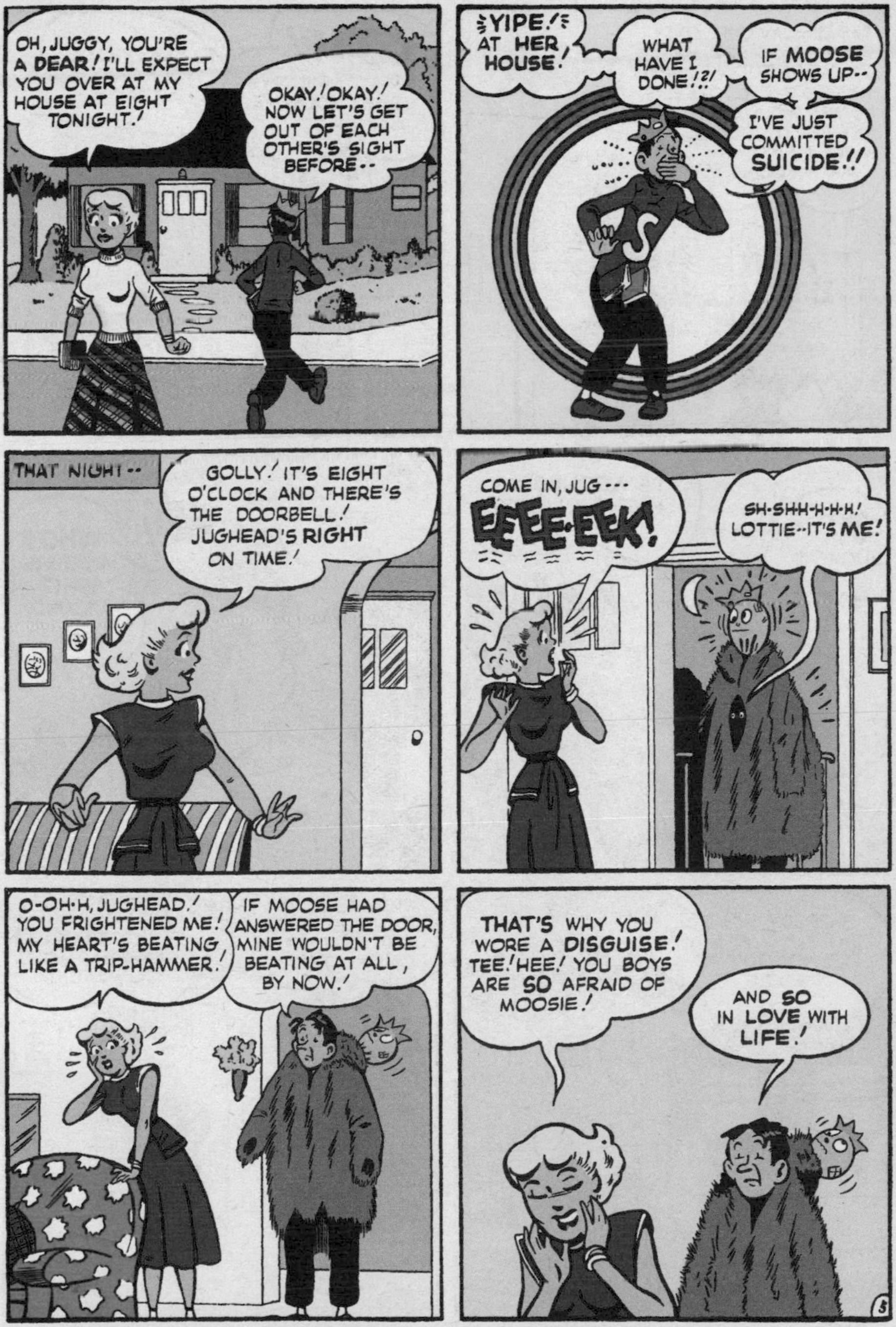
OH, JUGGY, YOU'RE A DEAR! I'LL EXPECT YOU OVER AT MY HOUSE AT EIGHT TONIGHT!
OKAY! OKAY! NOW LET'S GET OUT OF EACH OTHER'S SIGHT BEFORE--
YIPE! AT HER HOUSE!
WHAT HAVE I DONE!?!
IF MOOSE SHOWS UP--
I'VE JUST COMMITTED SUICIDE!!
THAT NIGHT--
GOLLY! IT'S EIGHT O'CLOCK AND THERE'S THE DOORBELL! JUGHEAD'S RIGHT ON TIME!
COME IN, JUG--- EEEEE-EEEK!
SH-SHH-H-H-H! LOTTIE--IT'S ME!
O-OH-H, JUGHEAD! YOU FRIGHTENED ME! MY HEART'S BEATING LIKE A TRIP-HAMMER!
IF MOOSE HAD ANSWERED THE DOOR, MINE WOULDN'T BE BEATING AT ALL, BY NOW!
THAT'S WHY YOU WORE A DISGUISE! TEE! HEE! YOU BOYS ARE SO AFRAID OF MOOSIE!
AND SO IN LOVE WITH LIFE!
5

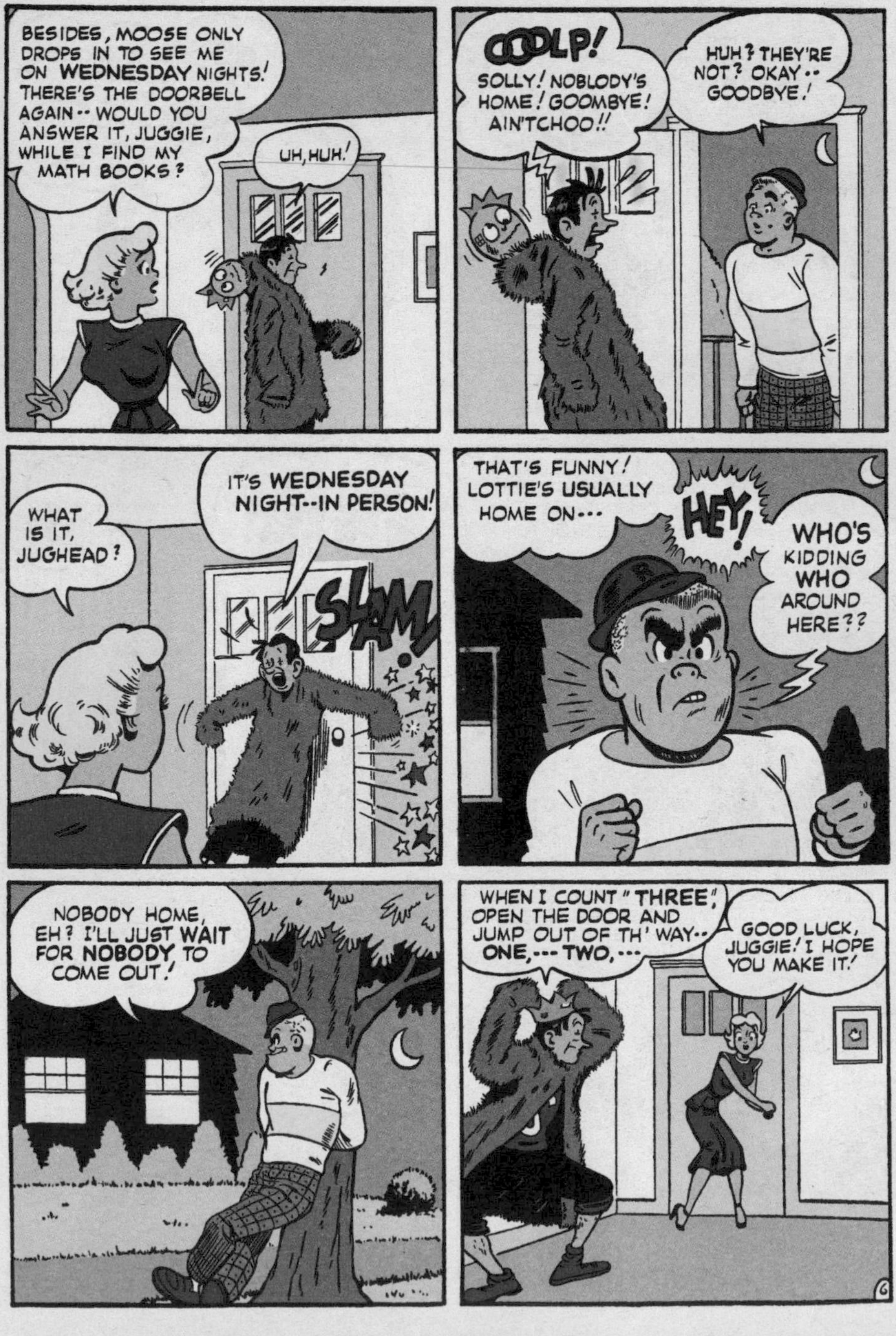
BESIDES, MOOSE ONLY DROPS IN TO SEE ME ON WEDNESDAY NIGHTS! THERE'S THE DOORBELL AGAIN -- WOULD YOU ANSWER IT, JUGGIE, WHILE I FIND MY MATH BOOKS?
UH, HUH!
GOOLP!
SOLLY! NOBLODY'S HOME! GOOMBYE! AIN'TCHOO!!
HUH? THEY'RE NOT? OKAY -- GOODBYE!
WHAT IS IT, JUGHEAD?
IT'S WEDNESDAY NIGHT--IN PERSON!
SLAM!
THAT'S FUNNY! LOTTIE'S USUALLY HOME ON---
HEY!
WHO'S KIDDING WHO AROUND HERE??
NOBODY HOME, EH? I'LL JUST WAIT FOR NOBODY TO COME OUT!
WHEN I COUNT "THREE", OPEN THE DOOR AND JUMP OUT OF TH' WAY-- ONE,--- TWO,---
GOOD LUCK, JUGGIE! I HOPE YOU MAKE IT!
6

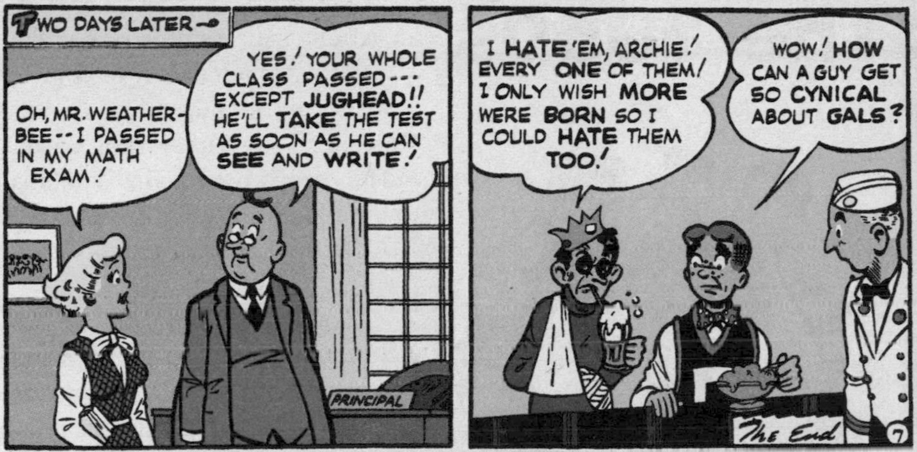
TWO DAYS LATER—
OH, MR. WEATHERBEE--I PASSED IN MY MATH EXAM!
YES! YOUR WHOLE CLASS PASSED--- EXCEPT JUGHEAD!! HE'LL TAKE THE TEST AS SOON AS HE CAN SEE AND WRITE!
PRINCIPAL
I HATE 'EM, ARCHIE! EVERY ONE OF THEM! I ONLY WISH MORE WERE BORN SO I COULD HATE THEM TOO!
WOW! HOW CAN A GUY GET SO CYNICAL ABOUT GALS?
The End
7

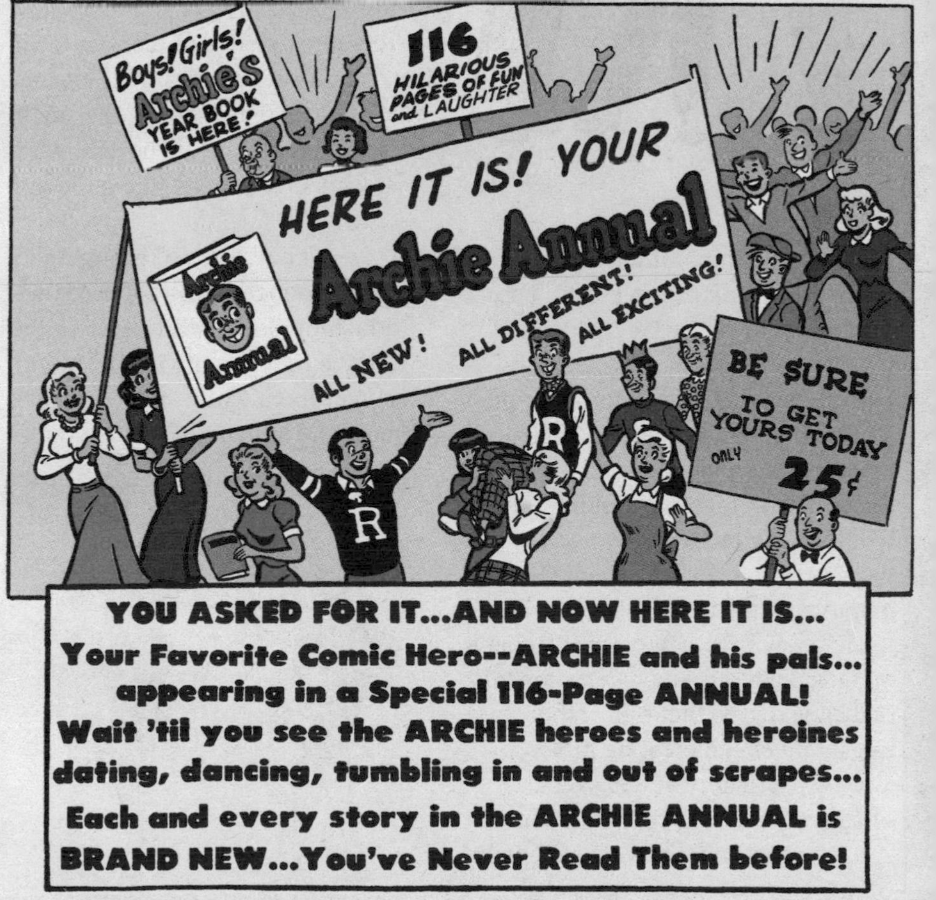
Boys! Girls! Archie's YEAR BOOK IS HERE!
116 HILARIOUS PAGES OF FUN and LAUGHTER
HERE IT IS! YOUR
Archie Annual
Archie Annual
ALL NEW!
ALL DIFFERENT!
ALL EXCITING!
BE SURE TO GET YOURS TODAY
ONLY 25¢

The 1950s

After a successful launch in the 1940s, the popularity of comics featuring Archie and his friends showed no signs of slowing down. The company capitalized on this popularity by adding even more Archie-related titles to its roster.

In other entertainment, movies were dominated by gritty guys and glamour gals. However, the biggest film stars of all were literally big—giant insects and dinosaurs viewed by scores of teens at local drive-in movie theaters. While teens flocked to the big screen, the small screen too had great success, with TV taking off like a rocket.

Most people think of teenagers when they think of the 1950s. The decade is considered a "golden era" for teens and it is easy to see why. Having weathered the storms of the 1930s and '40s, parents of 1950s teenagers were determined to provide the very best for their children; this led to giving teens "allowances." For the first time ever, this enabled the majority of teens to have "disposable income," which they promptly spent on fads, fashions and entertainment that appealed to them. In response, marketers began creating products aimed specifically at teenagers, effectively making consumerism "cool," and Archie was no exception!

The '50s also brought the introduction of famed Mattel fashion doll Barbie, who could have fit right in with Betty and Veronica,while "rock 'n' roll" became the anthem of 1950s youth.

The most noticeable change between the '40s and '50s Archie stories is the idea that the teens constitute a group of independent thinkers. Archie and his friends aren't rebellious, but in the 1950s there is a greater emphasis on solving their own teenage problems among themselves as opposed to merely having run-ins with their elders.

The romantic entanglements begun in the 1940s stories are made much more apparent in the 1950s, with the "eternal love triangle" scenarios playing an even greater role.

The love triangle would become the cornerstone of Archie Comics for years to come, culminating in two major event stories in the 1990s and 2000s that would provide the company and its main character with some of its greatest notoriety ever.

With the advent of "rebellious" rock 'n' roll and young Hollywood "bad boys" like James Dean, teenagers were often viewed as unruly and disobedient. Archie represented the flip side to this idea, showing the less dangerous side of the average suburban teenager as opposed to the rough and tumble "greasers" and gang "hoods." The idea of teens sharing "hangouts" like the local malt shop and drive-in as well as a shared love for movies and music targeted directly to them was emphasized in Archie Comics. Pop's Chok'lit Shop, with its friendly owner and updated jukebox, became a standard depiction of teens for the decade and beyond, and a familiar motif seen in TV shows and movies.

Ferocious Fems
Reggie #1, 1950
by George Frese

"He's a jerk, but at least he's got style!" What more do you need to know about Archie's very own master manipulator, Reggie Mantle? After tormenting Archie since his appearance in *Jackpot #5* (even though he wasn't named until #6) Reggie finally received his very own title. In "Ferocious Fems," Reggie gets the girls to take on a rival school in a game of football. However, like most of his schemes, this plan backfires and leaves him with more than hurt feelings!

--Joe Morciglio
Project Coordinator, Archie Comics

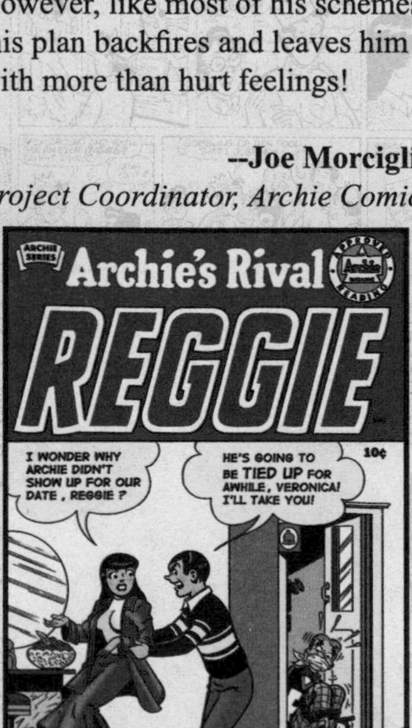
ARCHIE SERIES
Archie's Rival
REGGIE
10¢
I WONDER WHY ARCHIE DIDN'T SHOW UP FOR OUR DATE, REGGIE ?
HE'S GOING TO BE TIED UP FOR AWHILE, VERONICA! I'LL TAKE YOU!

Smell Bound
Ginger #1, 1950
by George Frese

A red-headed teen goes ga-ga over the opposite sex… and we don't mean Archie! In this lively gender-swap variation on Archie, Ginger takes the traditional Archie-Betty-Veronica love triangle a few steps further: she dates lots of different guys, and when we say "different," we mean it—from the nerdy Ickky to the gridiron hunk Whiz Baker, and every kind of guy in-between! In fact, the teens in Ginger's world all seem to date one another on a rotating basis, and therein lies the conflict, as the girls all maneuver to date the most desirable guys. A comedy of errors, the multitude of misunderstandings leads to much merriment.

--Paul Castiglia
Writer & archivist, Archie Comics

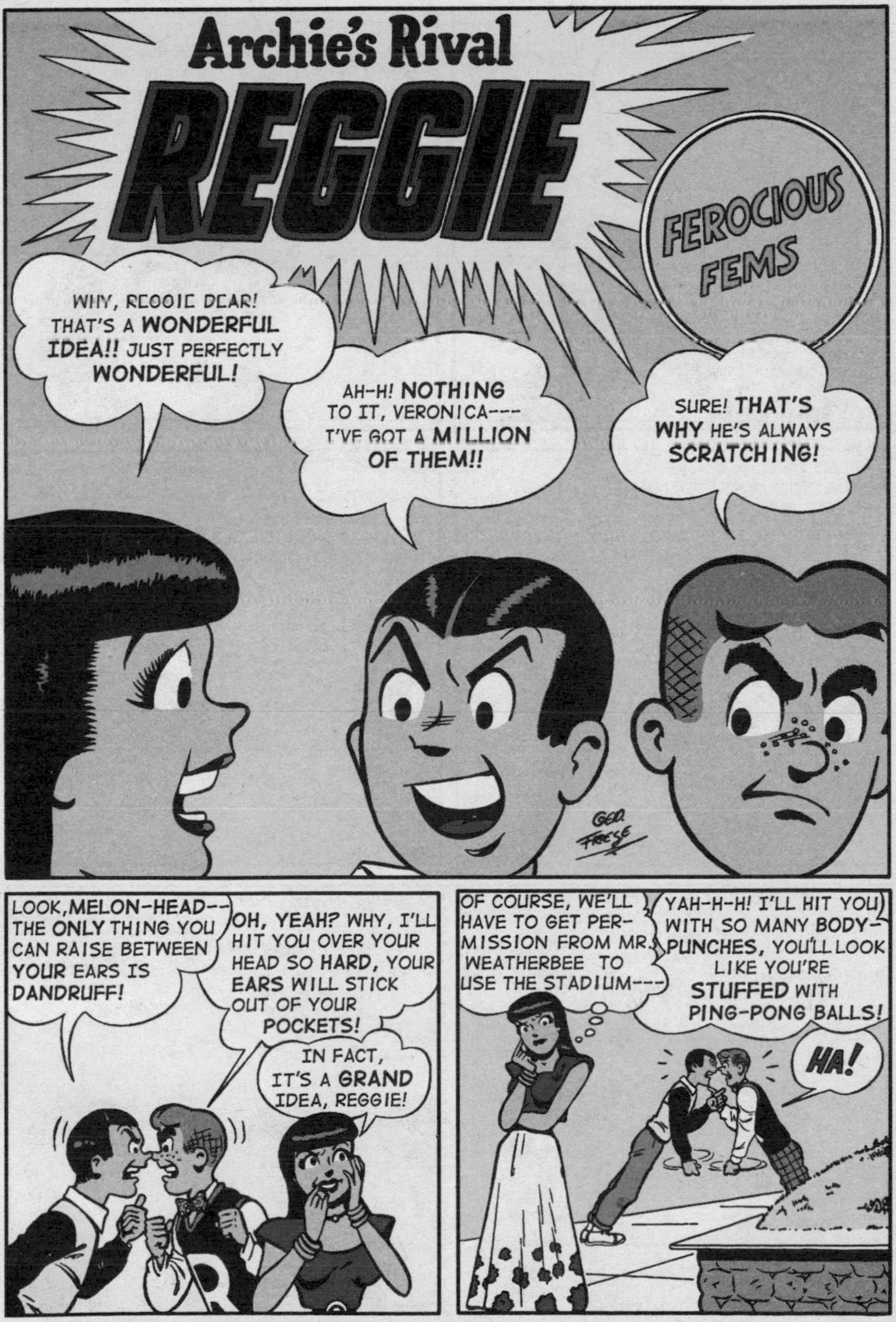

Archie's Rival
REGGIE
FEROCIOUS FEMS
WHY, REGGIE DEAR! THAT'S A WONDERFUL IDEA!! JUST PERFECTLY WONDERFUL!
AH-H! NOTHING TO IT, VERONICA--- I'VE GOT A MILLION OF THEM!!
SURE! THAT'S WHY HE'S ALWAYS SCRATCHING!
GEO. FRESE
LOOK, MELON-HEAD-- THE ONLY THING YOU CAN RAISE BETWEEN YOUR EARS IS DANDRUFF!
OH, YEAH? WHY, I'LL HIT YOU OVER YOUR HEAD SO HARD, YOUR EARS WILL STICK OUT OF YOUR POCKETS!
IN FACT, IT'S A GRAND IDEA, REGGIE!
OF COURSE, WE'LL HAVE TO GET PER-MISSION FROM MR. WEATHERBEE TO USE THE STADIUM---
YAH-H-H! I'LL HIT YOU WITH SO MANY BODY-PUNCHES, YOU'LL LOOK LIKE YOU'RE STUFFED WITH PING-PONG BALLS!
HA!

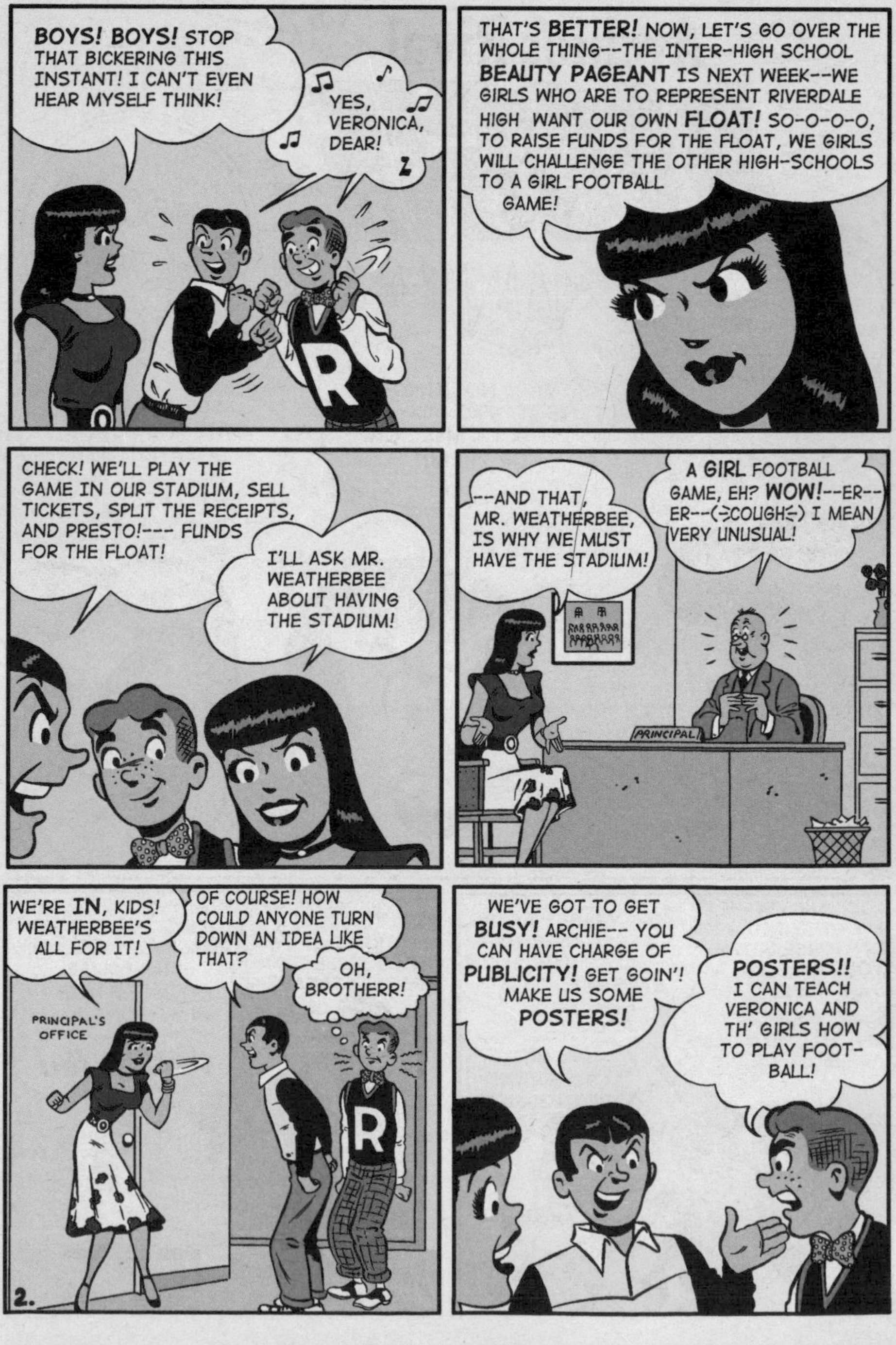
BOYS! BOYS! STOP THAT BICKERING THIS INSTANT! I CAN'T EVEN HEAR MYSELF THINK!
YES, VERONICA, DEAR!
Z
THAT'S BETTER! NOW, LET'S GO OVER THE WHOLE THING--THE INTER-HIGH SCHOOL BEAUTY PAGEANT IS NEXT WEEK--WE GIRLS WHO ARE TO REPRESENT RIVERDALE HIGH WANT OUR OWN FLOAT! SO-O-O-O, TO RAISE FUNDS FOR THE FLOAT, WE GIRLS WILL CHALLENGE THE OTHER HIGH-SCHOOLS TO A GIRL FOOTBALL GAME!
CHECK! WE'LL PLAY THE GAME IN OUR STADIUM, SELL TICKETS, SPLIT THE RECEIPTS, AND PRESTO!--- FUNDS FOR THE FLOAT!
I'LL ASK MR. WEATHERBEE ABOUT HAVING THE STADIUM!
--AND THAT, MR. WEATHERBEE, IS WHY WE MUST HAVE THE STADIUM!
A GIRL FOOTBALL GAME, EH? WOW!--ER--ER--(COUGH) I MEAN VERY UNUSUAL!
PRINCIPAL
WE'RE IN, KIDS! WEATHERBEE'S ALL FOR IT!
OF COURSE! HOW COULD ANYONE TURN DOWN AN IDEA LIKE THAT?
OH, BROTHERR!
PRINCIPAL'S OFFICE
2.
WE'VE GOT TO GET BUSY! ARCHIE-- YOU CAN HAVE CHARGE OF PUBLICITY! GET GOIN'! MAKE US SOME POSTERS!
POSTERS!! I CAN TEACH VERONICA AND TH' GIRLS HOW TO PLAY FOOT-BALL!

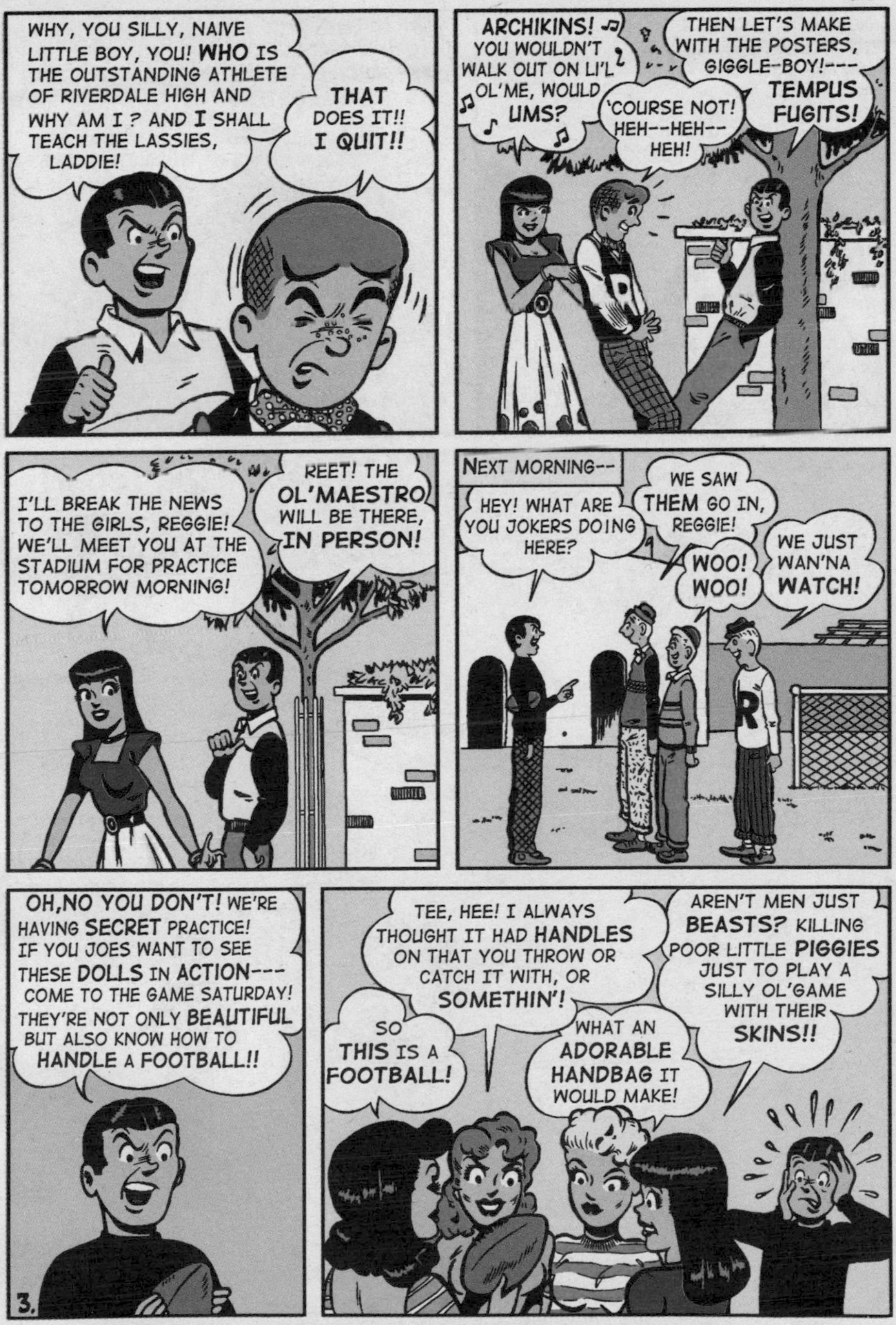
WHY, YOU SILLY, NAIVE LITTLE BOY, YOU! WHO IS THE OUTSTANDING ATHLETE OF RIVERDALE HIGH AND WHY AM I ? AND I SHALL TEACH THE LASSIES, LADDIE!
THAT DOES IT!! I QUIT!!
ARCHIKINS! YOU WOULDN'T WALK OUT ON LI'L OL'ME, WOULD UMS?
'COURSE NOT! HEH--HEH--HEH!
THEN LET'S MAKE WITH THE POSTERS, GIGGLE-BOY!--- TEMPUS FUGITS!
I'LL BREAK THE NEWS TO THE GIRLS, REGGIE! WE'LL MEET YOU AT THE STADIUM FOR PRACTICE TOMORROW MORNING!
REET! THE OL'MAESTRO WILL BE THERE, IN PERSON!
NEXT MORNING--
HEY! WHAT ARE YOU JOKERS DOING HERE?
WE SAW THEM GO IN, REGGIE!
WOO! WOO!
WE JUST WAN'NA WATCH!
OH,NO YOU DON'T! WE'RE HAVING SECRET PRACTICE! IF YOU JOES WANT TO SEE THESE DOLLS IN ACTION--- COME TO THE GAME SATURDAY! THEY'RE NOT ONLY BEAUTIFUL BUT ALSO KNOW HOW TO HANDLE A FOOTBALL!!
3.
SO THIS IS A FOOTBALL!
TEE, HEE! I ALWAYS THOUGHT IT HAD HANDLES ON THAT YOU THROW OR CATCH IT WITH, OR SOMETHIN'!
WHAT AN ADORABLE HANDBAG IT WOULD MAKE!
AREN'T MEN JUST BEASTS? KILLING POOR LITTLE PIGGIES JUST TO PLAY A SILLY OL'GAME WITH THEIR SKINS!!

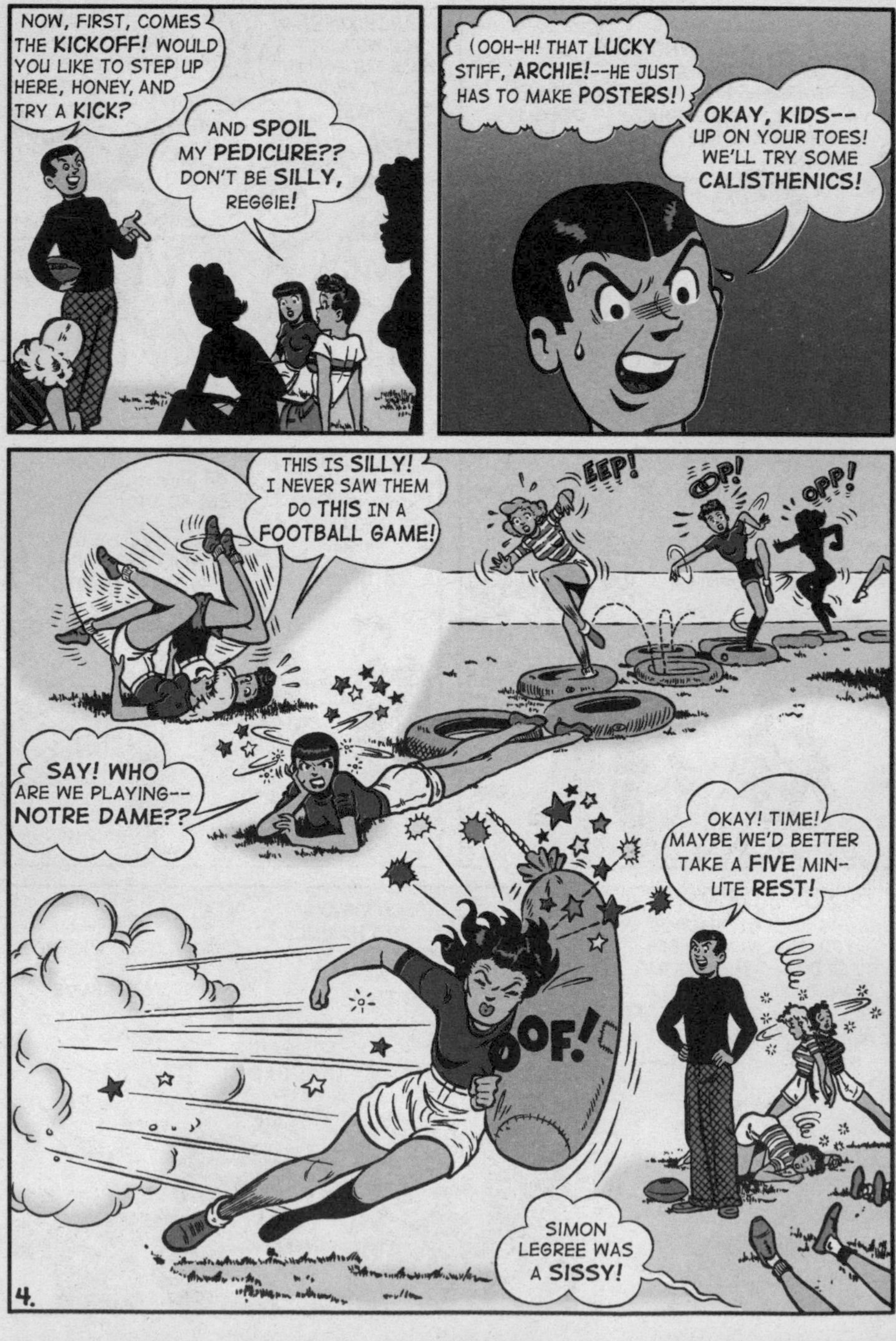
NOW, FIRST, COMES THE KICKOFF! WOULD YOU LIKE TO STEP UP HERE, HONEY, AND TRY A KICK?
AND SPOIL MY PEDICURE?? DON'T BE SILLY, REGGIE!
(OOH-H! THAT LUCKY STIFF, ARCHIE!--HE JUST HAS TO MAKE POSTERS!)
OKAY, KIDS-- UP ON YOUR TOES! WE'LL TRY SOME CALISTHENICS!
THIS IS SILLY! I NEVER SAW THEM DO THIS IN A FOOTBALL GAME!
EEP!
OOP!
OPP!
SAY! WHO ARE WE PLAYING-- NOTRE DAME??
OKAY! TIME! MAYBE WE'D BETTER TAKE A FIVE MIN-UTE REST!
OOF!
SIMON LEGREE WAS A SISSY!
4.

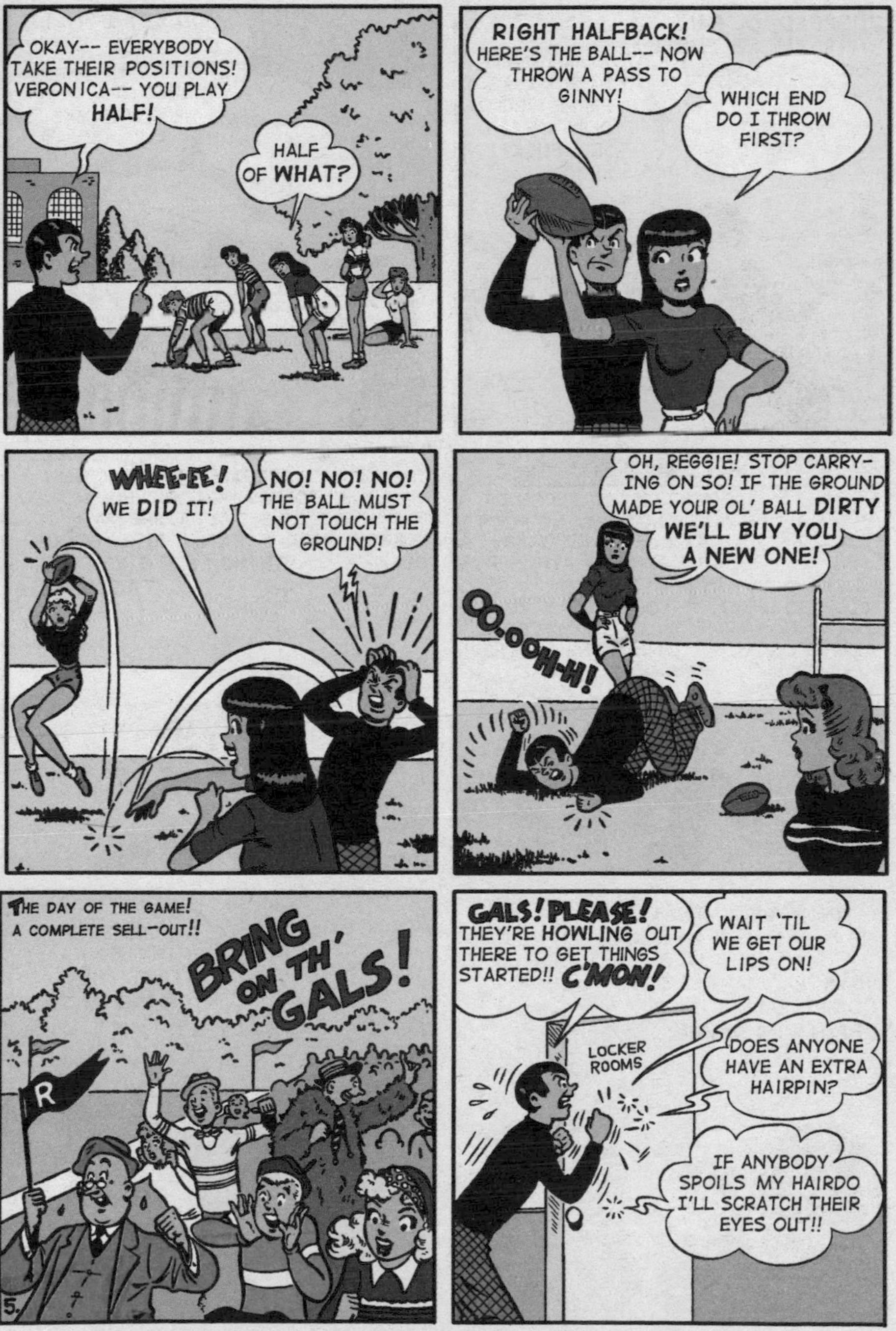
OKAY-- EVERYBODY TAKE THEIR POSITIONS! VERONICA-- YOU PLAY HALF!
HALF OF WHAT?
RIGHT HALFBACK! HERE'S THE BALL-- NOW THROW A PASS TO GINNY!
WHICH END DO I THROW FIRST?
WHEE-EE! WE DID IT!
NO! NO! NO! THE BALL MUST NOT TOUCH THE GROUND!
OH, REGGIE! STOP CARRYING ON SO! IF THE GROUND MADE YOUR OL' BALL DIRTY WE'LL BUY YOU A NEW ONE!
OO-OOH-H!
THE DAY OF THE GAME! A COMPLETE SELL-OUT!!
BRING ON TH' GALS!
R
5.
GALS! PLEASE! THEY'RE HOWLING OUT THERE TO GET THINGS STARTED!! C'MON!
WAIT 'TIL WE GET OUR LIPS ON!
LOCKER ROOMS
DOES ANYONE HAVE AN EXTRA HAIRPIN?
IF ANYBODY SPOILS MY HAIRDO I'LL SCRATCH THEIR EYES OUT!!

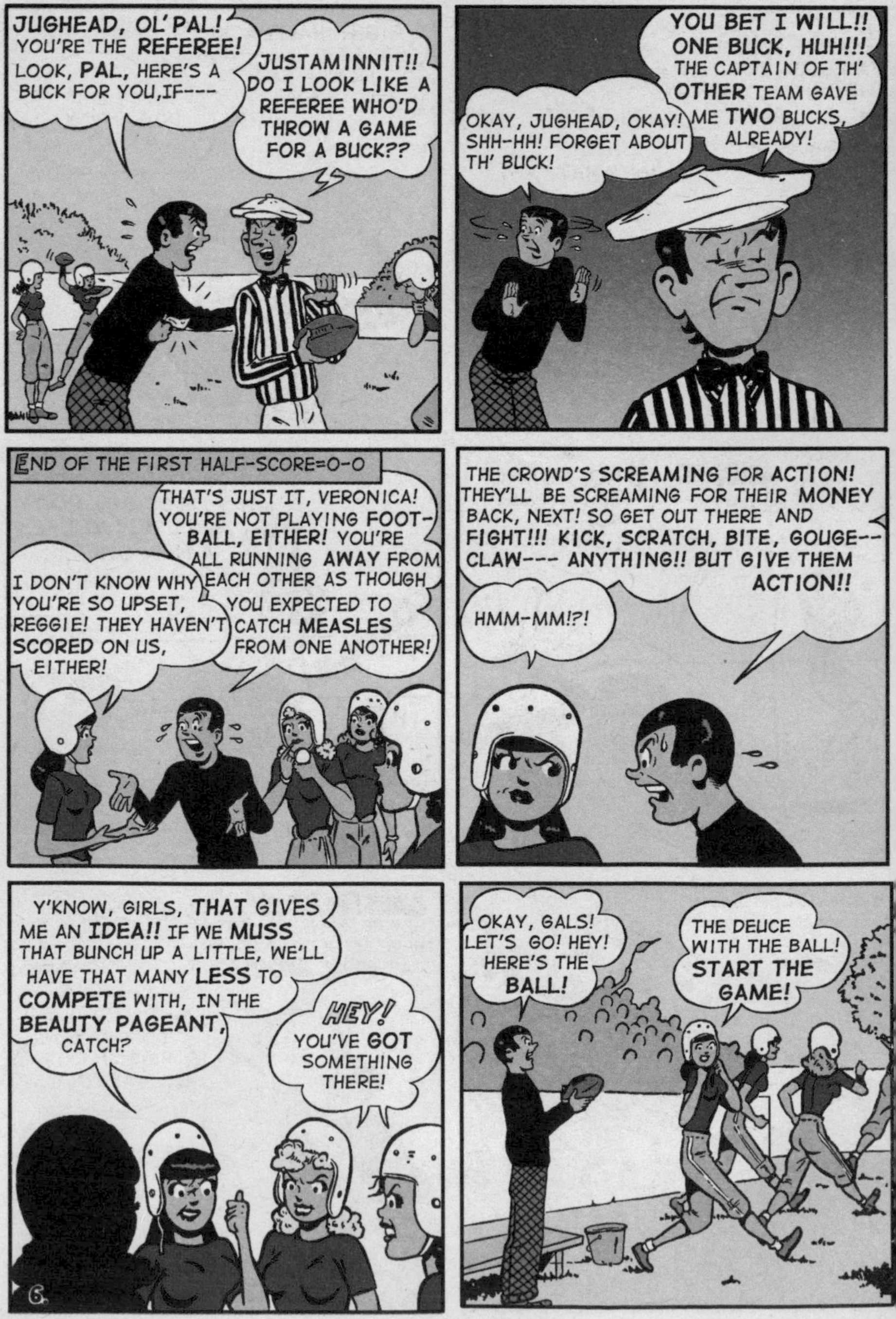
JUGHEAD, OL' PAL! YOU'RE THE REFEREE! LOOK, PAL, HERE'S A BUCK FOR YOU, IF---
JUSTAMINNIT!! DO I LOOK LIKE A REFEREE WHO'D THROW A GAME FOR A BUCK??
YOU BET I WILL!! ONE BUCK, HUH!!! THE CAPTAIN OF TH' OTHER TEAM GAVE ME TWO BUCKS, ALREADY!
OKAY, JUGHEAD, OKAY! SHH-HH! FORGET ABOUT TH' BUCK!
END OF THE FIRST HALF-SCORE=0-0
THAT'S JUST IT, VERONICA! YOU'RE NOT PLAYING FOOT-BALL, EITHER! YOU'RE ALL RUNNING AWAY FROM EACH OTHER AS THOUGH YOU EXPECTED TO CATCH MEASLES FROM ONE ANOTHER!
I DON'T KNOW WHY YOU'RE SO UPSET, REGGIE! THEY HAVEN'T SCORED ON US, EITHER!
THE CROWD'S SCREAMING FOR ACTION! THEY'LL BE SCREAMING FOR THEIR MONEY BACK, NEXT! SO GET OUT THERE AND FIGHT!!! KICK, SCRATCH, BITE, GOUGE-- CLAW--- ANYTHING!! BUT GIVE THEM ACTION!!
HMM-MM!?!
Y'KNOW, GIRLS, THAT GIVES ME AN IDEA!! IF WE MUSS THAT BUNCH UP A LITTLE, WE'LL HAVE THAT MANY LESS TO COMPETE WITH, IN THE BEAUTY PAGEANT, CATCH?
HEY! YOU'VE GOT SOMETHING THERE!
OKAY, GALS! LET'S GO! HEY! HERE'S THE BALL!
THE DEUCE WITH THE BALL! START THE GAME!

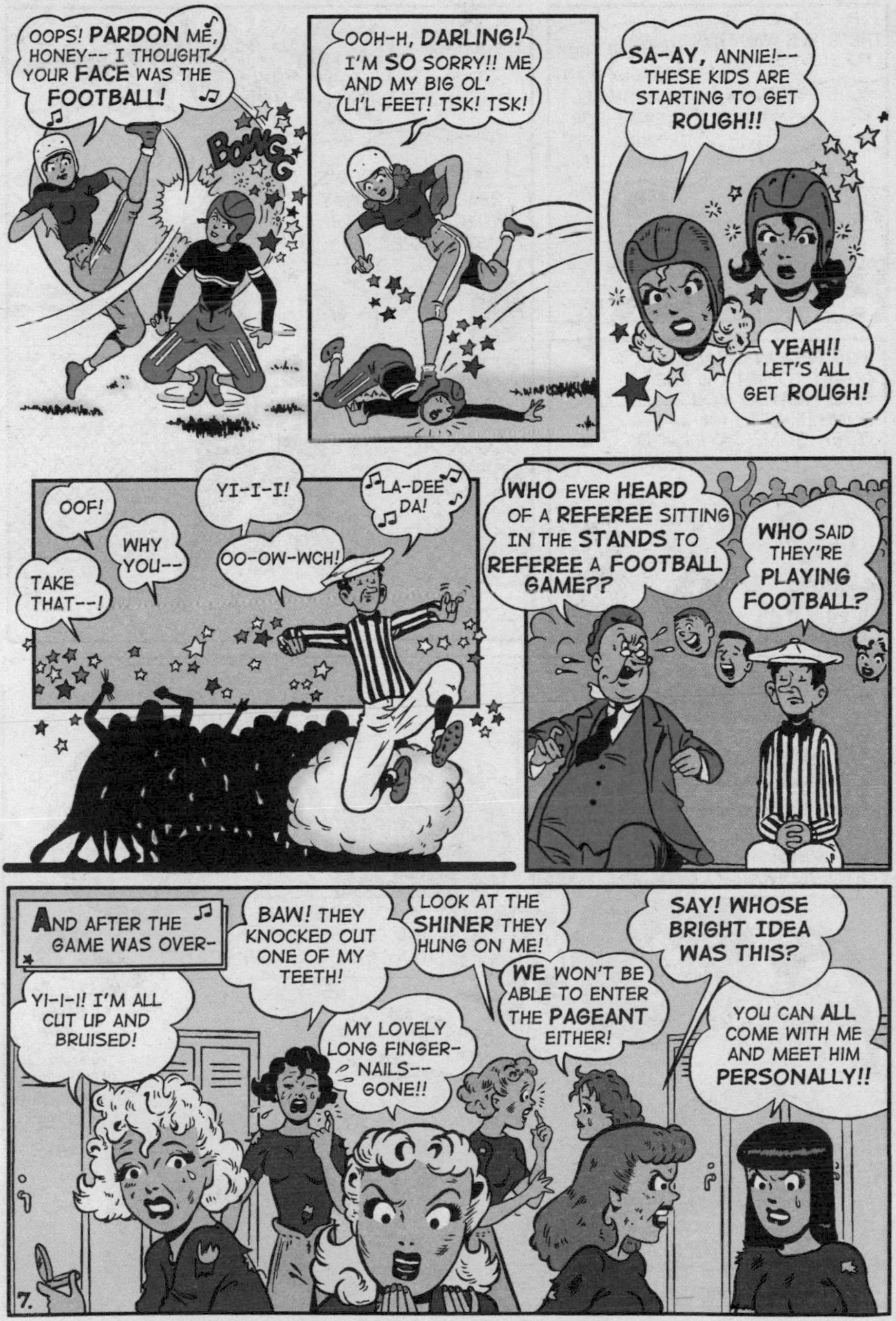
OOPS! PARDON ME, HONEY-- I THOUGHT YOUR FACE WAS THE FOOTBALL!
BOINGG
OOH-H, DARLING! I'M SO SORRY!! ME AND MY BIG OL' LI'L FEET! TSK! TSK!
SA-AY, ANNIE!-- THESE KIDS ARE STARTING TO GET ROUGH!!
YEAH!! LET'S ALL GET ROUGH!
OOF!
YI-I-I!
LA-DEE DA!
WHY YOU--
OO-OW-WCH!
TAKE THAT--!
WHO EVER HEARD OF A REFEREE SITTING IN THE STANDS TO REFEREE A FOOTBALL GAME??
WHO SAID THEY'RE PLAYING FOOTBALL?
AND AFTER THE GAME WAS OVER-
BAW! THEY KNOCKED OUT ONE OF MY TEETH!
LOOK AT THE SHINER THEY HUNG ON ME!
SAY! WHOSE BRIGHT IDEA WAS THIS?
YI-I-I! I'M ALL CUT UP AND BRUISED!
MY LOVELY LONG FINGER-NAILS-- GONE!!
WE WON'T BE ABLE TO ENTER THE PAGEANT EITHER!
YOU CAN ALL COME WITH ME AND MEET HIM PERSONALLY!!
7.

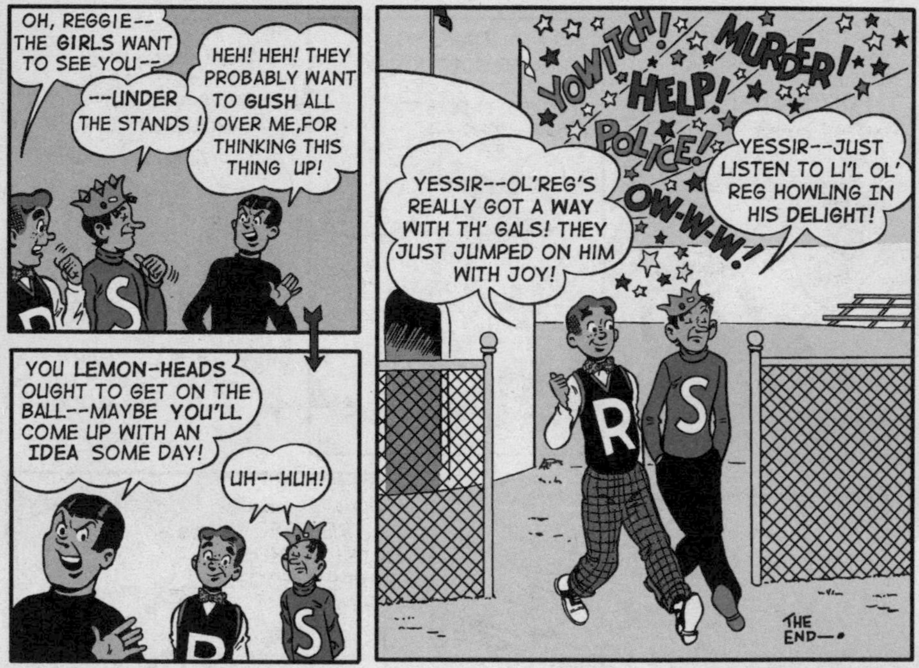
OH, REGGIE-- THE GIRLS WANT TO SEE YOU--
--UNDER THE STANDS!
HEH! HEH! THEY PROBABLY WANT TO GUSH ALL OVER ME,FOR THINKING THIS THING UP!
YOU LEMON-HEADS OUGHT TO GET ON THE BALL--MAYBE YOU'LL COME UP WITH AN IDEA SOME DAY!
UH--HUH!
YOWITCH!
MURDER!
HELP!
POLICE!
OW-W-W-W!
YESSIR--OL'REG'S REALLY GOT A WAY WITH TH' GALS! THEY JUST JUMPED ON HIM WITH JOY!
YESSIR--JUST LISTEN TO LI'L OL' REG HOWLING IN HIS DELIGHT!
THE END

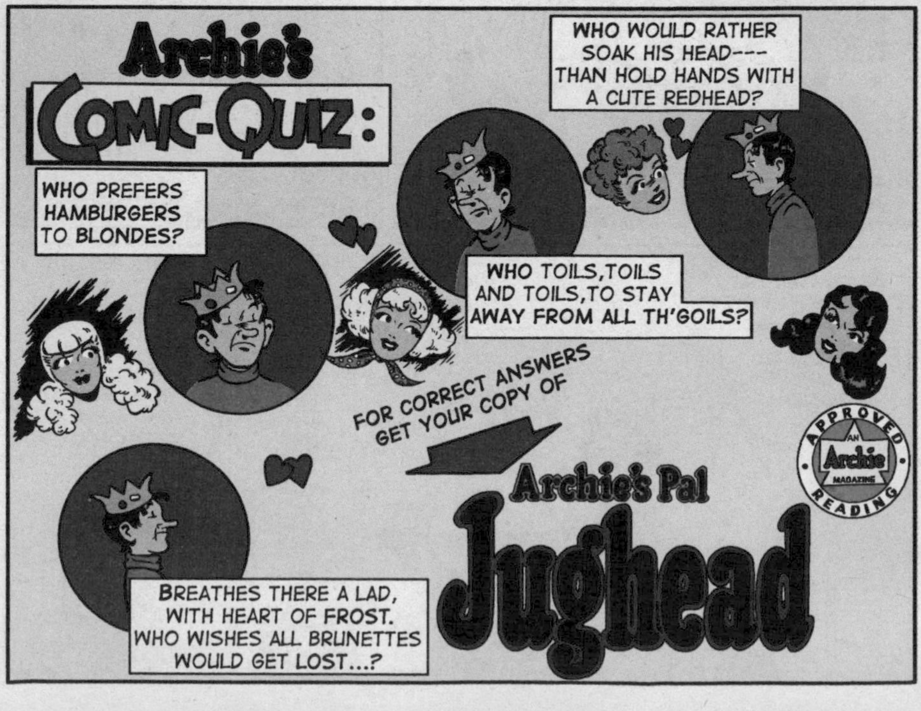
Archie's
COMIC-QUIZ:
WHO PREFERS HAMBURGERS TO BLONDES?
WHO TOILS,TOILS AND TOILS,TO STAY AWAY FROM ALL TH'GOILS?
WHO WOULD RATHER SOAK HIS HEAD--- THAN HOLD HANDS WITH A CUTE REDHEAD?
BREATHES THERE A LAD, WITH HEART OF FROST. WHO WISHES ALL BRUNETTES WOULD GET LOST...?
FOR CORRECT ANSWERS GET YOUR COPY OF
Archie's Pal
Jughead
APPROVED AN Archie MAGAZINE READING

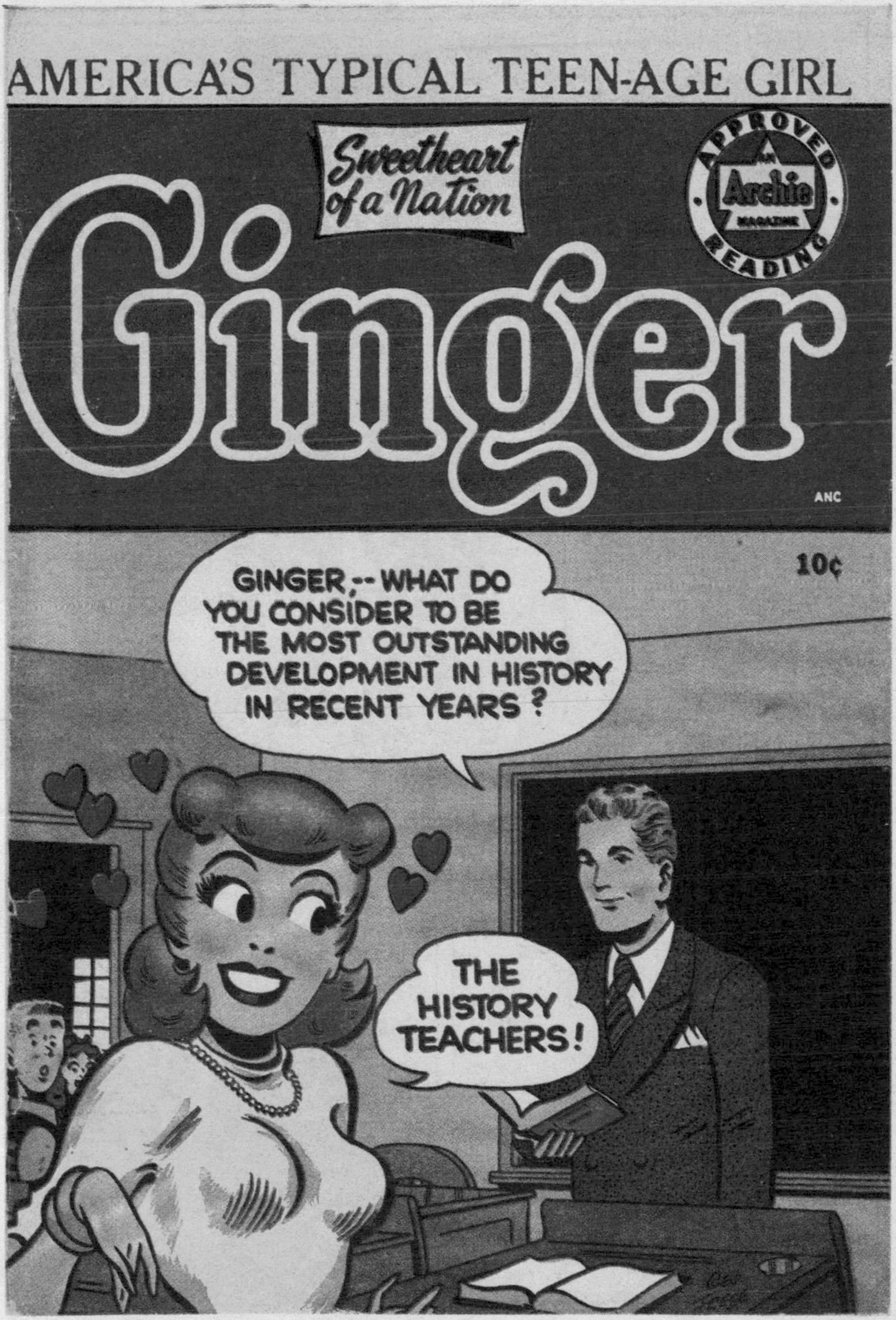

AMERICA'S TYPICAL TEEN-AGE GIRL
Sweetheart of a Nation
Ginger
APPROVED READING
AN Archie MAGAZINE
ANC
10¢
GINGER,-- WHAT DO YOU CONSIDER TO BE THE MOST OUTSTANDING DEVELOPMENT IN HISTORY IN RECENT YEARS?
THE HISTORY TEACHERS!

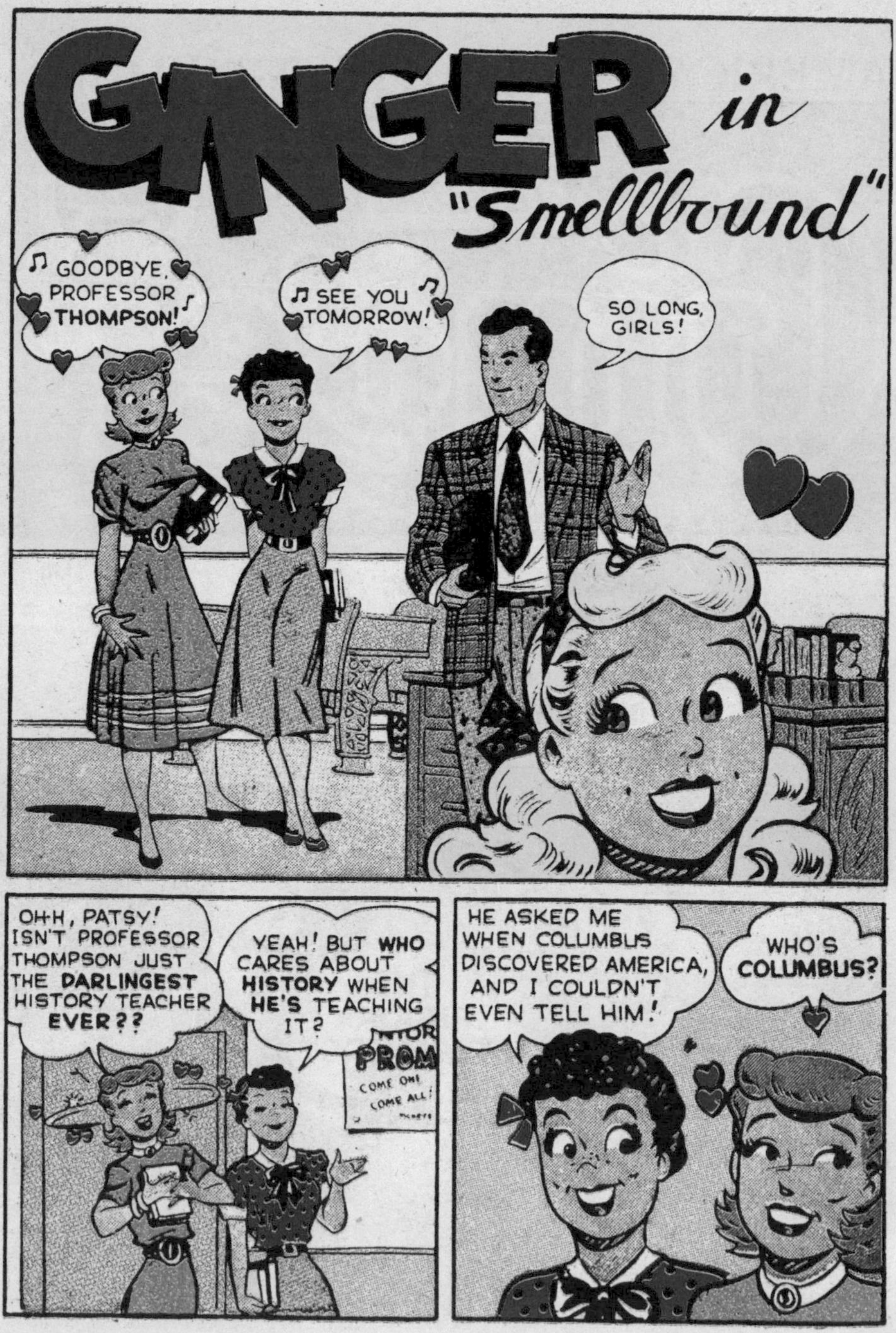
GINGER in "Smellbound"
♫ GOODBYE, PROFESSOR THOMPSON! ♪
♫ SEE YOU TOMORROW! ♪
SO LONG, GIRLS!
OH-H, PATSY! ISN'T PROFESSOR THOMPSON JUST THE DARLINGEST HISTORY TEACHER EVER??
YEAH! BUT WHO CARES ABOUT HISTORY WHEN HE'S TEACHING IT?
PROM
COME ON! COME ALL!
HE ASKED ME WHEN COLUMBUS DISCOVERED AMERICA, AND I COULDN'T EVEN TELL HIM!
WHO'S COLUMBUS?

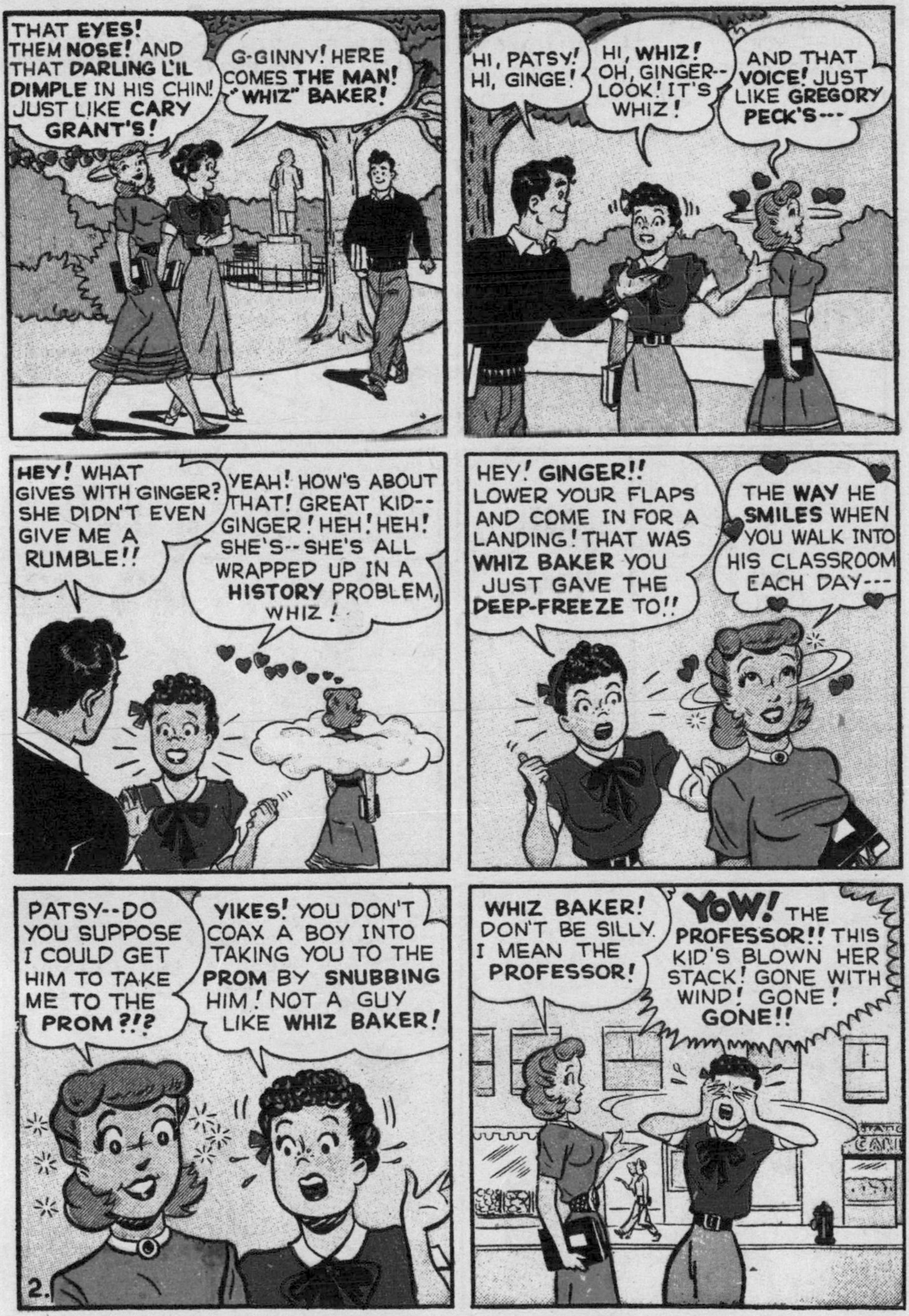
THAT EYES! THEM NOSE! AND THAT DARLING L'IL DIMPLE IN HIS CHIN! JUST LIKE CARY GRANT'S!
G-GINNY! HERE COMES THE MAN! "WHIZ" BAKER!
HI, PATSY! HI, GINGE!
HI, WHIZ! OH, GINGER-- LOOK! IT'S WHIZ!
AND THAT VOICE! JUST LIKE GREGORY PECK'S---
HEY! WHAT GIVES WITH GINGER? SHE DIDN'T EVEN GIVE ME A RUMBLE!!
YEAH! HOW'S ABOUT THAT! GREAT KID-- GINGER! HEH! HEH! SHE'S--SHE'S ALL WRAPPED UP IN A HISTORY PROBLEM, WHIZ!
HEY! GINGER!! LOWER YOUR FLAPS AND COME IN FOR A LANDING! THAT WAS WHIZ BAKER YOU JUST GAVE THE DEEP-FREEZE TO!!
THE WAY HE SMILES WHEN YOU WALK INTO HIS CLASSROOM EACH DAY---
PATSY--DO YOU SUPPOSE I COULD GET HIM TO TAKE ME TO THE PROM?!?
YIKES! YOU DON'T COAX A BOY INTO TAKING YOU TO THE PROM BY SNUBBING HIM! NOT A GUY LIKE WHIZ BAKER!
2.
WHIZ BAKER! DON'T BE SILLY. I MEAN THE PROFESSOR!
YOW! THE PROFESSOR!! THIS KID'S BLOWN HER STACK! GONE WITH WIND! GONE! GONE!!

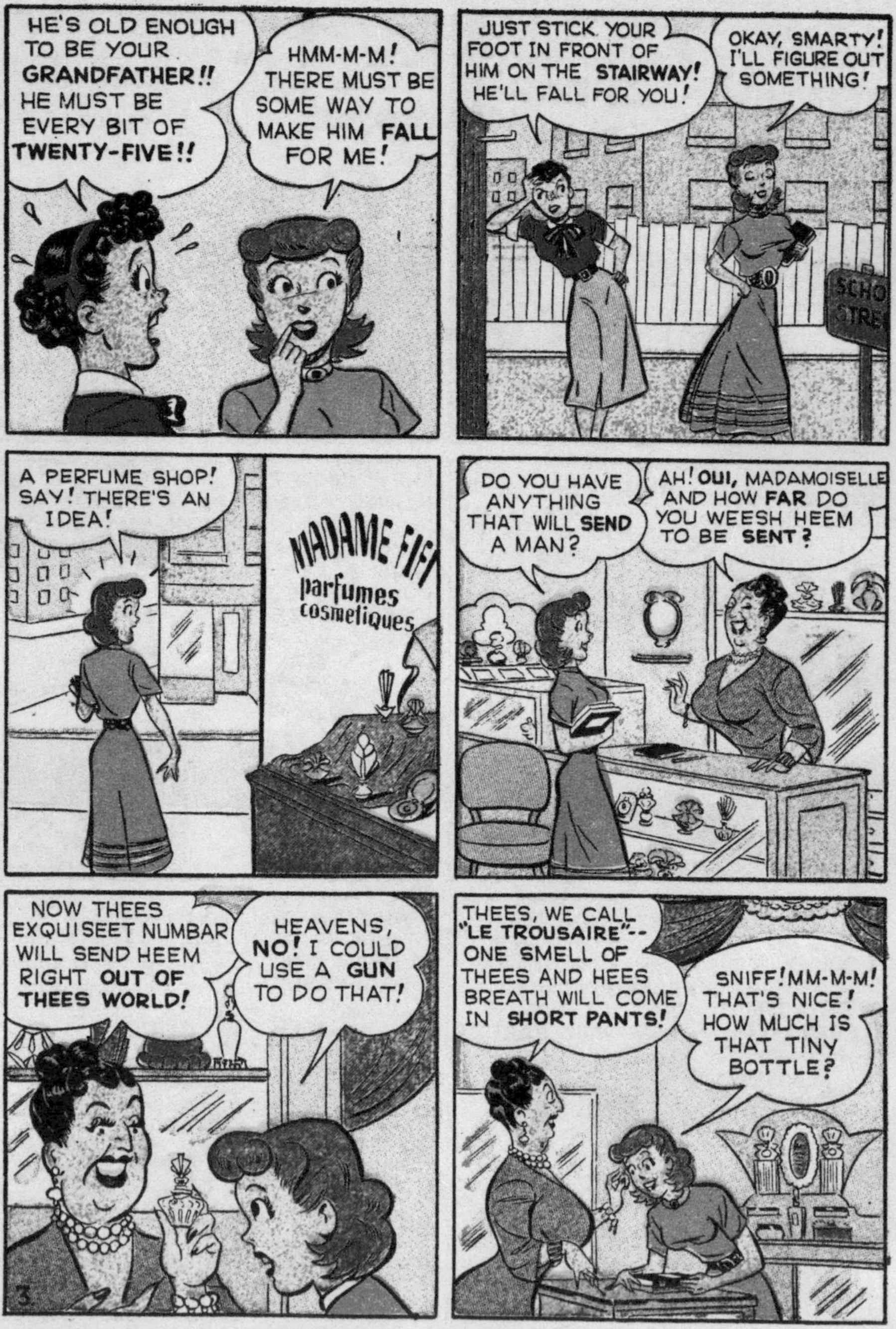
HE'S OLD ENOUGH TO BE YOUR **GRANDFATHER!!** HE MUST BE EVERY BIT OF **TWENTY-FIVE!!**
HMM-M-M! THERE MUST BE SOME WAY TO MAKE HIM **FALL** FOR ME!
JUST STICK YOUR FOOT IN FRONT OF HIM ON THE **STAIRWAY!** HE'LL FALL FOR YOU!
OKAY, SMARTY! I'LL FIGURE OUT SOMETHING!
A PERFUME SHOP! SAY! THERE'S AN IDEA!
MADAME FIFI
parfumes
cosmetiques
DO YOU HAVE ANYTHING THAT WILL **SEND** A MAN?
AH! **OUI,** MADAMOISELLE AND HOW **FAR** DO YOU WEESH HEEM TO BE **SENT?**
NOW THEES EXQUISEET NUMBAR WILL SEND HEEM RIGHT **OUT OF THEES WORLD!**
HEAVENS, **NO!** I COULD USE A **GUN** TO DO THAT!
THEES, WE CALL **"LE TROUSAIRE"**-- ONE SMELL OF THEES AND HEES BREATH WILL COME IN **SHORT PANTS!**
SNIFF! MM-M-M! THAT'S NICE! HOW MUCH IS THAT TINY BOTTLE?

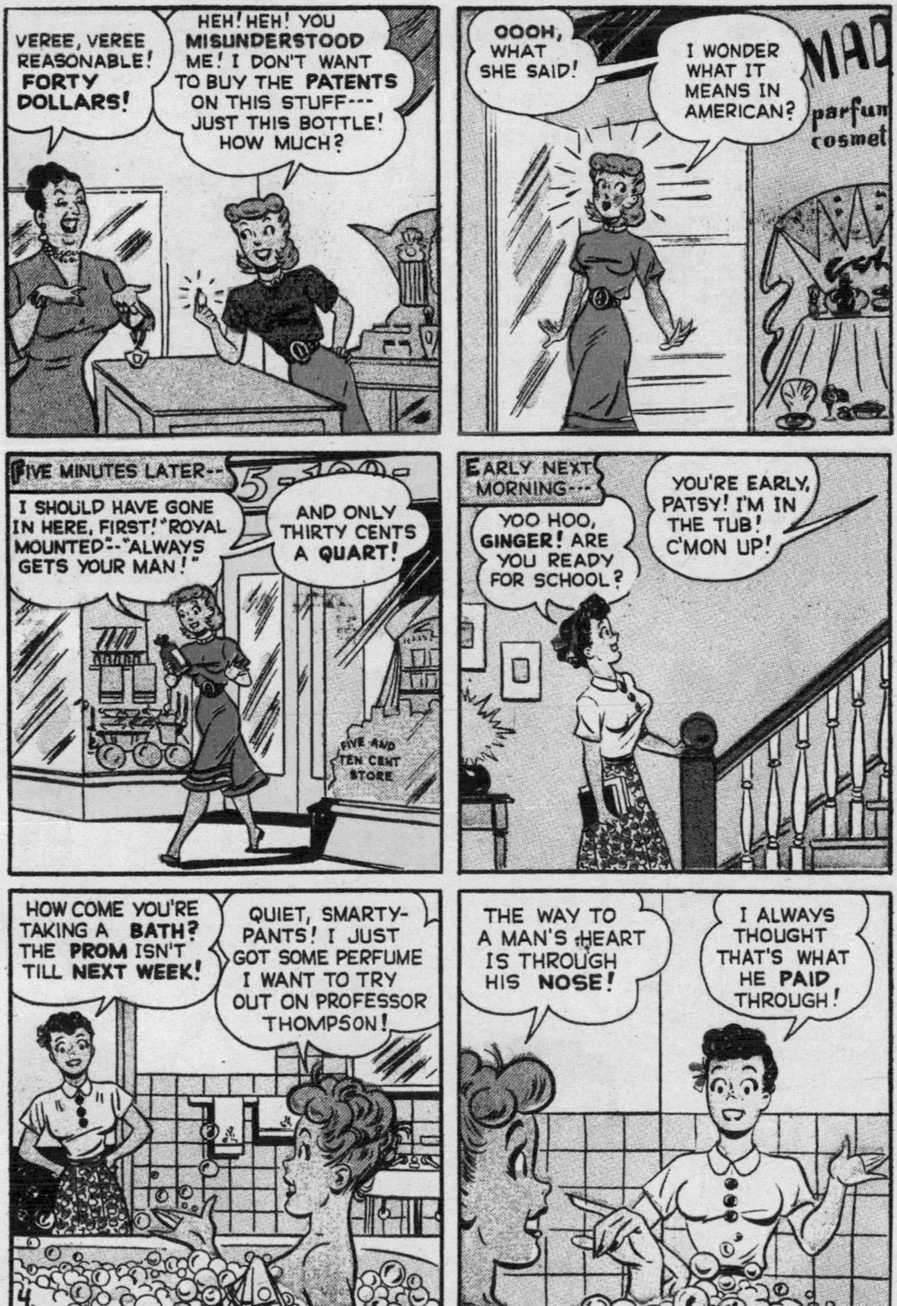
VEREE, VEREE REASONABLE! FORTY DOLLARS!
HEH! HEH! YOU MISUNDERSTOOD ME! I DON'T WANT TO BUY THE PATENTS ON THIS STUFF--- JUST THIS BOTTLE! HOW MUCH?
OOOH, WHAT SHE SAID!
I WONDER WHAT IT MEANS IN AMERICAN?
MAD
parfum
cosmet
FIVE MINUTES LATER--
I SHOULD HAVE GONE IN HERE, FIRST! "ROYAL MOUNTED"--"ALWAYS GETS YOUR MAN!"
AND ONLY THIRTY CENTS A QUART!
FIVE AND TEN CENT STORE
EARLY NEXT MORNING---
YOO HOO, GINGER! ARE YOU READY FOR SCHOOL?
YOU'RE EARLY, PATSY! I'M IN THE TUB! C'MON UP!
HOW COME YOU'RE TAKING A BATH? THE PROM ISN'T TILL NEXT WEEK!
QUIET, SMARTY-PANTS! I JUST GOT SOME PERFUME I WANT TO TRY OUT ON PROFESSOR THOMPSON!
4.
THE WAY TO A MAN'S HEART IS THROUGH HIS NOSE!
I ALWAYS THOUGHT THAT'S WHAT HE PAID THROUGH!

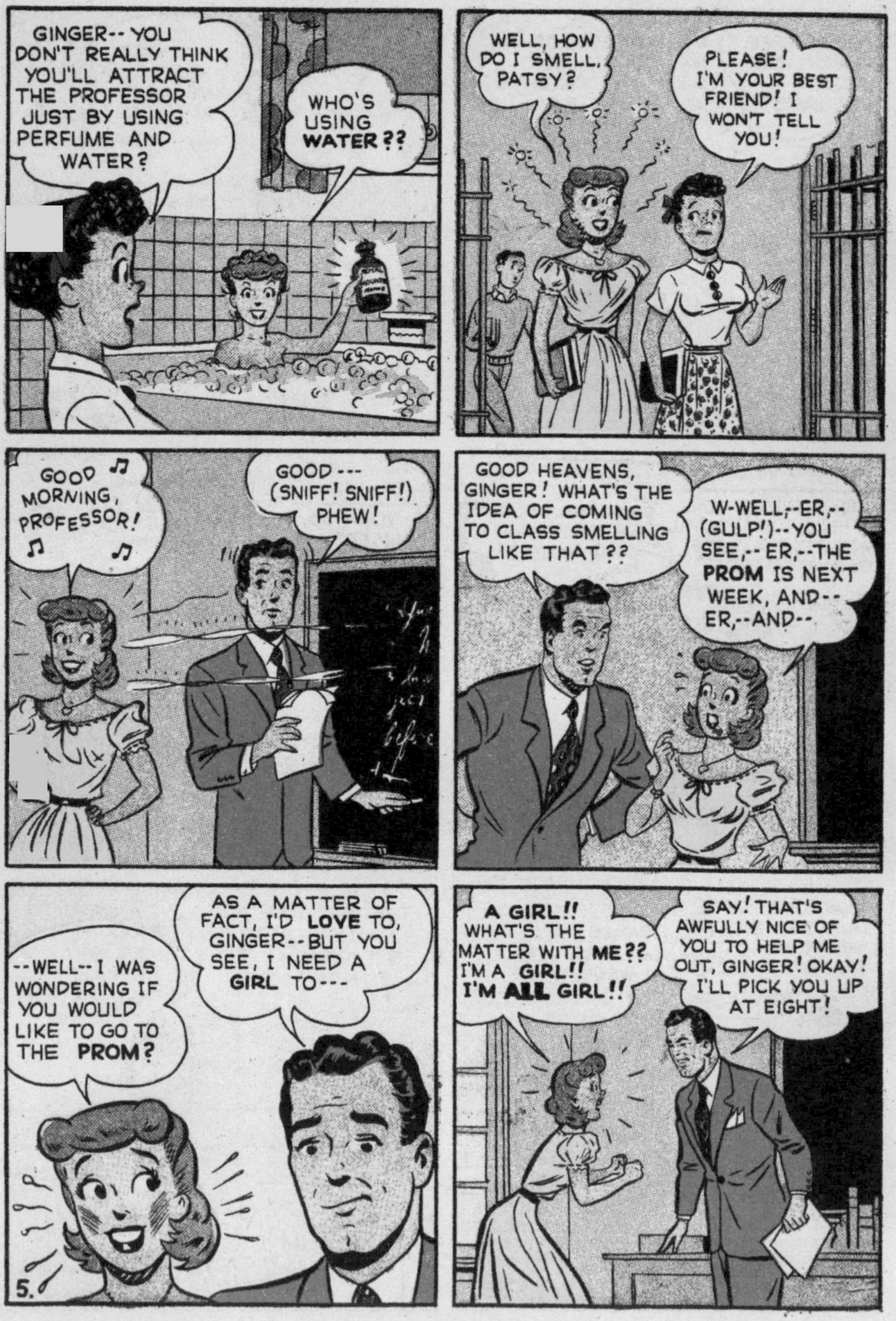
GINGER-- YOU DON'T REALLY THINK YOU'LL ATTRACT THE PROFESSOR JUST BY USING PERFUME AND WATER?
WHO'S USING WATER??
WELL, HOW DO I SMELL, PATSY?
PLEASE! I'M YOUR BEST FRIEND! I WON'T TELL YOU!
GOOD MORNING, PROFESSOR!
GOOD--- (SNIFF! SNIFF!) PHEW!
GOOD HEAVENS, GINGER! WHAT'S THE IDEA OF COMING TO CLASS SMELLING LIKE THAT??
W-WELL,-ER,-- (GULP!)--YOU SEE,-- ER,--THE PROM IS NEXT WEEK, AND-- ER,--AND--
--WELL--I WAS WONDERING IF YOU WOULD LIKE TO GO TO THE PROM?
AS A MATTER OF FACT, I'D LOVE TO, GINGER--BUT YOU SEE, I NEED A GIRL TO---
A GIRL!! WHAT'S THE MATTER WITH ME?? I'M A GIRL!! I'M ALL GIRL!!
SAY! THAT'S AWFULLY NICE OF YOU TO HELP ME OUT, GINGER! OKAY! I'LL PICK YOU UP AT EIGHT!
5.

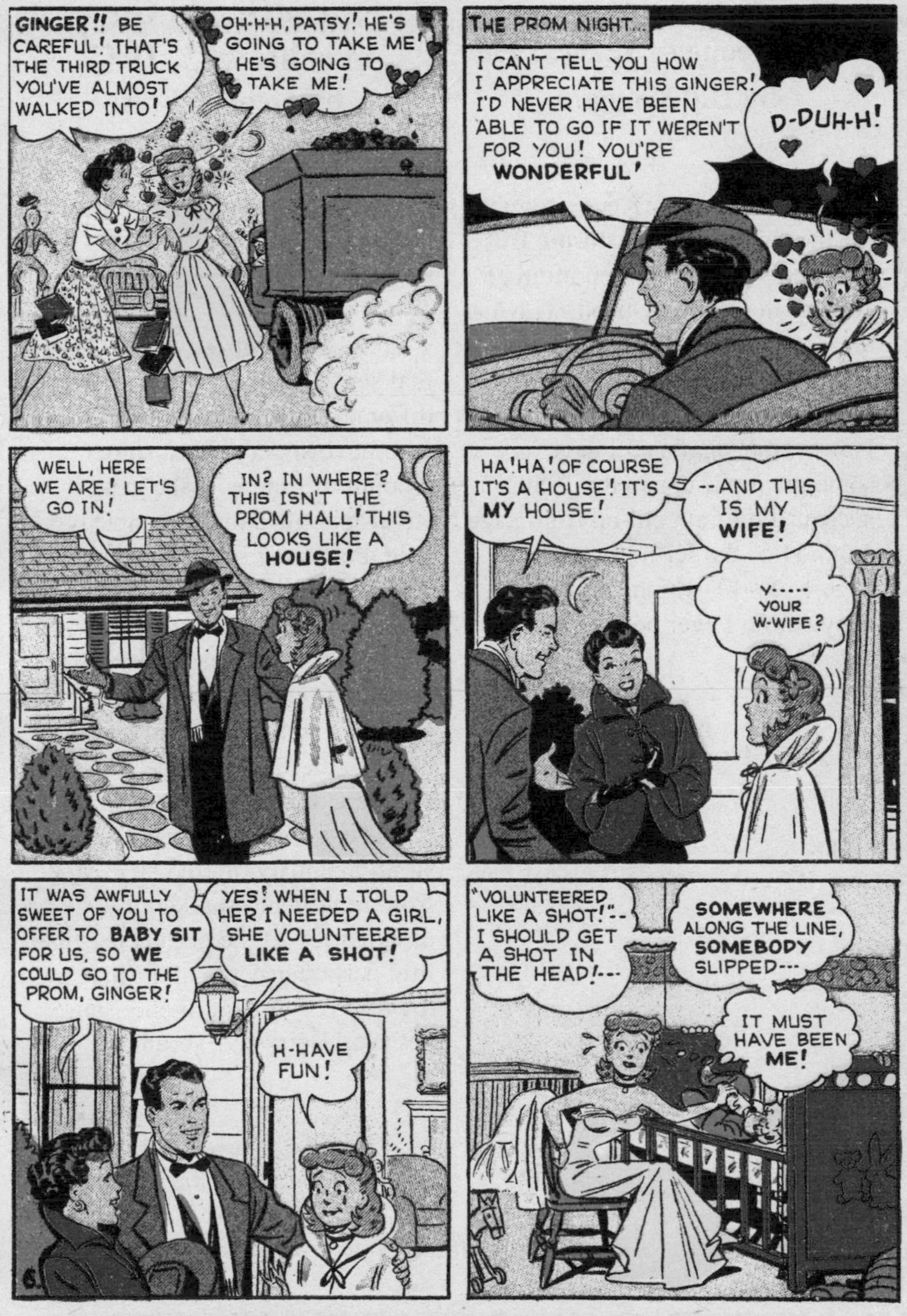
GINGER!! BE CAREFUL! THAT'S THE THIRD TRUCK YOU'VE ALMOST WALKED INTO!
OH-H-H, PATSY! HE'S GOING TO TAKE ME! HE'S GOING TO TAKE ME!
THE PROM NIGHT...
I CAN'T TELL YOU HOW I APPRECIATE THIS GINGER! I'D NEVER HAVE BEEN ABLE TO GO IF IT WEREN'T FOR YOU! YOU'RE WONDERFUL!
D-DUH-H!
WELL, HERE WE ARE! LET'S GO IN!
IN? IN WHERE? THIS ISN'T THE PROM HALL! THIS LOOKS LIKE A HOUSE!
HA! HA! OF COURSE IT'S A HOUSE! IT'S MY HOUSE!
--AND THIS IS MY WIFE!
Y---- YOUR W-WIFE?
IT WAS AWFULLY SWEET OF YOU TO OFFER TO BABY SIT FOR US, SO WE COULD GO TO THE PROM, GINGER!
YES! WHEN I TOLD HER I NEEDED A GIRL, SHE VOLUNTEERED LIKE A SHOT!
H-HAVE FUN!
"VOLUNTEERED LIKE A SHOT!"-- I SHOULD GET A SHOT IN THE HEAD!---
SOMEWHERE ALONG THE LINE, SOMEBODY SLIPPED---
IT MUST HAVE BEEN ME!

Pin-ups
Katy Keene #s 12-51, 1950
by Bill Woggon

My favorite Katy Keene comics are the early issues, featuring Bill Woggon's glamorous rendition of Katy as the Pin-up Queen, with his art at its best (before being toned down in the 1950s).

However, Woggon still gave us some great pin-ups in the 1950s, such as the Pirate pin-up from page 1 of #51 or the sci-fi pin-up from page 1 of #40, which was the first Katy comic I ever bought.

--Andrew Pepoy
Writer and illustrator,
Archie Comics

Touch and Go
Archie #63, 1953
by George Frese

Archie and Veronica take a trip to the cinema and have a "howling" good time!

Archie and I go way back. In that sense, at least, I'm not much different than the millions of fans who have spent at least some amount of time with the gang in Riverdale. As a kid, I anxiously read and re-read the adventures of Archie, Betty, Veronica, Jughead, Reggie, their friends, family and teachers. My mother would prepare a big, Jughead-esque plate of hamburgers, and I would dig into them and a huge stack of Archie Comics at the same time. It was a wonderful world that simultaneously offered an escape from reality and sparked my imagination of the perfect teenaged life, particularly the malt shop and the impossible task of choosing between Betty and Veronica.

--Steve Geppi
Founder,
Diamond Comic Distributors
Excerpted from his foreword in
Archie Americana: Best of the Eighties

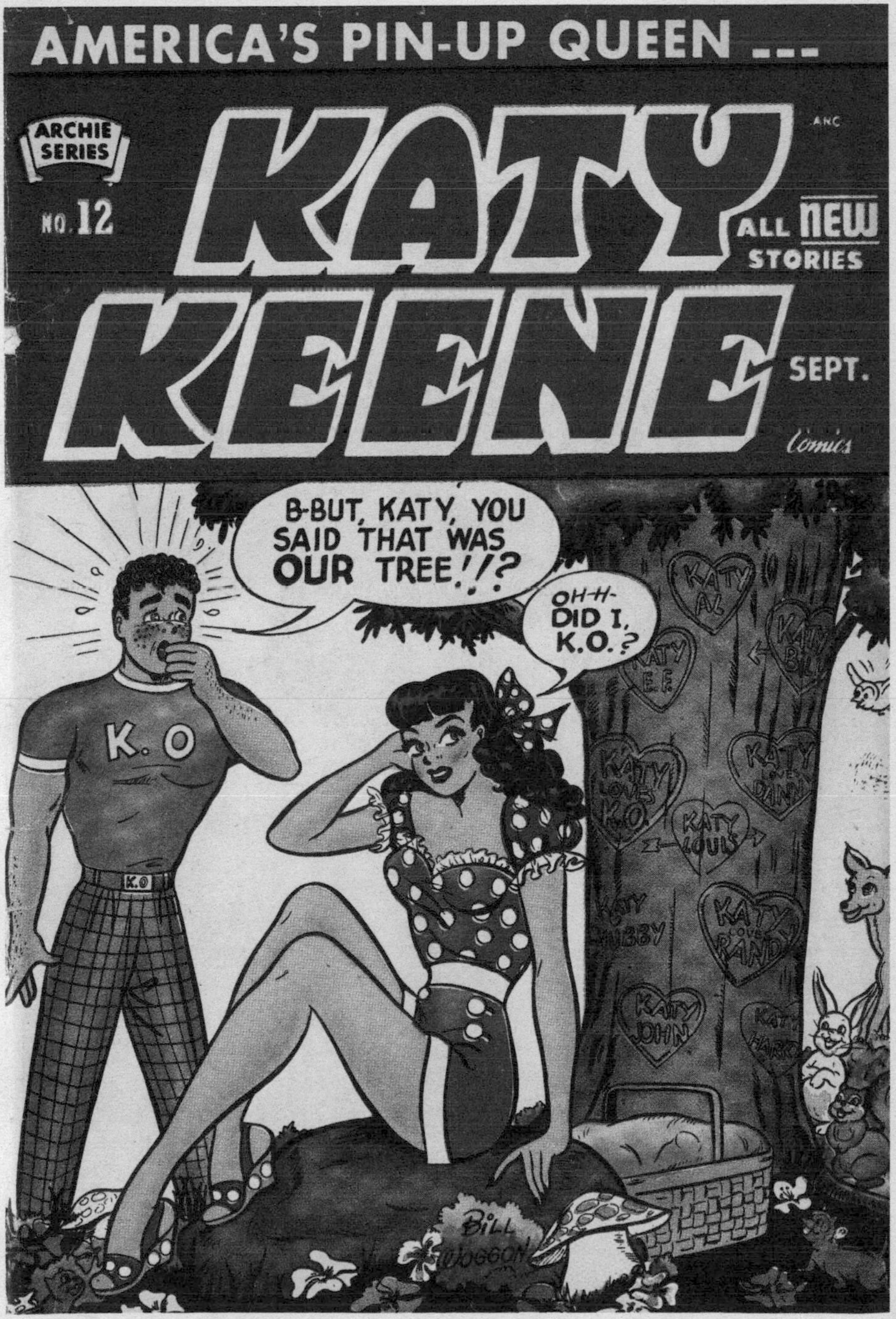
AMERICA'S PIN-UP QUEEN ....
ARCHIE SERIES
NO. 12
KATY KEENE
ALL NEW STORIES
SEPT.
Comics
B-BUT, KATY, YOU SAID THAT WAS OUR TREE!!?
OH-H- DID I, K.O.?
K.O
BILL WOGGON

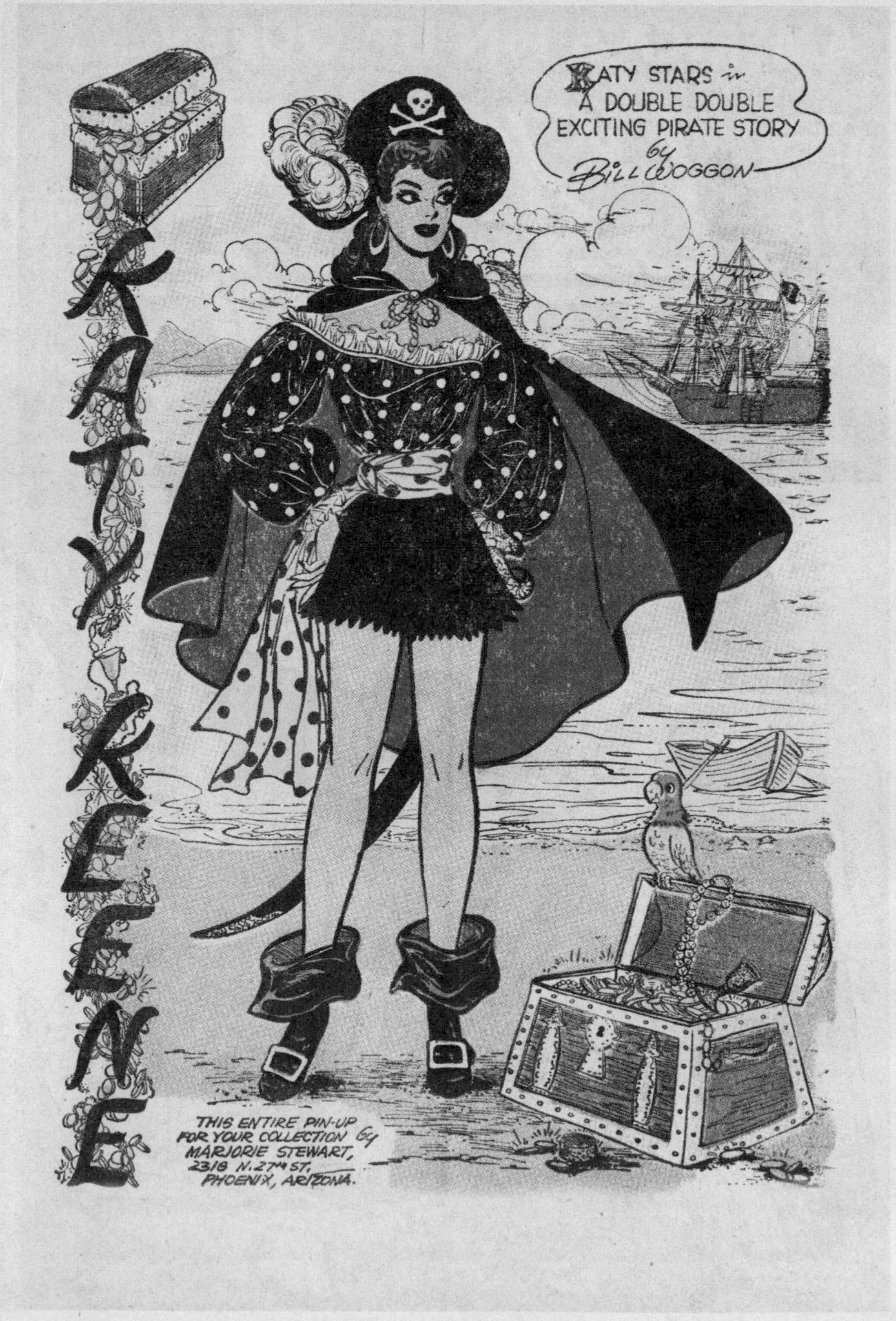
KATY STARS in
A DOUBLE DOUBLE
EXCITING PIRATE STORY
by
BILL WOGGON
KATY KEENE
THIS ENTIRE PIN-UP
FOR YOUR COLLECTION by
MARJORIE STEWART,
2318 N. 27th ST,
PHOENIX, ARIZONA.

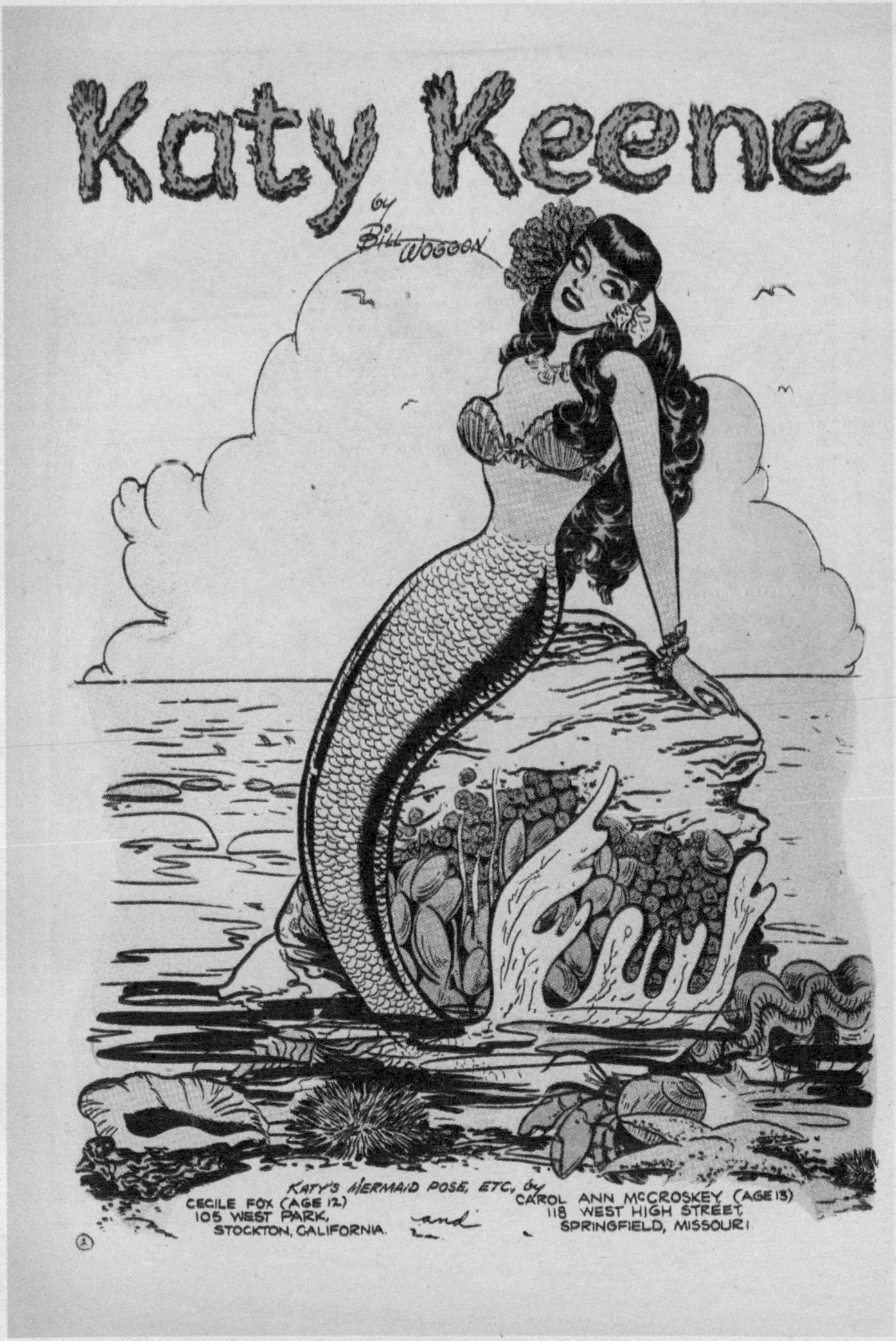
Katy Keene
by
Bill Woggon
Katy's Mermaid pose, etc. by
Cecile Fox (Age 12)
105 West Park,
Stockton, California.
and
Carol Ann McCroskey (Age 13)
118 West High Street,
Springfield, Missouri
1

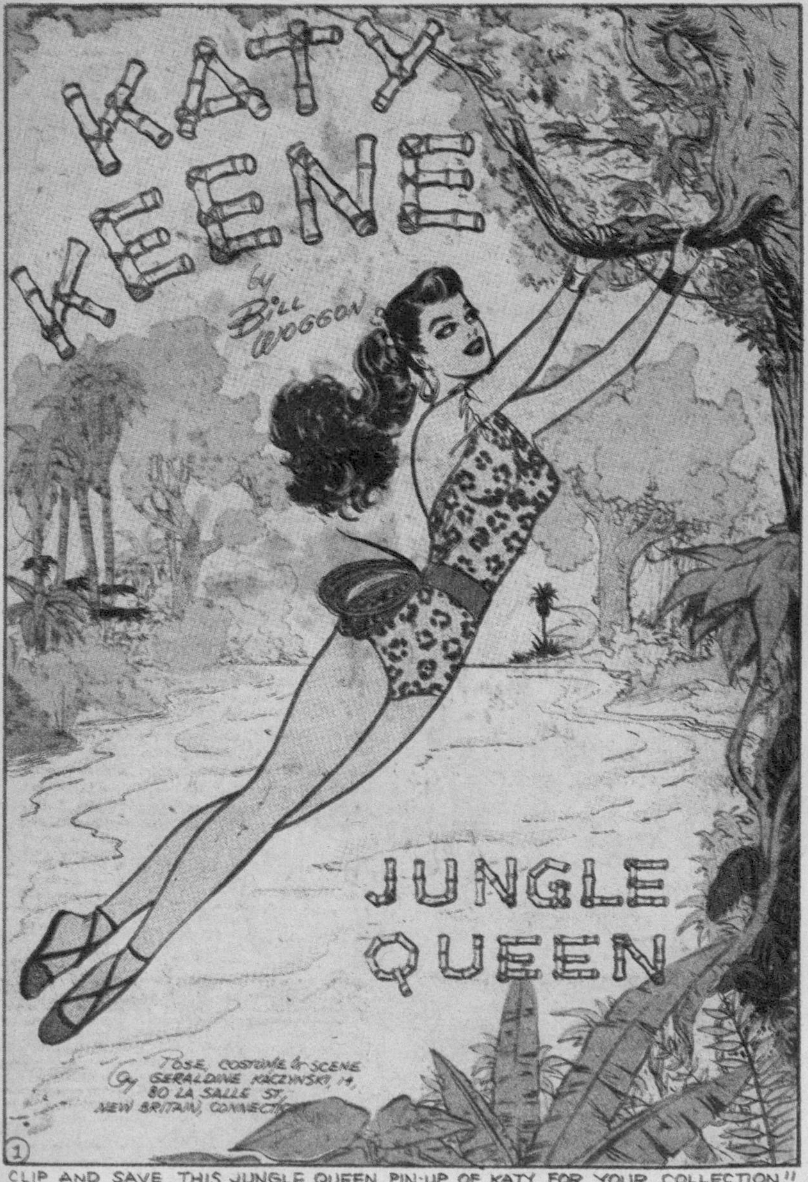
KATY KEENE
by Bill Woggon
JUNGLE QUEEN
POSE, COSTUME & SCENE
by GERALDINE KACZYNSKI, 14,
80 LA SALLE ST.,
NEW BRITAIN, CONNECTIC
1
CLIP AND SAVE THIS JUNGLE QUEEN PIN-UP OF KATY FOR YOUR COLLECTION!!

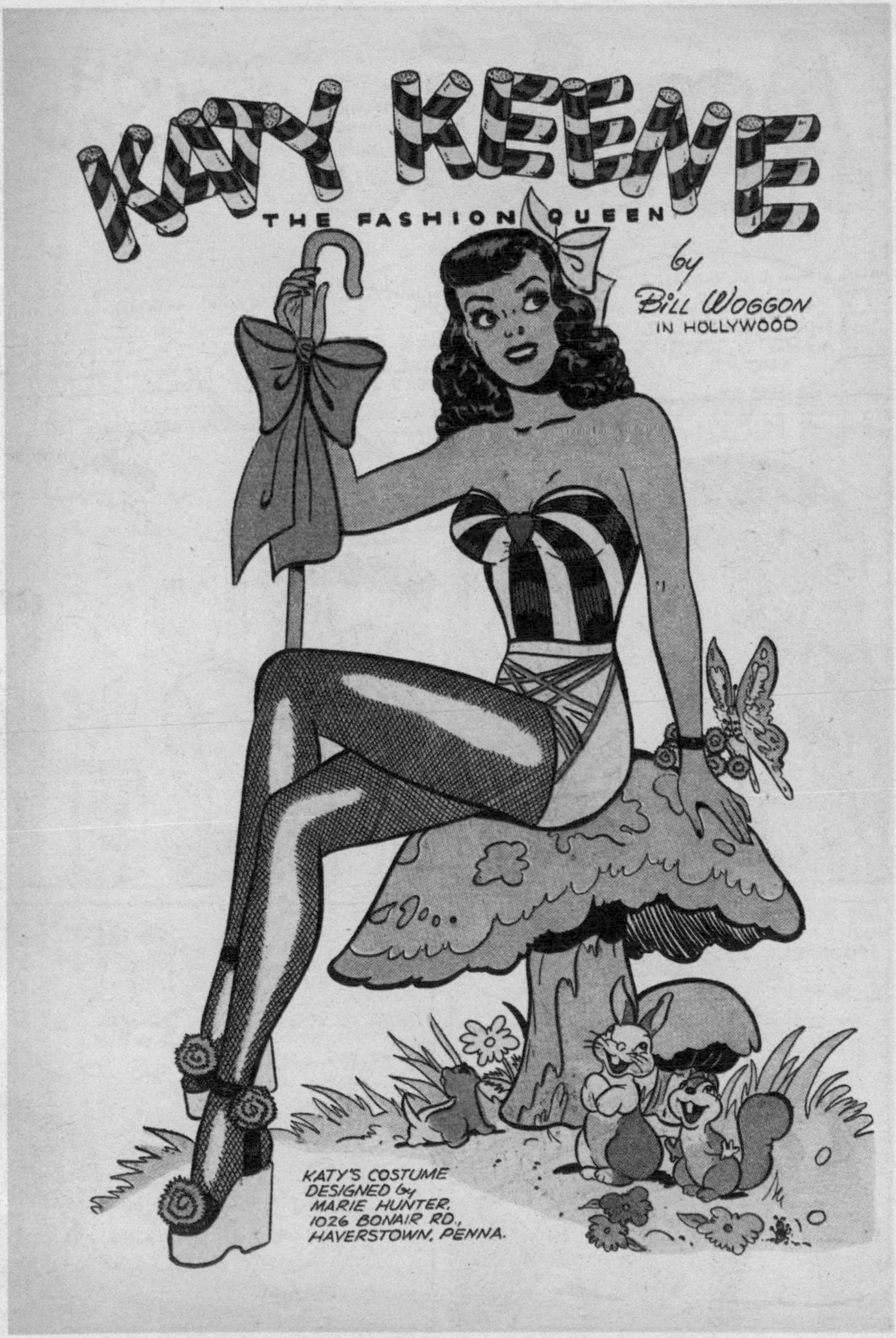
KATY KEENE
THE FASHION QUEEN
by
BILL WOGGON
IN HOLLYWOOD
KATY'S COSTUME
DESIGNED by
MARIE HUNTER,
1026 BONAIR RD.,
HAVERSTOWN, PENNA.

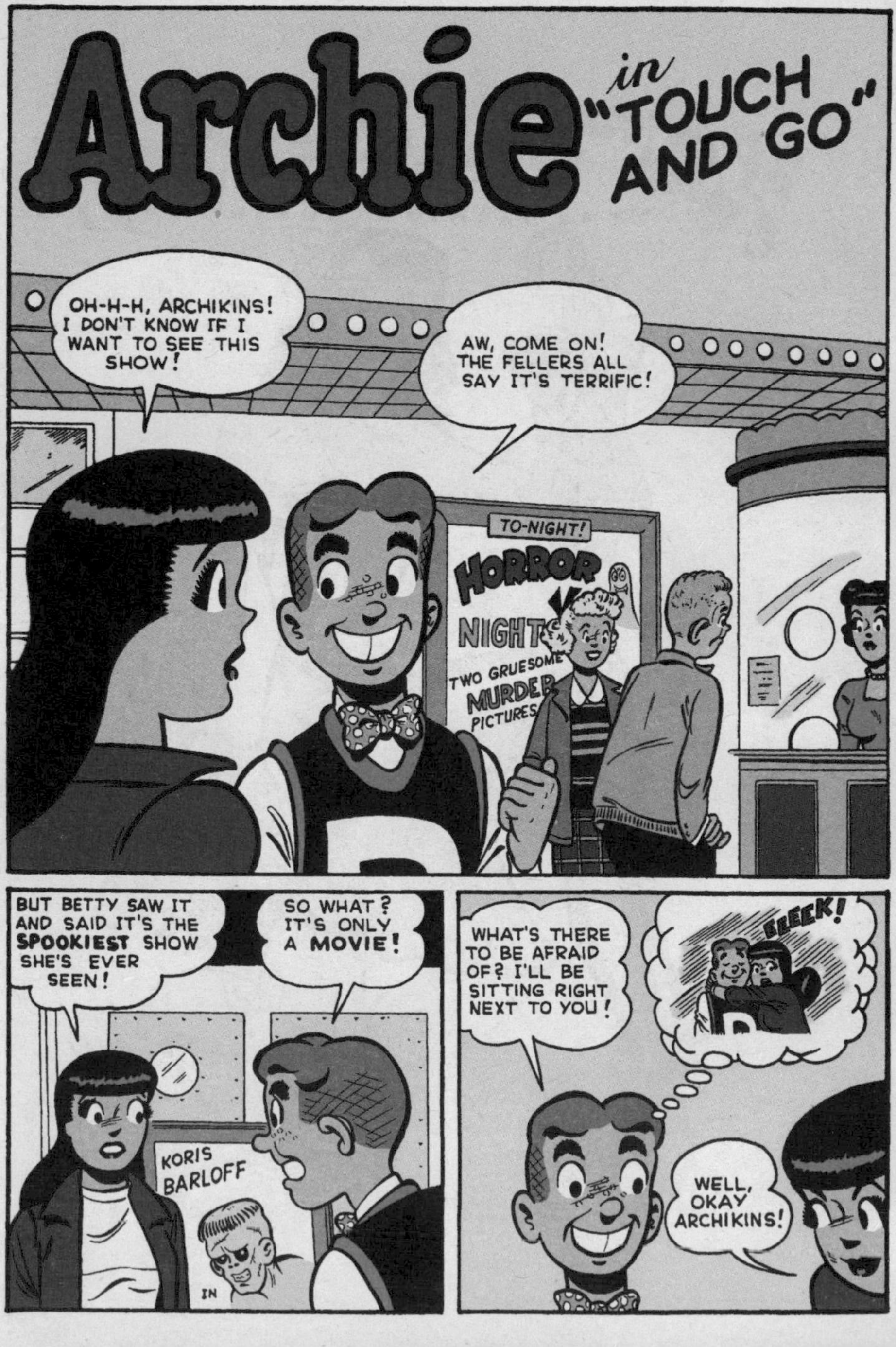
Archie in "TOUCH AND GO"
OH-H-H, ARCHIKINS! I DON'T KNOW IF I WANT TO SEE THIS SHOW!
AW, COME ON! THE FELLERS ALL SAY IT'S TERRIFIC!
TO-NIGHT!
HORROR NIGHT
TWO GRUESOME MURDER PICTURES
BUT BETTY SAW IT AND SAID IT'S THE SPOOKIEST SHOW SHE'S EVER SEEN!
SO WHAT? IT'S ONLY A MOVIE!
KORIS BARLOFF
IN
WHAT'S THERE TO BE AFRAID OF? I'LL BE SITTING RIGHT NEXT TO YOU!
EEEEK!
WELL, OKAY ARCHIKINS!

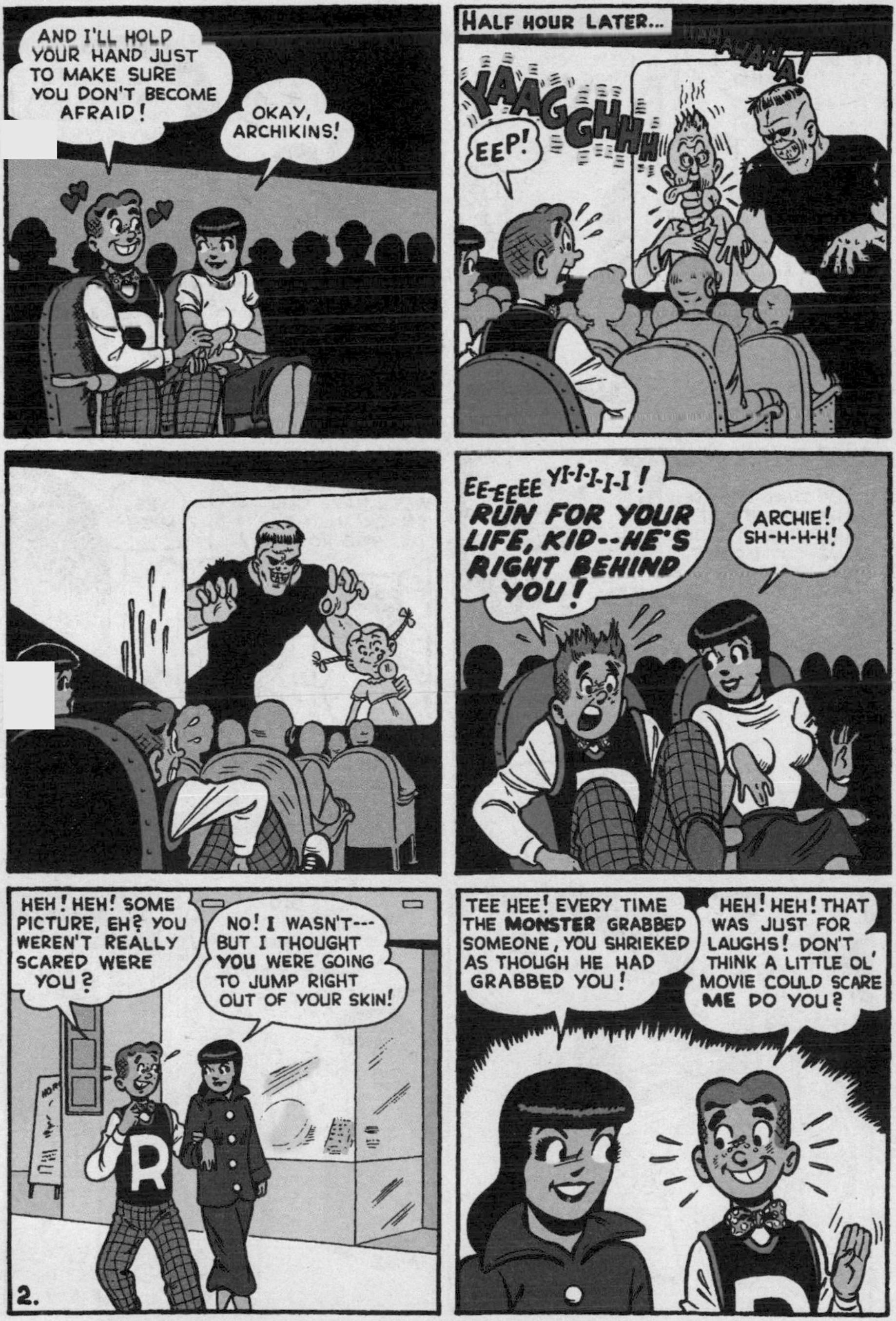
AND I'LL HOLD YOUR HAND JUST TO MAKE SURE YOU DON'T BECOME AFRAID!
OKAY, ARCHIKINS!
HALF HOUR LATER...
HAHAHAHA!
YAAGGHHH
EEP!
EE-EEEE YI-I-I-I-I!
RUN FOR YOUR LIFE, KID--HE'S RIGHT BEHIND YOU!
ARCHIE! SH-H-H-H!
HEH! HEH! SOME PICTURE, EH? YOU WEREN'T REALLY SCARED WERE YOU?
NO! I WASN'T--- BUT I THOUGHT YOU WERE GOING TO JUMP RIGHT OUT OF YOUR SKIN!
2.
TEE HEE! EVERY TIME THE MONSTER GRABBED SOMEONE, YOU SHRIEKED AS THOUGH HE HAD GRABBED YOU!
HEH! HEH! THAT WAS JUST FOR LAUGHS! DON'T THINK A LITTLE OL' MOVIE COULD SCARE ME DO YOU?

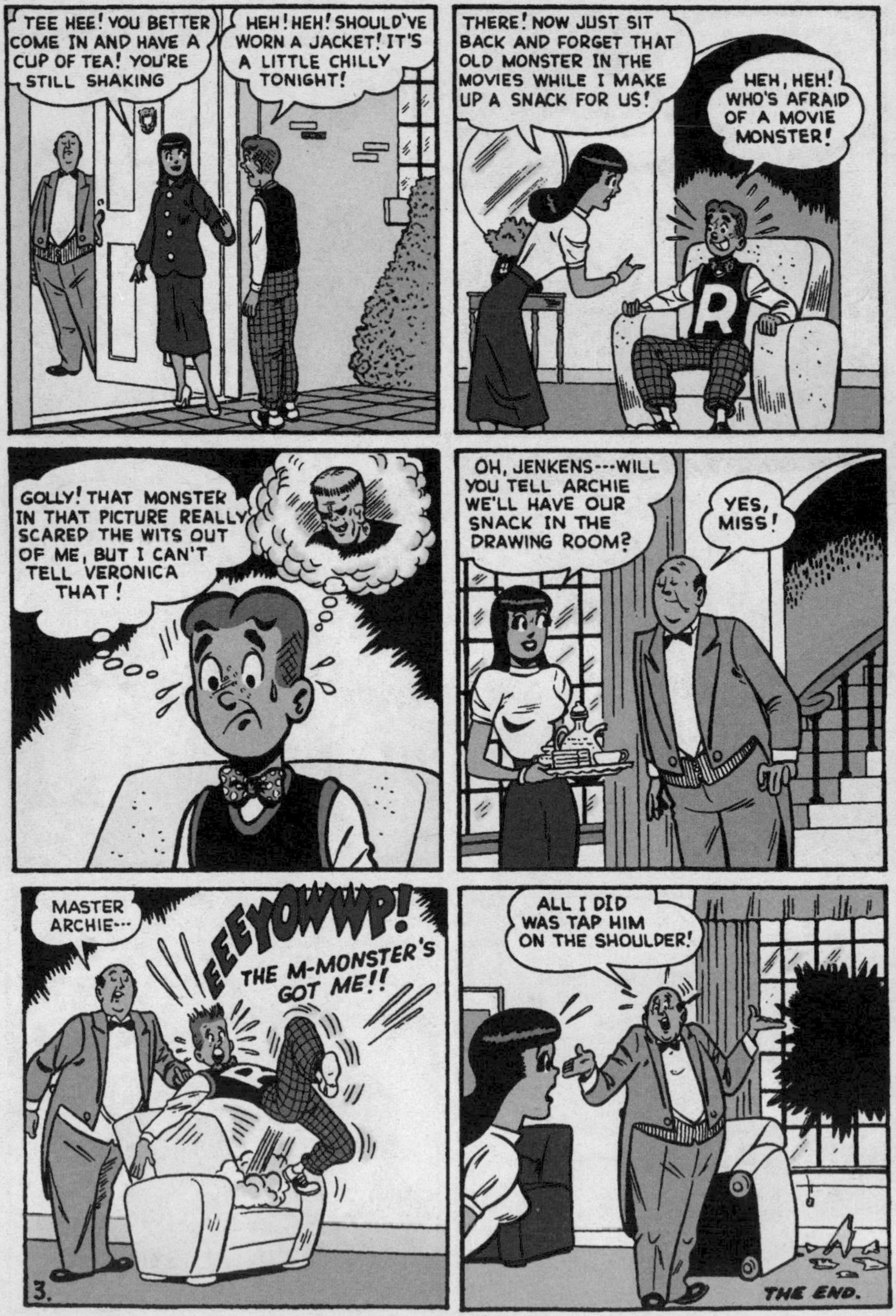
TEE HEE! YOU BETTER COME IN AND HAVE A CUP OF TEA! YOU'RE STILL SHAKING
HEH! HEH! SHOULD'VE WORN A JACKET! IT'S A LITTLE CHILLY TONIGHT!
THERE! NOW JUST SIT BACK AND FORGET THAT OLD MONSTER IN THE MOVIES WHILE I MAKE UP A SNACK FOR US!
HEH, HEH! WHO'S AFRAID OF A MOVIE MONSTER!
GOLLY! THAT MONSTER IN THAT PICTURE REALLY SCARED THE WITS OUT OF ME, BUT I CAN'T TELL VERONICA THAT!
OH, JENKENS---WILL YOU TELL ARCHIE WE'LL HAVE OUR SNACK IN THE DRAWING ROOM?
YES, MISS!
MASTER ARCHIE---
EEEYOWWP!
THE M-MONSTER'S GOT ME!!
3.
ALL I DID WAS TAP HIM ON THE SHOULDER!
THE END.

Love that Baby Sitting
Li'l Jinx #1, 1956
by Joe Edwards

This is a Joe Edwards story featuring Li'l Jinx, a cute girl who wanted to do what she wanted to do, that was first printed in 1956. Jinx would age over the course of the original strip's run to about 8 years old, so this very "Li'l Jinx" is a rarely seen treat. As a bonus, we see a glimpse of Jinx's mother, who would later all but disappear, as Li'l Jinx's relationship with her father became the focus of her home life.

--Suzannah Rowntree
Features Editor,
Life with Archie Magazine

Seal of Disapproval
Jughead #47, 1958
by Samm Schwartz

I like this story. It's got everything. It's got a seal and it has a monkey. Ha!

--Carlos Antunes
Editor, Archie Comics

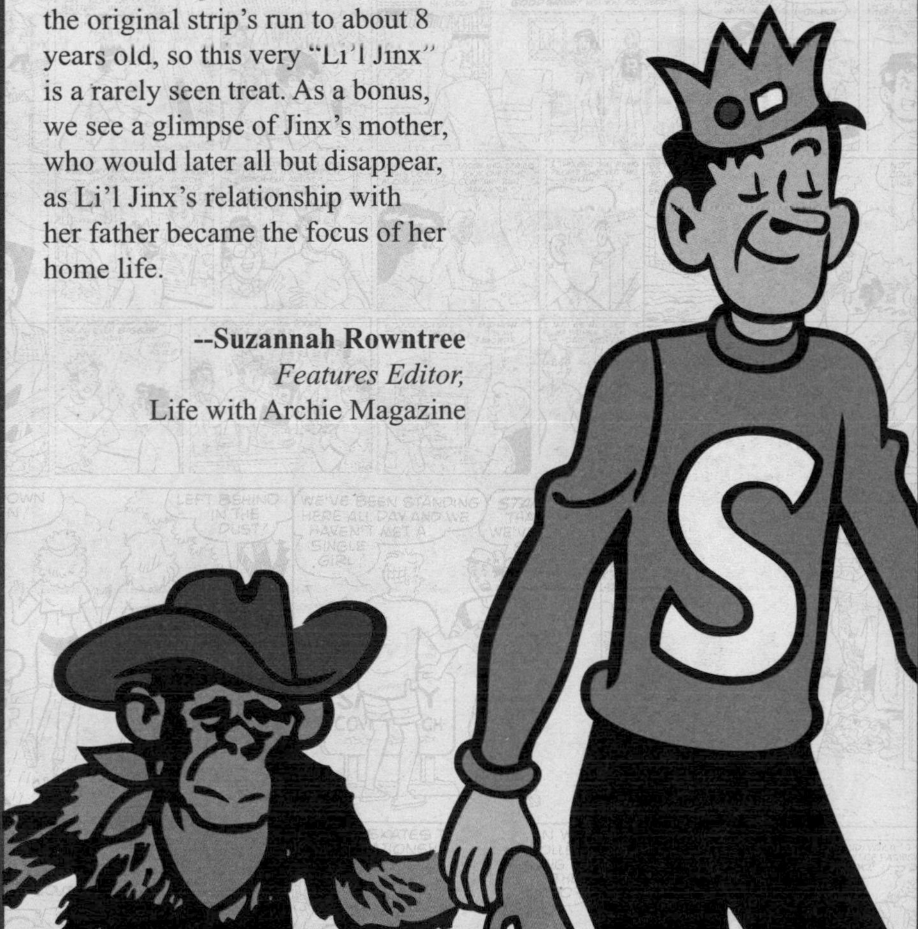

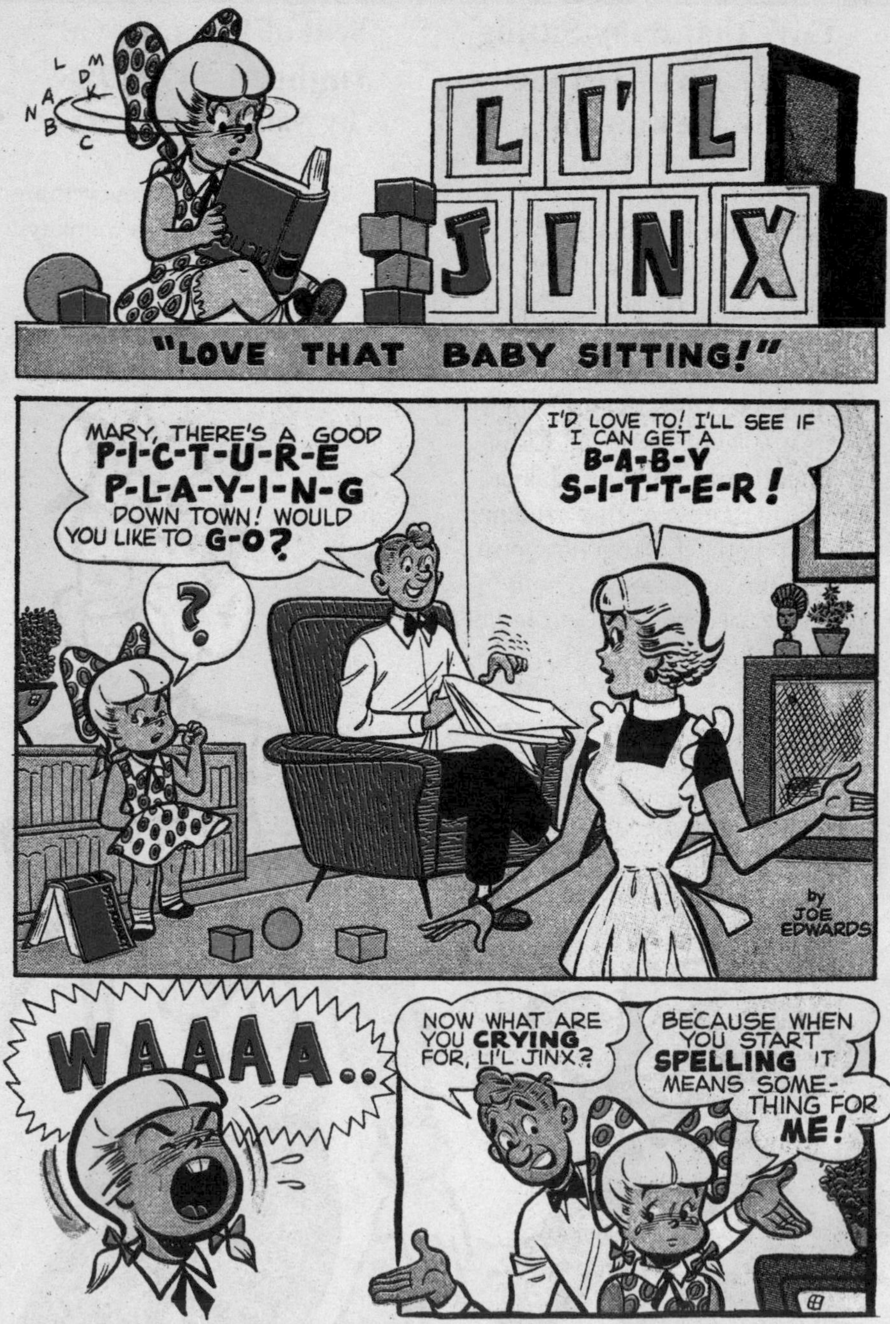
LI'L JINX
"LOVE THAT BABY SITTING!"
MARY, THERE'S A GOOD P-I-C-T-U-R-E P-L-A-Y-I-N-G DOWN TOWN! WOULD YOU LIKE TO G-O?
?
I'D LOVE TO! I'LL SEE IF I CAN GET A B-A-B-Y S-I-T-T-E-R!
by JOE EDWARDS
WAAAA..
NOW WHAT ARE YOU CRYING FOR, LI'L JINX?
BECAUSE WHEN YOU START SPELLING IT MEANS SOME-THING FOR ME!

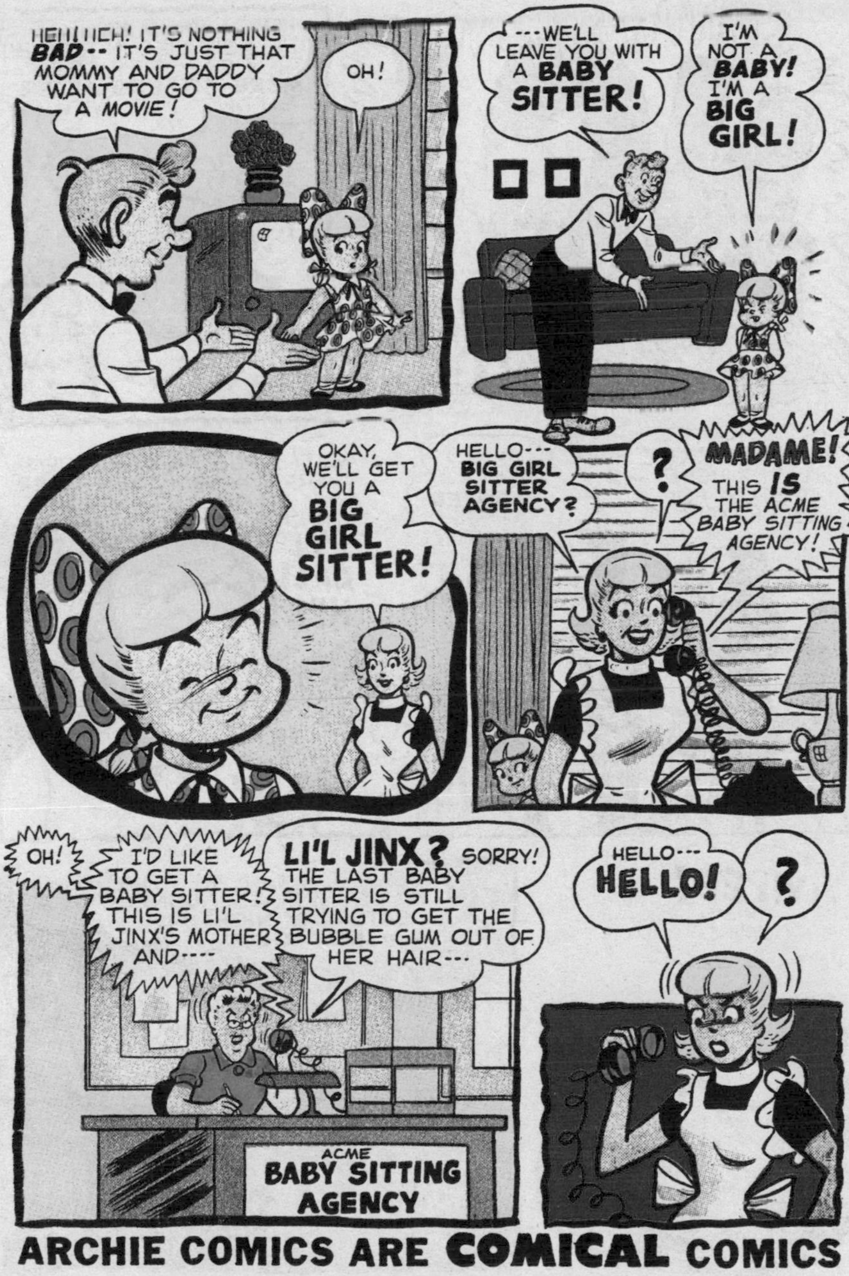
HEH! HEH! IT'S NOTHING BAD-- IT'S JUST THAT MOMMY AND DADDY WANT TO GO TO A MOVIE!
OH!
---WE'LL LEAVE YOU WITH A BABY SITTER!
I'M NOT A BABY! I'M A BIG GIRL!
OKAY, WE'LL GET YOU A BIG GIRL SITTER!
HELLO--- BIG GIRL SITTER AGENCY?
?
MADAME! THIS IS THE ACME BABY SITTING AGENCY!
OH!
I'D LIKE TO GET A BABY SITTER! THIS IS LI'L JINX'S MOTHER AND----
LI'L JINX? SORRY! THE LAST BABY SITTER IS STILL TRYING TO GET THE BUBBLE GUM OUT OF HER HAIR---
ACME BABY SITTING AGENCY
HELLO--- HELLO!
?
ARCHIE COMICS ARE COMICAL COMICS

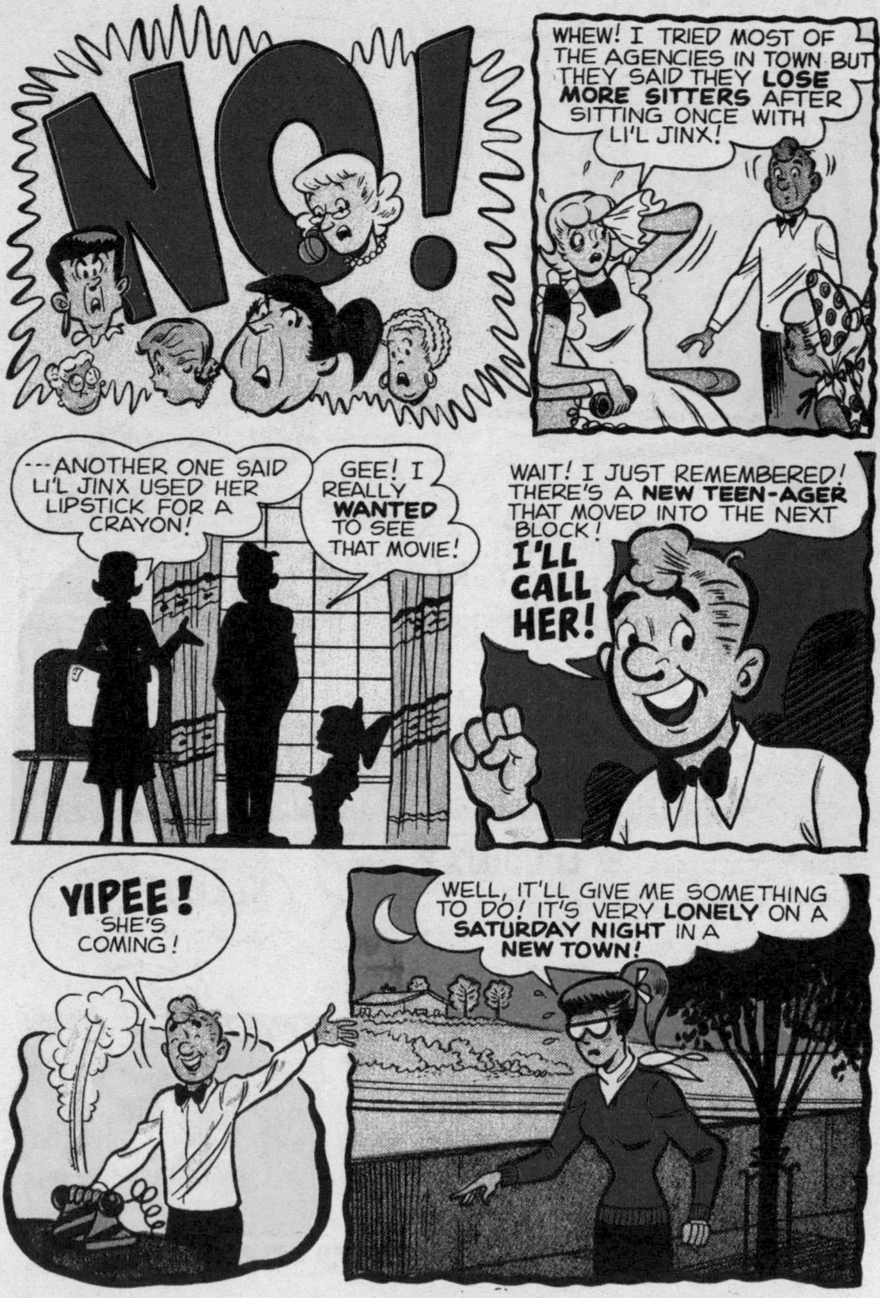
NO!
WHEW! I TRIED MOST OF THE AGENCIES IN TOWN BUT THEY SAID THEY LOSE MORE SITTERS AFTER SITTING ONCE WITH LI'L JINX!
---ANOTHER ONE SAID LI'L JINX USED HER LIPSTICK FOR A CRAYON!
GEE! I REALLY WANTED TO SEE THAT MOVIE!
WAIT! I JUST REMEMBERED! THERE'S A NEW TEEN-AGER THAT MOVED INTO THE NEXT BLOCK! I'LL CALL HER!
YIPEE! SHE'S COMING!
WELL, IT'LL GIVE ME SOMETHING TO DO! IT'S VERY LONELY ON A SATURDAY NIGHT IN A NEW TOWN!

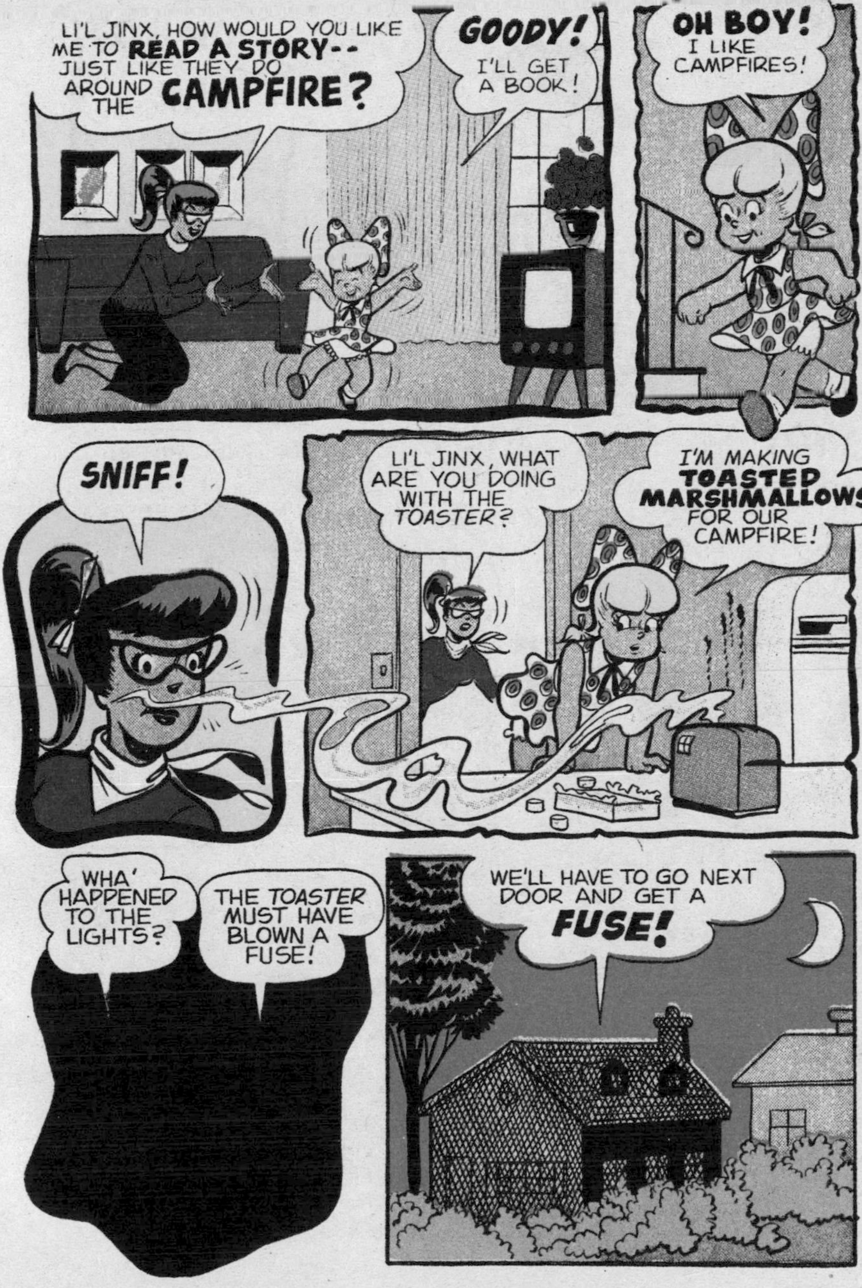
LI'L JINX, HOW WOULD YOU LIKE ME TO READ A STORY-- JUST LIKE THEY DO AROUND THE CAMPFIRE?
GOODY! I'LL GET A BOOK!
OH BOY! I LIKE CAMPFIRES!
SNIFF!
LI'L JINX, WHAT ARE YOU DOING WITH THE TOASTER?
I'M MAKING TOASTED MARSHMALLOWS! FOR OUR CAMPFIRE!
WHA' HAPPENED TO THE LIGHTS?
THE TOASTER MUST HAVE BLOWN A FUSE!
WE'LL HAVE TO GO NEXT DOOR AND GET A FUSE!

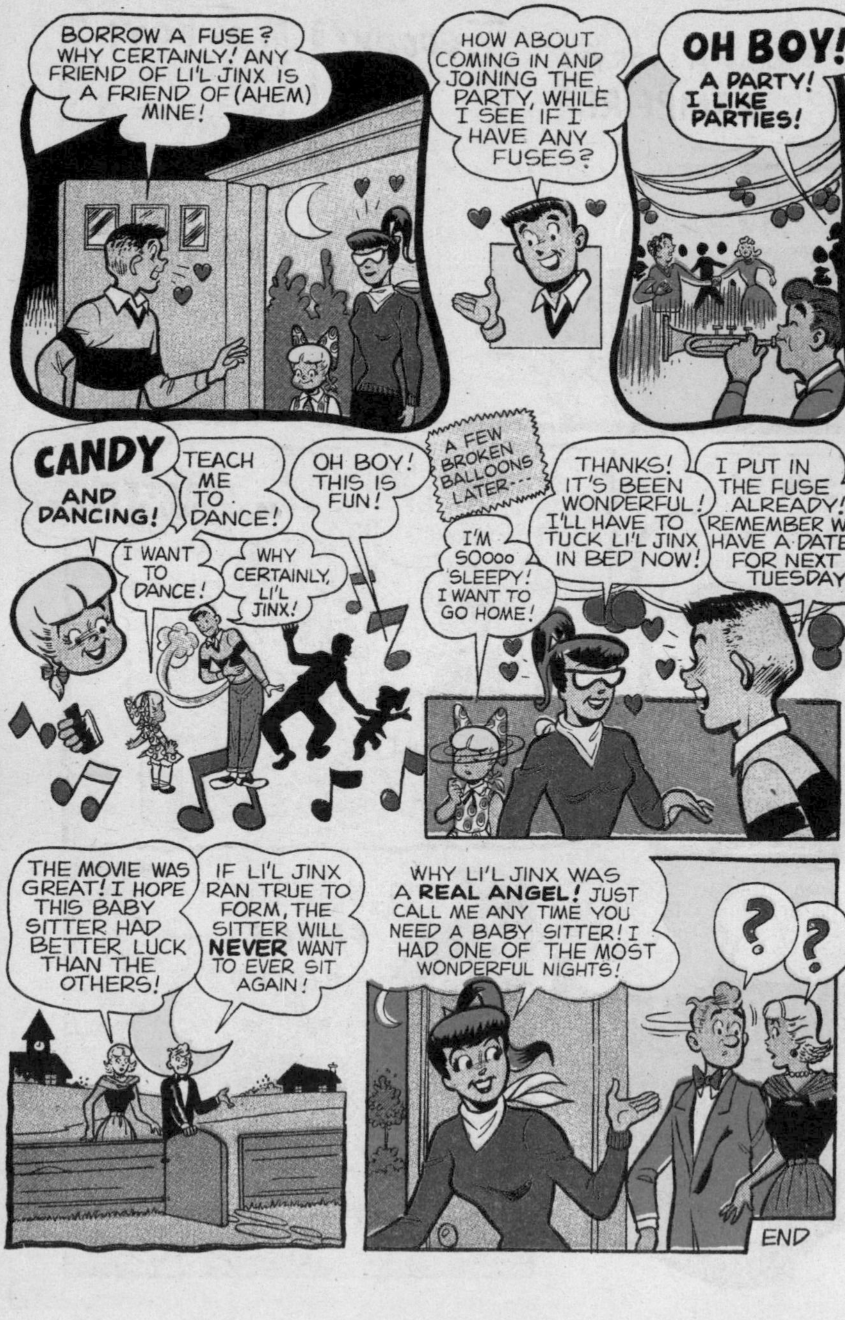
BORROW A FUSE? WHY CERTAINLY! ANY FRIEND OF LI'L JINX IS A FRIEND OF (AHEM) MINE!
HOW ABOUT COMING IN AND JOINING THE PARTY, WHILE I SEE IF I HAVE ANY FUSES?
OH BOY! A PARTY! I LIKE PARTIES!
CANDY AND DANCING!
TEACH ME TO DANCE!
I WANT TO DANCE!
WHY CERTAINLY, LI'L JINX!
OH BOY! THIS IS FUN!
A FEW BROKEN BALLOONS LATER---
I'M SOooo SLEEPY! I WANT TO GO HOME!
THANKS! IT'S BEEN WONDERFUL! I'LL HAVE TO TUCK LI'L JINX IN BED NOW!
I PUT IN THE FUSE ALREADY! REMEMBER WE HAVE A DATE FOR NEXT TUESDAY!
THE MOVIE WAS GREAT! I HOPE THIS BABY SITTER HAD BETTER LUCK THAN THE OTHERS!
IF LI'L JINX RAN TRUE TO FORM, THE SITTER WILL NEVER WANT TO EVER SIT AGAIN!
WHY LI'L JINX WAS A REAL ANGEL! JUST CALL ME ANY TIME YOU NEED A BABY SITTER! I HAD ONE OF THE MOST WONDERFUL NIGHTS!
?
?
END

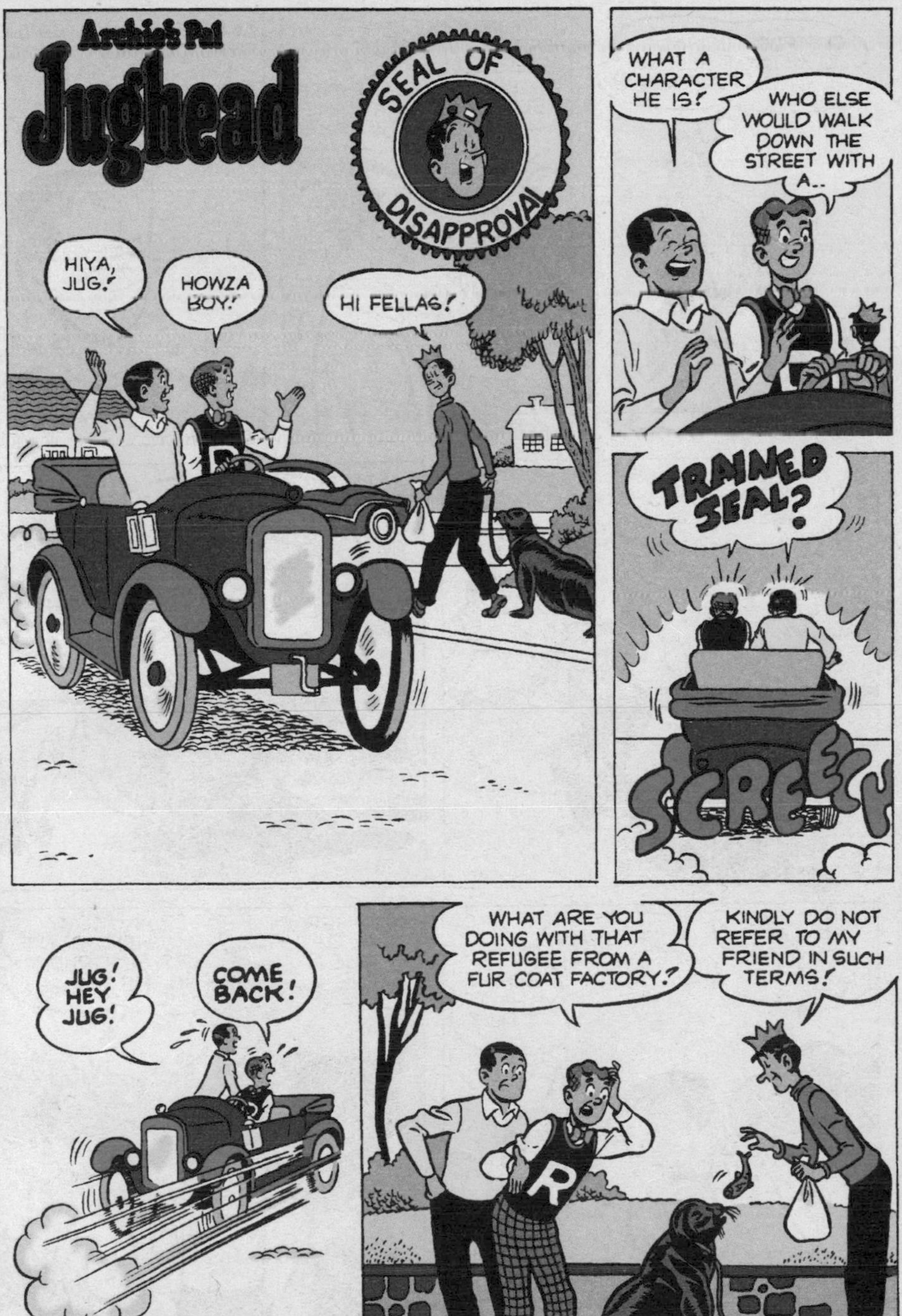
Archie's Pal
Jughead
SEAL OF DISAPPROVAL
HIYA, JUG!
HOWZA BOY!
HI FELLAS!
WHAT A CHARACTER HE IS!
WHO ELSE WOULD WALK DOWN THE STREET WITH A..
TRAINED SEAL?
SCREECH
JUG! HEY JUG!
COME BACK!
WHAT ARE YOU DOING WITH THAT REFUGEE FROM A FUR COAT FACTORY?
KINDLY DO NOT REFER TO MY FRIEND IN SUCH TERMS!

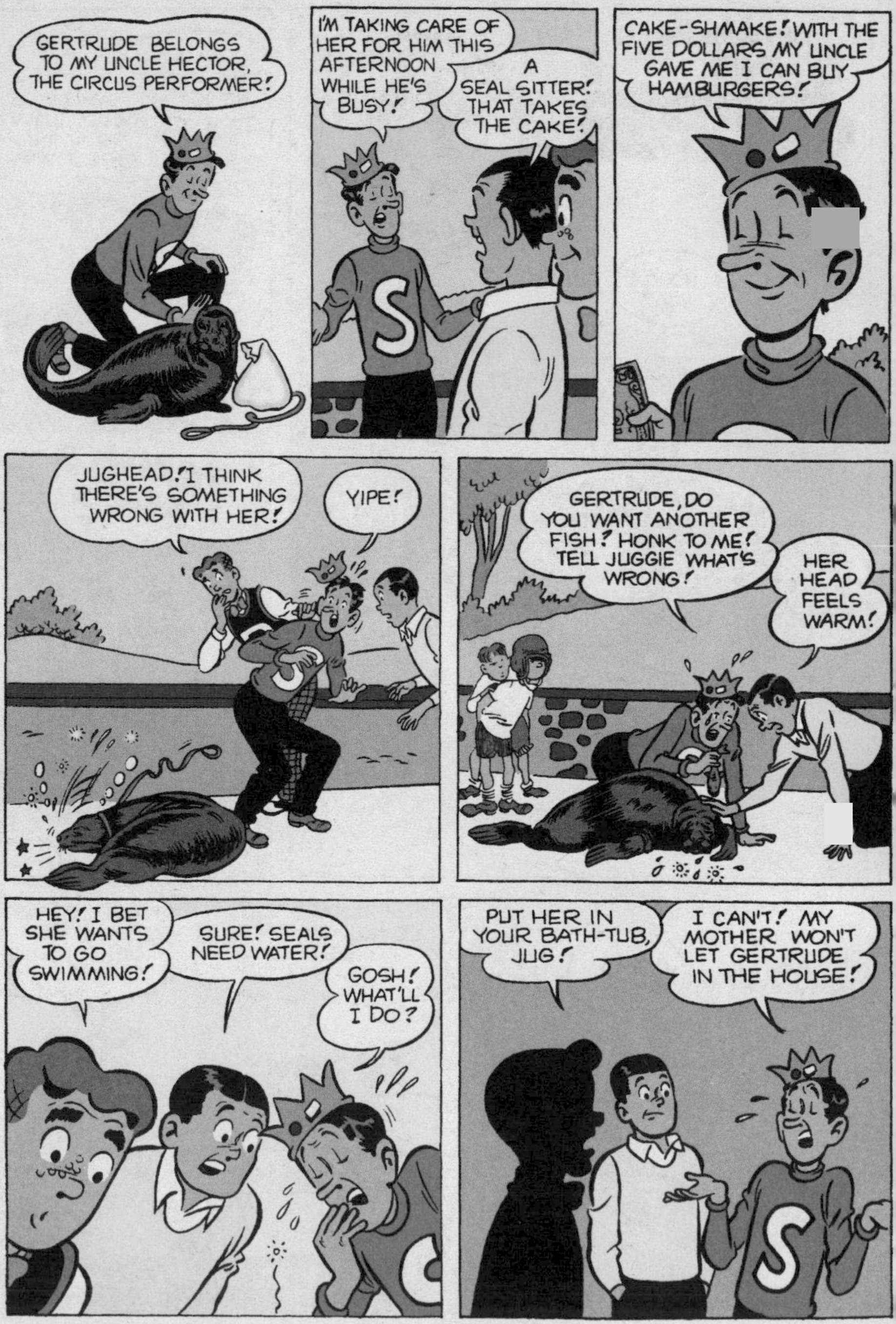
GERTRUDE BELONGS TO MY UNCLE HECTOR, THE CIRCUS PERFORMER!
I'M TAKING CARE OF HER FOR HIM THIS AFTERNOON WHILE HE'S BUSY!
A SEAL SITTER! THAT TAKES THE CAKE!
CAKE-SHMAKE! WITH THE FIVE DOLLARS MY UNCLE GAVE ME I CAN BUY HAMBURGERS!
JUGHEAD! I THINK THERE'S SOMETHING WRONG WITH HER!
YIPE!
GERTRUDE, DO YOU WANT ANOTHER FISH? HONK TO ME! TELL JUGGIE WHAT'S WRONG!
HER HEAD FEELS WARM!
HEY! I BET SHE WANTS TO GO SWIMMING!
SURE! SEALS NEED WATER!
GOSH! WHAT'LL I DO?
PUT HER IN YOUR BATH-TUB, JUG!
I CAN'T! MY MOTHER WON'T LET GERTRUDE IN THE HOUSE!

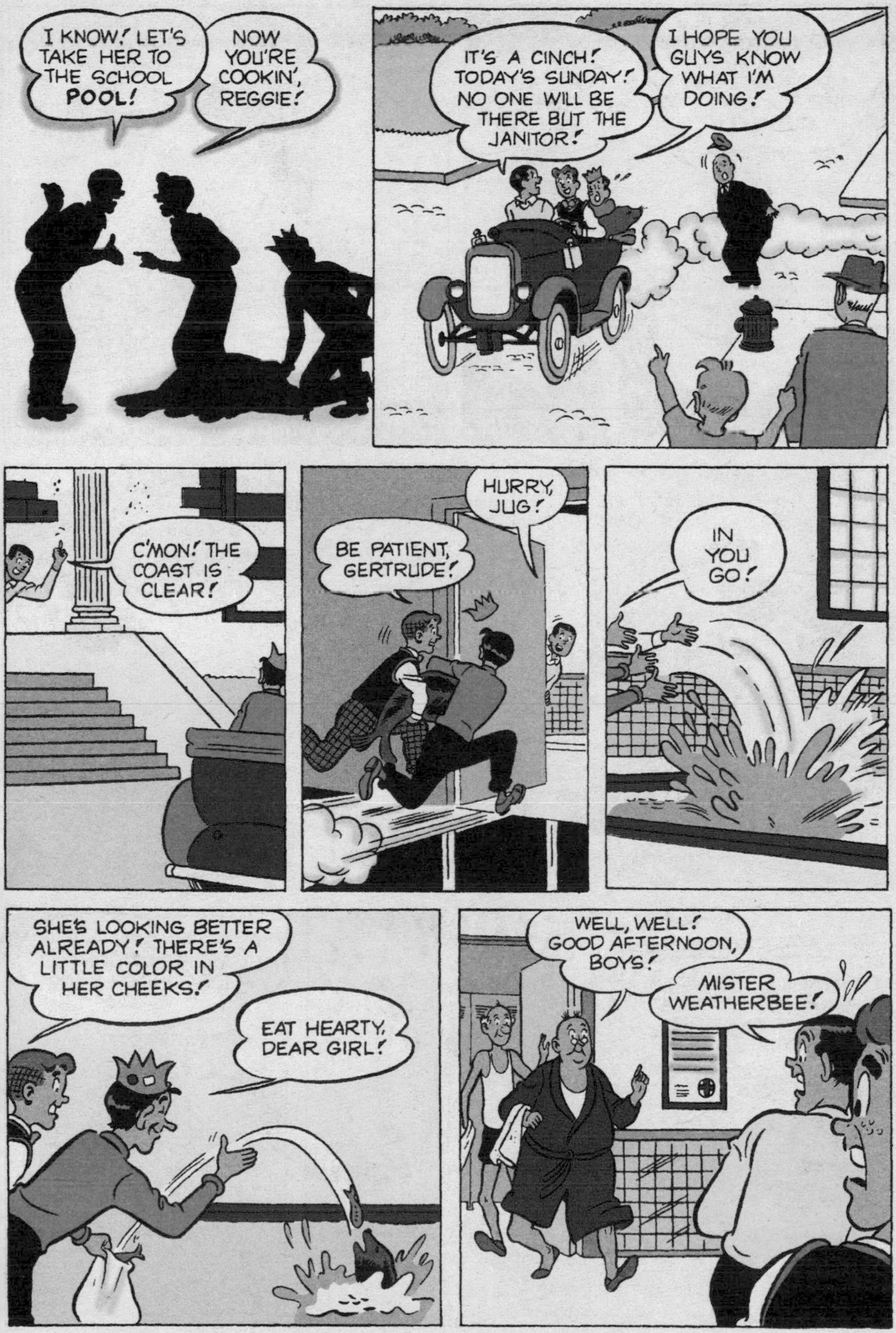
I KNOW! LET'S TAKE HER TO THE SCHOOL **POOL**!
NOW YOU'RE COOKIN', REGGIE!
IT'S A CINCH! TODAY'S SUNDAY! NO ONE WILL BE THERE BUT THE JANITOR!
I HOPE YOU GUYS KNOW WHAT I'M DOING!
C'MON! THE COAST IS CLEAR!
HURRY, JUG!
BE PATIENT, GERTRUDE!
IN YOU GO!
SHE'S LOOKING BETTER ALREADY! THERE'S A LITTLE COLOR IN HER CHEEKS!
EAT HEARTY, DEAR GIRL!
WELL, WELL! GOOD AFTERNOON, BOYS!
MISTER WEATHERBEE!

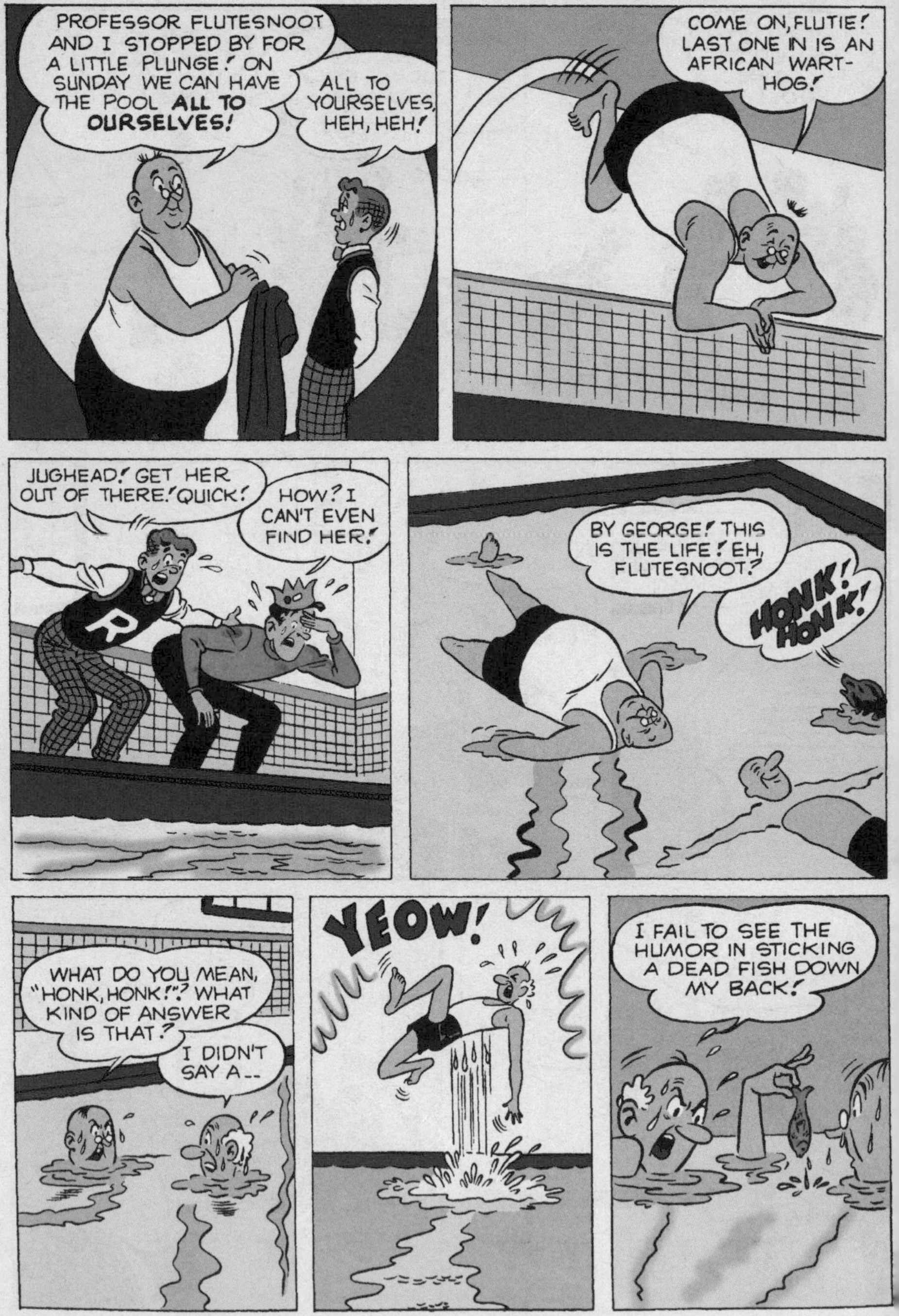
PROFESSOR FLUTESNOOT AND I STOPPED BY FOR A LITTLE PLUNGE! ON SUNDAY WE CAN HAVE THE POOL **ALL TO OURSELVES!**
ALL TO YOURSELVES, HEH, HEH!
COME ON, FLUTIE! LAST ONE IN IS AN AFRICAN WART-HOG!
JUGHEAD! GET HER OUT OF THERE! QUICK!
HOW? I CAN'T EVEN FIND HER!
BY GEORGE! THIS IS THE LIFE! EH, FLUTESNOOT?
HONK! HONK!
WHAT DO YOU MEAN, "HONK, HONK!"? WHAT KIND OF ANSWER IS THAT?
I DIDN'T SAY A--
YEOW!
I FAIL TO SEE THE HUMOR IN STICKING A DEAD FISH DOWN MY BACK!

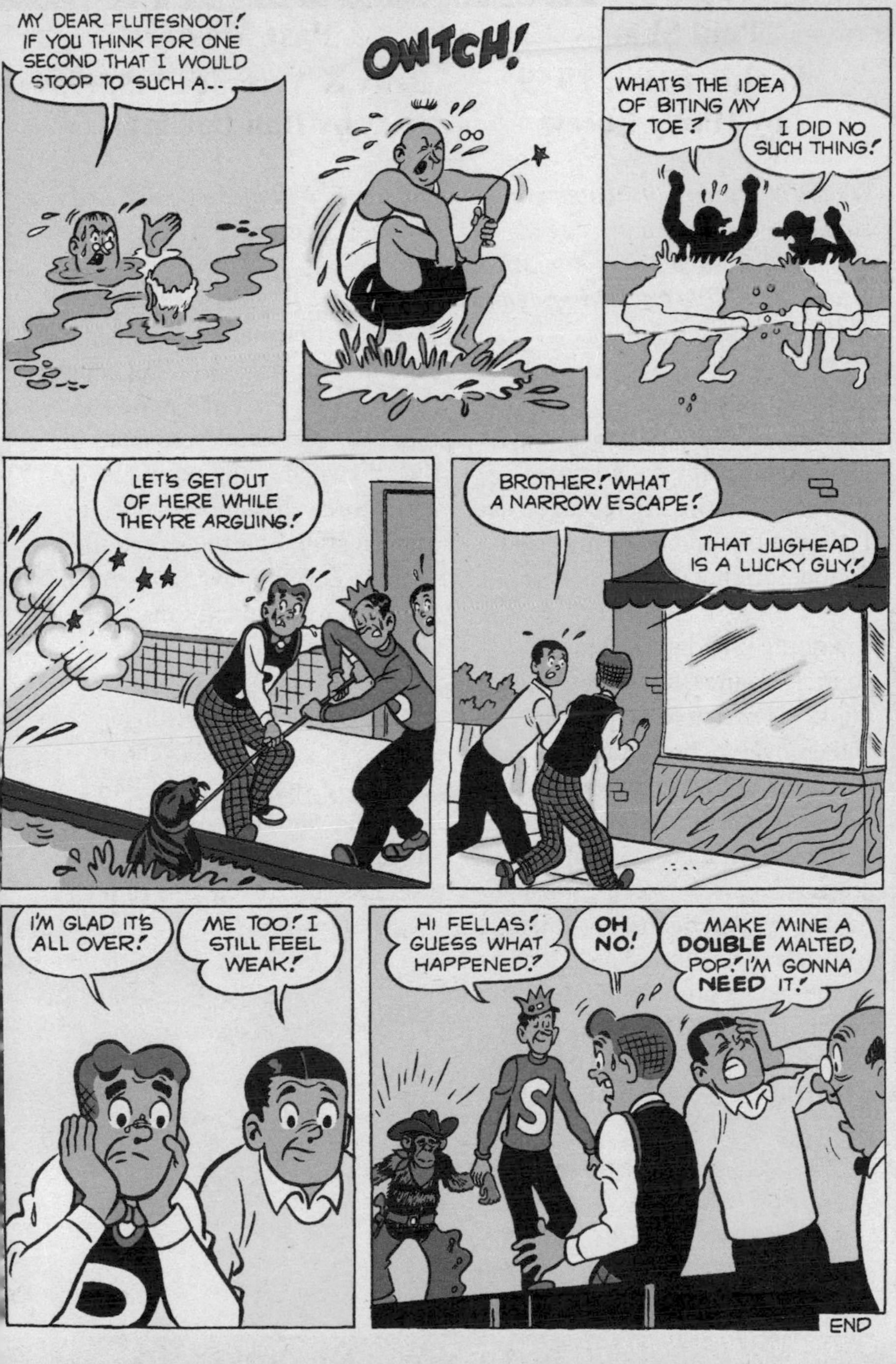
MY DEAR FLUTESNOOT! IF YOU THINK FOR ONE SECOND THAT I WOULD STOOP TO SUCH A..
OWTCH!
WHAT'S THE IDEA OF BITING MY TOE?
I DID NO SUCH THING!
LET'S GET OUT OF HERE WHILE THEY'RE ARGUING!
BROTHER! WHAT A NARROW ESCAPE!
THAT JUGHEAD IS A LUCKY GUY!
I'M GLAD IT'S ALL OVER!
ME TOO! I STILL FEEL WEAK!
HI FELLAS! GUESS WHAT HAPPENED?
OH NO!
MAKE MINE A DOUBLE MALTED, POP! I'M GONNA NEED IT!
END

Pool Sharks
Archie #103, 1959
by Harry Lucey

It's the beginning of summer, and Archie and Jughead are eager to enjoy Veronica's pool, but Mr. Lodge isn't quite finished prepping it for the new season...

I've spent a lot of hours in the company of Archie Andrews, Riverdale's premiere teenager, and I still count him one of my good fictional friends.

Literature—and even the comics are literature of a sort, I think—is meant to be pleasant and enjoyable, but I think it's also supposed to be useful, and Archie fulfilled a small but vital function in my life. In those painful, nerdy pre-teen years between eight and twelve, he and his friends (along with Dobie Gillis and his friends on the magic box) taught me how to live The Good Life as a teenager… if, that was, you were a fairly ordinary kid from small-town America.

--Stephen King
Bestselling American author, Excerpted from "The Importance of Being Archie", Archie Americana: Best of the Forties

Past Masters
Betty & Veronica #45, 1959
by Dan DeCarlo

Do gossip and history mix? find out in "Past Masters"!

I know I'm usually associated with superheroes, but—wouldja believe I'm also a big fan of Archie, Jughead, Betty and Veronica? I've always dug the crisp, clever, down-to-earth humor, the great cartoon style of artwork and the simple yet somehow outrageous story lines that always manage to hit close to home.

Archie Comics is more than a group of comic books. That seemingly eternal teenager and his world-famous pals are truly an American Institution—and I'm proud to declare I'm one of their biggest fans.

--Stan Lee
Legendary comic book writer and editor

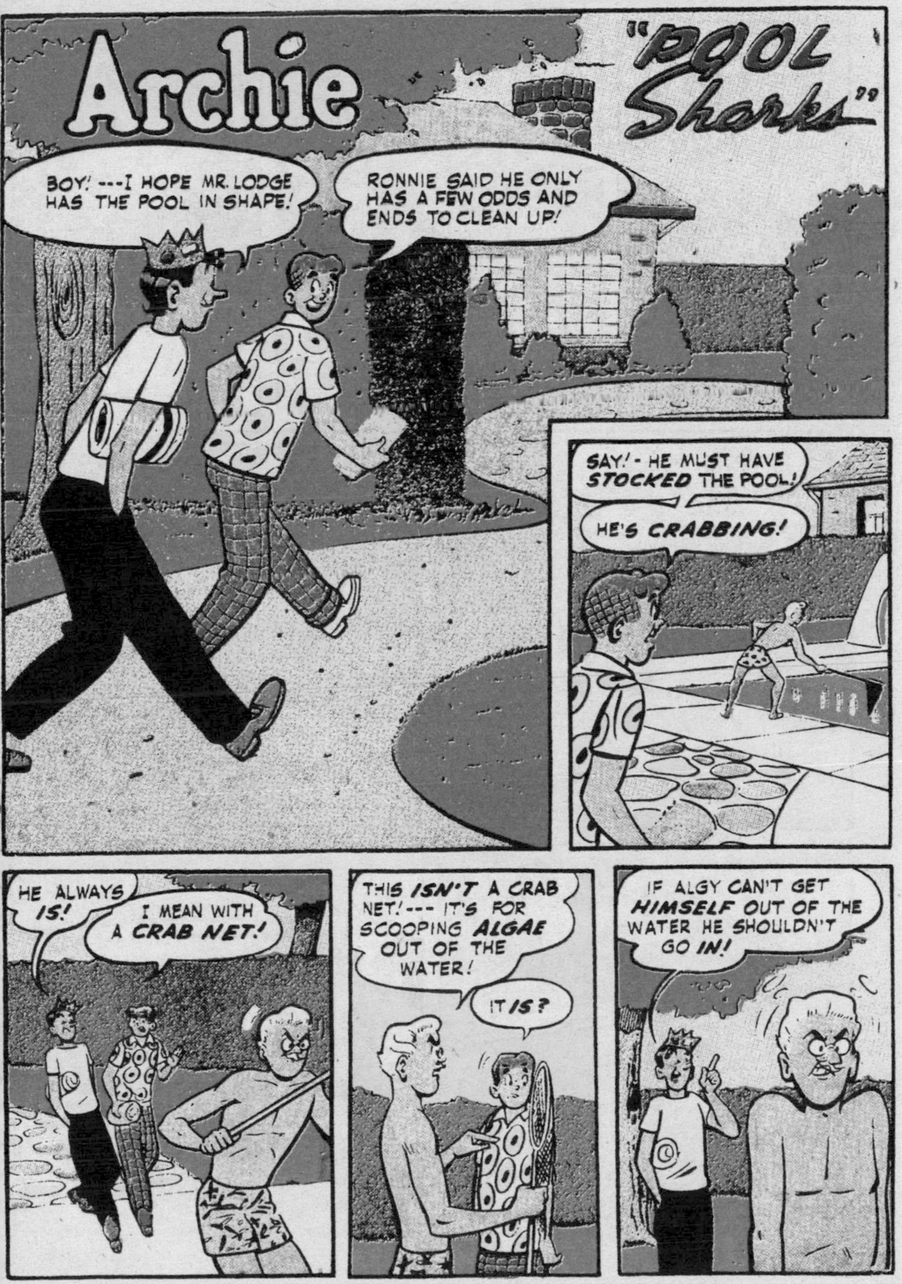
Archie
"POOL Sharks"
BOY! ---I HOPE MR. LODGE HAS THE POOL IN SHAPE!
RONNIE SAID HE ONLY HAS A FEW ODDS AND ENDS TO CLEAN UP!
SAY! - HE MUST HAVE STOCKED THE POOL!
HE'S CRABBING!
HE ALWAYS IS!
I MEAN WITH A CRAB NET!
THIS ISN'T A CRAB NET! --- IT'S FOR SCOOPING ALGAE OUT OF THE WATER!
IT IS?
IF ALGY CAN'T GET HIMSELF OUT OF THE WATER HE SHOULDN'T GO IN!

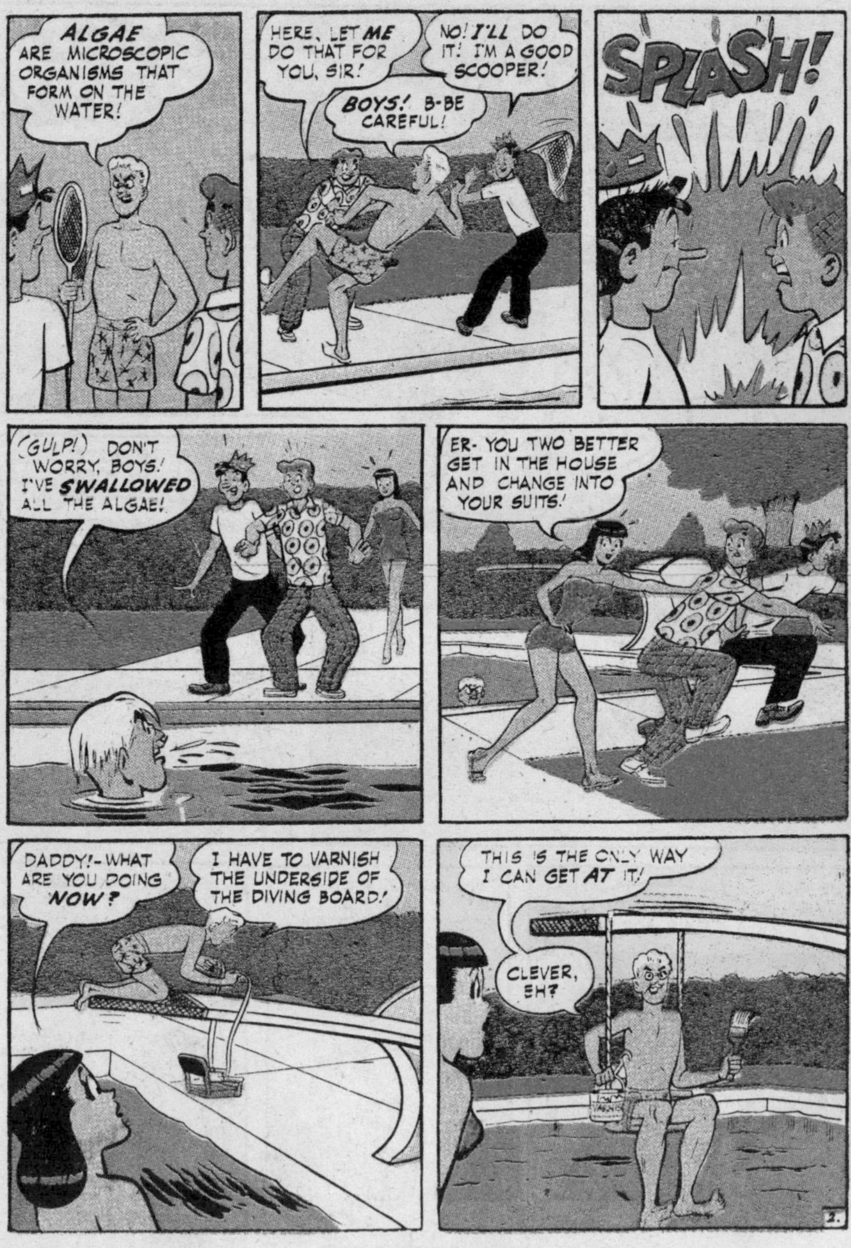
ALGAE ARE MICROSCOPIC ORGANISMS THAT FORM ON THE WATER!
HERE, LET ME DO THAT FOR YOU, SIR!
NO! I'LL DO IT! I'M A GOOD SCOOPER!
BOYS! B-BE CAREFUL!
SPLASH!
(GULP!) DON'T WORRY, BOYS! I'VE SWALLOWED ALL THE ALGAE!
ER- YOU TWO BETTER GET IN THE HOUSE AND CHANGE INTO YOUR SUITS!
DADDY!-WHAT ARE YOU DOING NOW?
I HAVE TO VARNISH THE UNDERSIDE OF THE DIVING BOARD!
THIS IS THE ONLY WAY I CAN GET AT IT!
CLEVER, EH?
2.

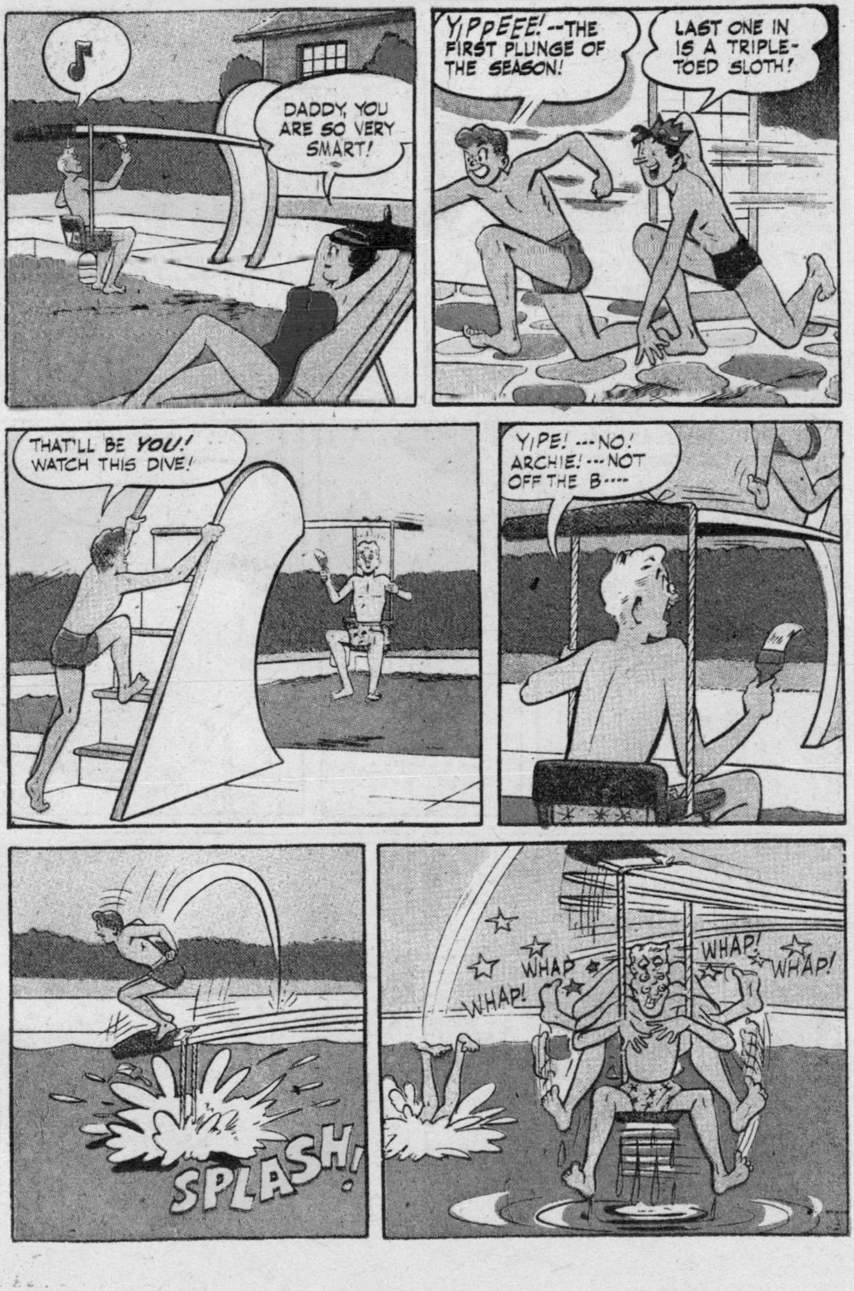
DADDY, YOU ARE SO VERY SMART!
YIPPEEE! --THE FIRST PLUNGE OF THE SEASON!
LAST ONE IN IS A TRIPLE-TOED SLOTH!
THAT'LL BE YOU! WATCH THIS DIVE!
YIPE! ---NO! ARCHIE! ---NOT OFF THE B----
SPLASH!
WHAP!
WHAP
WHAP!
WHAP!

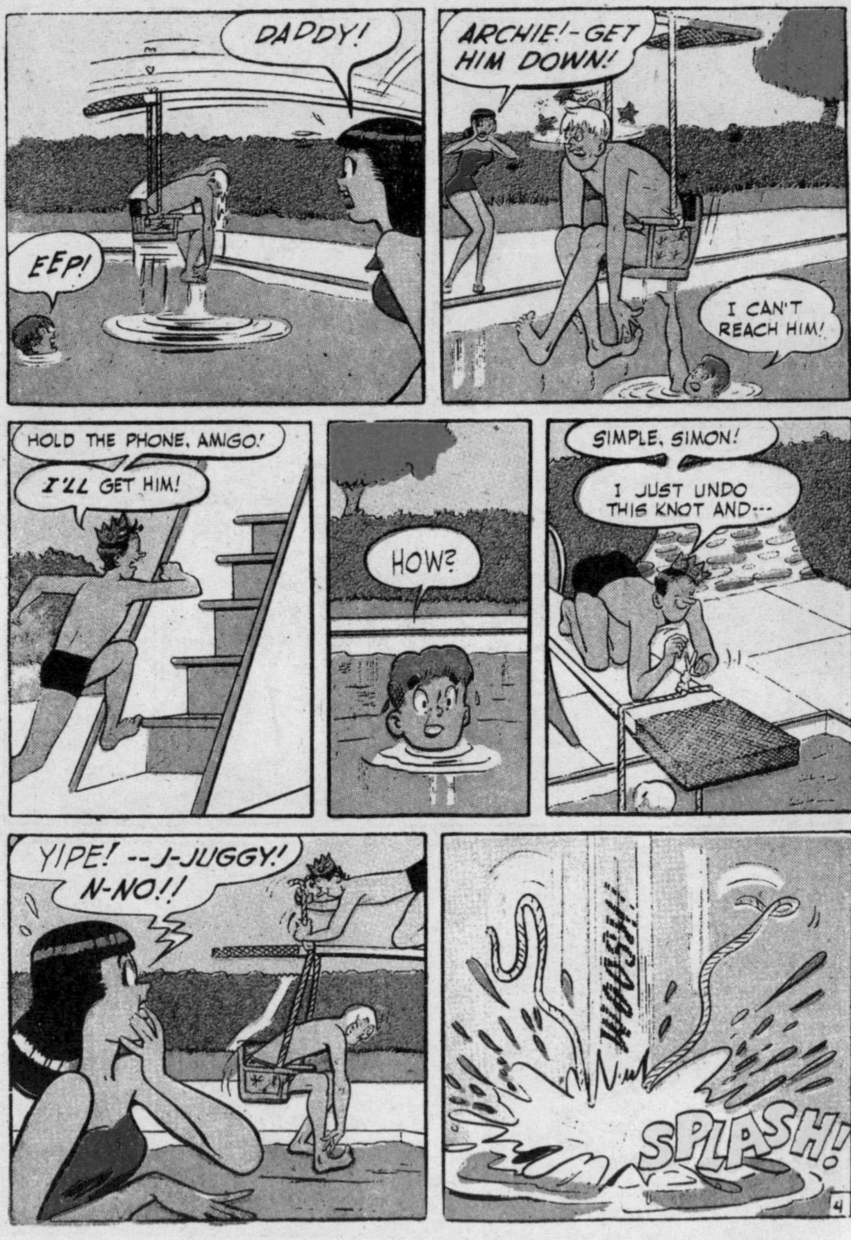
DADDY!
EEP!
ARCHIE!-GET HIM DOWN!
I CAN'T REACH HIM!
HOLD THE PHONE, AMIGO!
I'LL GET HIM!
HOW?
SIMPLE, SIMON!
I JUST UNDO THIS KNOT AND---
YIPE! --J-JUGGY! N-NO!!
WHOOSH!
SPLASH!
4

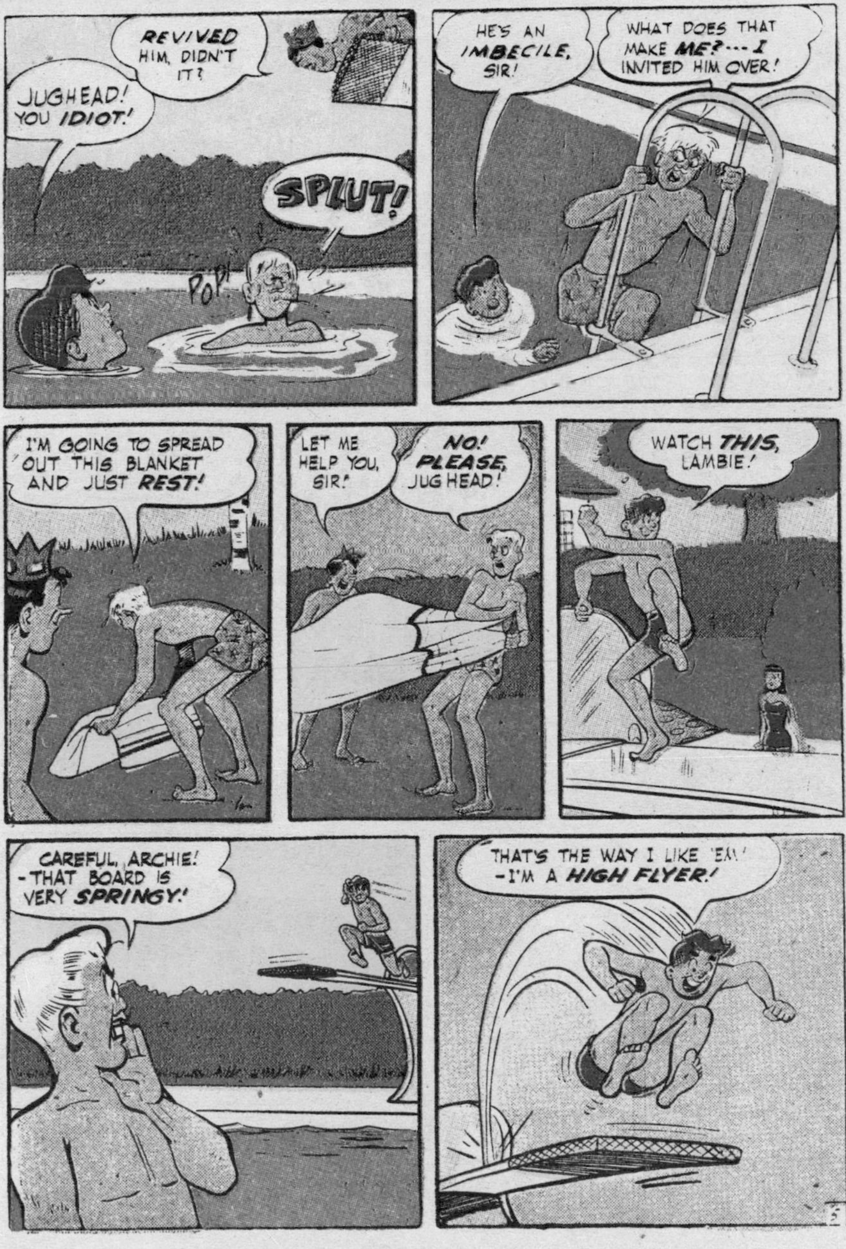
REVIVED HIM, DIDN'T IT?
JUGHEAD! YOU IDIOT!
SPLUT!
POP!
HE'S AN IMBECILE, SIR!
WHAT DOES THAT MAKE ME?--- I INVITED HIM OVER!
I'M GOING TO SPREAD OUT THIS BLANKET AND JUST REST!
LET ME HELP YOU, SIR!
NO! PLEASE, JUGHEAD!
WATCH THIS, LAMBIE!
CAREFUL, ARCHIE! -THAT BOARD IS VERY SPRINGY!
THAT'S THE WAY I LIKE 'EM! -I'M A HIGH FLYER!

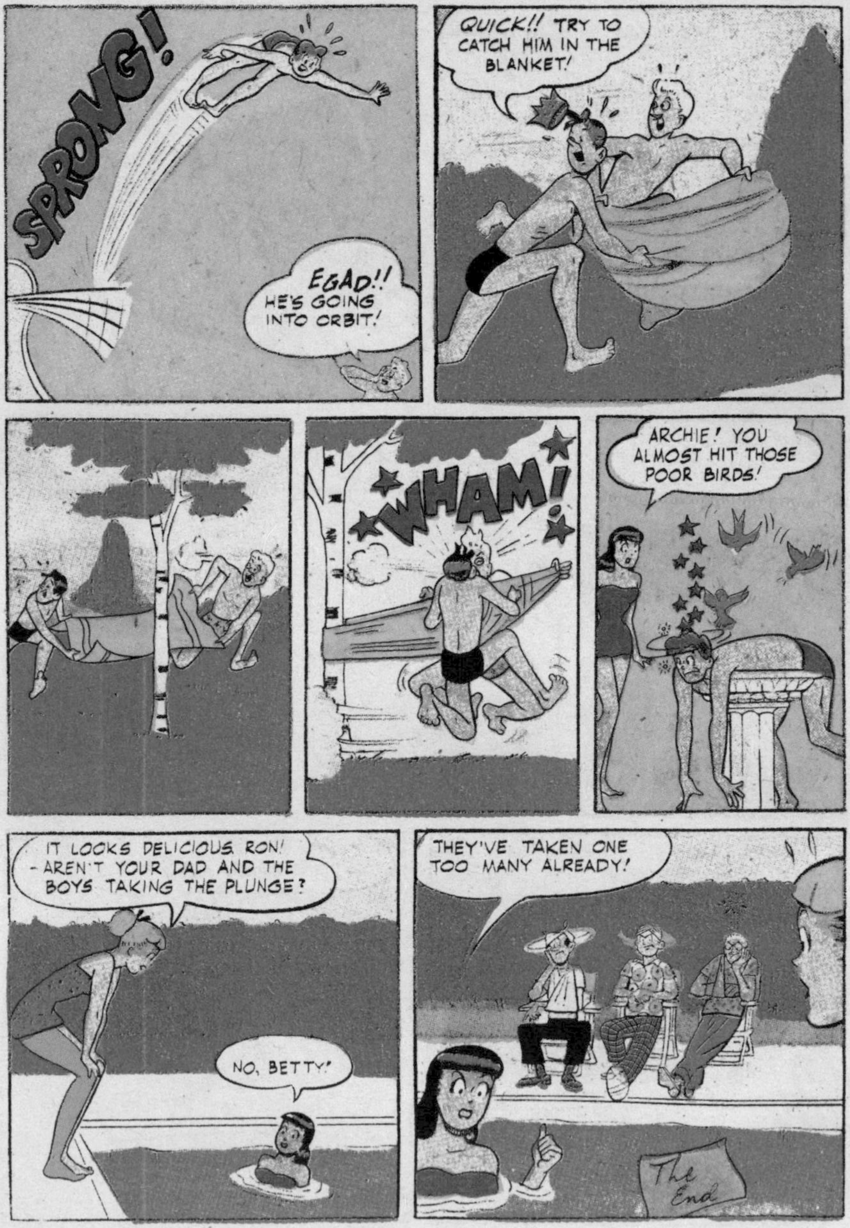
SPRONG!
EGAD!! HE'S GOING INTO ORBIT!
QUICK!! TRY TO CATCH HIM IN THE BLANKET!
WHAM!
ARCHIE! YOU ALMOST HIT THOSE POOR BIRDS!
IT LOOKS DELICIOUS, RON! - AREN'T YOUR DAD AND THE BOYS TAKING THE PLUNGE?
NO, BETTY!
THEY'VE TAKEN ONE TOO MANY ALREADY!
The End

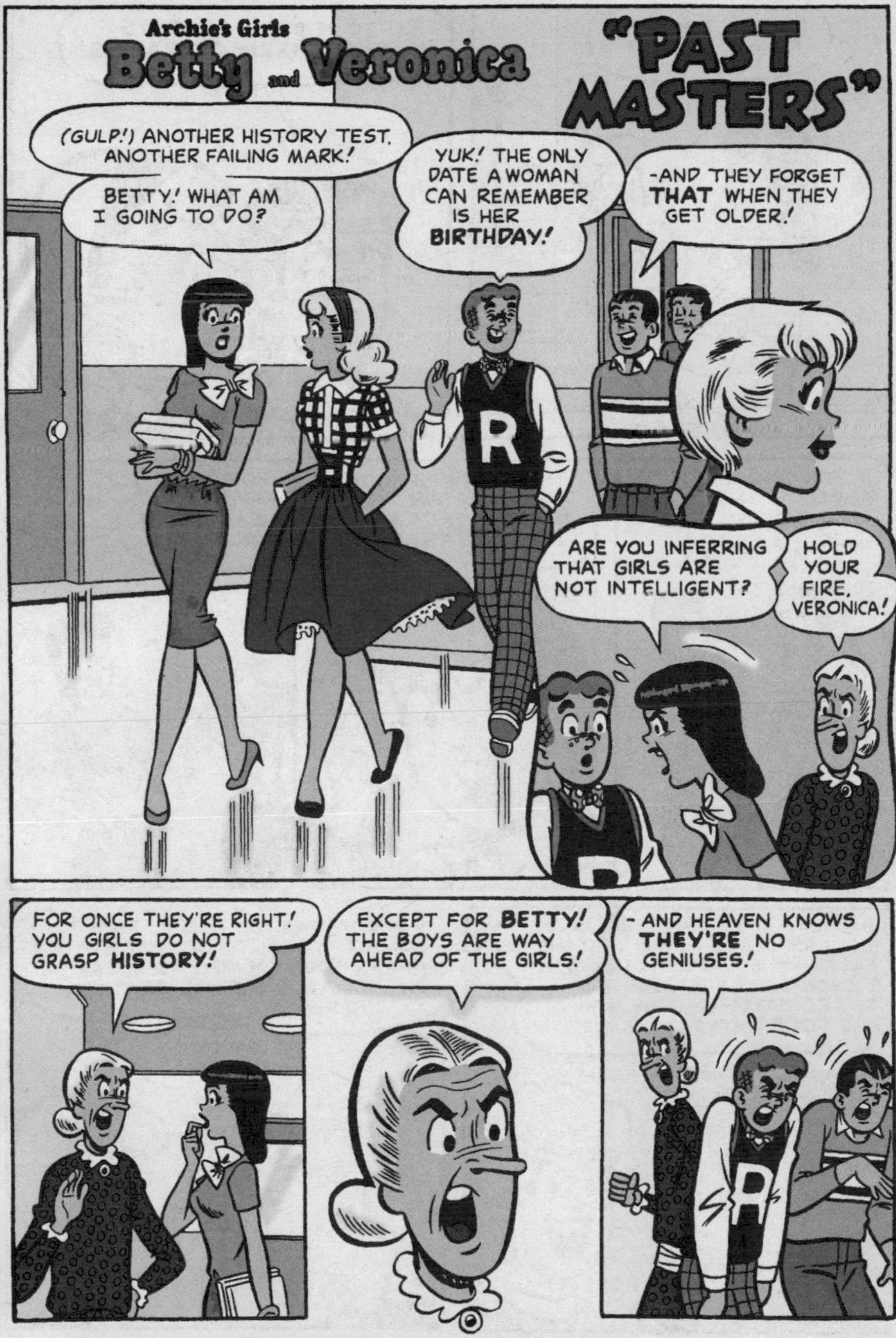
Archie's Girls
Betty and Veronica
"PAST MASTERS"
(GULP!) ANOTHER HISTORY TEST. ANOTHER FAILING MARK!
BETTY! WHAT AM I GOING TO DO?
YUK! THE ONLY DATE A WOMAN CAN REMEMBER IS HER BIRTHDAY!
-AND THEY FORGET THAT WHEN THEY GET OLDER!
ARE YOU INFERRING THAT GIRLS ARE NOT INTELLIGENT?
HOLD YOUR FIRE, VERONICA!
FOR ONCE THEY'RE RIGHT! YOU GIRLS DO NOT GRASP HISTORY!
EXCEPT FOR BETTY! THE BOYS ARE WAY AHEAD OF THE GIRLS!
- AND HEAVEN KNOWS THEY'RE NO GENIUSES!

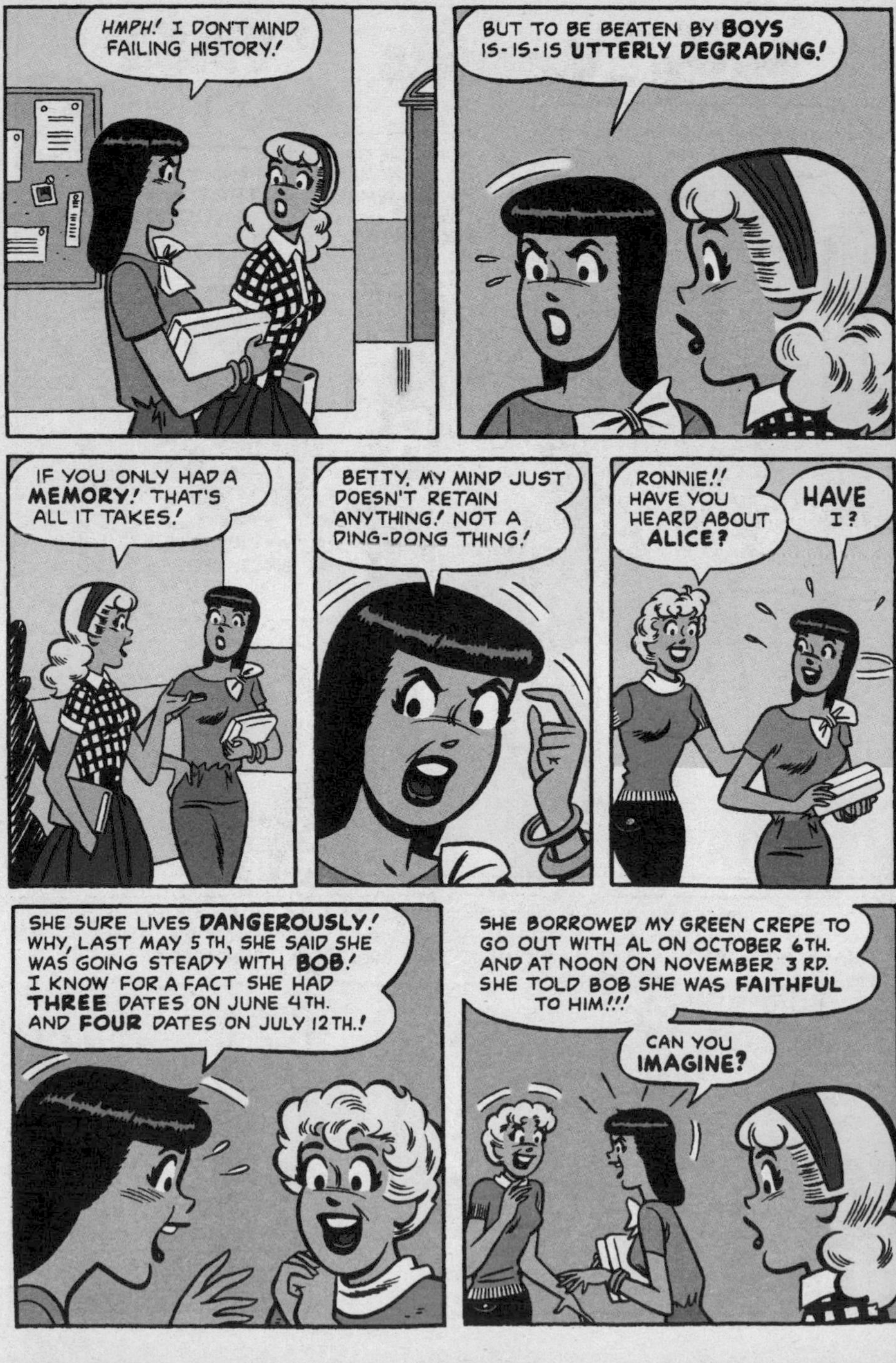
HMPH! I DON'T MIND FAILING HISTORY!
BUT TO BE BEATEN BY BOYS IS-IS-IS UTTERLY DEGRADING!
IF YOU ONLY HAD A MEMORY! THAT'S ALL IT TAKES!
BETTY, MY MIND JUST DOESN'T RETAIN ANYTHING! NOT A DING-DONG THING!
RONNIE!! HAVE YOU HEARD ABOUT ALICE?
HAVE I?
SHE SURE LIVES DANGEROUSLY! WHY, LAST MAY 5TH, SHE SAID SHE WAS GOING STEADY WITH BOB! I KNOW FOR A FACT SHE HAD THREE DATES ON JUNE 4TH. AND FOUR DATES ON JULY 12TH.!
SHE BORROWED MY GREEN CREPE TO GO OUT WITH AL ON OCTOBER 6TH. AND AT NOON ON NOVEMBER 3RD. SHE TOLD BOB SHE WAS FAITHFUL TO HIM!!!
CAN YOU IMAGINE?

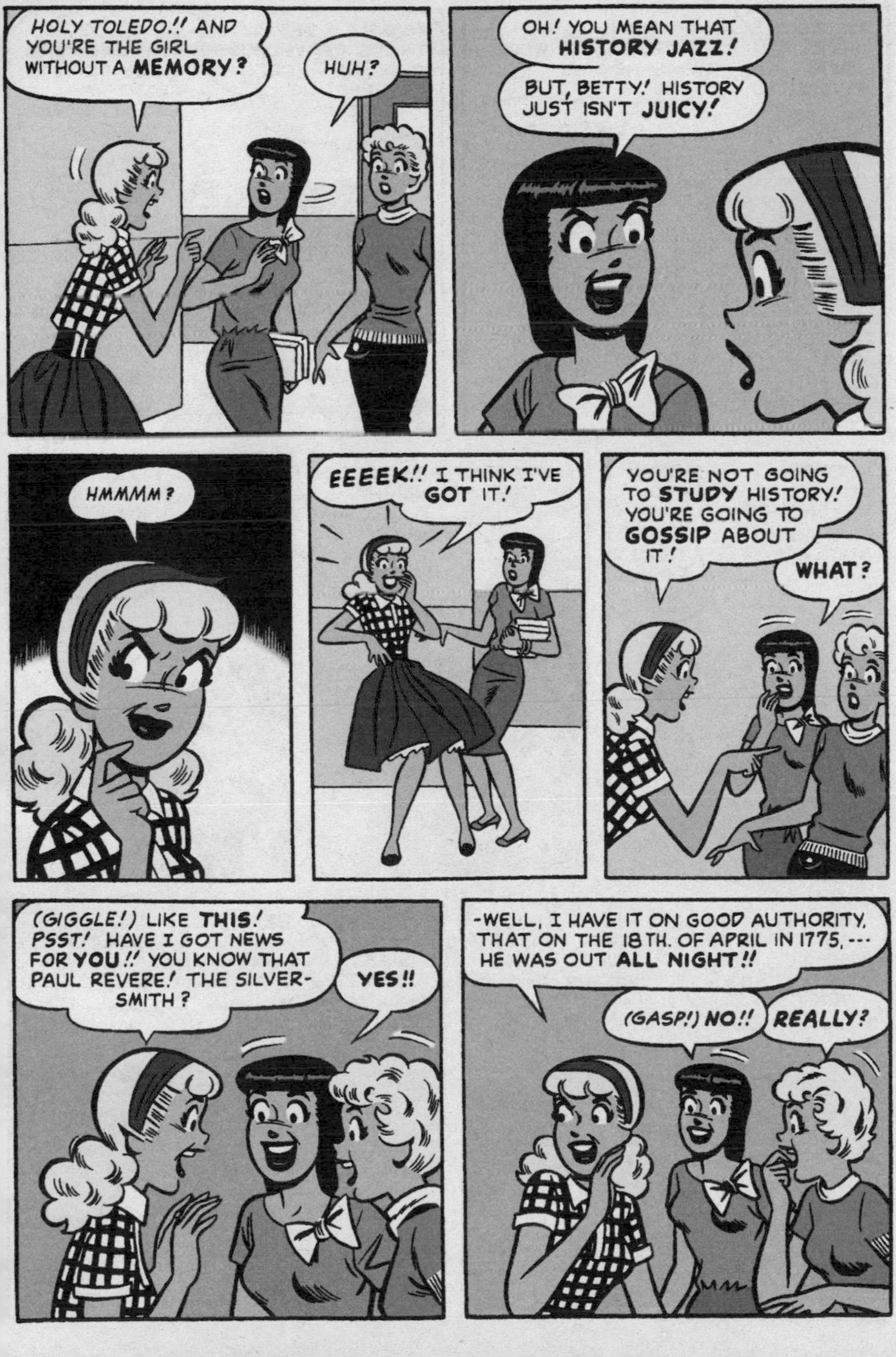
HOLY TOLEDO.!! AND YOU'RE THE GIRL WITHOUT A MEMORY?
HUH?
OH! YOU MEAN THAT HISTORY JAZZ!
BUT, BETTY! HISTORY JUST ISN'T JUICY!
HMMMM?
EEEEK!! I THINK I'VE GOT IT!
YOU'RE NOT GOING TO STUDY HISTORY! YOU'RE GOING TO GOSSIP ABOUT IT!
WHAT?
(GIGGLE!) LIKE THIS! PSST! HAVE I GOT NEWS FOR YOU!! YOU KNOW THAT PAUL REVERE! THE SILVER-SMITH?
YES!!
-WELL, I HAVE IT ON GOOD AUTHORITY, THAT ON THE 18TH. OF APRIL IN 1775, --- HE WAS OUT ALL NIGHT!!
(GASP!) NO!!
REALLY?

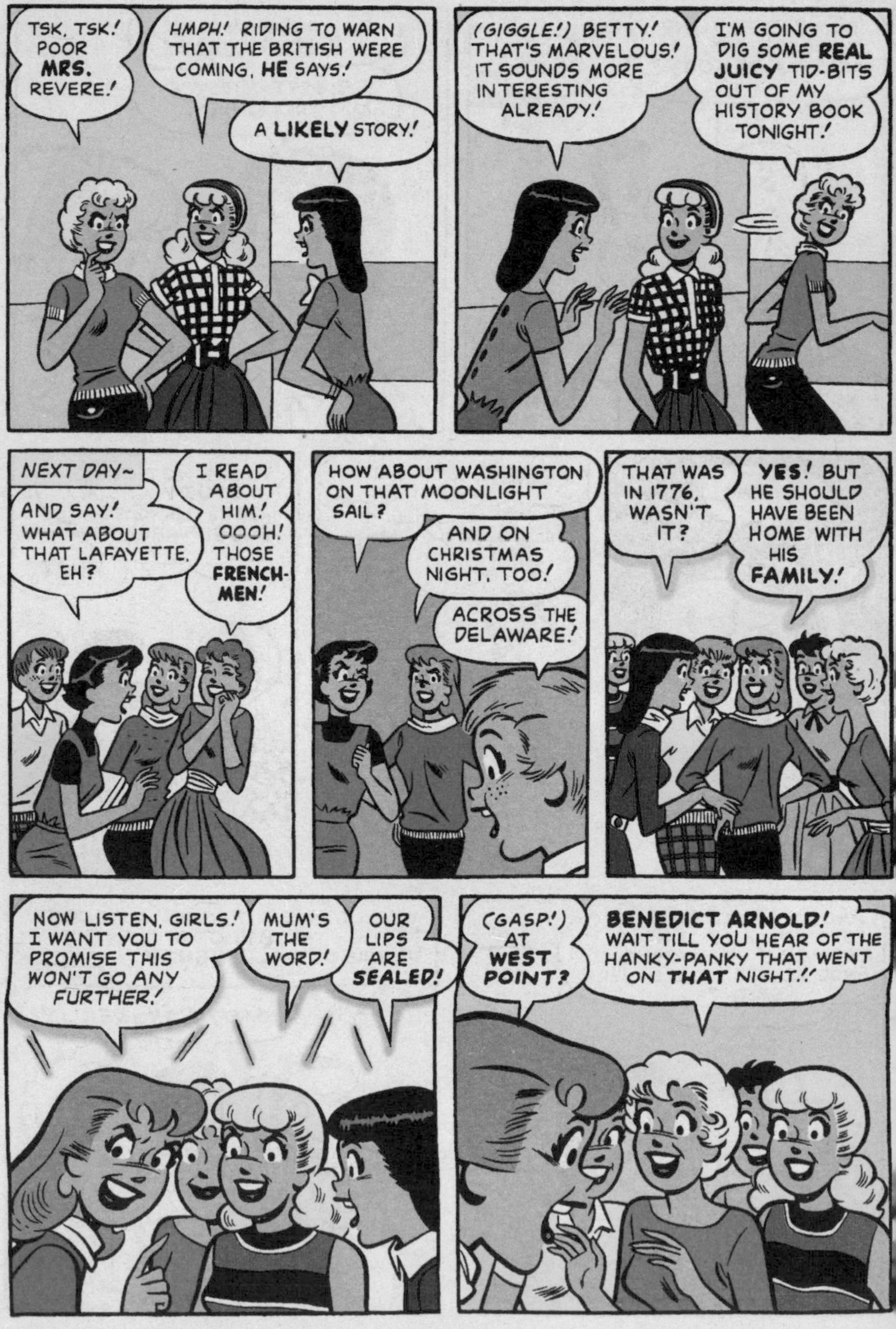
TSK, TSK! POOR MRS. REVERE!
HMPH! RIDING TO WARN THAT THE BRITISH WERE COMING, HE SAYS!
A LIKELY STORY!
(GIGGLE!) BETTY! THAT'S MARVELOUS! IT SOUNDS MORE INTERESTING ALREADY!
I'M GOING TO DIG SOME REAL JUICY TID-BITS OUT OF MY HISTORY BOOK TONIGHT!
NEXT DAY~
AND SAY! WHAT ABOUT THAT LAFAYETTE, EH?
I READ ABOUT HIM! OOOH! THOSE FRENCH-MEN!
HOW ABOUT WASHINGTON ON THAT MOONLIGHT SAIL?
AND ON CHRISTMAS NIGHT, TOO!
ACROSS THE DELAWARE!
THAT WAS IN 1776, WASN'T IT?
YES! BUT HE SHOULD HAVE BEEN HOME WITH HIS FAMILY!
NOW LISTEN, GIRLS! I WANT YOU TO PROMISE THIS WON'T GO ANY FURTHER!
MUM'S THE WORD!
OUR LIPS ARE SEALED!
(GASP!) AT WEST POINT?
BENEDICT ARNOLD! WAIT TILL YOU HEAR OF THE HANKY-PANKY THAT WENT ON THAT NIGHT!!

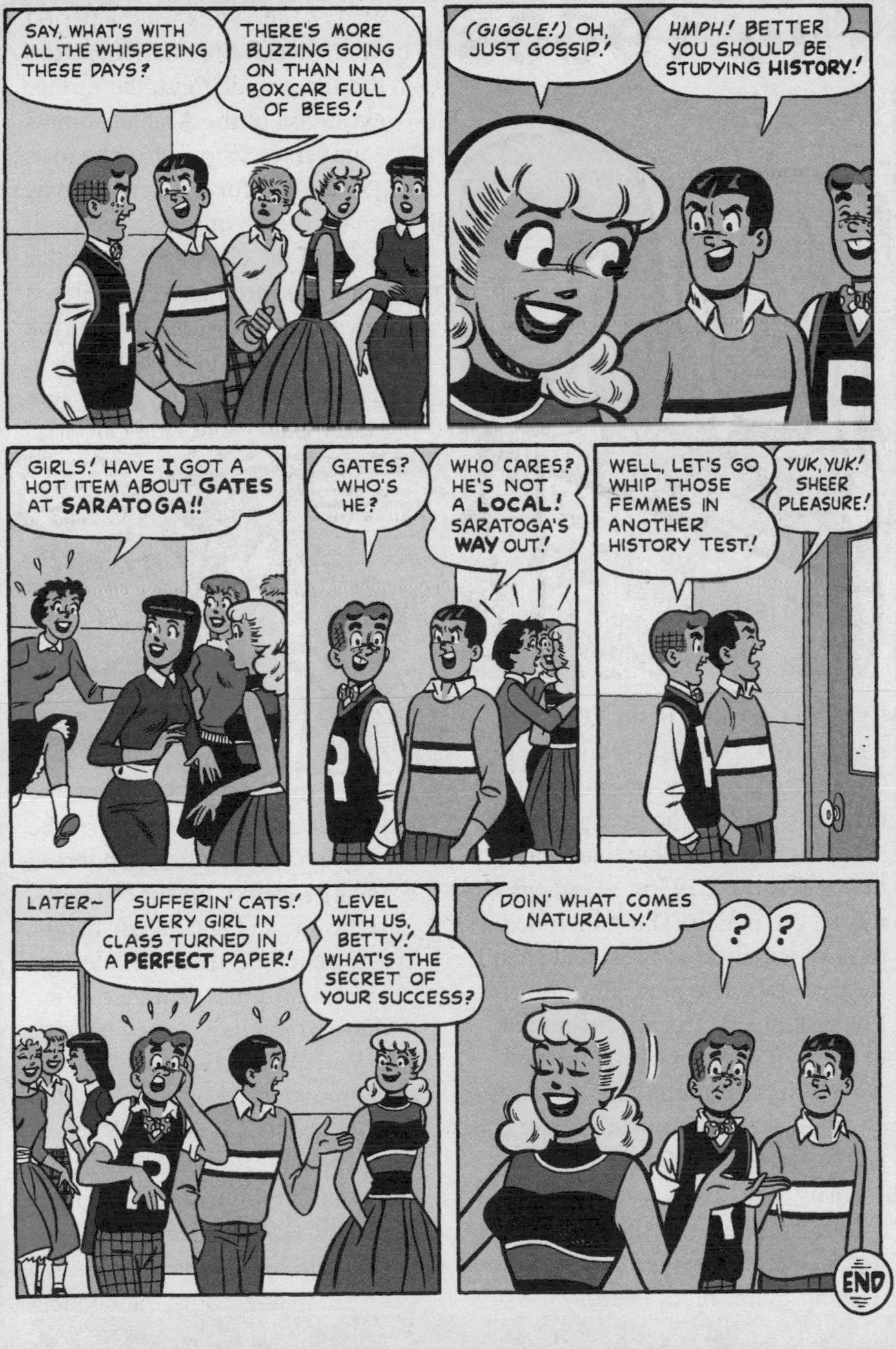
SAY, WHAT'S WITH ALL THE WHISPERING THESE DAYS?
THERE'S MORE BUZZING GOING ON THAN IN A BOXCAR FULL OF BEES!
(GIGGLE!) OH, JUST GOSSIP!
HMPH! BETTER YOU SHOULD BE STUDYING HISTORY!
GIRLS! HAVE I GOT A HOT ITEM ABOUT GATES AT SARATOGA!!
GATES? WHO'S HE?
WHO CARES? HE'S NOT A LOCAL! SARATOGA'S WAY OUT!
WELL, LET'S GO WHIP THOSE FEMMES IN ANOTHER HISTORY TEST!
YUK, YUK! SHEER PLEASURE!
LATER~
SUFFERIN' CATS! EVERY GIRL IN CLASS TURNED IN A PERFECT PAPER!
LEVEL WITH US, BETTY! WHAT'S THE SECRET OF YOUR SUCCESS?
DOIN' WHAT COMES NATURALLY!
? ?
END

The 1960s

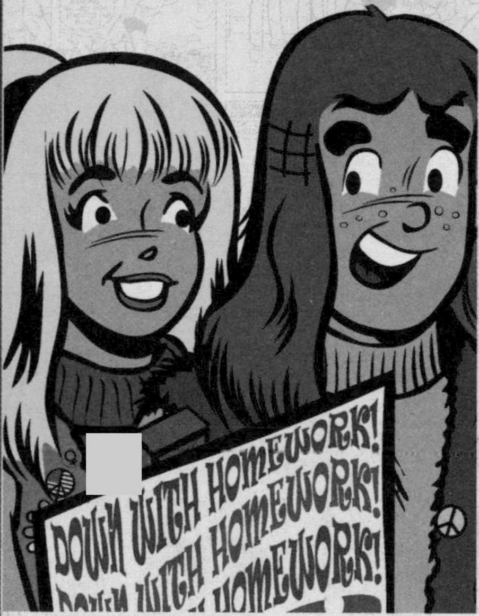
DOWN WITH HOMEWORK!
DOWN WITH HOMEWORK!

Of all the decades in the 20th century, none was filled with more dramatic change in America than the 1960s. While the decade began on a much calmer note than that of the "rebellious" 1950s, many events rocked the nation. These included the assassination of President John F. Kennedy, the rise and fall of Martin Luther King Jr., the advancements in the civil rights movement, Neil Armstrong becoming the first man on the moon, the colorful hippie era and America's involvement in the Vietnam War. These events left the nation – particularly the youth of the nation – often confused, divided and wanting their voices heard.

Just as the 1960s were a period of transition for the nation, so too did the decade mark the further evolution of the Archie Comics universe. Story-wise, the love triangle became further cemented as the primary theme of the series. Both the look of the characters and their personalities were more streamlined in this decade – a combination of the efforts of writers like Frank Doyle and George Gladir and artists like Harry Lucey and Dan DeCarlo.

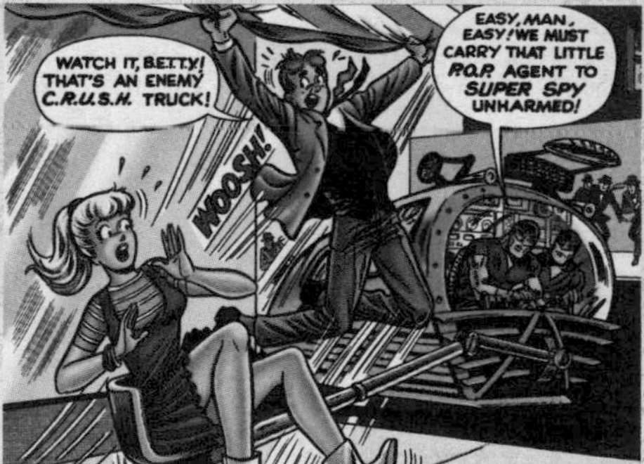
WATCH IT, BETTY! THAT'S AN ENEMY C.R.U.S.H. TRUCK!
EASY, MAN, EASY! WE MUST CARRY THAT LITTLE P.O.P. AGENT TO SUPER SPY UNHARMED!
WOOSH!

In terms of entertainment, the dangerous rock 'n' rollers of the '50s gave way to a pop music scene of squeaky clean teen idols, girl groups and surf music bands. Archie benefited from this change. They didn't just satirize the pop culture of the day… they became it! With James Bond all the rage on movie screens and *The Man from U.N.C.L.E.* a hit TV show, Archie and Betty became super spies, as The Man (and Girl) from R.I.V.E.R.D.A.L.E. Sitcoms about beautiful witches and genies, known as "magic-coms," abounded, giving the new Sabrina the Teenage Witch comic series an even bigger audience. The phenomenal success of TV's campy, pop art re-imagining of Batman led to renewed interest in superheroes. Archie not only revived the MLJ heroes of the '40s but also transformed Archie and his friends into campy crusaders like Pureheart the Powerful and Super Teen.

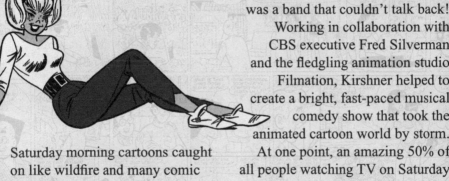

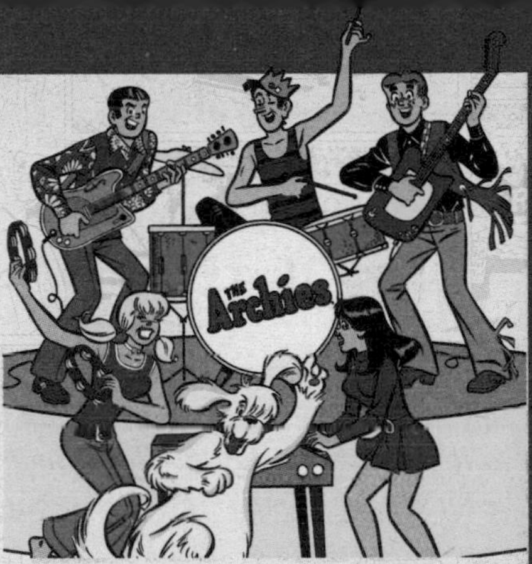
THE Archies

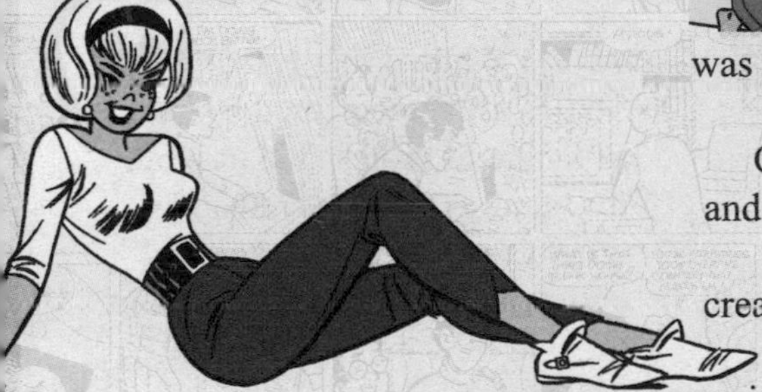

Saturday morning cartoons caught on like wildfire and many comic book characters benefited from being adapted for the small screen, including Archie and his friends. However, before his successful animated series, Archie and his friends almost debuted in live-action in 1964! Unfortunately, the series was never picked up. Meanwhile, music and TV producer Don Kirshner was fresh off his success in creating the Monkees. When the Monkees refused to record the latest song he brought them, Kirshner became inspired by one of his children's comics. The latest issue of *Life With Archie* depicted Archie's pop band called (naturally) The Archies—finally, here was a band that couldn't talk back! Working in collaboration with CBS executive Fred Silverman and the fledgling animation studio Filmation, Kirshner helped to create a bright, fast-paced musical comedy show that took the animated cartoon world by storm. At one point, an amazing 50% of all people watching TV on Saturday mornings were regularly tuned into *The Archie Show*! The music, with talented Ron Dante as the singing voice of Archie, was so catchy and fun that The Archies' songs began hitting the radio airwaves and climbing the pop charts.

In 1969, The Archies achieved the peak of their popularity: they had the number one most popular song of the year, "Sugar, Sugar" beating out The Beatles, the Rolling Stones and the Supremes! The dominance Archie and his friends achieved in the 1960s would carry over into the next decade.

Payola
Archie #109, 1960
by Frank Doyle
and Harry Lucey

In the late '50s and early '60s the radio industry struggled with allegations of "pay-to-play" deals with record companies, and Archie wasn't far behind. Speaking of behind, this classic story has an ending we wouldn't write today!

Our primary purpose in publishing the Archie series of comics magazines is to entertain the reader, with the poetic license which is allowed an author and an illustrator. Yet at the same time, we have tried to reflect problems of an American family in this nuclear and missile conscious world, and we have striven to maintain this balance through the medium of humor.

--John L. Goldwater
Archie Comics' founding publisher, editorial policy statement excerpt

The Interpreter
Archie #114, 1960
by Frank Doyle
and Harry Lucey

Archie discovers the value of Spanish class in this memorable story.

. . . While it is true that the Sixties are remembered by many as a time of protest and turmoil, for me it will always remain a time when young people were optimistic and enthusiastic about life and the future, a time when family values were the norm, as was having good, clean fun. My music and movies reflected these values—the same wholesome, family-oriented fun that Archie Comics portrays. To me, the beach pictures are like Archie Comics in that Betty, Veronica and Archie mirror the same qualities as characters portrayed by Annette [Funicello], me and whoever played the role of competing love interest.

--Frankie Avalon
Actor / Singer,
Excerpted from his introduction in Archie Americana: Best of the Sixties

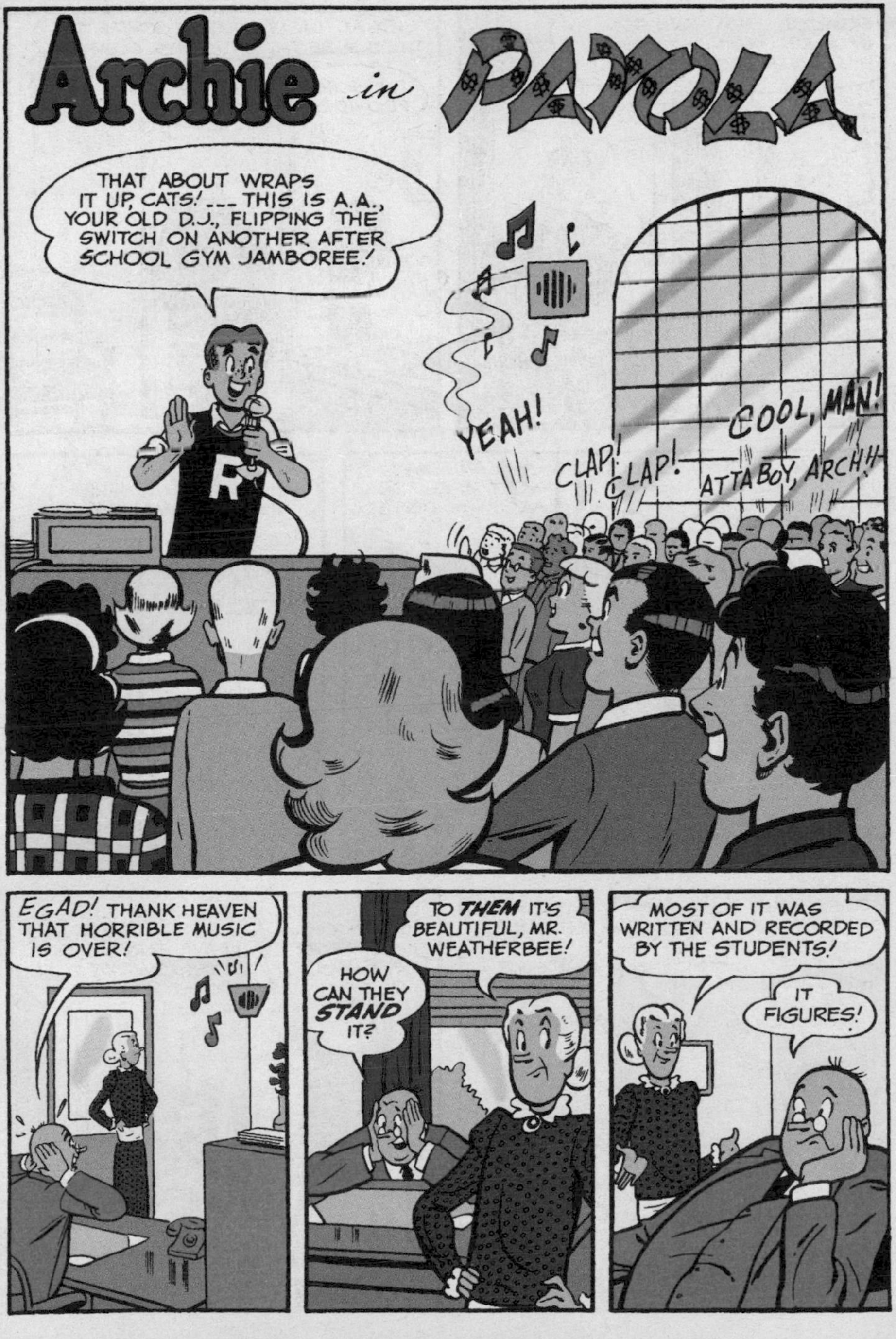
Archie in PAYOLA
THAT ABOUT WRAPS IT UP, CATS! --- THIS IS A.A., YOUR OLD D.J., FLIPPING THE SWITCH ON ANOTHER AFTER SCHOOL GYM JAMBOREE!
YEAH!
COOL, MAN!
CLAP! CLAP!
ATTA BOY, ARCH!!
EGAD! THANK HEAVEN THAT HORRIBLE MUSIC IS OVER!
HOW CAN THEY STAND IT?
TO THEM IT'S BEAUTIFUL, MR. WEATHERBEE!
MOST OF IT WAS WRITTEN AND RECORDED BY THE STUDENTS!
IT FIGURES!

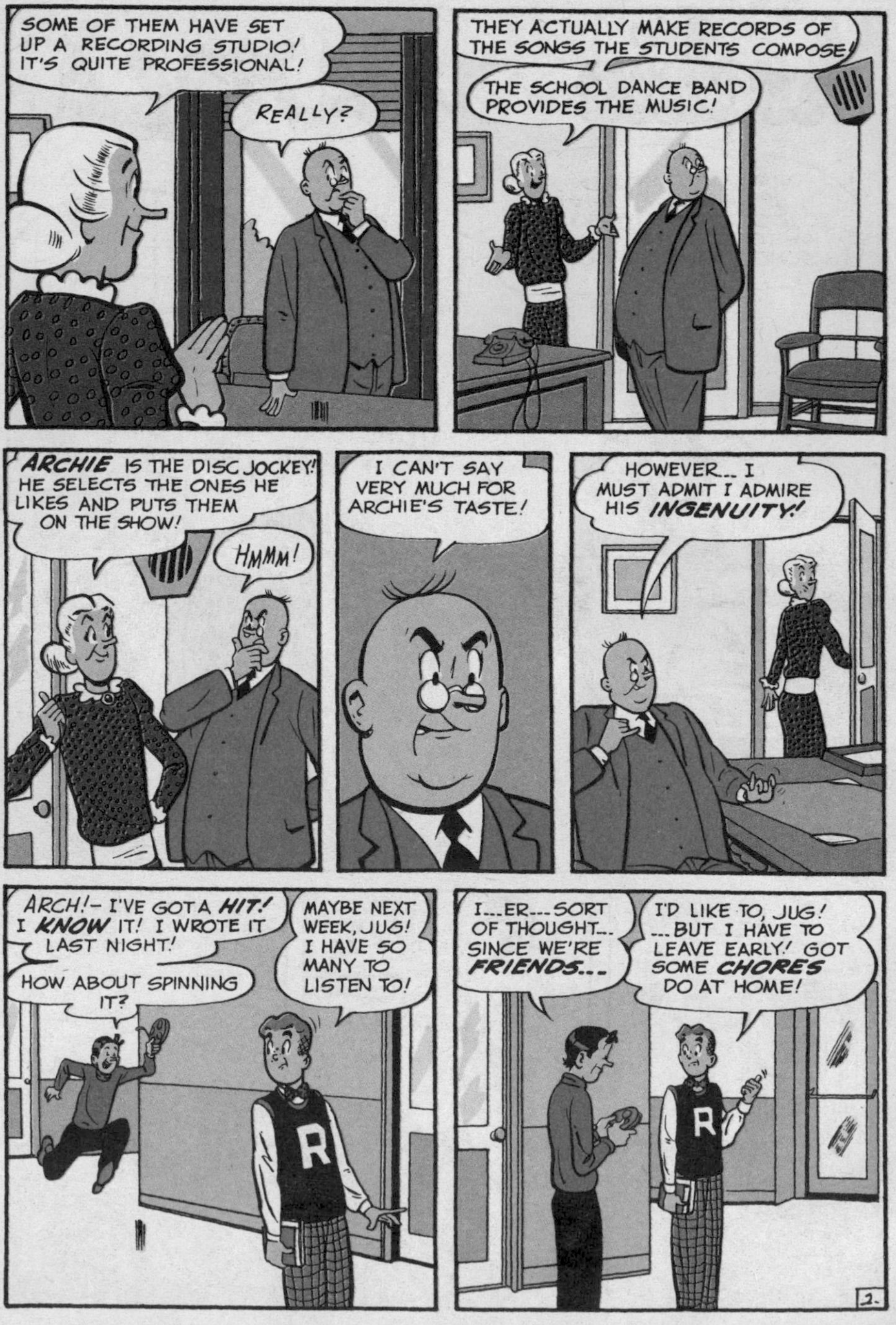
SOME OF THEM HAVE SET UP A RECORDING STUDIO! IT'S QUITE PROFESSIONAL!
REALLY?
THEY ACTUALLY MAKE RECORDS OF THE SONGS THE STUDENTS COMPOSE!
THE SCHOOL DANCE BAND PROVIDES THE MUSIC!
ARCHIE IS THE DISC JOCKEY! HE SELECTS THE ONES HE LIKES AND PUTS THEM ON THE SHOW!
HMMM!
I CAN'T SAY VERY MUCH FOR ARCHIE'S TASTE!
HOWEVER... I MUST ADMIT I ADMIRE HIS INGENUITY!
ARCH!– I'VE GOT A HIT! I KNOW IT! I WROTE IT LAST NIGHT!
HOW ABOUT SPINNING IT?
MAYBE NEXT WEEK, JUG! I HAVE SO MANY TO LISTEN TO!
I...ER...SORT OF THOUGHT... SINCE WE'RE FRIENDS...
I'D LIKE TO, JUG! ...BUT I HAVE TO LEAVE EARLY! GOT SOME CHORES DO AT HOME!
-2-

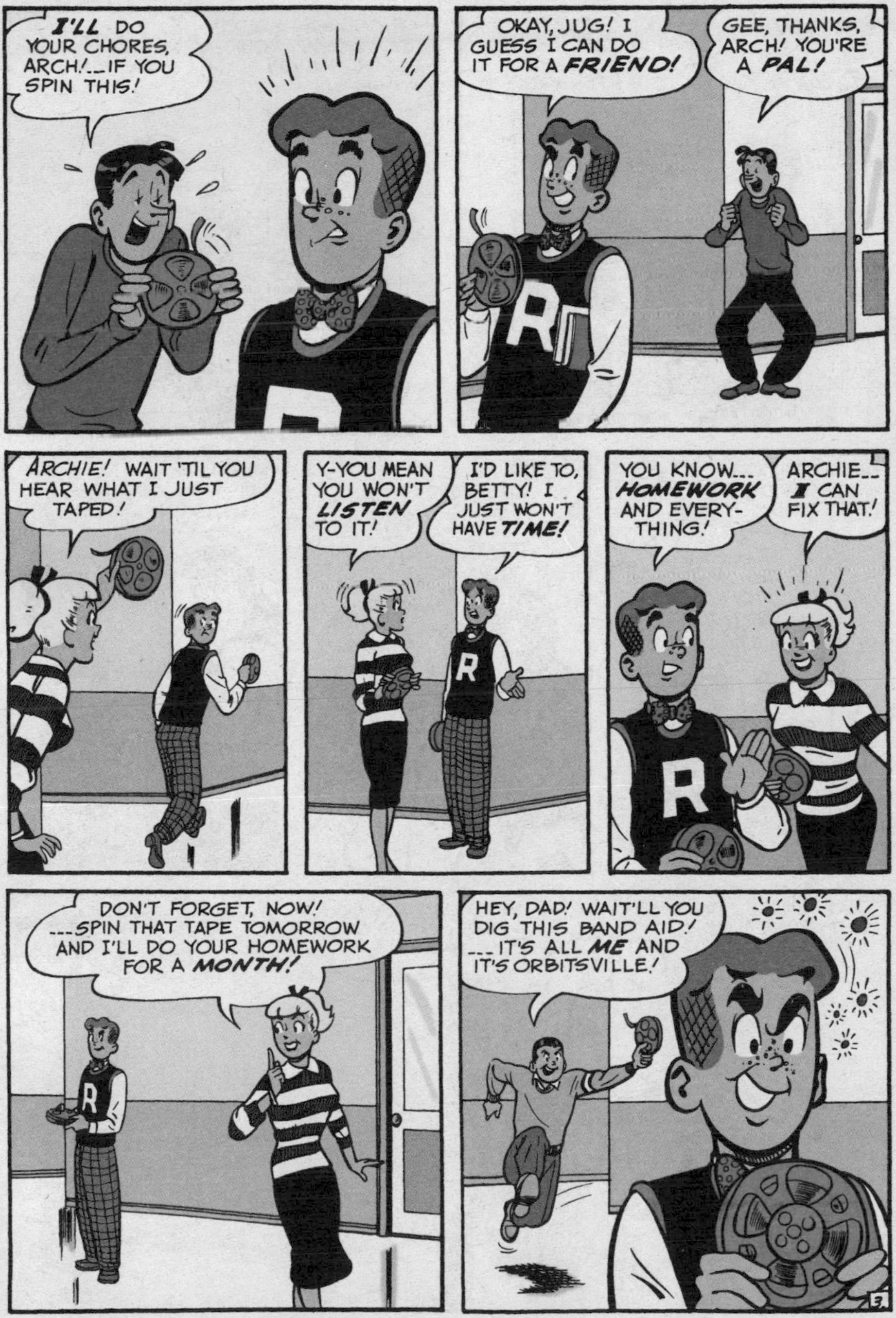
I'LL DO YOUR CHORES, ARCH!...IF YOU SPIN THIS!
OKAY, JUG! I GUESS I CAN DO IT FOR A FRIEND!
GEE, THANKS, ARCH! YOU'RE A PAL!
ARCHIE! WAIT 'TIL YOU HEAR WHAT I JUST TAPED!
Y-YOU MEAN YOU WON'T LISTEN TO IT!
I'D LIKE TO, BETTY! I JUST WON'T HAVE TIME!
YOU KNOW... HOMEWORK AND EVERY-THING!
ARCHIE... I CAN FIX THAT!
DON'T FORGET, NOW! ...SPIN THAT TAPE TOMORROW AND I'LL DO YOUR HOMEWORK FOR A MONTH!
HEY, DAD! WAIT'LL YOU DIG THIS BAND AID! ... IT'S ALL ME AND IT'S ORBITSVILLE!
3

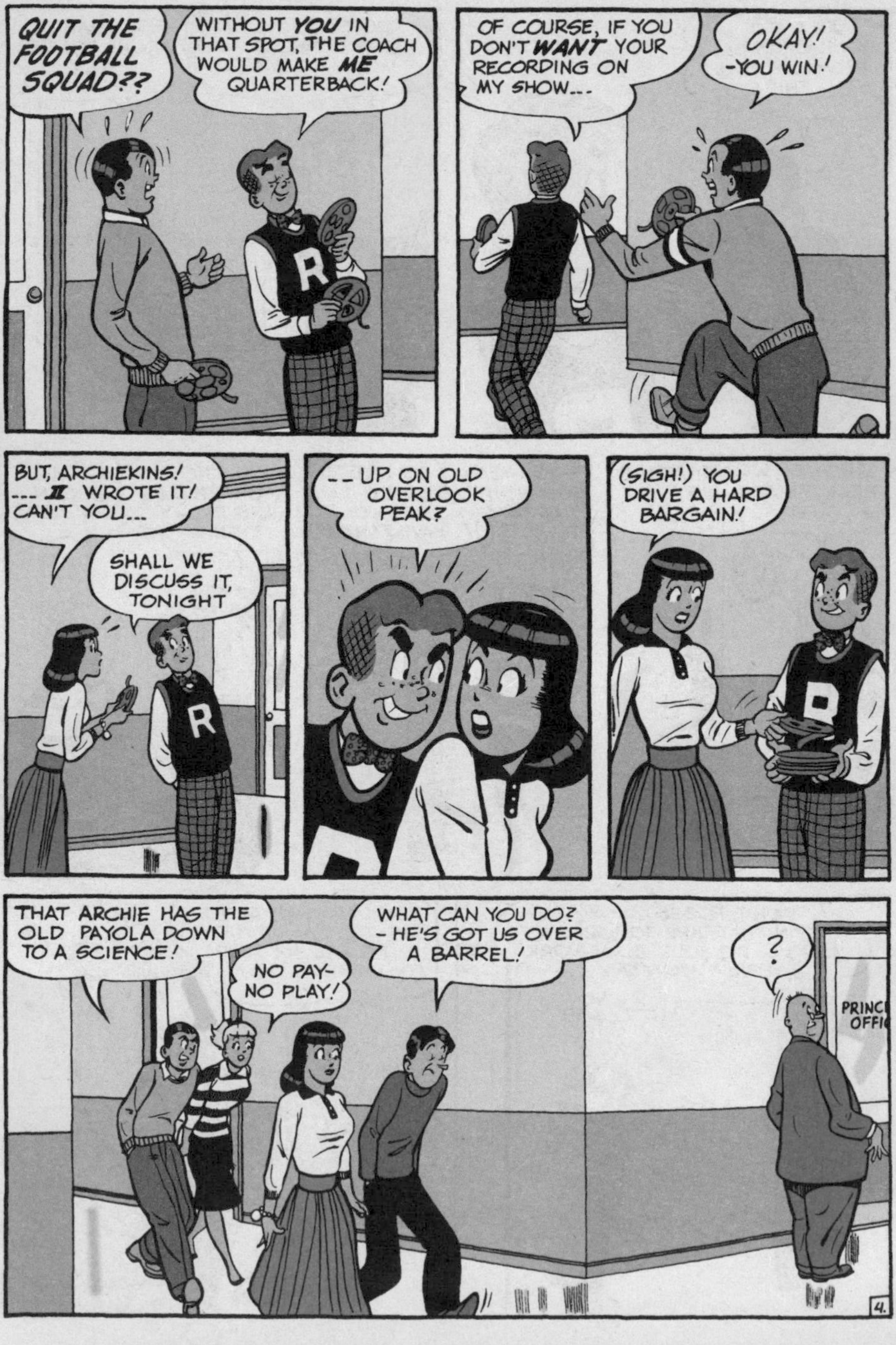
QUIT THE FOOTBALL SQUAD??
WITHOUT YOU IN THAT SPOT, THE COACH WOULD MAKE ME QUARTERBACK!
OF COURSE, IF YOU DON'T WANT YOUR RECORDING ON MY SHOW...
OKAY! -YOU WIN!
BUT, ARCHIEKINS! --- I WROTE IT! CAN'T YOU...
SHALL WE DISCUSS IT, TONIGHT
-- UP ON OLD OVERLOOK PEAK?
(SIGH!) YOU DRIVE A HARD BARGAIN!
THAT ARCHIE HAS THE OLD PAYOLA DOWN TO A SCIENCE!
NO PAY- NO PLAY!
WHAT CAN YOU DO? - HE'S GOT US OVER A BARREL!
?
4.

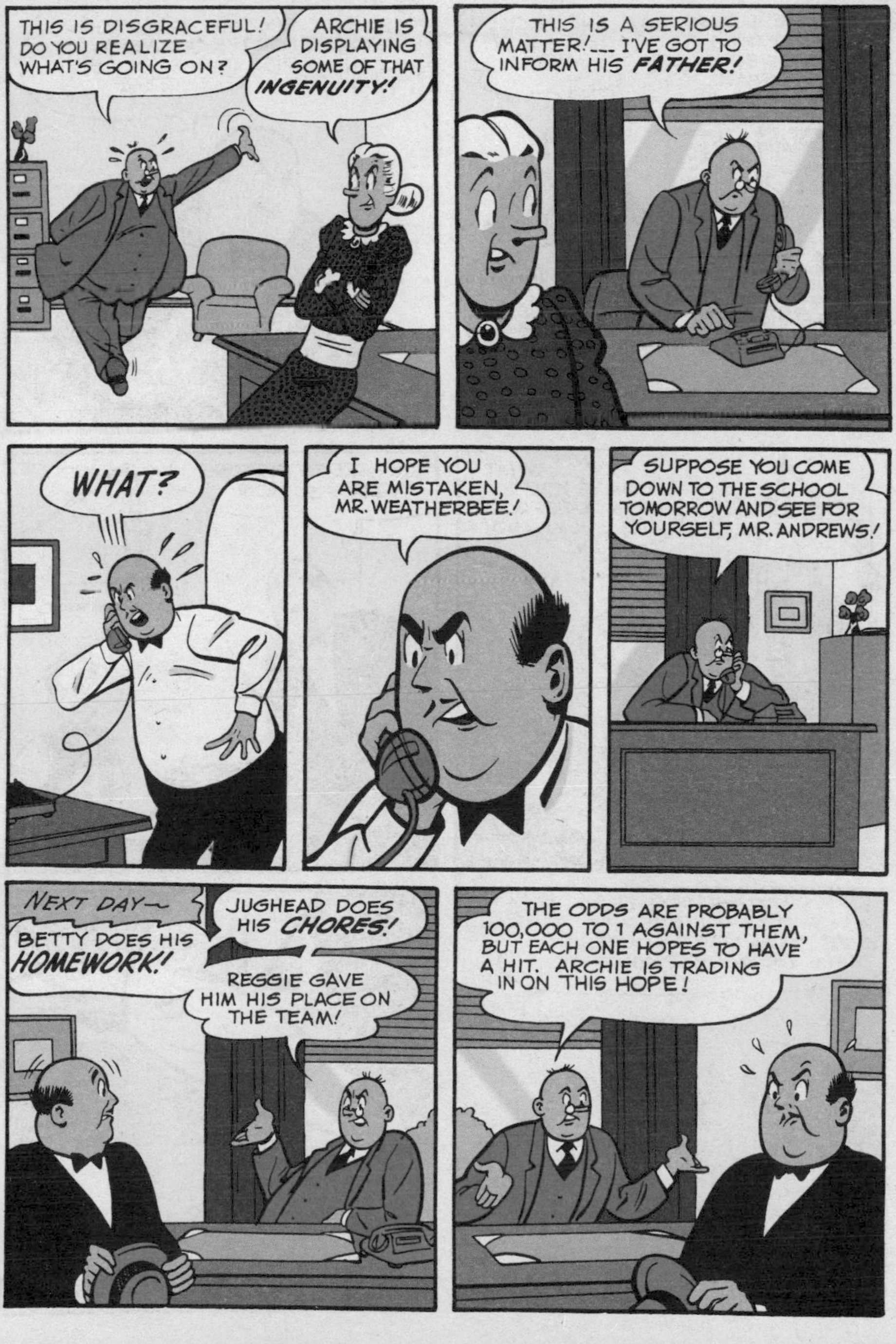
THIS IS DISGRACEFUL! DO YOU REALIZE WHAT'S GOING ON?
ARCHIE IS DISPLAYING SOME OF THAT INGENUITY!
THIS IS A SERIOUS MATTER!--- I'VE GOT TO INFORM HIS FATHER!
WHAT?
I HOPE YOU ARE MISTAKEN, MR. WEATHERBEE!
SUPPOSE YOU COME DOWN TO THE SCHOOL TOMORROW AND SEE FOR YOURSELF, MR. ANDREWS!
NEXT DAY—
BETTY DOES HIS HOMEWORK!
JUGHEAD DOES HIS CHORES!
REGGIE GAVE HIM HIS PLACE ON THE TEAM!
THE ODDS ARE PROBABLY 100,000 TO 1 AGAINST THEM, BUT EACH ONE HOPES TO HAVE A HIT. ARCHIE IS TRADING IN ON THIS HOPE!

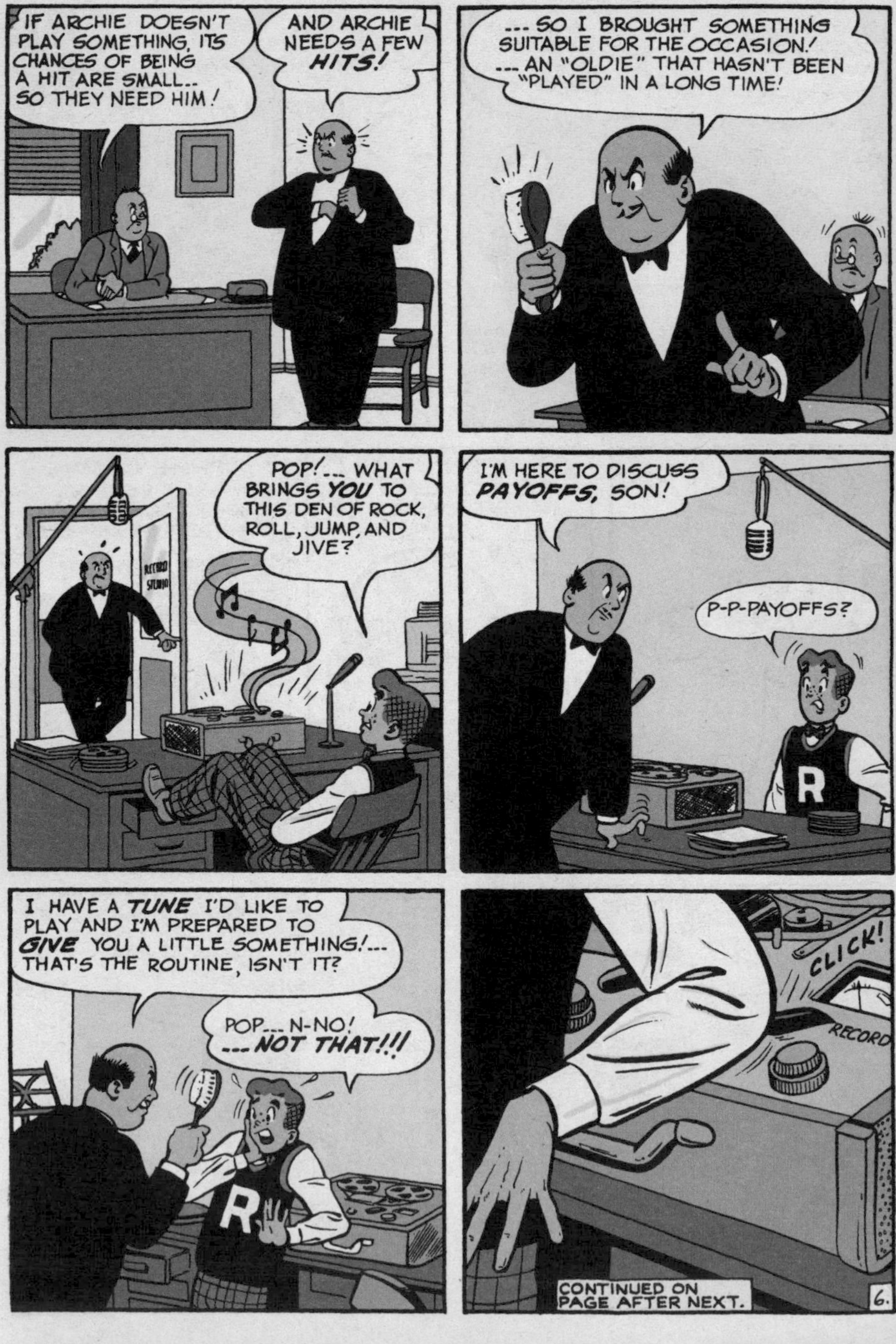
IF ARCHIE DOESN'T PLAY SOMETHING, ITS CHANCES OF BEING A HIT ARE SMALL.. SO THEY NEED HIM!
AND ARCHIE NEEDS A FEW HITS!
... SO I BROUGHT SOMETHING SUITABLE FOR THE OCCASION! ... AN "OLDIE" THAT HASN'T BEEN "PLAYED" IN A LONG TIME!
POP! ... WHAT BRINGS YOU TO THIS DEN OF ROCK, ROLL, JUMP, AND JIVE?
I'M HERE TO DISCUSS PAYOFFS, SON!
P-P-PAYOFFS?
I HAVE A TUNE I'D LIKE TO PLAY AND I'M PREPARED TO GIVE YOU A LITTLE SOMETHING! ... THAT'S THE ROUTINE, ISN'T IT?
POP... N-NO! ... NOT THAT!!!
CLICK!
RECORD
CONTINUED ON PAGE AFTER NEXT.
6.

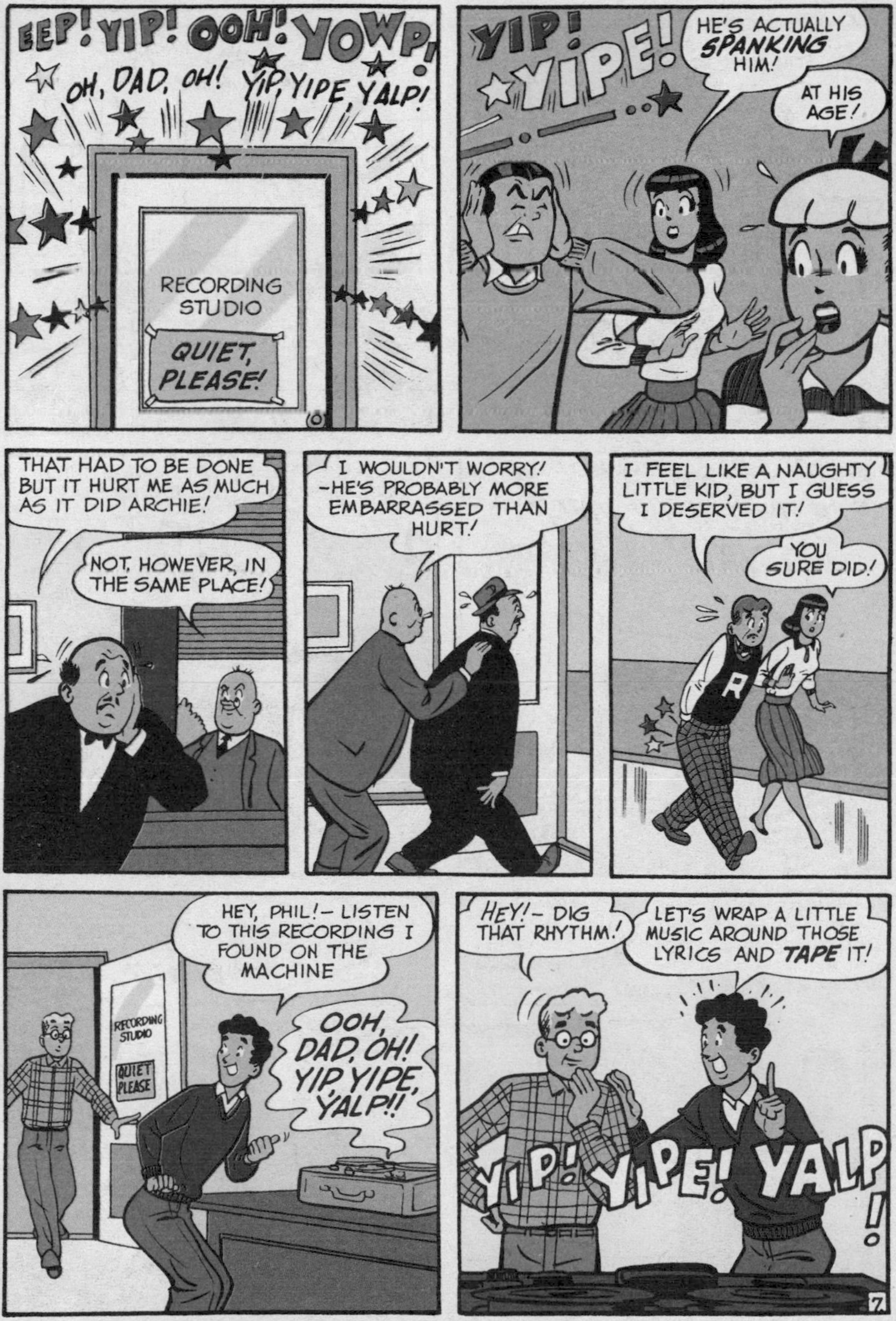
EEP! YIP! OOH! YOWP!
OH, DAD, OH! YIP, YIPE, YALP!
RECORDING STUDIO
QUIET, PLEASE!
YIP! YIPE!
HE'S ACTUALLY SPANKING HIM!
AT HIS AGE!
THAT HAD TO BE DONE BUT IT HURT ME AS MUCH AS IT DID ARCHIE!
NOT, HOWEVER, IN THE SAME PLACE!
I WOULDN'T WORRY! -HE'S PROBABLY MORE EMBARRASSED THAN HURT!
I FEEL LIKE A NAUGHTY LITTLE KID, BUT I GUESS I DESERVED IT!
YOU SURE DID!
HEY, PHIL!– LISTEN TO THIS RECORDING I FOUND ON THE MACHINE
OOH, DAD, OH! YIP, YIPE, YALP!!
RECORDING STUDIO
QUIET PLEASE
HEY!– DIG THAT RHYTHM!
LET'S WRAP A LITTLE MUSIC AROUND THOSE LYRICS AND TAPE IT!
YIP! YIPE! YALP!
7

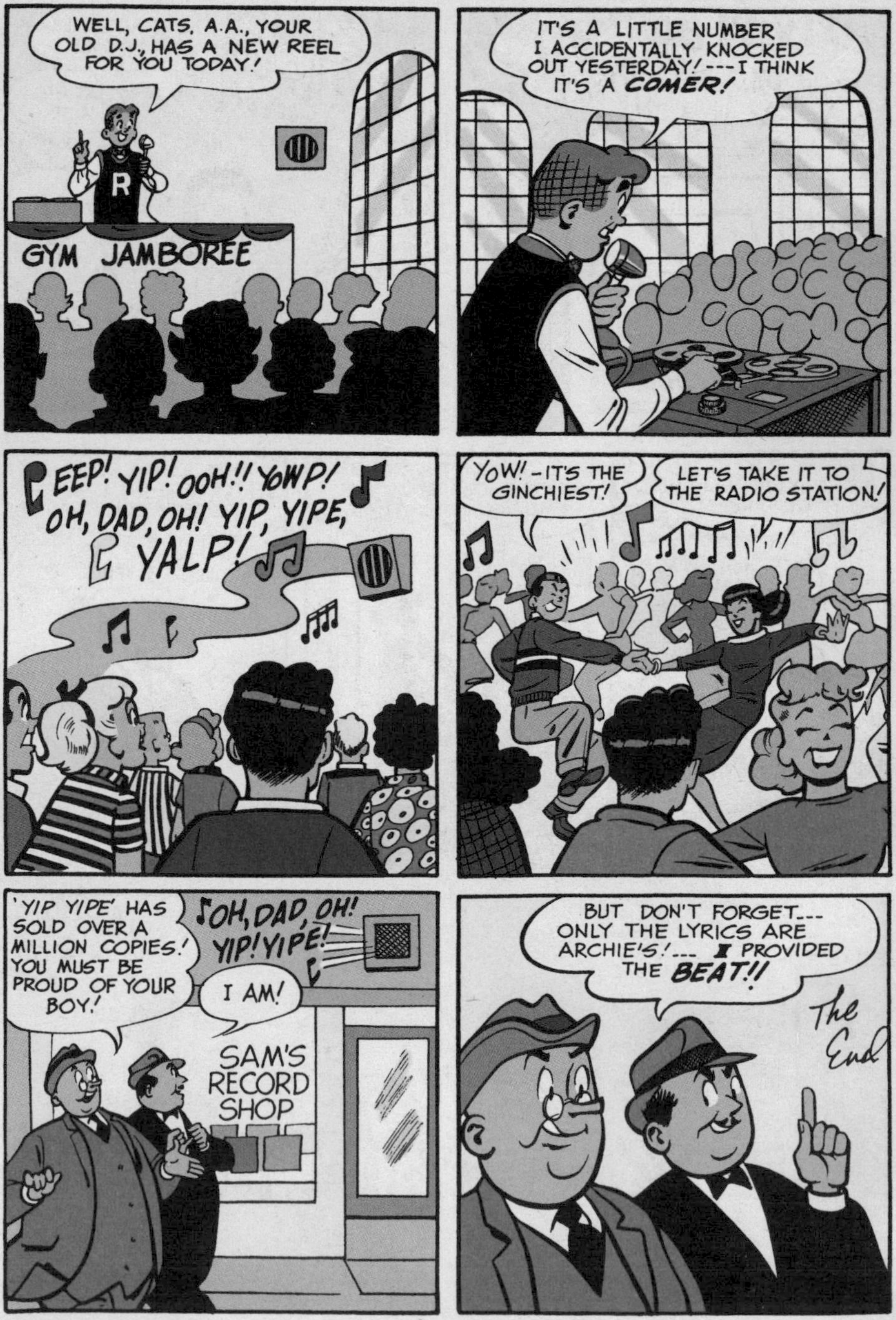
WELL, CATS, A.A., YOUR OLD D.J., HAS A NEW REEL FOR YOU TODAY!
GYM JAMBOREE
IT'S A LITTLE NUMBER I ACCIDENTALLY KNOCKED OUT YESTERDAY! ---I THINK IT'S A COMER!
EEP! YIP! OOH!! YOWP! OH, DAD, OH! YIP, YIPE, YALP!
YOW! -IT'S THE GINCHIEST!
LET'S TAKE IT TO THE RADIO STATION!
'YIP YIPE' HAS SOLD OVER A MILLION COPIES! YOU MUST BE PROUD OF YOUR BOY!
OH, DAD, OH! YIP! YIPE!
I AM!
SAM'S RECORD SHOP
BUT DON'T FORGET--- ONLY THE LYRICS ARE ARCHIE'S!--- I PROVIDED THE BEAT!!
The End

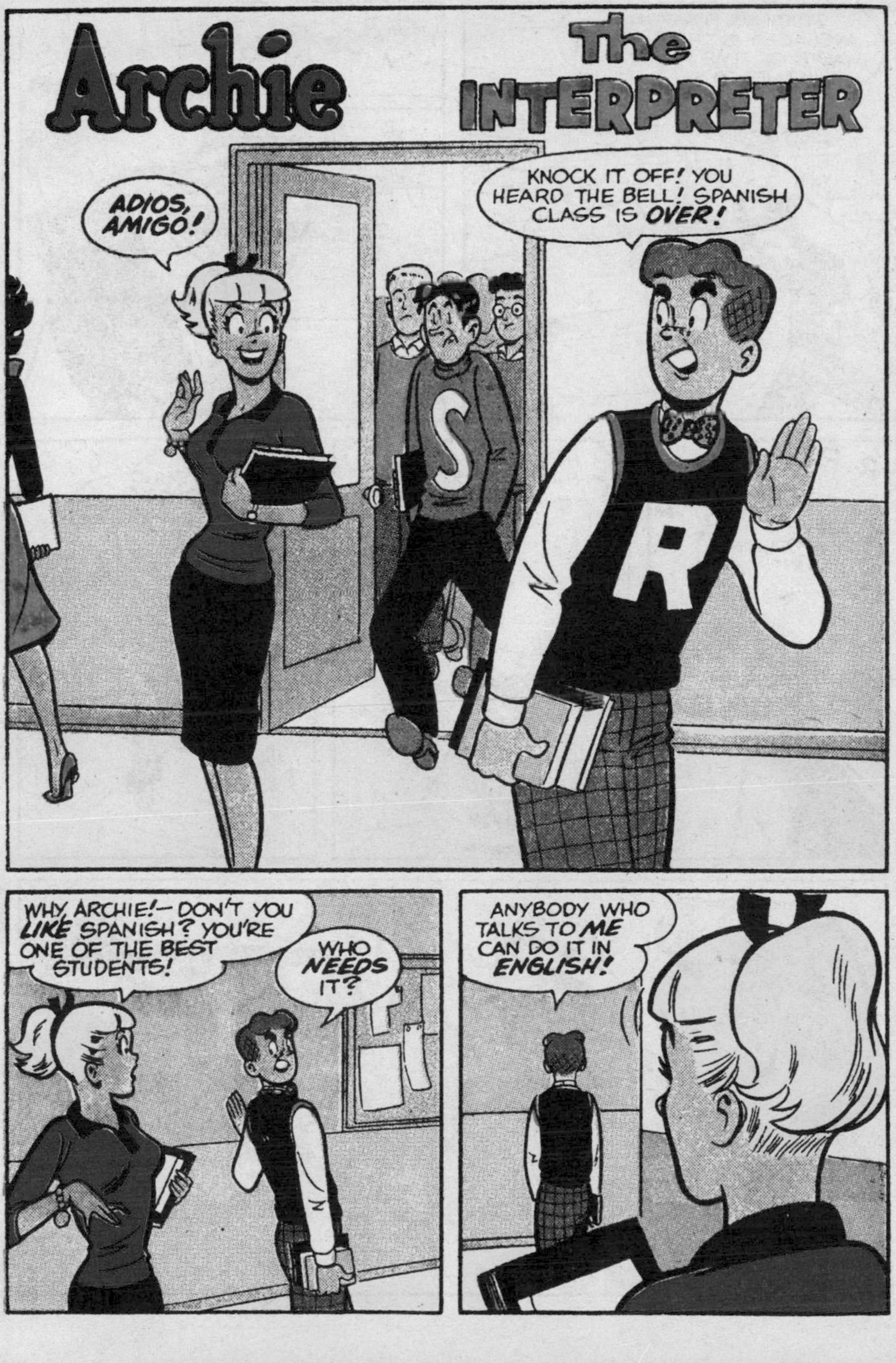
Archie
The INTERPRETER
ADIOS, AMIGO!
KNOCK IT OFF! YOU HEARD THE BELL! SPANISH CLASS IS OVER!
WHY, ARCHIE!— DON'T YOU LIKE SPANISH? YOU'RE ONE OF THE BEST STUDENTS!
WHO NEEDS IT?
ANYBODY WHO TALKS TO ME CAN DO IT IN ENGLISH!

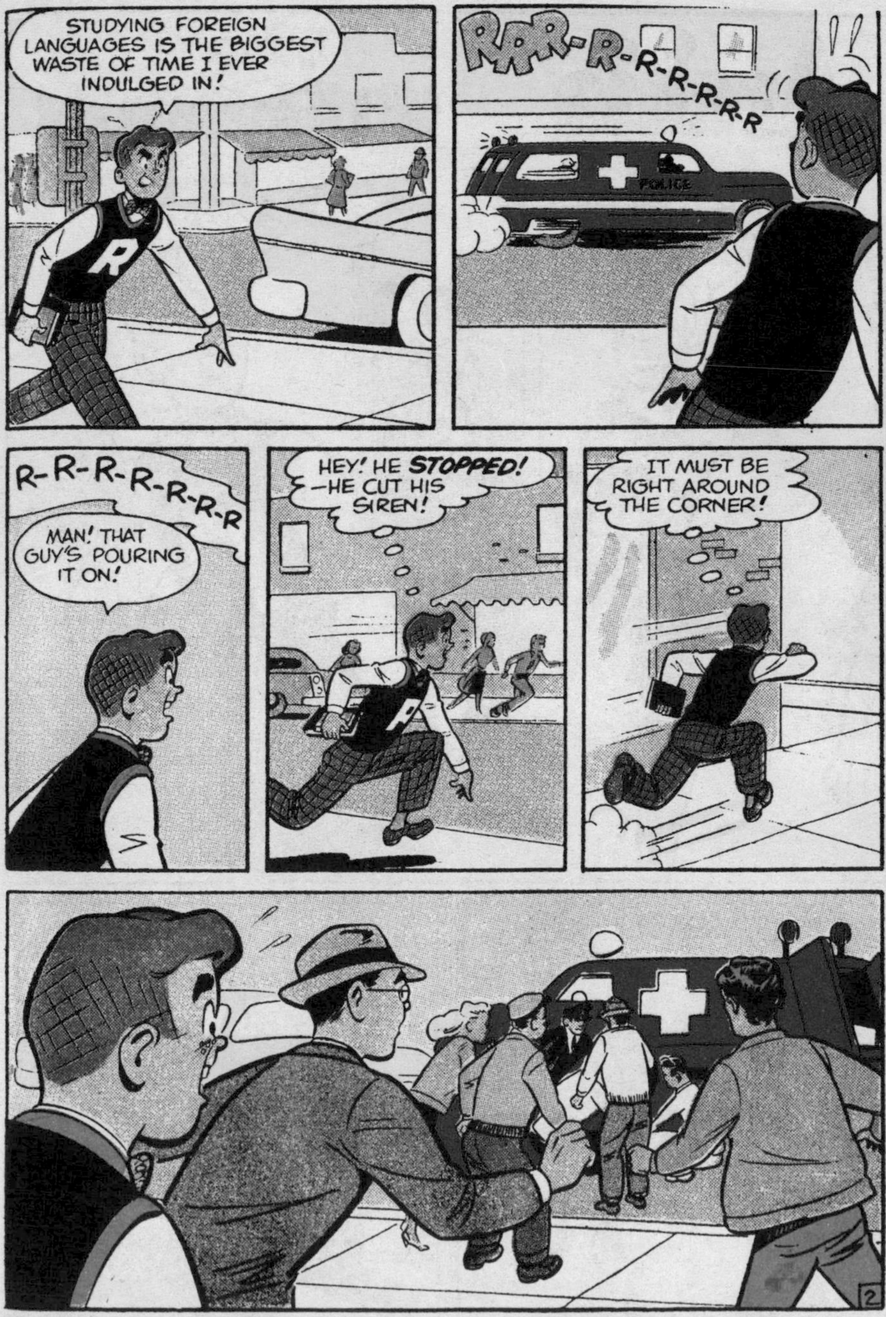
STUDYING FOREIGN LANGUAGES IS THE BIGGEST WASTE OF TIME I EVER INDULGED IN!
RRR-R-R-R-R-R-R
POLICE
R-R-R-R-R-R-R
MAN! THAT GUY'S POURING IT ON!
HEY! HE STOPPED! —HE CUT HIS SIREN!
IT MUST BE RIGHT AROUND THE CORNER!
2

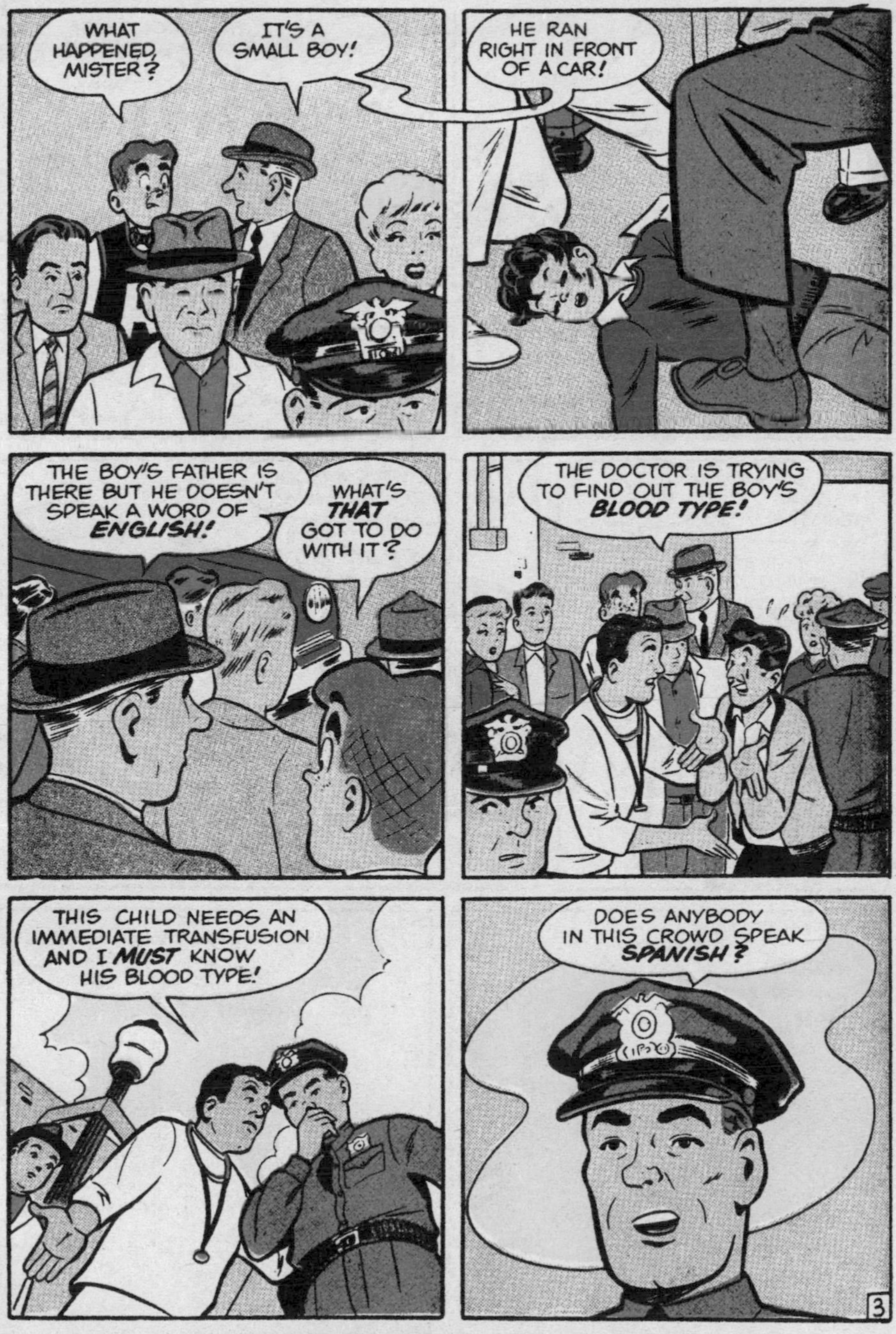
WHAT HAPPENED, MISTER?
IT'S A SMALL BOY!
HE RAN RIGHT IN FRONT OF A CAR!
THE BOY'S FATHER IS THERE BUT HE DOESN'T SPEAK A WORD OF ENGLISH!
WHAT'S THAT GOT TO DO WITH IT?
THE DOCTOR IS TRYING TO FIND OUT THE BOY'S BLOOD TYPE!
THIS CHILD NEEDS AN IMMEDIATE TRANSFUSION AND I MUST KNOW HIS BLOOD TYPE!
DOES ANYBODY IN THIS CROWD SPEAK SPANISH?
3

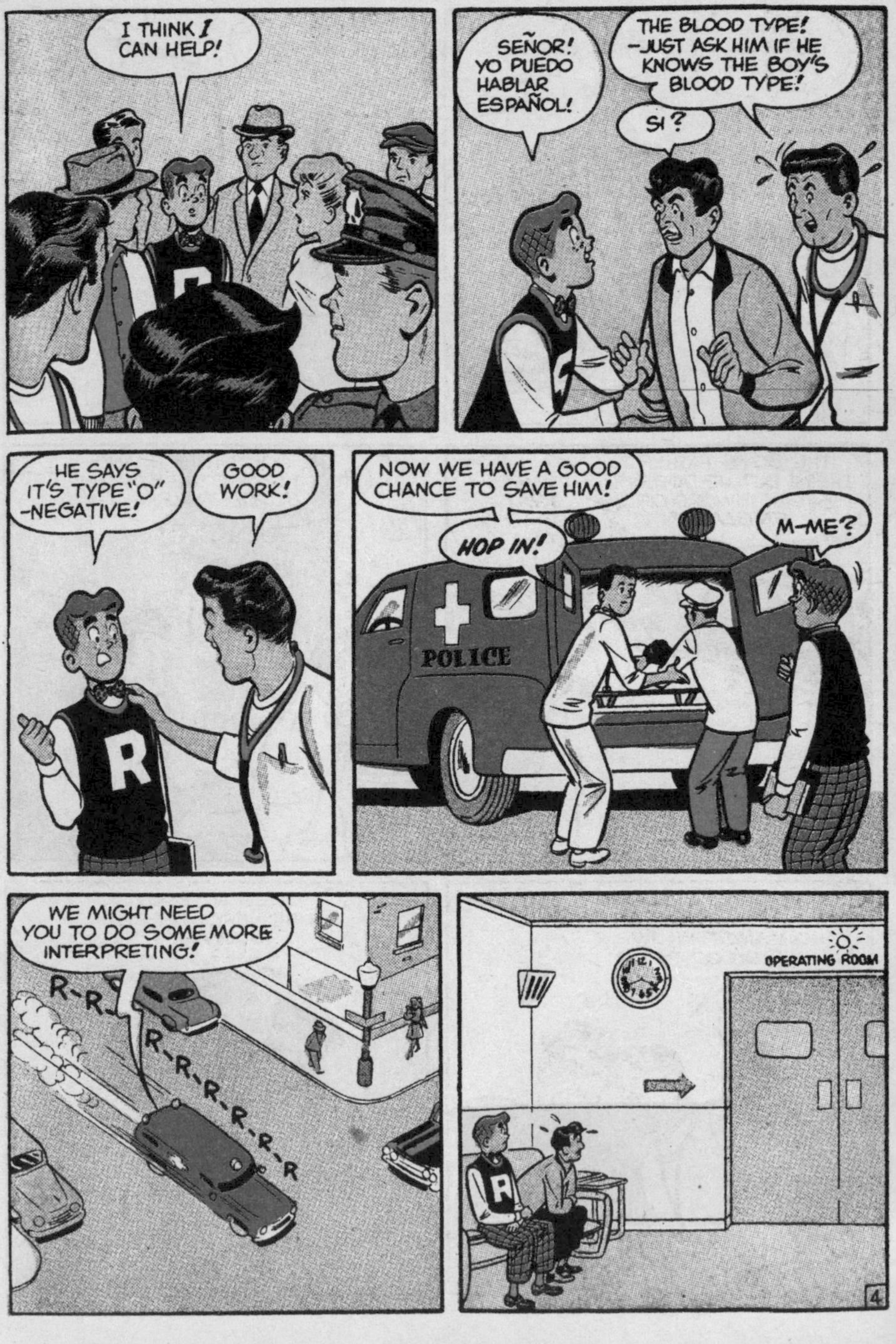
I THINK I CAN HELP!
SEÑOR! YO PUEDO HABLAR ESPAÑOL!
THE BLOOD TYPE! -JUST ASK HIM IF HE KNOWS THE BOY'S BLOOD TYPE!
SI?
HE SAYS IT'S TYPE "O" -NEGATIVE!
GOOD WORK!
NOW WE HAVE A GOOD CHANCE TO SAVE HIM!
HOP IN!
M-ME?
POLICE
WE MIGHT NEED YOU TO DO SOME MORE INTERPRETING!
R-R-
R-R-R-R-R-R
OPERATING ROOM
4

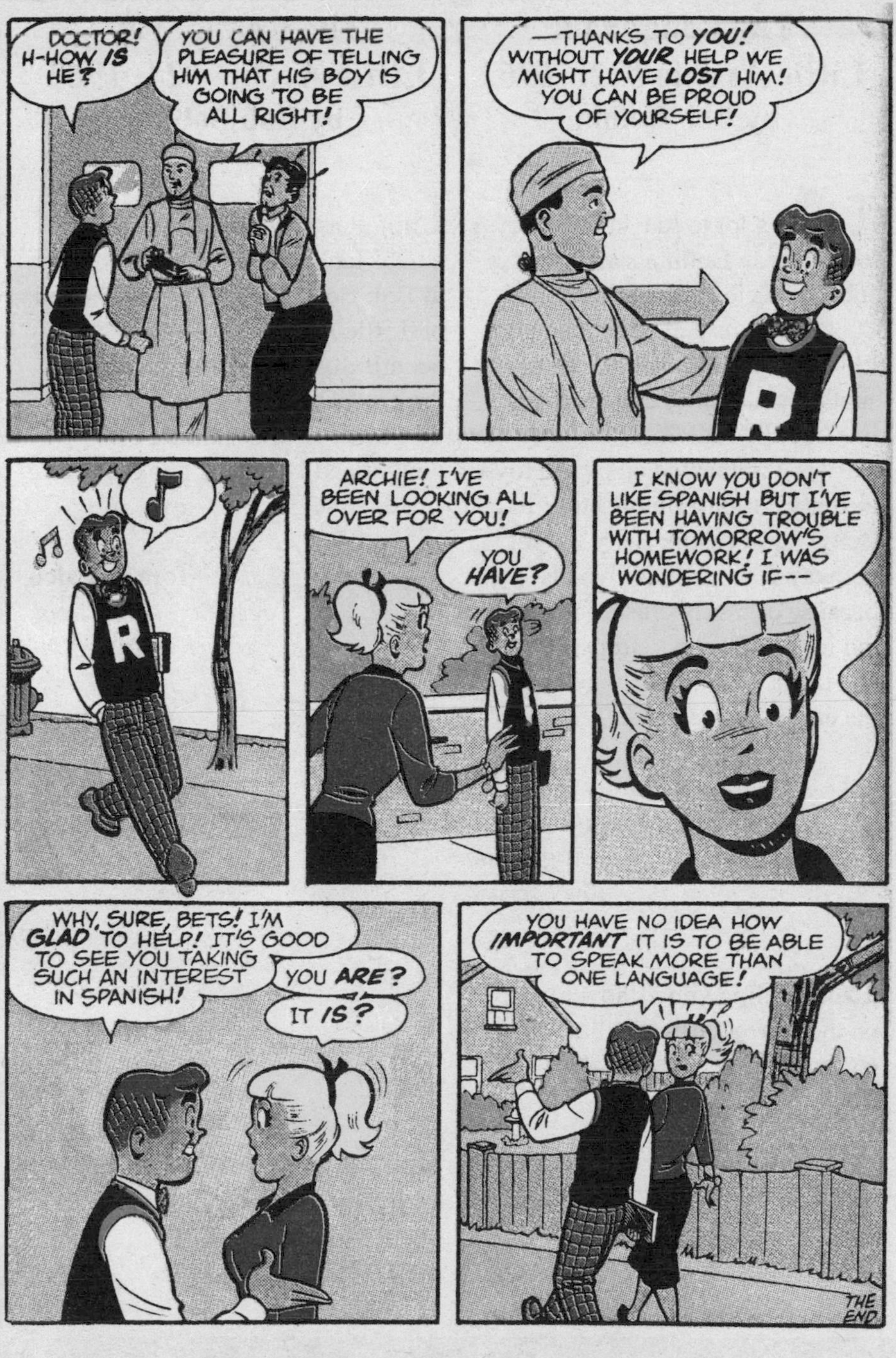
DOCTOR! H-HOW IS HE?
YOU CAN HAVE THE PLEASURE OF TELLING HIM THAT HIS BOY IS GOING TO BE ALL RIGHT!
—THANKS TO YOU! WITHOUT YOUR HELP WE MIGHT HAVE LOST HIM! YOU CAN BE PROUD OF YOURSELF!
R
R
ARCHIE! I'VE BEEN LOOKING ALL OVER FOR YOU!
YOU HAVE?
I KNOW YOU DON'T LIKE SPANISH BUT I'VE BEEN HAVING TROUBLE WITH TOMORROW'S HOMEWORK! I WAS WONDERING IF--
WHY, SURE, BETS! I'M GLAD TO HELP! IT'S GOOD TO SEE YOU TAKING SUCH AN INTEREST IN SPANISH!
YOU ARE?
IT IS?
YOU HAVE NO IDEA HOW IMPORTANT IT IS TO BE ABLE TO SPEAK MORE THAN ONE LANGUAGE!
THE END

The Long Walk
Little Archie #22, 1962
by Bob Bolling

There's a lot to like in this story. I like the way Bolling's art conveys subtle emotions through the use of expressions and body language. I like that it's sweeter and more subtle than a lot of comics from this time period. I like the way the story is commented on by the toys in Betty's room. But mostly I like Betty. I don't think Betty fought her way through those woods because of a silly crush. I think she did it because she's strong, brave, and determined. And I like that by the end... Archie agrees with me.

--Jimmy Gownley
Author and artist of the award-winning Amelia Rules! *graphic novel series.*

Bob Bolling knows how to tug on those heartstrings without being corny. And you feel for poor Little Betty in this story.

--Dan Parent
Writer and illustrator, Archie Comics

The Gentle Way
Little Archie #24, 1962
by Bob Bolling

I might as well come clean. I am a total fanboy geek when it comes to Bob Bolling and the work he did on Little Archie. The stories were beautifully crafted and exquisitely drawn. "The Gentle Way" is the first Little Archie comic I ever bought and I've been hooked ever since.

--Tom DeFalco
Legendary comic book writer and editor

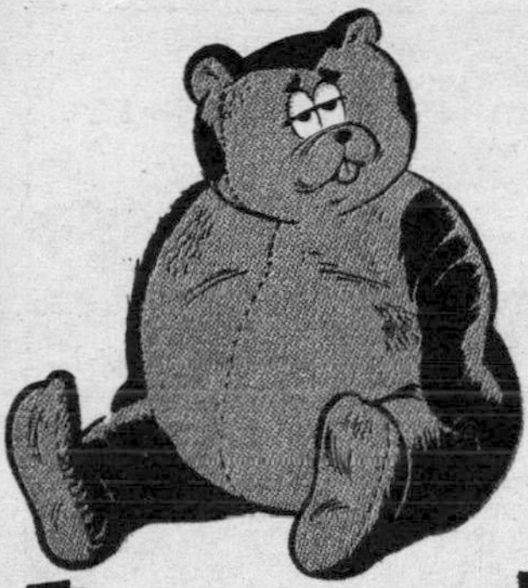

THE PANDA IS
NOT EXACTLY DUMB

BUT HIS BRAINS ARE
AT A MINIMUM

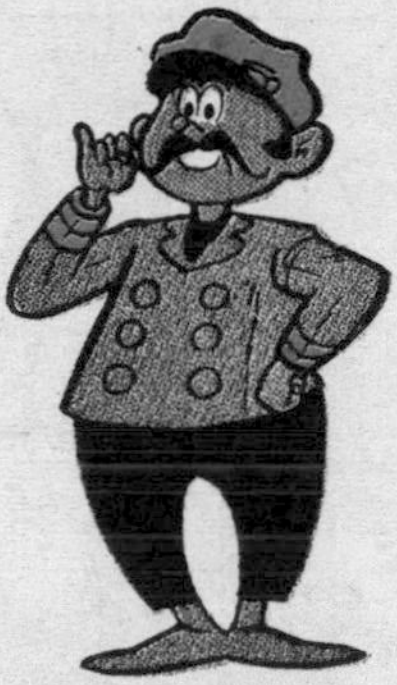

NOW THE CAP'N'S BRAINS
ARE NOT DELETED

BUT, BOY! HE'S
CERTAINLY CONCEITED

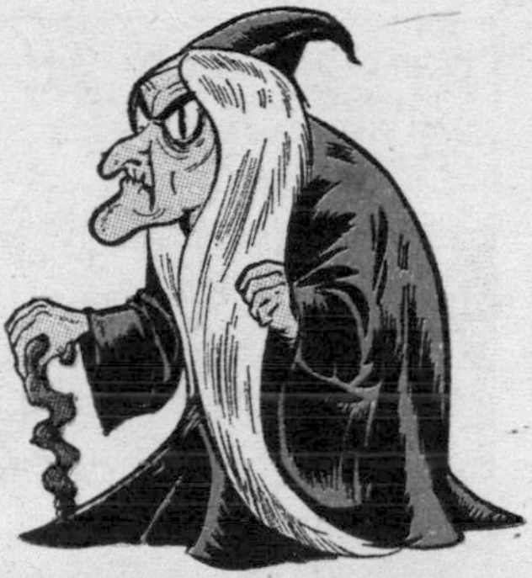

THIS WITCH'S LOT IS
NOT A HAPPY ONE

BUT BRAINS SHE'S
GOT BY THE TON

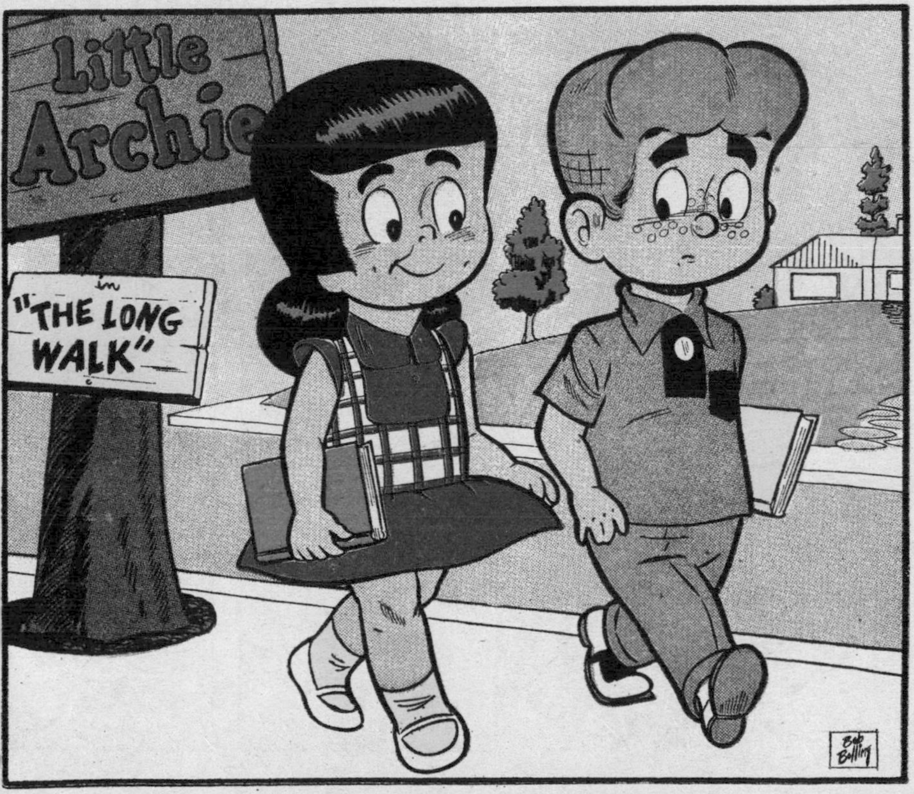
Little Archie
in
"THE LONG WALK"
Bob Bolling

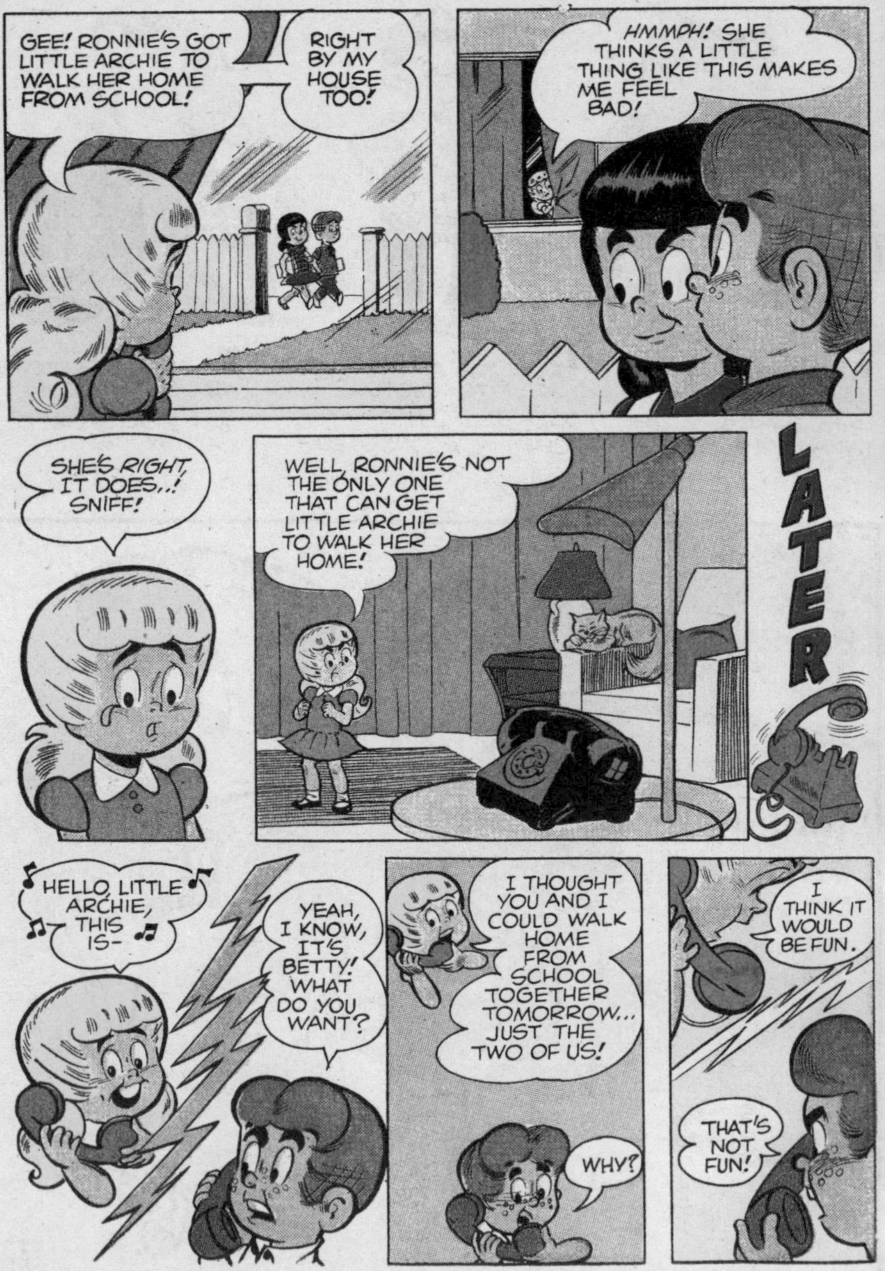
GEE! RONNIE'S GOT LITTLE ARCHIE TO WALK HER HOME FROM SCHOOL!
RIGHT BY MY HOUSE TOO!
HMMPH! SHE THINKS A LITTLE THING LIKE THIS MAKES ME FEEL BAD!
SHE'S RIGHT, IT DOES..! SNIFF!
WELL, RONNIE'S NOT THE ONLY ONE THAT CAN GET LITTLE ARCHIE TO WALK HER HOME!
LATER
HELLO, LITTLE ARCHIE, THIS IS-
YEAH, I KNOW, IT'S BETTY! WHAT DO YOU WANT?
I THOUGHT YOU AND I COULD WALK HOME FROM SCHOOL TOGETHER TOMORROW... JUST THE TWO OF US!
WHY?
I THINK IT WOULD BE FUN.
THAT'S NOT FUN!

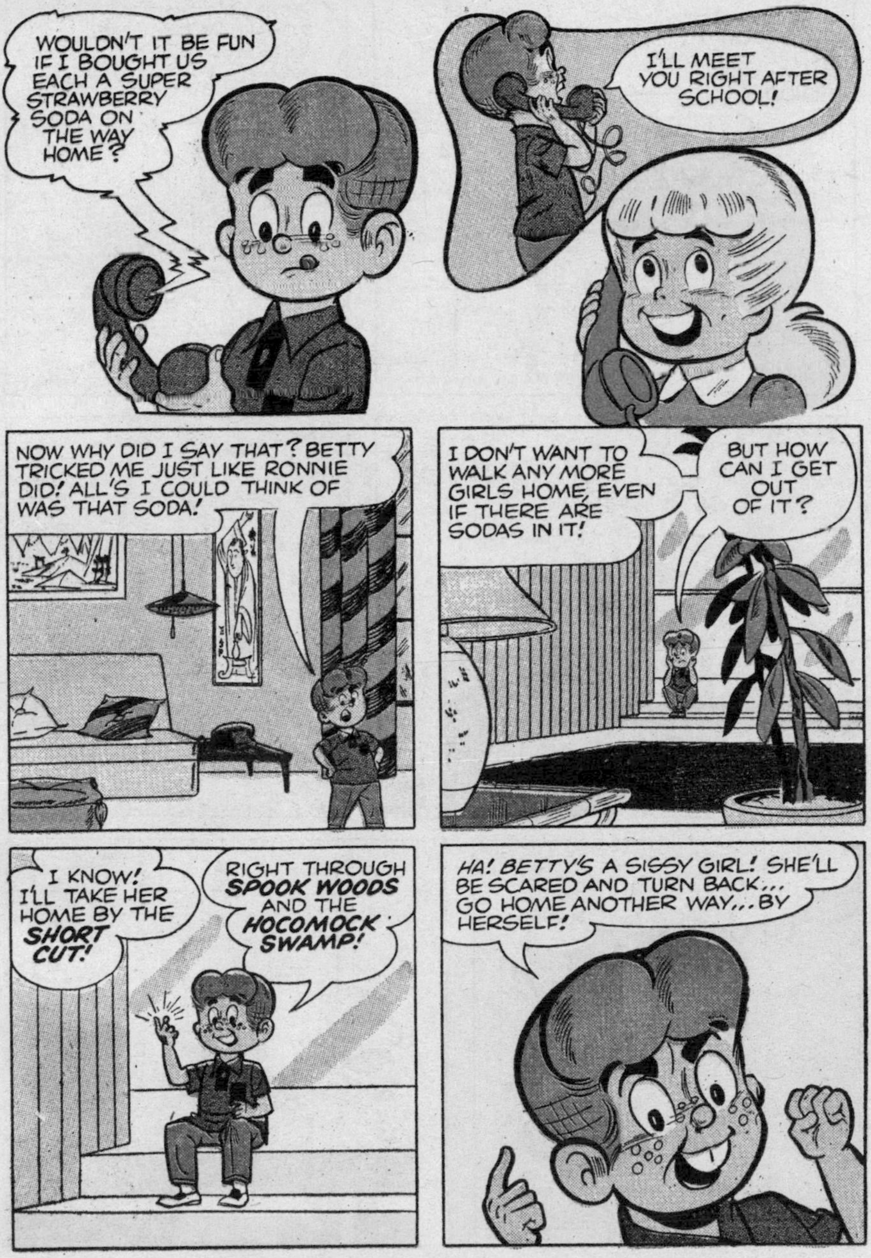
WOULDN'T IT BE FUN IF I BOUGHT US EACH A SUPER STRAWBERRY SODA ON THE WAY HOME?
I'LL MEET YOU RIGHT AFTER SCHOOL!
NOW WHY DID I SAY THAT? BETTY TRICKED ME JUST LIKE RONNIE DID! ALL'S I COULD THINK OF WAS THAT SODA!
I DON'T WANT TO WALK ANY MORE GIRLS HOME, EVEN IF THERE ARE SODAS IN IT!
BUT HOW CAN I GET OUT OF IT?
I KNOW! I'LL TAKE HER HOME BY THE SHORT CUT!
RIGHT THROUGH SPOOK WOODS AND THE HOCOMOCK SWAMP!
HA! BETTY'S A SISSY GIRL! SHE'LL BE SCARED AND TURN BACK... GO HOME ANOTHER WAY... BY HERSELF!

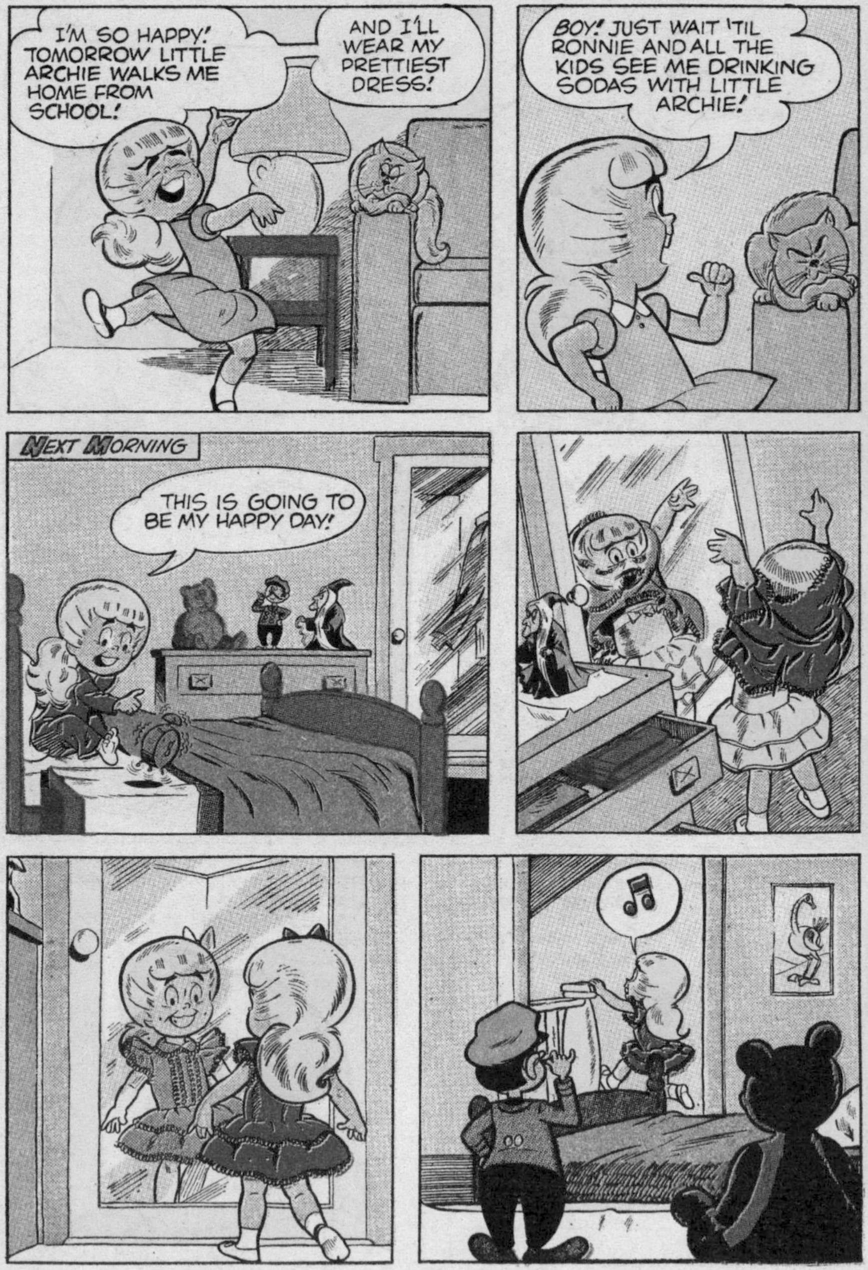
I'M SO HAPPY! TOMORROW LITTLE ARCHIE WALKS ME HOME FROM SCHOOL!
AND I'LL WEAR MY PRETTIEST DRESS!
BOY! JUST WAIT 'TIL RONNIE AND ALL THE KIDS SEE ME DRINKING SODAS WITH LITTLE ARCHIE!
NEXT MORNING
THIS IS GOING TO BE MY HAPPY DAY!

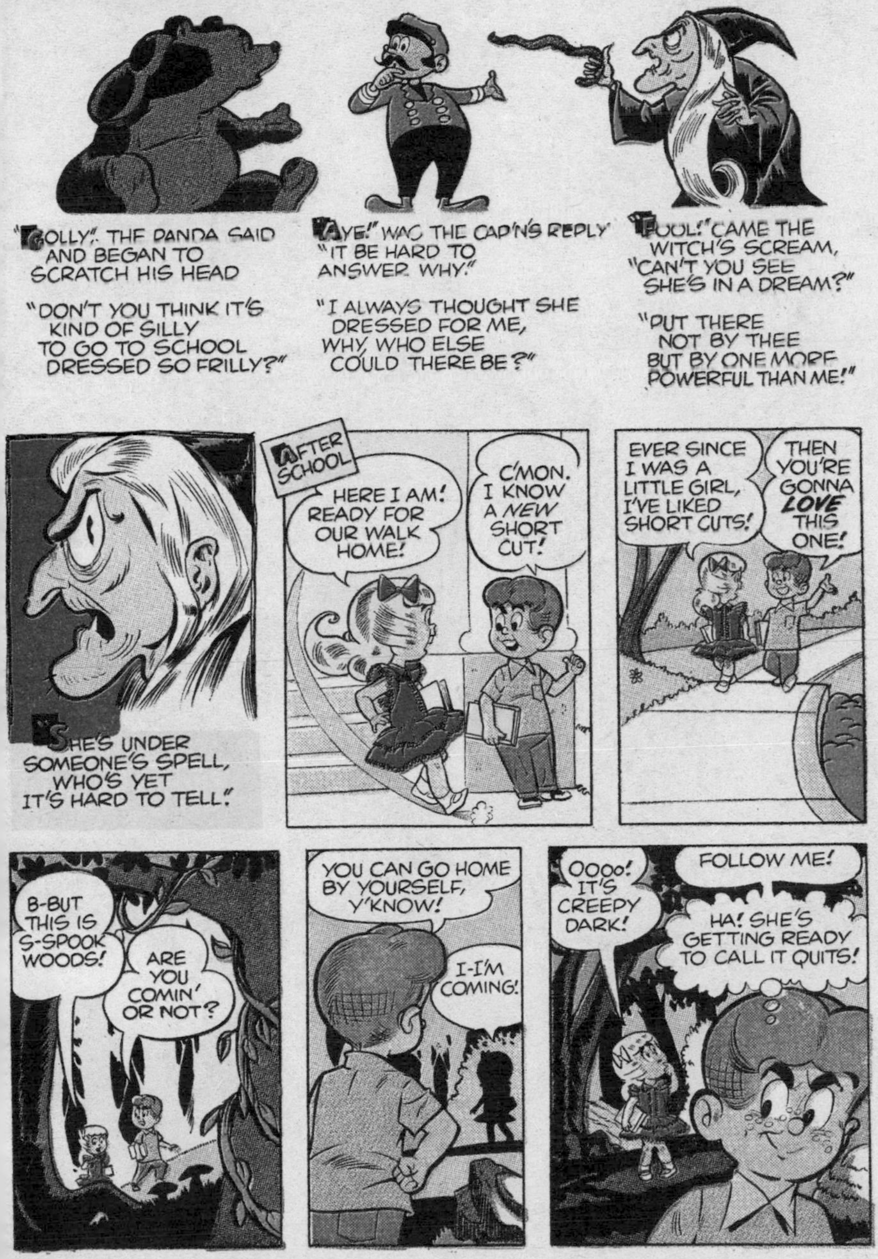
"GOLLY!" THE PANDA SAID AND BEGAN TO SCRATCH HIS HEAD
"DON'T YOU THINK IT'S KIND OF SILLY TO GO TO SCHOOL DRESSED SO FRILLY?"
"AYE!" WAS THE CAP'N'S REPLY "IT BE HARD TO ANSWER WHY."
"I ALWAYS THOUGHT SHE DRESSED FOR ME, WHY, WHO ELSE COULD THERE BE?"
"FOOL!" CAME THE WITCH'S SCREAM, "CAN'T YOU SEE SHE'S IN A DREAM?"
"PUT THERE NOT BY THEE BUT BY ONE MORE POWERFUL THAN ME!"
"SHE'S UNDER SOMEONE'S SPELL, WHO'S YET IT'S HARD TO TELL."
AFTER SCHOOL
HERE I AM! READY FOR OUR WALK HOME!
C'MON. I KNOW A NEW SHORT CUT!
EVER SINCE I WAS A LITTLE GIRL, I'VE LIKED SHORT CUTS!
THEN YOU'RE GONNA LOVE THIS ONE!
B-BUT THIS IS S-SPOOK WOODS!
ARE YOU COMIN' OR NOT?
YOU CAN GO HOME BY YOURSELF, Y'KNOW!
I-I'M COMING!
OOOo! IT'S CREEPY DARK!
FOLLOW ME!
HA! SHE'S GETTING READY TO CALL IT QUITS!

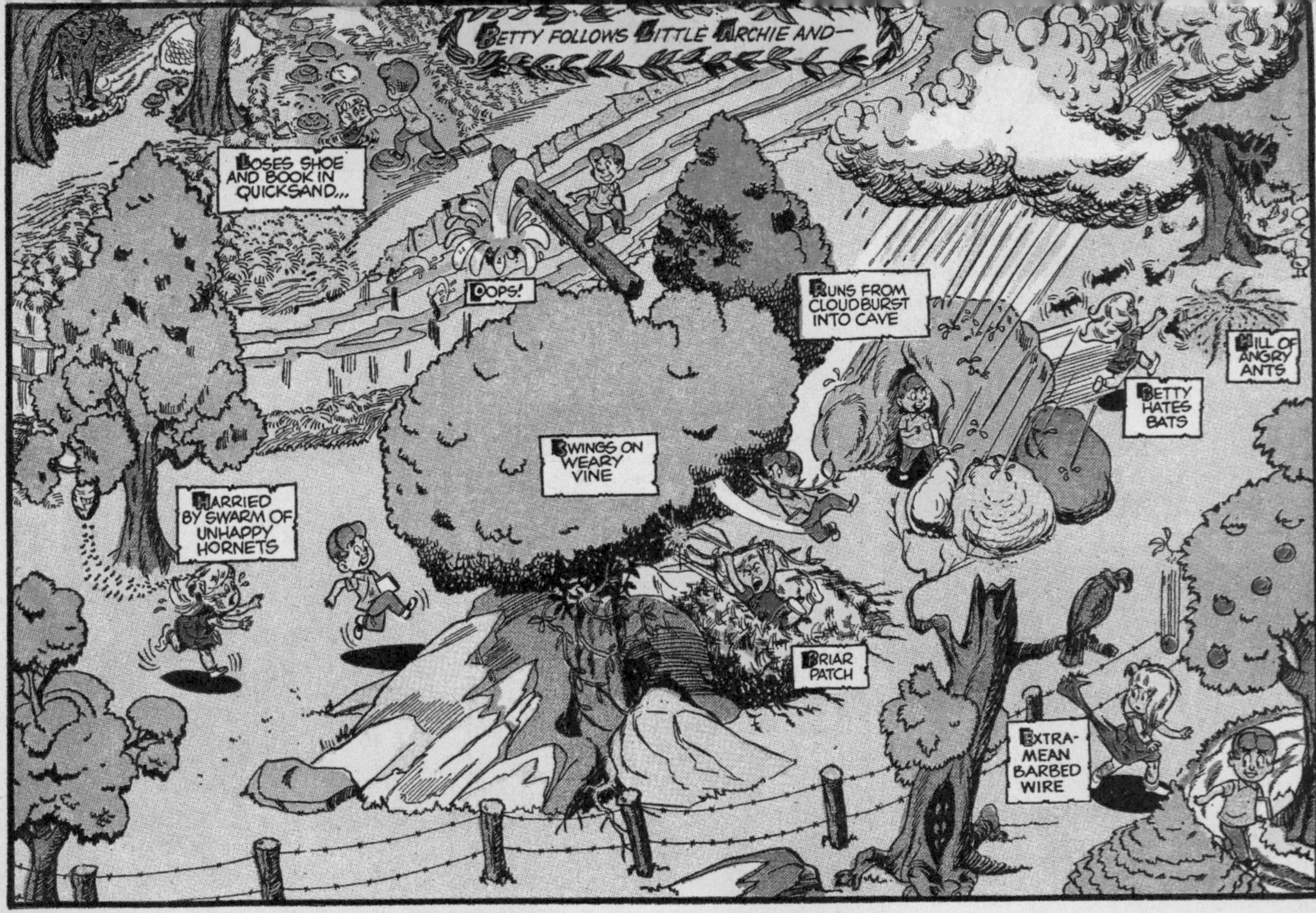
BETTY FOLLOWS LITTLE ARCHIE AND—
LOSES SHOE AND BOOK IN QUICKSAND...
OOPS!
RUNS FROM CLOUDBURST INTO CAVE
HILL OF ANGRY ANTS
BETTY HATES BATS
SWINGS ON WEARY VINE
HARRIED BY SWARM OF UNHAPPY HORNETS
BRIAR PATCH
EXTRA-MEAN BARBED WIRE

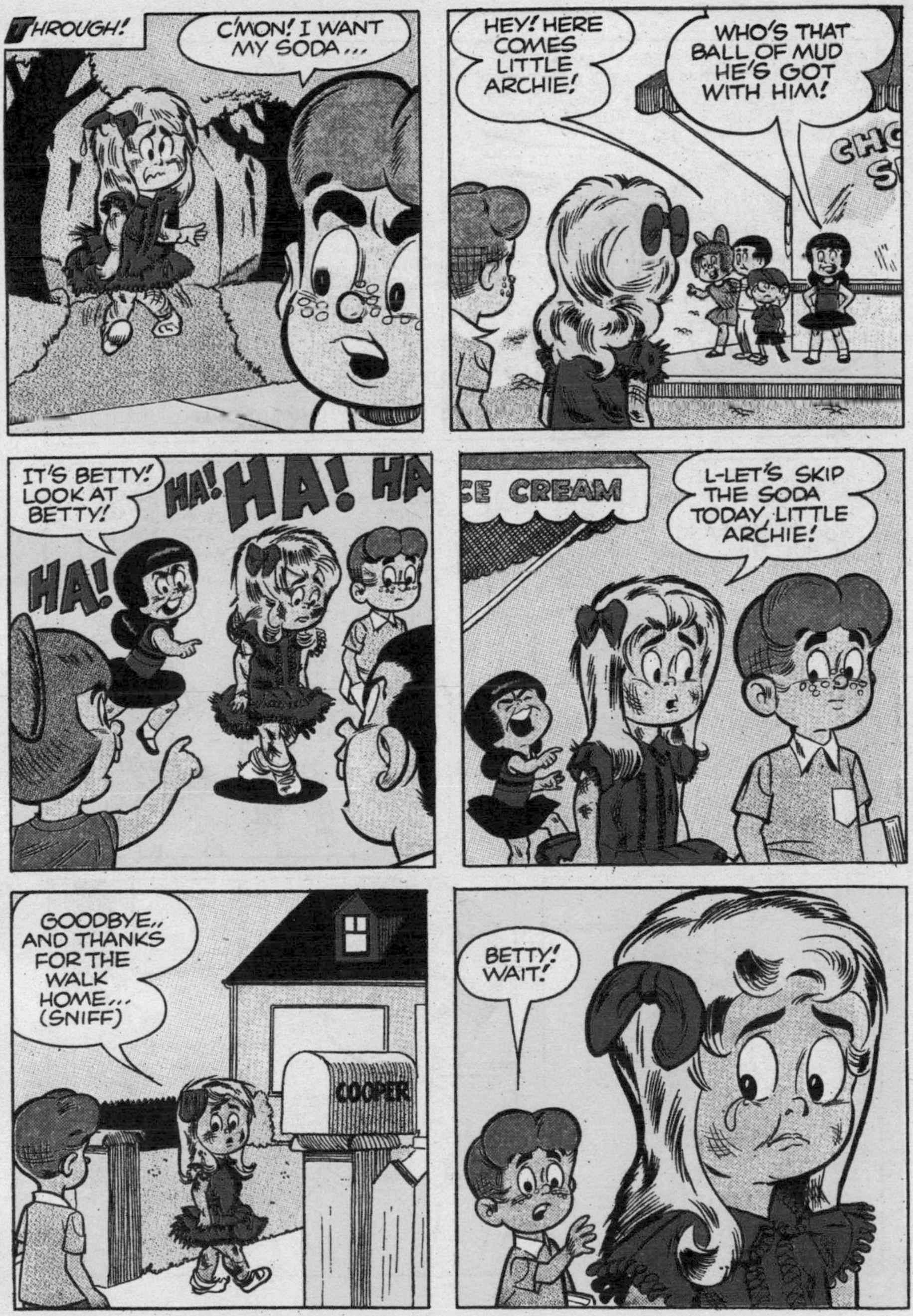
THROUGH!
C'MON! I WANT MY SODA...
HEY! HERE COMES LITTLE ARCHIE!
WHO'S THAT BALL OF MUD HE'S GOT WITH HIM!
IT'S BETTY! LOOK AT BETTY!
HA! HA! HA
HA!
SE CREAM
L-LET'S SKIP THE SODA TODAY, LITTLE ARCHIE!
GOODBYE,, AND THANKS FOR THE WALK HOME,.. (SNIFF)
COOPER
BETTY! WAIT!

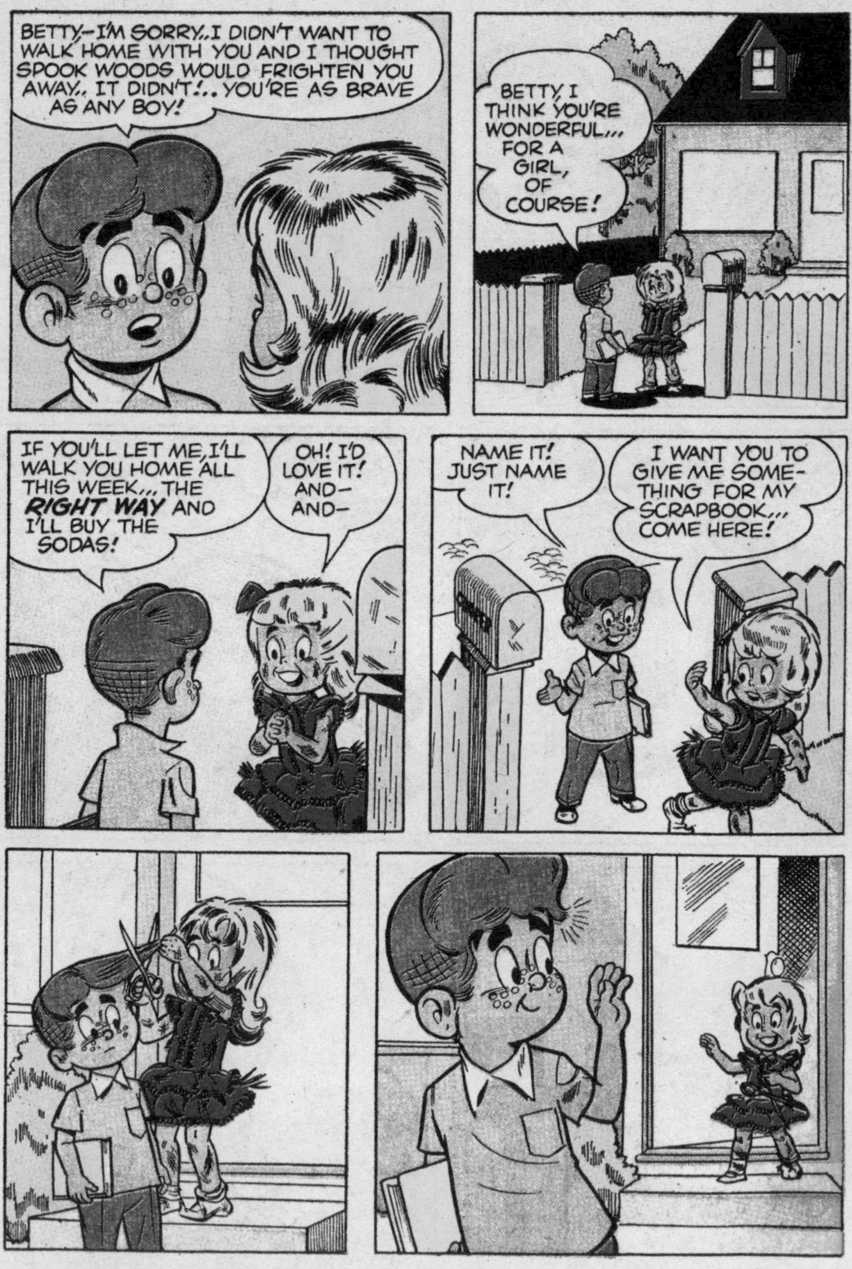
BETTY,—I'M SORRY,.I DIDN'T WANT TO WALK HOME WITH YOU AND I THOUGHT SPOOK WOODS WOULD FRIGHTEN YOU AWAY.. IT DIDN'T!.. YOU'RE AS BRAVE AS ANY BOY!
BETTY, I THINK YOU'RE WONDERFUL,,, FOR A GIRL, OF COURSE!
IF YOU'LL LET ME, I'LL WALK YOU HOME ALL THIS WEEK,,, THE RIGHT WAY AND I'LL BUY THE SODAS!
OH! I'D LOVE IT! AND— AND—
NAME IT! JUST NAME IT!
I WANT YOU TO GIVE ME SOME-THING FOR MY SCRAPBOOK,,, COME HERE!

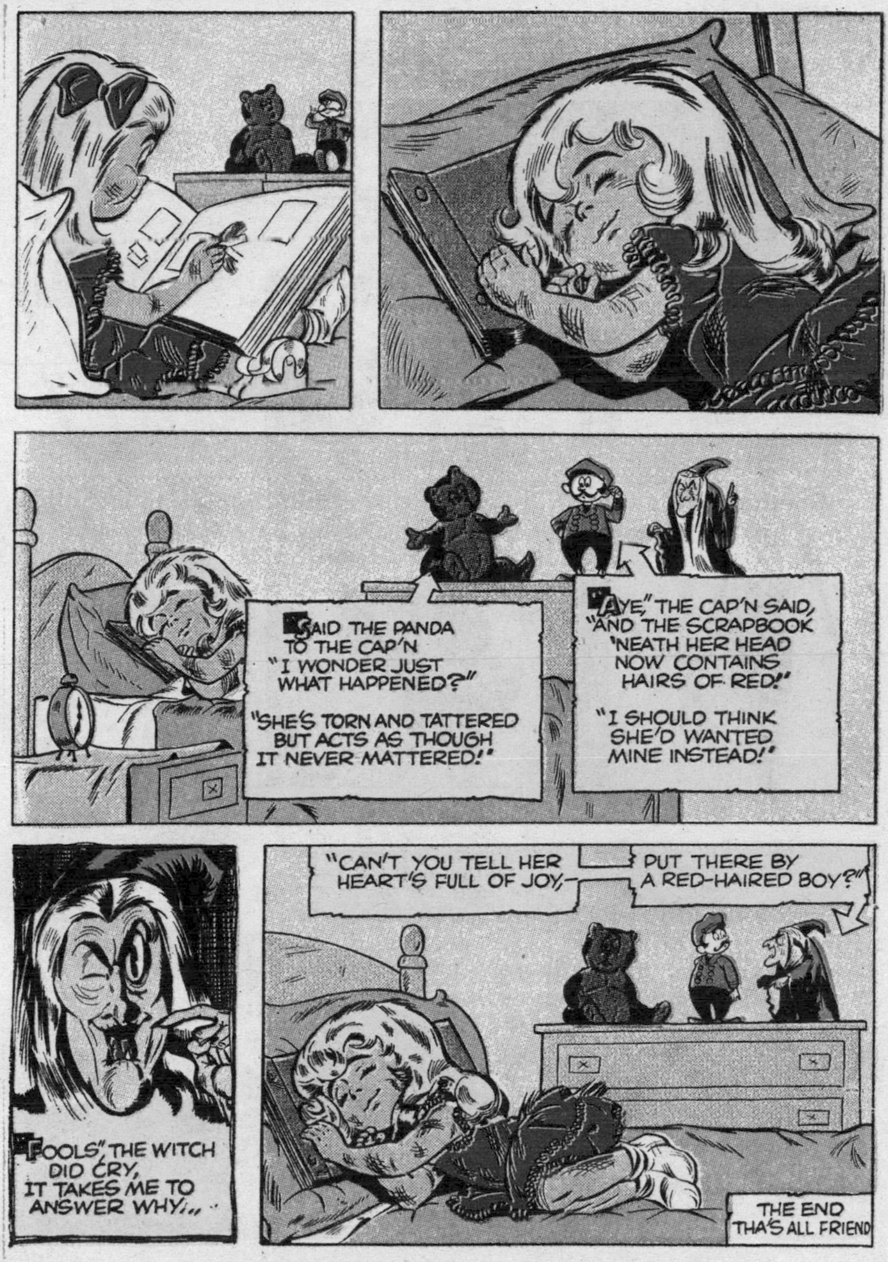
SAID THE PANDA TO THE CAP'N "I WONDER JUST WHAT HAPPENED?"
"SHE'S TORN AND TATTERED BUT ACTS AS THOUGH IT NEVER MATTERED!"
"AYE," THE CAP'N SAID, "AND THE SCRAPBOOK 'NEATH HER HEAD NOW CONTAINS HAIRS OF RED!"
"I SHOULD THINK SHE'D WANTED MINE INSTEAD!"
"FOOLS," THE WITCH DID CRY, IT TAKES ME TO ANSWER WHY...
"CAN'T YOU TELL HER HEART'S FULL OF JOY,—
PUT THERE BY A RED-HAIRED BOY?"
THE END THA'S ALL FRIEND

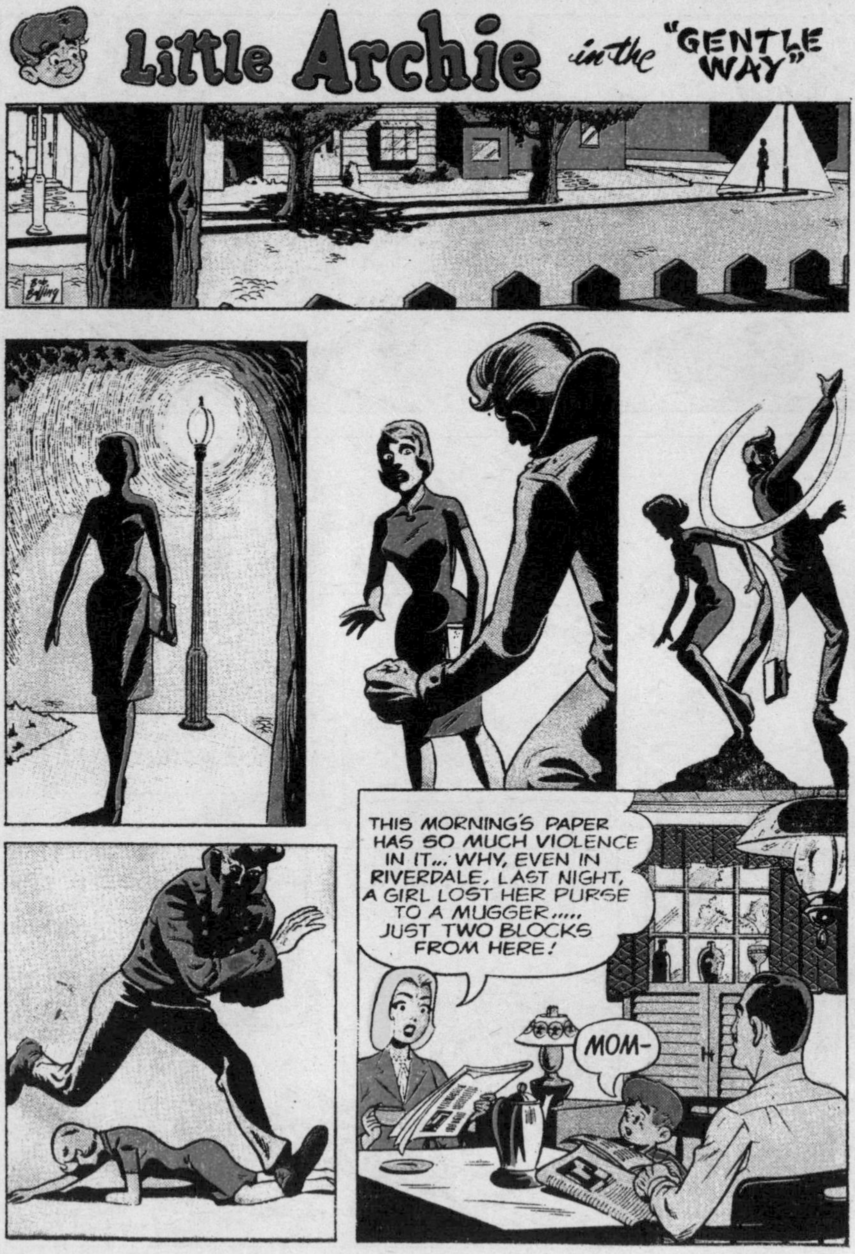
Little Archie in the "GENTLE WAY"
THIS MORNING'S PAPER HAS SO MUCH VIOLENCE IN IT... WHY, EVEN IN RIVERDALE, LAST NIGHT, A GIRL LOST HER PURSE TO A MUGGER..... JUST TWO BLOCKS FROM HERE!
MOM-

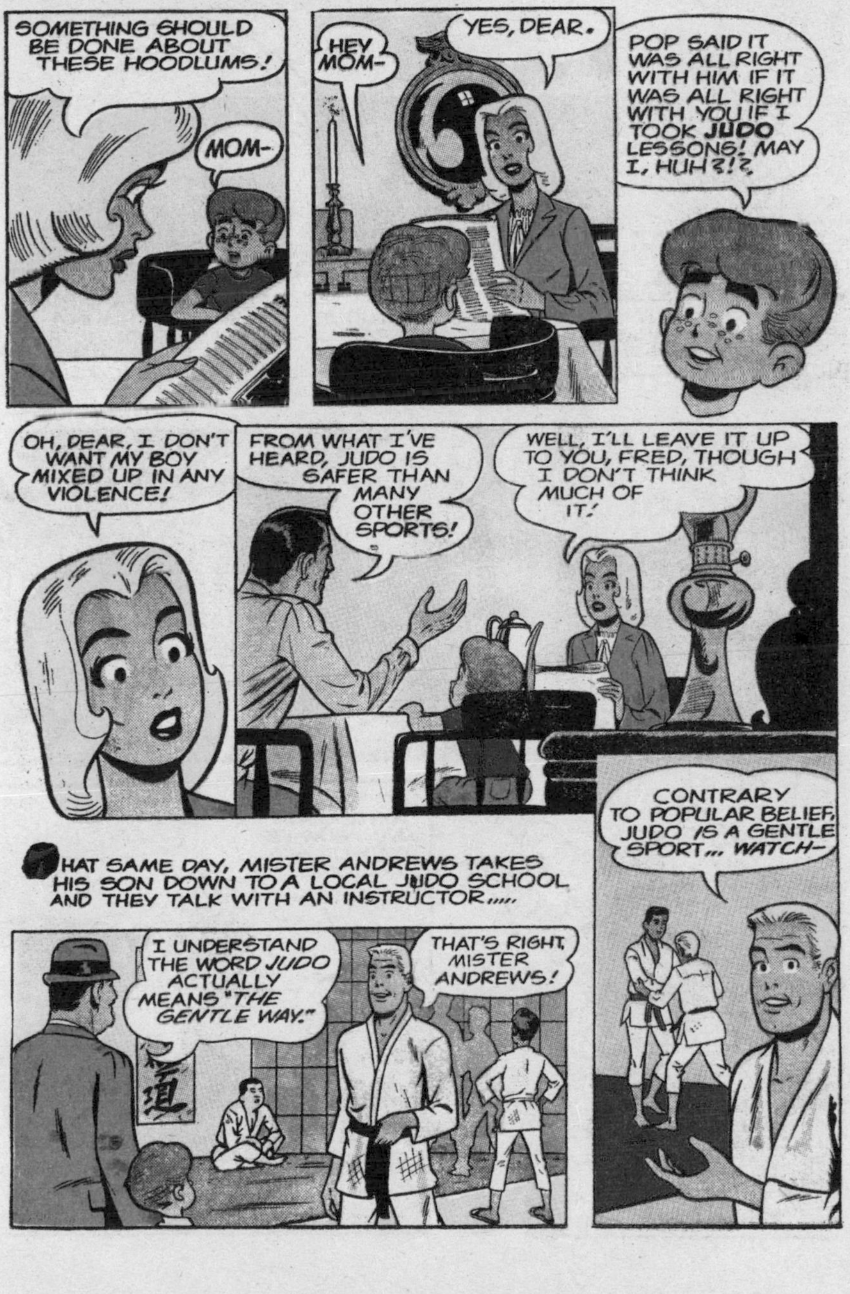
SOMETHING SHOULD BE DONE ABOUT THESE HOODLUMS!
MOM-
HEY MOM-
YES, DEAR.
POP SAID IT WAS ALL RIGHT WITH HIM IF IT WAS ALL RIGHT WITH YOU IF I TOOK **JUDO** LESSONS! MAY I, HUH?!?
OH, DEAR, I DON'T WANT MY BOY MIXED UP IN ANY VIOLENCE!
FROM WHAT I'VE HEARD, JUDO IS SAFER THAN MANY OTHER SPORTS!
WELL, I'LL LEAVE IT UP TO YOU, FRED, THOUGH I DON'T THINK MUCH OF IT!
THAT SAME DAY, MISTER ANDREWS TAKES HIS SON DOWN TO A LOCAL JUDO SCHOOL AND THEY TALK WITH AN INSTRUCTOR.....
I UNDERSTAND THE WORD *JUDO* ACTUALLY MEANS *"THE GENTLE WAY."*
THAT'S RIGHT, MISTER ANDREWS!
CONTRARY TO POPULAR BELIEF, JUDO *IS* A GENTLE SPORT... *WATCH-*

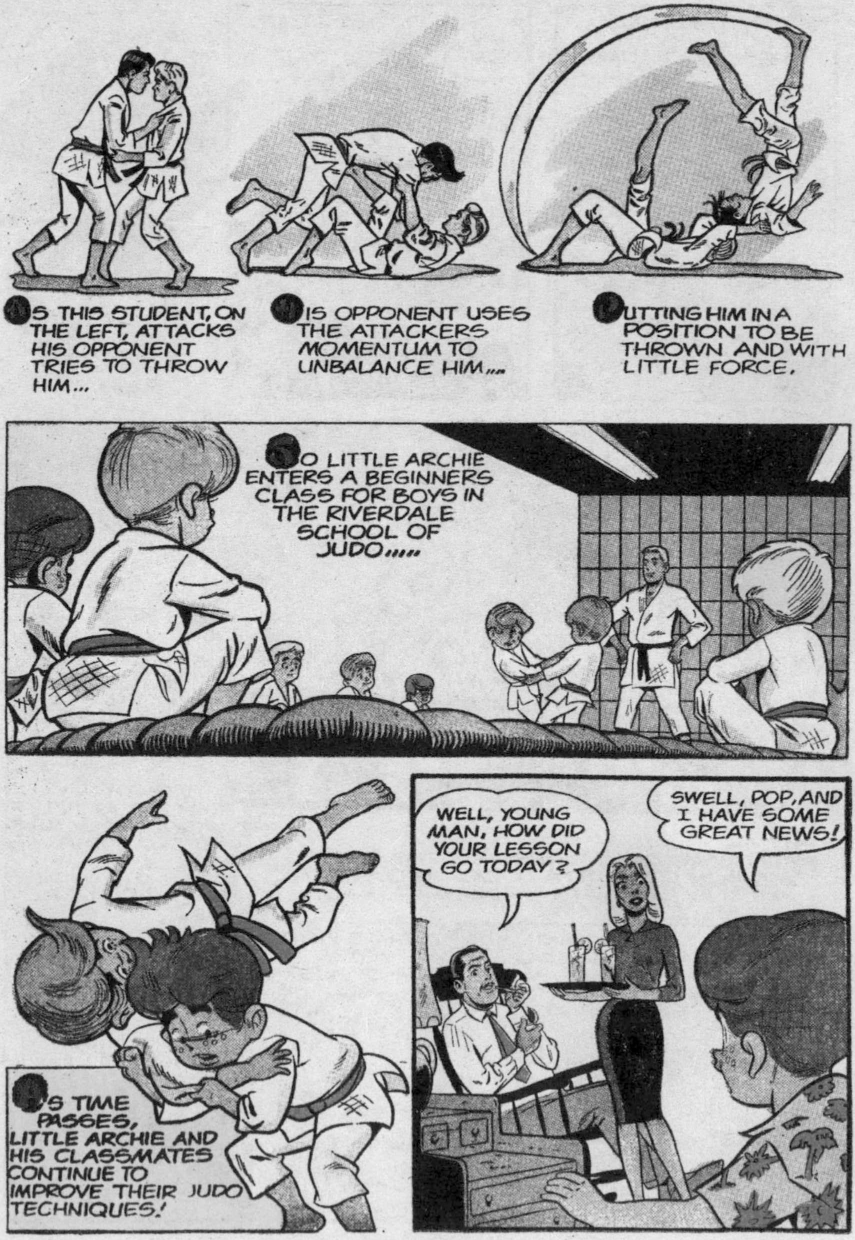
S THIS STUDENT, ON THE LEFT, ATTACKS HIS OPPONENT TRIES TO THROW HIM...
IS OPPONENT USES THE ATTACKERS MOMENTUM TO UNBALANCE HIM....
UTTING HIM IN A POSITION TO BE THROWN AND WITH LITTLE FORCE.
O LITTLE ARCHIE ENTERS A BEGINNERS CLASS FOR BOYS IN THE RIVERDALE SCHOOL OF JUDO.....
S TIME PASSES, LITTLE ARCHIE AND HIS CLASSMATES CONTINUE TO IMPROVE THEIR JUDO TECHNIQUES!
WELL, YOUNG MAN, HOW DID YOUR LESSON GO TODAY?
SWELL, POP, AND I HAVE SOME GREAT NEWS!

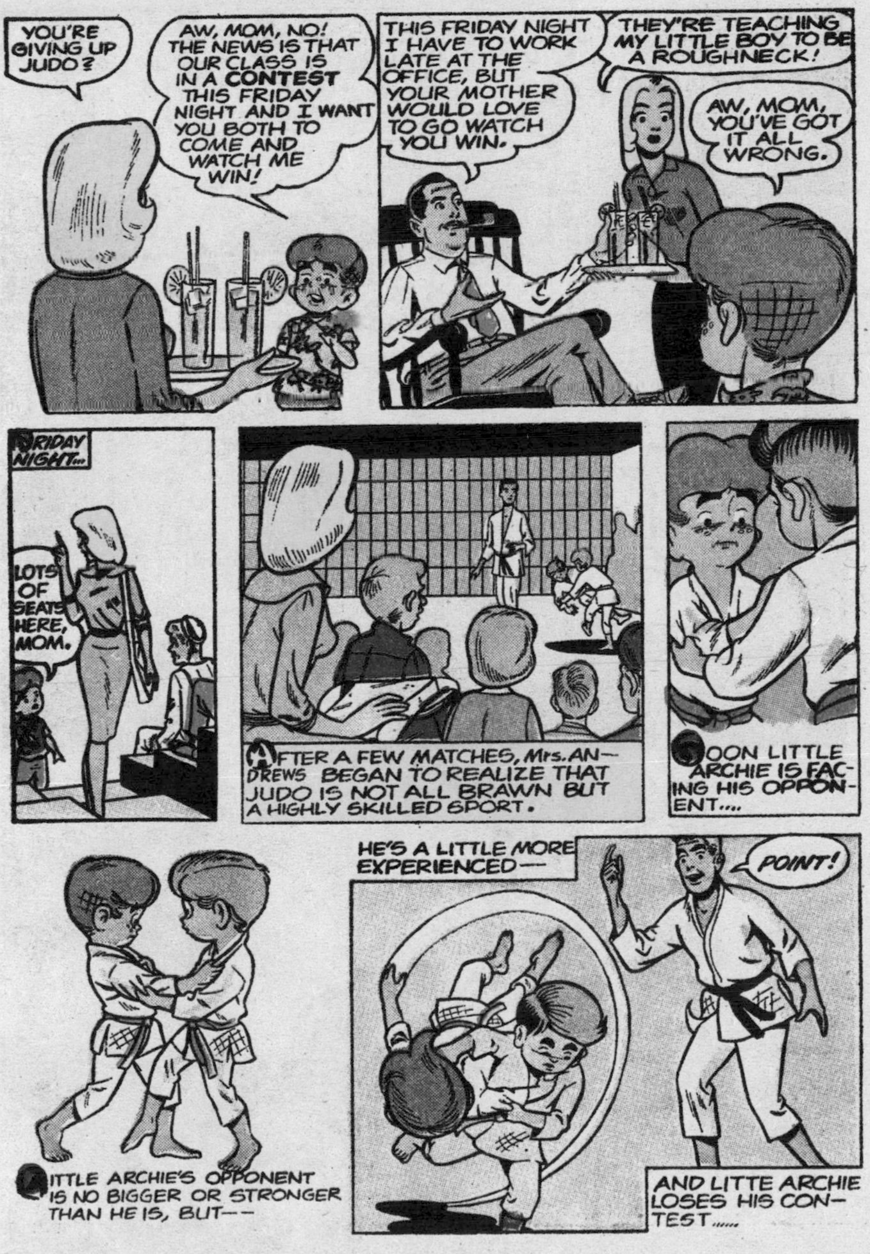
YOU'RE GIVING UP JUDO?
AW, MOM, NO! THE NEWS IS THAT OUR CLASS IS IN A CONTEST THIS FRIDAY NIGHT AND I WANT YOU BOTH TO COME AND WATCH ME WIN!
THIS FRIDAY NIGHT I HAVE TO WORK LATE AT THE OFFICE, BUT YOUR MOTHER WOULD LOVE TO GO WATCH YOU WIN.
THEY'RE TEACHING MY LITTLE BOY TO BE A ROUGHNECK!
AW, MOM, YOU'VE GOT IT ALL WRONG.
FRIDAY NIGHT...
LOTS OF SEATS HERE, MOM.
AFTER A FEW MATCHES, Mrs. ANDREWS BEGAN TO REALIZE THAT JUDO IS NOT ALL BRAWN BUT A HIGHLY SKILLED SPORT.
SOON LITTLE ARCHIE IS FACING HIS OPPONENT....
LITTLE ARCHIE'S OPPONENT IS NO BIGGER OR STRONGER THAN HE IS, BUT--
HE'S A LITTLE MORE EXPERIENCED--
POINT!
AND LITTE ARCHIE LOSES HIS CONTEST......

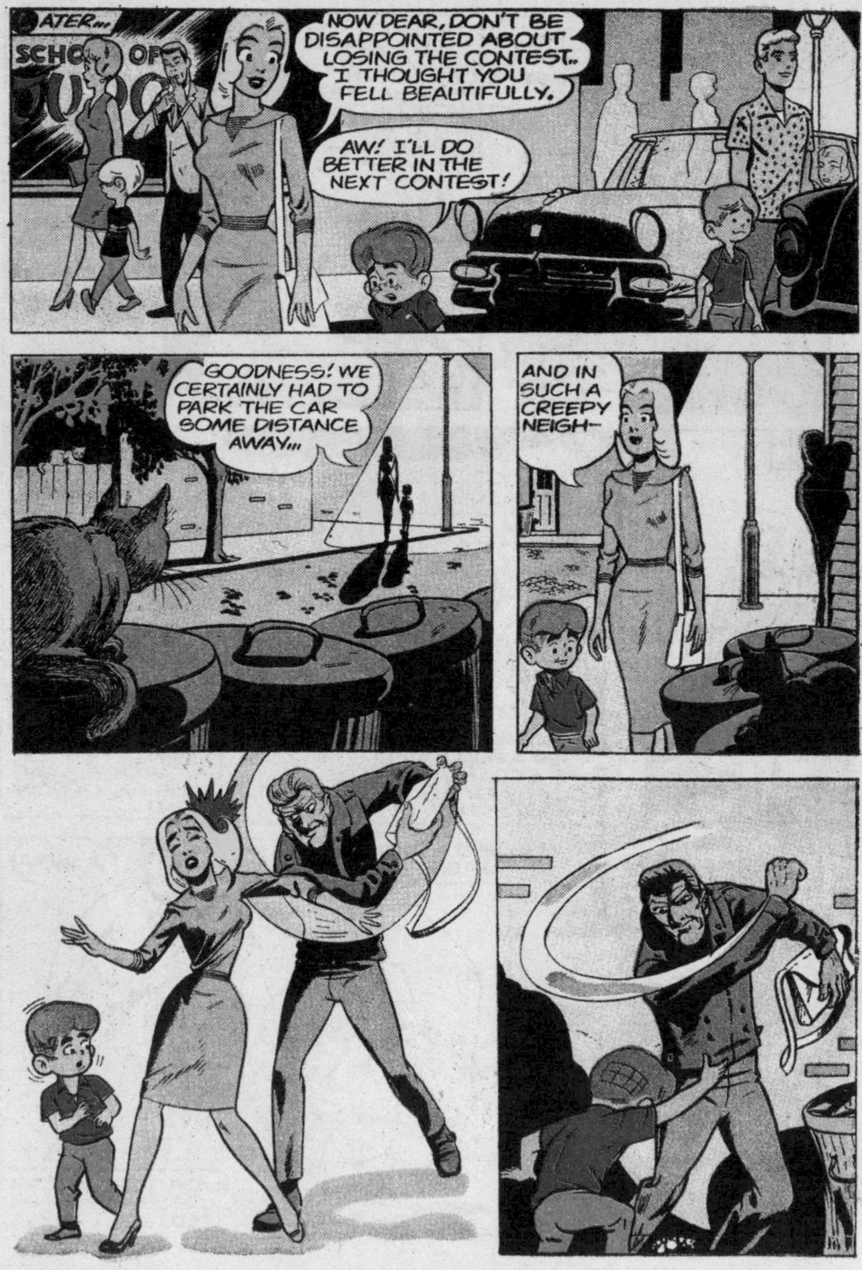
LATER...
SCHO OF JUDO
NOW DEAR, DON'T BE DISAPPOINTED ABOUT LOSING THE CONTEST.. I THOUGHT YOU FELL BEAUTIFULLY.
AW! I'LL DO BETTER IN THE NEXT CONTEST!
GOODNESS! WE CERTAINLY HAD TO PARK THE CAR SOME DISTANCE AWAY...
AND IN SUCH A CREEPY NEIGH--

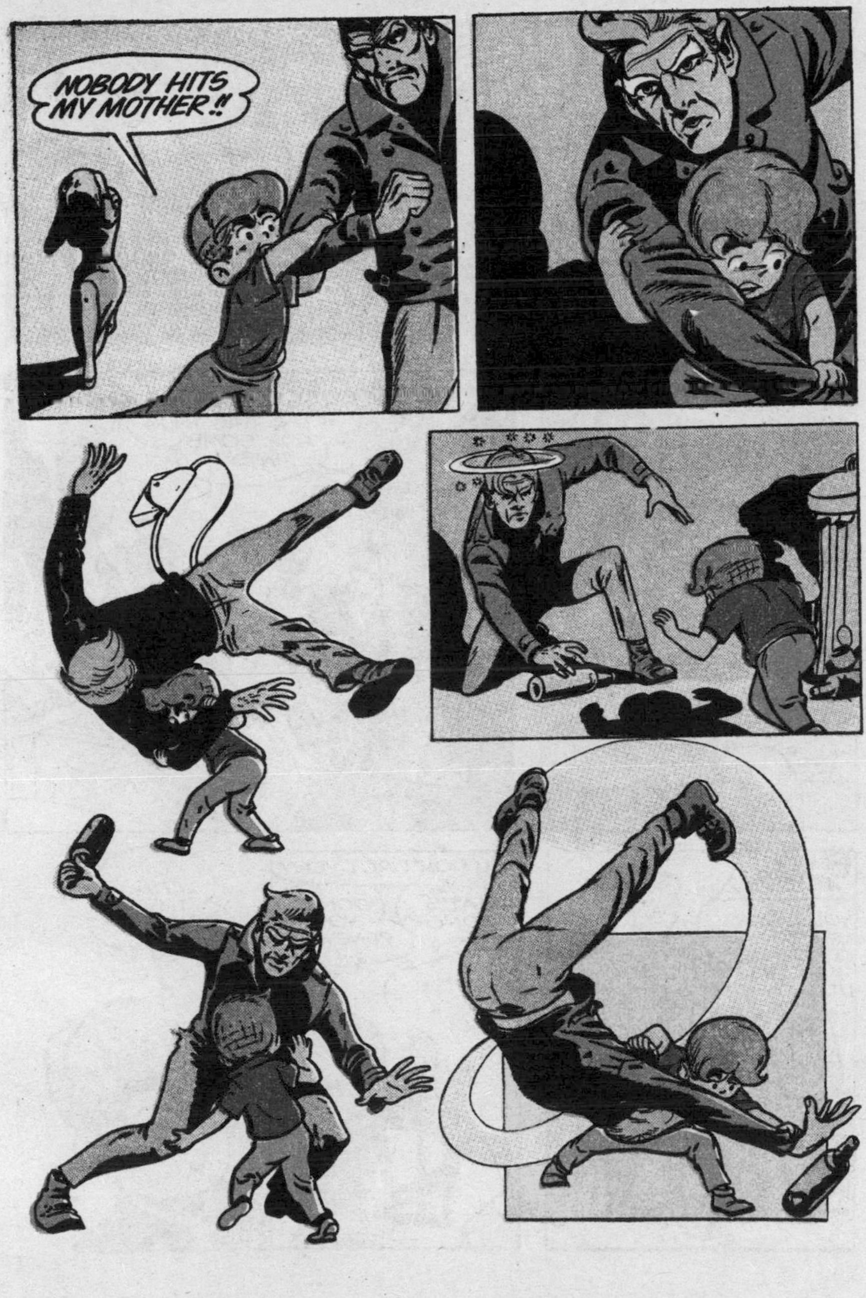
NOBODY HITS MY MOTHER !!

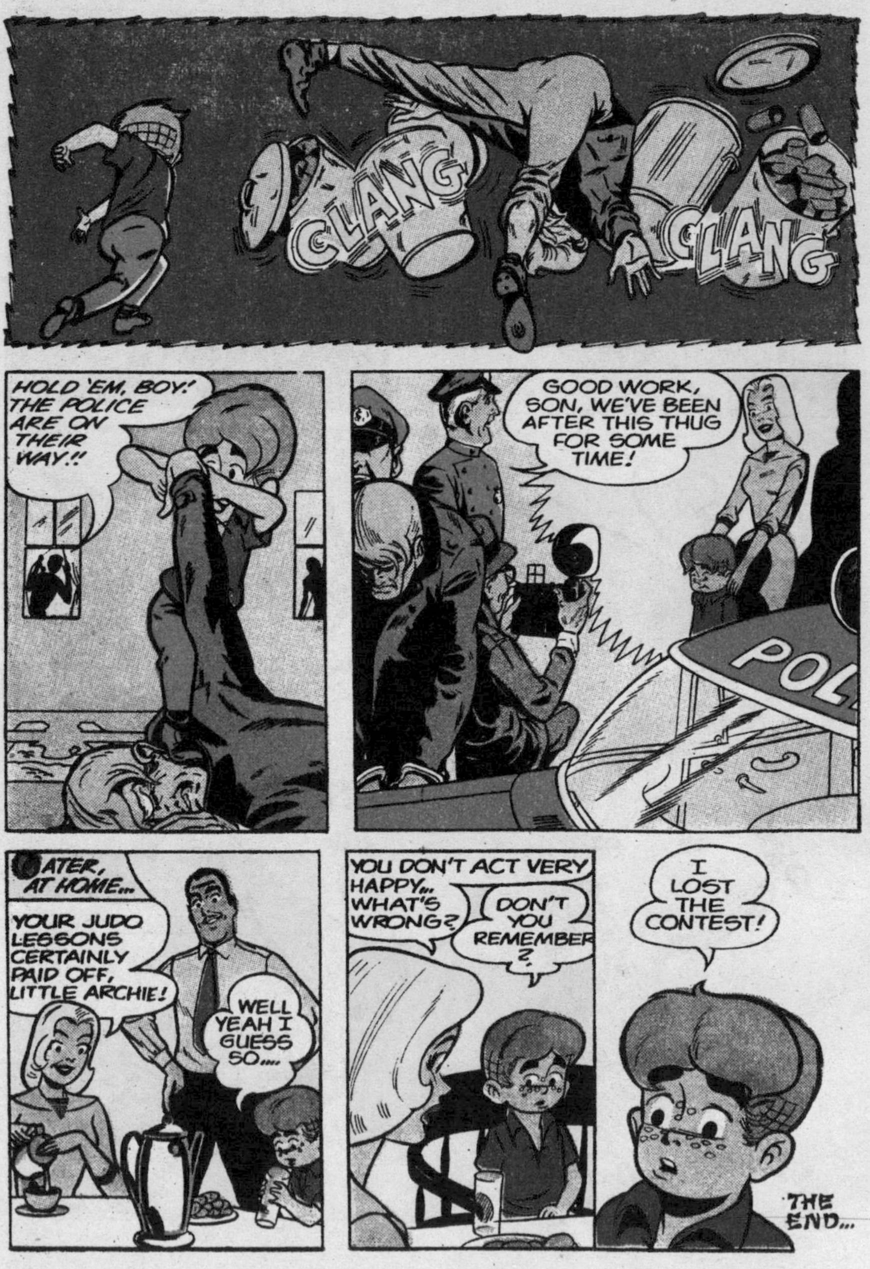
CLANG
CLANG
HOLD 'EM, BOY! THE POLICE ARE ON THEIR WAY!!
GOOD WORK, SON, WE'VE BEEN AFTER THIS THUG FOR SOME TIME!
POLI
LATER, AT HOME...
YOUR JUDO LESSONS CERTAINLY PAID OFF, LITTLE ARCHIE!
WELL YEAH I GUESS SO....
YOU DON'T ACT VERY HAPPY... WHAT'S WRONG?
DON'T YOU REMEMBER?
I LOST THE CONTEST!
THE END...

Sabrina the Teenage Witch
Archie's Mad House #22, 1962
by George Gladir
and Dan DeCarlo

A favorite story of mine was the one in which I created Sabrina (*Archie's Mad House #22*, October 1962). No one would guess at the time that this six-pager would one day lead to an animated TV show and later to a long-running live TV series.

Dan DeCarlo illustrated this one, and Sabrina owes much of her success to his masterful artwork.

--George Gladir
Writer, Archie Comics

Loser's Luck
Betty & Veronica #98, 1964
by Dan DeCarlo

As a little girl growing up in Reno, Nevada, I loved to keep up with the comic book exploits of Archie Andrews and his two favorite girls, Betty & Veronica. For me, Betty Cooper was more than just the product of an artist's imagination, she was the quintessential girl-next-door, a model I aspired to. Little did I know that I'd have the opportunity to portray another iconic girl-next-door, Mary Ann Summers.

Mary Ann acted as one of the rudders of the ship on Gilligan's Island. She was an enthusiastic leader, effective at getting everyone to do his or her part. In the same way, Betty Cooper is a stabilizing influence in Archie and the gang's lives. It is a Midwestern, small-town ethic that Mary Ann, Betty and myself share—a patriotic, never-give-up approach to life.

--Dawn Wells
Mary Ann on Gilligan's Island,
Excerpted from her foreword to
Betty & Veronica Summer Fun.

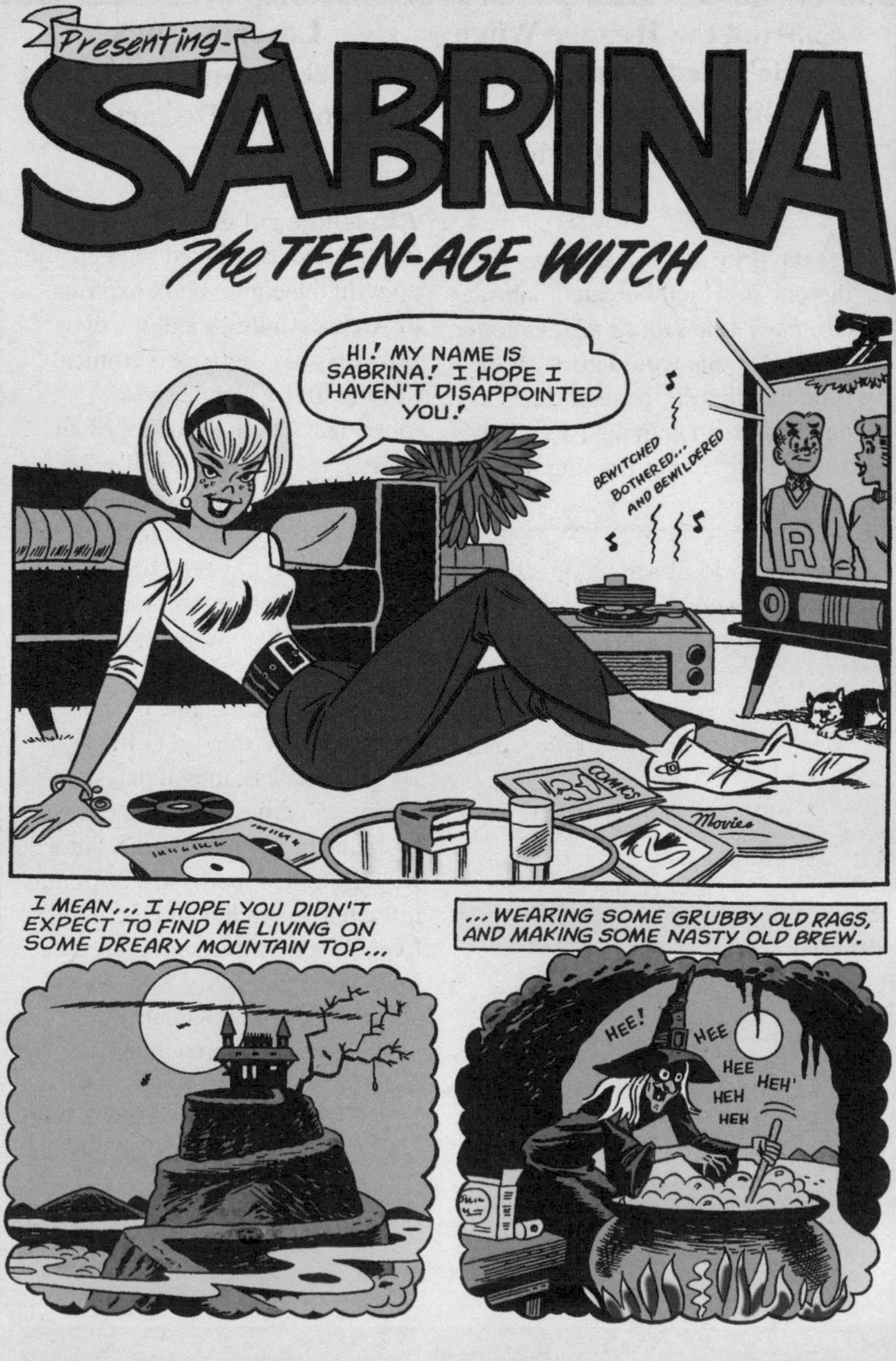
Presenting-
SABRINA
The TEEN-AGE WITCH
HI! MY NAME IS SABRINA! I HOPE I HAVEN'T DISAPPOINTED YOU!
BEWITCHED BOTHERED... AND BEWILDERED
COMICS
Movies
I MEAN... I HOPE YOU DIDN'T EXPECT TO FIND ME LIVING ON SOME DREARY MOUNTAIN TOP...
...WEARING SOME GRUBBY OLD RAGS, AND MAKING SOME NASTY OLD BREW.
HEE! HEE HEE HEH' HEH HEH

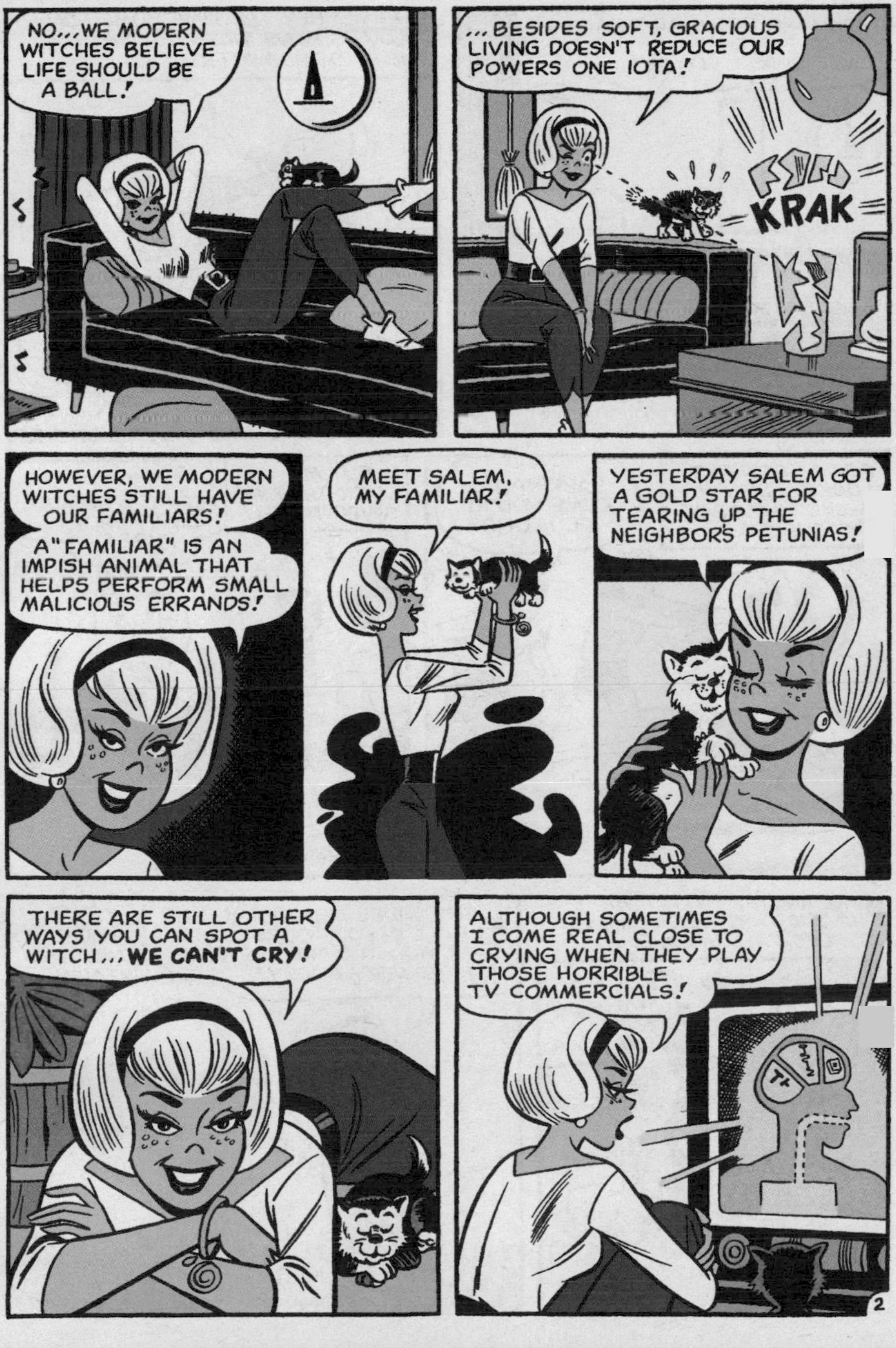
NO...WE MODERN WITCHES BELIEVE LIFE SHOULD BE A BALL!
...BESIDES SOFT, GRACIOUS LIVING DOESN'T REDUCE OUR POWERS ONE IOTA!
KRAK
HOWEVER, WE MODERN WITCHES STILL HAVE OUR FAMILIARS!
A "FAMILIAR" IS AN IMPISH ANIMAL THAT HELPS PERFORM SMALL MALICIOUS ERRANDS!
MEET SALEM, MY FAMILIAR!
YESTERDAY SALEM GOT A GOLD STAR FOR TEARING UP THE NEIGHBOR'S PETUNIAS!
THERE ARE STILL OTHER WAYS YOU CAN SPOT A WITCH... **WE CAN'T CRY!**
ALTHOUGH SOMETIMES I COME REAL CLOSE TO CRYING WHEN THEY PLAY THOSE HORRIBLE TV COMMERCIALS!
2

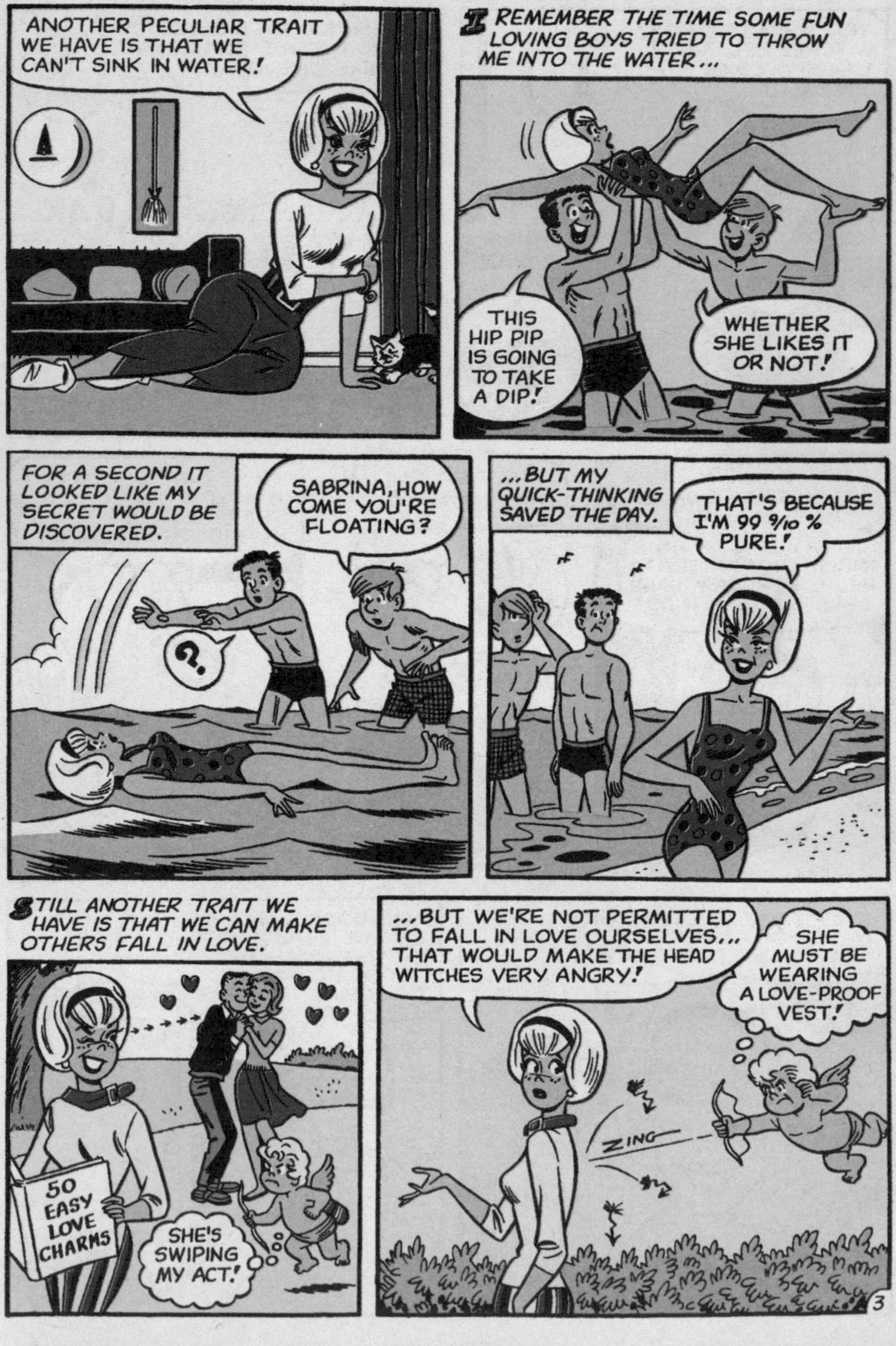
ANOTHER PECULIAR TRAIT WE HAVE IS THAT WE CAN'T SINK IN WATER!
I REMEMBER THE TIME SOME FUN LOVING BOYS TRIED TO THROW ME INTO THE WATER...
THIS HIP PIP IS GOING TO TAKE A DIP!
WHETHER SHE LIKES IT OR NOT!
FOR A SECOND IT LOOKED LIKE MY SECRET WOULD BE DISCOVERED.
SABRINA, HOW COME YOU'RE FLOATING?
?
...BUT MY QUICK-THINKING SAVED THE DAY.
THAT'S BECAUSE I'M 99 9/10 % PURE!
STILL ANOTHER TRAIT WE HAVE IS THAT WE CAN MAKE OTHERS FALL IN LOVE.
50 EASY LOVE CHARMS
SHE'S SWIPING MY ACT!
...BUT WE'RE NOT PERMITTED TO FALL IN LOVE OURSELVES... THAT WOULD MAKE THE HEAD WITCHES VERY ANGRY!
SHE MUST BE WEARING A LOVE-PROOF VEST!
ZING
3

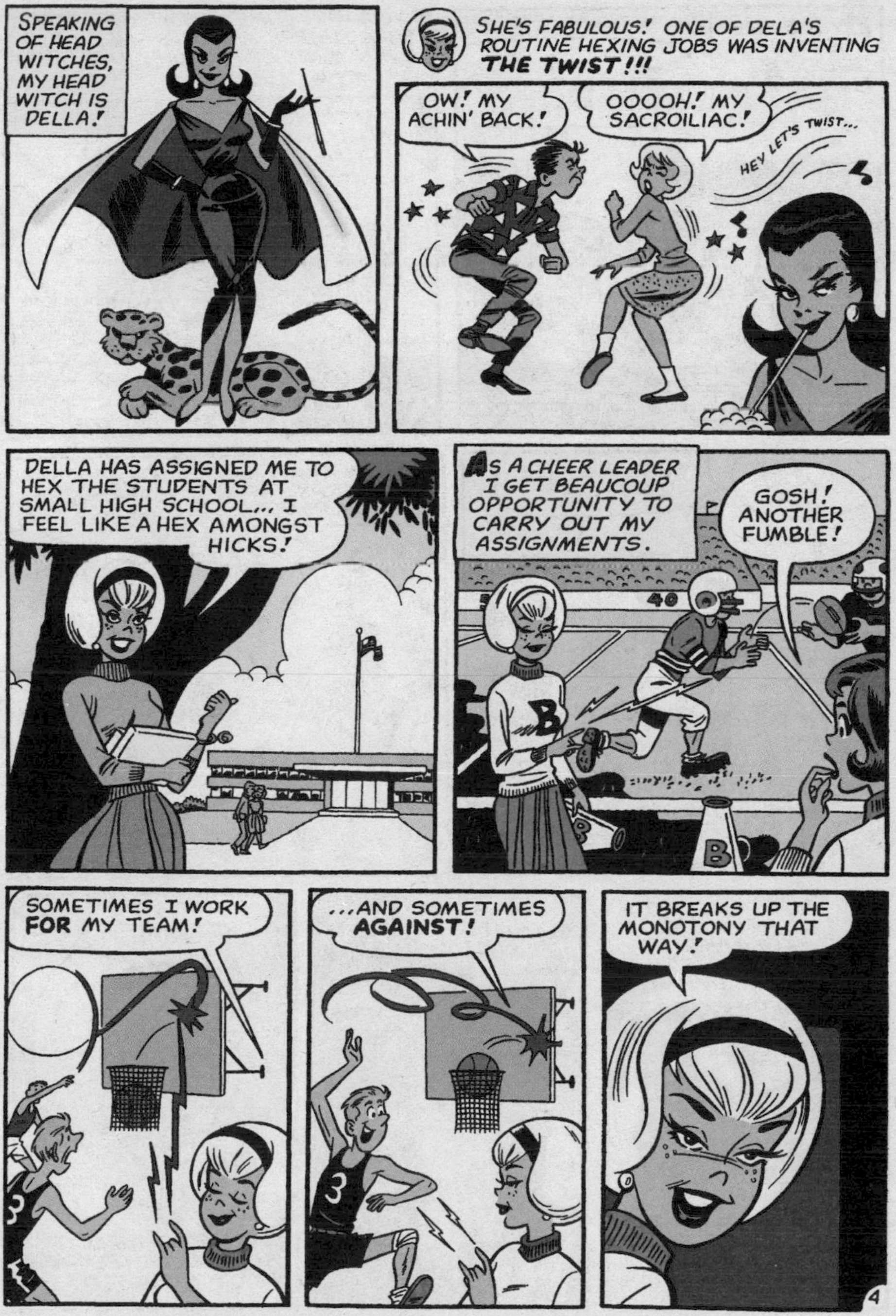
SPEAKING OF HEAD WITCHES, MY HEAD WITCH IS DELLA!
SHE'S FABULOUS! ONE OF DELA'S ROUTINE HEXING JOBS WAS INVENTING THE TWIST!!!
OW! MY ACHIN' BACK!
OOOOH! MY SACROILIAC!
HEY LET'S TWIST...
DELLA HAS ASSIGNED ME TO HEX THE STUDENTS AT SMALL HIGH SCHOOL... I FEEL LIKE A HEX AMONGST HICKS!
AS A CHEER LEADER I GET BEAUCOUP OPPORTUNITY TO CARRY OUT MY ASSIGNMENTS.
GOSH! ANOTHER FUMBLE!
SOMETIMES I WORK FOR MY TEAM!
...AND SOMETIMES AGAINST!
IT BREAKS UP THE MONOTONY THAT WAY!
4

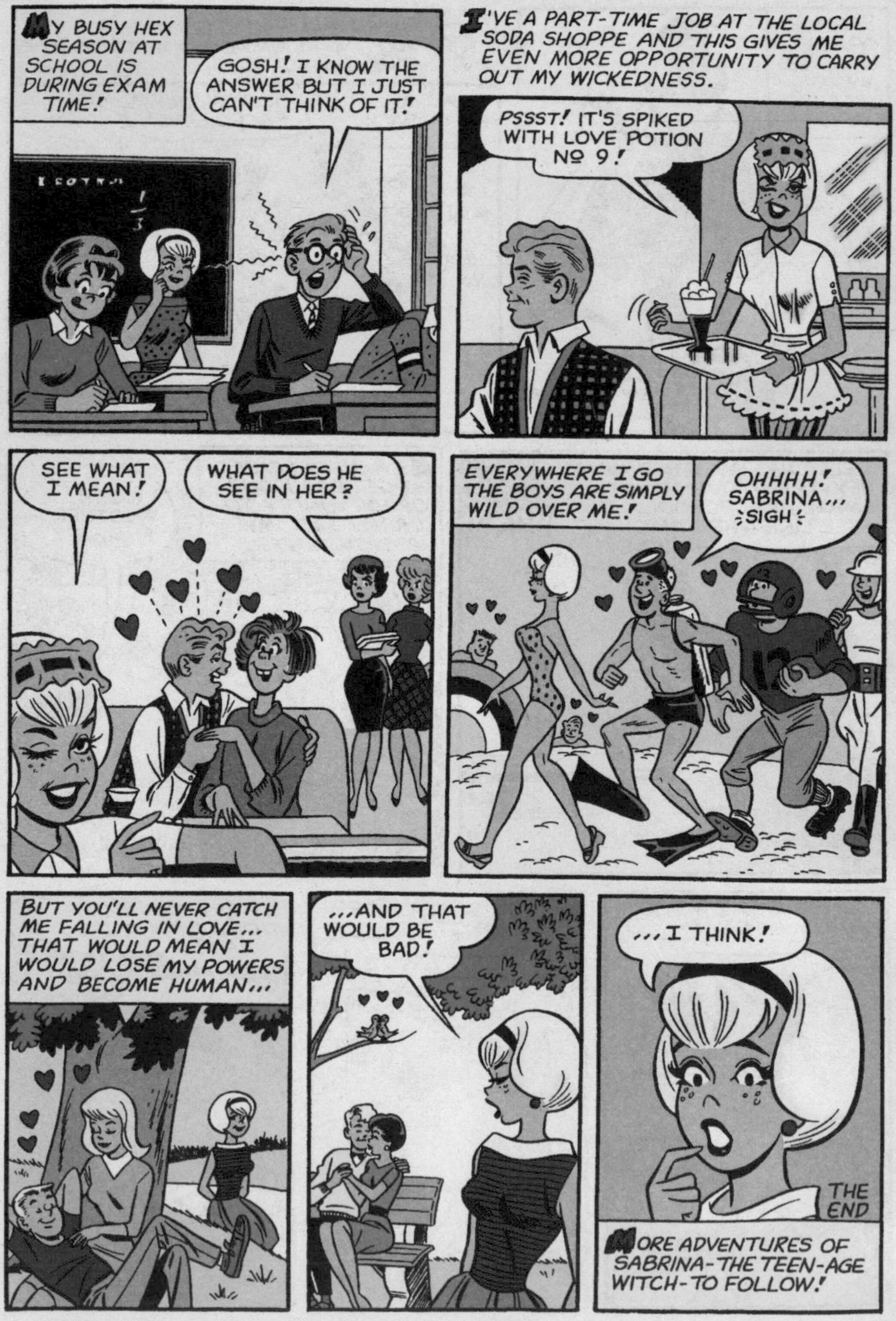
MY BUSY HEX SEASON AT SCHOOL IS DURING EXAM TIME!
GOSH! I KNOW THE ANSWER BUT I JUST CAN'T THINK OF IT!
I'VE A PART-TIME JOB AT THE LOCAL SODA SHOPPE AND THIS GIVES ME EVEN MORE OPPORTUNITY TO CARRY OUT MY WICKEDNESS.
PSSST! IT'S SPIKED WITH LOVE POTION № 9!
SEE WHAT I MEAN!
WHAT DOES HE SEE IN HER?
EVERYWHERE I GO THE BOYS ARE SIMPLY WILD OVER ME!
OHHHH! SABRINA... SIGH
BUT YOU'LL NEVER CATCH ME FALLING IN LOVE... THAT WOULD MEAN I WOULD LOSE MY POWERS AND BECOME HUMAN...
...AND THAT WOULD BE BAD!
...I THINK!
THE END
MORE ADVENTURES OF SABRINA-THE TEEN-AGE WITCH-TO FOLLOW!

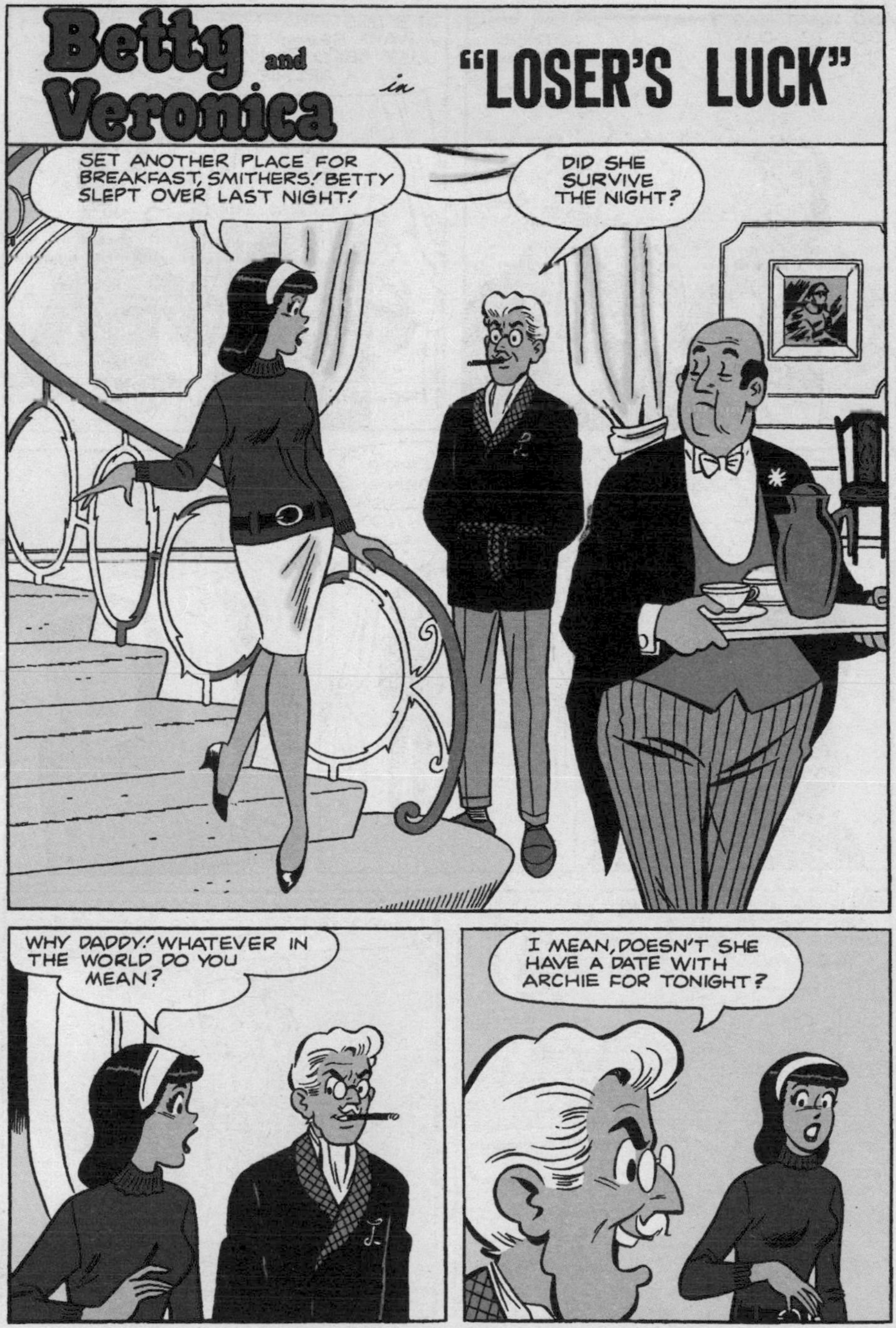
Betty and Veronica in
"LOSER'S LUCK"
SET ANOTHER PLACE FOR BREAKFAST, SMITHERS! BETTY SLEPT OVER LAST NIGHT!
DID SHE SURVIVE THE NIGHT?
WHY DADDY! WHATEVER IN THE WORLD DO YOU MEAN?
I MEAN, DOESN'T SHE HAVE A DATE WITH ARCHIE FOR TONIGHT?

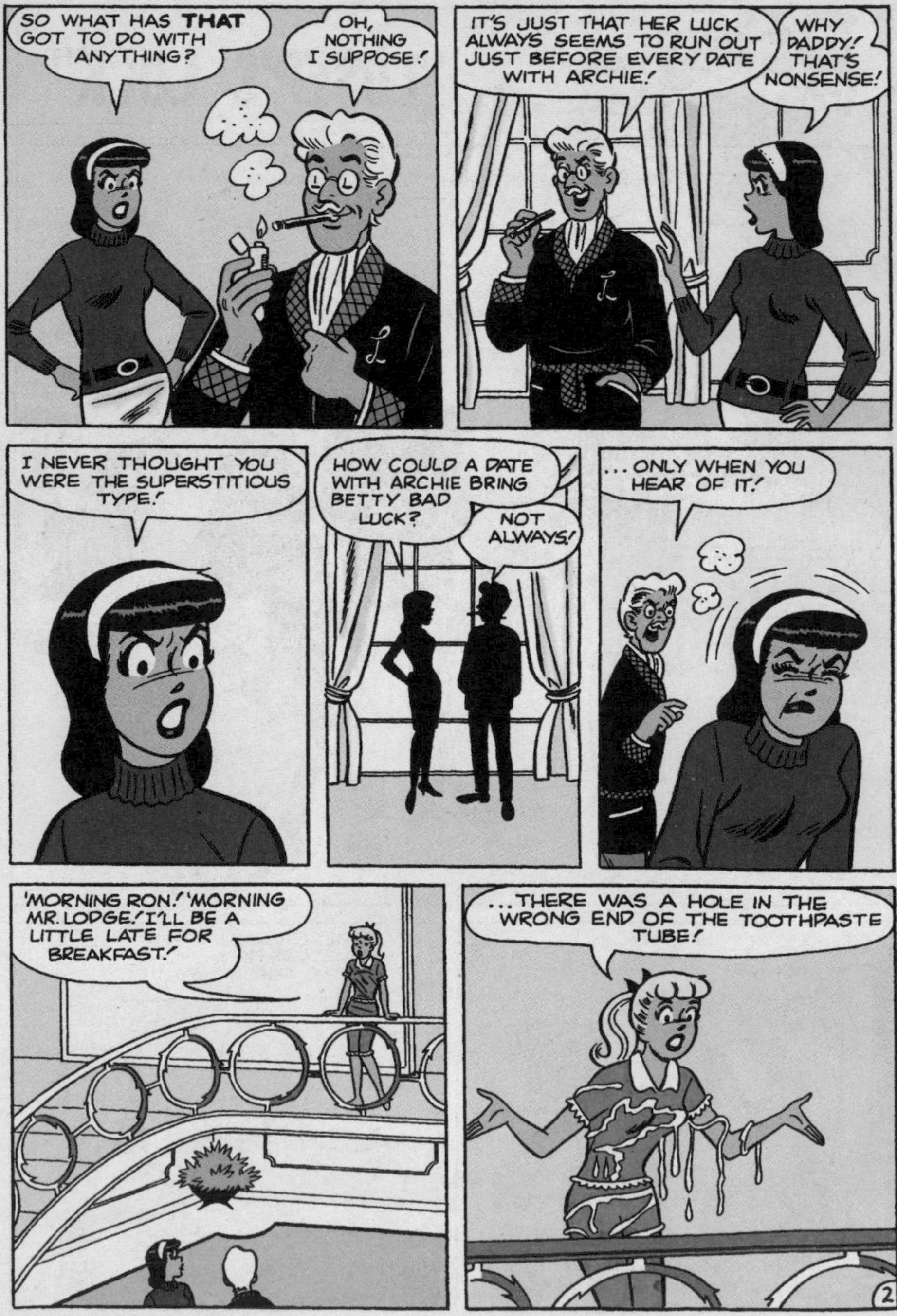
SO WHAT HAS **THAT** GOT TO DO WITH ANYTHING?
OH, NOTHING I SUPPOSE!
IT'S JUST THAT HER LUCK ALWAYS SEEMS TO RUN OUT JUST BEFORE EVERY DATE WITH ARCHIE!
WHY DADDY! THAT'S NONSENSE!
I NEVER THOUGHT YOU WERE THE SUPERSTITIOUS TYPE!
HOW COULD A DATE WITH ARCHIE BRING BETTY BAD LUCK?
NOT ALWAYS!
...ONLY WHEN YOU HEAR OF IT!
'MORNING RON! 'MORNING MR. LODGE! I'LL BE A LITTLE LATE FOR BREAKFAST!
...THERE WAS A HOLE IN THE WRONG END OF THE TOOTHPASTE TUBE!

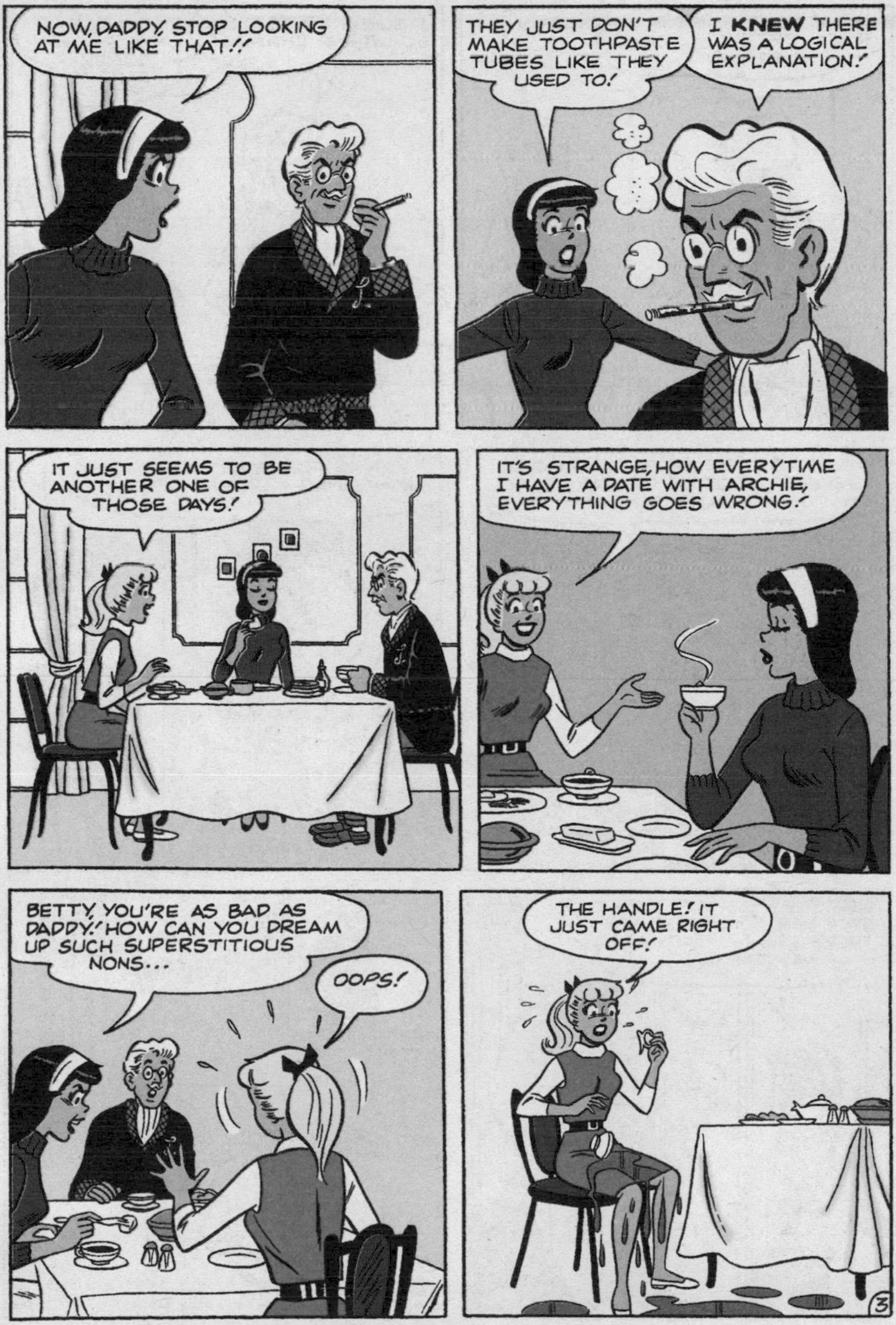
NOW, DADDY, STOP LOOKING AT ME LIKE THAT!!
THEY JUST DON'T MAKE TOOTHPASTE TUBES LIKE THEY USED TO!
I KNEW THERE WAS A LOGICAL EXPLANATION!
IT JUST SEEMS TO BE ANOTHER ONE OF THOSE DAYS!
IT'S STRANGE, HOW EVERYTIME I HAVE A DATE WITH ARCHIE, EVERYTHING GOES WRONG!
BETTY, YOU'RE AS BAD AS DADDY! HOW CAN YOU DREAM UP SUCH SUPERSTITIOUS NONS...
OOPS!
THE HANDLE! IT JUST CAME RIGHT OFF!
3

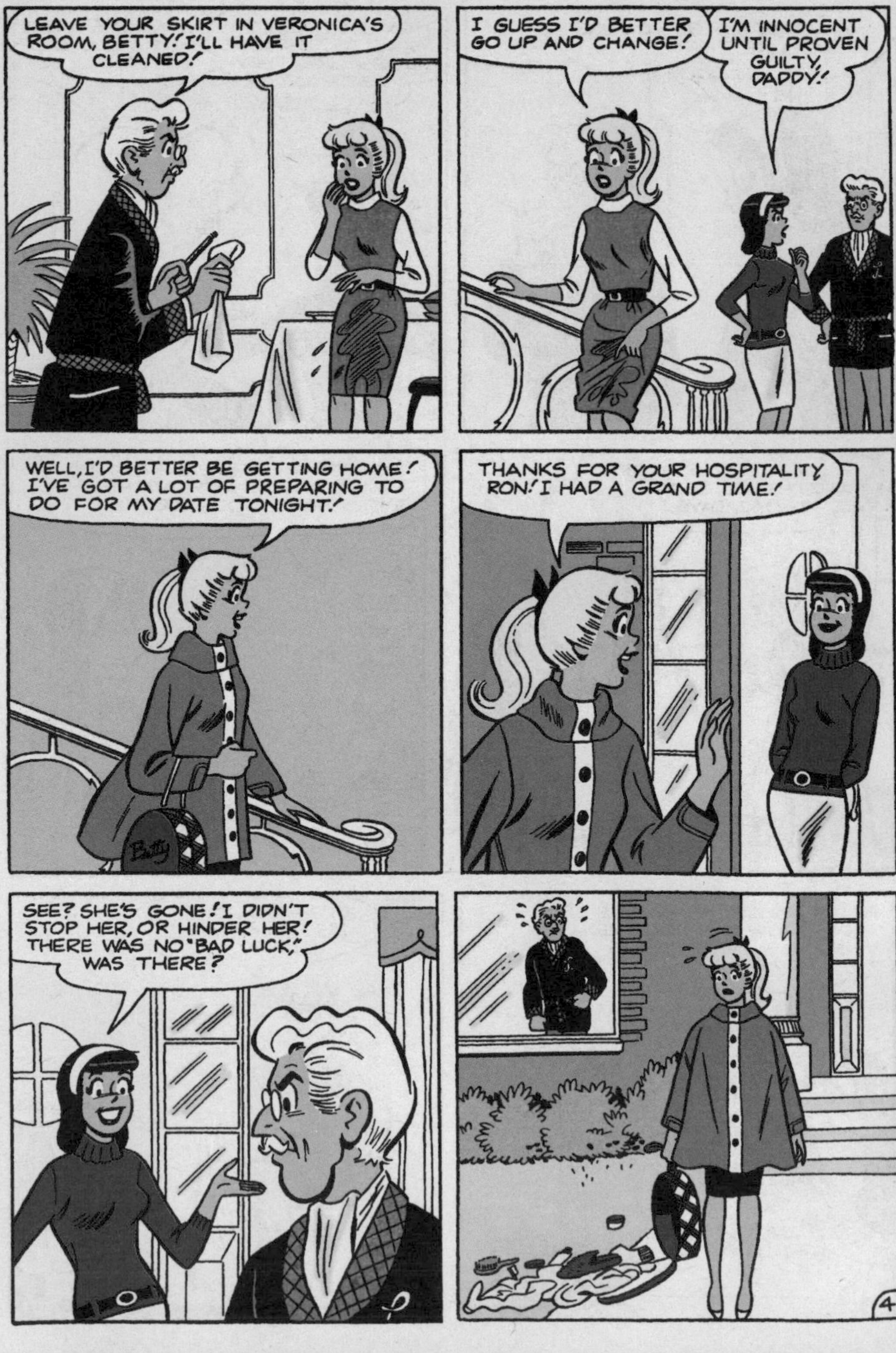
LEAVE YOUR SKIRT IN VERONICA'S ROOM, BETTY! I'LL HAVE IT CLEANED!
I GUESS I'D BETTER GO UP AND CHANGE!
I'M INNOCENT UNTIL PROVEN GUILTY, DADDY!
WELL, I'D BETTER BE GETTING HOME! I'VE GOT A LOT OF PREPARING TO DO FOR MY DATE TONIGHT!
Betty
THANKS FOR YOUR HOSPITALITY, RON! I HAD A GRAND TIME!
SEE? SHE'S GONE! I DIDN'T STOP HER, OR HINDER HER! THERE WAS NO "BAD LUCK," WAS THERE?
4

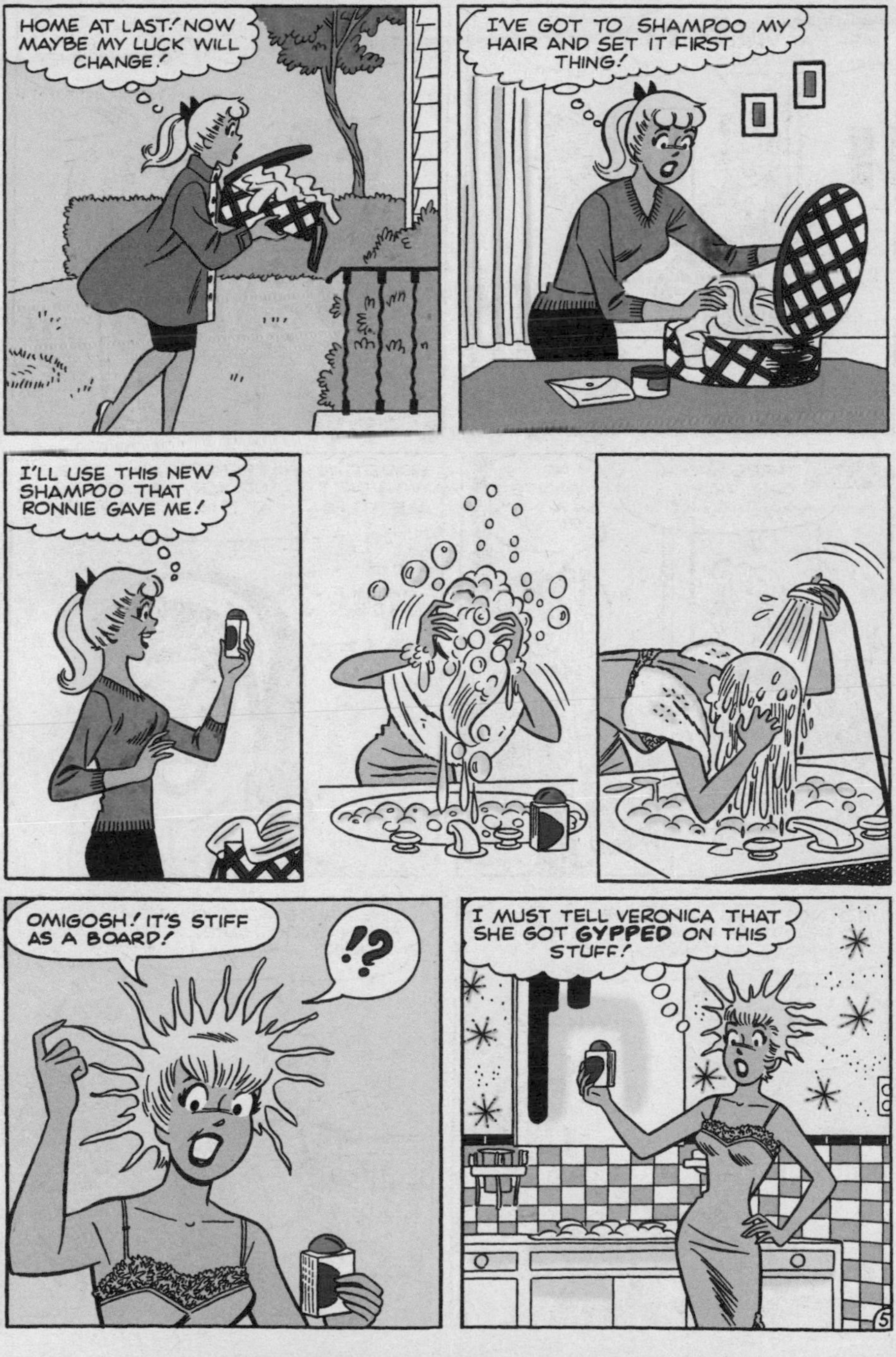
HOME AT LAST! NOW MAYBE MY LUCK WILL CHANGE!
I'VE GOT TO SHAMPOO MY HAIR AND SET IT FIRST THING!
I'LL USE THIS NEW SHAMPOO THAT RONNIE GAVE ME!
OMIGOSH! IT'S STIFF AS A BOARD!
!?
I MUST TELL VERONICA THAT SHE GOT **GYPPED** ON THIS STUFF!
5

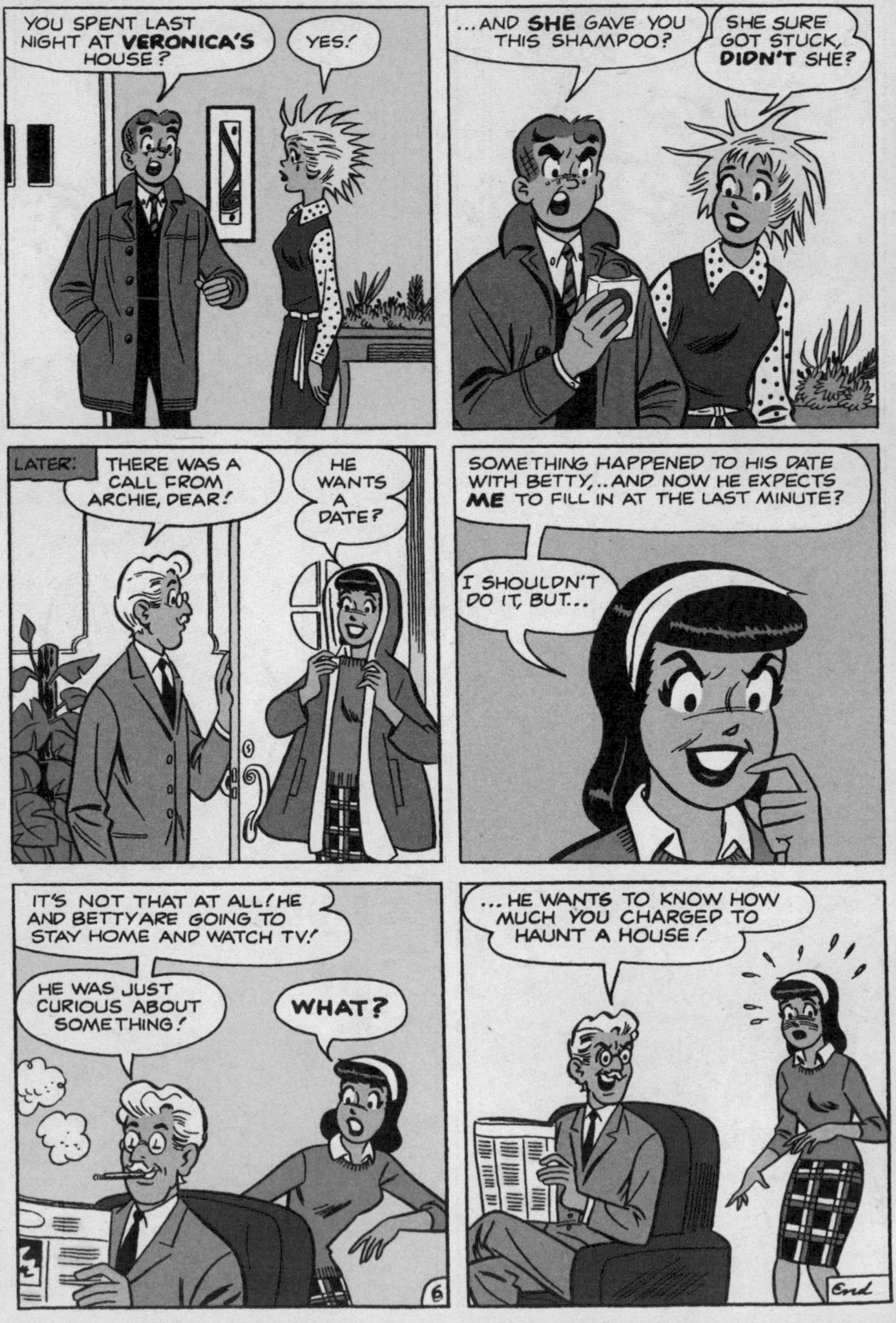
YOU SPENT LAST NIGHT AT VERONICA'S HOUSE?
YES!
...AND SHE GAVE YOU THIS SHAMPOO?
SHE SURE GOT STUCK, DIDN'T SHE?
LATER:
THERE WAS A CALL FROM ARCHIE, DEAR!
HE WANTS A DATE?
SOMETHING HAPPENED TO HIS DATE WITH BETTY,..AND NOW HE EXPECTS ME TO FILL IN AT THE LAST MINUTE?
I SHOULDN'T DO IT, BUT...
IT'S NOT THAT AT ALL! HE AND BETTYARE GOING TO STAY HOME AND WATCH TV!
HE WAS JUST CURIOUS ABOUT SOMETHING!
WHAT?
6
...HE WANTS TO KNOW HOW MUCH YOU CHARGED TO HAUNT A HOUSE!
End

Measure Up
Archie #148, 1964
by Frank Doyle
and Harry Lucey

What is really nice about working at Archie is the generational feel to the staff, especially the freelancer staff. Many of the artists, writers and so on have been working with Archie for years and in some cases decades. Early on in my career at Archie, most of the artists still came to the office every week to turn in their work. One week they were all laughing and talking about this one story. They were acting it out! Grown men, grizzled vets talking about this story from years ago. I had to find it and read it. This is that story. If ever there was just one Archie story you need to read, this is it.

--**Mike Pellerito**
President, Archie Comics

Pussy Footing
Josie #45, 1969
by Dan DeCarlo

One summer morning, when I was about five years old, I remember my father calling me into the living room and seeing a big stack of comics on the table that he'd bought for me. One of the books was the 1993 48-page special of Josie & the Pussycats. My favorite story of the bunch was "Pussy Footing," which introduced the girls' cat suits!

Dan DeCarlo's art was so easy on the eyes, and each character showed their personality on their leopard-patterned sleeve! I loved the cat suit gimmick, and I remember actually writing a letter to Archie Comics asking if they could form a real Josie and the Pussycats band, one that would put out albums and go on tour!

I'm still waiting…

--**Pat Woodruff**
Digital Publishing Coordinator,
Archie Comics

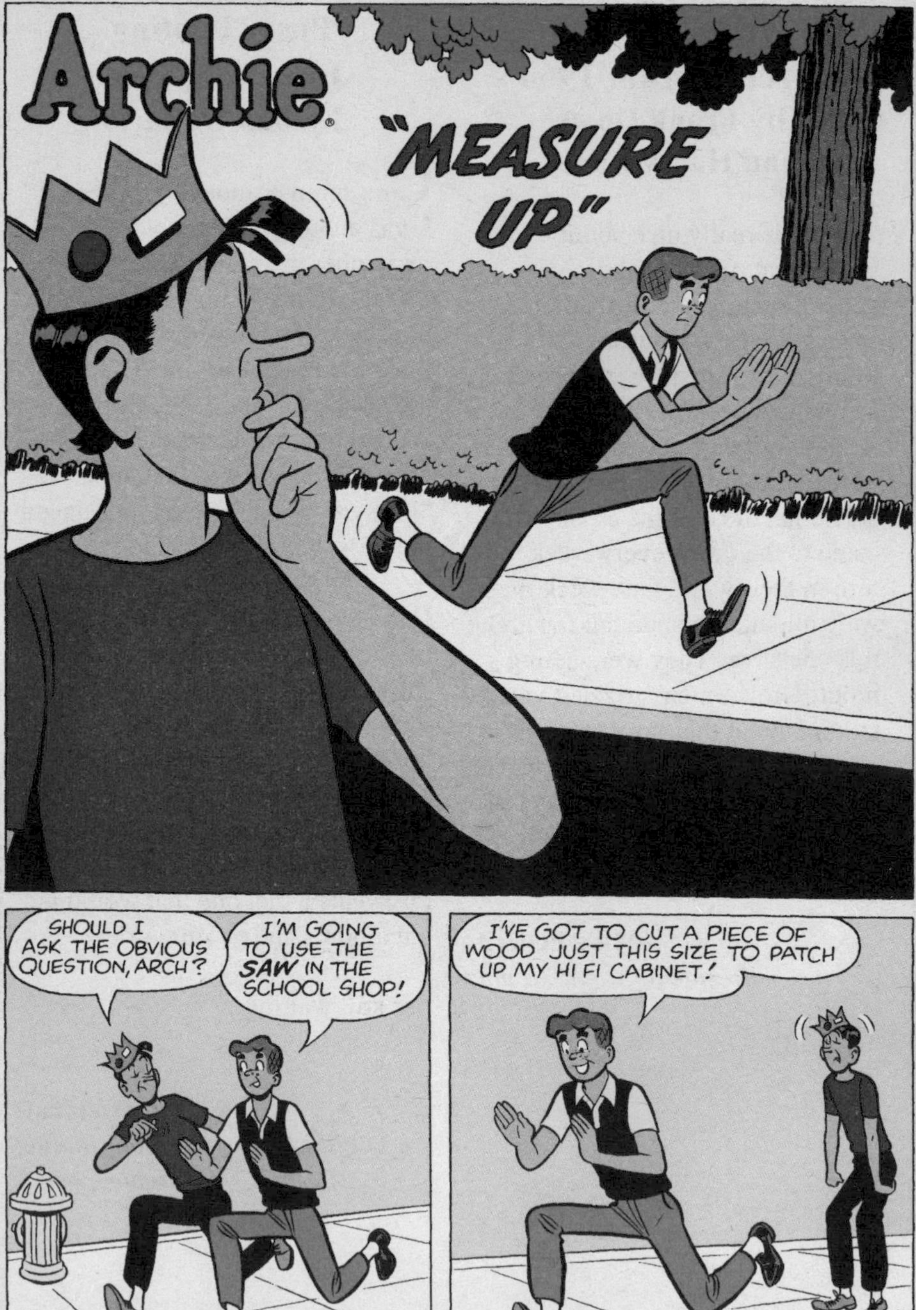
Archie
"MEASURE UP"
SHOULD I ASK THE OBVIOUS QUESTION, ARCH?
I'M GOING TO USE THE SAW IN THE SCHOOL SHOP!
I'VE GOT TO CUT A PIECE OF WOOD JUST THIS SIZE TO PATCH UP MY HI FI CABINET!

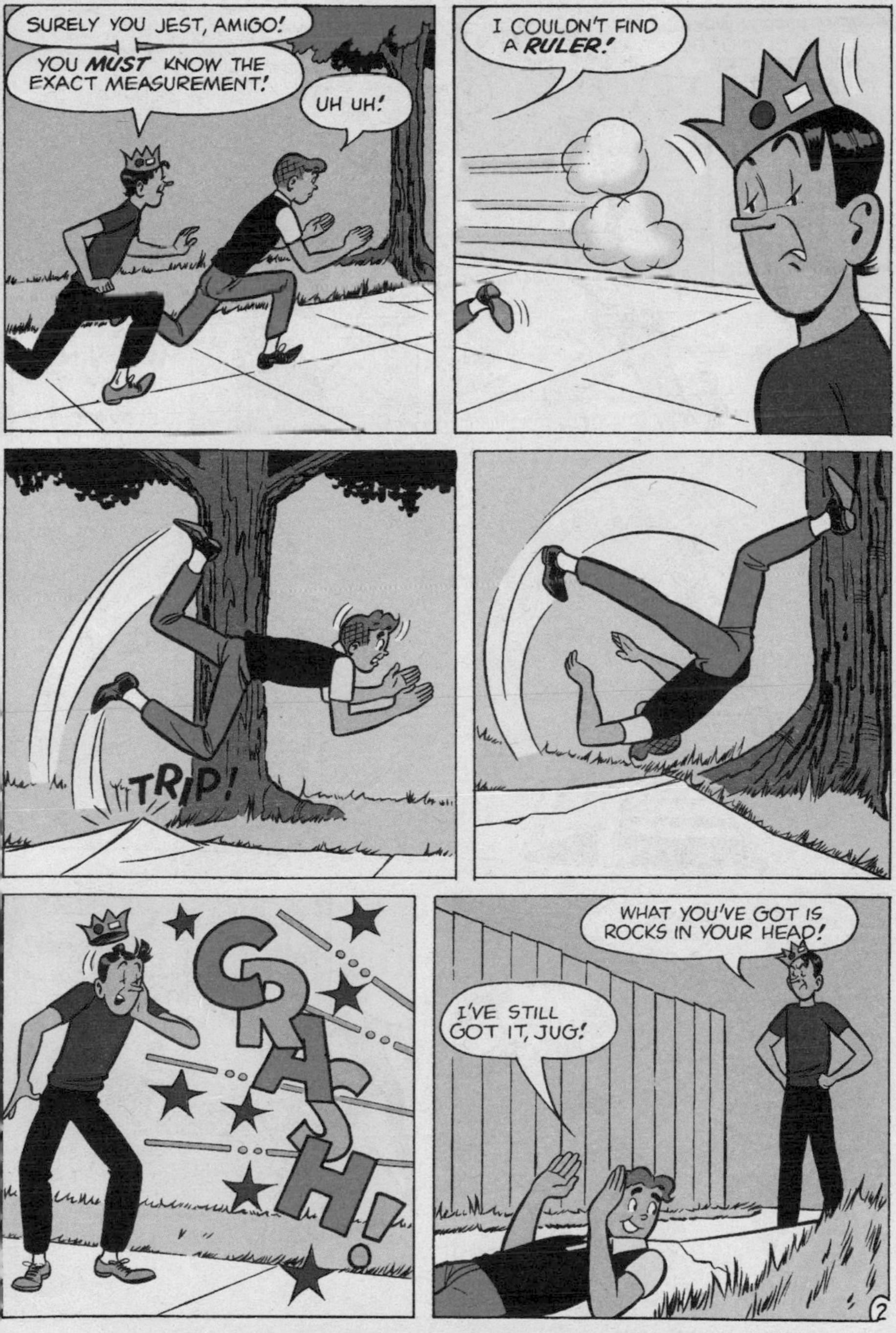
SURELY YOU JEST, AMIGO!
YOU MUST KNOW THE EXACT MEASUREMENT!
UH UH!
I COULDN'T FIND A RULER!
TRIP!
CRASH!
WHAT YOU'VE GOT IS ROCKS IN YOUR HEAD!
I'VE STILL GOT IT, JUG!
2

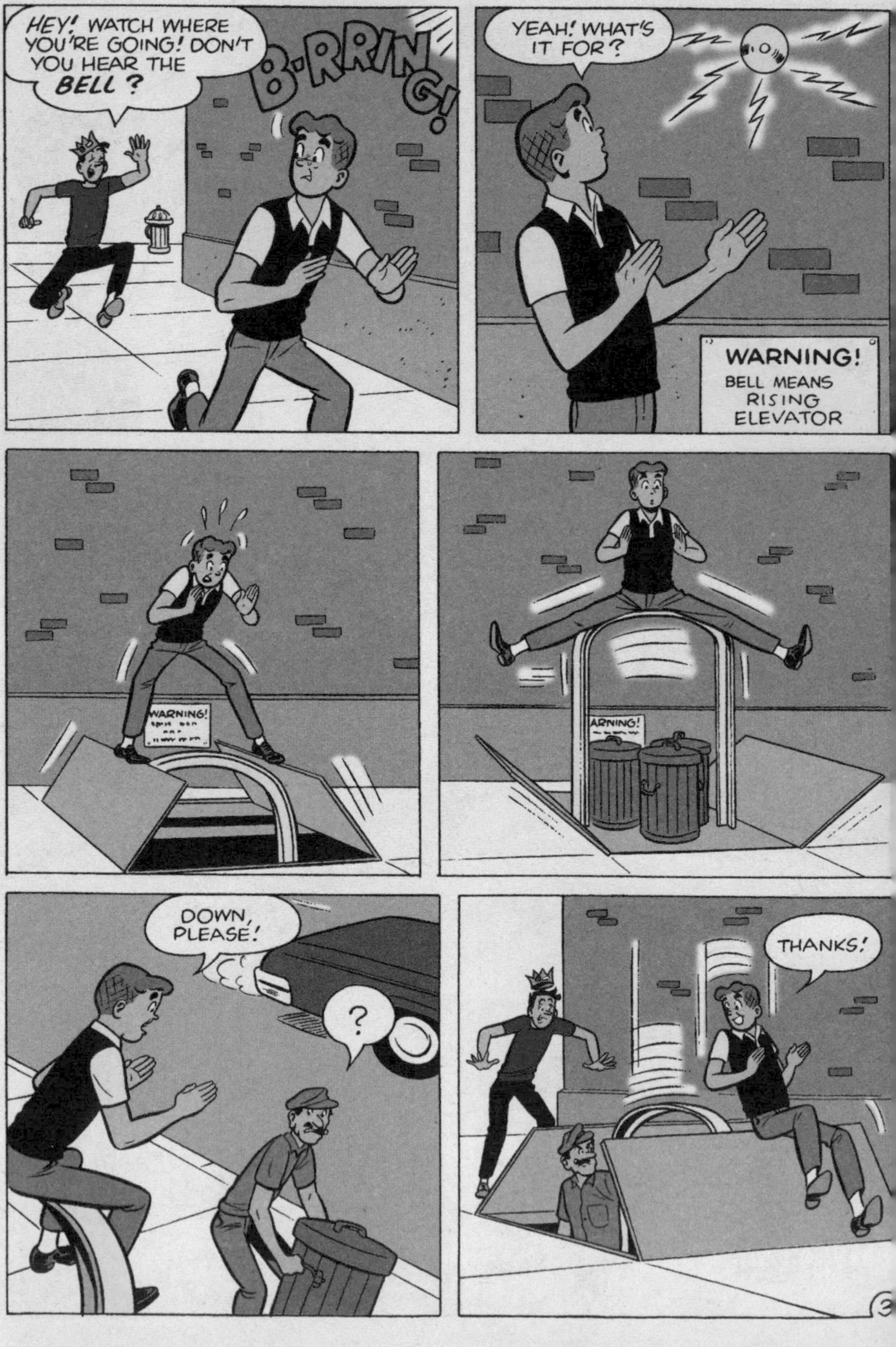
HEY! WATCH WHERE YOU'RE GOING! DON'T YOU HEAR THE BELL?
B-RRING!
YEAH! WHAT'S IT FOR?
WARNING!
BELL MEANS RISING ELEVATOR
WARNING!
WARNING!
DOWN, PLEASE!
?
THANKS!

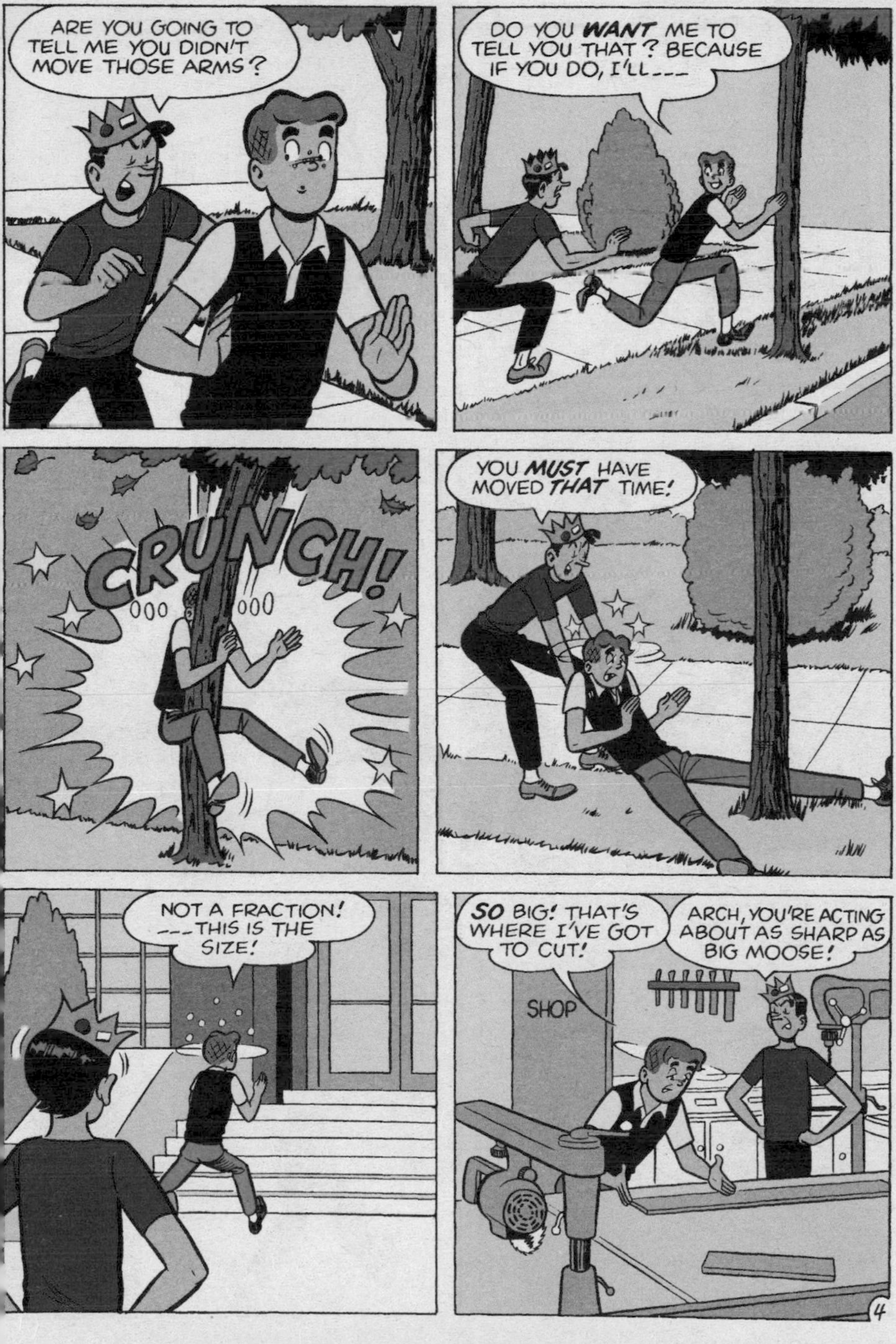
ARE YOU GOING TO TELL ME YOU DIDN'T MOVE THOSE ARMS?
DO YOU WANT ME TO TELL YOU THAT? BECAUSE IF YOU DO, I'LL---
CRUNCH!
OOO
OOO
YOU MUST HAVE MOVED THAT TIME!
NOT A FRACTION! ---THIS IS THE SIZE!
SO BIG! THAT'S WHERE I'VE GOT TO CUT!
ARCH, YOU'RE ACTING ABOUT AS SHARP AS BIG MOOSE!
SHOP
4

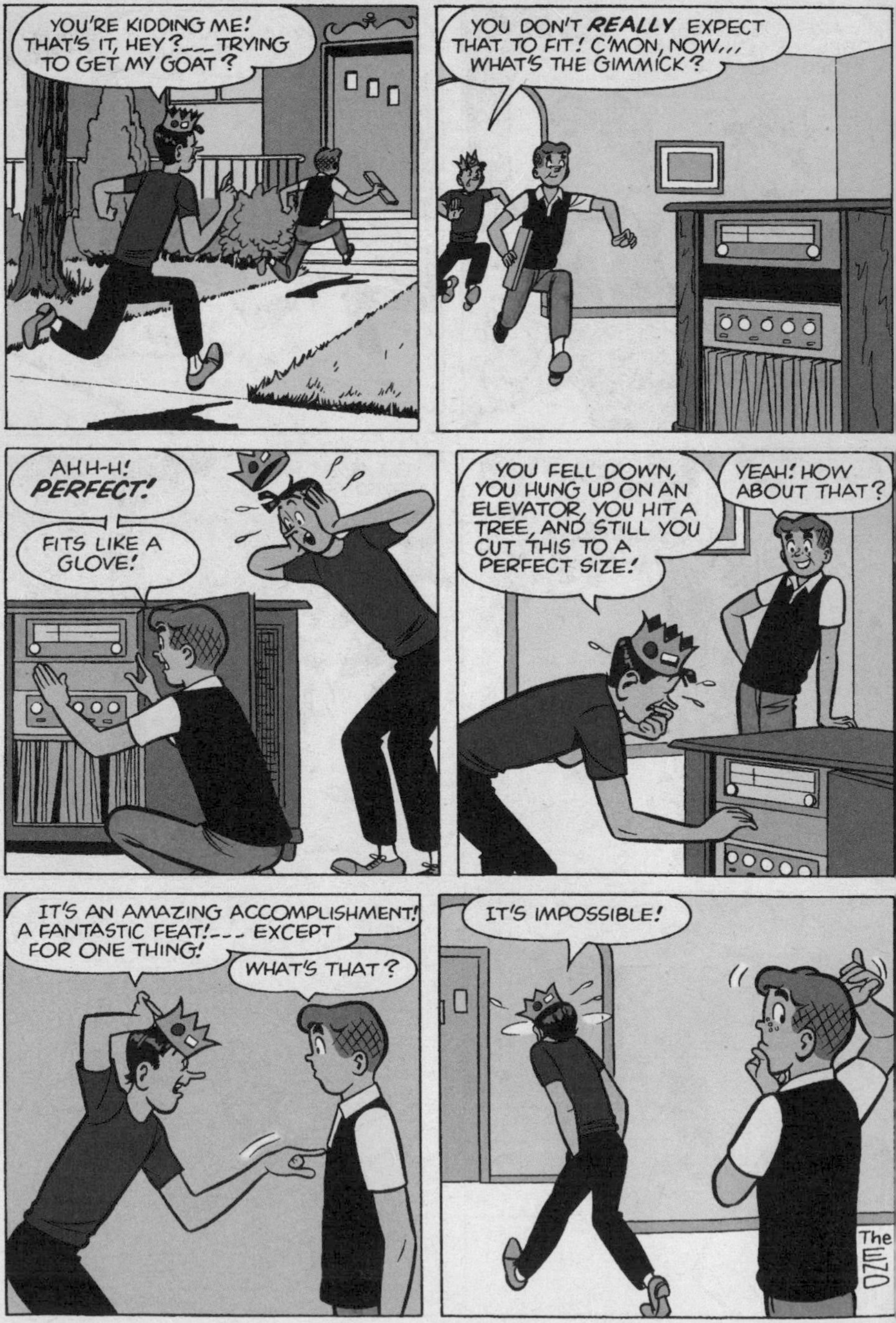
YOU'RE KIDDING ME! THAT'S IT, HEY?--- TRYING TO GET MY GOAT?
YOU DON'T REALLY EXPECT THAT TO FIT! C'MON, NOW,,, WHAT'S THE GIMMICK?
AHH-H! PERFECT!
FITS LIKE A GLOVE!
YOU FELL DOWN, YOU HUNG UP ON AN ELEVATOR, YOU HIT A TREE, AND STILL YOU CUT THIS TO A PERFECT SIZE!
YEAH! HOW ABOUT THAT?
IT'S AN AMAZING ACCOMPLISHMENT! A FANTASTIC FEAT!--- EXCEPT FOR ONE THING!
WHAT'S THAT?
IT'S IMPOSSIBLE!
The END

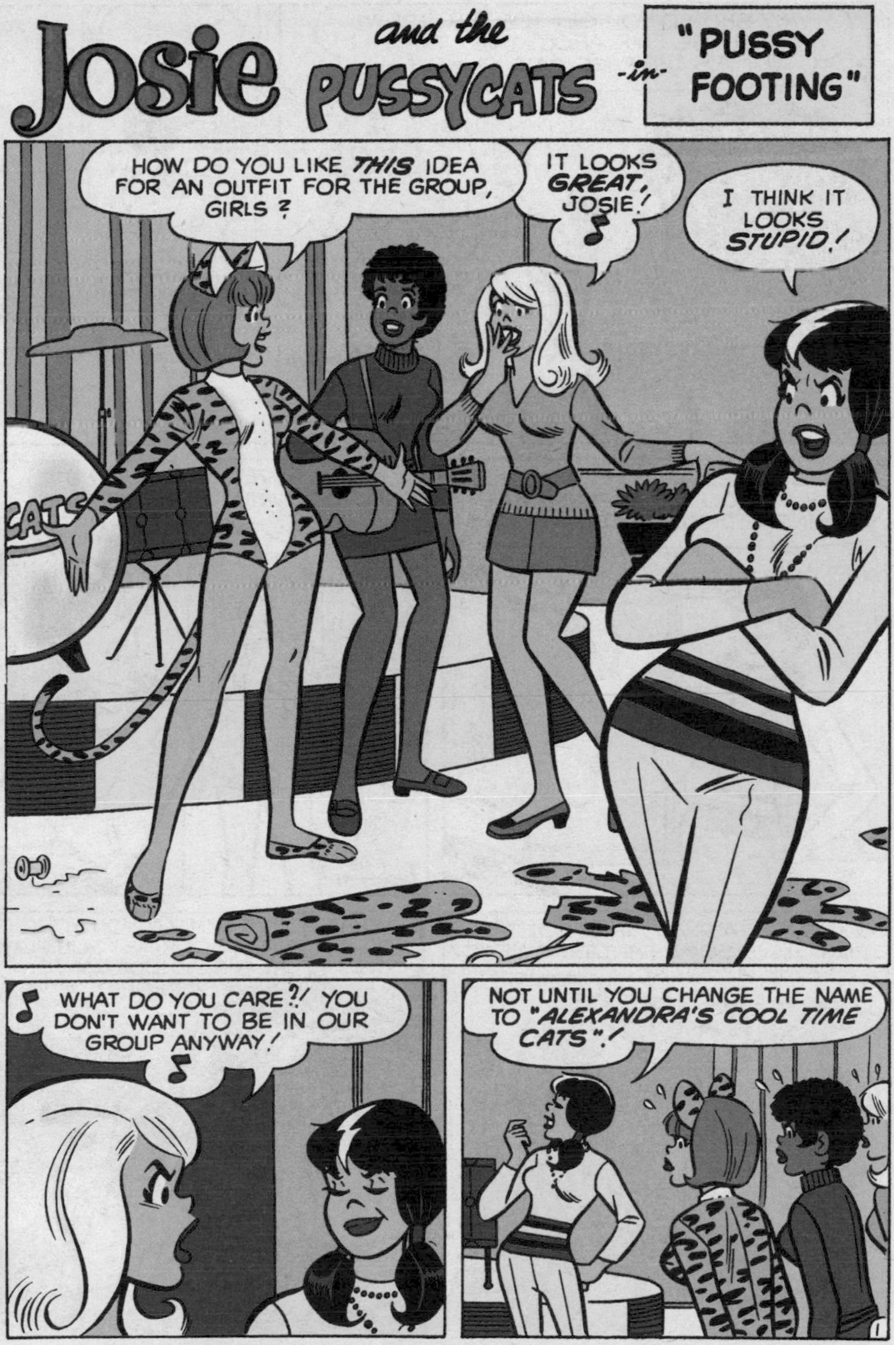
Josie and the PUSSYCATS -in- "PUSSY FOOTING"
HOW DO YOU LIKE THIS IDEA FOR AN OUTFIT FOR THE GROUP, GIRLS ?
IT LOOKS GREAT, JOSIE!
I THINK IT LOOKS STUPID!
CATS
WHAT DO YOU CARE?! YOU DON'T WANT TO BE IN OUR GROUP ANYWAY!
NOT UNTIL YOU CHANGE THE NAME TO "ALEXANDRA'S COOL TIME CATS"!
1

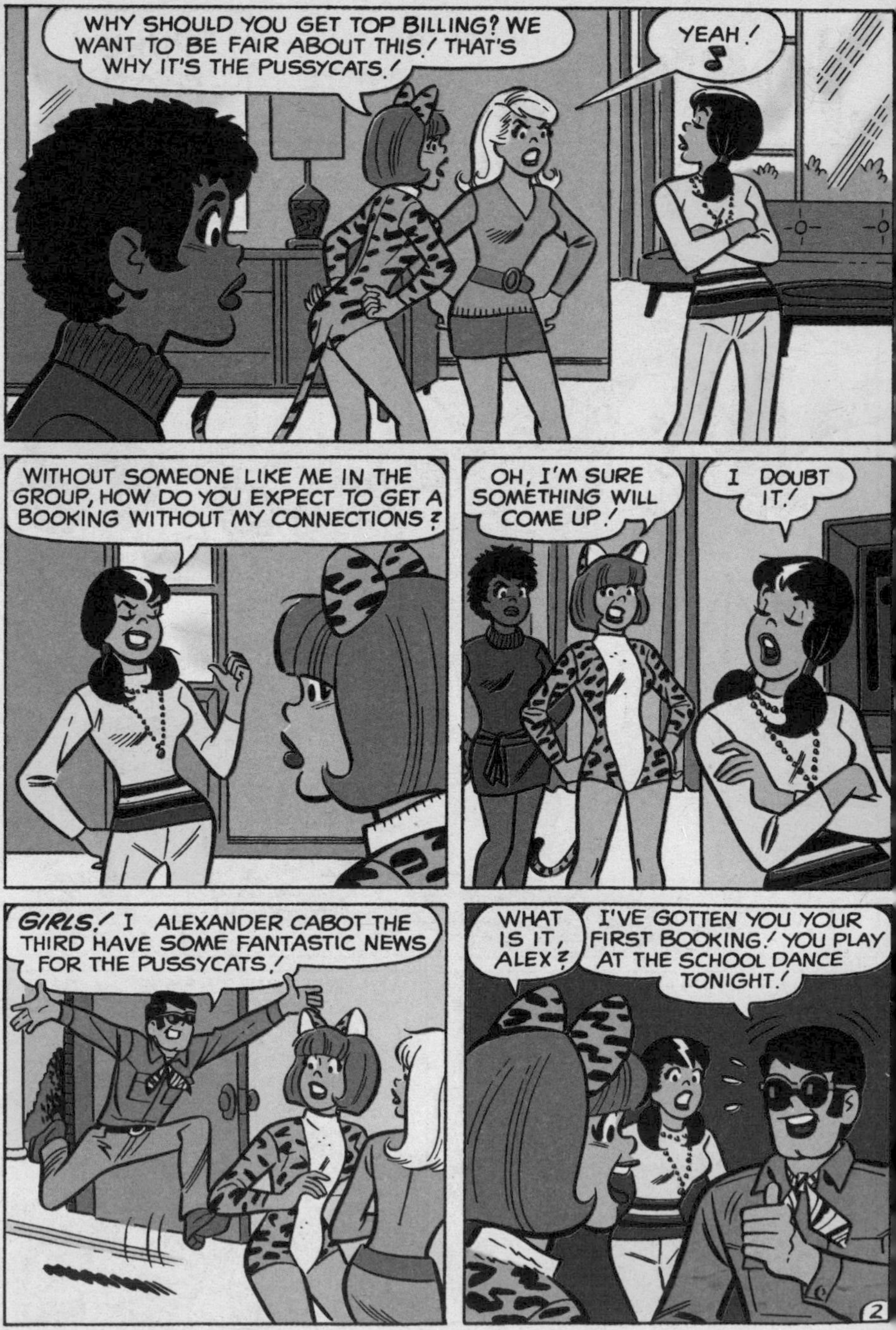
WHY SHOULD YOU GET TOP BILLING? WE WANT TO BE FAIR ABOUT THIS! THAT'S WHY IT'S THE PUSSYCATS!
YEAH!
WITHOUT SOMEONE LIKE ME IN THE GROUP, HOW DO YOU EXPECT TO GET A BOOKING WITHOUT MY CONNECTIONS?
OH, I'M SURE SOMETHING WILL COME UP!
I DOUBT IT!
GIRLS! I ALEXANDER CABOT THE THIRD HAVE SOME FANTASTIC NEWS FOR THE PUSSYCATS!
WHAT IS IT, ALEX?
I'VE GOTTEN YOU YOUR FIRST BOOKING! YOU PLAY AT THE SCHOOL DANCE TONIGHT!
2

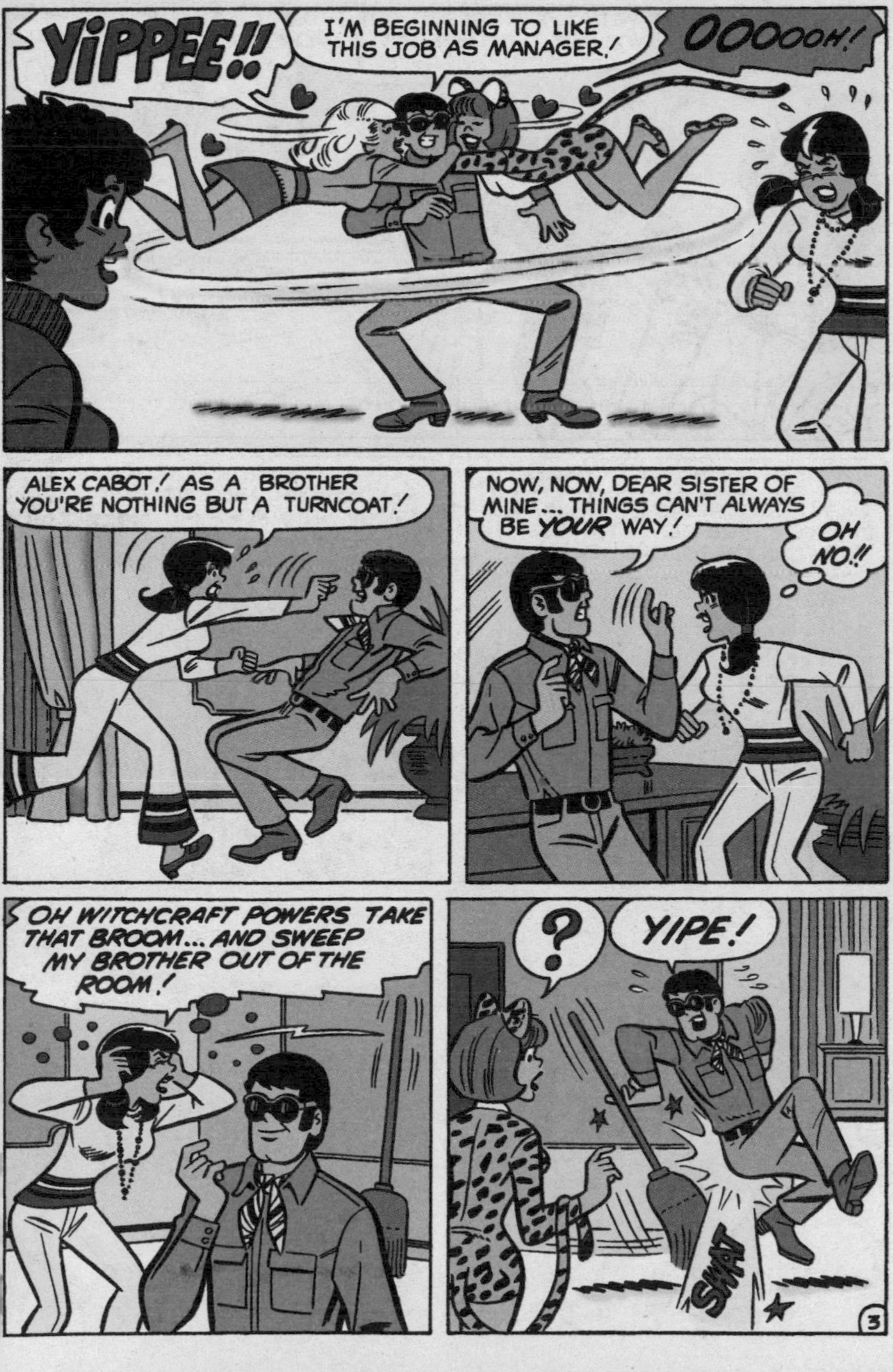
YIPPEE!!
I'M BEGINNING TO LIKE THIS JOB AS MANAGER!
OOOOOOH!
ALEX CABOT! AS A BROTHER YOU'RE NOTHING BUT A TURNCOAT!
NOW, NOW, DEAR SISTER OF MINE... THINGS CAN'T ALWAYS BE YOUR WAY!
OH NO!!
OH WITCHCRAFT POWERS TAKE THAT BROOM... AND SWEEP MY BROTHER OUT OF THE ROOM!
?
YIPE!
SWAT
3

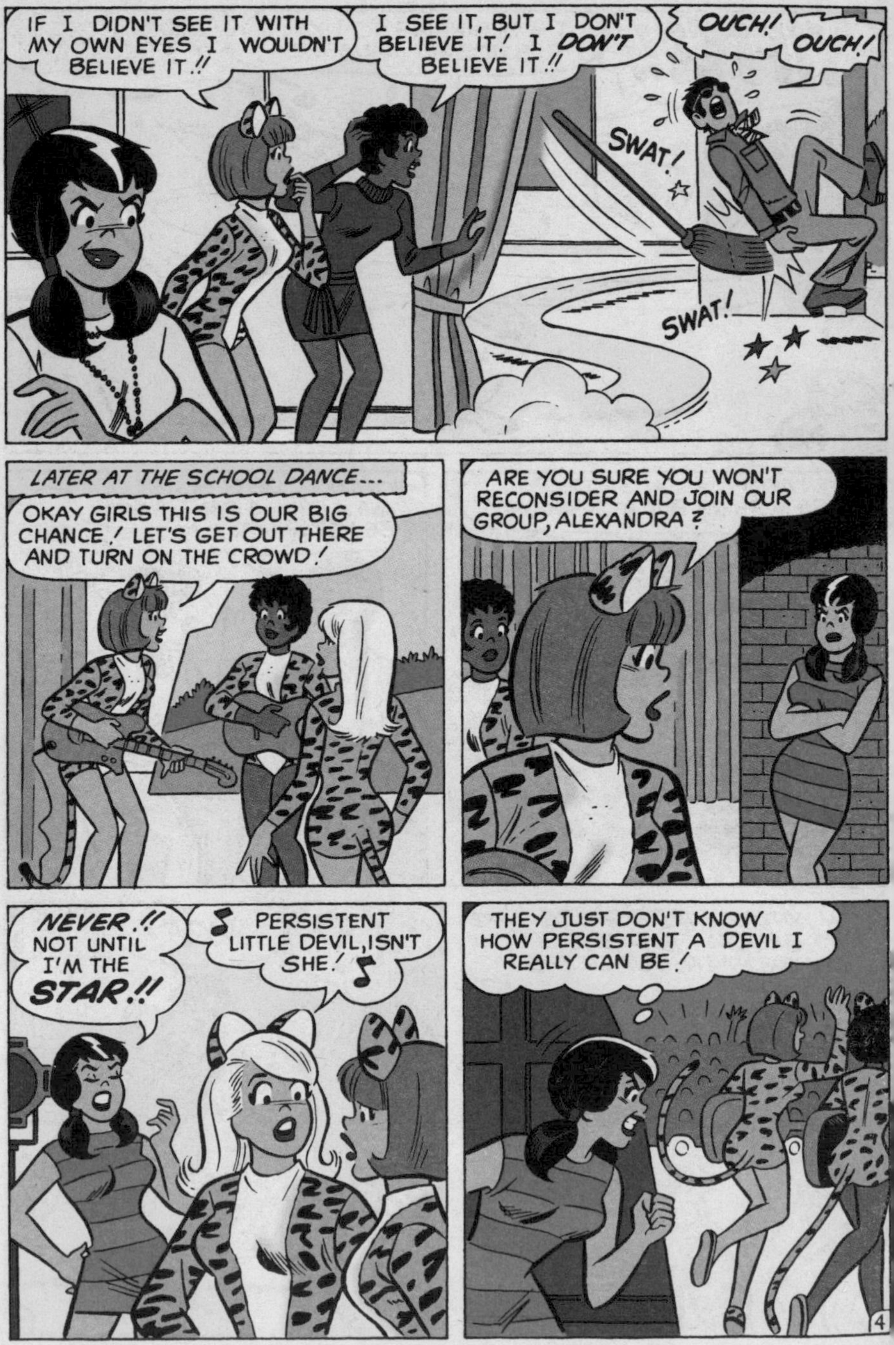
IF I DIDN'T SEE IT WITH MY OWN EYES I WOULDN'T BELIEVE IT.!!
I SEE IT, BUT I DON'T BELIEVE IT! I DON'T BELIEVE IT.!!
OUCH!
OUCH!
SWAT!
SWAT!
LATER AT THE SCHOOL DANCE...
OKAY GIRLS THIS IS OUR BIG CHANCE! LET'S GET OUT THERE AND TURN ON THE CROWD!
ARE YOU SURE YOU WON'T RECONSIDER AND JOIN OUR GROUP, ALEXANDRA?
NEVER.!! NOT UNTIL I'M THE STAR.!!
PERSISTENT LITTLE DEVIL, ISN'T SHE!
THEY JUST DON'T KNOW HOW PERSISTENT A DEVIL I REALLY CAN BE!
4

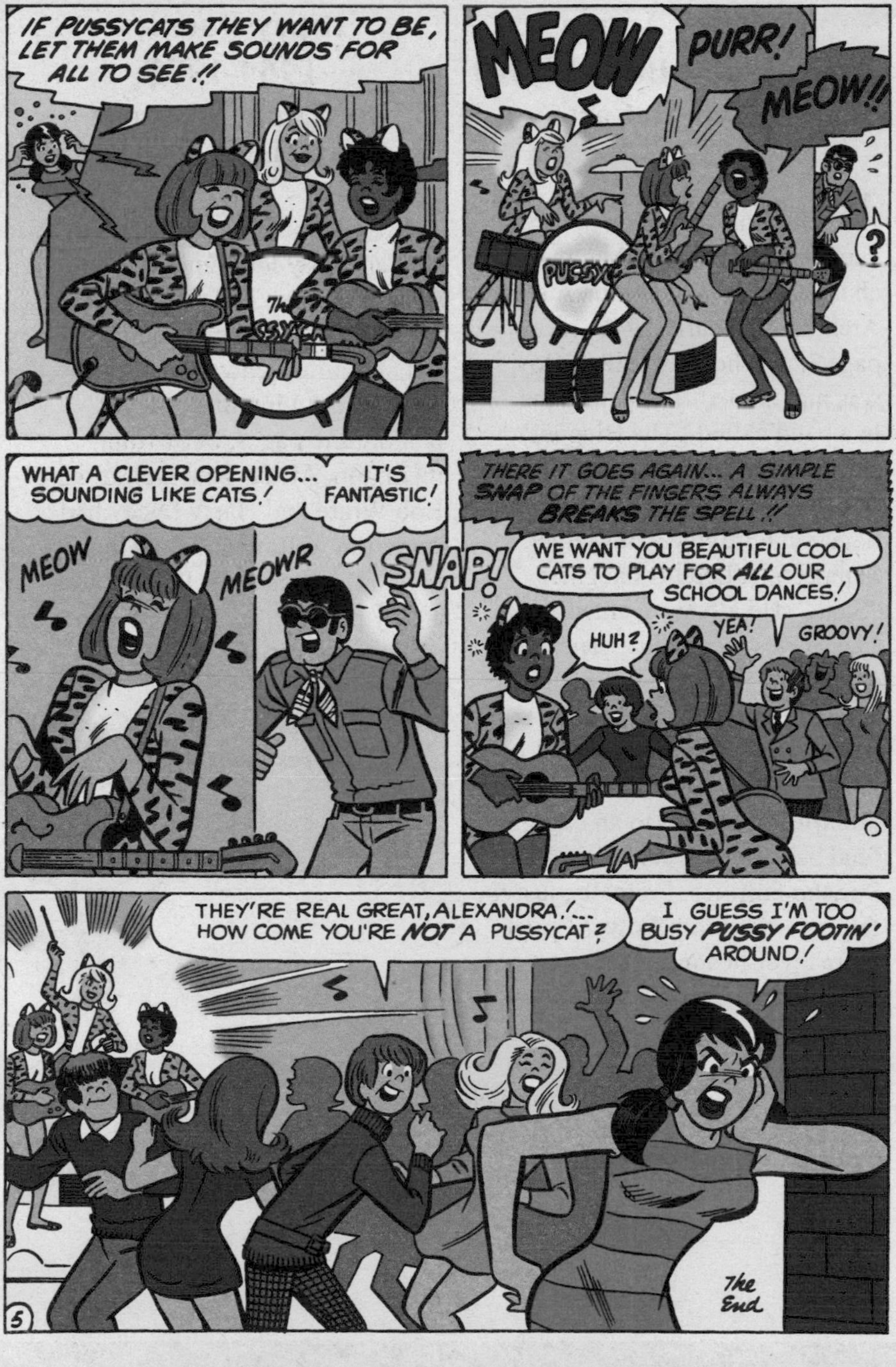
IF PUSSYCATS THEY WANT TO BE, LET THEM MAKE SOUNDS FOR ALL TO SEE.!!
MEOW
PURR!
MEOW!!
?
WHAT A CLEVER OPENING... SOUNDING LIKE CATS.!
IT'S FANTASTIC!
MEOW
MEOWR
SNAP!
THERE IT GOES AGAIN... A SIMPLE SNAP OF THE FINGERS ALWAYS BREAKS THE SPELL.!!
WE WANT YOU BEAUTIFUL COOL CATS TO PLAY FOR ALL OUR SCHOOL DANCES!
HUH?
YEA!
GROOVY!
THEY'RE REAL GREAT, ALEXANDRA!... HOW COME YOU'RE NOT A PUSSYCAT?
I GUESS I'M TOO BUSY PUSSY FOOTIN' AROUND!
The End
5

Enemy Action
That Wilkin Boy #2, 1969
by Dan DeCarlo

That Wilkin Boy is an updated version of Wilbur Wilkin, the character who actually pre-dated Archie in the early 1940s (see page 32). The new Wilkin Boy was nicknamed Bingo and was in a band called "The Bingoes" (following the success of The Archies). Bingo has a girlfriend, Samantha Smythe. Her father, Sampson, called his daughter "Sam." He always wanted a son. The stories were edgy, especially where Mr. Smythe was involved. He was depicted as sort of an Archie Bunker (two years before Archie Bunker's debut in *All in the Family*), which led to an ongoing feud between the Wilkin and Smythe families. Actually, just the fathers—the mothers were much more level-headed. However, poor Bingo and Samantha were always caught in the middle.

--**Victor Gorelick**
*Co-President/Editor-in-Chief,
Archie Comics*

Dipsy Doodles
1969-1975
by Samm Schwartz
and Dan DeCarlo

Dipsy Doodles were originally conceived by longtime Archie writer George Gladir as filler pages for the Jughead comic. Artist Samm Schwartz not only enjoyed drawing these clever pantomime pages, but writing them, too. Artists Dan DeCarlo, Bob White and Harry Lucey had some fun writing and drawing Dipsy Doodles as well. This was a very popular feature with our readers and artists.

--**Victor Gorelick**
*Co-President/Editor-in-Chief,
Archie Comics*

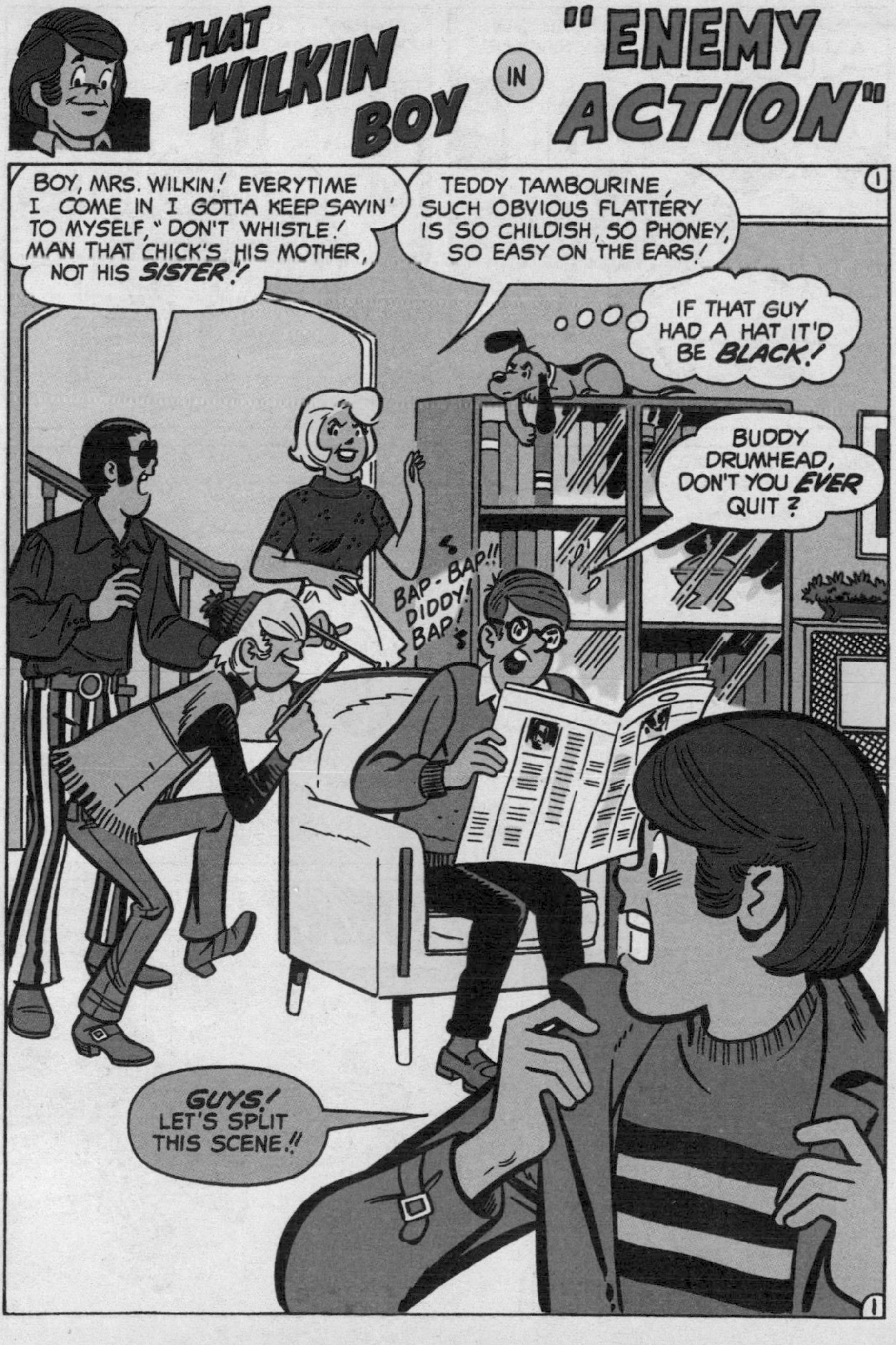
THAT WILKIN BOY IN "ENEMY ACTION"
BOY, MRS. WILKIN! EVERYTIME I COME IN I GOTTA KEEP SAYIN' TO MYSELF, "DON'T WHISTLE! MAN THAT CHICK'S HIS MOTHER, NOT HIS SISTER"!
TEDDY TAMBOURINE, SUCH OBVIOUS FLATTERY IS SO CHILDISH, SO PHONEY, SO EASY ON THE EARS!
IF THAT GUY HAD A HAT IT'D BE BLACK!
BUDDY DRUMHEAD, DON'T YOU EVER QUIT?
BAP-BAP!! DIDDY BAP!
GUYS! LET'S SPLIT THIS SCENE!!

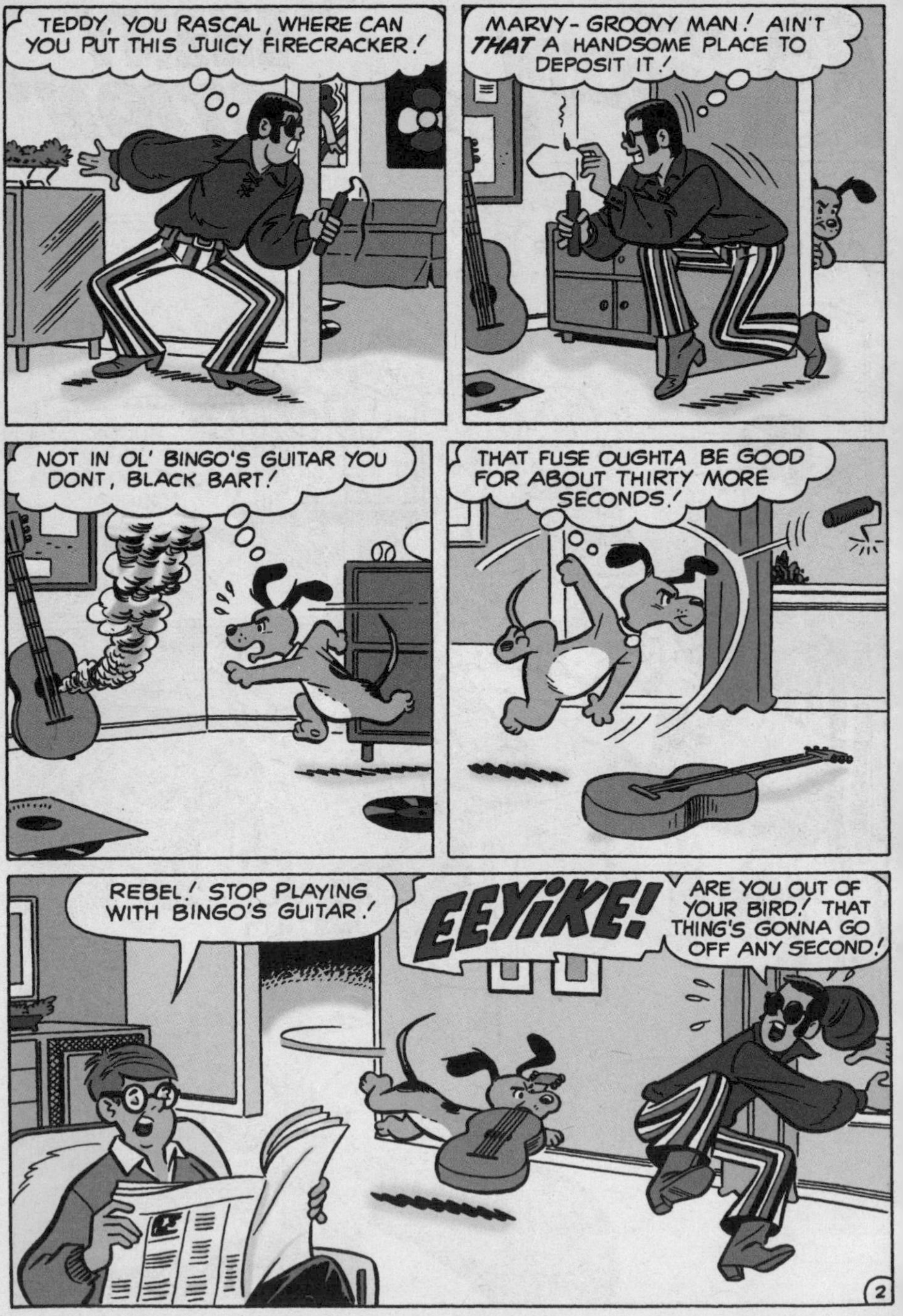
TEDDY, YOU RASCAL, WHERE CAN YOU PUT THIS JUICY FIRECRACKER!
MARVY-GROOVY MAN! AIN'T THAT A HANDSOME PLACE TO DEPOSIT IT!
NOT IN OL' BINGO'S GUITAR YOU DONT, BLACK BART!
THAT FUSE OUGHTA BE GOOD FOR ABOUT THIRTY MORE SECONDS!
REBEL! STOP PLAYING WITH BINGO'S GUITAR!
EEYIKE!
ARE YOU OUT OF YOUR BIRD! THAT THING'S GONNA GO OFF ANY SECOND!
2

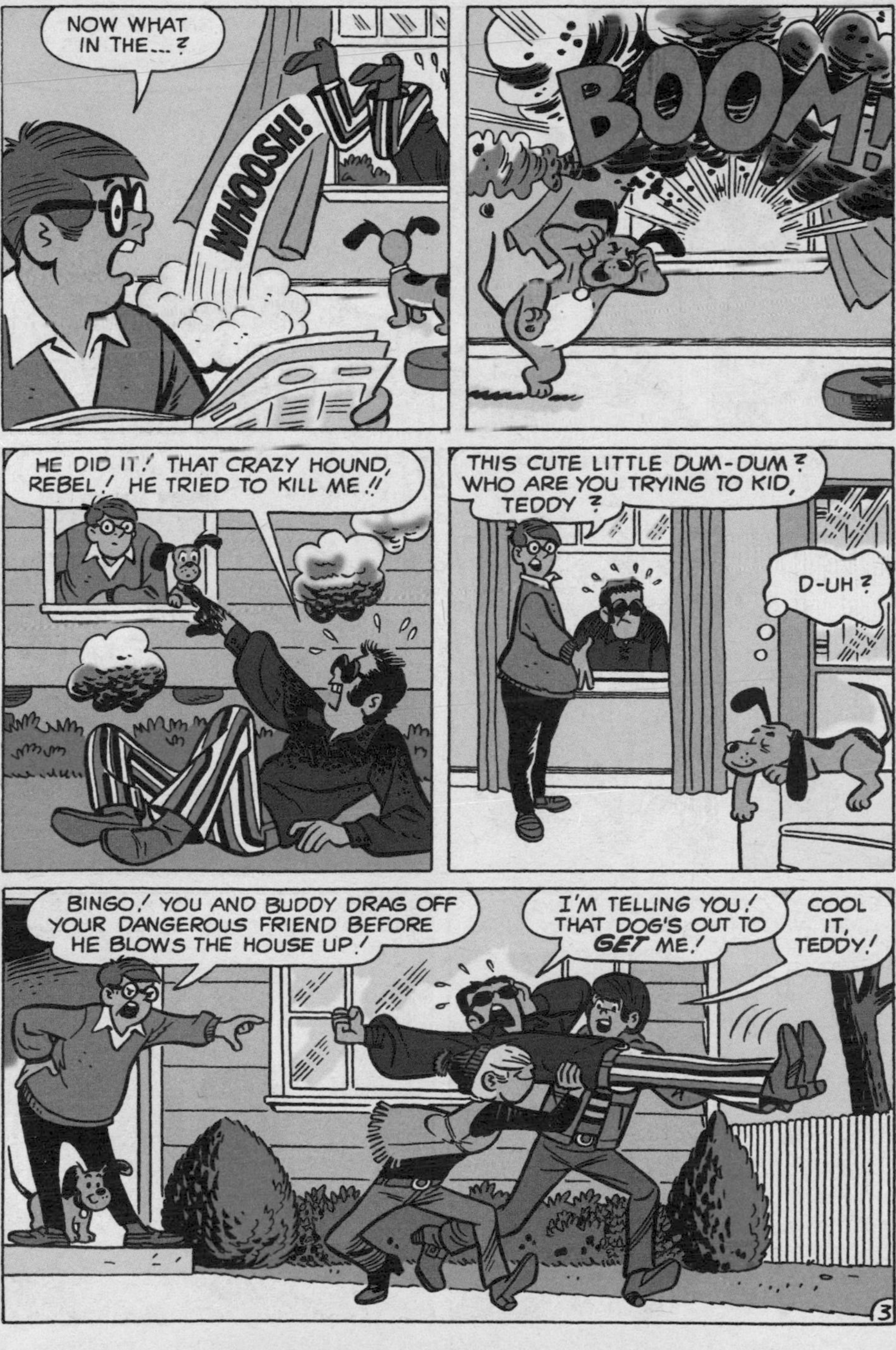
NOW WHAT IN THE...?
WHOOSH!
BOOM!
HE DID IT! THAT CRAZY HOUND, REBEL! HE TRIED TO KILL ME!!
THIS CUTE LITTLE DUM-DUM? WHO ARE YOU TRYING TO KID, TEDDY?
D-UH?
BINGO! YOU AND BUDDY DRAG OFF YOUR DANGEROUS FRIEND BEFORE HE BLOWS THE HOUSE UP!
I'M TELLING YOU! THAT DOG'S OUT TO GET ME!
COOL IT, TEDDY!
3

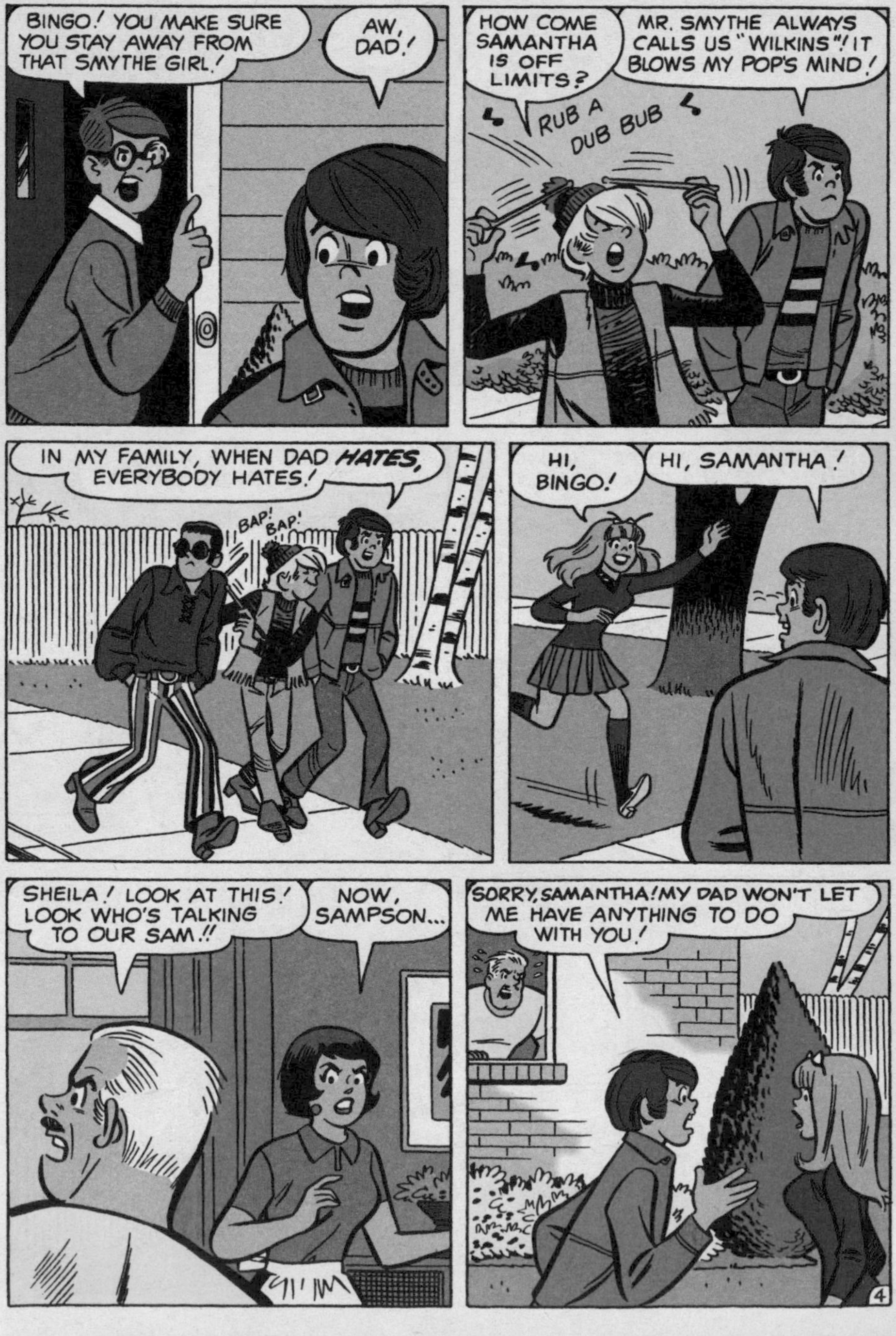
BINGO! YOU MAKE SURE YOU STAY AWAY FROM THAT SMYTHE GIRL!
AW, DAD!
HOW COME SAMANTHA IS OFF LIMITS?
MR. SMYTHE ALWAYS CALLS US "WILKINS"! IT BLOWS MY POP'S MIND!
RUB A DUB BUB
IN MY FAMILY, WHEN DAD HATES, EVERYBODY HATES!
BAP! BAP!
HI, BINGO!
HI, SAMANTHA!
SHEILA! LOOK AT THIS! LOOK WHO'S TALKING TO OUR SAM!!
NOW, SAMPSON...
SORRY, SAMANTHA! MY DAD WON'T LET ME HAVE ANYTHING TO DO WITH YOU!
4

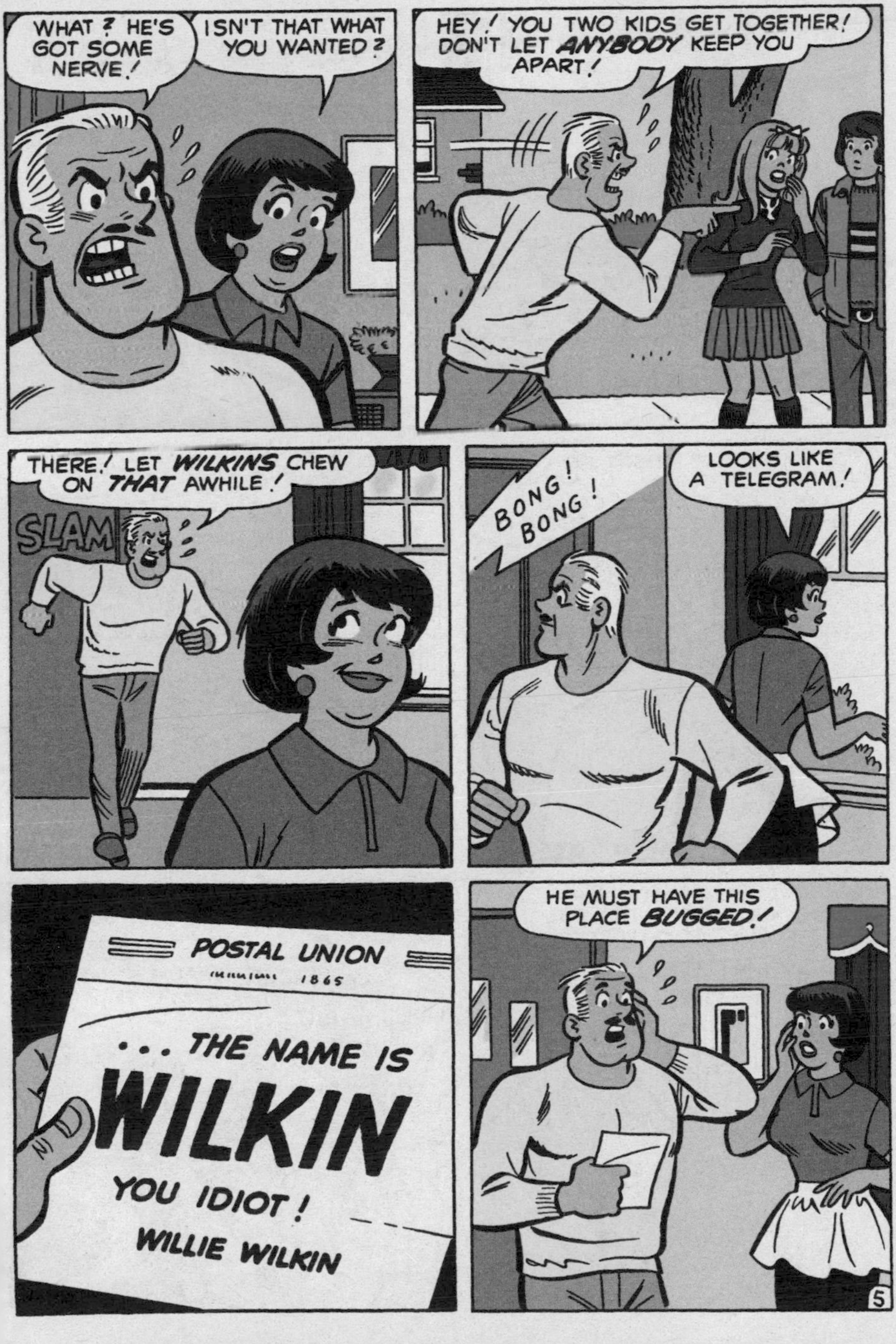
WHAT ? HE'S GOT SOME NERVE!
ISN'T THAT WHAT YOU WANTED ?
HEY! YOU TWO KIDS GET TOGETHER! DON'T LET ANYBODY KEEP YOU APART!
THERE! LET WILKINS CHEW ON THAT AWHILE!
SLAM
BONG! BONG!
LOOKS LIKE A TELEGRAM!
POSTAL UNION
1865
... THE NAME IS
WILKIN
YOU IDIOT!
WILLIE WILKIN
HE MUST HAVE THIS PLACE BUGGED!
5

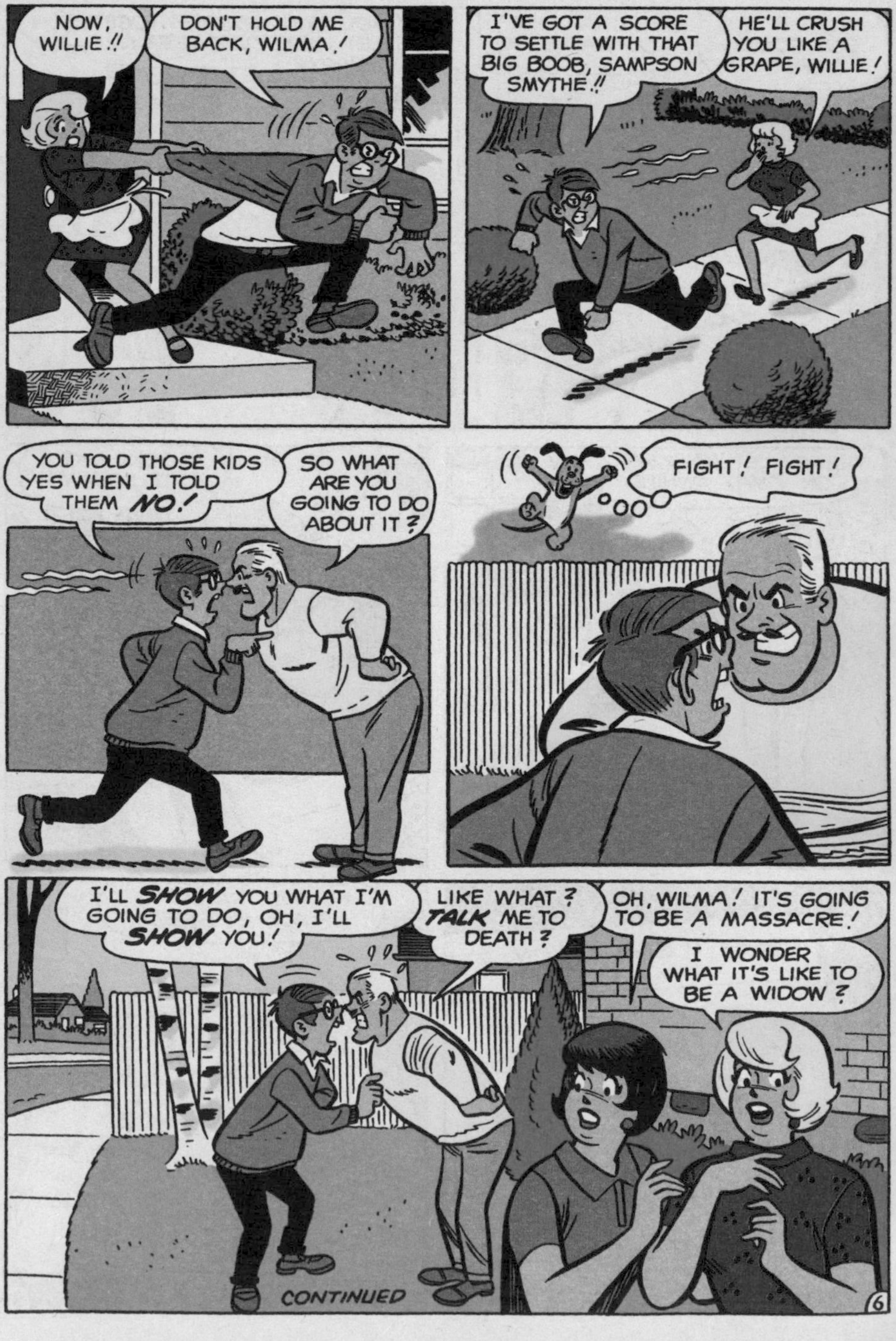
NOW, WILLIE.!!
DON'T HOLD ME BACK, WILMA.!
I'VE GOT A SCORE TO SETTLE WITH THAT BIG BOOB, SAMPSON SMYTHE.!!
HE'LL CRUSH YOU LIKE A GRAPE, WILLIE!
YOU TOLD THOSE KIDS YES WHEN I TOLD THEM NO!
SO WHAT ARE YOU GOING TO DO ABOUT IT?
FIGHT! FIGHT!
I'LL SHOW YOU WHAT I'M GOING TO DO, OH, I'LL SHOW YOU!
LIKE WHAT? TALK ME TO DEATH?
OH, WILMA! IT'S GOING TO BE A MASSACRE!
I WONDER WHAT IT'S LIKE TO BE A WIDOW?
CONTINUED
6

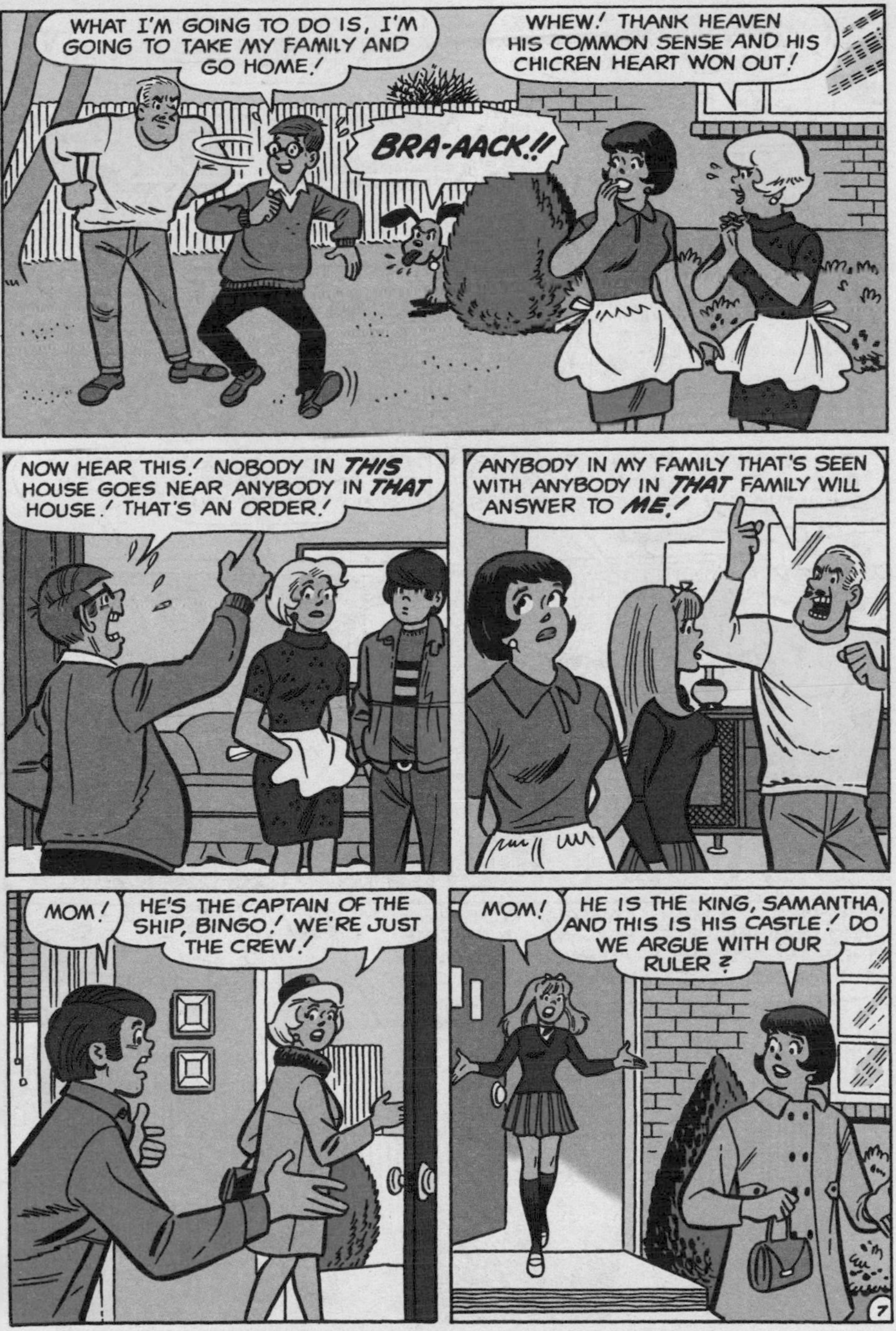
WHAT I'M GOING TO DO IS, I'M GOING TO TAKE MY FAMILY AND GO HOME!
WHEW! THANK HEAVEN HIS COMMON SENSE AND HIS CHICREN HEART WON OUT!
BRA-AACK!!
NOW HEAR THIS! NOBODY IN THIS HOUSE GOES NEAR ANYBODY IN THAT HOUSE! THAT'S AN ORDER!
ANYBODY IN MY FAMILY THAT'S SEEN WITH ANYBODY IN THAT FAMILY WILL ANSWER TO ME!
MOM!
HE'S THE CAPTAIN OF THE SHIP, BINGO! WE'RE JUST THE CREW!
MOM!
HE IS THE KING, SAMANTHA, AND THIS IS HIS CASTLE! DO WE ARGUE WITH OUR RULER?
7

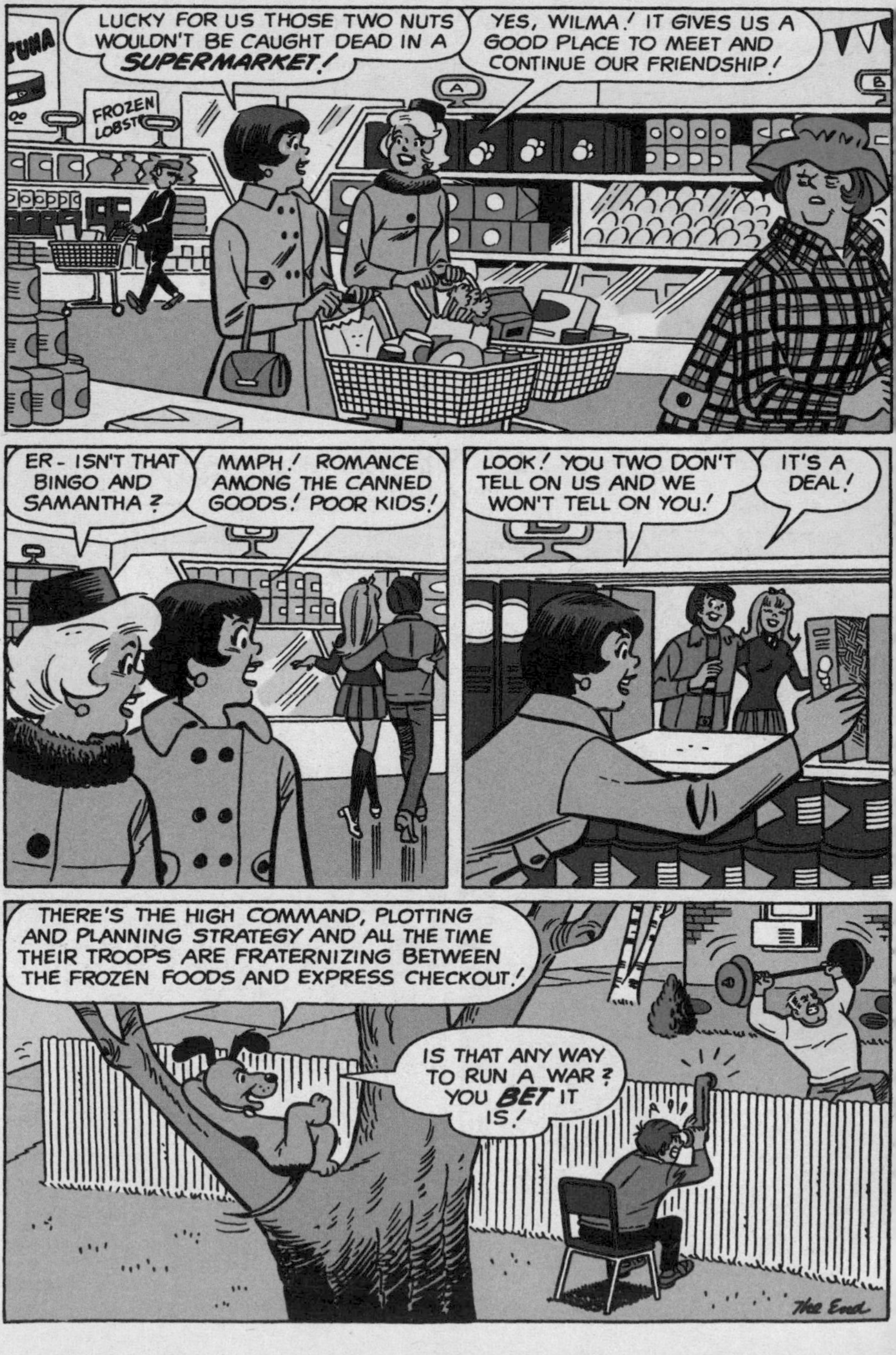
LUCKY FOR US THOSE TWO NUTS WOULDN'T BE CAUGHT DEAD IN A SUPERMARKET!
YES, WILMA! IT GIVES US A GOOD PLACE TO MEET AND CONTINUE OUR FRIENDSHIP!
TUNA
FROZEN LOBST
A
B
ER- ISN'T THAT BINGO AND SAMANTHA?
MMPH! ROMANCE AMONG THE CANNED GOODS! POOR KIDS!
LOOK! YOU TWO DON'T TELL ON US AND WE WON'T TELL ON YOU!
IT'S A DEAL!
THERE'S THE HIGH COMMAND, PLOTTING AND PLANNING STRATEGY AND ALL THE TIME THEIR TROOPS ARE FRATERNIZING BETWEEN THE FROZEN FOODS AND EXPRESS CHECKOUT!
IS THAT ANY WAY TO RUN A WAR? YOU BET IT IS!

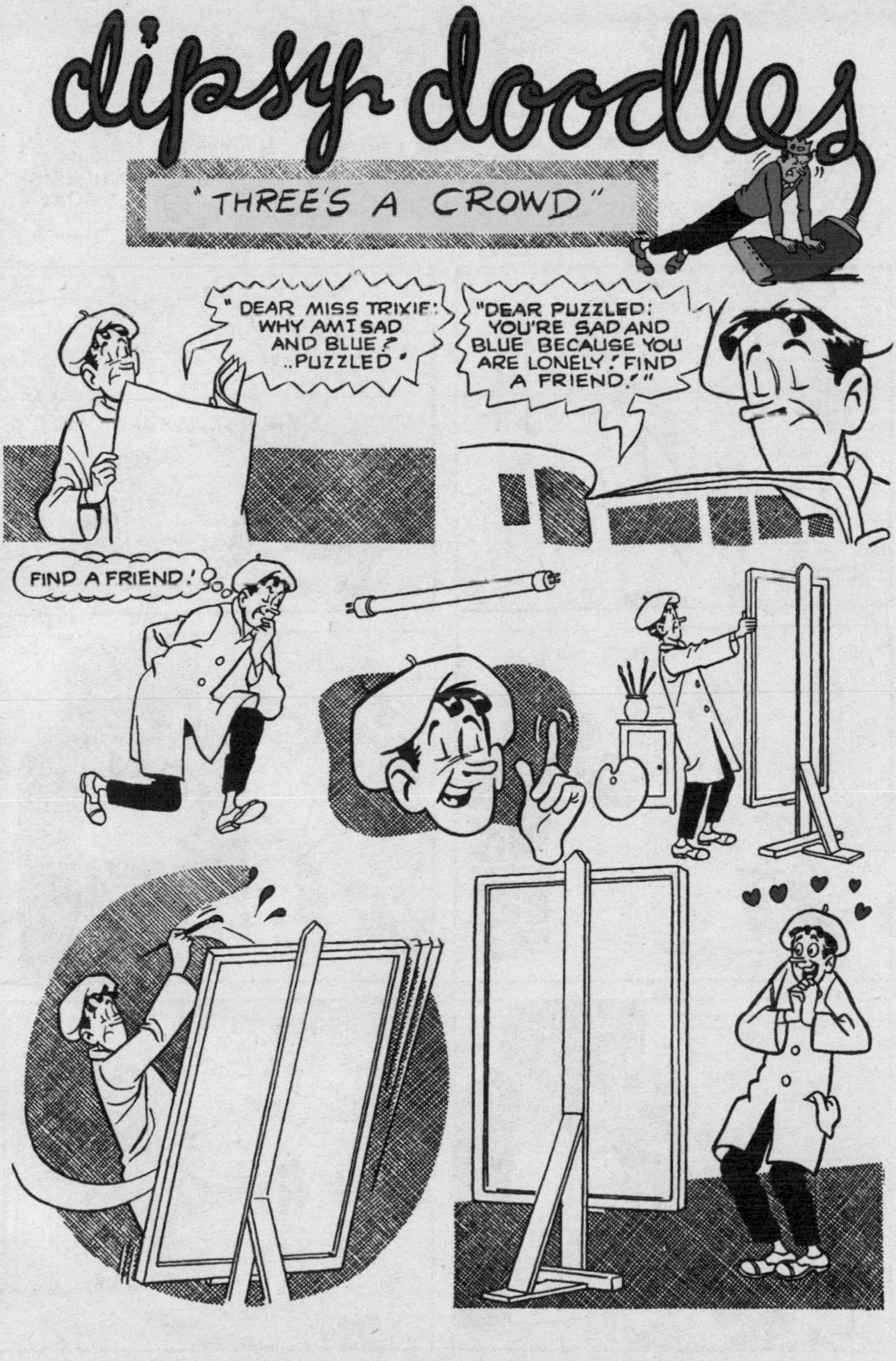
dipsy doodles
"THREE'S A CROWD"
"DEAR MISS TRIXIE: WHY AM I SAD AND BLUE? ..PUZZLED"
"DEAR PUZZLED: YOU'RE SAD AND BLUE BECAUSE YOU ARE LONELY! FIND A FRIEND!"
FIND A FRIEND!

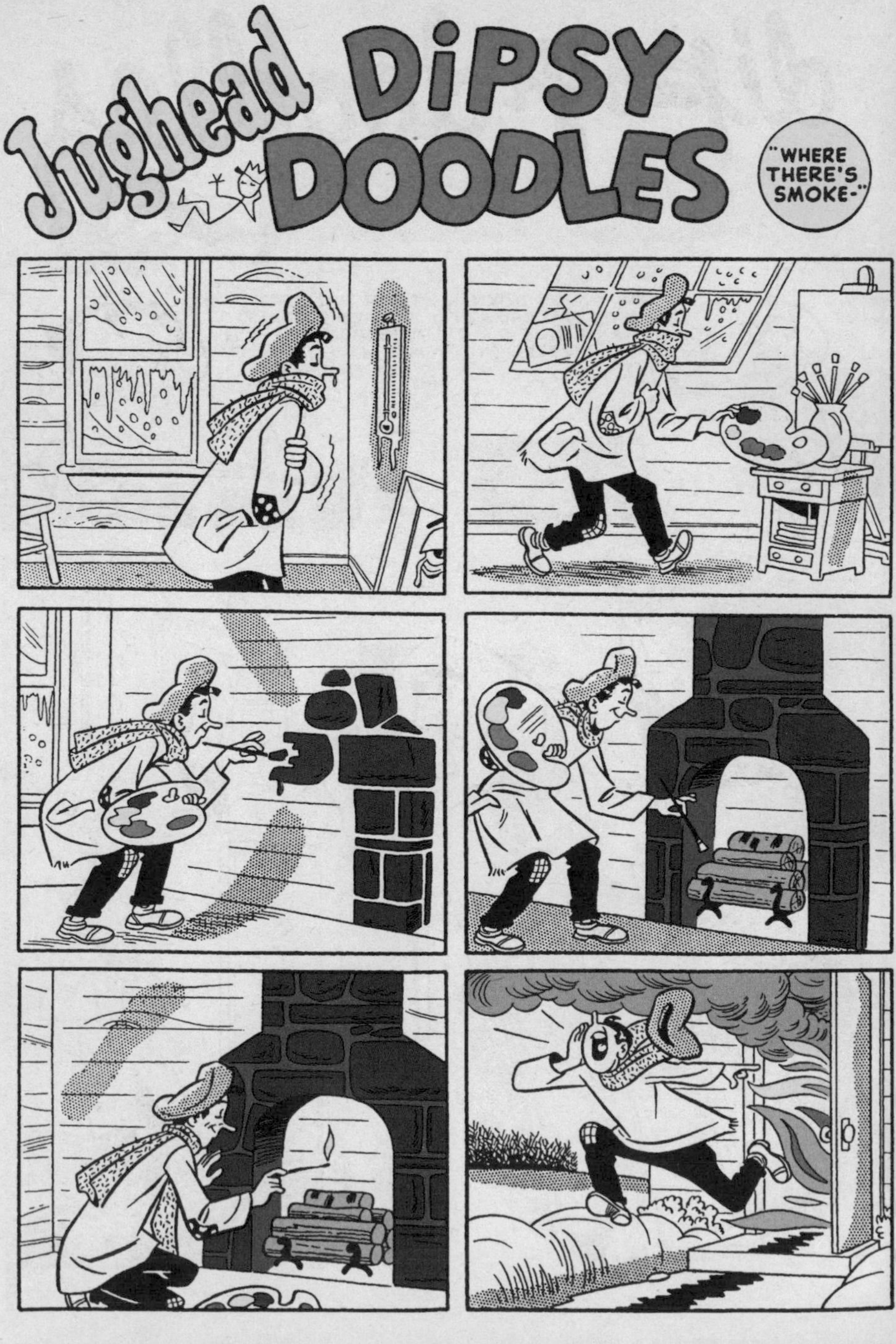
Jughead
DiPSY DOODLES
"WHERE THERE'S SMOKE-"

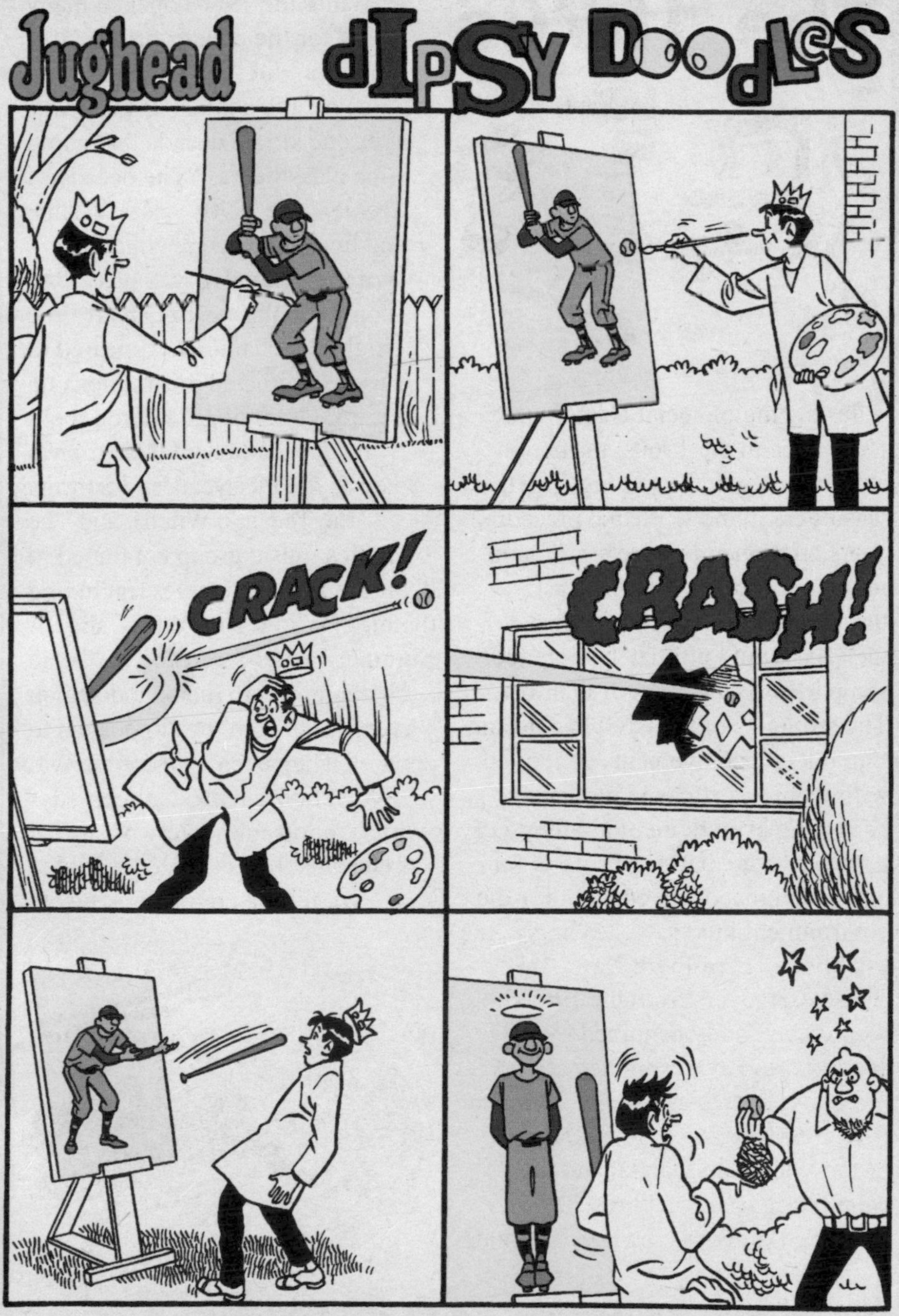
Jughead
dIpSY DooodLes
CRACK!
CRASH!

The 1970s

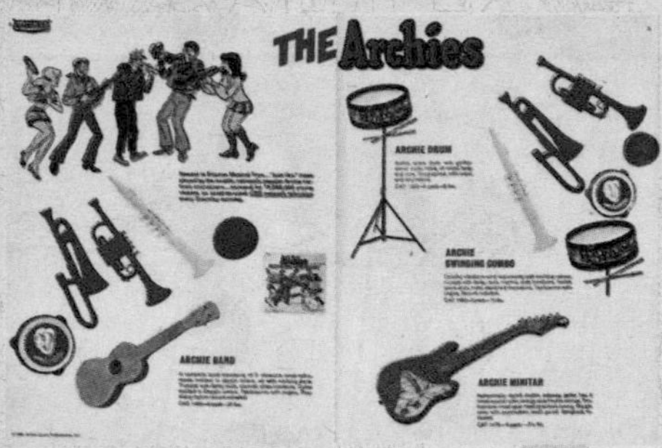
THE Archies

While the 1960s opened many doors for the country in the '70s, so too did it influence the fate of Archie comics. If there was ever one single decade that could be classified as "The decade of Archie," the 1970s was it! Archie and his friends were at the height of their popularity. Sales of the comic books were at an all-time high, the characters appeared in various animated incarnations on Saturday morning TV throughout the decade (as did their friends Josie & the Pussycats and Sabrina the Teenage Witch), and The Archies music group continued to chart albums and singles (including the hits "Who's Your Baby" and "A Summer Prayer for Peace"). Archie characters were merchandised on everything from toys to posters to apparel. They even appeared in two live-action TV musical-comedy-variety pilots, ultimately broadcast as specials. It was indeed a golden era for the comic book teens!

After the major social changes that took place in the 1960s, the nation strived to regain its footing. The task wasn't easy, and while the preceding years continued to have a profound influence on the 1970s (at least through the first half of the decade), the '70s would ultimately embrace some identifying traits of their own. The struggles of the Civil Rights and Equal Rights movements continued, with women's rights in particular becoming even more of a rallying cry throughout the nation. Protests for peace continued and concern for the environment increased, leading to the establishment of Earth Day.

These carryovers from the 1960s would eventually be joined by new concerns and events in the nation, including the resignation of President Richard M. Nixon in the aftermath of the Watergate scandal and the celebration of the nation's 200th birthday (known as the Bicentennial).

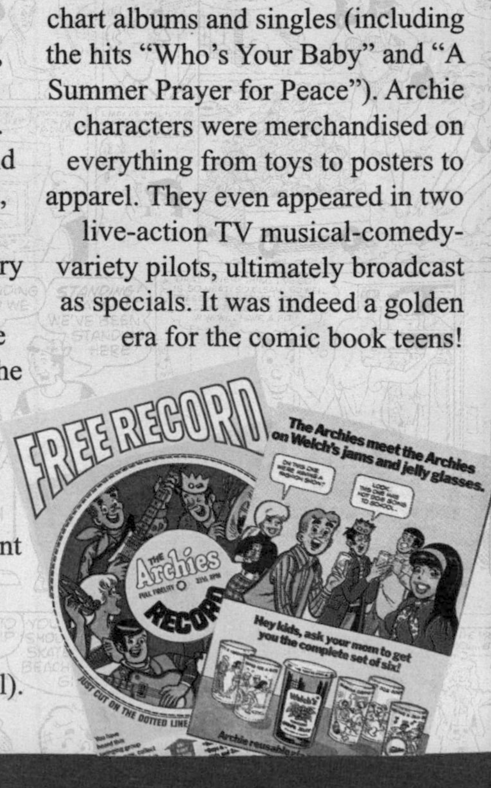
FREE RECORD
The Archies meet the Archies on Welch's jams and jelly glasses.
The Archies
RECORD
Hey kids, ask your mom to get you the complete set of six!
JUST CUT ON THE DOTTED LINE

Entertainment in the 1970s had a bit of something for everyone. While pop singles remained hits with pre-teens, the further development of guitar-based music led to the increased popularity of album rock among teens. Several movies in the '70s depicted teens coming of age in previous decades, most notably the movie adaptation of the hit Broadway musical *Grease* and the sitcom *Happy Days*. In the midst of it all, Archie and his friends prevailed and built an enduring entertainment empire of their own.

The influence of *The Archie Show* on the comics helped contribute to the further streamlining of the characters. There was a greater focus on the core archetypical traits of the cast, such as the scheming of Veronica and Reggie, the sweetness of Betty and the uniqueness of Jughead.

The popularity of the cartoons and The Archies music group along with the dominance of Archie Comics on the newsstand made for an unbeatable combination. Archie was showing up in places he'd never been before, including cereal box promotions, a pilot Archie restaurant, and even a licensed series of custom comics.

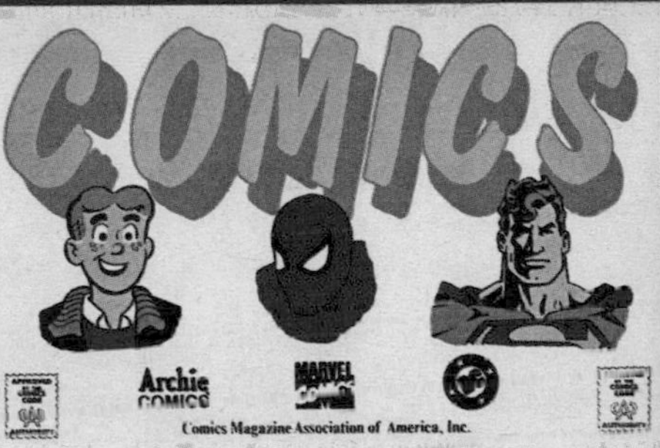
COMICS
Archie COMICS
MARVEL
Comics Magazine Association of America, Inc.

Alongside DC and Marvel, Archie Comics were so popular on the newsstands that images of Archie often appeared on spinner racks with Superman and Spider-Man. Archie and his "boss," John L. Goldwater, were leading forces keeping the CMAA (Comics Magazine Association of America) running like a well-oiled machine. When the decade brought the rise of comic conventions and comic shops, Archie came along for the ride and courted new fans into the next decade. The decade is often referred to as "the swingin' Seventies," and nobody swung along on a bigger wave of popularity than Archie!

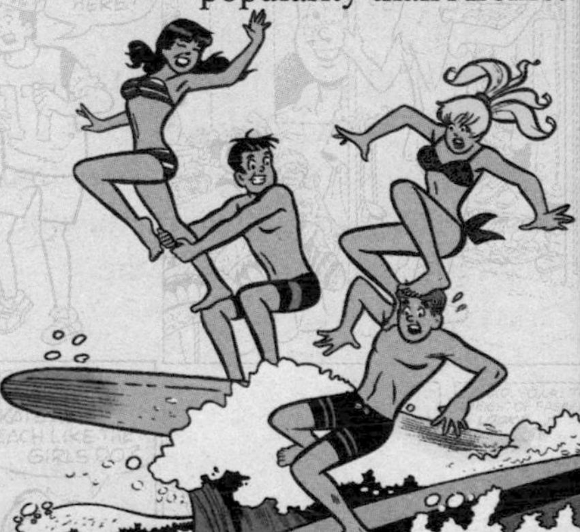

Icebreaker
Jughead #178, 1970
by Al Hartley

There was a certain starkness to Al Hartley's version of the Archie gang. Hartley's Archie often seemed like an anguished soul; plenty of teeth clenching and fist clutching. His Veronica was a bit more callous; his Moose a bit more vacant, his Reggie a bit more heartless—and his Jughead seemed to positively luxuriate in his oddballness. In the Hot Dog story, "Icebreaker," it seems not to have crossed Jug's mind that he should look for a human skating partner. People, especially female people, carry more baggage than he's interested in dealing with, so choosing his pet Hot Dog for the purpose is his Occam's Razor solution. Other storytellers might have made Jughead's selection of his dog for his "date" the nonsensical punchline that the story builds to. With Hartley, it's the starting point, with the actions that follow nudging Jughead reluctantly back toward the realm of the conventional.

--Craig Boldman
Writer, Archie Comics

First Love
Jughead #192, 1971
by Samm Schwartz

Samm Schwartz, my favorite of the classic Jughead artists, did work that was simple and stylish. His characters carried themselves with an amped-up body English that could've been borrowed from Art Carney's Ed Norton and always enlivened a story. "First Love," prehistoric setting aside, is six pages of conversation (the only essential action in the story is the climactic kiss on page four). Samm was never one for pages of talking heads, though. He adds a few bits of business, such as Jughead's spontaneous invention of the sport of stickball, to ensure that the discussion never drags. That one of those "bits of business" is a dinosaur attack(!), which happens and then passes without derailing the plot, demonstrates just how deft Samm was at his brand of comics sleight-of-hand.

--Craig Boldman
Writer, Archie Comics

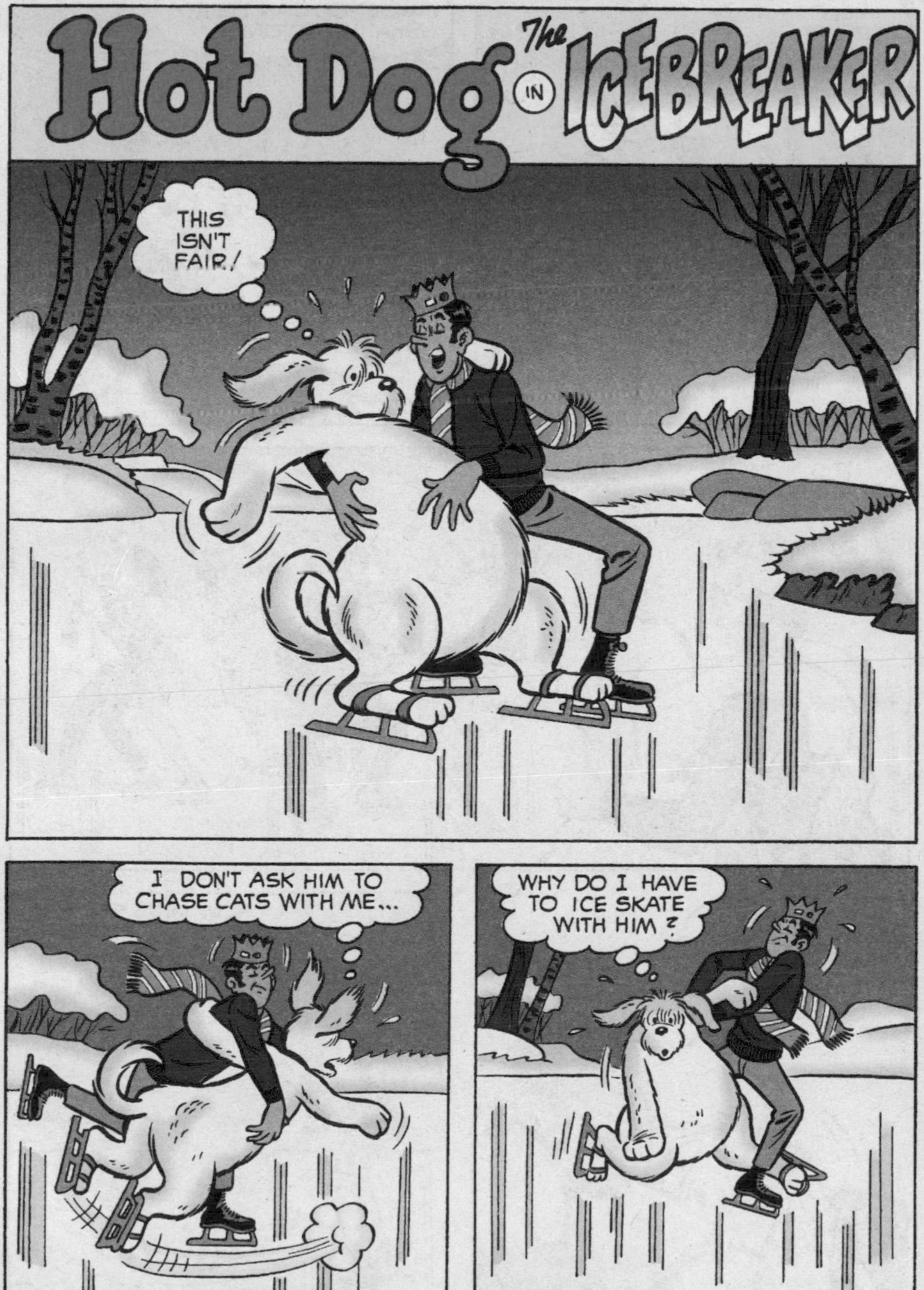
Hot Dog
IN
The ICEBREAKER
THIS ISN'T FAIR!
I DON'T ASK HIM TO CHASE CATS WITH ME...
WHY DO I HAVE TO ICE SKATE WITH HIM?

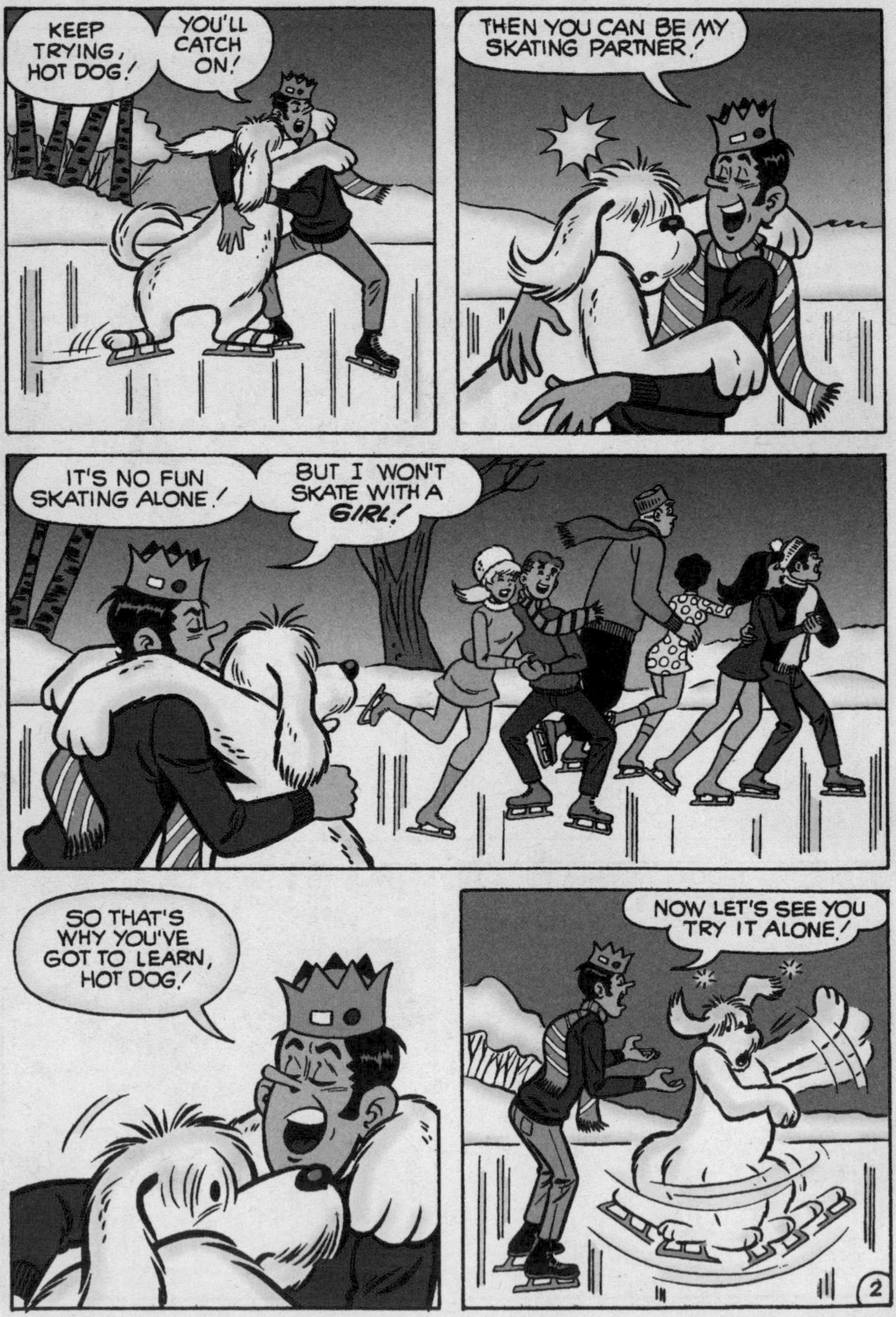
KEEP TRYING, HOT DOG!
YOU'LL CATCH ON!
THEN YOU CAN BE MY SKATING PARTNER!
IT'S NO FUN SKATING ALONE!
BUT I WON'T SKATE WITH A GIRL!
SO THAT'S WHY YOU'VE GOT TO LEARN, HOT DOG!
NOW LET'S SEE YOU TRY IT ALONE!
2

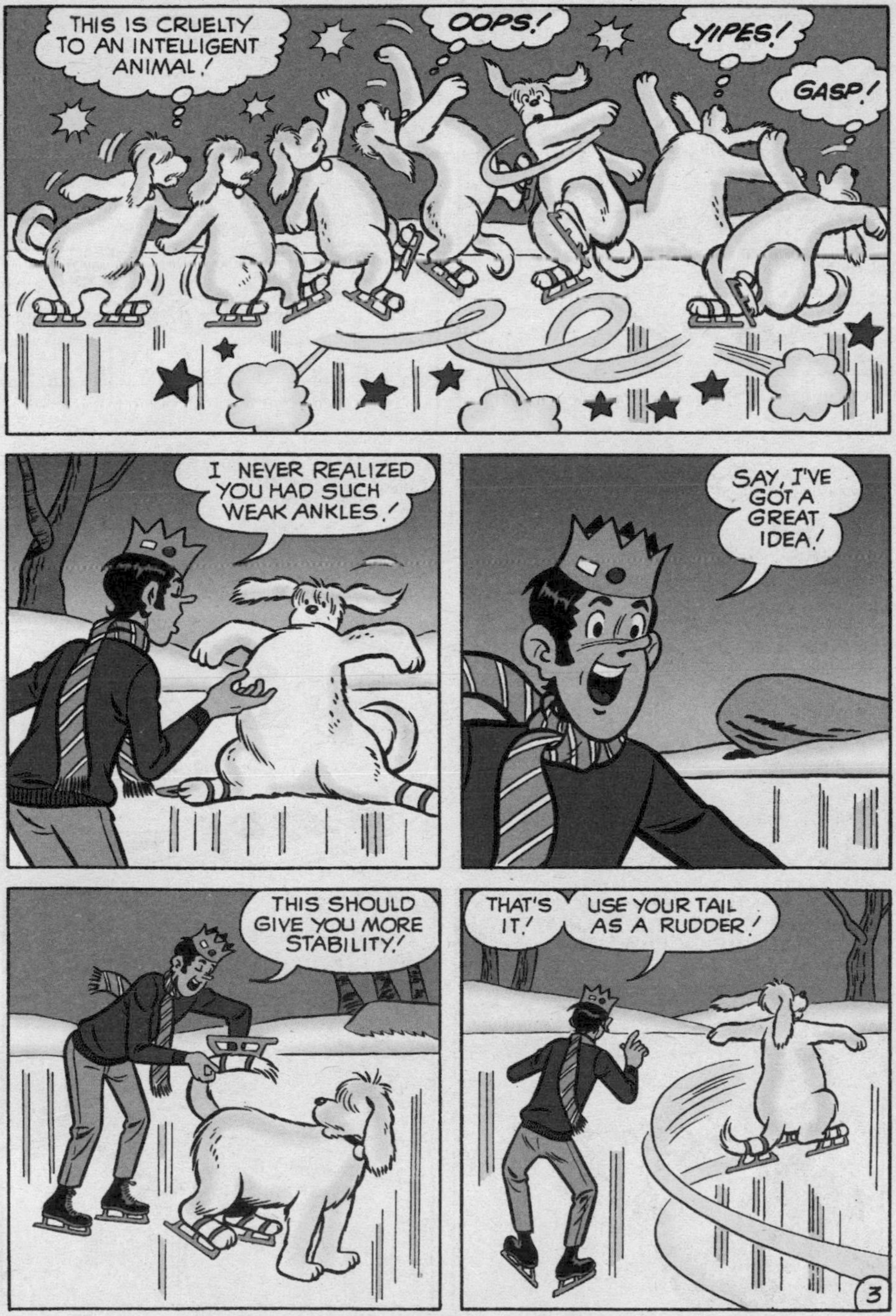
THIS IS CRUELTY TO AN INTELLIGENT ANIMAL!
OOPS!
YIPES!
GASP!
I NEVER REALIZED YOU HAD SUCH WEAK ANKLES!
SAY, I'VE GOT A GREAT IDEA!
THIS SHOULD GIVE YOU MORE STABILITY!
THAT'S IT!
USE YOUR TAIL AS A RUDDER!
3

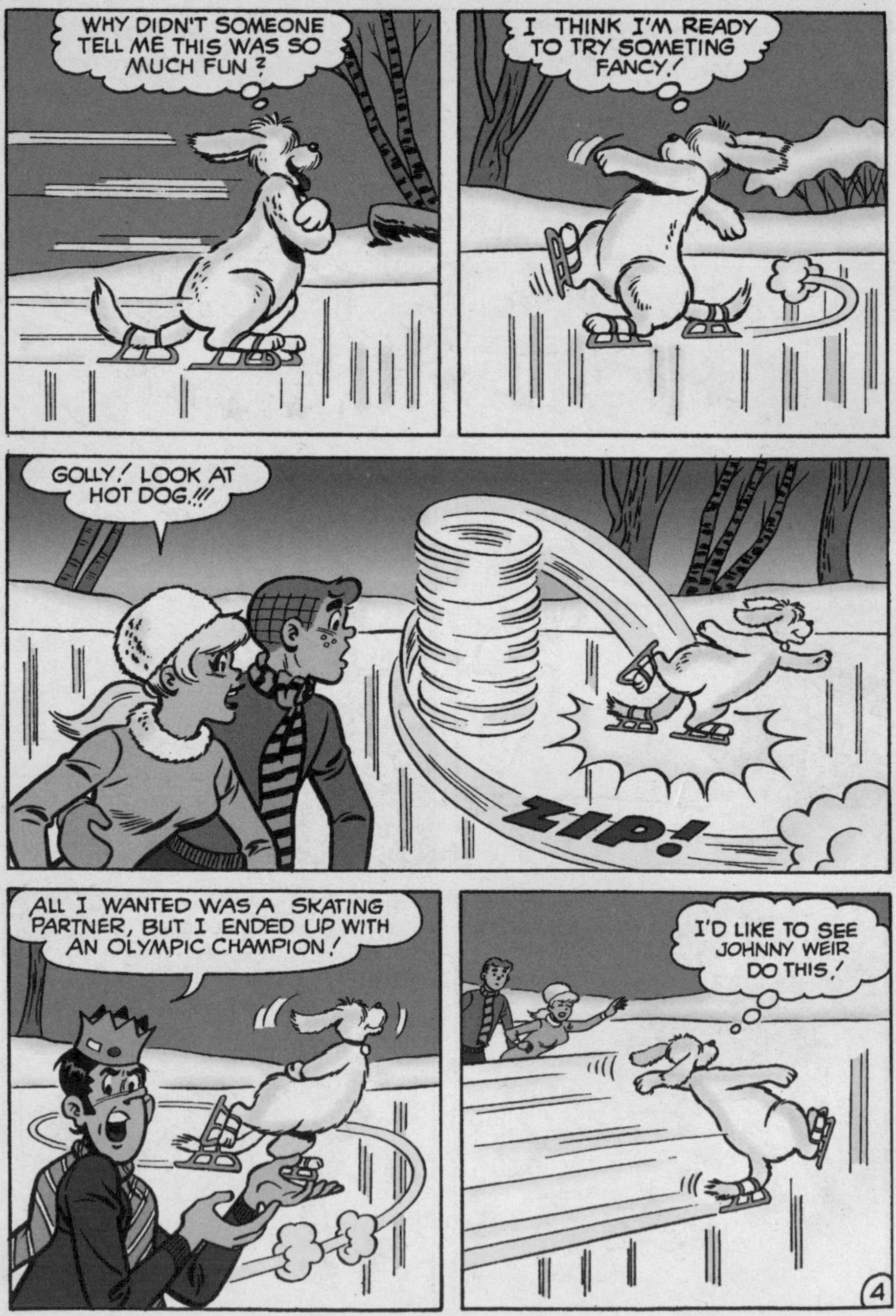
WHY DIDN'T SOMEONE TELL ME THIS WAS SO MUCH FUN?
I THINK I'M READY TO TRY SOMETING FANCY!
GOLLY! LOOK AT HOT DOG!!!
ZIP!
ALL I WANTED WAS A SKATING PARTNER, BUT I ENDED UP WITH AN OLYMPIC CHAMPION!
I'D LIKE TO SEE JOHNNY WEIR DO THIS!
4

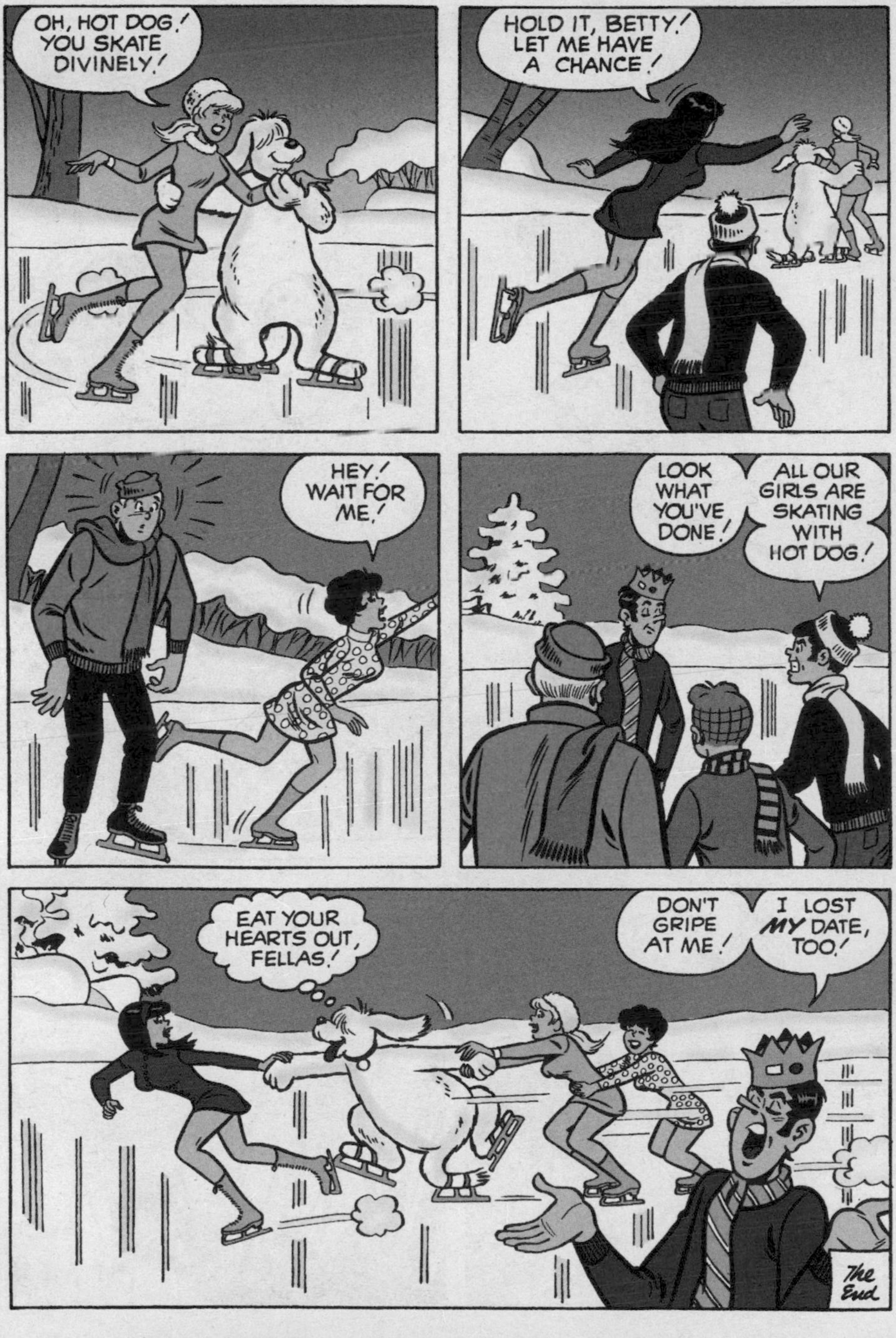
OH, HOT DOG! YOU SKATE DIVINELY!
HOLD IT, BETTY! LET ME HAVE A CHANCE!
HEY! WAIT FOR ME!
LOOK WHAT YOU'VE DONE!
ALL OUR GIRLS ARE SKATING WITH HOT DOG!
EAT YOUR HEARTS OUT, FELLAS!
DON'T GRIPE AT ME!
I LOST MY DATE, TOO!
The End

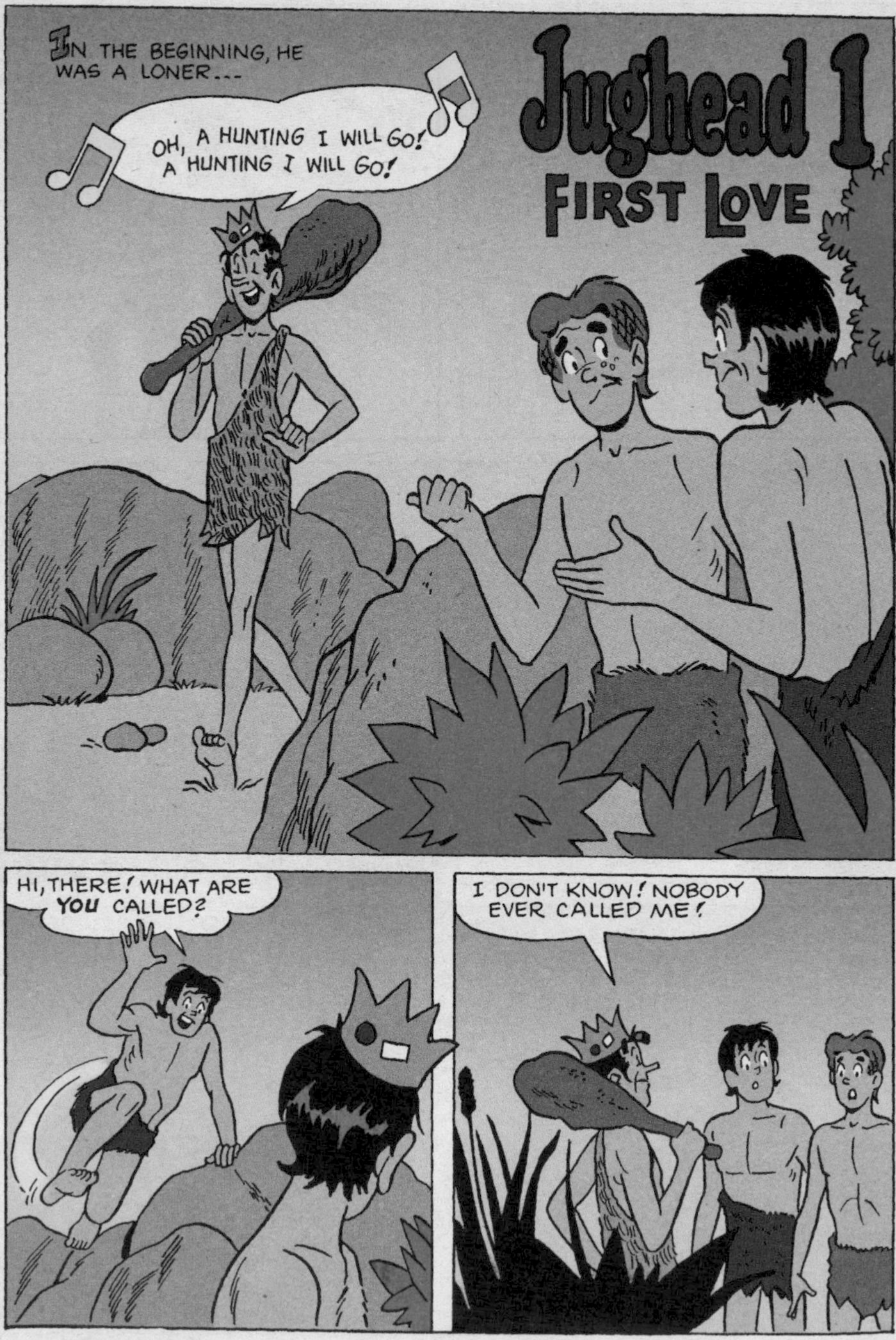
IN THE BEGINNING, HE WAS A LONER...
Jughead 1
FIRST LOVE
OH, A HUNTING I WILL GO! A HUNTING I WILL GO!
HI, THERE! WHAT ARE YOU CALLED?
I DON'T KNOW! NOBODY EVER CALLED ME!

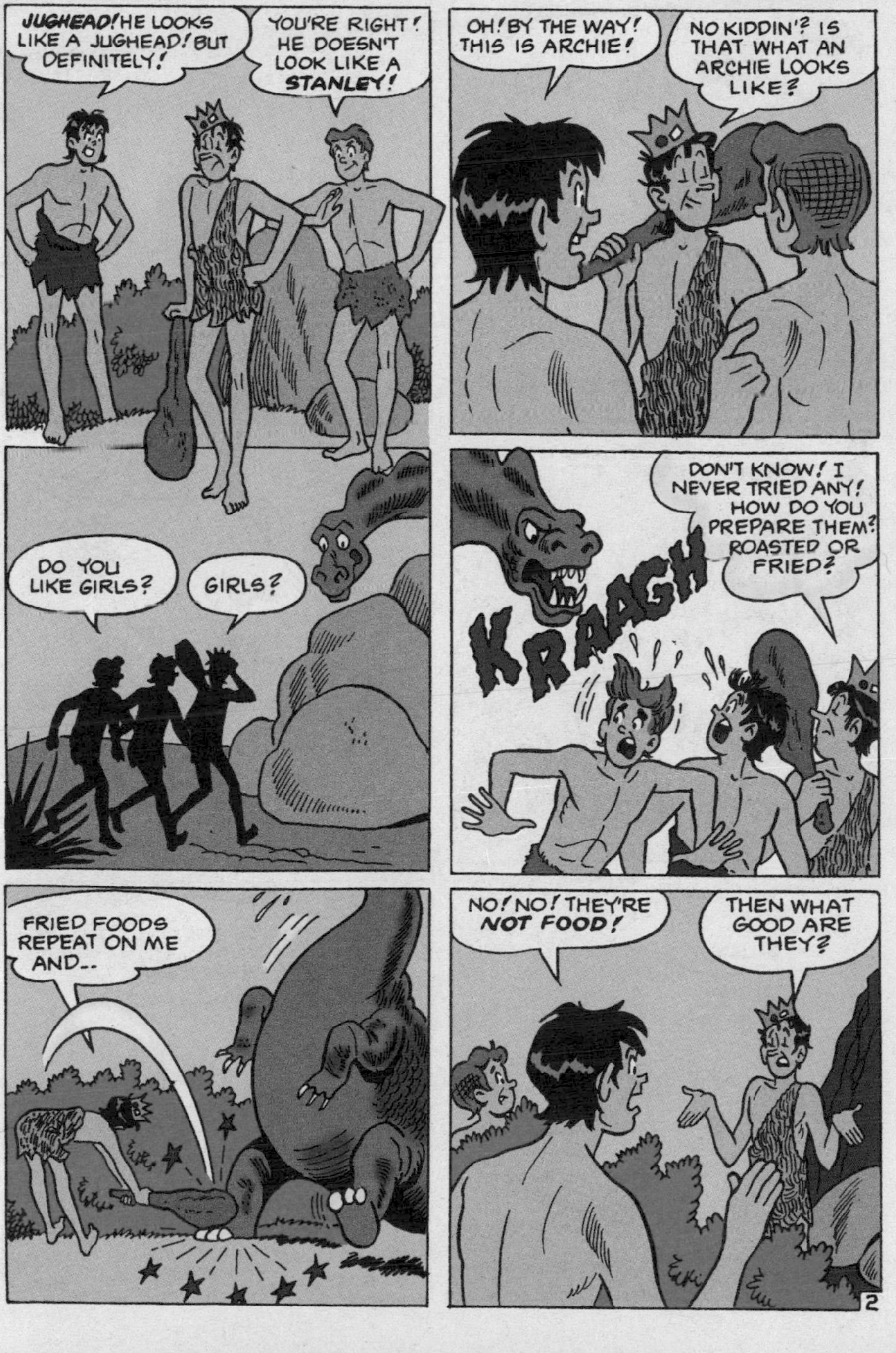
JUGHEAD! HE LOOKS LIKE A JUGHEAD! BUT DEFINITELY!
YOU'RE RIGHT! HE DOESN'T LOOK LIKE A STANLEY!
OH! BY THE WAY! THIS IS ARCHIE!
NO KIDDIN'? IS THAT WHAT AN ARCHIE LOOKS LIKE?
DO YOU LIKE GIRLS?
GIRLS?
KRAAGH
DON'T KNOW! I NEVER TRIED ANY! HOW DO YOU PREPARE THEM? ROASTED OR FRIED?
FRIED FOODS REPEAT ON ME AND..
NO! NO! THEY'RE NOT FOOD!
THEN WHAT GOOD ARE THEY?
2

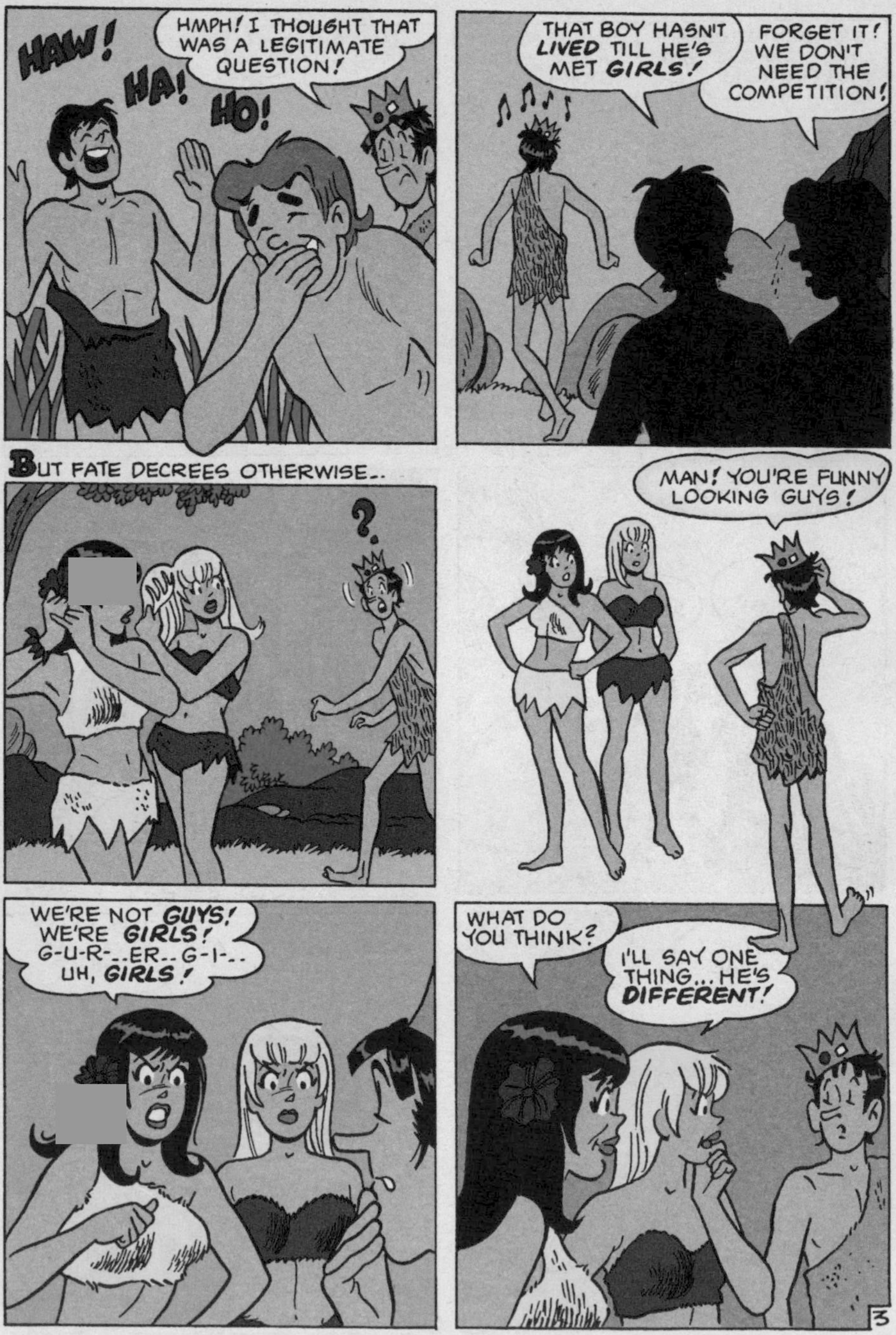
HAW!
HA!
HO!
HMPH! I THOUGHT THAT WAS A LEGITIMATE QUESTION!
THAT BOY HASN'T LIVED TILL HE'S MET GIRLS!
FORGET IT! WE DON'T NEED THE COMPETITION!
BUT FATE DECREES OTHERWISE..
?
MAN! YOU'RE FUNNY LOOKING GUYS!
WE'RE NOT GUYS! WE'RE GIRLS! G-U-R-..ER..G-I-.. UH, GIRLS!
WHAT DO YOU THINK?
I'LL SAY ONE THING... HE'S DIFFERENT!
3

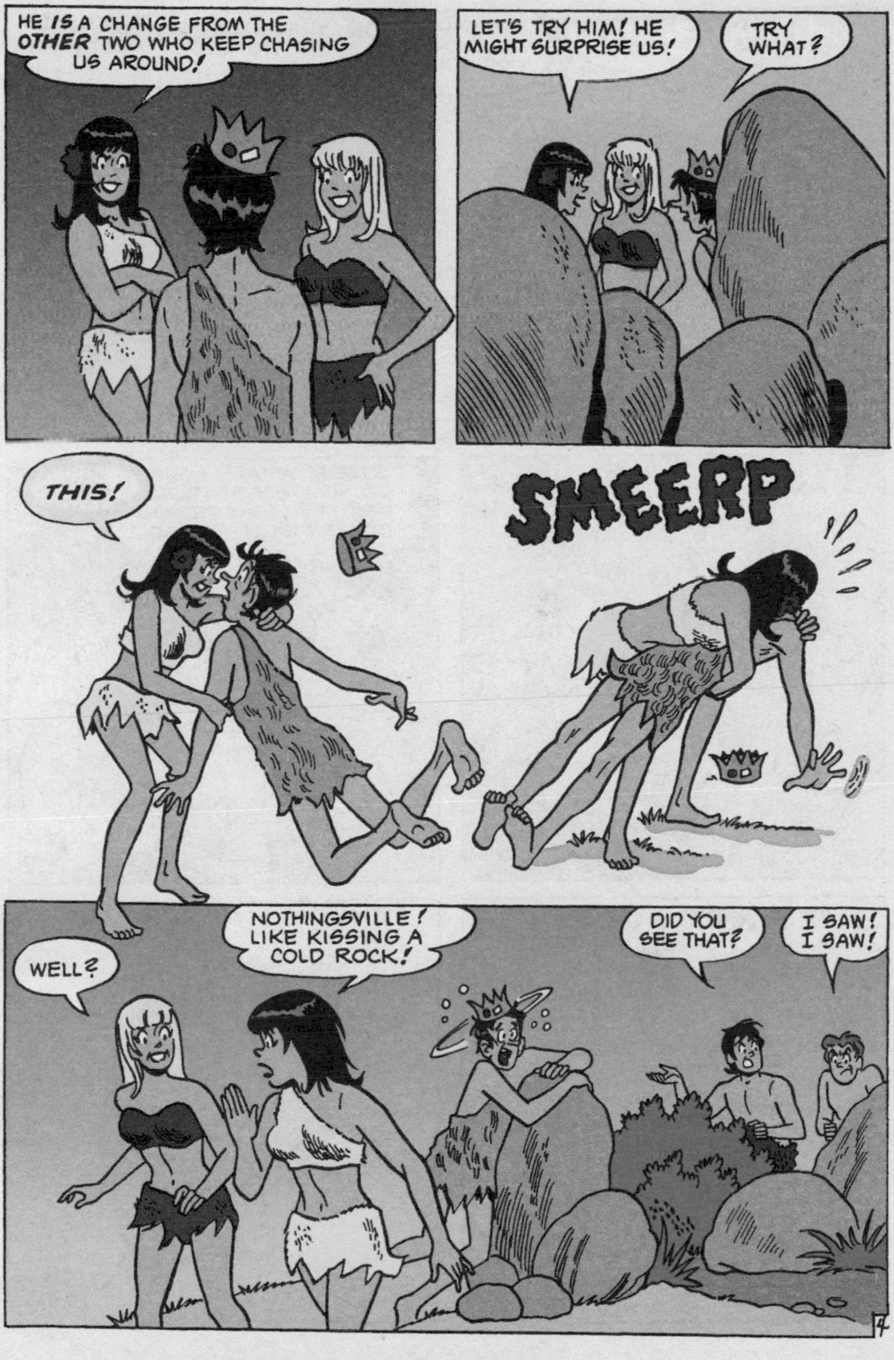
HE IS A CHANGE FROM THE OTHER TWO WHO KEEP CHASING US AROUND!
LET'S TRY HIM! HE MIGHT SURPRISE US!
TRY WHAT?
THIS!
SMEERP
WELL?
NOTHINGSVILLE! LIKE KISSING A COLD ROCK!
DID YOU SEE THAT?
I SAW! I SAW!
4

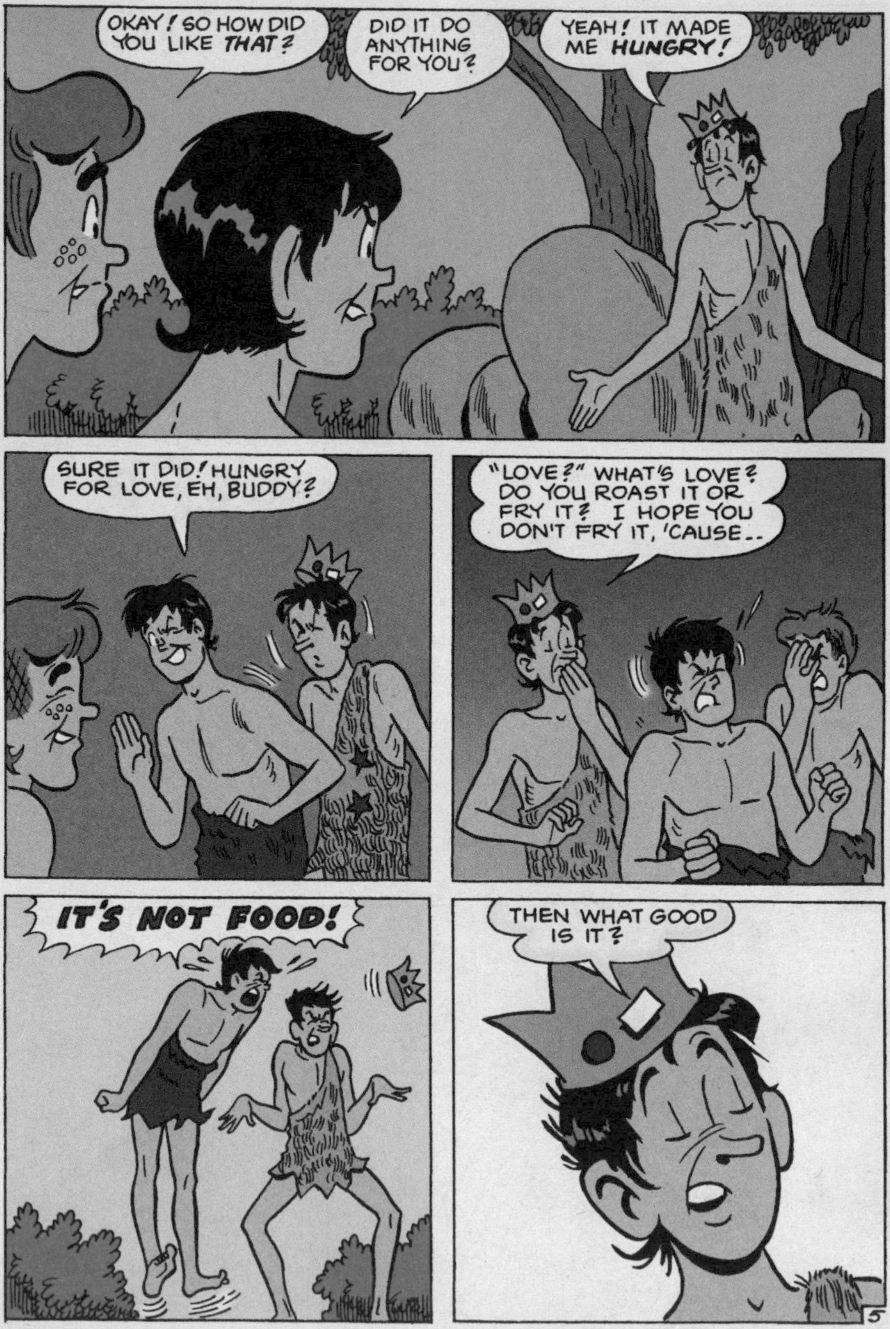
OKAY! SO HOW DID YOU LIKE THAT?
DID IT DO ANYTHING FOR YOU?
YEAH! IT MADE ME HUNGRY!
SURE IT DID! HUNGRY FOR LOVE, EH, BUDDY?
"LOVE?" WHAT'S LOVE? DO YOU ROAST IT OR FRY IT? I HOPE YOU DON'T FRY IT, 'CAUSE..
IT'S NOT FOOD!
THEN WHAT GOOD IS IT?

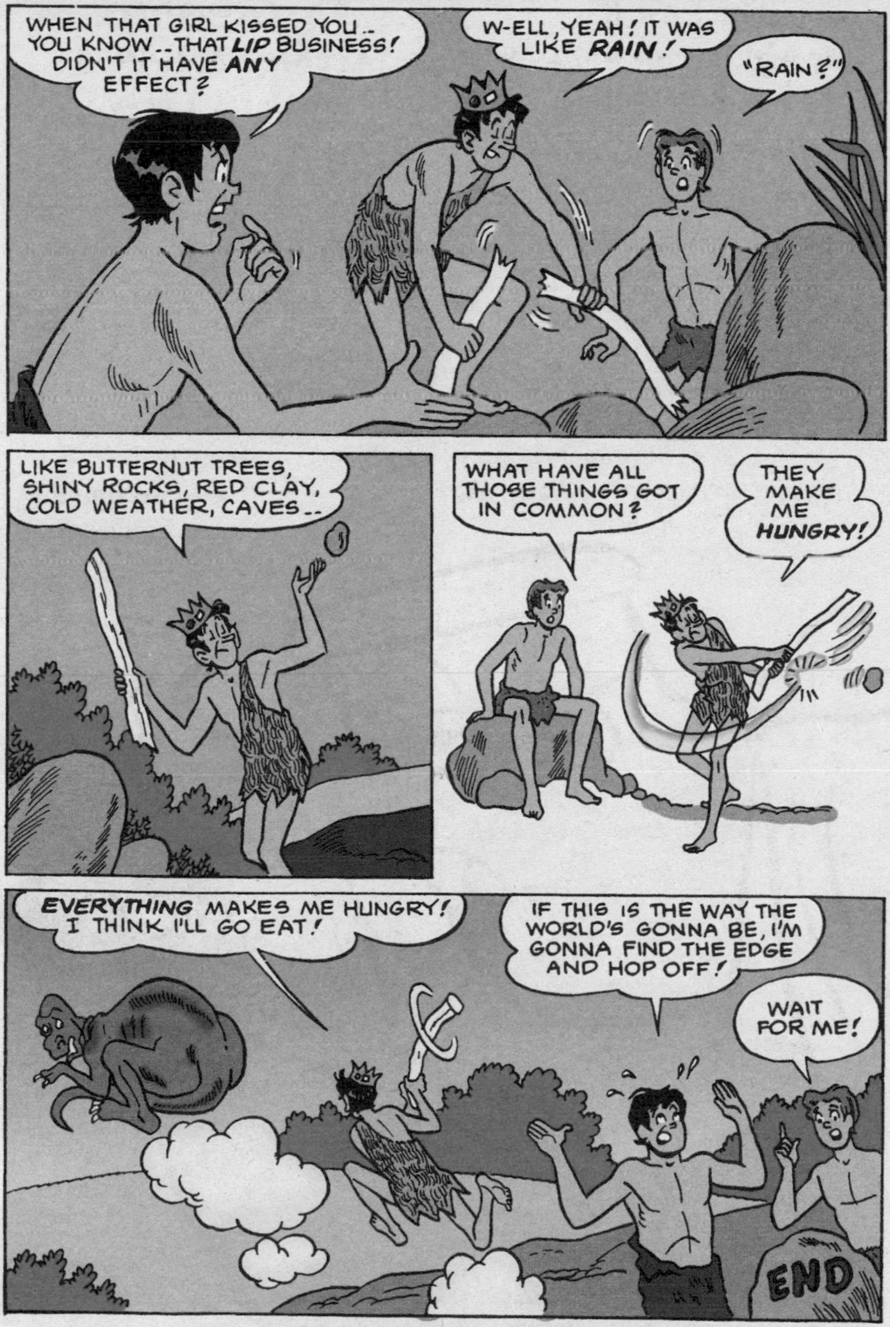
WHEN THAT GIRL KISSED YOU.. YOU KNOW..THAT LIP BUSINESS! DIDN'T IT HAVE ANY EFFECT?
W-ELL, YEAH! IT WAS LIKE RAIN!
"RAIN?"
LIKE BUTTERNUT TREES, SHINY ROCKS, RED CLAY, COLD WEATHER, CAVES..
WHAT HAVE ALL THOSE THINGS GOT IN COMMON?
THEY MAKE ME HUNGRY!
EVERYTHING MAKES ME HUNGRY! I THINK I'LL GO EAT!
IF THIS IS THE WAY THE WORLD'S GONNA BE, I'M GONNA FIND THE EDGE AND HOP OFF!
WAIT FOR ME!
END

The Last Kiss
Life with Archie #120, 1972
by Bob Bolling

Bob Bolling!!! This is an unusual Archie tale with beautiful, soft artwork. It's a sweet, romantic story that I think could happen in the real world—a great story for any hopeless romantic like me!

--Jack Copley
Official Archie Comics Historian

The Organizers
Archie #224, 1973
by Harry Lucey

Archie and Reggie hatch a scheme for the perfect dance at Riverdale High School.

Archie has always been the king. To have Betty and Veronica fight over him...endlessly... proves me right!

--Gene Simmons
Lead singer, KISS

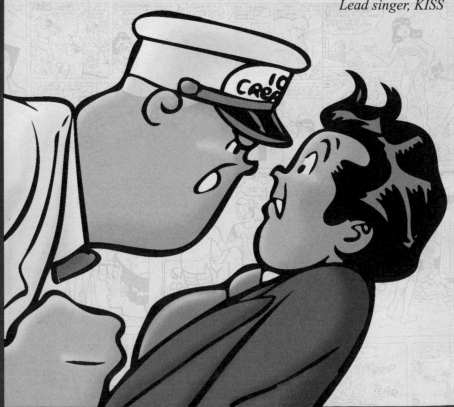

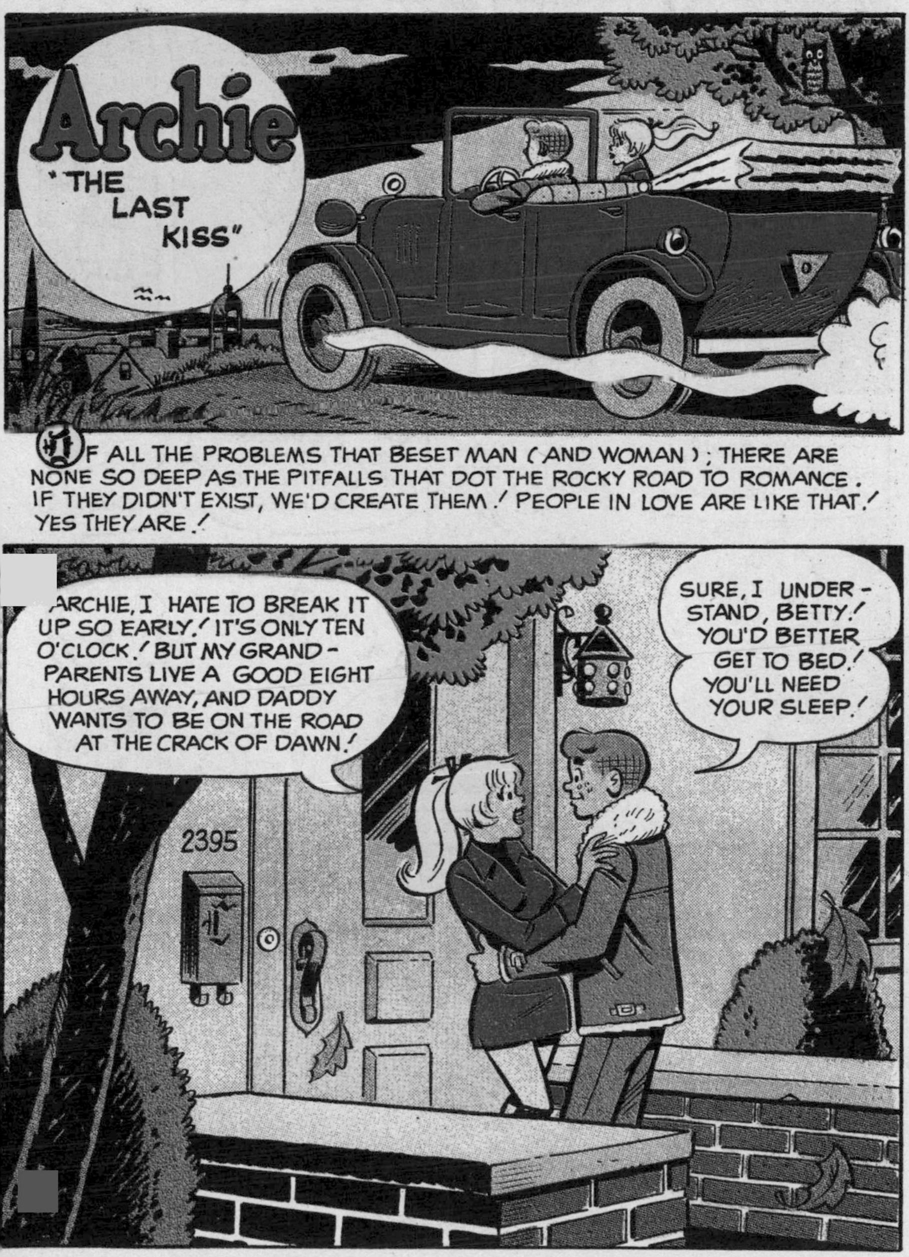
Archie
"THE LAST KISS"
OF ALL THE PROBLEMS THAT BESET MAN (AND WOMAN); THERE ARE NONE SO DEEP AS THE PITFALLS THAT DOT THE ROCKY ROAD TO ROMANCE. IF THEY DIDN'T EXIST, WE'D CREATE THEM! PEOPLE IN LOVE ARE LIKE THAT! YES THEY ARE!
ARCHIE, I HATE TO BREAK IT UP SO EARLY! IT'S ONLY TEN O'CLOCK! BUT MY GRAND-PARENTS LIVE A GOOD EIGHT HOURS AWAY, AND DADDY WANTS TO BE ON THE ROAD AT THE CRACK OF DAWN!
SURE, I UNDER-STAND, BETTY! YOU'D BETTER GET TO BED! YOU'LL NEED YOUR SLEEP!
2395

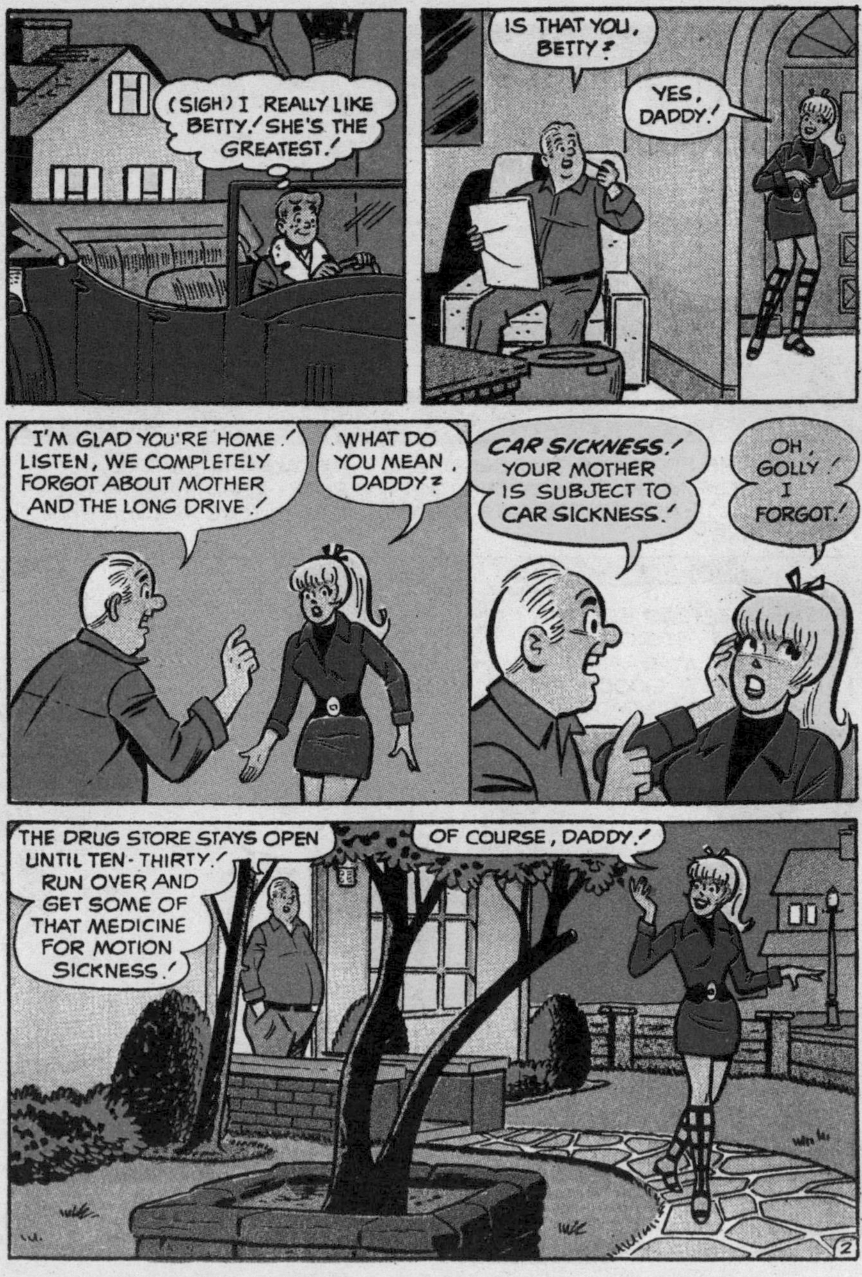
(SIGH) I REALLY LIKE BETTY! SHE'S THE GREATEST!
IS THAT YOU, BETTY?
YES, DADDY!
I'M GLAD YOU'RE HOME! LISTEN, WE COMPLETELY FORGOT ABOUT MOTHER AND THE LONG DRIVE!
WHAT DO YOU MEAN, DADDY?
CAR SICKNESS! YOUR MOTHER IS SUBJECT TO CAR SICKNESS!
OH, GOLLY! I FORGOT!
THE DRUG STORE STAYS OPEN UNTIL TEN-THIRTY! RUN OVER AND GET SOME OF THAT MEDICINE FOR MOTION SICKNESS!
OF COURSE, DADDY!
2

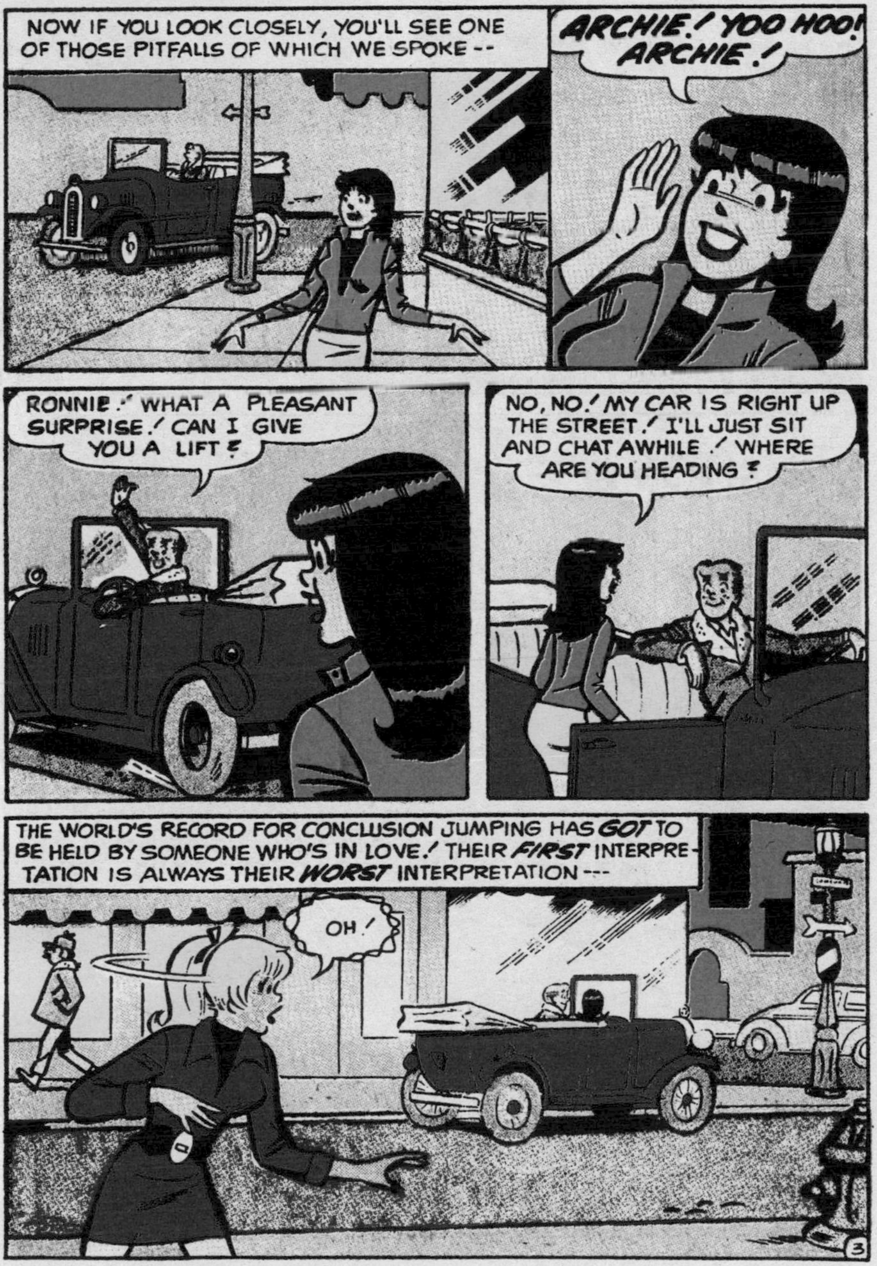
NOW IF YOU LOOK CLOSELY, YOU'LL SEE ONE OF THOSE PITFALLS OF WHICH WE SPOKE --
ARCHIE.! YOO HOO! ARCHIE.!
RONNIE.! WHAT A PLEASANT SURPRISE.! CAN I GIVE YOU A LIFT?
NO, NO.! MY CAR IS RIGHT UP THE STREET.! I'LL JUST SIT AND CHAT AWHILE.! WHERE ARE YOU HEADING?
THE WORLD'S RECORD FOR CONCLUSION JUMPING HAS GOT TO BE HELD BY SOMEONE WHO'S IN LOVE.! THEIR FIRST INTERPRETATION IS ALWAYS THEIR WORST INTERPRETATION ---
OH!
3

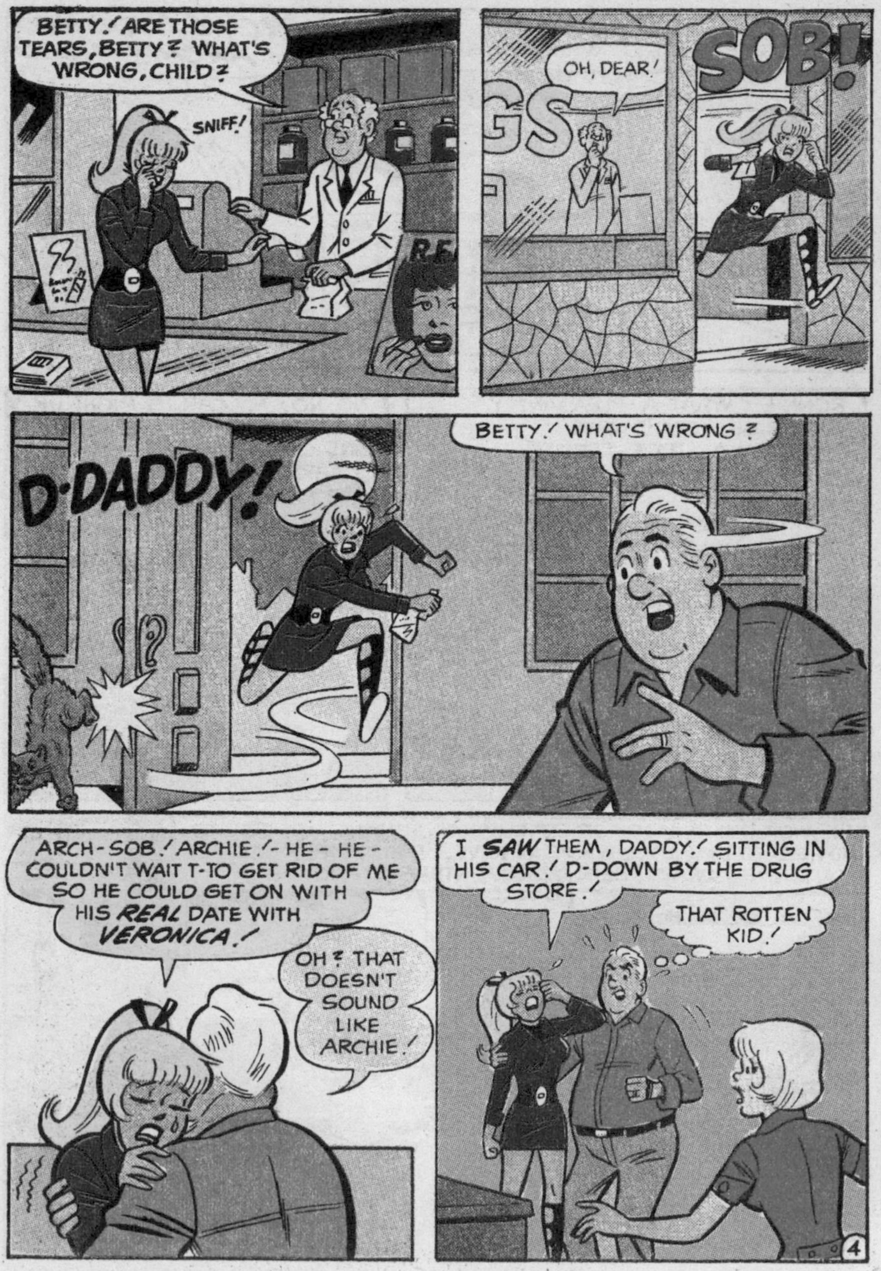
BETTY! ARE THOSE TEARS, BETTY? WHAT'S WRONG, CHILD?
SNIFF!
OH, DEAR!
SOB!
D-DADDY!
BETTY! WHAT'S WRONG?
ARCH-SOB! ARCHIE!- HE - HE - COULDN'T WAIT T-TO GET RID OF ME SO HE COULD GET ON WITH HIS REAL DATE WITH VERONICA!
OH? THAT DOESN'T SOUND LIKE ARCHIE!
I SAW THEM, DADDY! SITTING IN HIS CAR! D-DOWN BY THE DRUG STORE!
THAT ROTTEN KID!
4

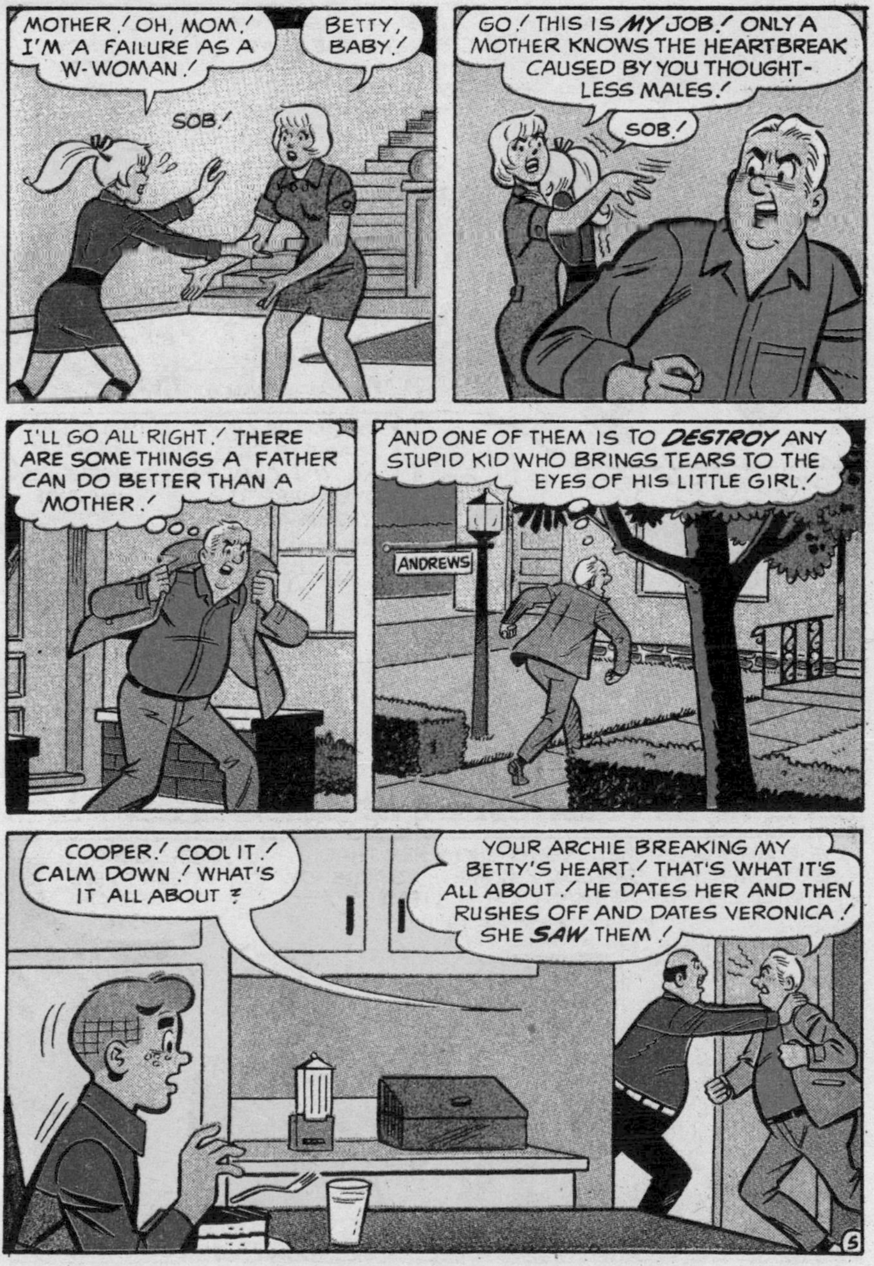
MOTHER! OH, MOM! I'M A FAILURE AS A W-WOMAN!
BETTY, BABY!
SOB!
GO! THIS IS MY JOB! ONLY A MOTHER KNOWS THE HEARTBREAK CAUSED BY YOU THOUGHT-LESS MALES!
SOB!
I'LL GO ALL RIGHT! THERE ARE SOME THINGS A FATHER CAN DO BETTER THAN A MOTHER!
AND ONE OF THEM IS TO DESTROY ANY STUPID KID WHO BRINGS TEARS TO THE EYES OF HIS LITTLE GIRL!
ANDREWS
COOPER! COOL IT! CALM DOWN! WHAT'S IT ALL ABOUT?
YOUR ARCHIE BREAKING MY BETTY'S HEART! THAT'S WHAT IT'S ALL ABOUT! HE DATES HER AND THEN RUSHES OFF AND DATES VERONICA! SHE SAW THEM!
5

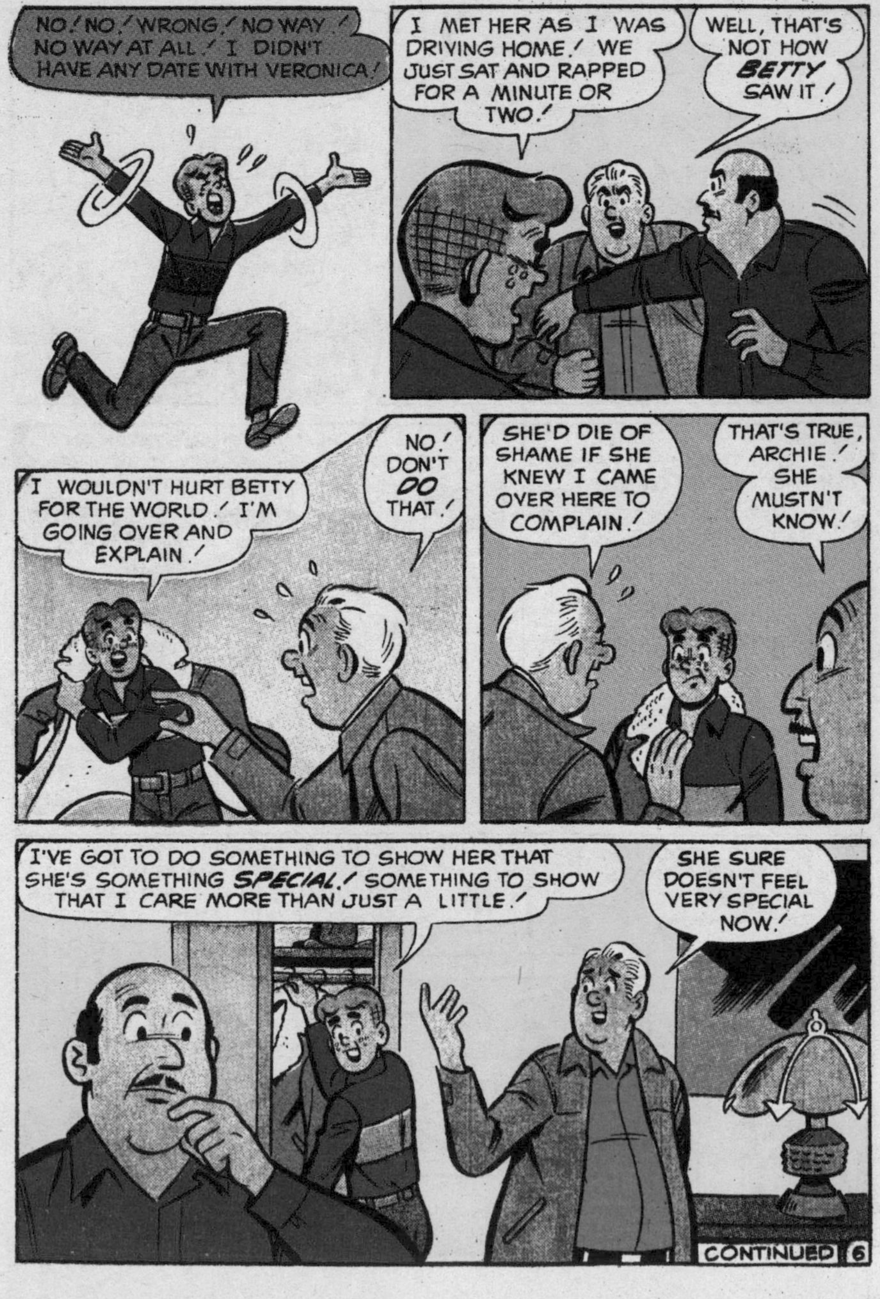
NO! NO! WRONG! NO WAY! NO WAY AT ALL! I DIDN'T HAVE ANY DATE WITH VERONICA!
I MET HER AS I WAS DRIVING HOME! WE JUST SAT AND RAPPED FOR A MINUTE OR TWO!
WELL, THAT'S NOT HOW BETTY SAW IT!
I WOULDN'T HURT BETTY FOR THE WORLD! I'M GOING OVER AND EXPLAIN!
NO! DON'T DO THAT!
SHE'D DIE OF SHAME IF SHE KNEW I CAME OVER HERE TO COMPLAIN!
THAT'S TRUE, ARCHIE! SHE MUSTN'T KNOW!
I'VE GOT TO DO SOMETHING TO SHOW HER THAT SHE'S SOMETHING SPECIAL! SOMETHING TO SHOW THAT I CARE MORE THAN JUST A LITTLE!
SHE SURE DOESN'T FEEL VERY SPECIAL NOW!
CONTINUED 6

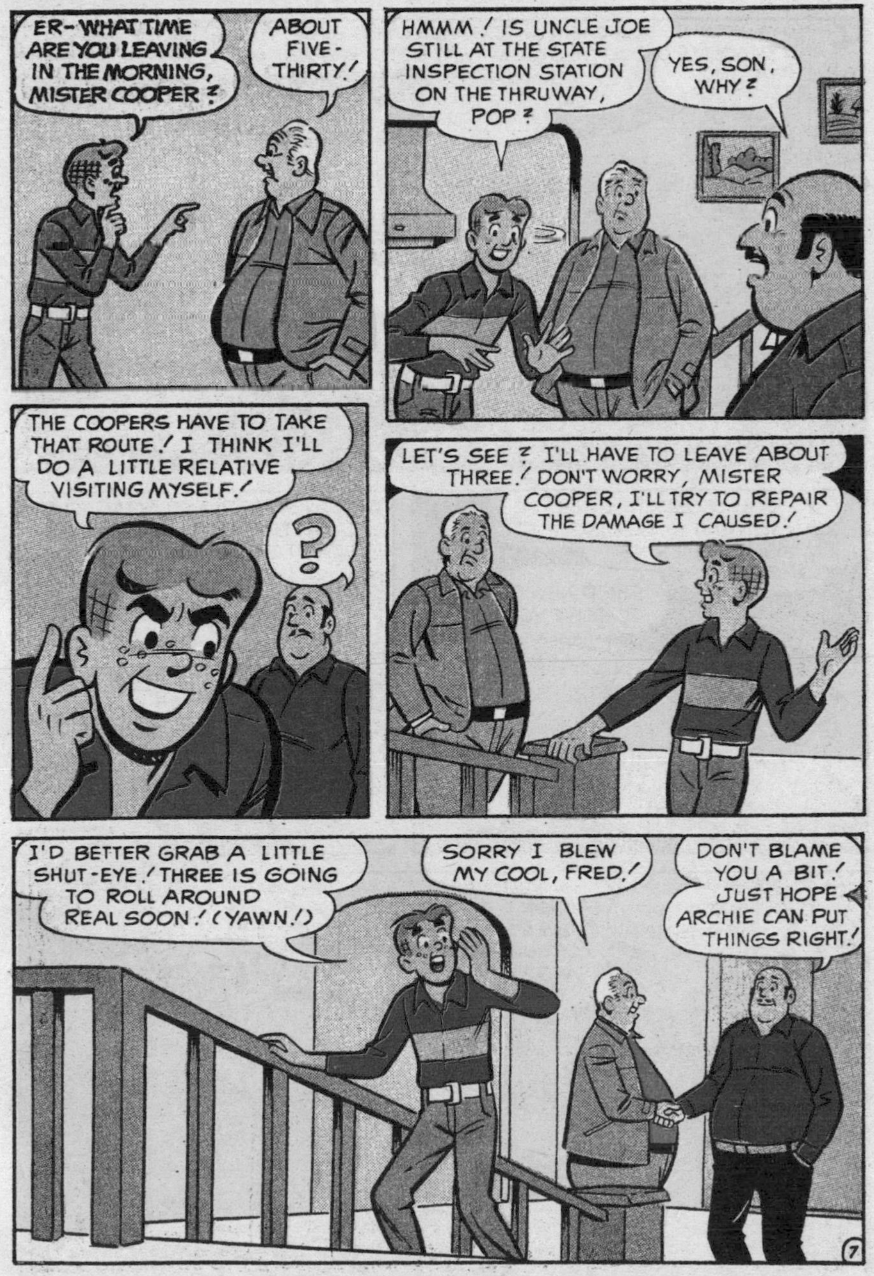
ER- WHAT TIME ARE YOU LEAVING IN THE MORNING, MISTER COOPER ?
ABOUT FIVE-THIRTY!
HMMM! IS UNCLE JOE STILL AT THE STATE INSPECTION STATION ON THE THRUWAY, POP ?
YES, SON, WHY ?
THE COOPERS HAVE TO TAKE THAT ROUTE! I THINK I'LL DO A LITTLE RELATIVE VISITING MYSELF!
?
LET'S SEE ? I'LL HAVE TO LEAVE ABOUT THREE! DON'T WORRY, MISTER COOPER, I'LL TRY TO REPAIR THE DAMAGE I CAUSED!
I'D BETTER GRAB A LITTLE SHUT-EYE! THREE IS GOING TO ROLL AROUND REAL SOON! (YAWN!)
SORRY I BLEW MY COOL, FRED!
DON'T BLAME YOU A BIT! JUST HOPE ARCHIE CAN PUT THINGS RIGHT!
7

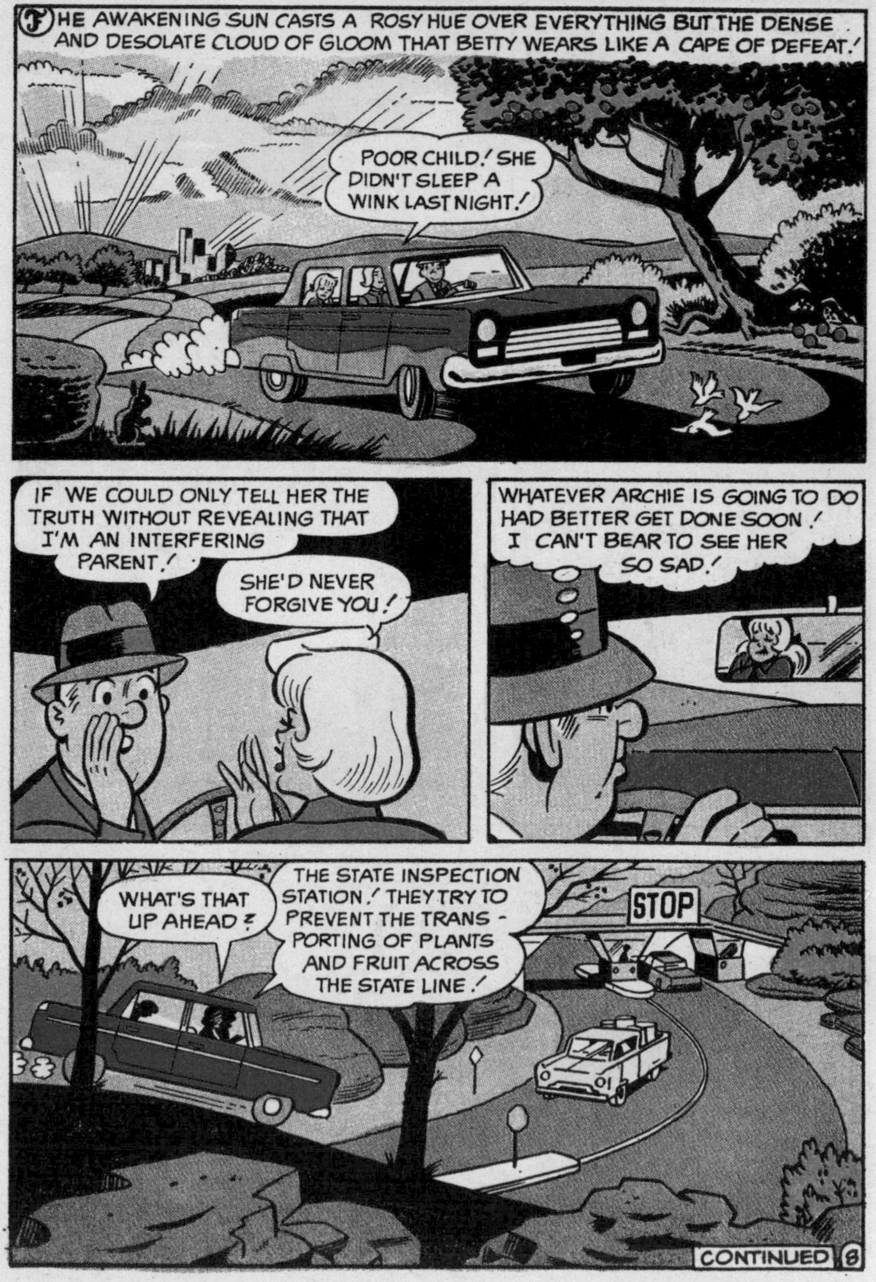
THE AWAKENING SUN CASTS A ROSY HUE OVER EVERYTHING BUT THE DENSE AND DESOLATE CLOUD OF GLOOM THAT BETTY WEARS LIKE A CAPE OF DEFEAT!
POOR CHILD! SHE DIDN'T SLEEP A WINK LAST NIGHT!
IF WE COULD ONLY TELL HER THE TRUTH WITHOUT REVEALING THAT I'M AN INTERFERING PARENT!
SHE'D NEVER FORGIVE YOU!
WHATEVER ARCHIE IS GOING TO DO HAD BETTER GET DONE SOON! I CAN'T BEAR TO SEE HER SO SAD!
WHAT'S THAT UP AHEAD?
THE STATE INSPECTION STATION! THEY TRY TO PREVENT THE TRANS - PORTING OF PLANTS AND FRUIT ACROSS THE STATE LINE!
STOP
CONTINUED
8

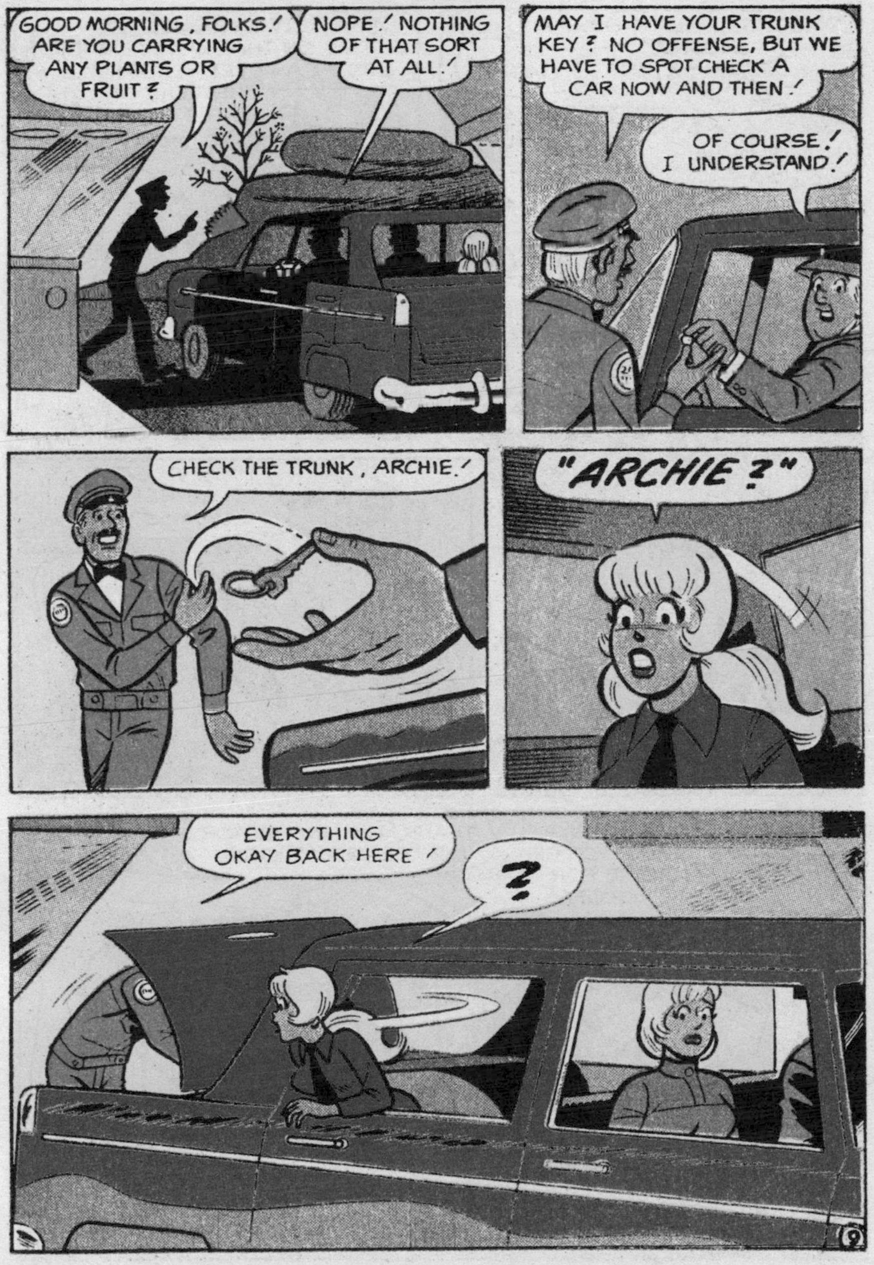
GOOD MORNING, FOLKS! ARE YOU CARRYING ANY PLANTS OR FRUIT?
NOPE! NOTHING OF THAT SORT AT ALL!
MAY I HAVE YOUR TRUNK KEY? NO OFFENSE, BUT WE HAVE TO SPOT CHECK A CAR NOW AND THEN!
OF COURSE! I UNDERSTAND!
CHECK THE TRUNK, ARCHIE!
"ARCHIE?"
EVERYTHING OKAY BACK HERE!
?
9

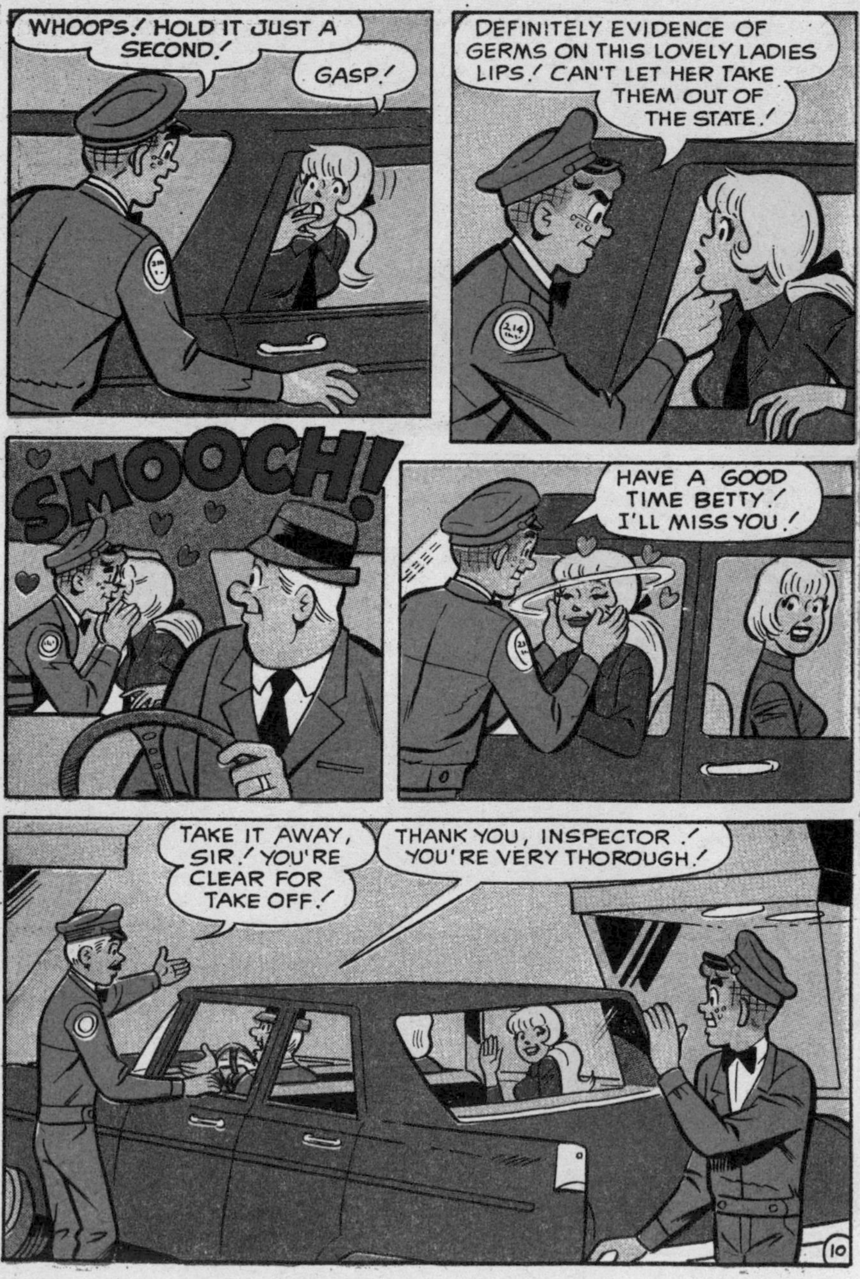
WHOOPS! HOLD IT JUST A SECOND!
GASP!
DEFINITELY EVIDENCE OF GERMS ON THIS LOVELY LADIES LIPS! CAN'T LET HER TAKE THEM OUT OF THE STATE!
SMOOCH!
HAVE A GOOD TIME BETTY! I'LL MISS YOU!
TAKE IT AWAY, SIR! YOU'RE CLEAR FOR TAKE OFF!
THANK YOU, INSPECTOR! YOU'RE VERY THOROUGH!
10

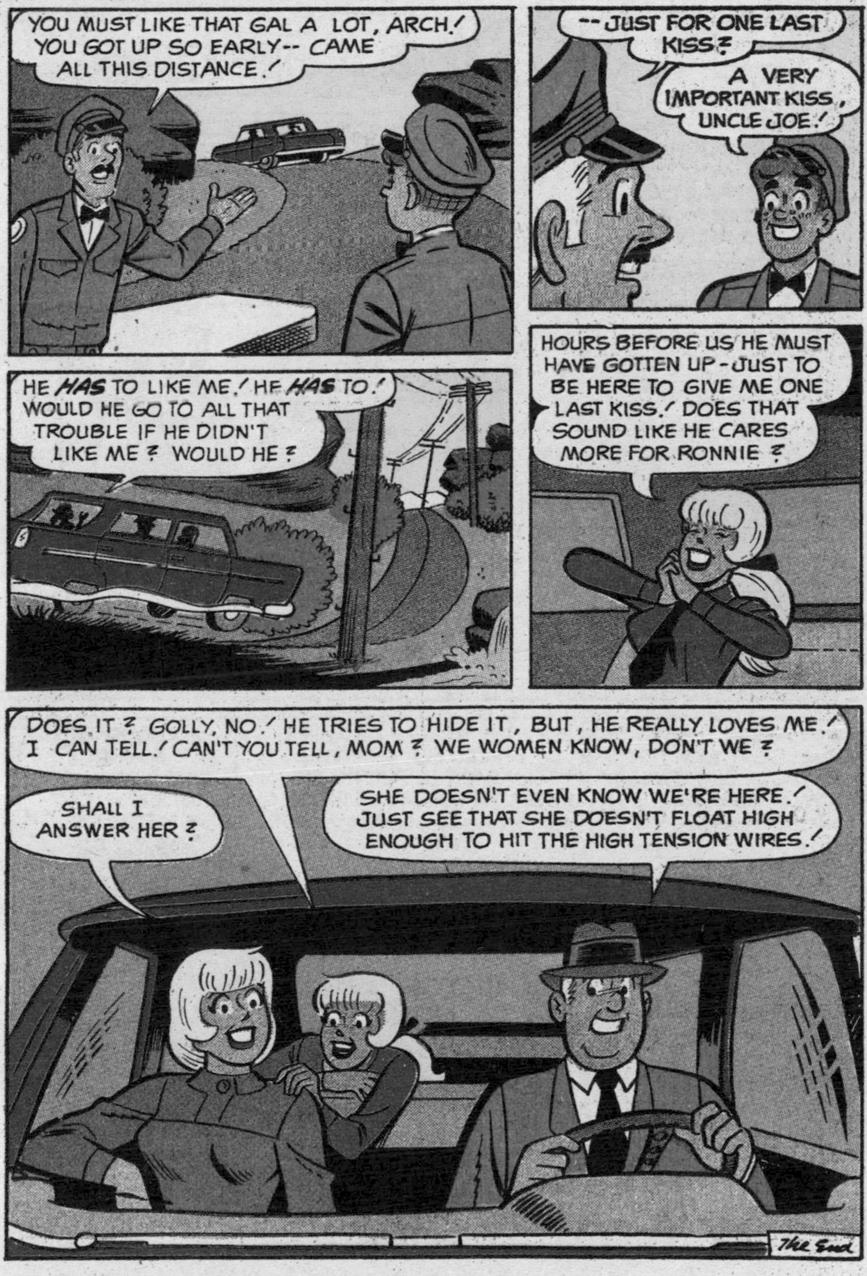
YOU MUST LIKE THAT GAL A LOT, ARCH! YOU GOT UP SO EARLY-- CAME ALL THIS DISTANCE!
-- JUST FOR ONE LAST KISS?
A VERY IMPORTANT KISS, UNCLE JOE!
HE HAS TO LIKE ME! HE HAS TO! WOULD HE GO TO ALL THAT TROUBLE IF HE DIDN'T LIKE ME? WOULD HE?
HOURS BEFORE US HE MUST HAVE GOTTEN UP - JUST TO BE HERE TO GIVE ME ONE LAST KISS! DOES THAT SOUND LIKE HE CARES MORE FOR RONNIE?
DOES IT? GOLLY, NO! HE TRIES TO HIDE IT, BUT, HE REALLY LOVES ME! I CAN TELL! CAN'T YOU TELL, MOM? WE WOMEN KNOW, DON'T WE?
SHALL I ANSWER HER?
SHE DOESN'T EVEN KNOW WE'RE HERE! JUST SEE THAT SHE DOESN'T FLOAT HIGH ENOUGH TO HIT THE HIGH TENSION WIRES!
The End

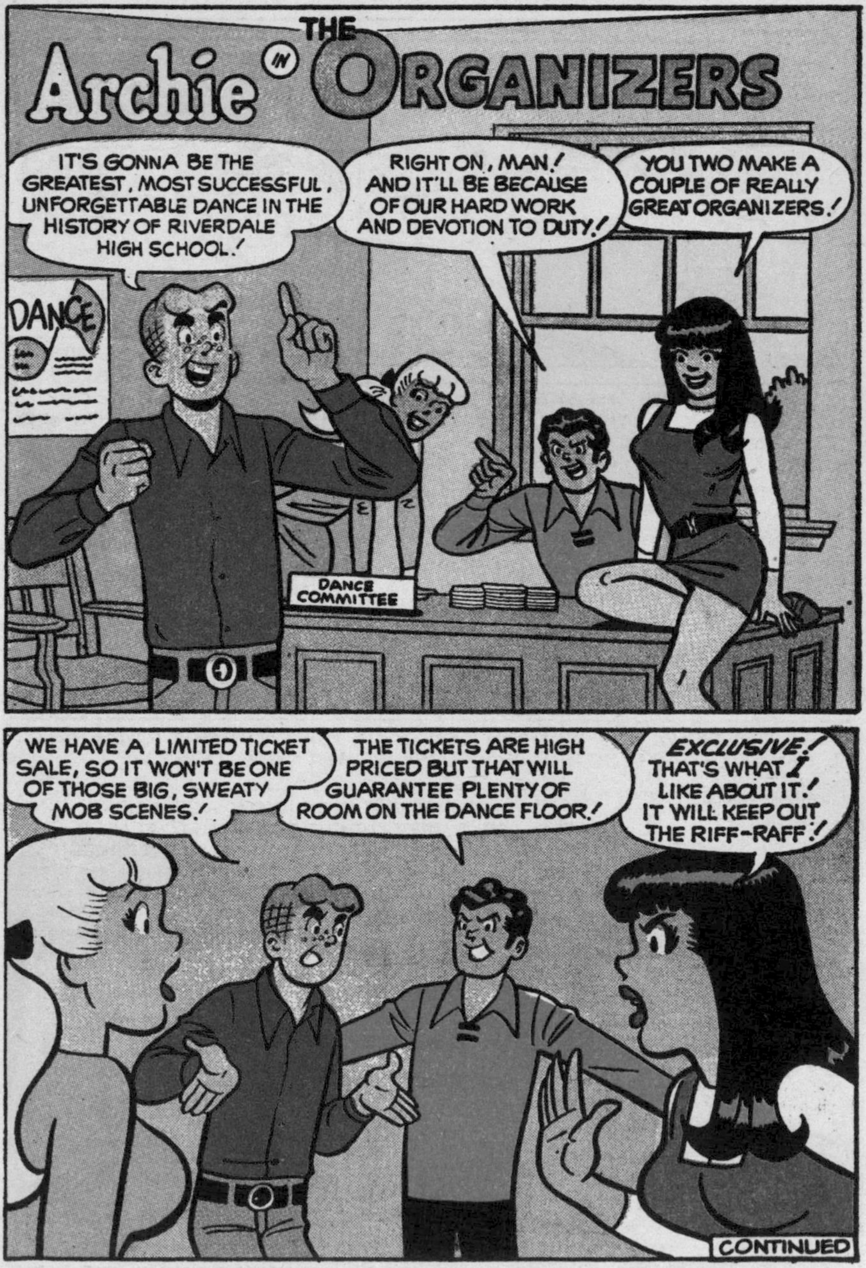
Archie in THE ORGANIZERS
IT'S GONNA BE THE GREATEST, MOST SUCCESSFUL, UNFORGETTABLE DANCE IN THE HISTORY OF RIVERDALE HIGH SCHOOL!
RIGHT ON, MAN! AND IT'LL BE BECAUSE OF OUR HARD WORK AND DEVOTION TO DUTY!
YOU TWO MAKE A COUPLE OF REALLY GREAT ORGANIZERS!
DANCE
DANCE COMMITTEE
WE HAVE A LIMITED TICKET SALE, SO IT WON'T BE ONE OF THOSE BIG, SWEATY MOB SCENES!
THE TICKETS ARE HIGH PRICED BUT THAT WILL GUARANTEE PLENTY OF ROOM ON THE DANCE FLOOR!
EXCLUSIVE! THAT'S WHAT I LIKE ABOUT IT! IT WILL KEEP OUT THE RIFF-RAFF!
CONTINUED

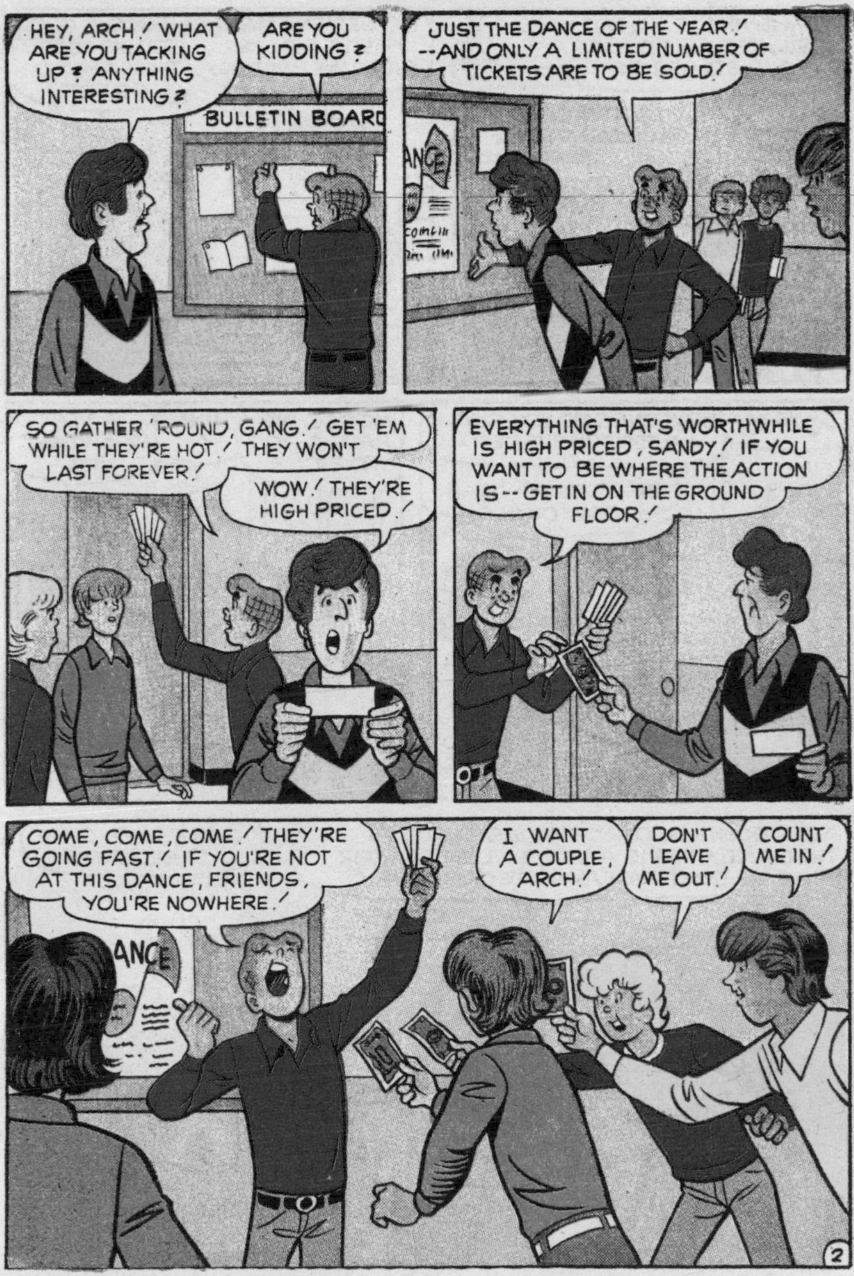
HEY, ARCH! WHAT ARE YOU TACKING UP? ANYTHING INTERESTING?
ARE YOU KIDDING?
BULLETIN BOARD
JUST THE DANCE OF THE YEAR! --AND ONLY A LIMITED NUMBER OF TICKETS ARE TO BE SOLD!
SO GATHER 'ROUND, GANG! GET 'EM WHILE THEY'RE HOT! THEY WON'T LAST FOREVER!
WOW! THEY'RE HIGH PRICED!
EVERYTHING THAT'S WORTHWHILE IS HIGH PRICED, SANDY! IF YOU WANT TO BE WHERE THE ACTION IS--GET IN ON THE GROUND FLOOR!
COME, COME, COME! THEY'RE GOING FAST! IF YOU'RE NOT AT THIS DANCE, FRIENDS, YOU'RE NOWHERE!
I WANT A COUPLE, ARCH!
DON'T LEAVE ME OUT!
COUNT ME IN!
2

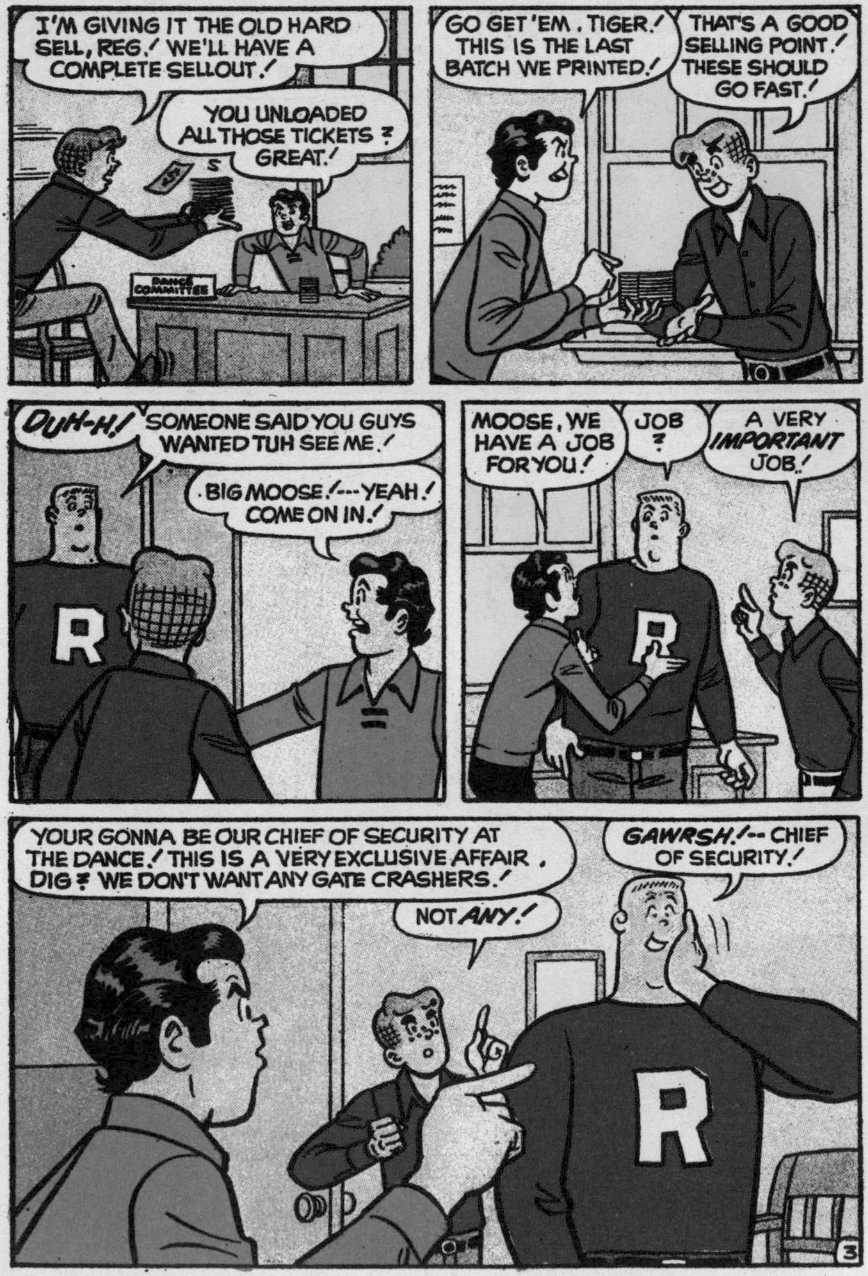
I'M GIVING IT THE OLD HARD SELL, REG.! WE'LL HAVE A COMPLETE SELLOUT!
YOU UNLOADED ALL THOSE TICKETS? GREAT!
DANCE COMMITTEE
GO GET 'EM, TIGER! THIS IS THE LAST BATCH WE PRINTED!
THAT'S A GOOD SELLING POINT! THESE SHOULD GO FAST!
DUH-H!
SOMEONE SAID YOU GUYS WANTED TUH SEE ME!
BIG MOOSE!--- YEAH! COME ON IN!
MOOSE, WE HAVE A JOB FOR YOU!
JOB?
A VERY *IMPORTANT* JOB!
YOUR GONNA BE OUR CHIEF OF SECURITY AT THE DANCE! THIS IS A VERY EXCLUSIVE AFFAIR, DIG? WE DON'T WANT ANY GATE CRASHERS!
NOT *ANY*!
GAWRSH!-- CHIEF OF SECURITY!
3

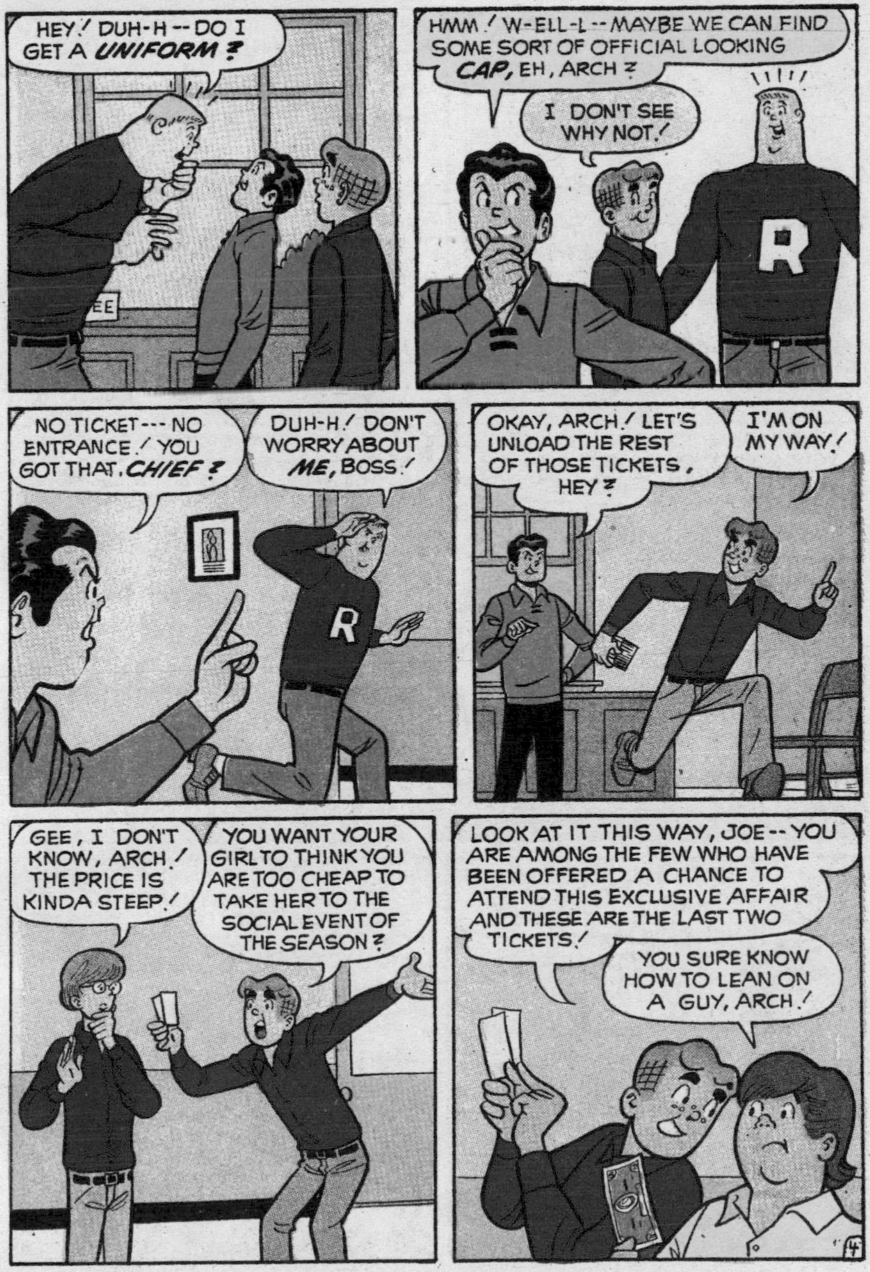
HEY! DUH-H -- DO I GET A *UNIFORM* ?
HMM! W-ELL-L -- MAYBE WE CAN FIND SOME SORT OF OFFICIAL LOOKING *CAP*, EH, ARCH ?
I DON'T SEE WHY NOT!
NO TICKET --- NO ENTRANCE! YOU GOT THAT, *CHIEF* ?
DUH-H! DON'T WORRY ABOUT *ME*, BOSS!
OKAY, ARCH! LET'S UNLOAD THE REST OF THOSE TICKETS, HEY ?
I'M ON MY WAY!
GEE, I DON'T KNOW, ARCH! THE PRICE IS KINDA STEEP!
YOU WANT YOUR GIRL TO THINK YOU ARE TOO CHEAP TO TAKE HER TO THE SOCIAL EVENT OF THE SEASON ?
LOOK AT IT THIS WAY, JOE -- YOU ARE AMONG THE FEW WHO HAVE BEEN OFFERED A CHANCE TO ATTEND THIS EXCLUSIVE AFFAIR AND THESE ARE THE LAST TWO TICKETS!
YOU SURE KNOW HOW TO LEAN ON A GUY, ARCH!
4

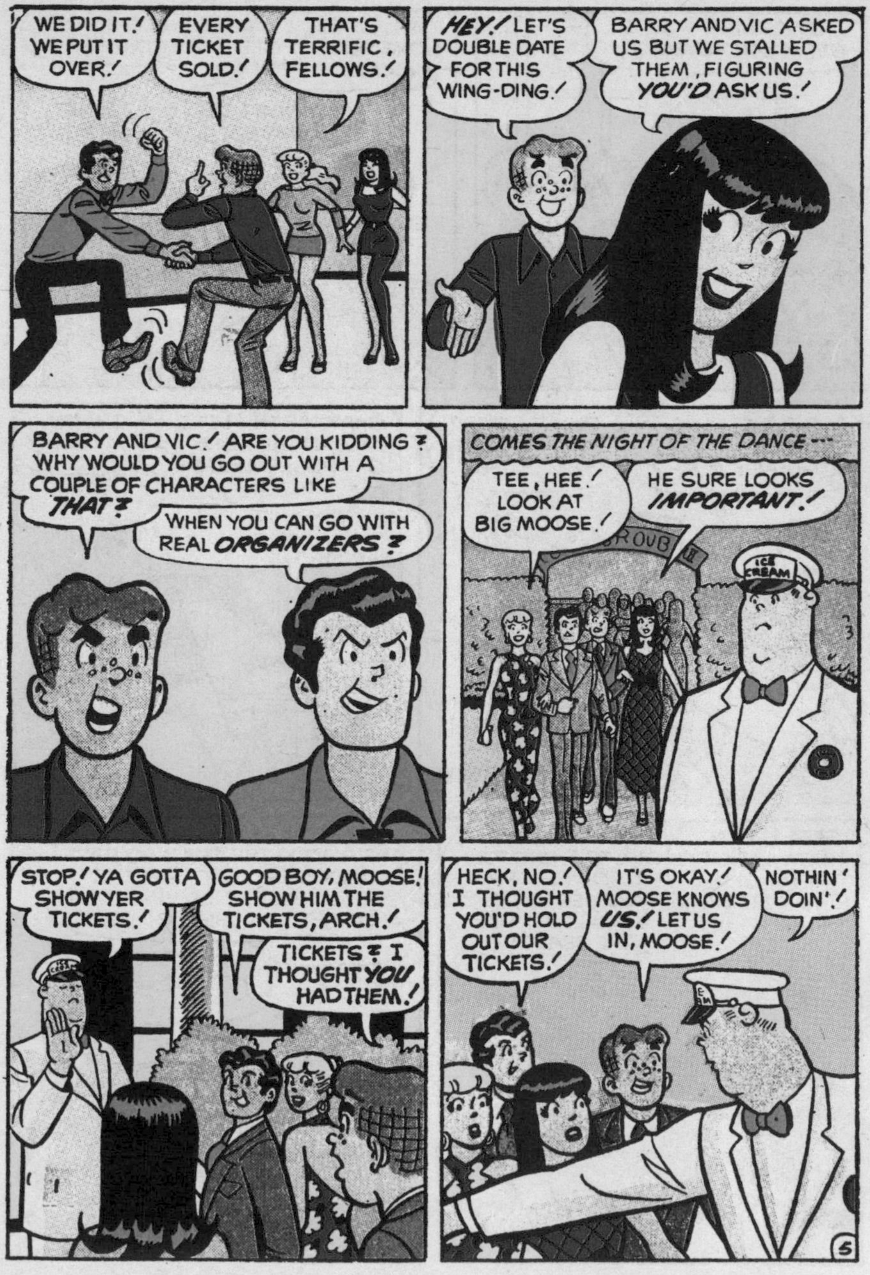
WE DID IT.! WE PUT IT OVER.!
EVERY TICKET SOLD.!
THAT'S TERRIFIC, FELLOWS.!
HEY.! LET'S DOUBLE DATE FOR THIS WING-DING.!
BARRY AND VIC ASKED US BUT WE STALLED THEM, FIGURING YOU'D ASK US.!
BARRY AND VIC.! ARE YOU KIDDING? WHY WOULD YOU GO OUT WITH A COUPLE OF CHARACTERS LIKE THAT?
WHEN YOU CAN GO WITH REAL ORGANIZERS?
COMES THE NIGHT OF THE DANCE---
TEE, HEE.! LOOK AT BIG MOOSE.!
HE SURE LOOKS IMPORTANT.!
ICE CREAM
STOP.! YA GOTTA SHOW YER TICKETS.!
GOOD BOY, MOOSE.! SHOW HIM THE TICKETS, ARCH.!
TICKETS? I THOUGHT YOU HAD THEM.!
HECK, NO.! I THOUGHT YOU'D HOLD OUT OUR TICKETS.!
IT'S OKAY.! MOOSE KNOWS US.! LET US IN, MOOSE.!
NOTHIN' DOIN'.!
5

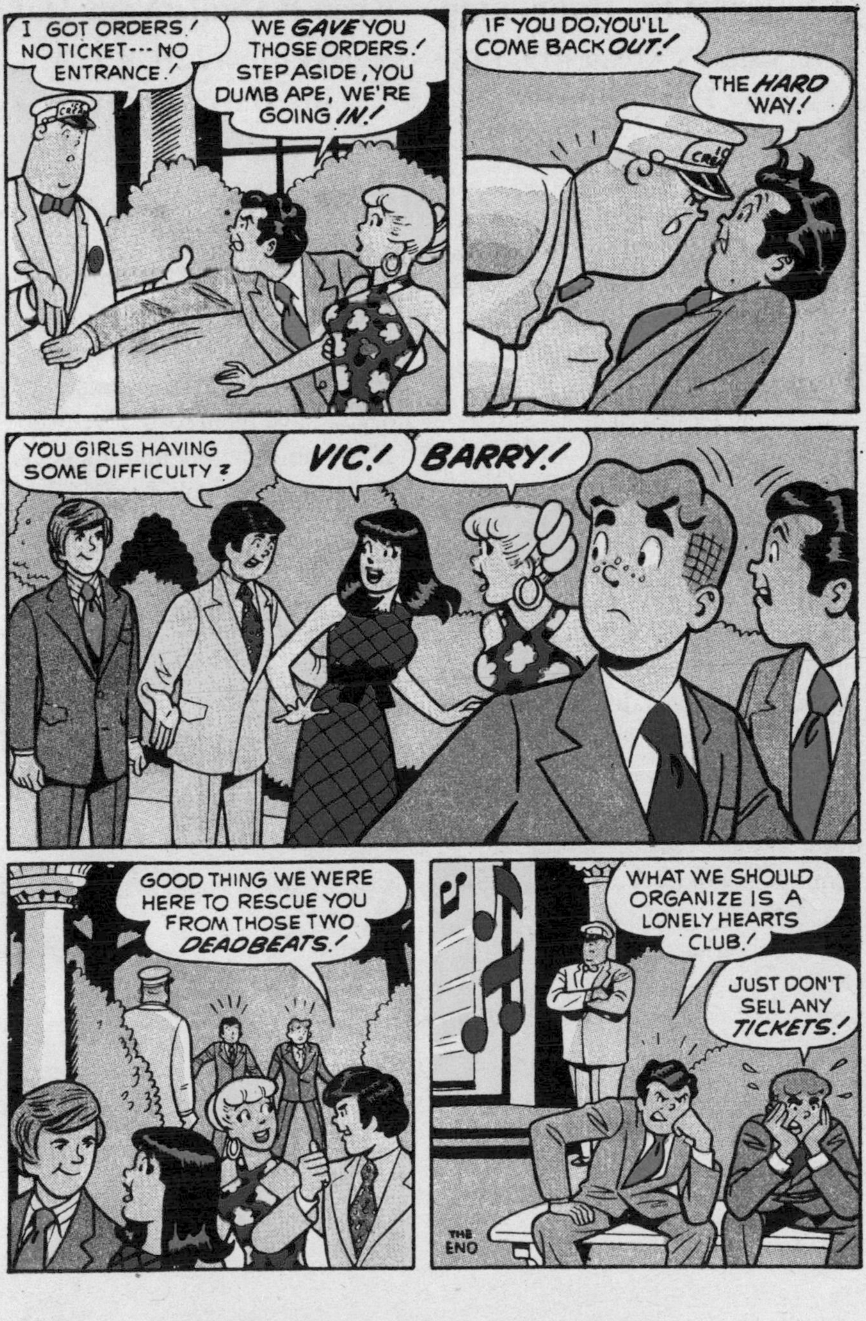
I GOT ORDERS! NO TICKET--- NO ENTRANCE!
WE GAVE YOU THOSE ORDERS! STEP ASIDE, YOU DUMB APE, WE'RE GOING IN!
IF YOU DO, YOU'LL COME BACK OUT!
THE HARD WAY!
YOU GIRLS HAVING SOME DIFFICULTY?
VIC!
BARRY!
GOOD THING WE WERE HERE TO RESCUE YOU FROM THOSE TWO DEADBEATS!
WHAT WE SHOULD ORGANIZE IS A LONELY HEARTS CLUB!
JUST DON'T SELL ANY TICKETS!
THE END

A Share of the Happening
Everything's Archie #29, 1973
by Harry Lucey

This story brings back vivid memories of my childhood. For the first time, Archie and the Gang were popular in other media. Actually, they were a smash hit! The Archies had the #1 selling song in the United States, "Sugar Sugar," Archie was the #1 cartoon on television on Saturday morning, and Archie was the most popular kids' comic book. Archie was the King of all Media! This story, of which my father was so proud—shows Archie enjoying his success. Generally, my father did not discuss the business much when he came home—but he was so proud of the success of the TV show and the music, that this story reminds me of Archie at its height, when "Everything's Archie" was absolutely true.

--**Jon Goldwater**
Co-CEO, Archie Comics

Keep It Under Your Hat
Archie #228, 1973
by Harry Lucey

Harry Lucey!!!! "Keep It Under Your Hat" is a funny story with awesome artwork! This story still makes me giggle just thinking about it! When people ask me "Why Archie?" this is an excellent story to have them read. I've used it many times before and it's never failed to make people laugh!

--**Jack Copley**
Official Archie Comics Historian

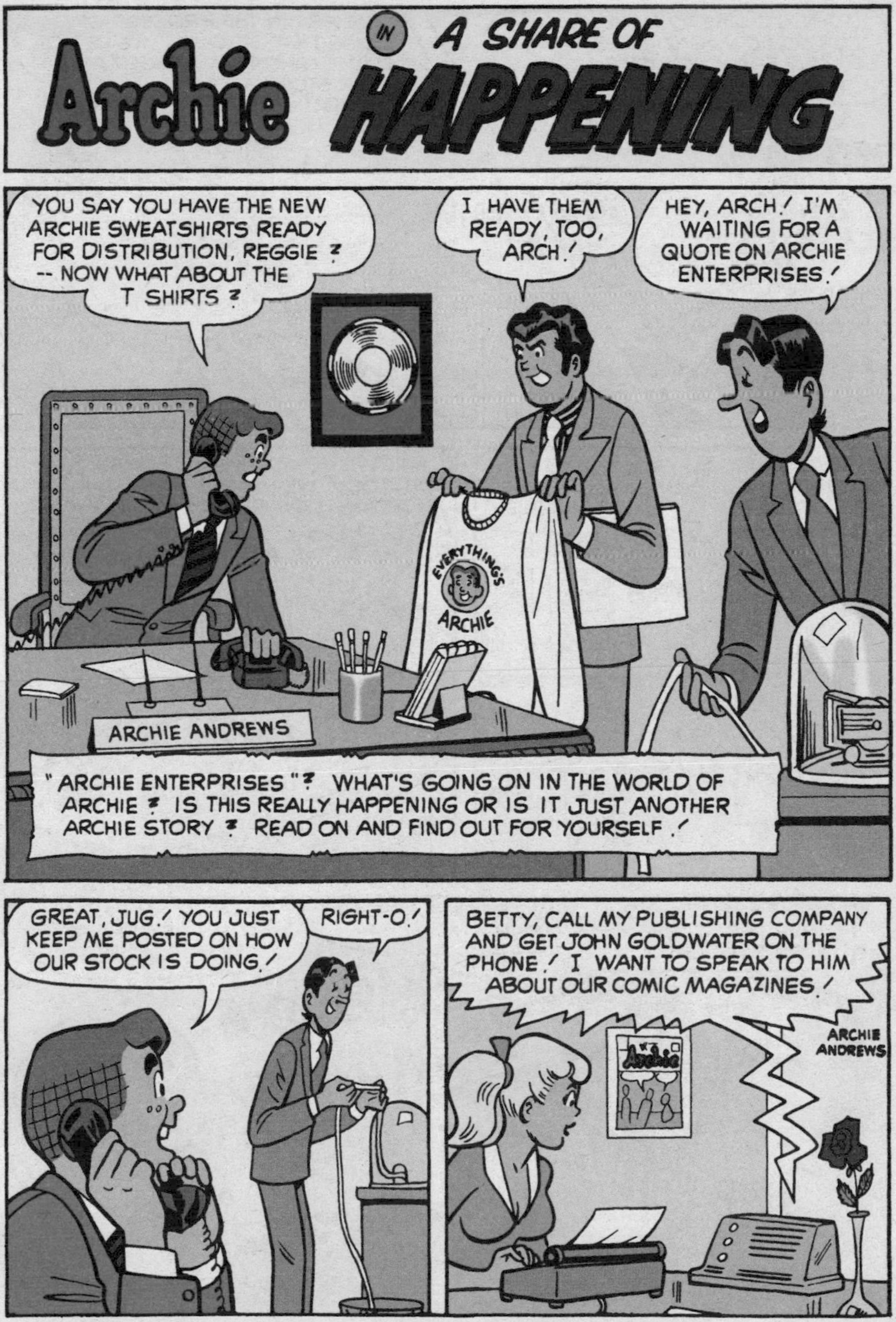
Archie
IN
A SHARE OF HAPPENING
YOU SAY YOU HAVE THE NEW ARCHIE SWEATSHIRTS READY FOR DISTRIBUTION, REGGIE ? -- NOW WHAT ABOUT THE T SHIRTS ?
I HAVE THEM READY, TOO, ARCH!
HEY, ARCH! I'M WAITING FOR A QUOTE ON ARCHIE ENTERPRISES!
EVERYTHING'S ARCHIE
ARCHIE ANDREWS
"ARCHIE ENTERPRISES"? WHAT'S GOING ON IN THE WORLD OF ARCHIE? IS THIS REALLY HAPPENING OR IS IT JUST ANOTHER ARCHIE STORY? READ ON AND FIND OUT FOR YOURSELF!
GREAT, JUG! YOU JUST KEEP ME POSTED ON HOW OUR STOCK IS DOING!
RIGHT-O!
BETTY, CALL MY PUBLISHING COMPANY AND GET JOHN GOLDWATER ON THE PHONE! I WANT TO SPEAK TO HIM ABOUT OUR COMIC MAGAZINES!
ARCHIE ANDREWS
Archie

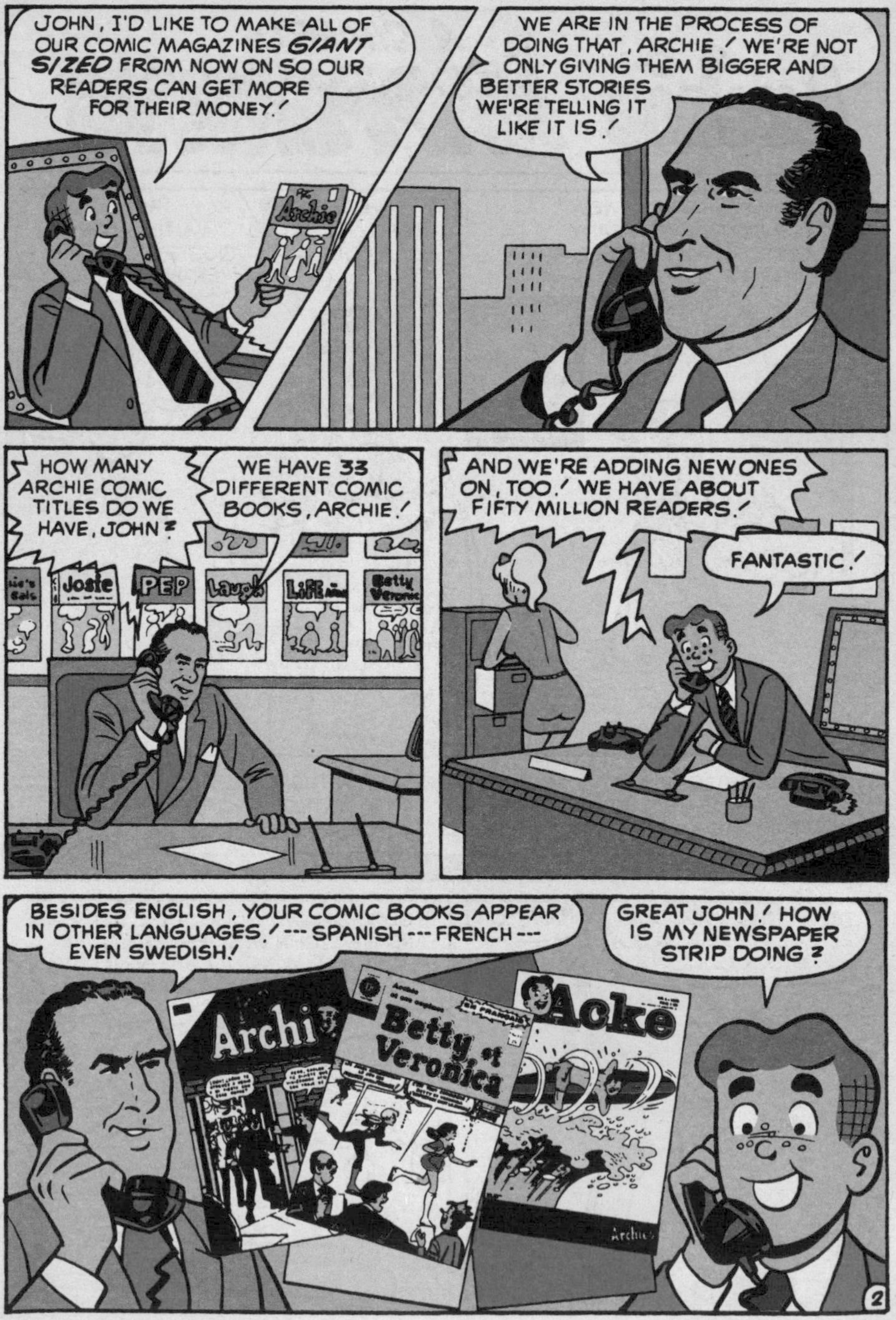
JOHN, I'D LIKE TO MAKE ALL OF OUR COMIC MAGAZINES *GIANT SIZED* FROM NOW ON SO OUR READERS CAN GET MORE FOR THEIR MONEY!
WE ARE IN THE PROCESS OF DOING THAT, ARCHIE! WE'RE NOT ONLY GIVING THEM BIGGER AND BETTER STORIES WE'RE TELLING IT LIKE IT IS!
HOW MANY ARCHIE COMIC TITLES DO WE HAVE, JOHN?
WE HAVE 33 DIFFERENT COMIC BOOKS, ARCHIE!
Josie
PEP
Laugh
Life
Betty Veronica
AND WE'RE ADDING NEW ONES ON, TOO! WE HAVE ABOUT FIFTY MILLION READERS!
FANTASTIC!
BESIDES ENGLISH, YOUR COMIC BOOKS APPEAR IN OTHER LANGUAGES! --- SPANISH --- FRENCH --- EVEN SWEDISH!
GREAT JOHN! HOW IS MY NEWSPAPER STRIP DOING?
Archi
Betty et Veronica
Acke
2

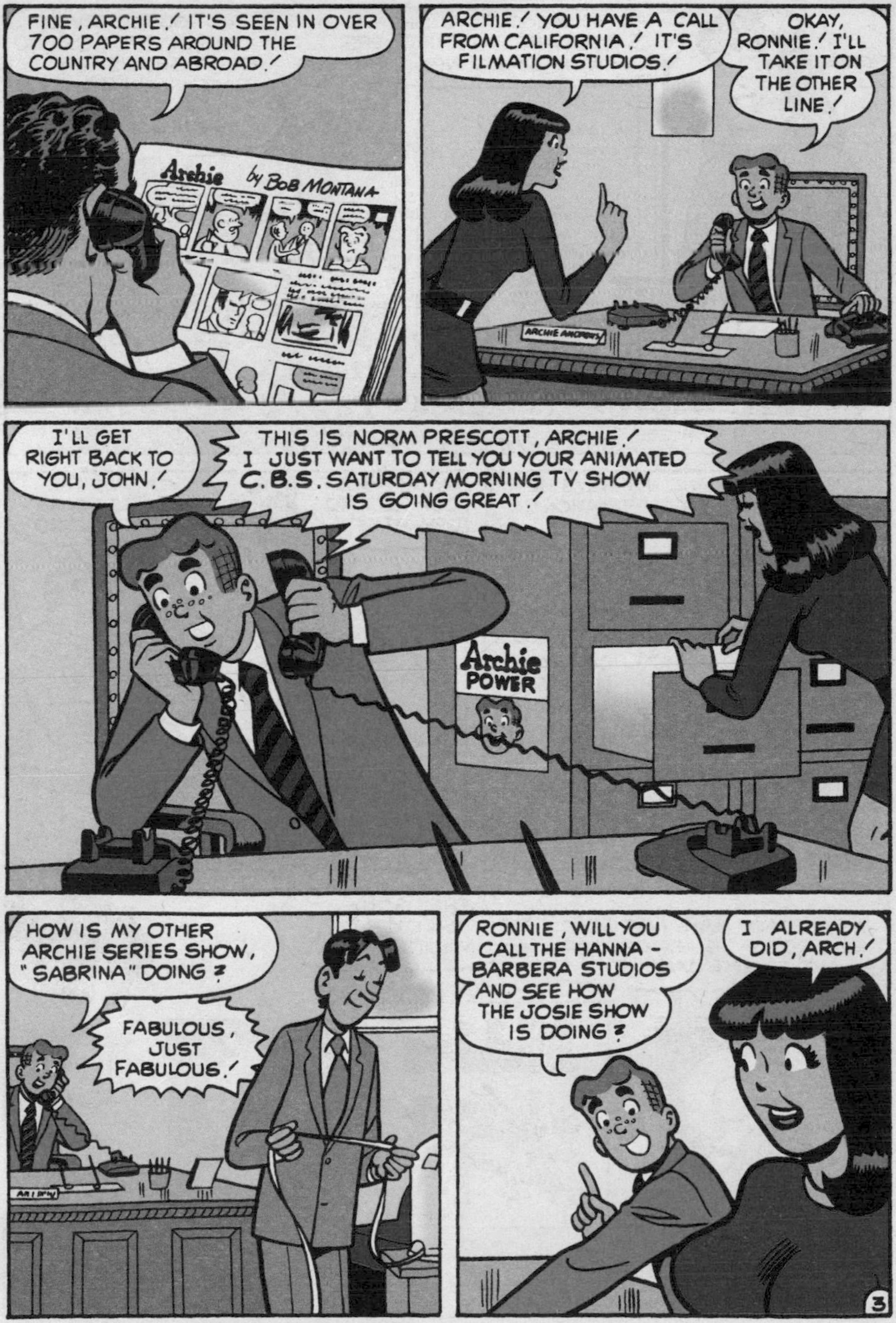
FINE, ARCHIE! IT'S SEEN IN OVER 700 PAPERS AROUND THE COUNTRY AND ABROAD!
Archie by BOB MONTANA
ARCHIE! YOU HAVE A CALL FROM CALIFORNIA! IT'S FILMATION STUDIOS!
OKAY, RONNIE! I'LL TAKE IT ON THE OTHER LINE!
ARCHIE ANDREWS
I'LL GET RIGHT BACK TO YOU, JOHN!
THIS IS NORM PRESCOTT, ARCHIE! I JUST WANT TO TELL YOU YOUR ANIMATED C.B.S. SATURDAY MORNING TV SHOW IS GOING GREAT!
Archie POWER
HOW IS MY OTHER ARCHIE SERIES SHOW, "SABRINA" DOING?
FABULOUS, JUST FABULOUS!
RONNIE, WILL YOU CALL THE HANNA-BARBERA STUDIOS AND SEE HOW THE JOSIE SHOW IS DOING?
I ALREADY DID, ARCH!
3

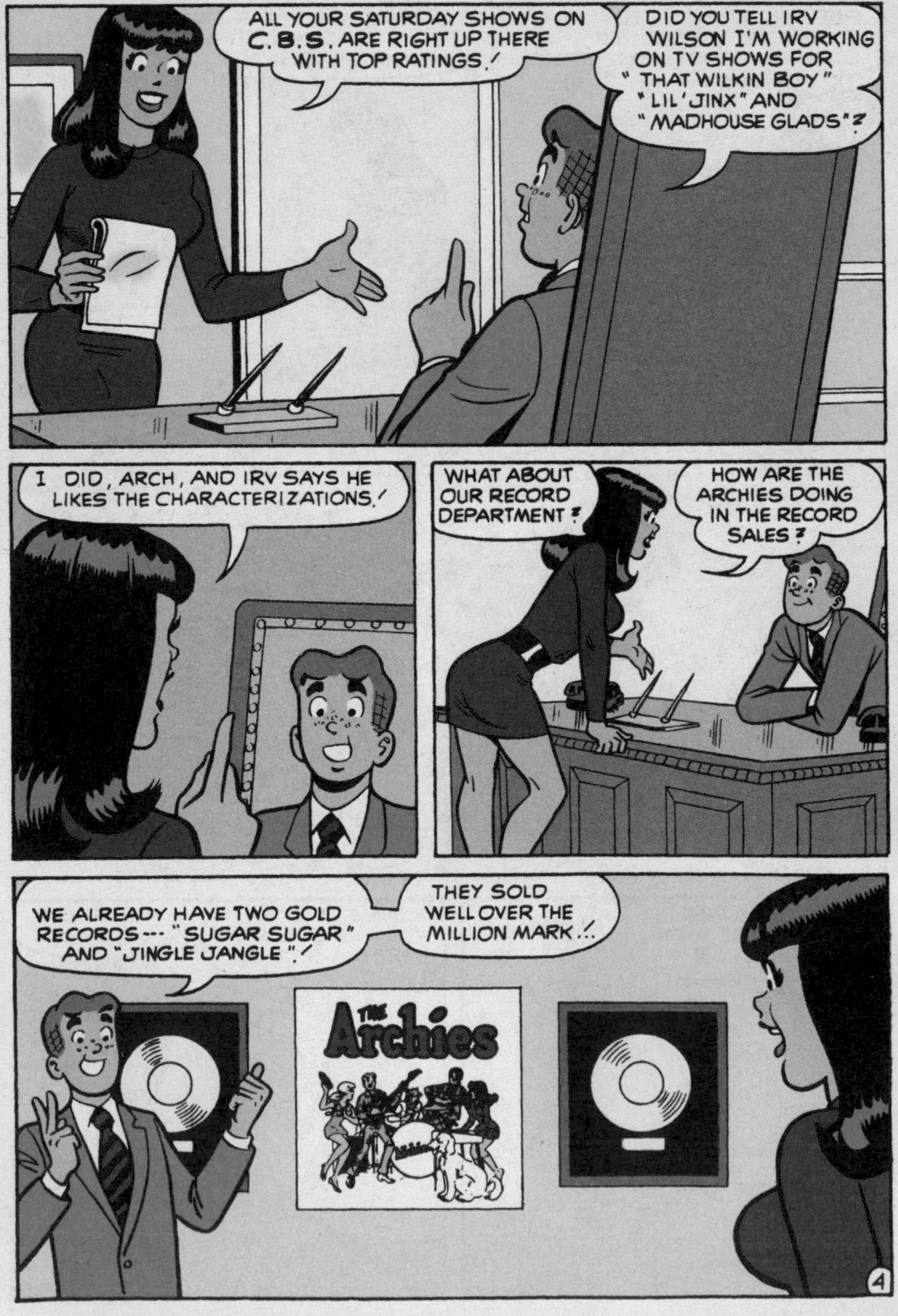
ALL YOUR SATURDAY SHOWS ON C.B.S. ARE RIGHT UP THERE WITH TOP RATINGS!
DID YOU TELL IRV WILSON I'M WORKING ON TV SHOWS FOR "THAT WILKIN BOY" "LIL' JINX" AND "MADHOUSE GLADS"?
I DID, ARCH, AND IRV SAYS HE LIKES THE CHARACTERIZATIONS!
WHAT ABOUT OUR RECORD DEPARTMENT?
HOW ARE THE ARCHIES DOING IN THE RECORD SALES?
WE ALREADY HAVE TWO GOLD RECORDS--- "SUGAR SUGAR" AND "JINGLE JANGLE"!
THEY SOLD WELL OVER THE MILLION MARK!!
THE Archies
4

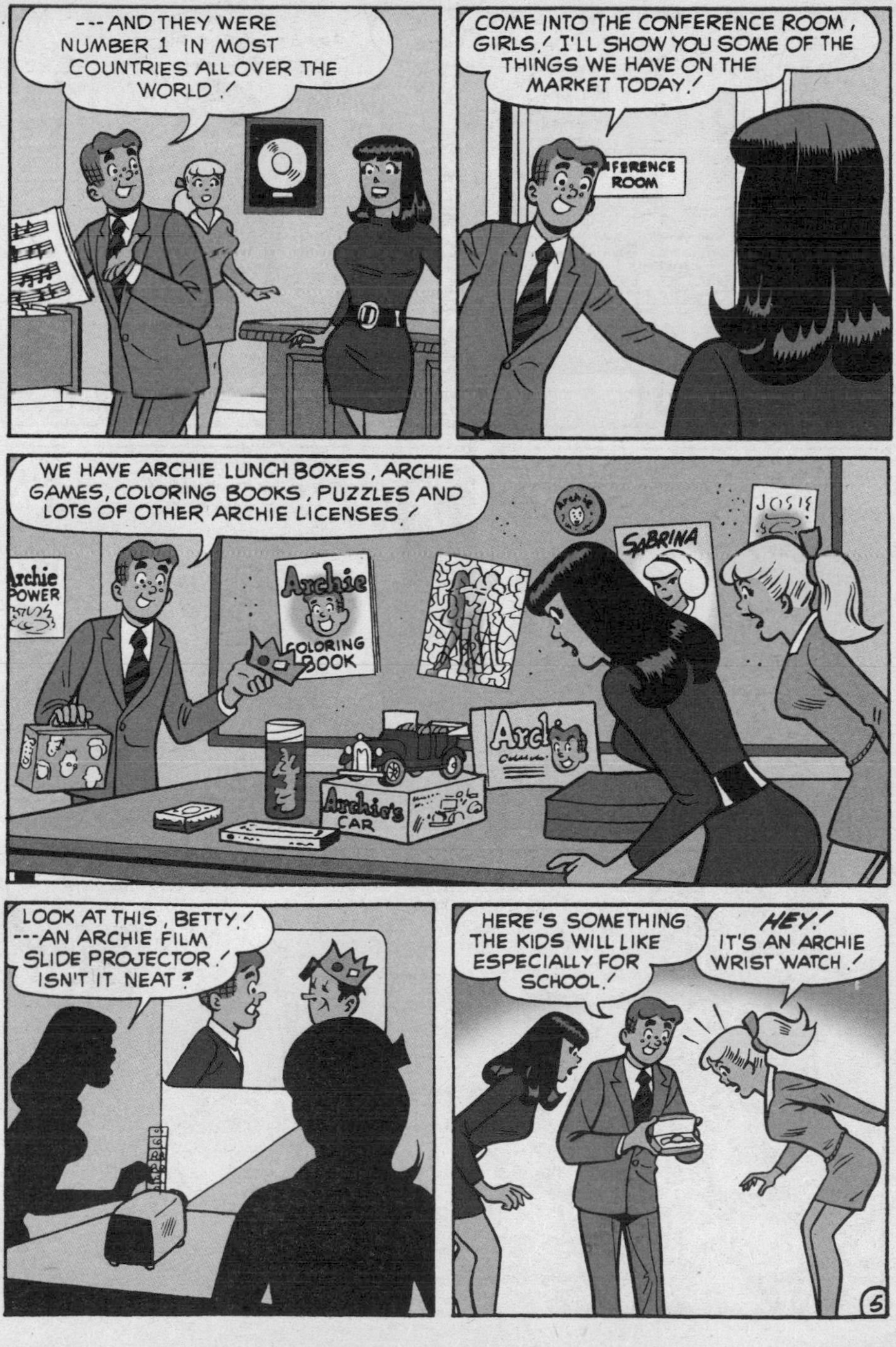
---AND THEY WERE NUMBER 1 IN MOST COUNTRIES ALL OVER THE WORLD!
COME INTO THE CONFERENCE ROOM, GIRLS! I'LL SHOW YOU SOME OF THE THINGS WE HAVE ON THE MARKET TODAY!
FERENCE ROOM
WE HAVE ARCHIE LUNCH BOXES, ARCHIE GAMES, COLORING BOOKS, PUZZLES AND LOTS OF OTHER ARCHIE LICENSES!
Archie POWER
Archie COLORING BOOK
SABRINA
JOSIE
Archie's CAR
LOOK AT THIS, BETTY! ---AN ARCHIE FILM SLIDE PROJECTOR! ISN'T IT NEAT?
HERE'S SOMETHING THE KIDS WILL LIKE ESPECIALLY FOR SCHOOL!
HEY! IT'S AN ARCHIE WRIST WATCH!
5

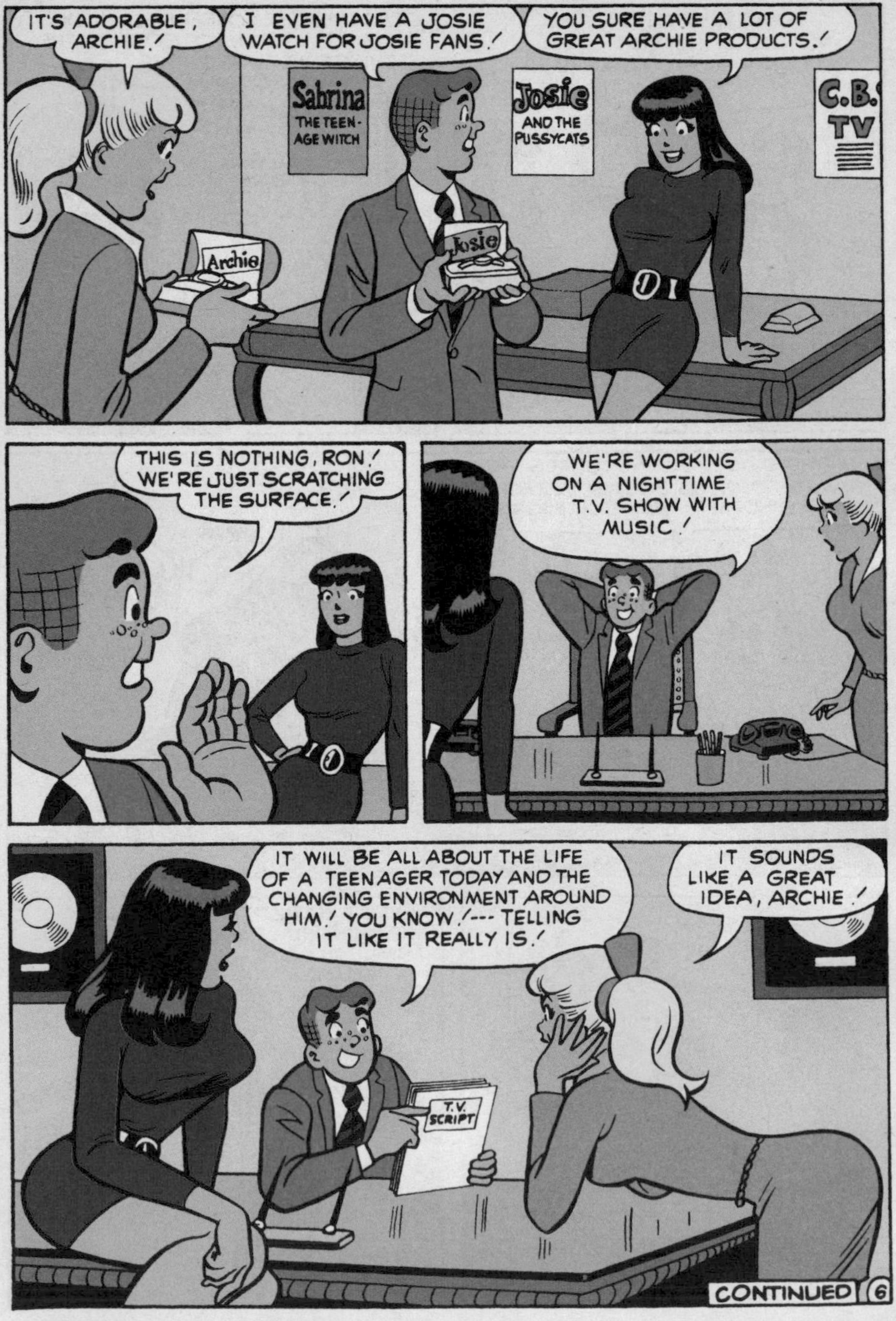
IT'S ADORABLE, ARCHIE.!
I EVEN HAVE A JOSIE WATCH FOR JOSIE FANS.!
YOU SURE HAVE A LOT OF GREAT ARCHIE PRODUCTS.!
Sabrina THE TEEN-AGE WITCH
Josie AND THE PUSSYCATS
C.B.S TV
Archie
Josie
THIS IS NOTHING, RON.! WE'RE JUST SCRATCHING THE SURFACE.!
WE'RE WORKING ON A NIGHTTIME T.V. SHOW WITH MUSIC.!
IT WILL BE ALL ABOUT THE LIFE OF A TEENAGER TODAY AND THE CHANGING ENVIRONMENT AROUND HIM.! YOU KNOW.!--- TELLING IT LIKE IT REALLY IS.!
IT SOUNDS LIKE A GREAT IDEA, ARCHIE.!
T.V. SCRIPT
CONTINUED
6

JUG, YOU TELL THEM ABOUT THE IDEA YOU LIKE THE BEST.!

OH, BOY.! MY MOUTH WATERS JUST *THINKING* ABOUT IT.!

SLURP!

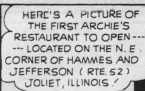

HERE'S A PICTURE OF THE FIRST ARCHIE'S RESTAURANT TO OPEN --- --- LOCATED ON THE N.E. CORNER OF HAMMES AND JEFFERSON (RTE. 52) JOLIET, ILLINOIS.!

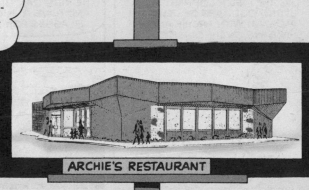

ARCHIE'S RESTAURANT

IT WILL FEATURE JUGHEAD'S PIE A LA MODE AND ANY ICE CREAM CONCOCTION YOU CAN THINK OF.!

WOW!

GOLLY.! I JUST CAN'T WAIT, ARCHIE.! I THINK IT'S A SUPER IDEA.!

7

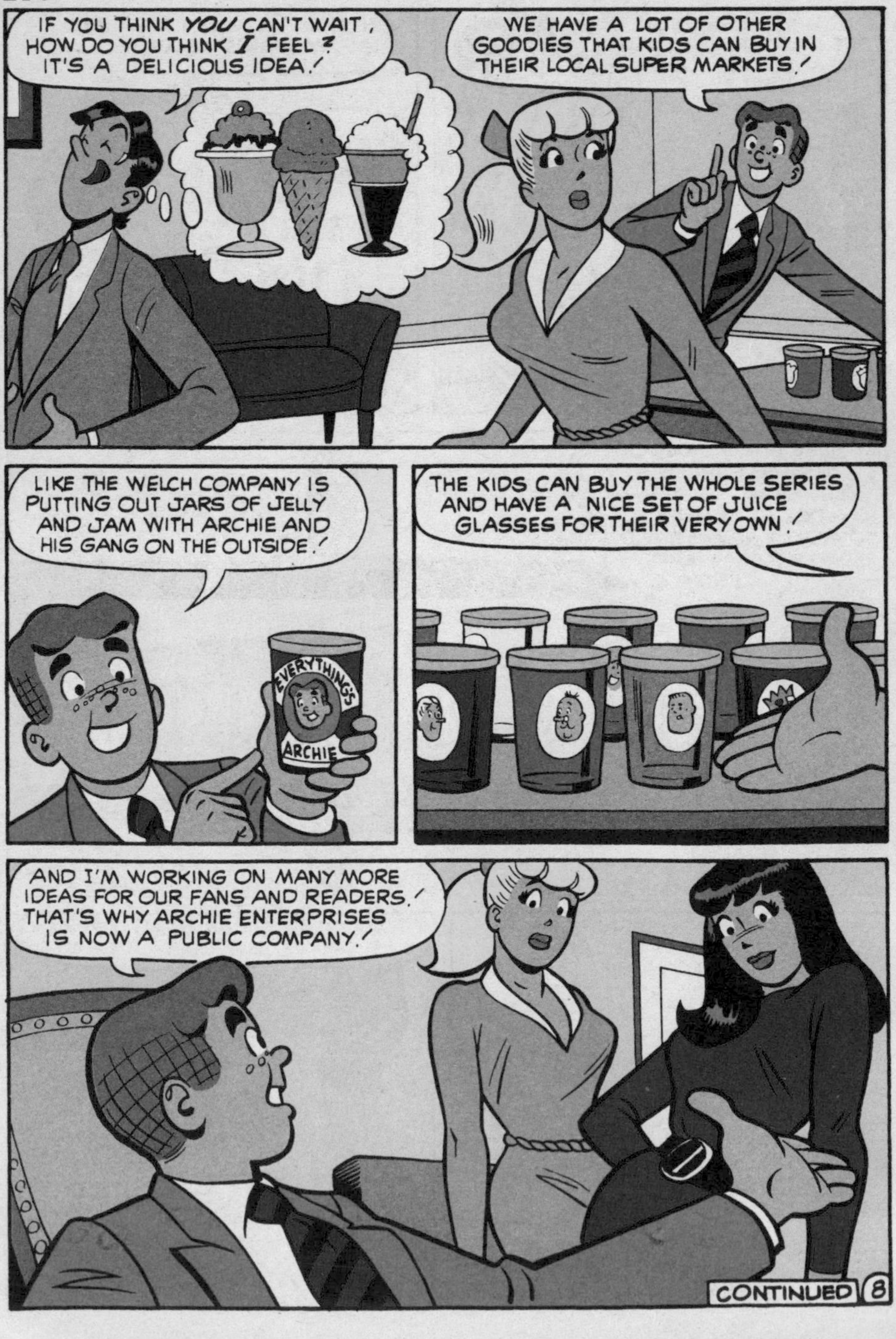
IF YOU THINK YOU CAN'T WAIT, HOW DO YOU THINK I FEEL? IT'S A DELICIOUS IDEA!
WE HAVE A LOT OF OTHER GOODIES THAT KIDS CAN BUY IN THEIR LOCAL SUPER MARKETS!
LIKE THE WELCH COMPANY IS PUTTING OUT JARS OF JELLY AND JAM WITH ARCHIE AND HIS GANG ON THE OUTSIDE!
EVERYTHING'S ARCHIE
THE KIDS CAN BUY THE WHOLE SERIES AND HAVE A NICE SET OF JUICE GLASSES FOR THEIR VERY OWN!
AND I'M WORKING ON MANY MORE IDEAS FOR OUR FANS AND READERS! THAT'S WHY ARCHIE ENTERPRISES IS NOW A PUBLIC COMPANY!
CONTINUED
8

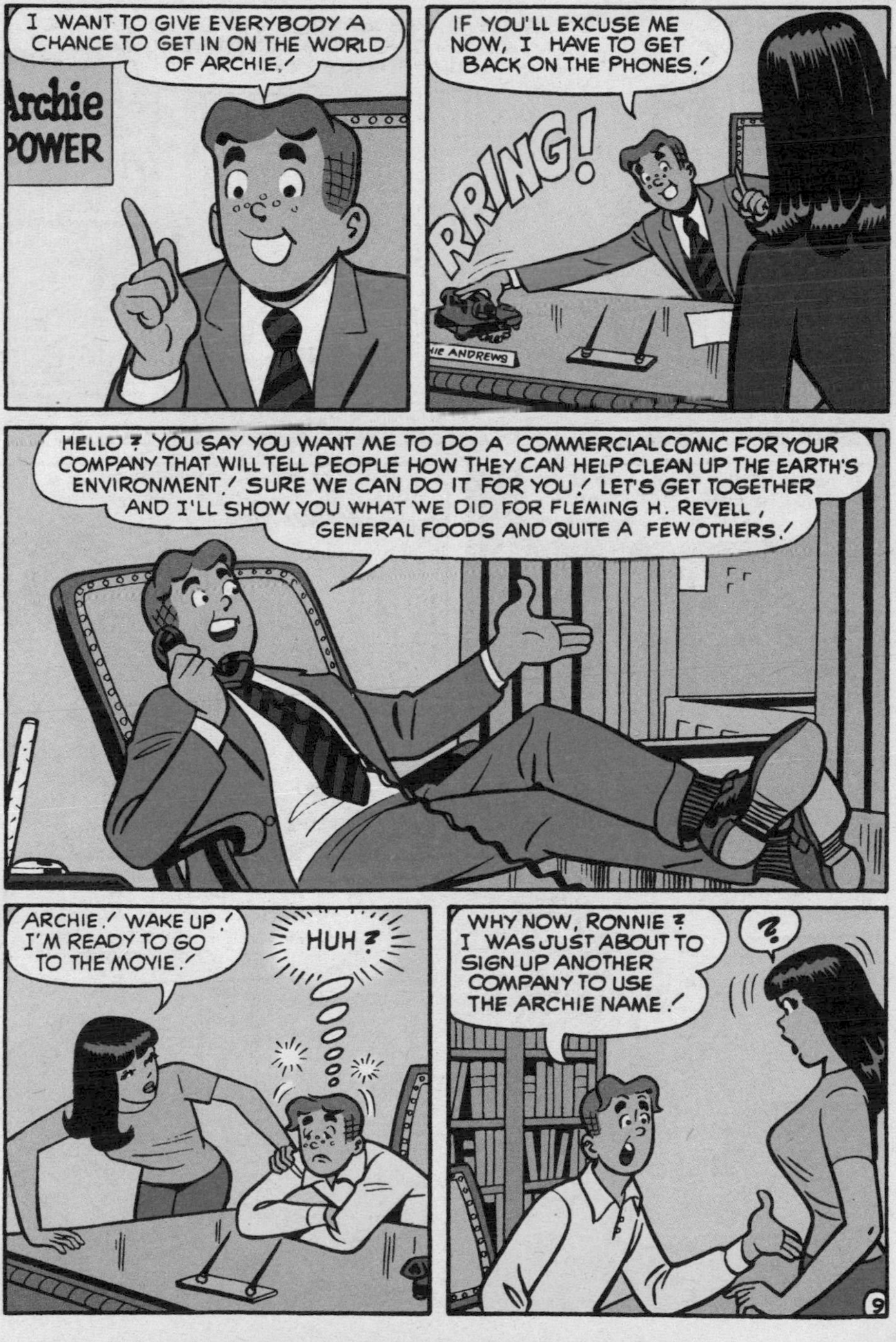
I WANT TO GIVE EVERYBODY A CHANCE TO GET IN ON THE WORLD OF ARCHIE!
Archie POWER
IF YOU'LL EXCUSE ME NOW, I HAVE TO GET BACK ON THE PHONES!
RRING!
HELLO? YOU SAY YOU WANT ME TO DO A COMMERCIAL COMIC FOR YOUR COMPANY THAT WILL TELL PEOPLE HOW THEY CAN HELP CLEAN UP THE EARTH'S ENVIRONMENT! SURE WE CAN DO IT FOR YOU! LET'S GET TOGETHER AND I'LL SHOW YOU WHAT WE DID FOR FLEMING H. REVELL, GENERAL FOODS AND QUITE A FEW OTHERS!
ARCHIE! WAKE UP! I'M READY TO GO TO THE MOVIE!
HUH?
WHY NOW, RONNIE? I WAS JUST ABOUT TO SIGN UP ANOTHER COMPANY TO USE THE ARCHIE NAME!
?
9

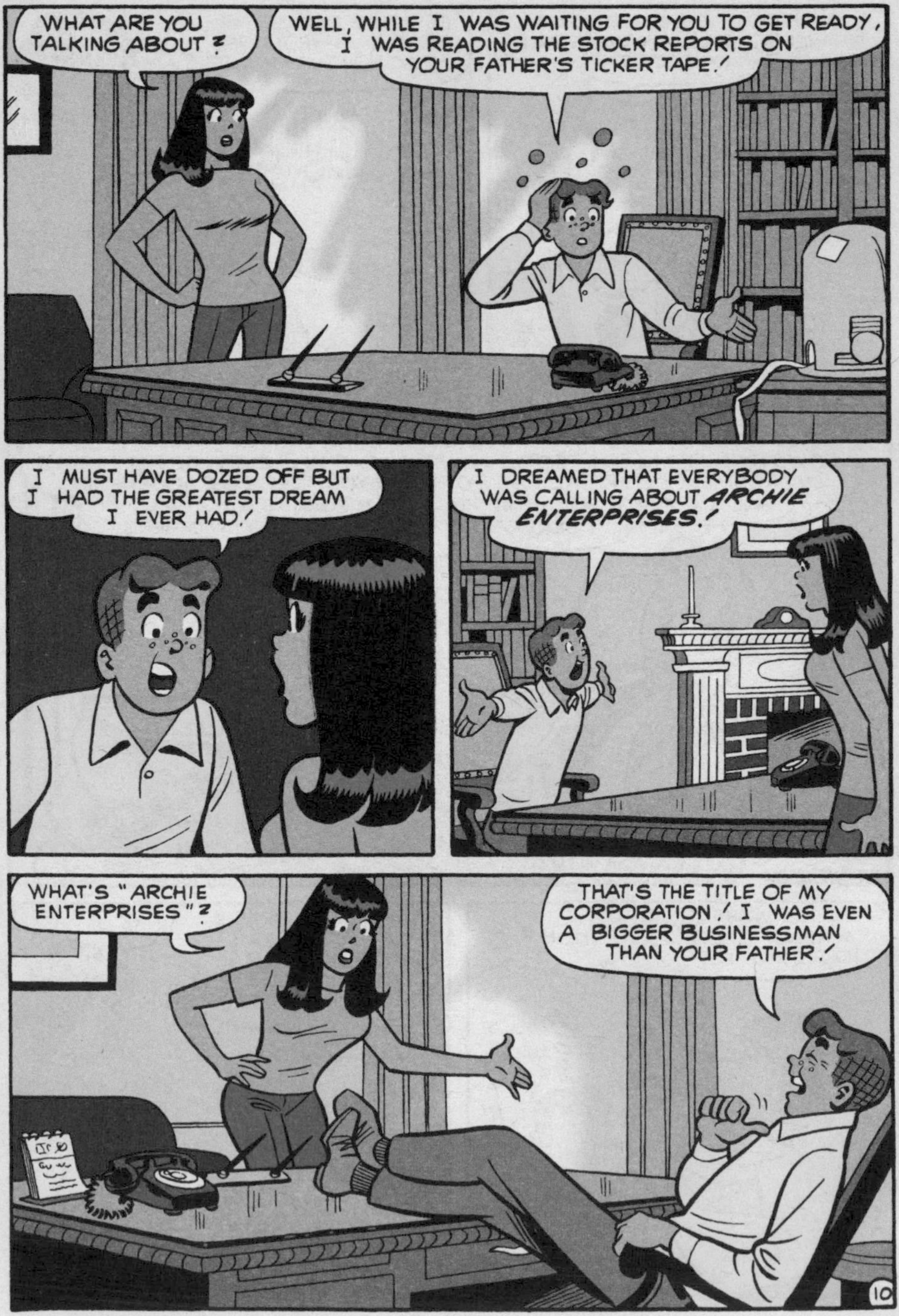
WHAT ARE YOU TALKING ABOUT ?
WELL, WHILE I WAS WAITING FOR YOU TO GET READY, I WAS READING THE STOCK REPORTS ON YOUR FATHER'S TICKER TAPE!
I MUST HAVE DOZED OFF BUT I HAD THE GREATEST DREAM I EVER HAD!
I DREAMED THAT EVERYBODY WAS CALLING ABOUT ARCHIE ENTERPRISES!
WHAT'S "ARCHIE ENTERPRISES"?
THAT'S THE TITLE OF MY CORPORATION! I WAS EVEN A BIGGER BUSINESSMAN THAN YOUR FATHER!
10

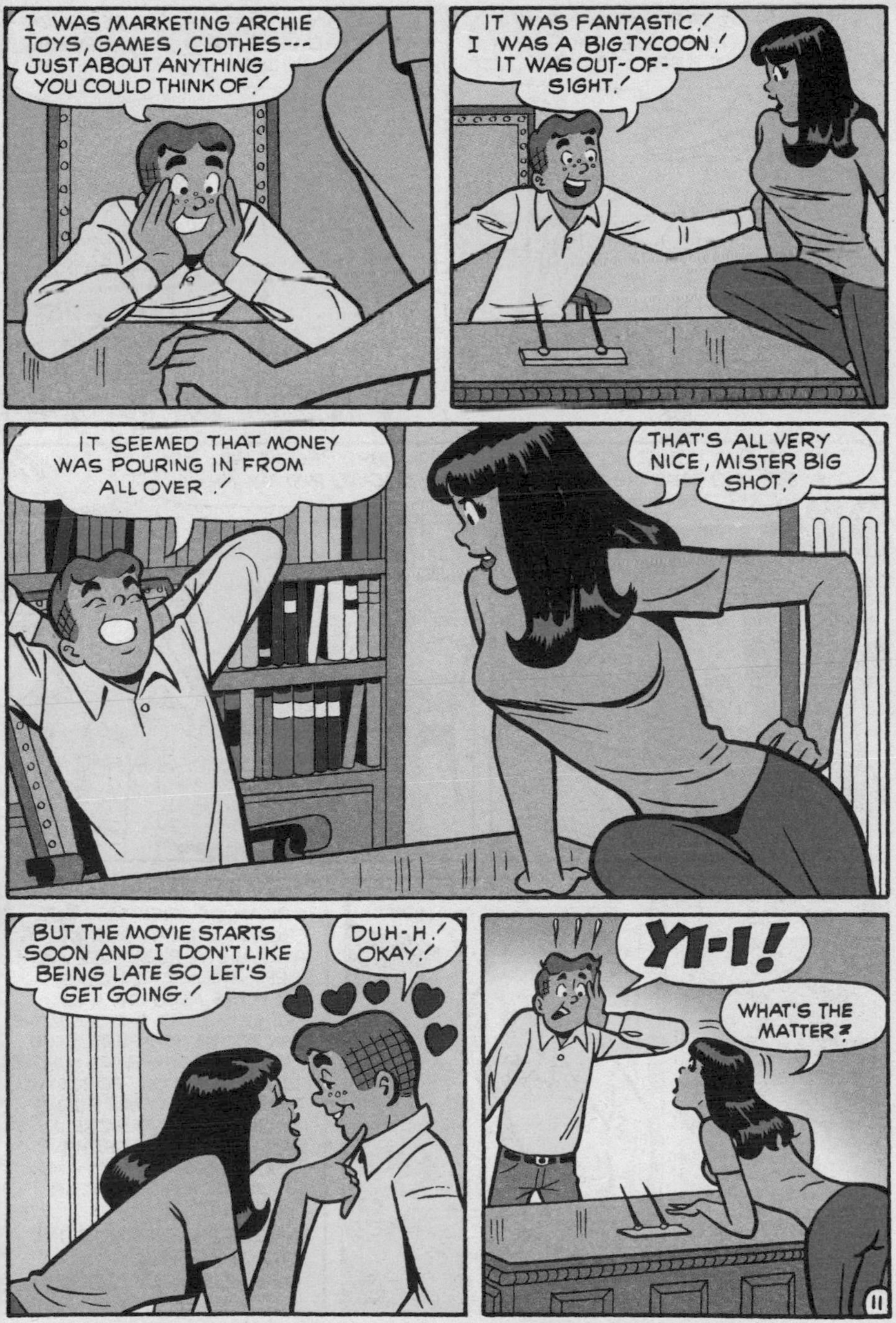
I WAS MARKETING ARCHIE TOYS, GAMES, CLOTHES--- JUST ABOUT ANYTHING YOU COULD THINK OF!
IT WAS FANTASTIC! I WAS A BIG TYCOON! IT WAS OUT-OF-SIGHT!
IT SEEMED THAT MONEY WAS POURING IN FROM ALL OVER!
THAT'S ALL VERY NICE, MISTER BIG SHOT!
BUT THE MOVIE STARTS SOON AND I DON'T LIKE BEING LATE SO LET'S GET GOING!
DUH-H! OKAY!
YI-I!
WHAT'S THE MATTER?
11

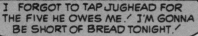

I FORGOT TO TAP JUGHEAD FOR THE FIVE HE OWES ME.! I'M GONNA BE SHORT OF BREAD TONIGHT.!

ER... DO YOU SUPPOSE YOU COULD LEND ME A FEW BUCKS?

A FEW BUCKS? I HAVE A MUCH BETTER IDEA!

WHY DON'T YOU JUST GO BACK TO SLEEP AND TAKE ME OUT IN YOUR DREAMS?

I'M SURE REGGIE WILL BE *GLAD* TO PAY MY WAY!

PLEASANT DREAMS!

BAH! WOMEN! WHAT DO THEY KNOW ABOUT SUCCESS?

SLAM!

THIS MAY HAVE BEEN A DREAM OF ARCHIE'S, BUT ARCHIE ENTERPRISES, INC. IS A REAL LIVE PUBLIC COMPANY. THERE ARE ARCHIE LICENSES, TV SHOWS, RECORDS AND ARCHIE IS SYNDICATED IN MORE THAN 700 NEWSPAPERS, PLUS MANY OTHER SURPRISES FOR THE FUTURE! AND DON'T FORGET ALL THOSE ARCHIE COMIC BOOKS. IF YOU WOULD LIKE MORE IN-SIDE STUFF ABOUT ARCHIE ENTERPRISES, WRITE IN AND LET US KNOW! SEND YOUR LETTERS TO:

ARCHIE ENTERPRISES, INC.
1116 FIRST AVE.
NEW YORK, N.Y. 10021

Archie "KEEP IT UNDER YOUR HAT"

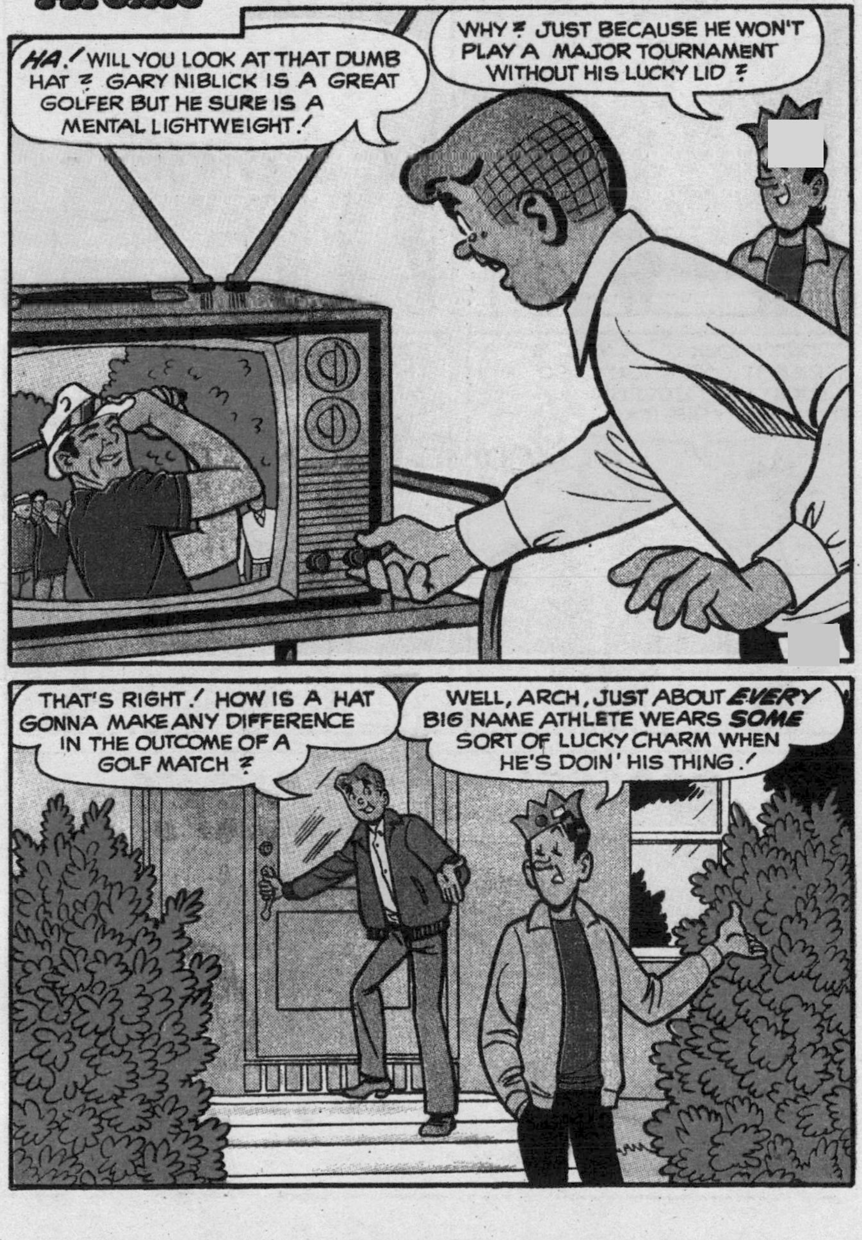
HA! WILL YOU LOOK AT THAT DUMB HAT? GARY NIBLICK IS A GREAT GOLFER BUT HE SURE IS A MENTAL LIGHTWEIGHT!
WHY? JUST BECAUSE HE WON'T PLAY A MAJOR TOURNAMENT WITHOUT HIS LUCKY LID?
THAT'S RIGHT! HOW IS A HAT GONNA MAKE ANY DIFFERENCE IN THE OUTCOME OF A GOLF MATCH?
WELL, ARCH, JUST ABOUT EVERY BIG NAME ATHLETE WEARS SOME SORT OF LUCKY CHARM WHEN HE'S DOIN' HIS THING!

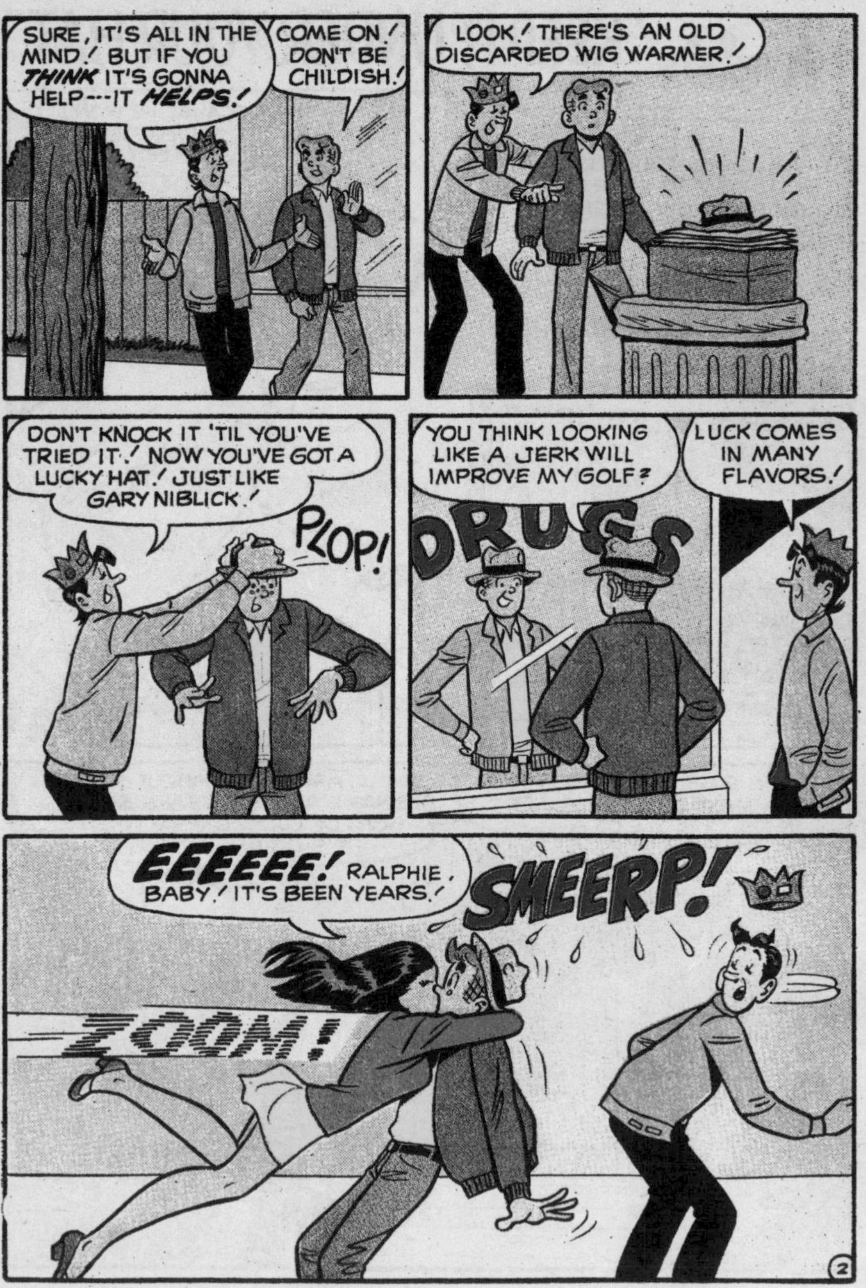
SURE, IT'S ALL IN THE MIND! BUT IF YOU THINK IT'S GONNA HELP---IT HELPS!
COME ON! DON'T BE CHILDISH!
LOOK! THERE'S AN OLD DISCARDED WIG WARMER!
DON'T KNOCK IT 'TIL YOU'VE TRIED IT! NOW YOU'VE GOT A LUCKY HAT! JUST LIKE GARY NIBLICK!
PLOP!
YOU THINK LOOKING LIKE A JERK WILL IMPROVE MY GOLF?
LUCK COMES IN MANY FLAVORS!
DRUGS
EEEEEE! RALPHIE, BABY! IT'S BEEN YEARS!
SMEERP!
ZOOM!
2

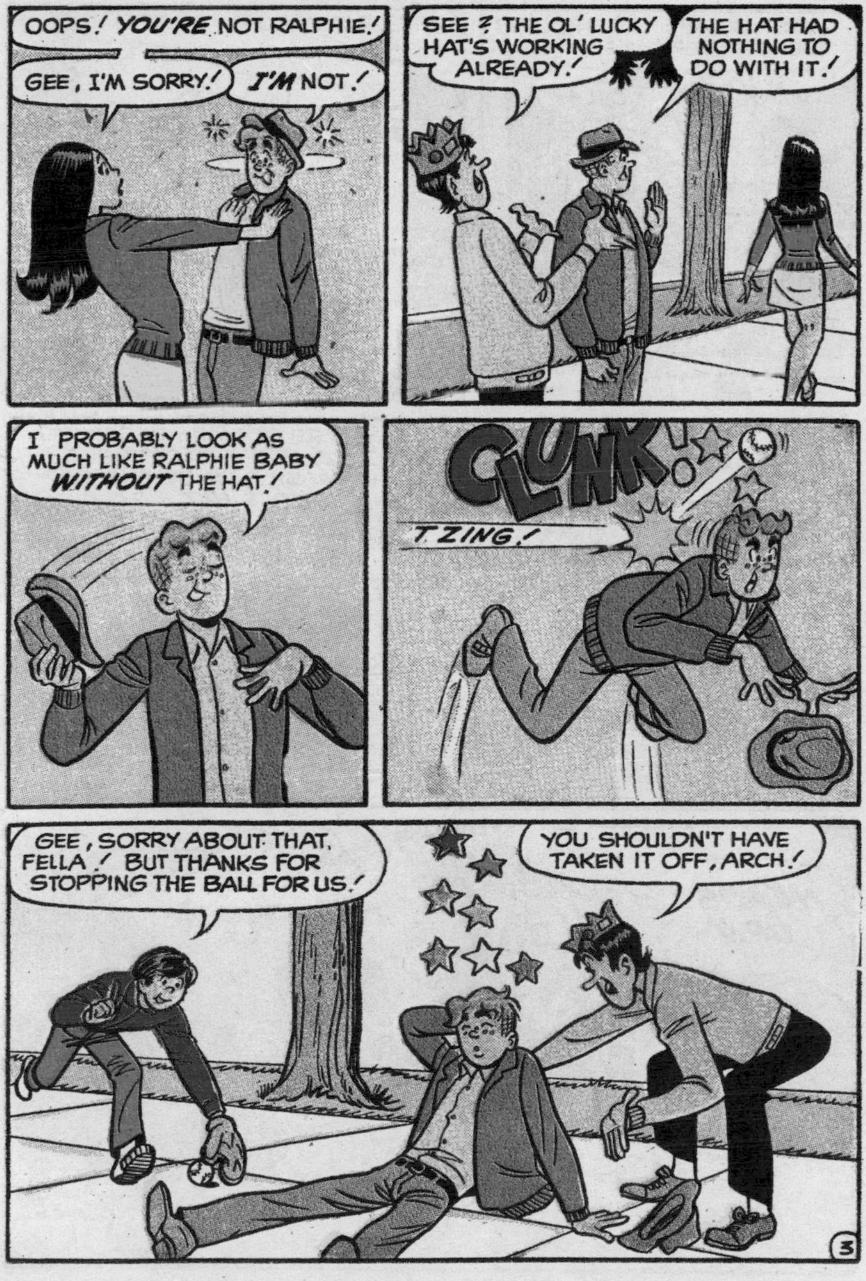
OOPS! YOU'RE NOT RALPHIE!
GEE, I'M SORRY!
I'M NOT!
SEE? THE OL' LUCKY HAT'S WORKING ALREADY!
THE HAT HAD NOTHING TO DO WITH IT!
I PROBABLY LOOK AS MUCH LIKE RALPHIE BABY WITHOUT THE HAT!
CLONK!
TZING!
GEE, SORRY ABOUT THAT, FELLA! BUT THANKS FOR STOPPING THE BALL FOR US!
YOU SHOULDN'T HAVE TAKEN IT OFF, ARCH!
3

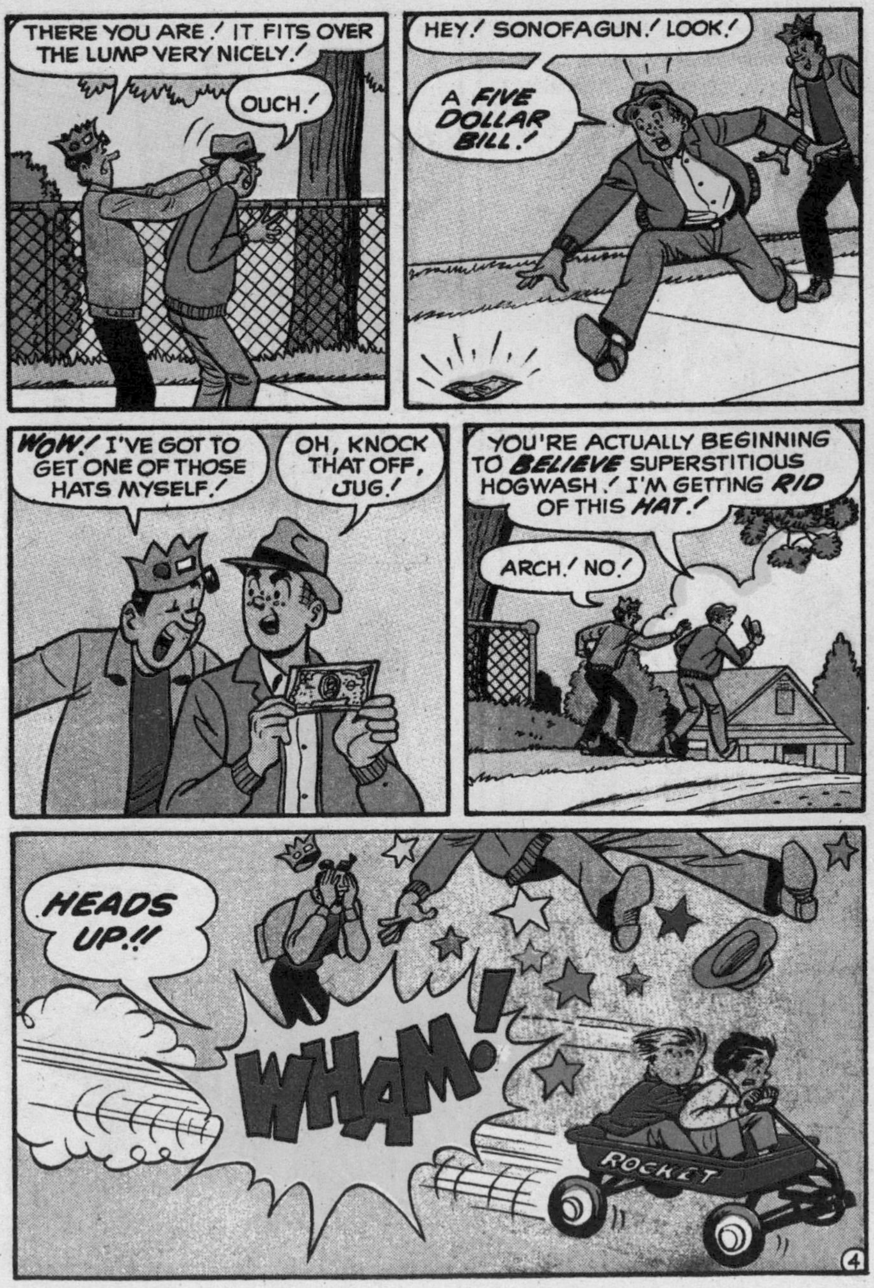
THERE YOU ARE.! IT FITS OVER THE LUMP VERY NICELY.!
OUCH.!
HEY.! SONOFAGUN.! LOOK.!
A FIVE DOLLAR BILL.!
WOW.! I'VE GOT TO GET ONE OF THOSE HATS MYSELF.!
OH, KNOCK THAT OFF, JUG.!
YOU'RE ACTUALLY BEGINNING TO BELIEVE SUPERSTITIOUS HOGWASH.! I'M GETTING RID OF THIS HAT.!
ARCH.! NO.!
HEADS UP.!!
WHAM!
ROCKET
4

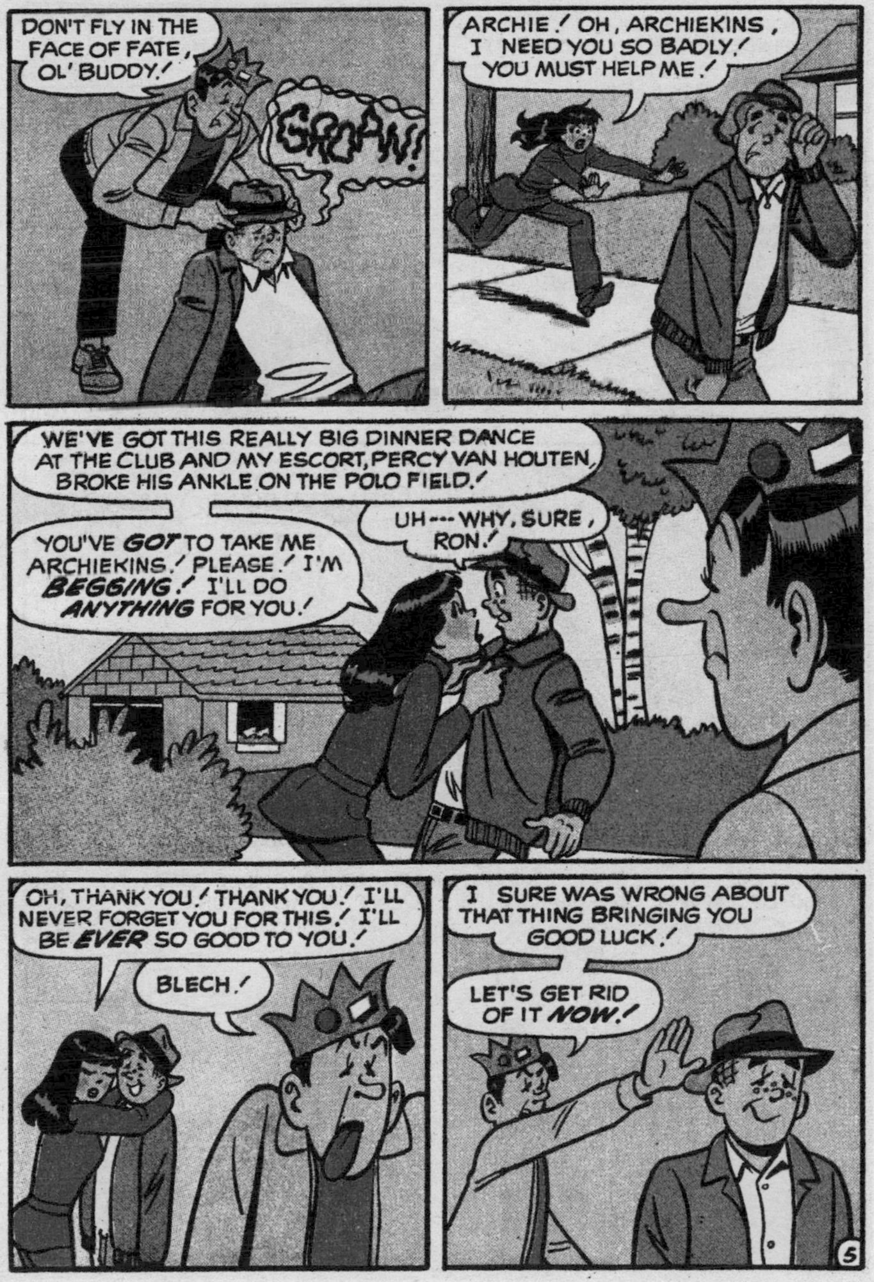
DON'T FLY IN THE FACE OF FATE, OL' BUDDY!
GROAN!
ARCHIE! OH, ARCHIEKINS, I NEED YOU SO BADLY! YOU MUST HELP ME!
WE'VE GOT THIS REALLY BIG DINNER DANCE AT THE CLUB AND MY ESCORT, PERCY VAN HOUTEN, BROKE HIS ANKLE ON THE POLO FIELD!
YOU'VE GOT TO TAKE ME ARCHIEKINS! PLEASE! I'M BEGGING! I'LL DO ANYTHING FOR YOU!
UH--- WHY, SURE, RON!
OH, THANK YOU! THANK YOU! I'LL NEVER FORGET YOU FOR THIS! I'LL BE EVER SO GOOD TO YOU!
BLECH!
I SURE WAS WRONG ABOUT THAT THING BRINGING YOU GOOD LUCK!
LET'S GET RID OF IT NOW!
5

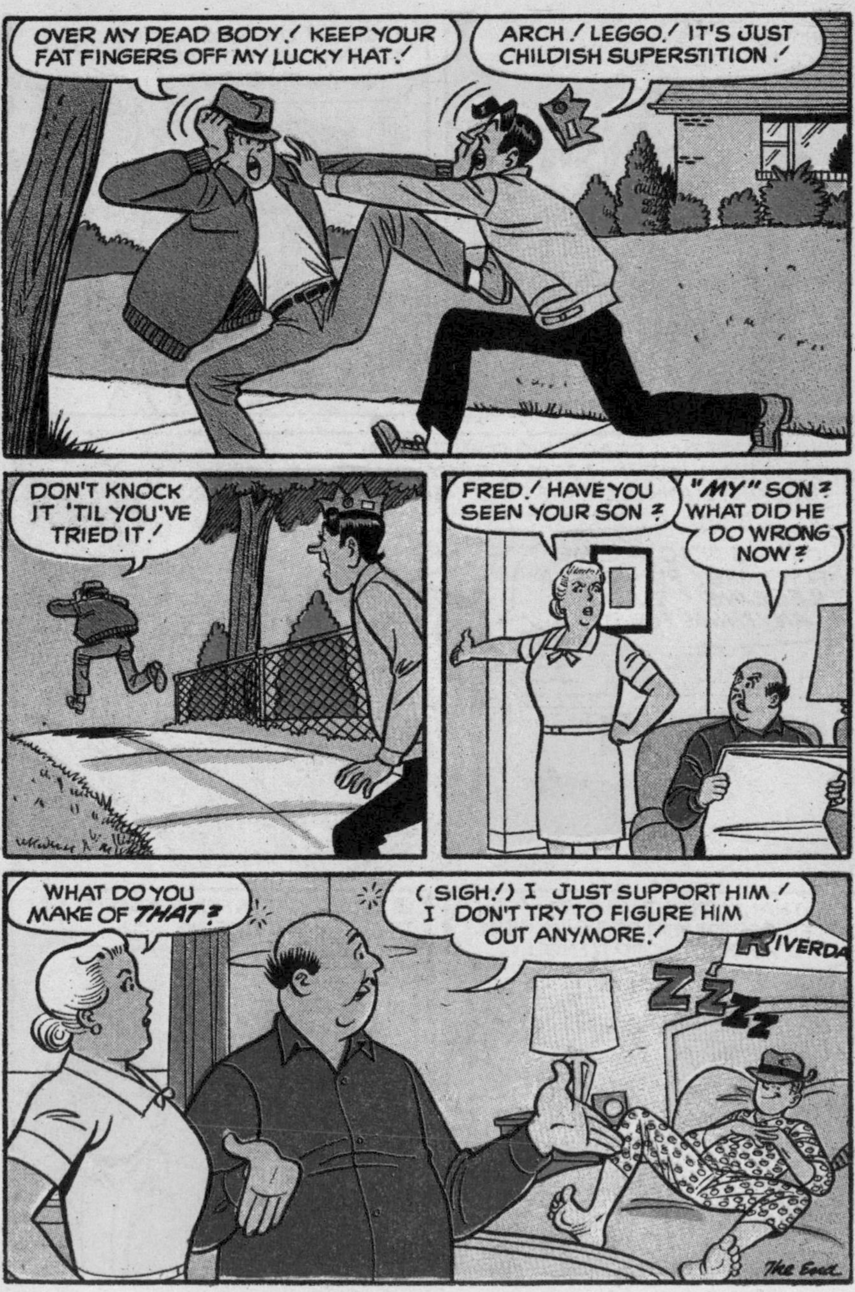
OVER MY DEAD BODY! KEEP YOUR FAT FINGERS OFF MY LUCKY HAT!
ARCH! LEGGO! IT'S JUST CHILDISH SUPERSTITION!
DON'T KNOCK IT 'TIL YOU'VE TRIED IT!
FRED! HAVE YOU SEEN YOUR SON?
"MY" SON? WHAT DID HE DO WRONG NOW?
WHAT DO YOU MAKE OF THAT?
(SIGH!) I JUST SUPPORT HIM! I DON'T TRY TO FIGURE HIM OUT ANYMORE!
RIVERDA
ZZZZ
The End

You Came a Long Way, Baby
Archie #228, 1973
by Dan DeCarlo
and Rudy Lapick

Reading this story again after so many years brought me back to a time when you wouldn't want to do anything considered not feminine. This was before Title Nine! Believe it or not, this kind of story really would have been considered progressive, not so much for Archie Comics, but the actual subject around the dinner table. Women's rights were a big irritation to a lot of people, not only men. The fact was women weren't even close to equal, in pay or civil rights. Sexual harassment was considered your own fault. And since you weren't a man and supporting a family you were paid less. A lot less. Even to be recognized as Ms. like Miss Grundy at the end was quite huge. Weatherbee was such a great guy in this story, you could believe he had a daughter who wanted to play sports or go to college or something outrageous like that.

--Ellen Leonforte
Senior Art Director, Archie Comics

Name That Tune
Archie Giant Series #470, 1978
by Frank Doyle
and Dan DeCarlo

"Stomp fritter polly wok, kittatinny koo!"? Yeah, no clue either. It's hard to pinpoint what exactly clicked in my seven-year-old brain when I discovered this story in *Betty and Veronica Double Digest #10* -- coincidentally, my first comic ever. Was it the masterful Dan DeCarlo artwork – perfectly choreographed, beautifully drawn and looking effortless? Or was it the fun, youthful and downright funny Frank Doyle script that crackled with comedic energy every time the Gang interacted? Or the idea of Archie and Jughead trading lyrics and made-up songs to a frustrated and bemused Betty and Veronica? I didn't know then. I'm still not sure now. But from that moment on, I was totally and unabashedly hooked on the adventures of Archie and the gang – and it's provided me with years of joy and memories. So, thanks Dan and Frank. I owe you one.

--Alex Segura
Executive Director of Publicity & Marketing, Archie Comics

Betty and Veronica in "YOU CAME A LONG WAY, BABY..

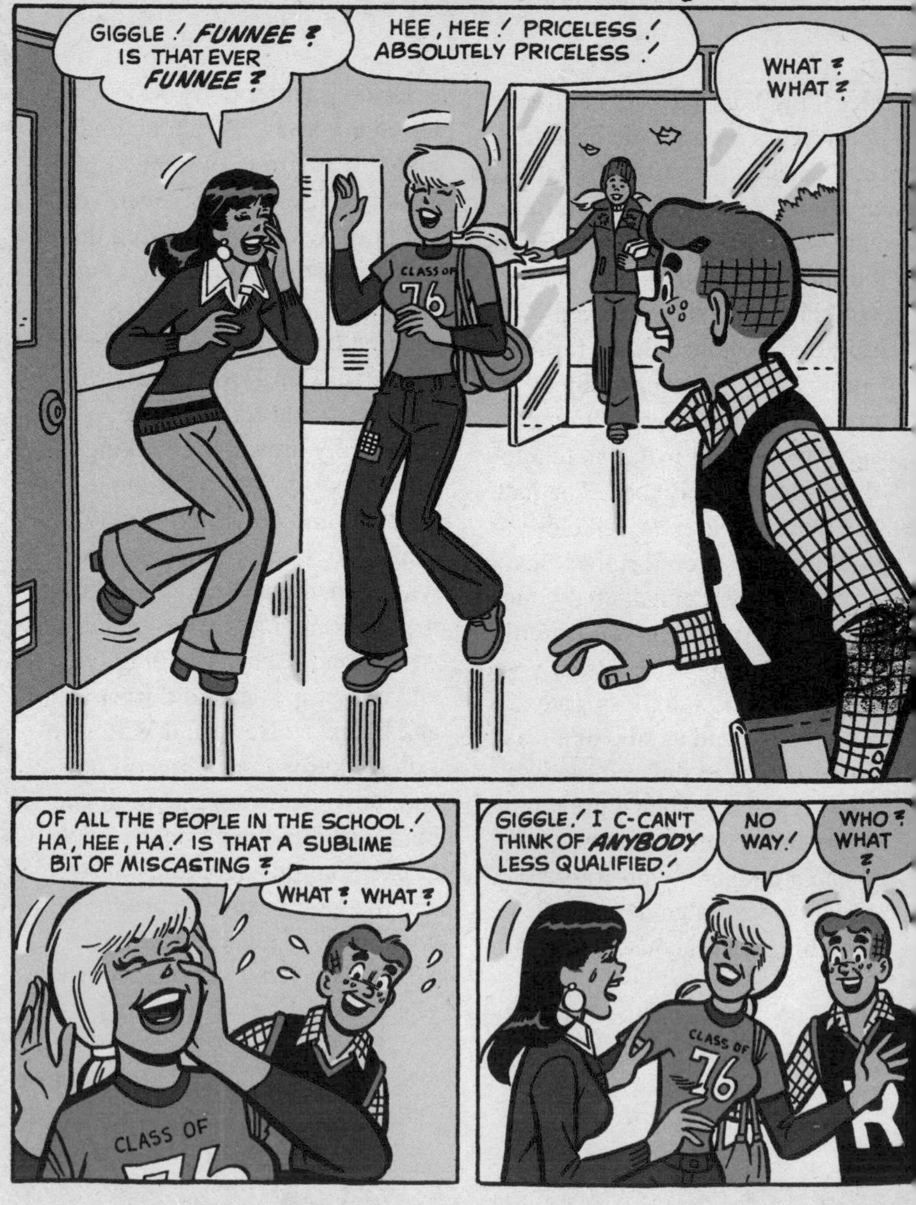
GIGGLE! FUNNEE? IS THAT EVER FUNNEE?
HEE, HEE! PRICELESS! ABSOLUTELY PRICELESS!
WHAT? WHAT?
OF ALL THE PEOPLE IN THE SCHOOL! HA, HEE, HA! IS THAT A SUBLIME BIT OF MISCASTING?
WHAT? WHAT?
GIGGLE! I C-CAN'T THINK OF ANYBODY LESS QUALIFIED!
NO WAY!
WHO? WHAT?

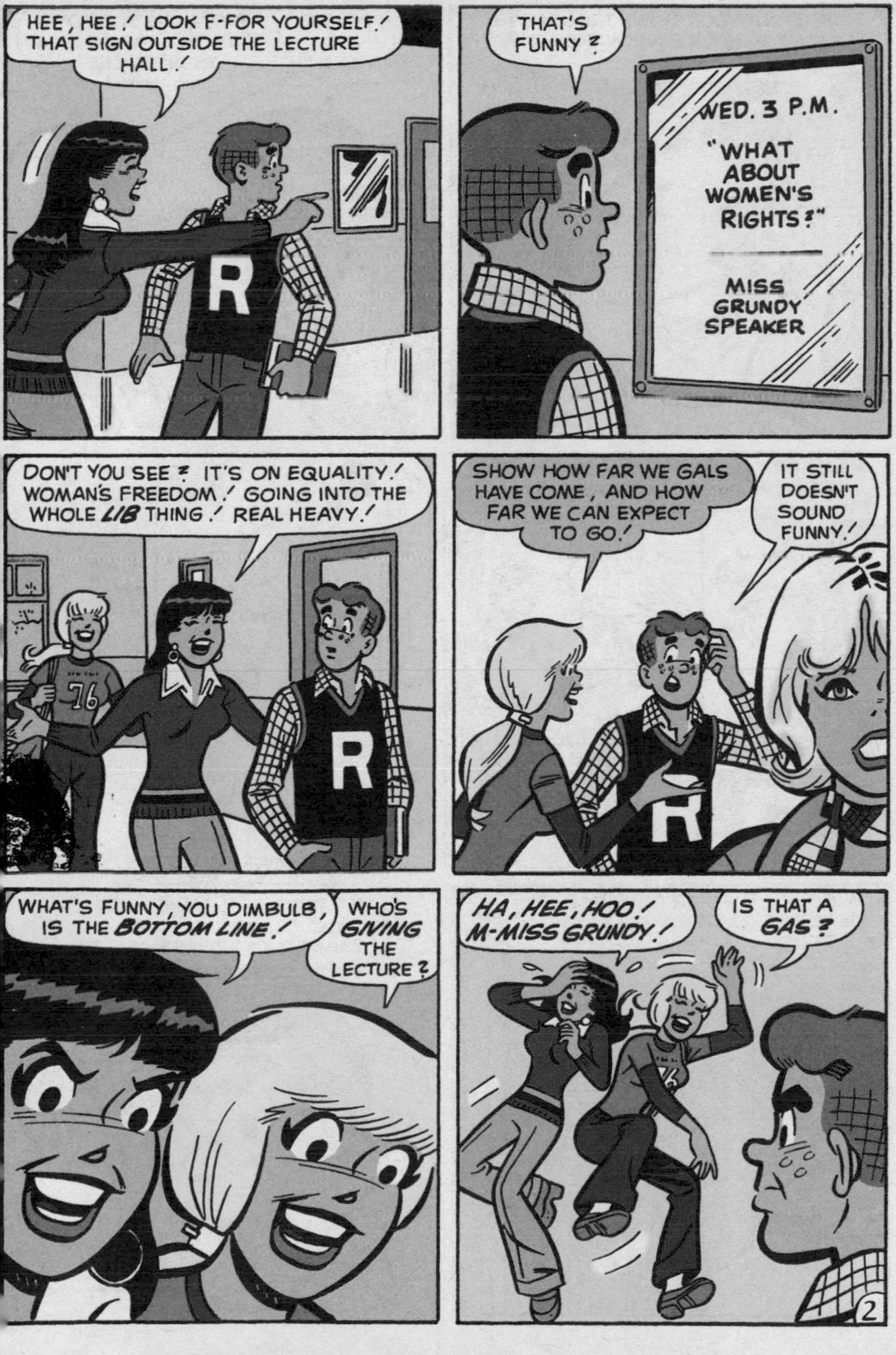
HEE, HEE! LOOK F-FOR YOURSELF! THAT SIGN OUTSIDE THE LECTURE HALL!
THAT'S FUNNY?
WED. 3 P.M.
"WHAT ABOUT WOMEN'S RIGHTS?"
MISS GRUNDY SPEAKER
DON'T YOU SEE? IT'S ON EQUALITY! WOMAN'S FREEDOM! GOING INTO THE WHOLE LIB THING! REAL HEAVY!
76
SHOW HOW FAR WE GALS HAVE COME, AND HOW FAR WE CAN EXPECT TO GO!
IT STILL DOESN'T SOUND FUNNY!
WHAT'S FUNNY, YOU DIMBULB, IS THE BOTTOM LINE!
WHO'S GIVING THE LECTURE?
HA, HEE, HOO! M-MISS GRUNDY!
IS THAT A GAS?
2

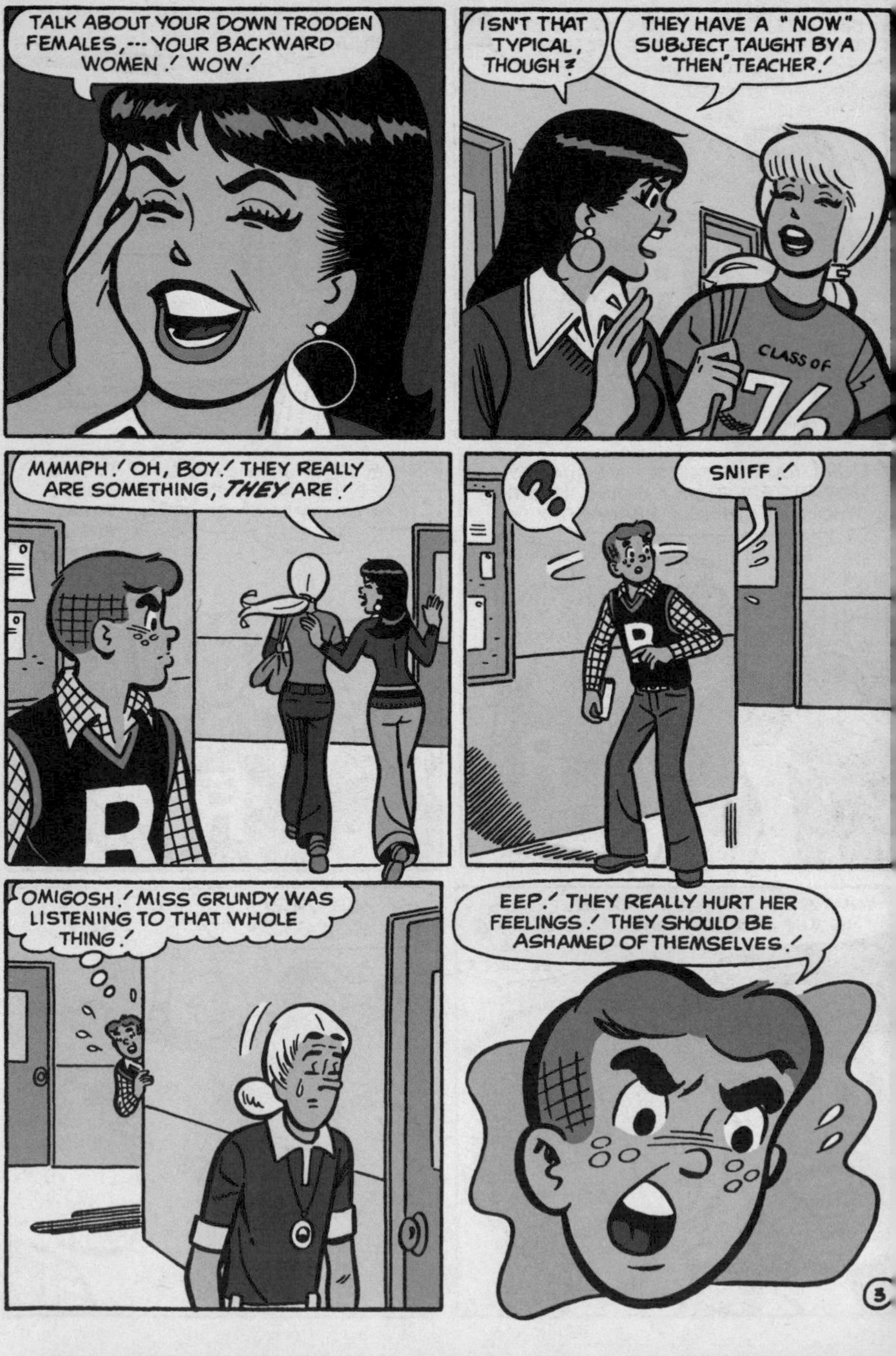
TALK ABOUT YOUR DOWN TRODDEN FEMALES,--- YOUR BACKWARD WOMEN! WOW!
ISN'T THAT TYPICAL, THOUGH?
THEY HAVE A "NOW" SUBJECT TAUGHT BY A "THEN" TEACHER!
CLASS OF 76
MMMPH! OH, BOY! THEY REALLY ARE SOMETHING, THEY ARE!
?
SNIFF!
OMIGOSH! MISS GRUNDY WAS LISTENING TO THAT WHOLE THING!
EEP! THEY REALLY HURT HER FEELINGS! THEY SHOULD BE ASHAMED OF THEMSELVES!
3

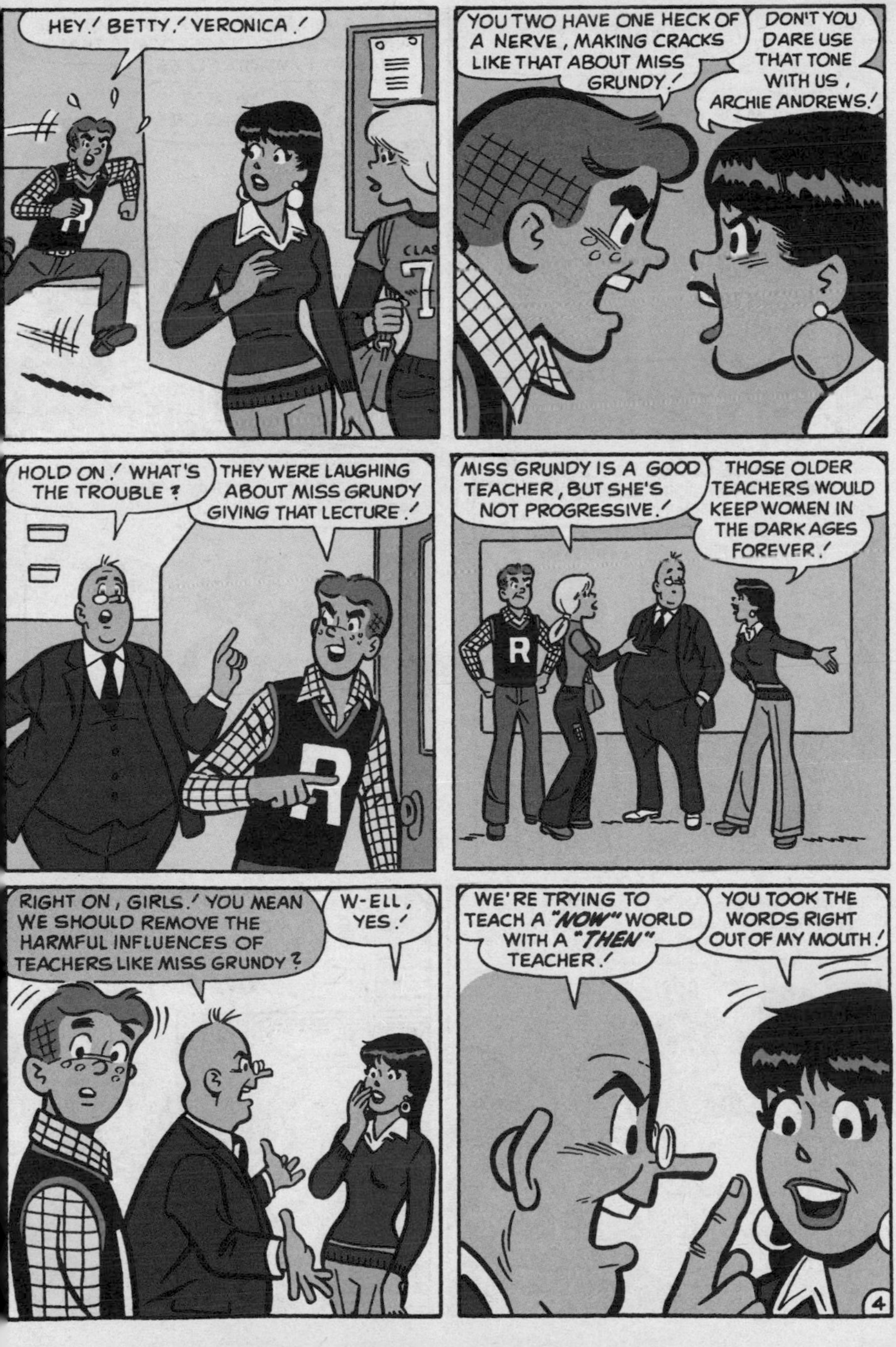
HEY! BETTY! VERONICA!
YOU TWO HAVE ONE HECK OF A NERVE, MAKING CRACKS LIKE THAT ABOUT MISS GRUNDY!
DON'T YOU DARE USE THAT TONE WITH US, ARCHIE ANDREWS!
HOLD ON! WHAT'S THE TROUBLE?
THEY WERE LAUGHING ABOUT MISS GRUNDY GIVING THAT LECTURE!
MISS GRUNDY IS A GOOD TEACHER, BUT SHE'S NOT PROGRESSIVE!
THOSE OLDER TEACHERS WOULD KEEP WOMEN IN THE DARK AGES FOREVER!
RIGHT ON, GIRLS! YOU MEAN WE SHOULD REMOVE THE HARMFUL INFLUENCES OF TEACHERS LIKE MISS GRUNDY?
W-ELL, YES!
WE'RE TRYING TO TEACH A "NOW" WORLD WITH A "THEN" TEACHER!
YOU TOOK THE WORDS RIGHT OUT OF MY MOUTH!
4

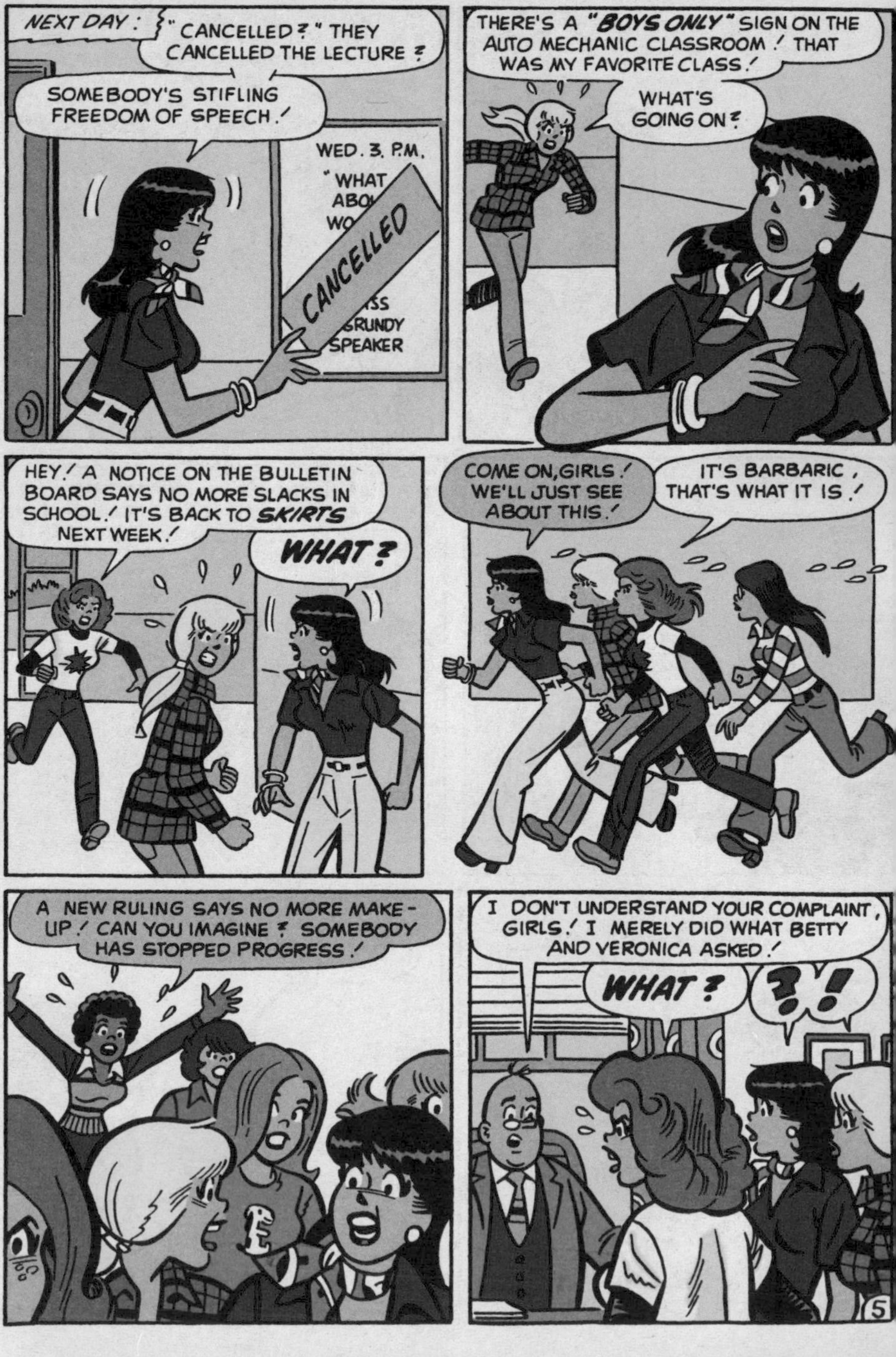
NEXT DAY:
"CANCELLED?" THEY CANCELLED THE LECTURE?
SOMEBODY'S STIFLING FREEDOM OF SPEECH!
WED. 3. P.M.
"WHAT ABO WO
CANCELLED
SS GRUNDY SPEAKER
THERE'S A "BOYS ONLY" SIGN ON THE AUTO MECHANIC CLASSROOM! THAT WAS MY FAVORITE CLASS!
WHAT'S GOING ON?
HEY! A NOTICE ON THE BULLETIN BOARD SAYS NO MORE SLACKS IN SCHOOL! IT'S BACK TO SKIRTS NEXT WEEK!
WHAT?
COME ON, GIRLS! WE'LL JUST SEE ABOUT THIS!
IT'S BARBARIC, THAT'S WHAT IT IS!
A NEW RULING SAYS NO MORE MAKE-UP! CAN YOU IMAGINE? SOMEBODY HAS STOPPED PROGRESS!
I DON'T UNDERSTAND YOUR COMPLAINT, GIRLS! I MERELY DID WHAT BETTY AND VERONICA ASKED!
WHAT?
?!
5

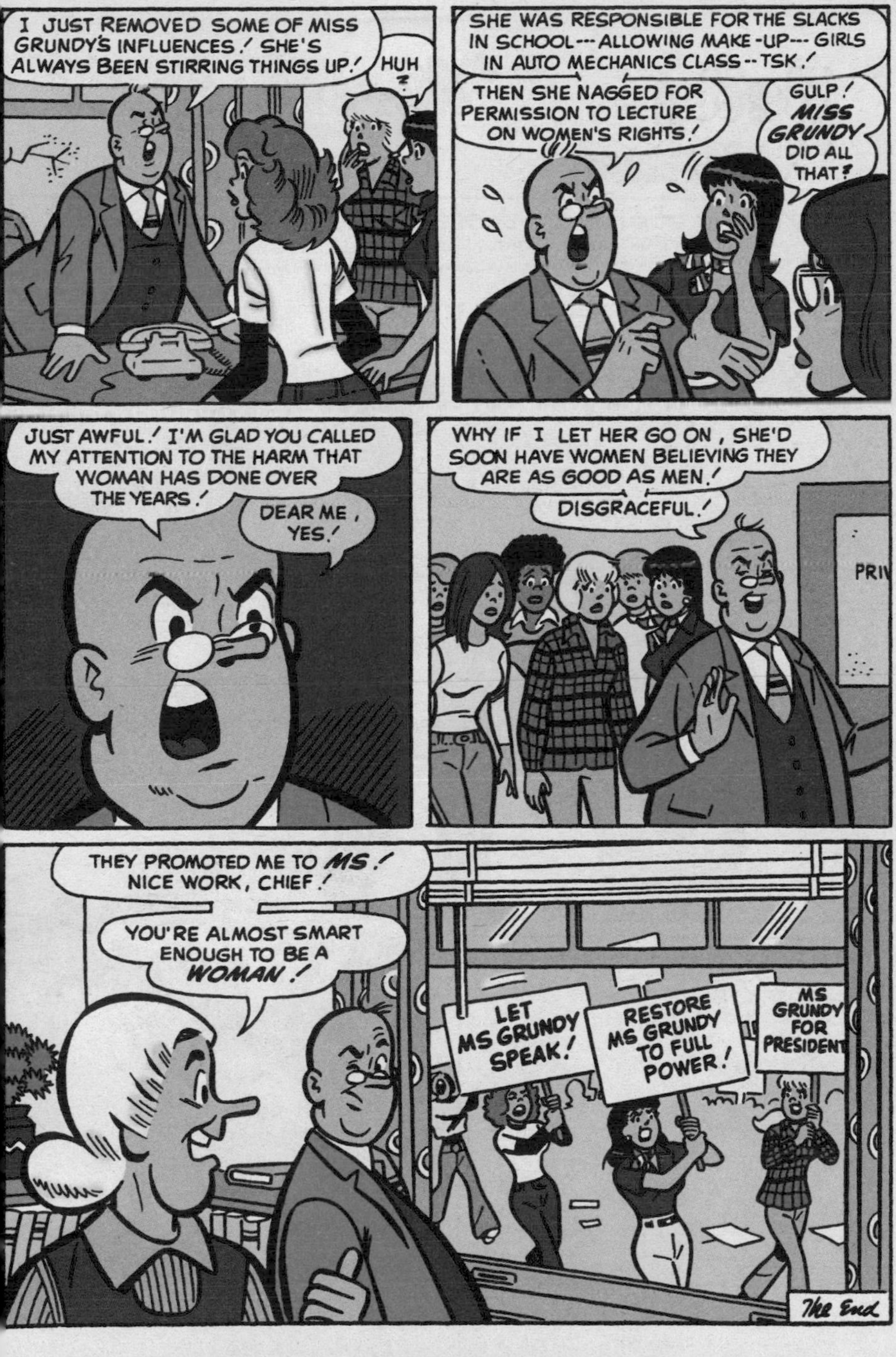
I JUST REMOVED SOME OF MISS GRUNDY'S INFLUENCES! SHE'S ALWAYS BEEN STIRRING THINGS UP!
HUH?
SHE WAS RESPONSIBLE FOR THE SLACKS IN SCHOOL--- ALLOWING MAKE-UP--- GIRLS IN AUTO MECHANICS CLASS -- TSK!
THEN SHE NAGGED FOR PERMISSION TO LECTURE ON WOMEN'S RIGHTS!
GULP! MISS GRUNDY DID ALL THAT?
JUST AWFUL! I'M GLAD YOU CALLED MY ATTENTION TO THE HARM THAT WOMAN HAS DONE OVER THE YEARS!
DEAR ME, YES!
WHY IF I LET HER GO ON, SHE'D SOON HAVE WOMEN BELIEVING THEY ARE AS GOOD AS MEN!
DISGRACEFUL!
PRIV
THEY PROMOTED ME TO MS! NICE WORK, CHIEF!
YOU'RE ALMOST SMART ENOUGH TO BE A WOMAN!
LET MS GRUNDY SPEAK!
RESTORE MS GRUNDY TO FULL POWER!
MS GRUNDY FOR PRESIDENT
The End

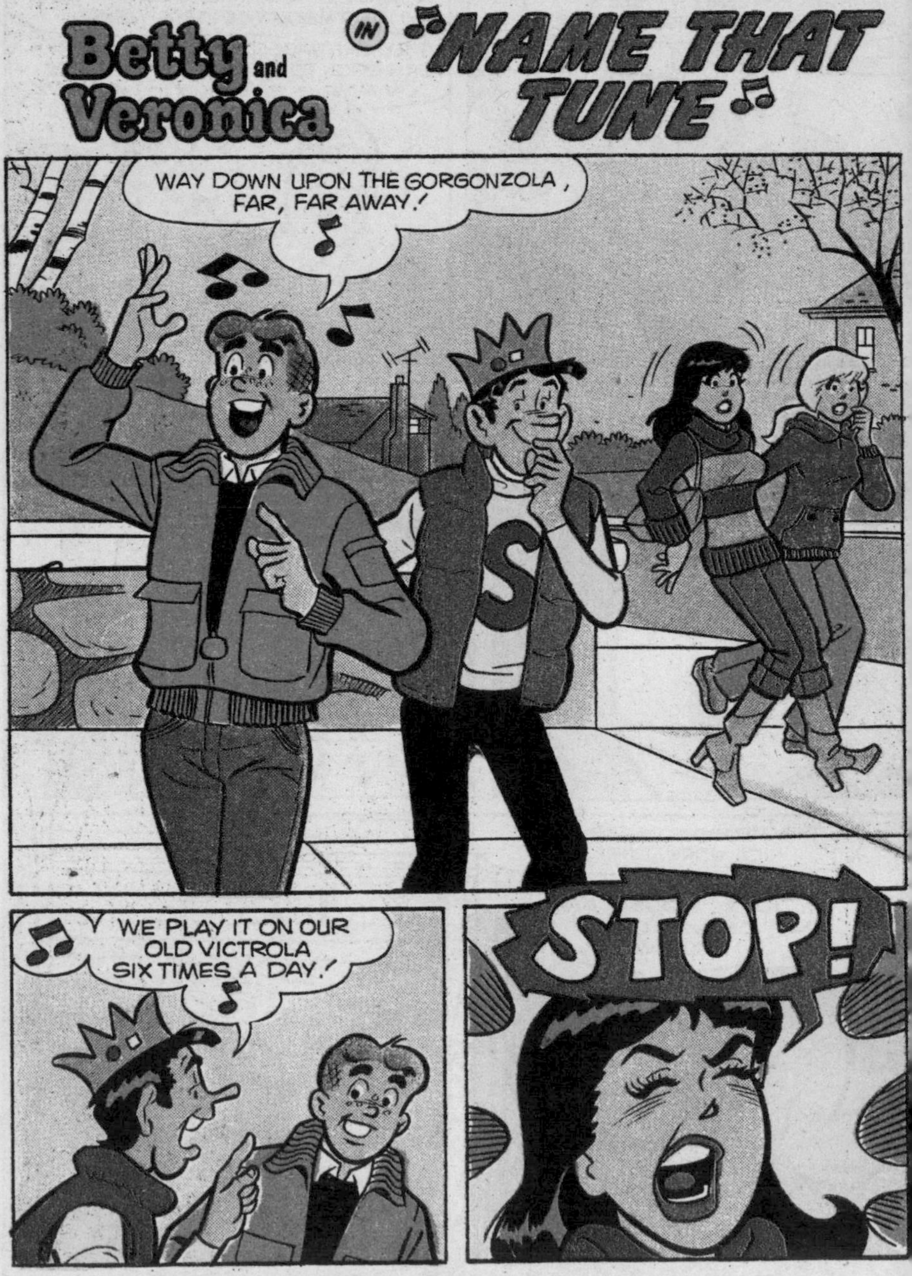
Betty and Veronica
IN
"NAME THAT TUNE"
WAY DOWN UPON THE GORGONZOLA, FAR, FAR AWAY!
WE PLAY IT ON OUR OLD VICTROLA SIX TIMES A DAY!
STOP!

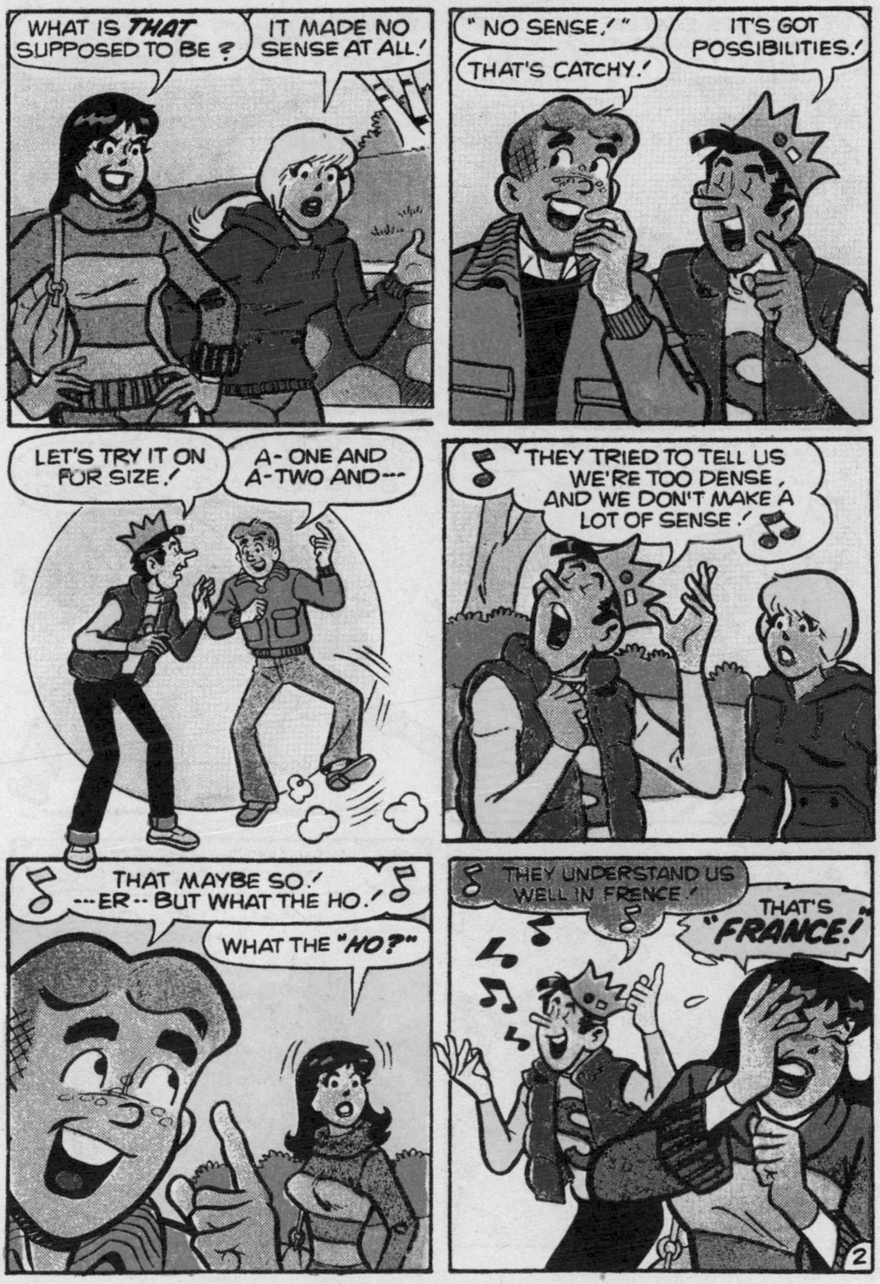
WHAT IS THAT SUPPOSED TO BE ?
IT MADE NO SENSE AT ALL!
"NO SENSE!"
THAT'S CATCHY!
IT'S GOT POSSIBILITIES!
LET'S TRY IT ON FOR SIZE!
A-ONE AND A-TWO AND---
THEY TRIED TO TELL US WE'RE TOO DENSE, AND WE DON'T MAKE A LOT OF SENSE!
THAT MAYBE SO! ---ER-- BUT WHAT THE HO!
WHAT THE "HO?"
THEY UNDERSTAND US WELL IN FRENCE!
THAT'S "FRANCE!"
2

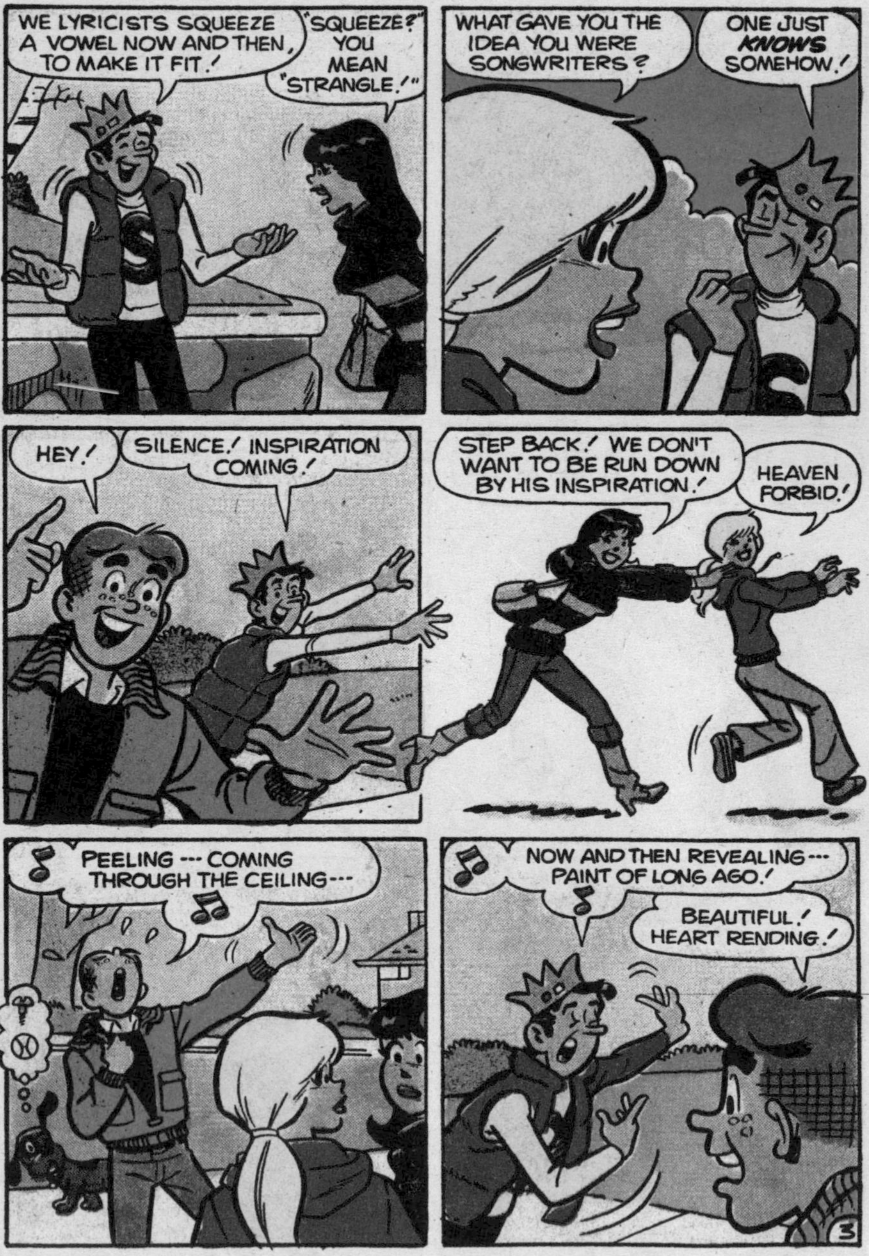
WE LYRICISTS SQUEEZE A VOWEL NOW AND THEN, TO MAKE IT FIT!
"SQUEEZE?" YOU MEAN "STRANGLE!"
WHAT GAVE YOU THE IDEA YOU WERE SONGWRITERS?
ONE JUST KNOWS SOMEHOW!
HEY!
SILENCE! INSPIRATION COMING!
STEP BACK! WE DON'T WANT TO BE RUN DOWN BY HIS INSPIRATION!
HEAVEN FORBID!
PEELING --- COMING THROUGH THE CEILING ---
NOW AND THEN REVEALING --- PAINT OF LONG AGO!
BEAUTIFUL! HEART RENDING!
3

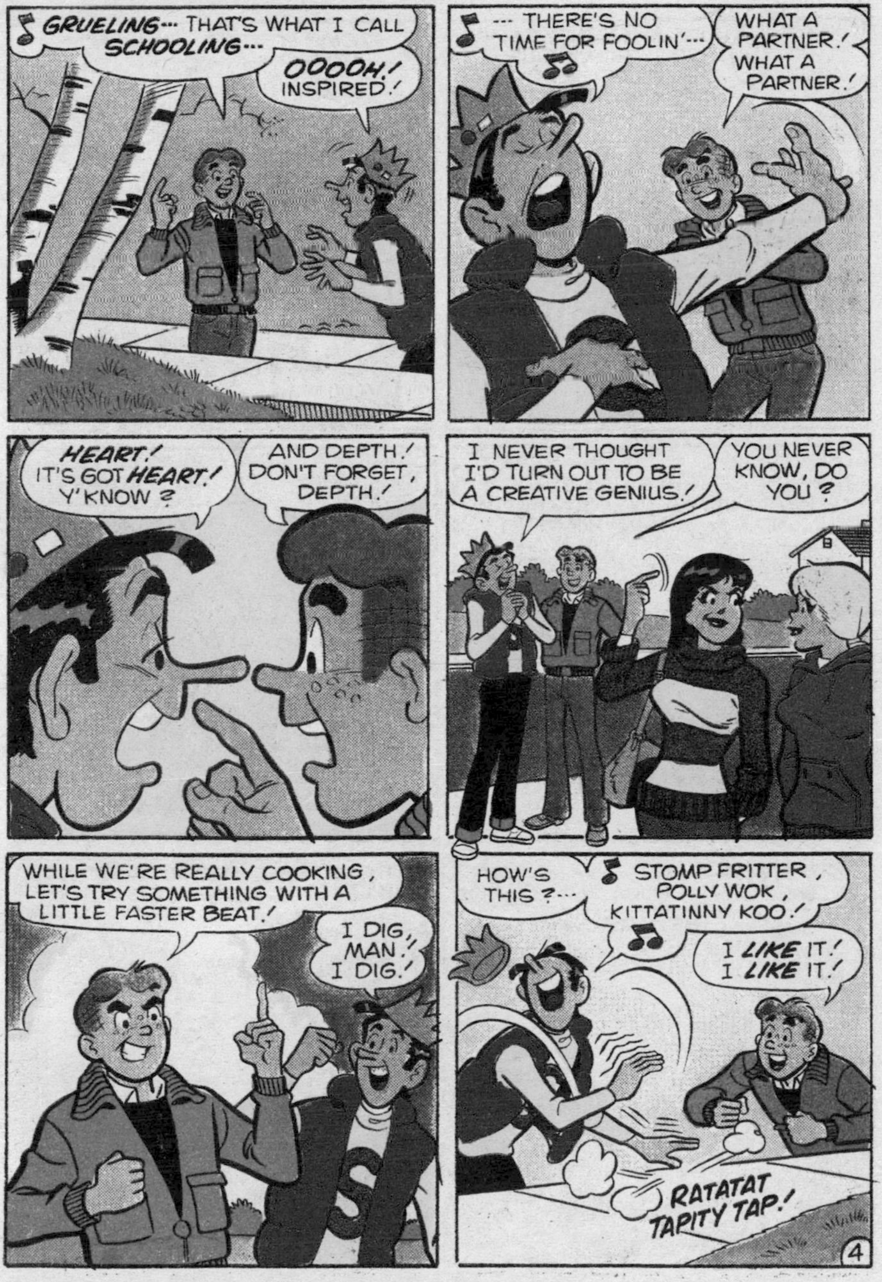
GRUELING... THAT'S WHAT I CALL SCHOOLING...
OOOOH! INSPIRED!
--- THERE'S NO TIME FOR FOOLIN'---
WHAT A PARTNER! WHAT A PARTNER!
HEART! IT'S GOT HEART! Y'KNOW ?
AND DEPTH! DON'T FORGET, DEPTH!
I NEVER THOUGHT I'D TURN OUT TO BE A CREATIVE GENIUS!
YOU NEVER KNOW, DO YOU ?
WHILE WE'RE REALLY COOKING, LET'S TRY SOMETHING WITH A LITTLE FASTER BEAT!
I DIG, MAN. I DIG!
HOW'S THIS ?...
STOMP FRITTER, POLLY WOK, KITTATINNY KOO!
I LIKE IT! I LIKE IT!
RATATAT TAPITY TAP!
4

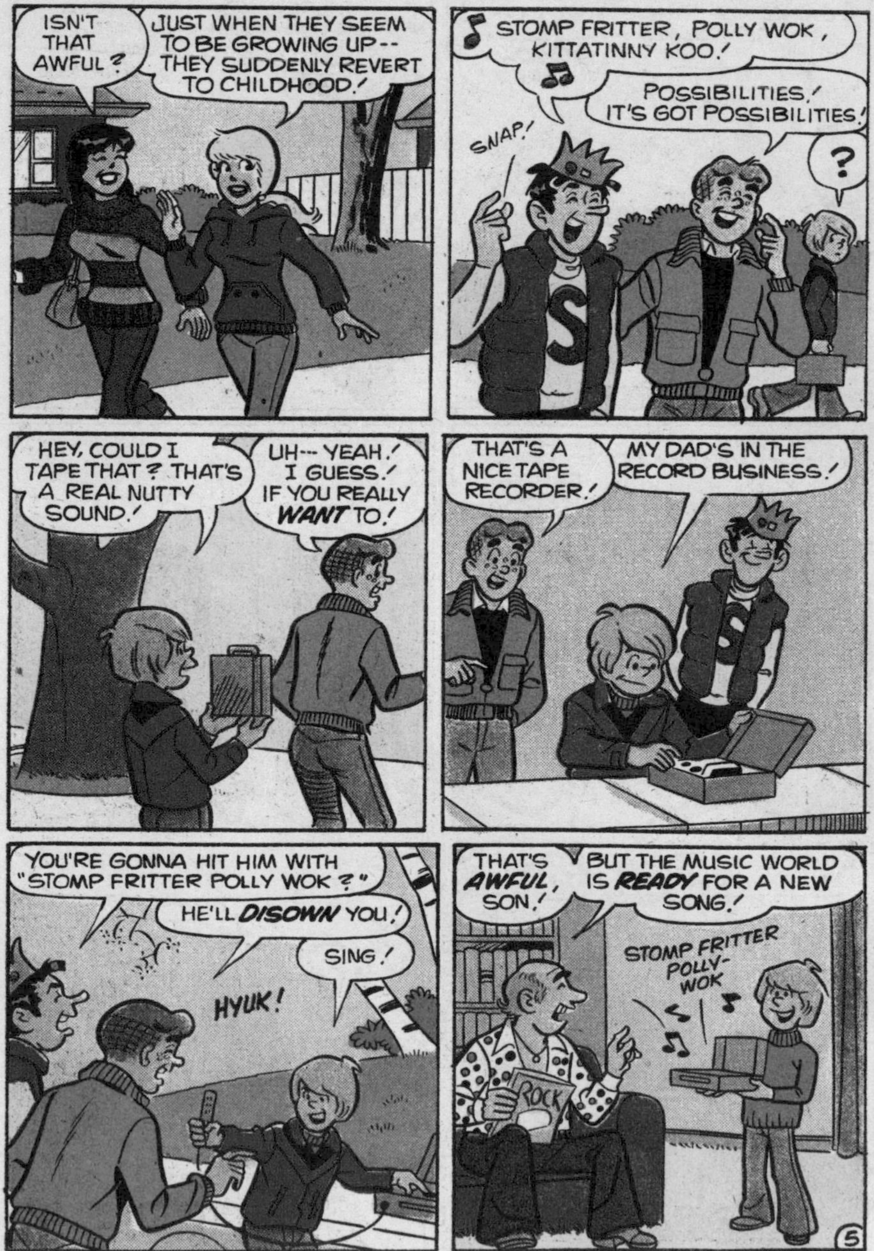
ISN'T THAT AWFUL?
JUST WHEN THEY SEEM TO BE GROWING UP-- THEY SUDDENLY REVERT TO CHILDHOOD!
STOMP FRITTER, POLLY WOK, KITTATINNY KOO!
SNAP!
POSSIBILITIES! IT'S GOT POSSIBILITIES!
?
HEY, COULD I TAPE THAT? THAT'S A REAL NUTTY SOUND!
UH-- YEAH! I GUESS! IF YOU REALLY WANT TO!
THAT'S A NICE TAPE RECORDER!
MY DAD'S IN THE RECORD BUSINESS!
YOU'RE GONNA HIT HIM WITH "STOMP FRITTER POLLY WOK?"
HE'LL DISOWN YOU!
SING!
HYUK!
THAT'S AWFUL, SON!
BUT THE MUSIC WORLD IS READY FOR A NEW SONG!
STOMP FRITTER POLLY-WOK
ROCK
5

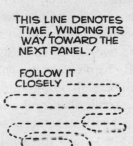

THIS LINE DENOTES TIME, WINDING ITS WAY TOWARD THE NEXT PANEL!

FOLLOW IT CLOSELY ------

---AND NOW, THE LATEST NUMBER TO CLAW ITS WAY ONTO THE CHARTS---

"STOMP FRITTER!"

"STOMP FRITTER?"

LIKE IN ARCHIE AND JUGGIE?

STOMP FRITTER POLLY WOK KITTATINNY KOO!

POM BOOZLE, SNICKER FRITZ?

SAK GNOM WING WOK?

OR MAYBE "WOK WING?"

DAY BY DAY, SMITHERS, THEY GET HARDER TO UNDERSTAND!

IMPOSSIBLE, SIR!

The End

The 1980s

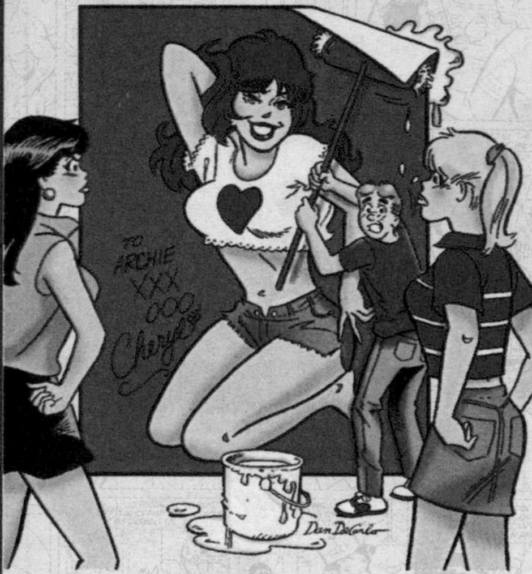
TO ARCHIE XXX OOO Cheryl
Dan DeCarlo

The ’80s marked several major shifts at Archie, including some behind-the-scenes changes, such as the second generation of what became a two-family business, with Richard Goldwater and Michael Silberkleit now guiding the company. Archie also continued to experiment with its comics and digests.The writers and artists continued to adapt the characters to changing standards and fashions. Whether sporting the “preppie” look or “new wave” styles, the fashions were brighter and crazier. Perhaps most ambitious of all was Cheryl Blossom, a new arrival in Riverdale—and a new rival to Betty & Veronica for Archie!

If the ’60s were about social upheaval and the ’70s were about making sense of the ’60s, then the ’80s were an about face, as many prospered and embraced excess and good times. Perhaps more than any prior decade, the ’80s saw the manufacture of non-essential goods. In many ways, it was a contradiction, as there were still some real, serious concerns in the nation. During President Reagan’s term, tensions were heightened as the arms race between the U.S. and the U.S.S.R. accelerated. Despite the ills facing the nation, many maintained a “live it up” attitude, and for many a certain optimism and national pride resulted from the collapse of the Soviet Union and the fall of the Berlin Wall.

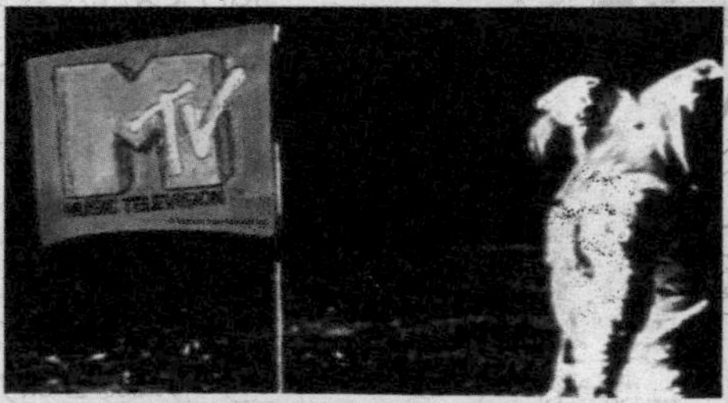
MTV
MUSIC TELEVISION

Just as in the 1970s, the double-sided nature of the times led to various forms of entertainment. In the world of music, listeners could choose between socially conscious acts or simply entertaining ones… and watch music videos of all of the above on the newly launched MTV. In contrast to the happy-time party vibe were the sci-fi films of the era that reflected the real-life nuclear worries lurking beneath the surface. There was still room for fun, though—filmmaker Stephen Spielberg rose to even greater prominence with a string of films he directed or produced that courted families with fun, adventure and thrills.

By the end of the decade Archie introduced a few experimental titles, like the sci-fi-esque *Archie 3000* which placed the teens in the far-off future, *Faculty Funnies,* which found the teachers gaining super powers and *Dilton's Strange Science* adding a sci-fi twist worthy of atomic scare '50s monster films. The final year of the '80s also found Archie take on a series that they licensed from elsewhere—the *Teenage Mutant Ninja Turtles,* which would become a lucrative success for Archie through the first half of the next decade.

While the Archie characters were the undisputed champs of Saturday morning TV in the 1970s, other characters and shows arose in the 1980s to take their place. Archie and his friends would return to the airwaves in 1987 in *The New Archies*, a new animated series produced by DIC that updated the look of the cast and placed them in junior high. Two other changes from the original cartoons included Veronica's voice changing from that of a southern belle to a California valley girl, and Dilton being replaced by a similar African-American character named Eugene.

All in all, the Archie Comics of the '80s served to introduce the characters to new readers while satisfying long-time fans, and paved the way for the following decade's golden anniversary.

True to Type
Sabrina #58, 1980
by Dan DeCarlo,
Rudy Lapick
and Bill Yoshida

Sabrina's creators, writer George Gladir and artist Dan DeCarlo, brought a whole new spin to the idea of what a witch was in pop-culture. Gone was the old, green-faced hag with black robes and missing teeth, and in was a stylish, bubbly teen whose attempts at magic didn't always match her good intentions. This story is a perfect example of who Sabrina is in a nutshell: fun, positive and mischievous, as well as just a teensy bit careless with her spells! Like a real teen, Sabrina is a little defiant with her elders, but she always proves that her heart is in the right place. And, of course, there's magic with comedic and unexpected results! That's why stories like this are timeless, and will never go out of style—Sabrina herself is a shining example of a well-rounded character who can make people laugh while enjoying the possibilities (and mishaps) that magic can create.

--Tania Del Rio
Writer, Sabrina the Teenage Witch

E.T. Travesty
Archie #322, 1983
by Dan DeCarlo Jr.,
Jimmy DeCarlo
and Bill Yoshida

Ah… the '80s… Big hair, glam rock and Ronald Reagan. What a combination! We saw movies like *Back to the Future, E.T.* and *Chariots of Fire*. We heard Madonna and Bon Jovi for the first time. We witnessed the collapse of the Berlin Wall and the rise of pop culture icons. It was quite the decade. Standing strong in the midst of it all was Archie.

--Glenn Scarpelli
Alex Handris on TV sitcom One Day at a Time *and son of longtime Archie artist Henry Scarpelli, excerpted from his foreword to* Archie Americana: Best of the Eighties Book 2

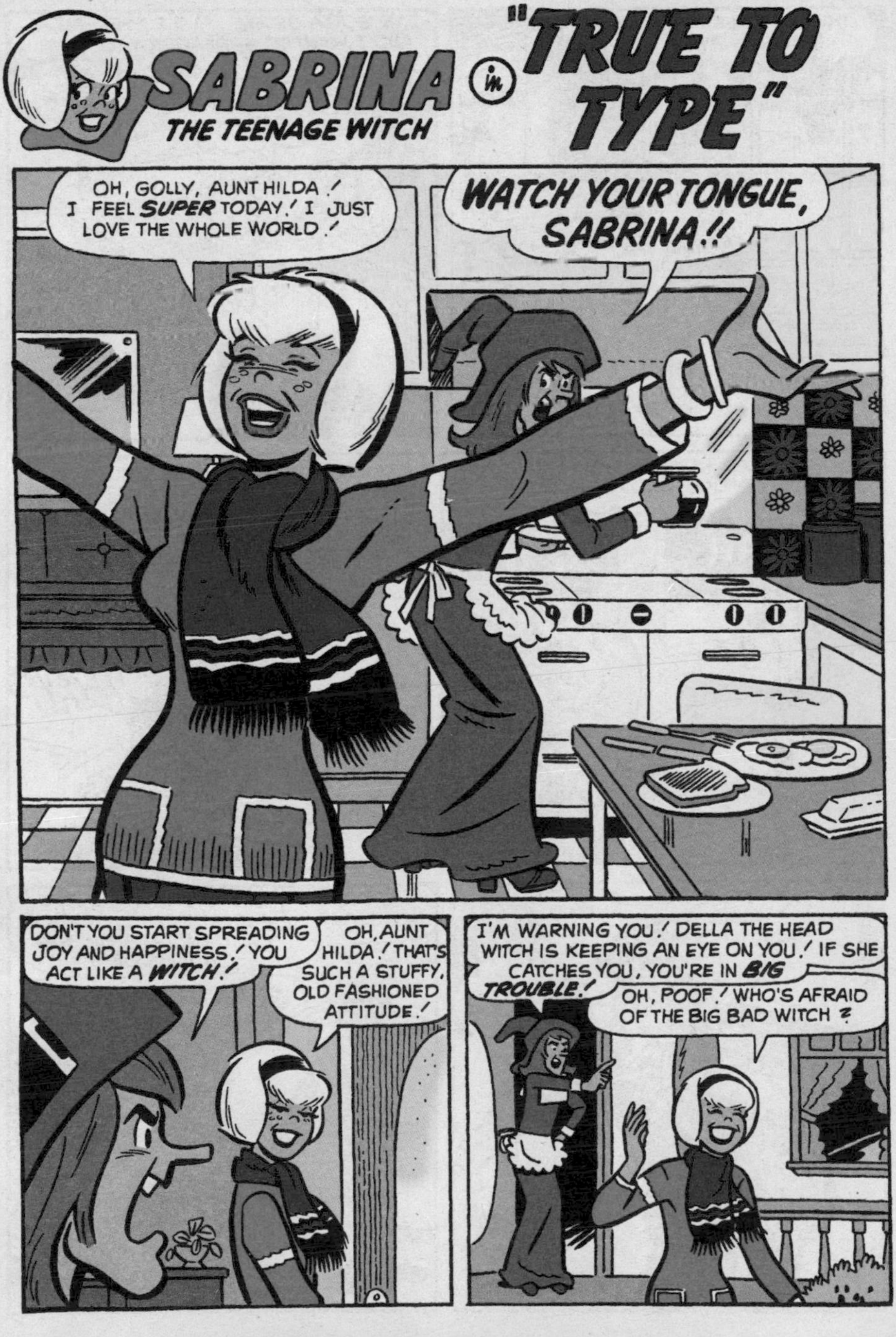
SABRINA THE TEENAGE WITCH in "TRUE TO TYPE"
OH, GOLLY, AUNT HILDA! I FEEL SUPER TODAY! I JUST LOVE THE WHOLE WORLD!
WATCH YOUR TONGUE, SABRINA!!
DON'T YOU START SPREADING JOY AND HAPPINESS! YOU ACT LIKE A WITCH!
OH, AUNT HILDA! THAT'S SUCH A STUFFY, OLD FASHIONED ATTITUDE!
I'M WARNING YOU! DELLA THE HEAD WITCH IS KEEPING AN EYE ON YOU! IF SHE CATCHES YOU, YOU'RE IN BIG TROUBLE!
OH, POOF! WHO'S AFRAID OF THE BIG BAD WITCH?

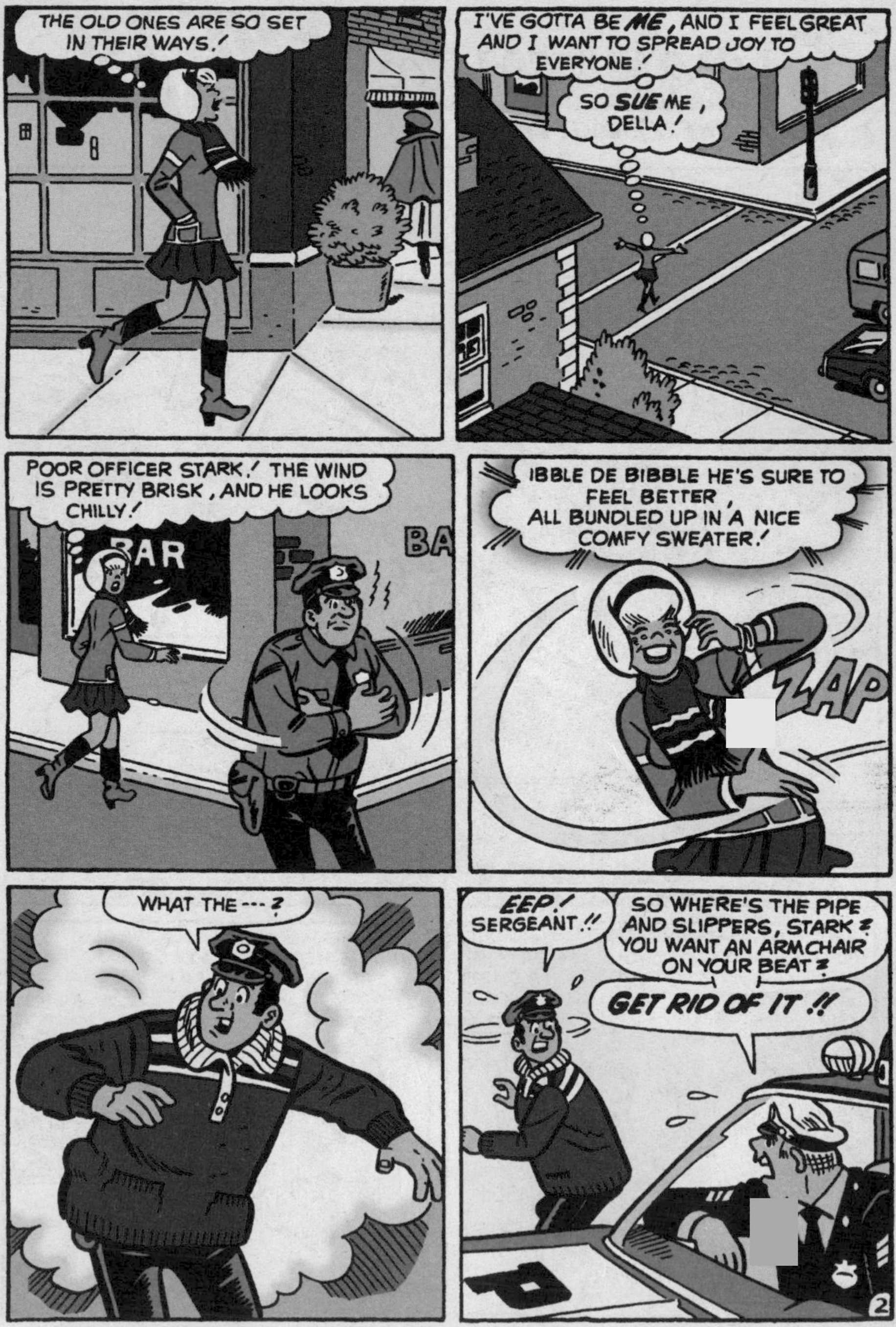
THE OLD ONES ARE SO SET IN THEIR WAYS.!
I'VE GOTTA BE ME, AND I FEEL GREAT AND I WANT TO SPREAD JOY TO EVERYONE.!
SO SUE ME, DELLA!
POOR OFFICER STARK.! THE WIND IS PRETTY BRISK, AND HE LOOKS CHILLY!
BAR
BA
IBBLE DE BIBBLE HE'S SURE TO FEEL BETTER, ALL BUNDLED UP IN A NICE COMFY SWEATER.!
ZAP
WHAT THE---?
EEP! SERGEANT.!!
SO WHERE'S THE PIPE AND SLIPPERS, STARK? YOU WANT AN ARMCHAIR ON YOUR BEAT?
GET RID OF IT.!!
2

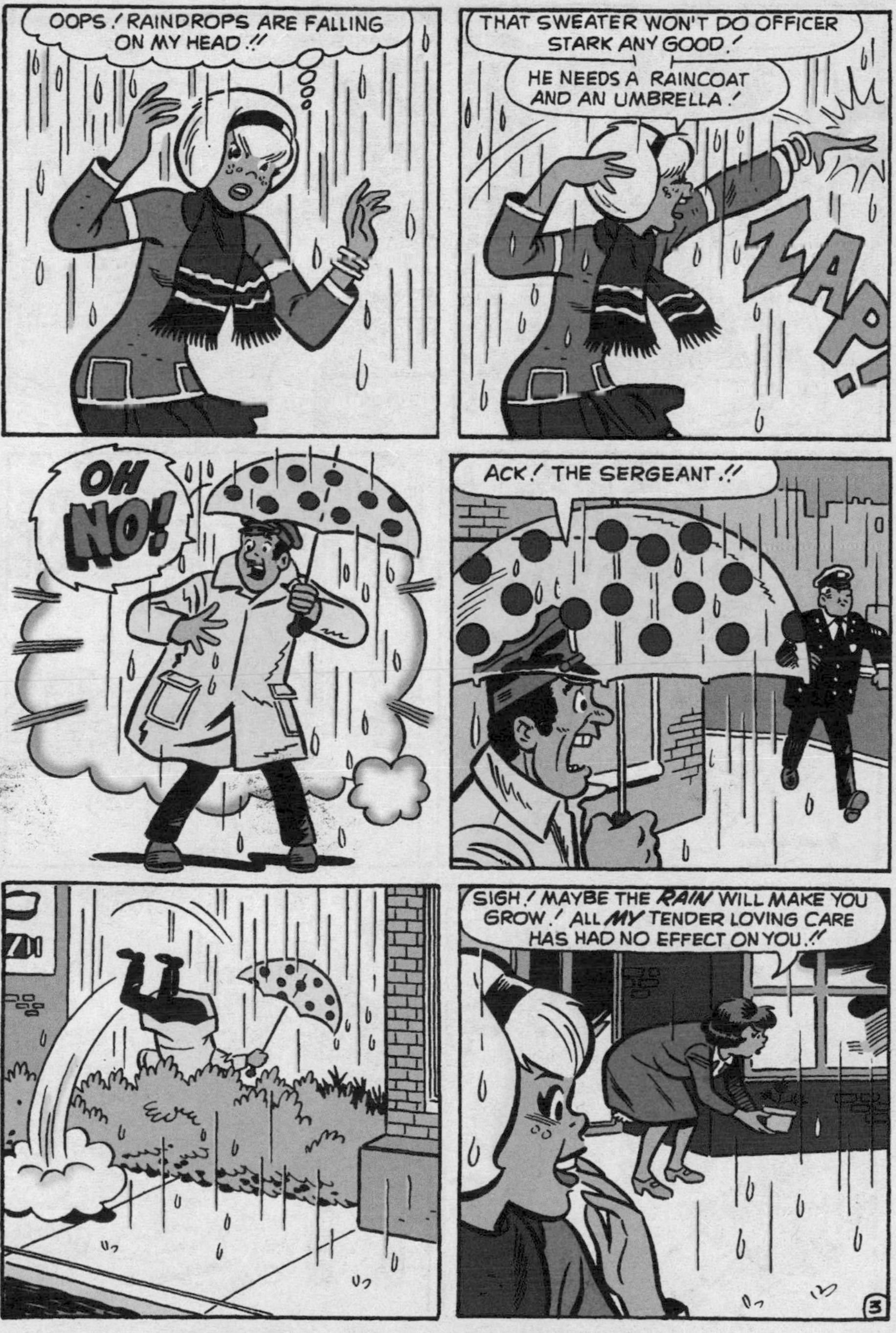
OOPS! RAINDROPS ARE FALLING ON MY HEAD!!
THAT SWEATER WON'T DO OFFICER STARK ANY GOOD!
HE NEEDS A RAINCOAT AND AN UMBRELLA!
ZAP!!
OH NO!
ACK! THE SERGEANT!!
SIGH! MAYBE THE RAIN WILL MAKE YOU GROW! ALL MY TENDER LOVING CARE HAS HAD NO EFFECT ON YOU!!
3

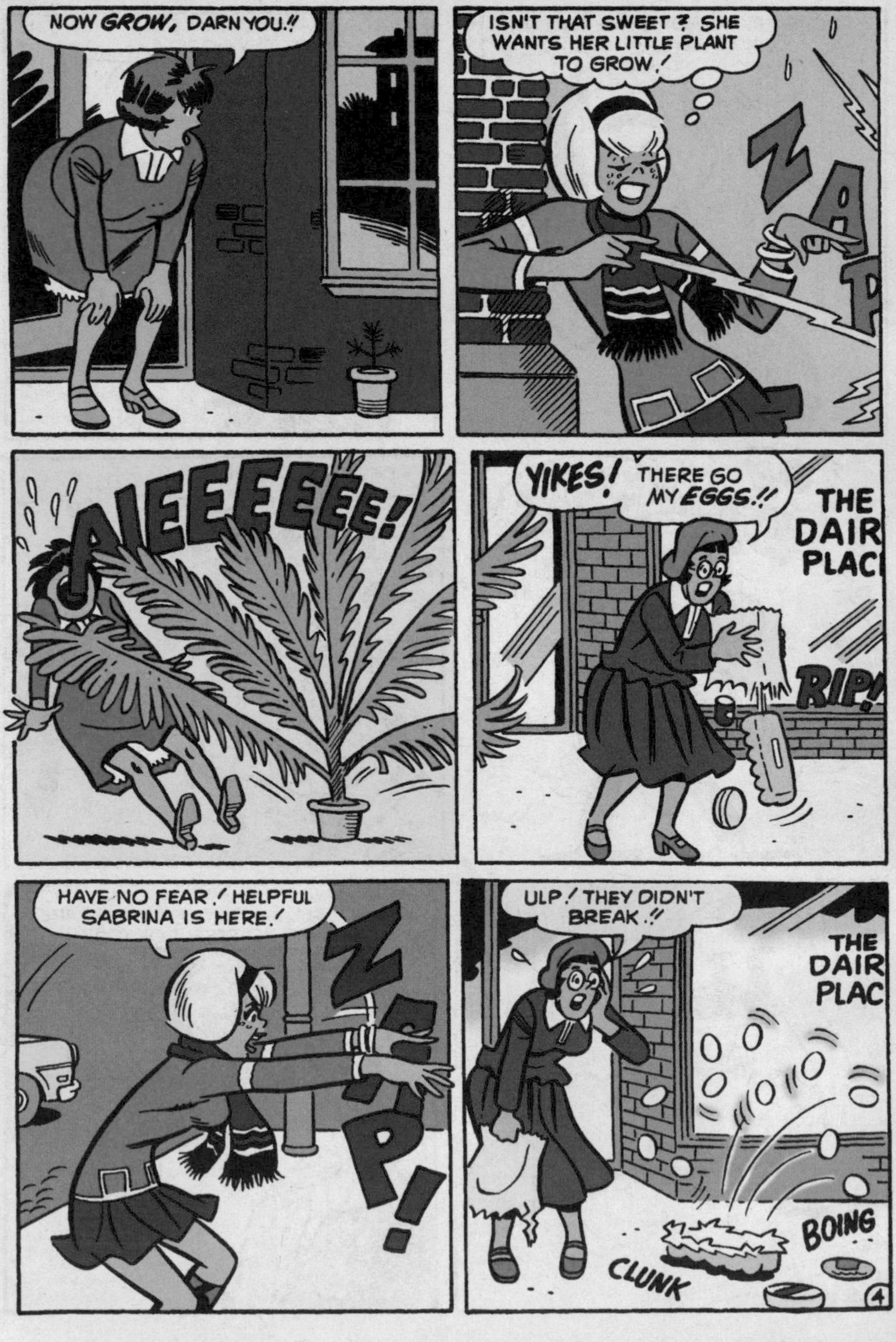
NOW GROW, DARN YOU.!!
ISN'T THAT SWEET ? SHE WANTS HER LITTLE PLANT TO GROW!
ZAP
AIEEEEEEE!
YIKES! THERE GO MY EGGS.!!
THE DAIR PLAC
RIP!
HAVE NO FEAR! HELPFUL SABRINA IS HERE!
ZAP!
ULP! THEY DIDN'T BREAK.!!
THE DAIR PLAC
BOING
CLUNK
4

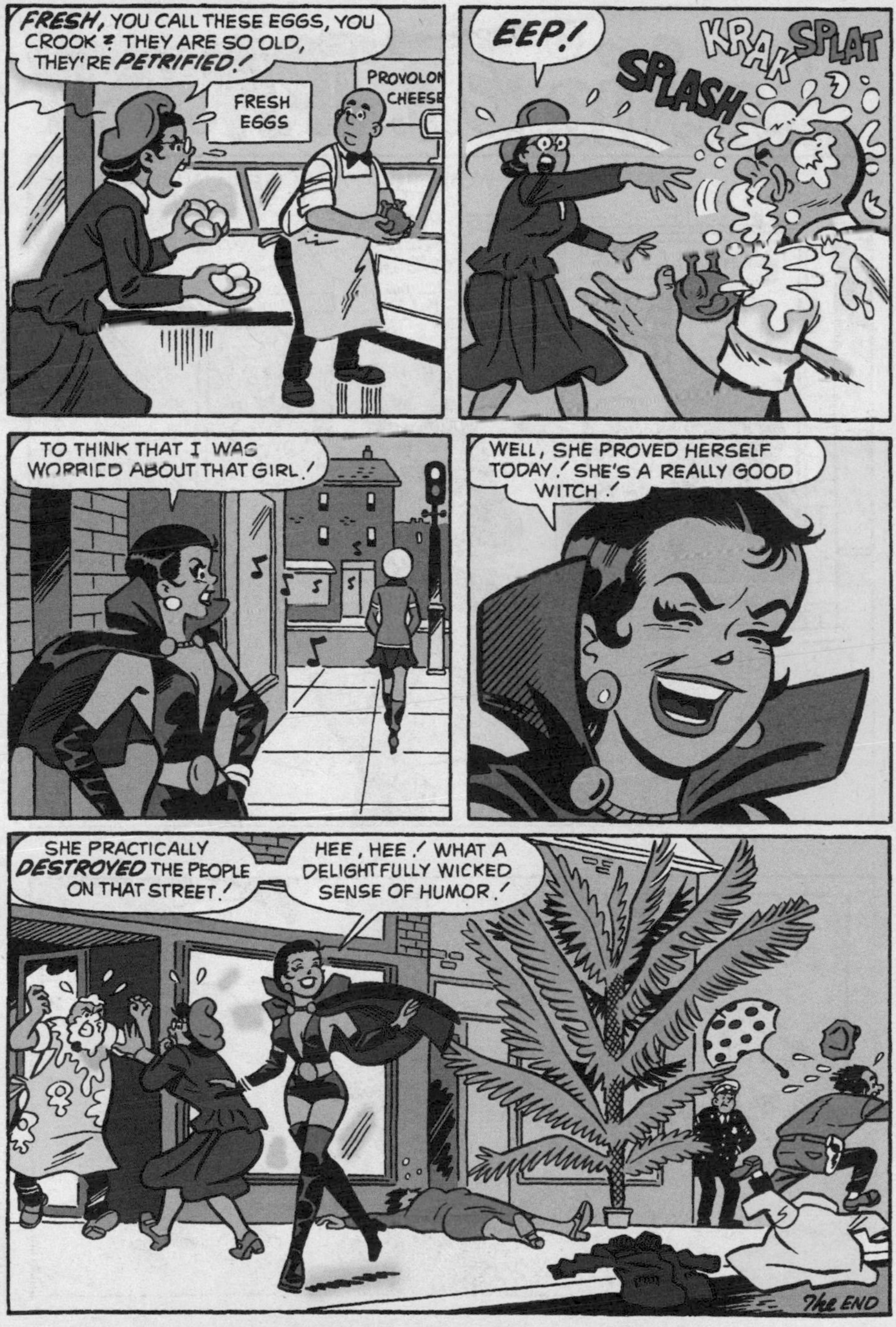

FRESH, YOU CALL THESE EGGS, YOU CROOK? THEY ARE SO OLD, THEY'RE PETRIFIED!
FRESH EGGS
PROVOLON CHEESE
EEP!
KRAK
SPLAT
SPLASH
TO THINK THAT I WAS WORRIED ABOUT THAT GIRL!
WELL, SHE PROVED HERSELF TODAY! SHE'S A REALLY GOOD WITCH!
SHE PRACTICALLY DESTROYED THE PEOPLE ON THAT STREET!
HEE, HEE! WHAT A DELIGHTFULLY WICKED SENSE OF HUMOR!
The END

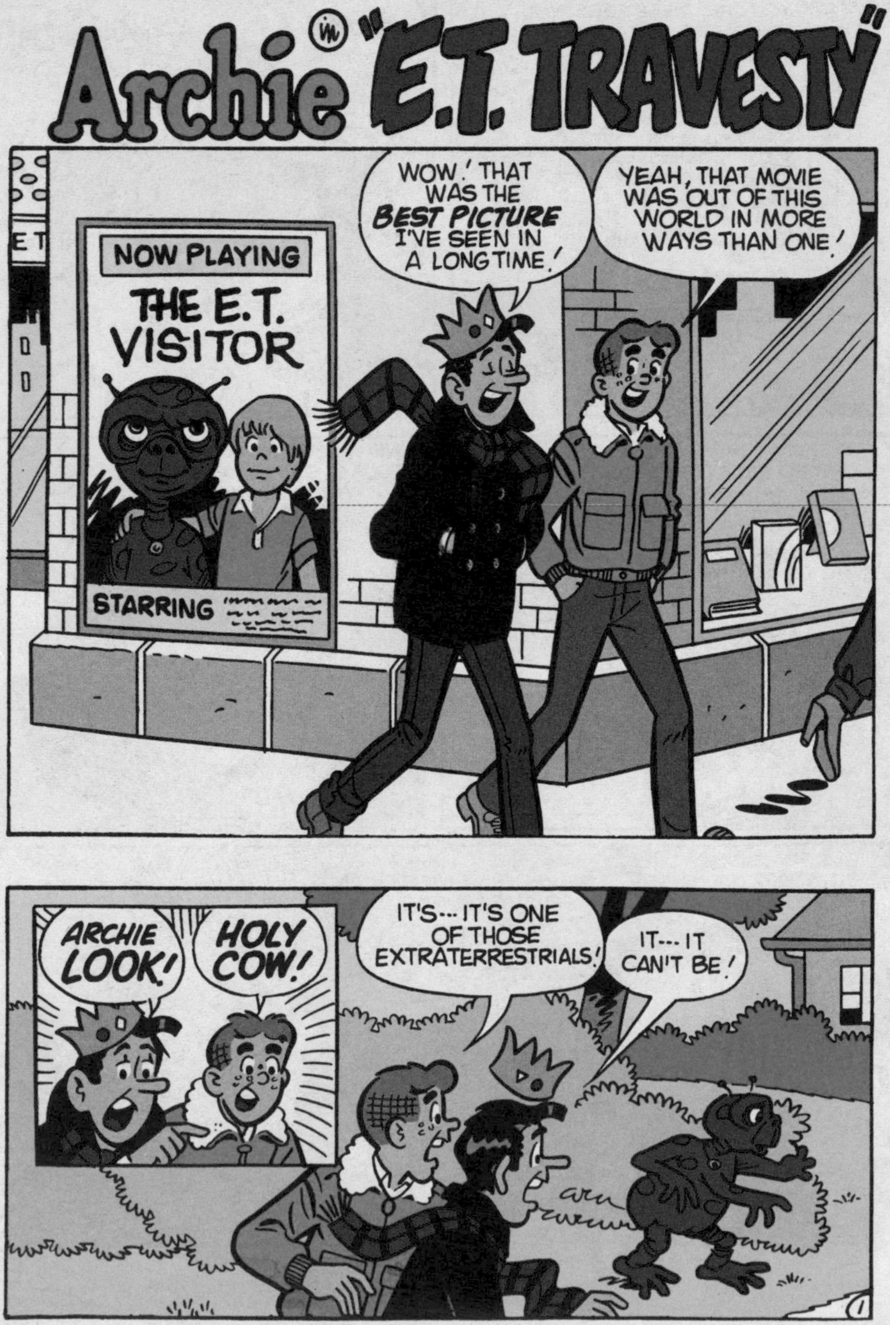
Archie in "E.T. TRAVESTY"
NOW PLAYING
THE E.T. VISITOR
STARRING
WOW! THAT WAS THE BEST PICTURE I'VE SEEN IN A LONG TIME!
YEAH, THAT MOVIE WAS OUT OF THIS WORLD IN MORE WAYS THAN ONE!
ARCHIE LOOK!
HOLY COW!
IT'S--- IT'S ONE OF THOSE EXTRATERRESTRIALS!
IT--- IT CAN'T BE!
1

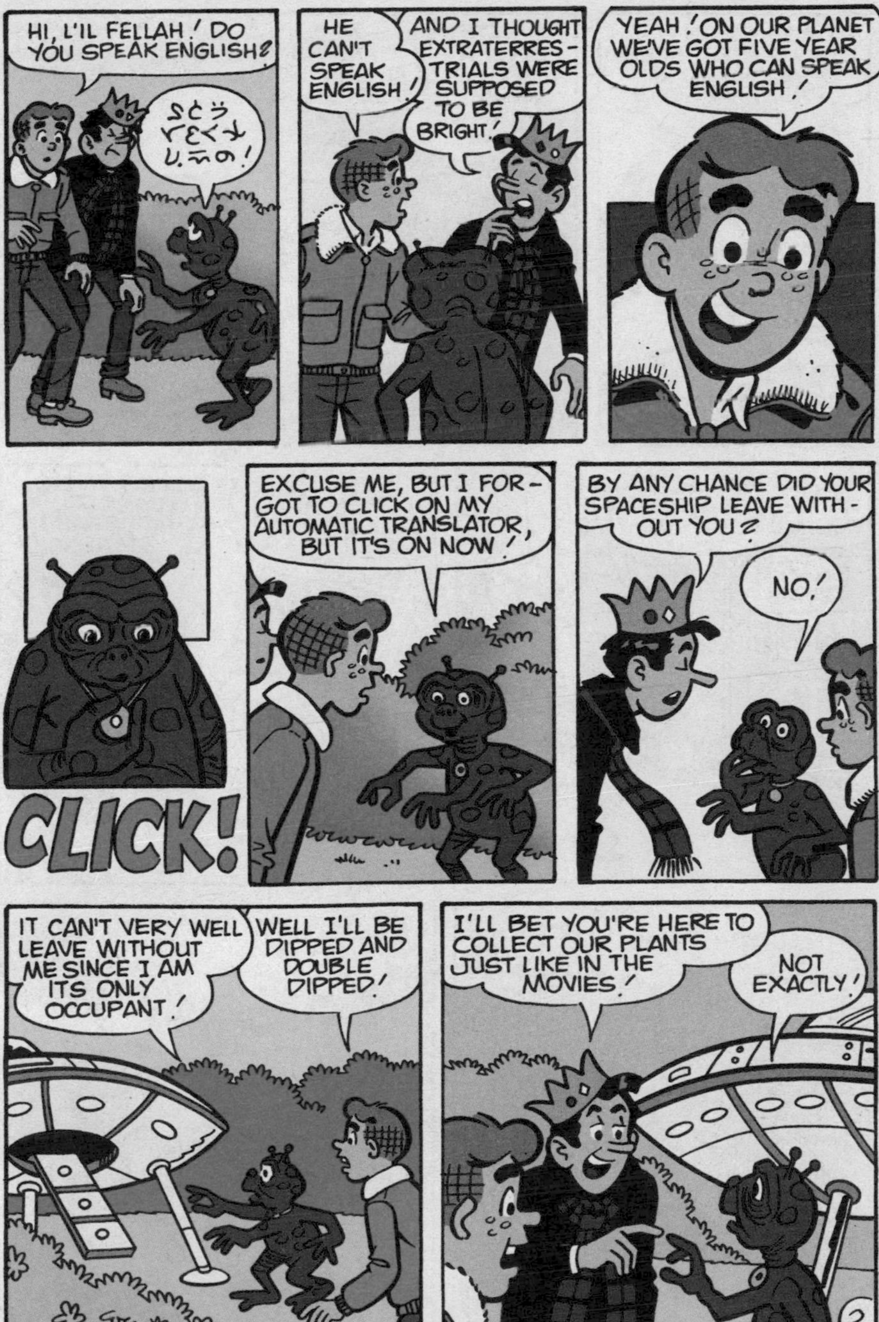
HI, L'IL FELLAH! DO YOU SPEAK ENGLISH?
HE CAN'T SPEAK ENGLISH!
AND I THOUGHT EXTRATERRES-TRIALS WERE SUPPOSED TO BE BRIGHT!
YEAH! ON OUR PLANET WE'VE GOT FIVE YEAR OLDS WHO CAN SPEAK ENGLISH!
CLICK!
EXCUSE ME, BUT I FOR-GOT TO CLICK ON MY AUTOMATIC TRANSLATOR, BUT IT'S ON NOW!
BY ANY CHANCE DID YOUR SPACESHIP LEAVE WITH-OUT YOU?
NO!
IT CAN'T VERY WELL LEAVE WITHOUT ME SINCE I AM ITS ONLY OCCUPANT!
WELL I'LL BE DIPPED AND DOUBLE DIPPED!
I'LL BET YOU'RE HERE TO COLLECT OUR PLANTS JUST LIKE IN THE MOVIES!
NOT EXACTLY!
2

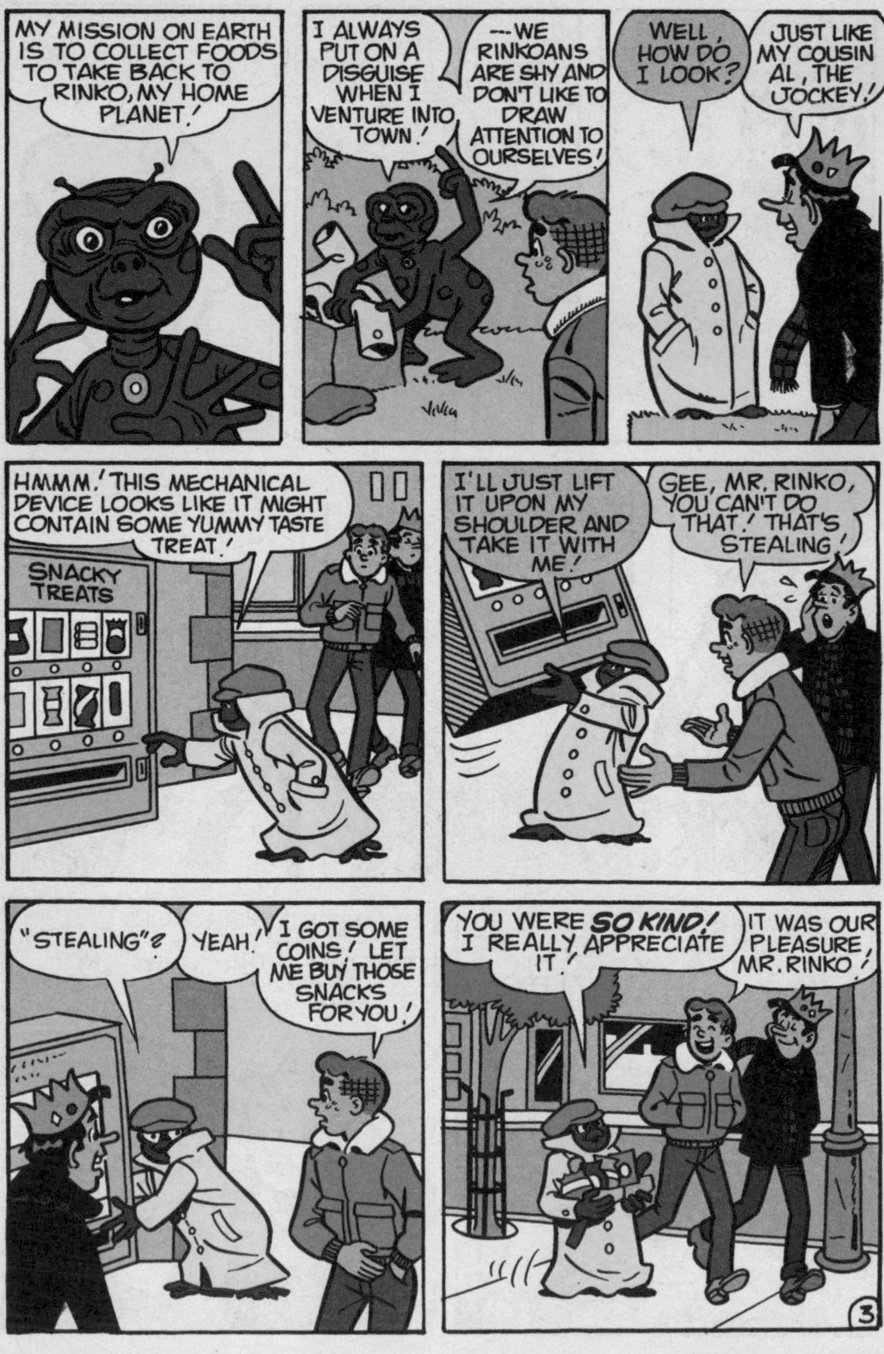
MY MISSION ON EARTH IS TO COLLECT FOODS TO TAKE BACK TO RINKO, MY HOME PLANET!
I ALWAYS PUT ON A DISGUISE WHEN I VENTURE INTO TOWN!
---WE RINKOANS ARE SHY AND DON'T LIKE TO DRAW ATTENTION TO OURSELVES!
WELL, HOW DO I LOOK?
JUST LIKE MY COUSIN AL, THE JOCKEY!
HMMM! THIS MECHANICAL DEVICE LOOKS LIKE IT MIGHT CONTAIN SOME YUMMY TASTE TREAT!
SNACKY TREATS
I'LL JUST LIFT IT UPON MY SHOULDER AND TAKE IT WITH ME!
GEE, MR. RINKO, YOU CAN'T DO THAT! THAT'S STEALING!
"STEALING"?
YEAH!
I GOT SOME COINS! LET ME BUY THOSE SNACKS FOR YOU!
YOU WERE SO KIND! I REALLY APPRECIATE IT!
IT WAS OUR PLEASURE, MR. RINKO!
3

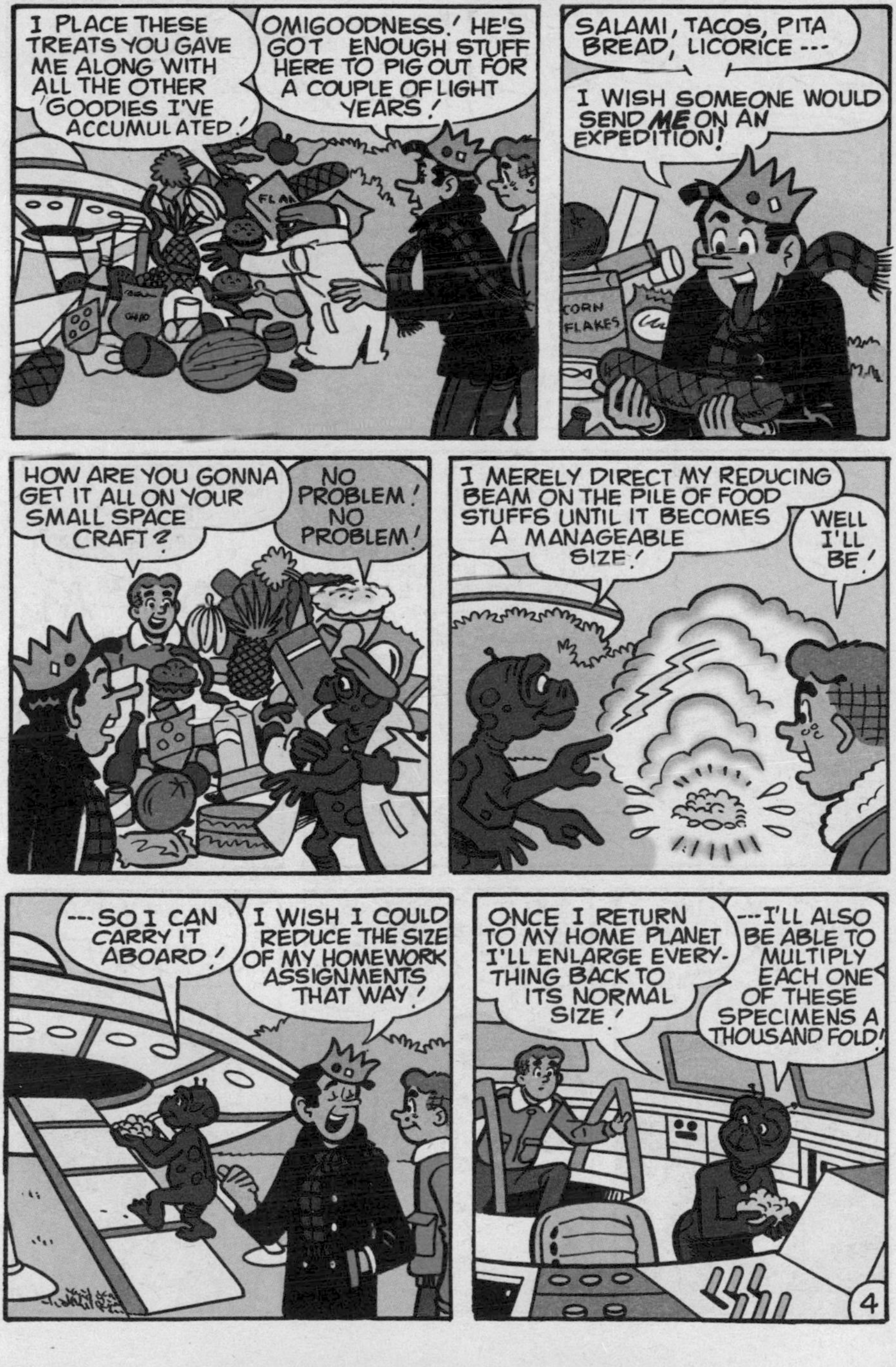
I PLACE THESE TREATS YOU GAVE ME ALONG WITH ALL THE OTHER GOODIES I'VE ACCUMULATED!
OMIGOODNESS! HE'S GOT ENOUGH STUFF HERE TO PIG OUT FOR A COUPLE OF LIGHT YEARS!
SALAMI, TACOS, PITA BREAD, LICORICE ---
I WISH SOMEONE WOULD SEND ME ON AN EXPEDITION!
CORN FLAKES
HOW ARE YOU GONNA GET IT ALL ON YOUR SMALL SPACE CRAFT?
NO PROBLEM! NO PROBLEM!
I MERELY DIRECT MY REDUCING BEAM ON THE PILE OF FOOD STUFFS UNTIL IT BECOMES A MANAGEABLE SIZE!
WELL I'LL BE!
--- SO I CAN CARRY IT ABOARD!
I WISH I COULD REDUCE THE SIZE OF MY HOMEWORK ASSIGNMENTS THAT WAY!
ONCE I RETURN TO MY HOME PLANET I'LL ENLARGE EVERYTHING BACK TO ITS NORMAL SIZE!
---I'LL ALSO BE ABLE TO MULTIPLY EACH ONE OF THESE SPECIMENS A THOUSAND FOLD!
4

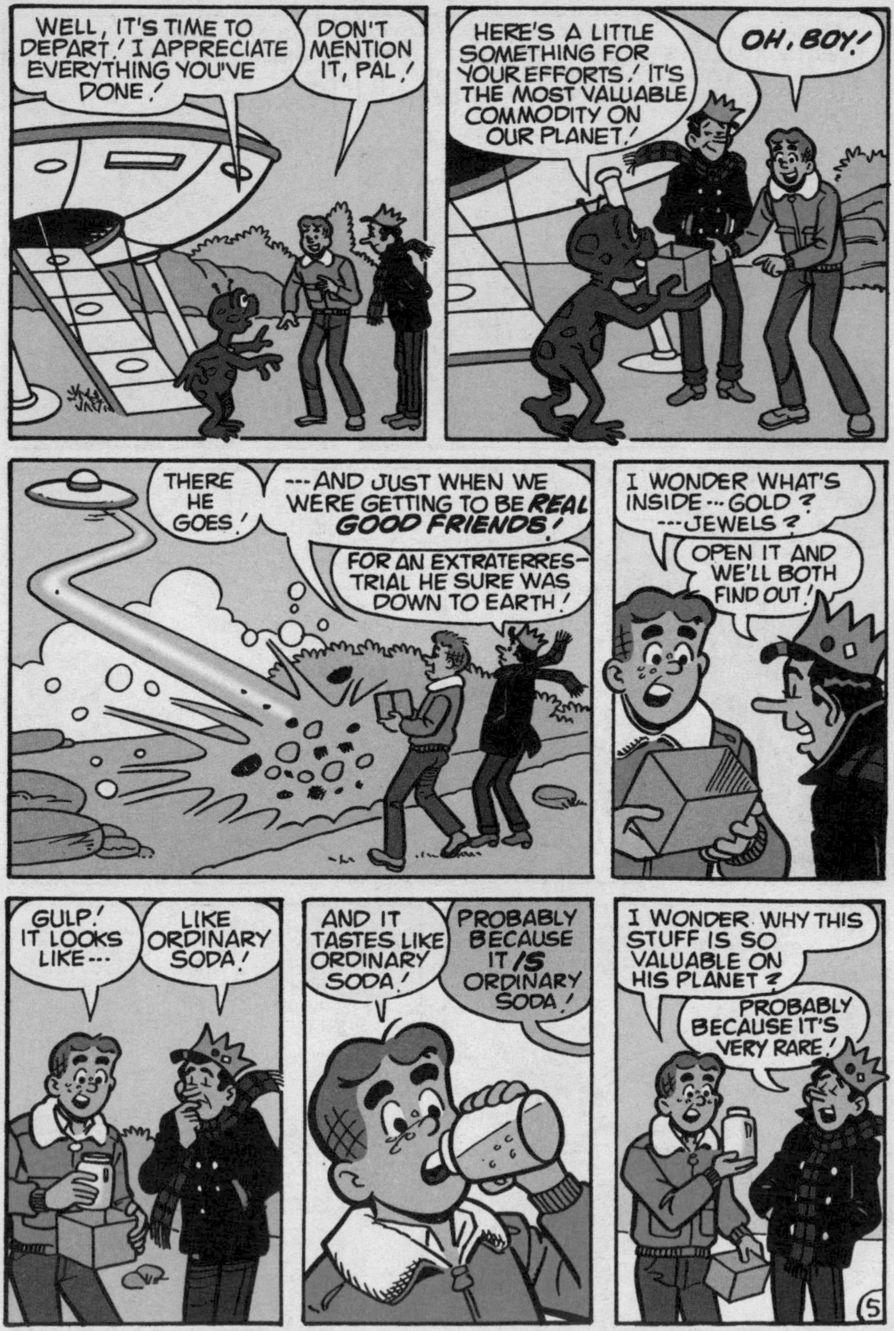
WELL, IT'S TIME TO DEPART! I APPRECIATE EVERYTHING YOU'VE DONE!
DON'T MENTION IT, PAL!
HERE'S A LITTLE SOMETHING FOR YOUR EFFORTS! IT'S THE MOST VALUABLE COMMODITY ON OUR PLANET!
OH, BOY!
THERE HE GOES!
---AND JUST WHEN WE WERE GETTING TO BE REAL GOOD FRIENDS!
FOR AN EXTRATERRES-TRIAL HE SURE WAS DOWN TO EARTH!
I WONDER WHAT'S INSIDE---GOLD? ---JEWELS?
OPEN IT AND WE'LL BOTH FIND OUT!
GULP! IT LOOKS LIKE---
LIKE ORDINARY SODA!
AND IT TASTES LIKE ORDINARY SODA!
PROBABLY BECAUSE IT IS ORDINARY SODA!
I WONDER WHY THIS STUFF IS SO VALUABLE ON HIS PLANET?
PROBABLY BECAUSE IT'S VERY RARE!
5

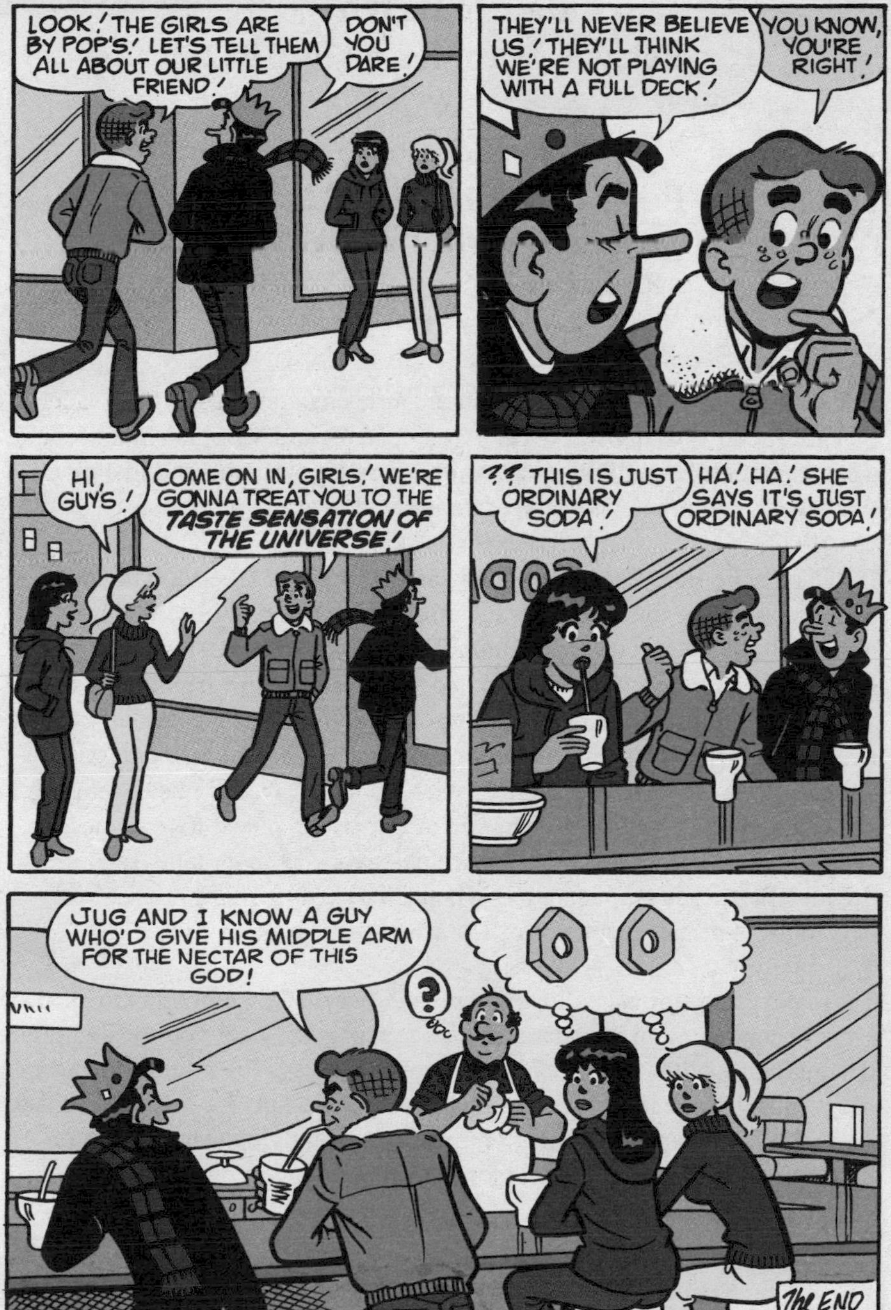
LOOK! THE GIRLS ARE BY POP'S! LET'S TELL THEM ALL ABOUT OUR LITTLE FRIEND!
DON'T YOU DARE!
THEY'LL NEVER BELIEVE US! THEY'LL THINK WE'RE NOT PLAYING WITH A FULL DECK!
YOU KNOW, YOU'RE RIGHT!
HI, GUYS!
COME ON IN, GIRLS! WE'RE GONNA TREAT YOU TO THE *TASTE SENSATION OF THE UNIVERSE!*
?? THIS IS JUST ORDINARY SODA!
HA! HA! SHE SAYS IT'S JUST ORDINARY SODA!
JUG AND I KNOW A GUY WHO'D GIVE HIS MIDDLE ARM FOR THE NECTAR OF THIS GOD!
?
The END

Dare to Be Bare
Betty & Veronica #320, 1982
&
Fast & Loose
Betty & Veronica #322, 1983
by Frank Doyle, Dan DeCarlo,
Rudy Lapick and Bill Yoshida

Wow, Cheryl Blossom. Talk about a game changer. Just when readers thought the love triangle between Archie, Betty and Veronica had become a constant, enter one of the most controversial, polarizing and just plain fun new characters to visit Riverdale in, well, ever.

In "Dare to be Bare," readers get an early glimpse at Cheryl, who turns up the volume on the spoiled-brat-with-good-looks role Veronica had previously laid claim to. Beautifully illustrated by the master, Dan DeCarlo, readers know from page one that this girl isn't from down the street. She's from another planet altogether. Paired with her equally edgy twin brother Jason, the Blossoms would be a compelling and entertaining addition to the Riverdale gang for years—one that would raise eyebrows, stir laughter and change the dynamic of one of the oldest love stories in comics. Her presence would shift Archie's world most notably over a decade after her first appearance, when Cheryl came roaring back into Riverdale as part of the historic "Love Showdown" storyline.

These next two stories, collecting two of Cheryl's key moments in her early history, sum up the character in a few pages: She's Veronica without the qualms, a sultry new love interest for the always lovable Archie and a dangerous wrench thrown into a dynamic readers may have started to take for granted. Oh, and did I mention most of her early appearances were drawn by Dan DeCarlo? What more incentive would you need? Trust me, you're in for a treat.

--Alex Segura
Executive Director of Publicity & Marketing,
Archie Comics

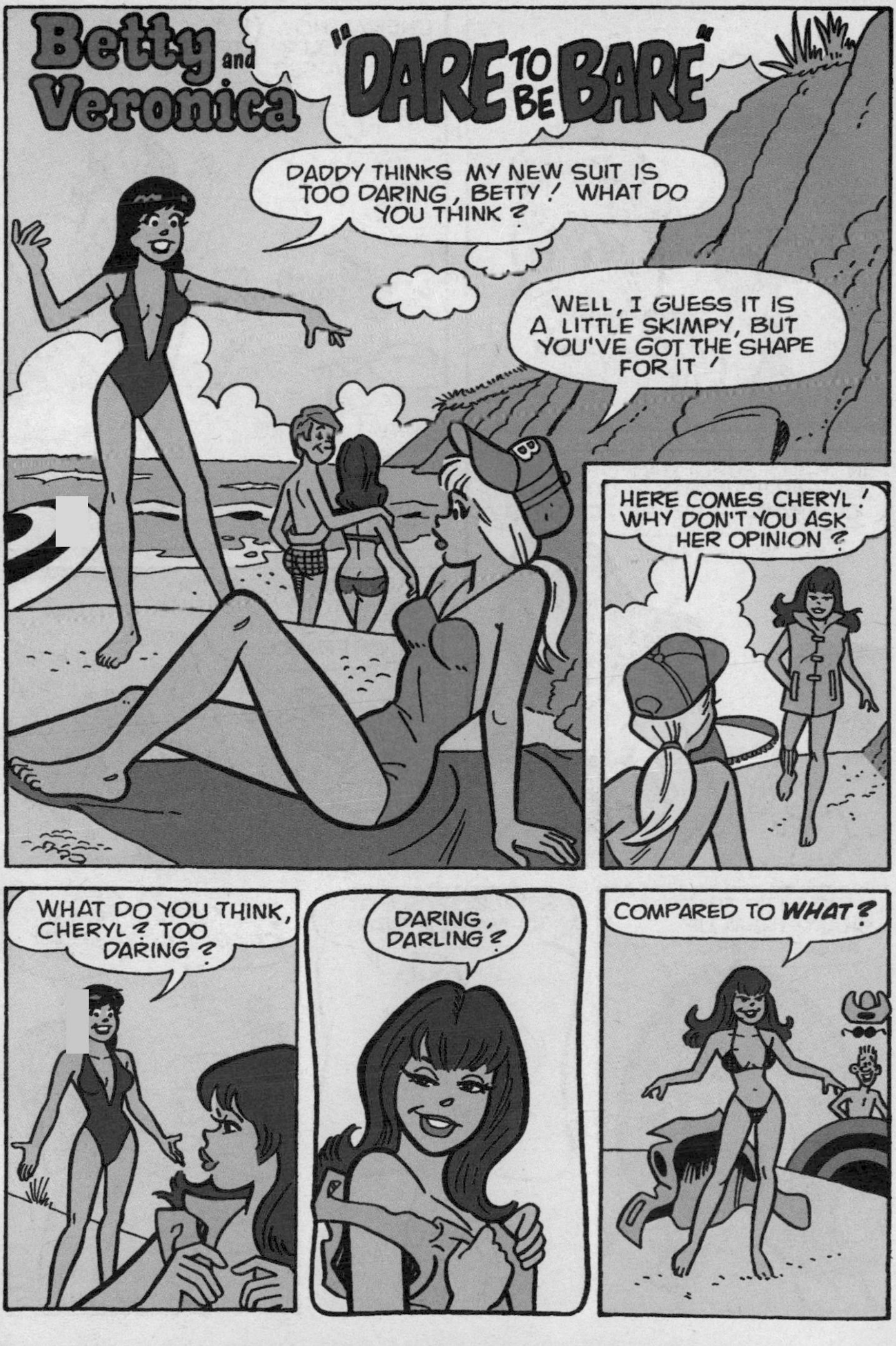
Betty and Veronica
"DARE TO BE BARE"
DADDY THINKS MY NEW SUIT IS TOO DARING, BETTY! WHAT DO YOU THINK?
WELL, I GUESS IT IS A LITTLE SKIMPY, BUT YOU'VE GOT THE SHAPE FOR IT!
HERE COMES CHERYL! WHY DON'T YOU ASK HER OPINION?
WHAT DO YOU THINK, CHERYL? TOO DARING?
DARING, DARLING?
COMPARED TO WHAT?

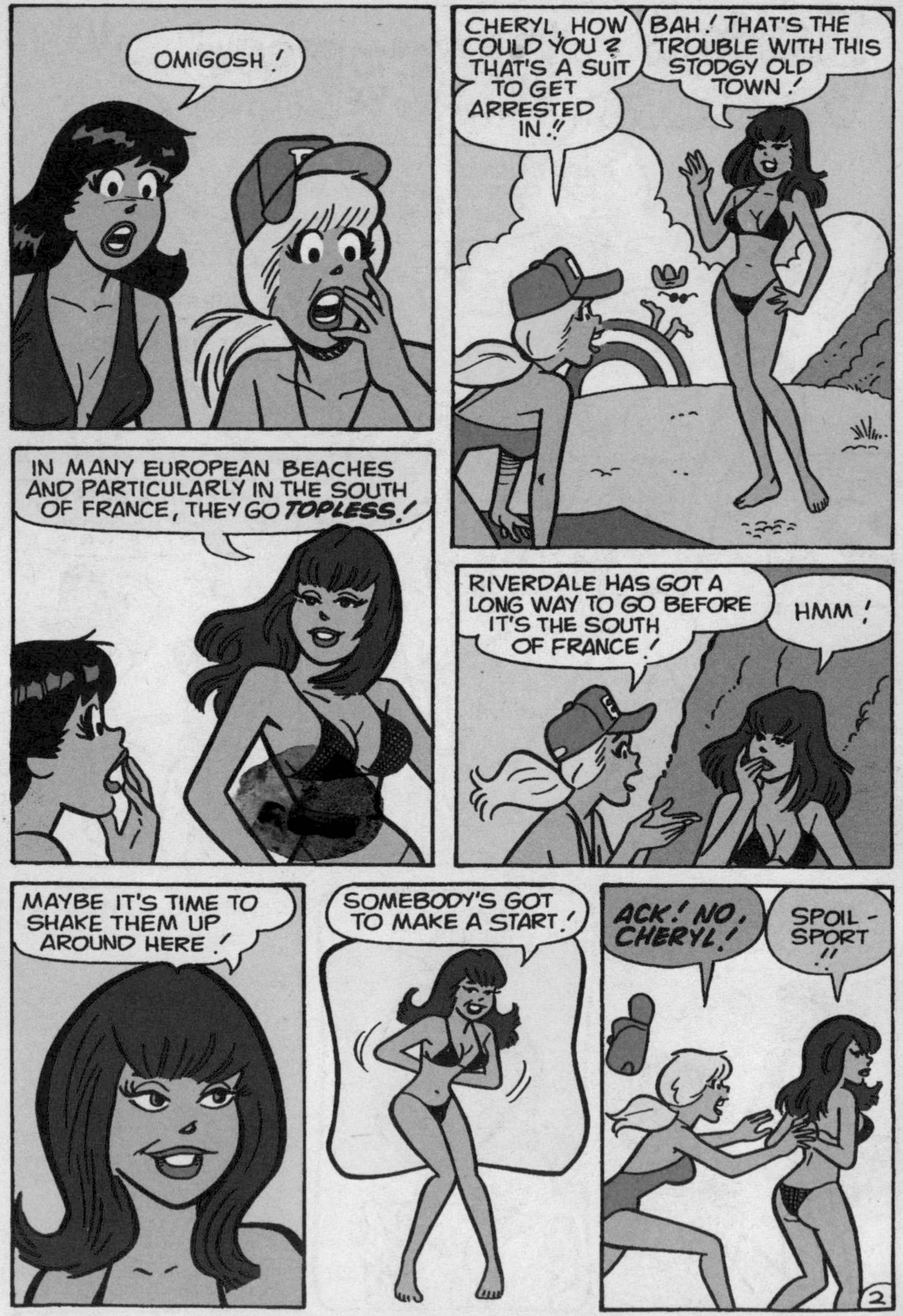
OMIGOSH!
CHERYL, HOW COULD YOU? THAT'S A SUIT TO GET ARRESTED IN.!!
BAH! THAT'S THE TROUBLE WITH THIS STODGY OLD TOWN!
IN MANY EUROPEAN BEACHES AND PARTICULARLY IN THE SOUTH OF FRANCE, THEY GO TOPLESS!
RIVERDALE HAS GOT A LONG WAY TO GO BEFORE IT'S THE SOUTH OF FRANCE!
HMM!
MAYBE IT'S TIME TO SHAKE THEM UP AROUND HERE!
SOMEBODY'S GOT TO MAKE A START!
ACK! NO, CHERYL!
SPOIL-SPORT!!
2

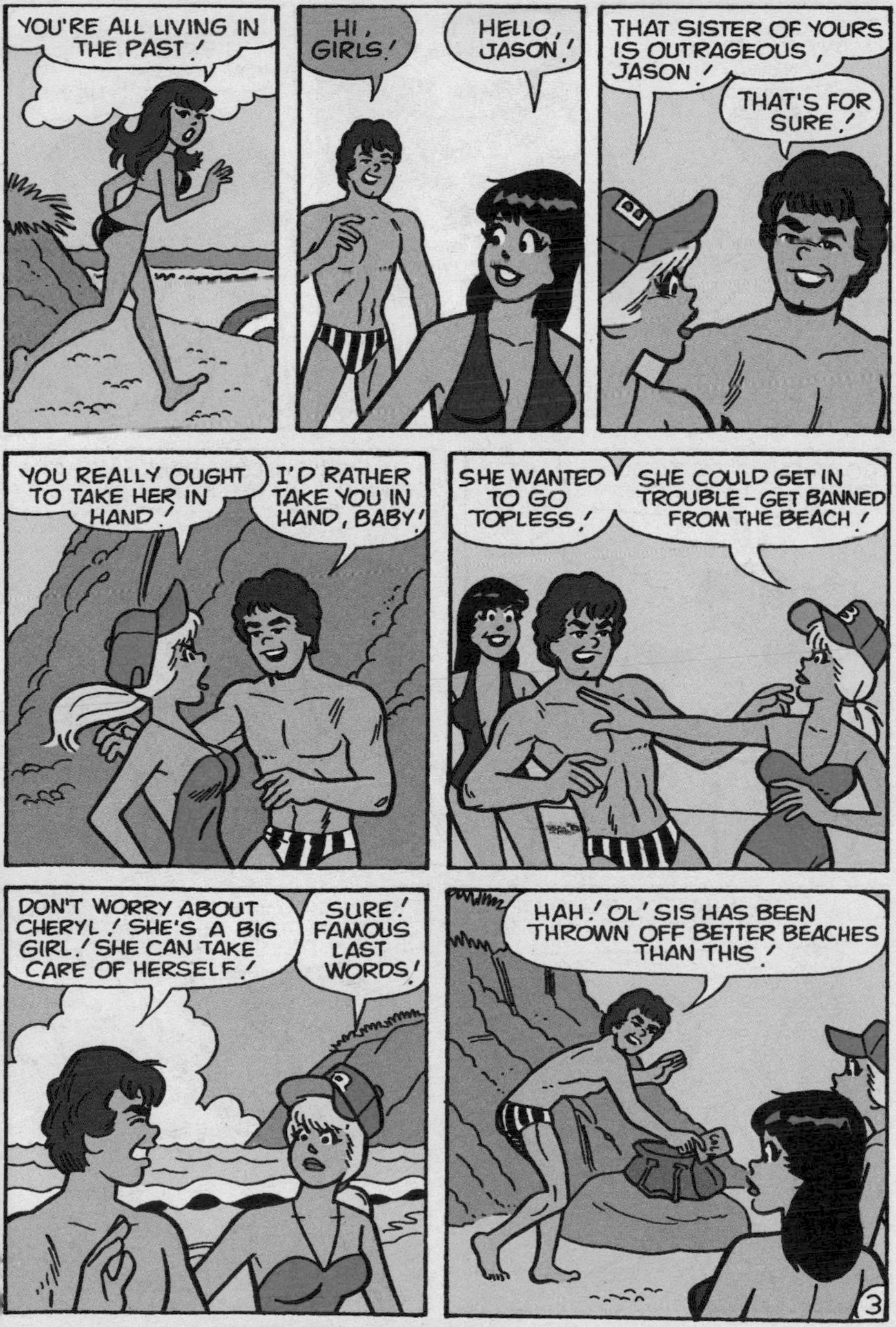
YOU'RE ALL LIVING IN THE PAST!
HI, GIRLS!
HELLO, JASON!
THAT SISTER OF YOURS IS OUTRAGEOUS, JASON!
THAT'S FOR SURE!
YOU REALLY OUGHT TO TAKE HER IN HAND!
I'D RATHER TAKE YOU IN HAND, BABY!
SHE WANTED TO GO TOPLESS!
SHE COULD GET IN TROUBLE - GET BANNED FROM THE BEACH!
DON'T WORRY ABOUT CHERYL! SHE'S A BIG GIRL! SHE CAN TAKE CARE OF HERSELF!
SURE! FAMOUS LAST WORDS!
HAH! OL' SIS HAS BEEN THROWN OFF BETTER BEACHES THAN THIS!
3

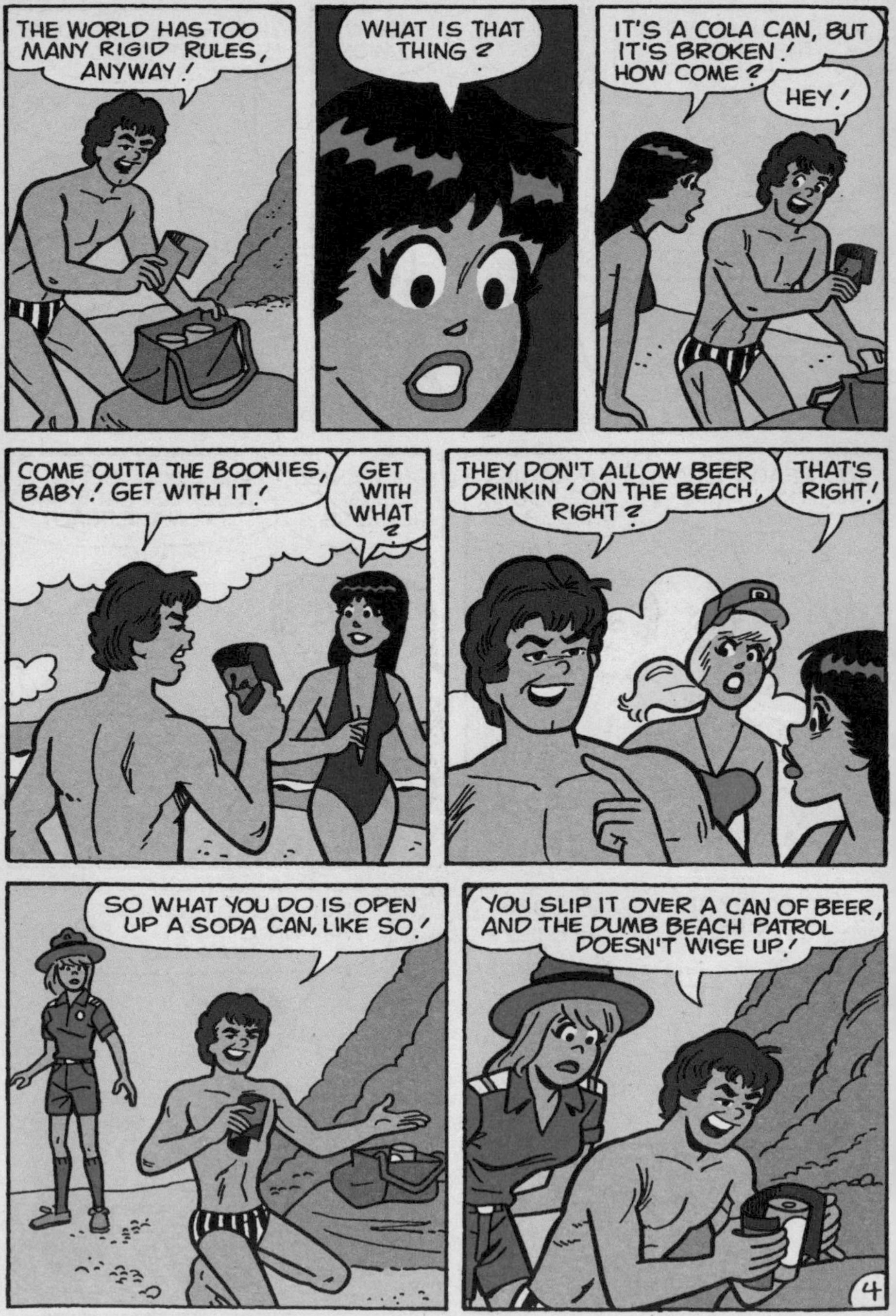
THE WORLD HAS TOO MANY RIGID RULES, ANYWAY!
WHAT IS THAT THING?
IT'S A COLA CAN, BUT IT'S BROKEN! HOW COME?
HEY!
COME OUTTA THE BOONIES, BABY! GET WITH IT!
GET WITH WHAT?
THEY DON'T ALLOW BEER DRINKIN' ON THE BEACH, RIGHT?
THAT'S RIGHT!
SO WHAT YOU DO IS OPEN UP A SODA CAN, LIKE SO!
YOU SLIP IT OVER A CAN OF BEER, AND THE DUMB BEACH PATROL DOESN'T WISE UP!
4

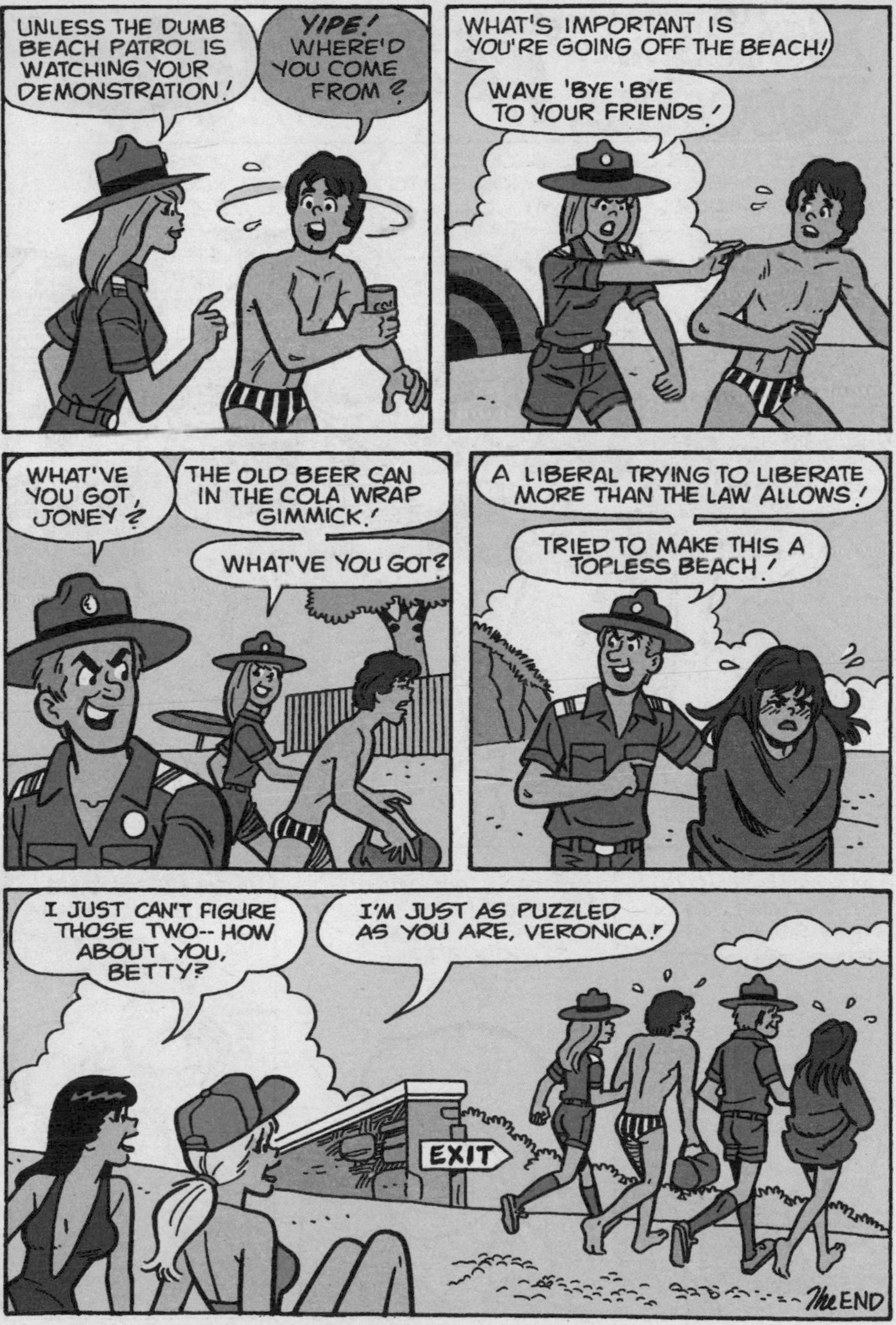
UNLESS THE DUMB BEACH PATROL IS WATCHING YOUR DEMONSTRATION!
YIPE! WHERE'D YOU COME FROM?
WHAT'S IMPORTANT IS YOU'RE GOING OFF THE BEACH!
WAVE 'BYE 'BYE TO YOUR FRIENDS!
WHAT'VE YOU GOT, JONEY?
THE OLD BEER CAN IN THE COLA WRAP GIMMICK!
WHAT'VE YOU GOT?
A LIBERAL TRYING TO LIBERATE MORE THAN THE LAW ALLOWS!
TRIED TO MAKE THIS A TOPLESS BEACH!
I JUST CAN'T FIGURE THOSE TWO-- HOW ABOUT YOU, BETTY?
I'M JUST AS PUZZLED AS YOU ARE, VERONICA!
EXIT
The END

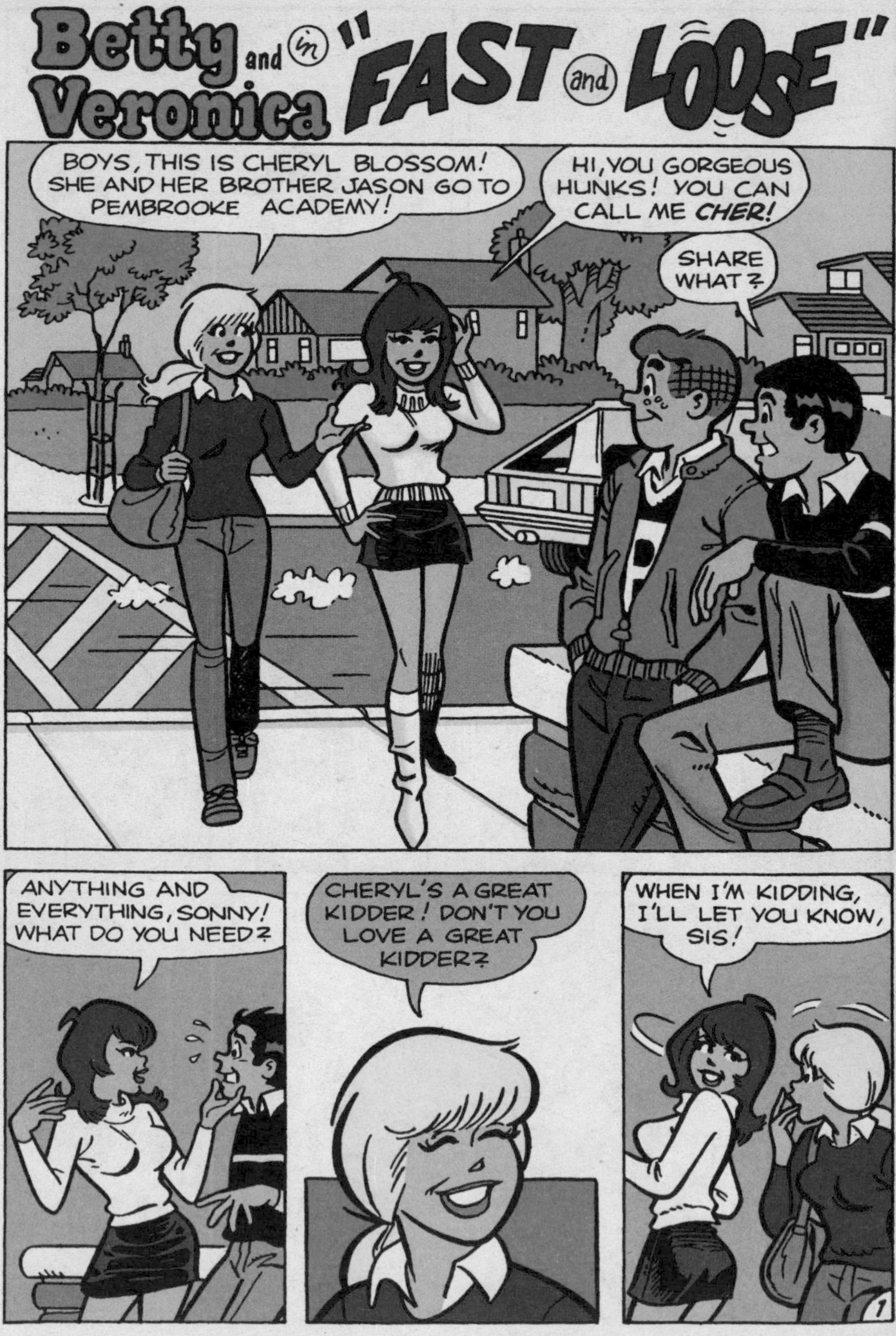
Betty and Veronica
in "FAST and LOOSE"
BOYS, THIS IS CHERYL BLOSSOM! SHE AND HER BROTHER JASON GO TO PEMBROOKE ACADEMY!
HI, YOU GORGEOUS HUNKS! YOU CAN CALL ME CHER!
SHARE WHAT?
ANYTHING AND EVERYTHING, SONNY! WHAT DO YOU NEED?
CHERYL'S A GREAT KIDDER! DON'T YOU LOVE A GREAT KIDDER?
WHEN I'M KIDDING, I'LL LET YOU KNOW, SIS!
1

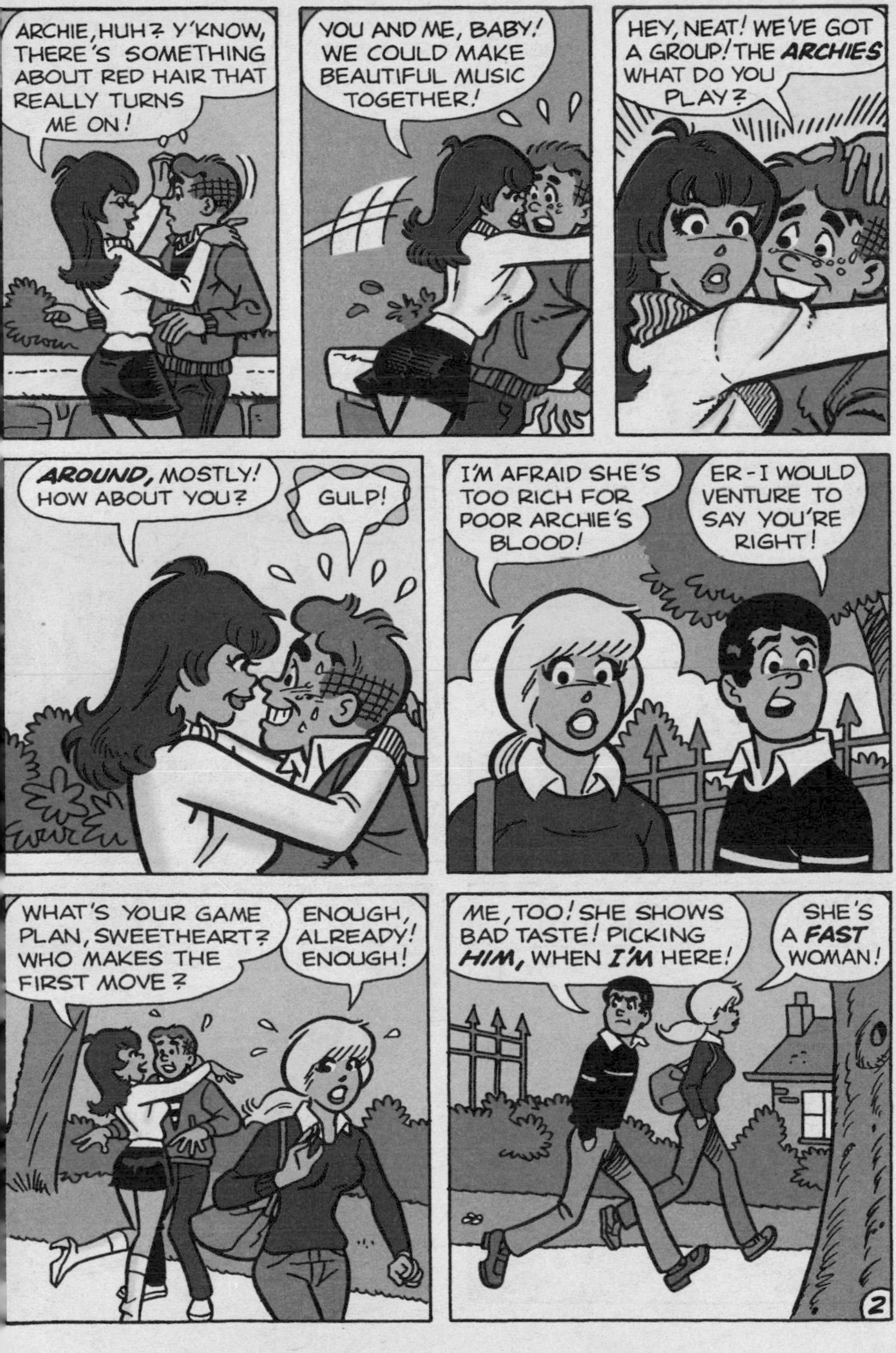
ARCHIE, HUH? Y'KNOW, THERE'S SOMETHING ABOUT RED HAIR THAT REALLY TURNS ME ON!
YOU AND ME, BABY! WE COULD MAKE BEAUTIFUL MUSIC TOGETHER!
HEY, NEAT! WE'VE GOT A GROUP! THE **ARCHIES** WHAT DO YOU PLAY?
AROUND, MOSTLY! HOW ABOUT YOU?
GULP!
I'M AFRAID SHE'S TOO RICH FOR POOR ARCHIE'S BLOOD!
ER-I WOULD VENTURE TO SAY YOU'RE RIGHT!
WHAT'S YOUR GAME PLAN, SWEETHEART? WHO MAKES THE FIRST MOVE?
ENOUGH, ALREADY! ENOUGH!
ME, TOO! SHE SHOWS BAD TASTE! PICKING ***HIM,*** WHEN ***I'M*** HERE!
SHE'S A ***FAST*** WOMAN!
2

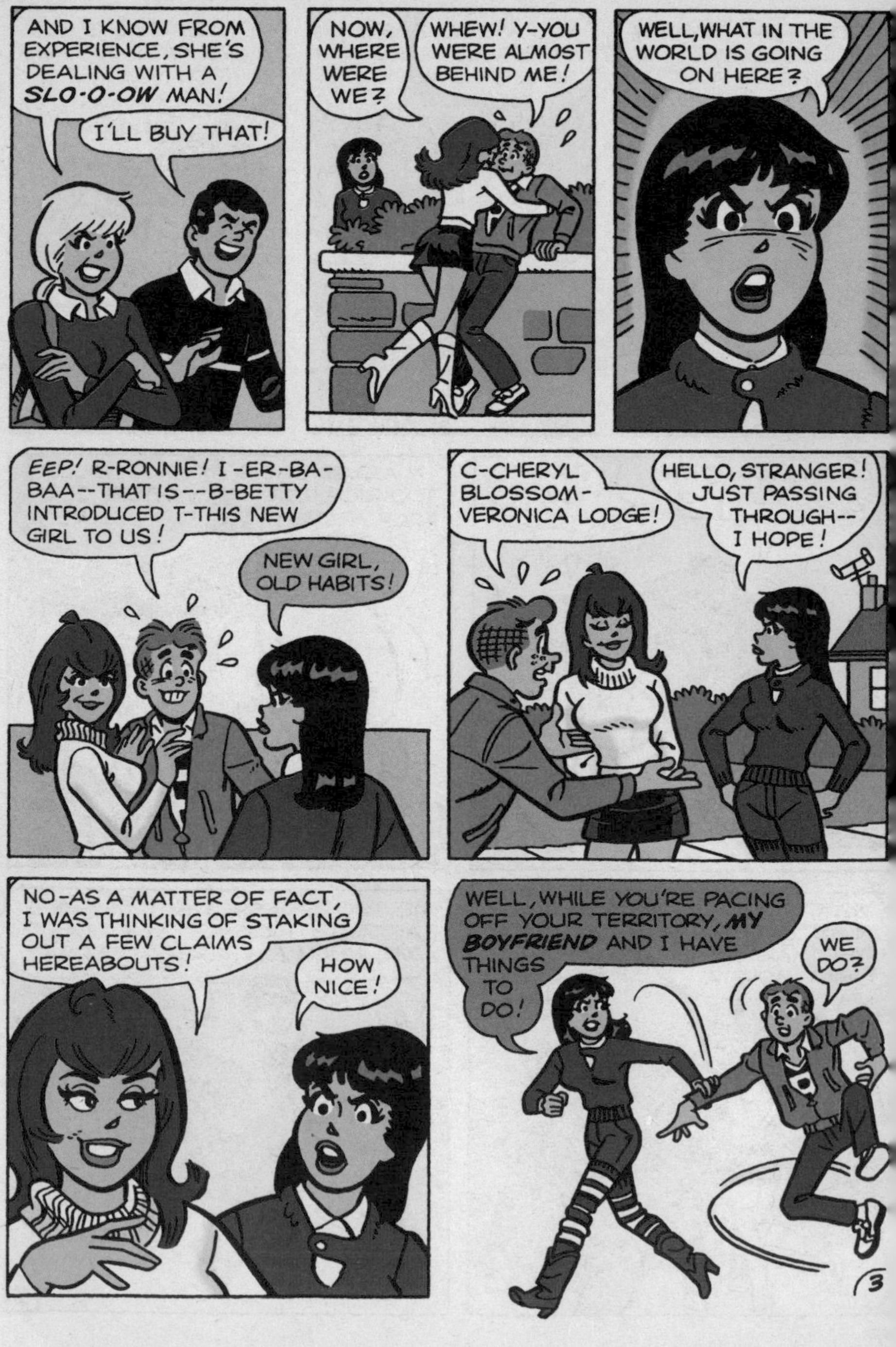
AND I KNOW FROM EXPERIENCE, SHE'S DEALING WITH A SLO-O-OW MAN!
I'LL BUY THAT!
NOW, WHERE WERE WE?
WHEW! Y-YOU WERE ALMOST BEHIND ME!
WELL, WHAT IN THE WORLD IS GOING ON HERE?
EEP! R-RONNIE! I-ER-BA-BAA--THAT IS--B-BETTY INTRODUCED T-THIS NEW GIRL TO US!
NEW GIRL, OLD HABITS!
C-CHERYL BLOSSOM-VERONICA LODGE!
HELLO, STRANGER! JUST PASSING THROUGH--I HOPE!
NO-AS A MATTER OF FACT, I WAS THINKING OF STAKING OUT A FEW CLAIMS HEREABOUTS!
HOW NICE!
WELL, WHILE YOU'RE PACING OFF YOUR TERRITORY, MY BOYFRIEND AND I HAVE THINGS TO DO!
WE DO?
3

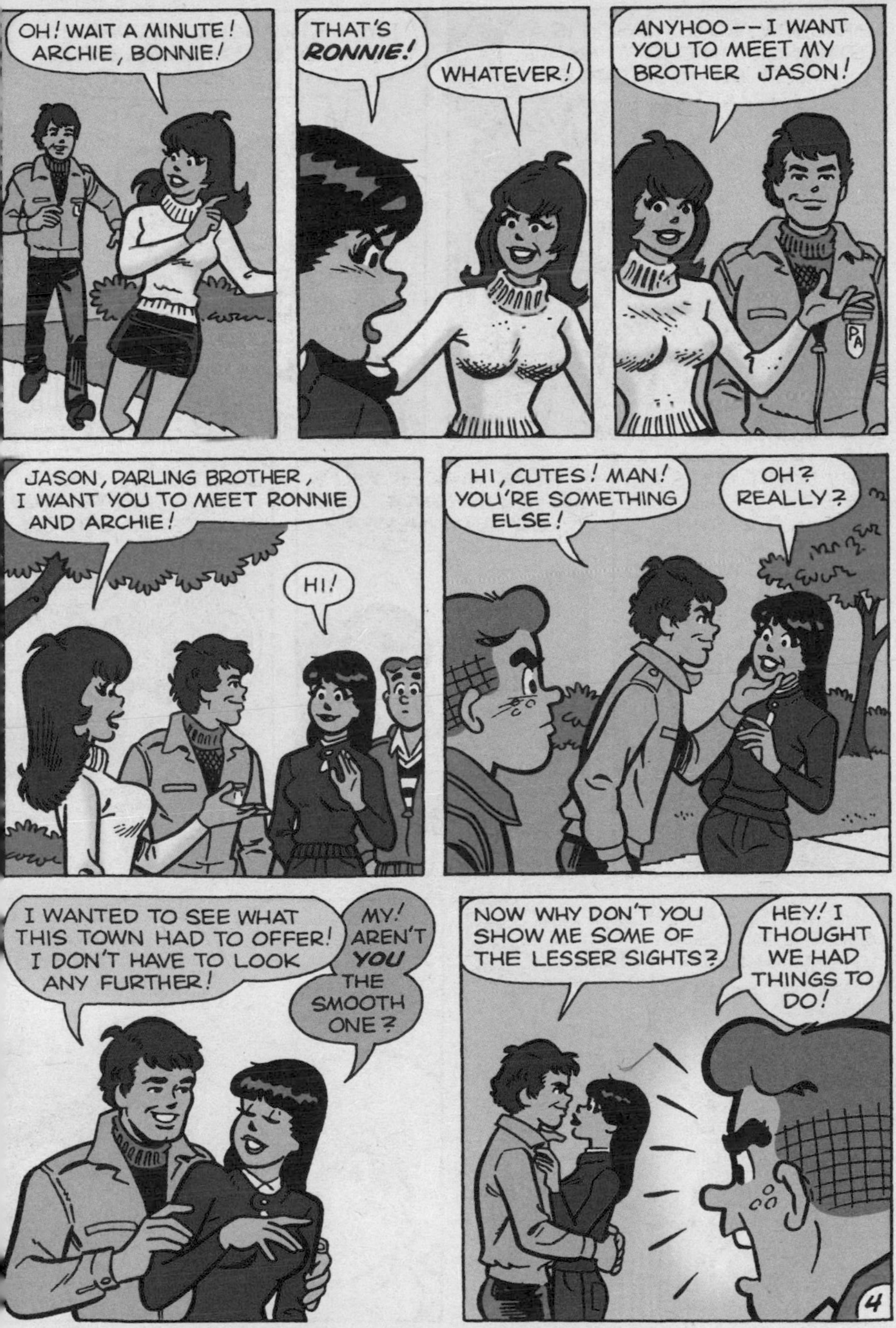
OH! WAIT A MINUTE! ARCHIE, BONNIE!
THAT'S RONNIE!
WHATEVER!
ANYHOO -- I WANT YOU TO MEET MY BROTHER JASON!
JASON, DARLING BROTHER, I WANT YOU TO MEET RONNIE AND ARCHIE!
HI!
HI, CUTES! MAN! YOU'RE SOMETHING ELSE!
OH? REALLY?
I WANTED TO SEE WHAT THIS TOWN HAD TO OFFER! I DON'T HAVE TO LOOK ANY FURTHER!
MY! AREN'T YOU THE SMOOTH ONE?
NOW WHY DON'T YOU SHOW ME SOME OF THE LESSER SIGHTS?
HEY! I THOUGHT WE HAD THINGS TO DO!
4

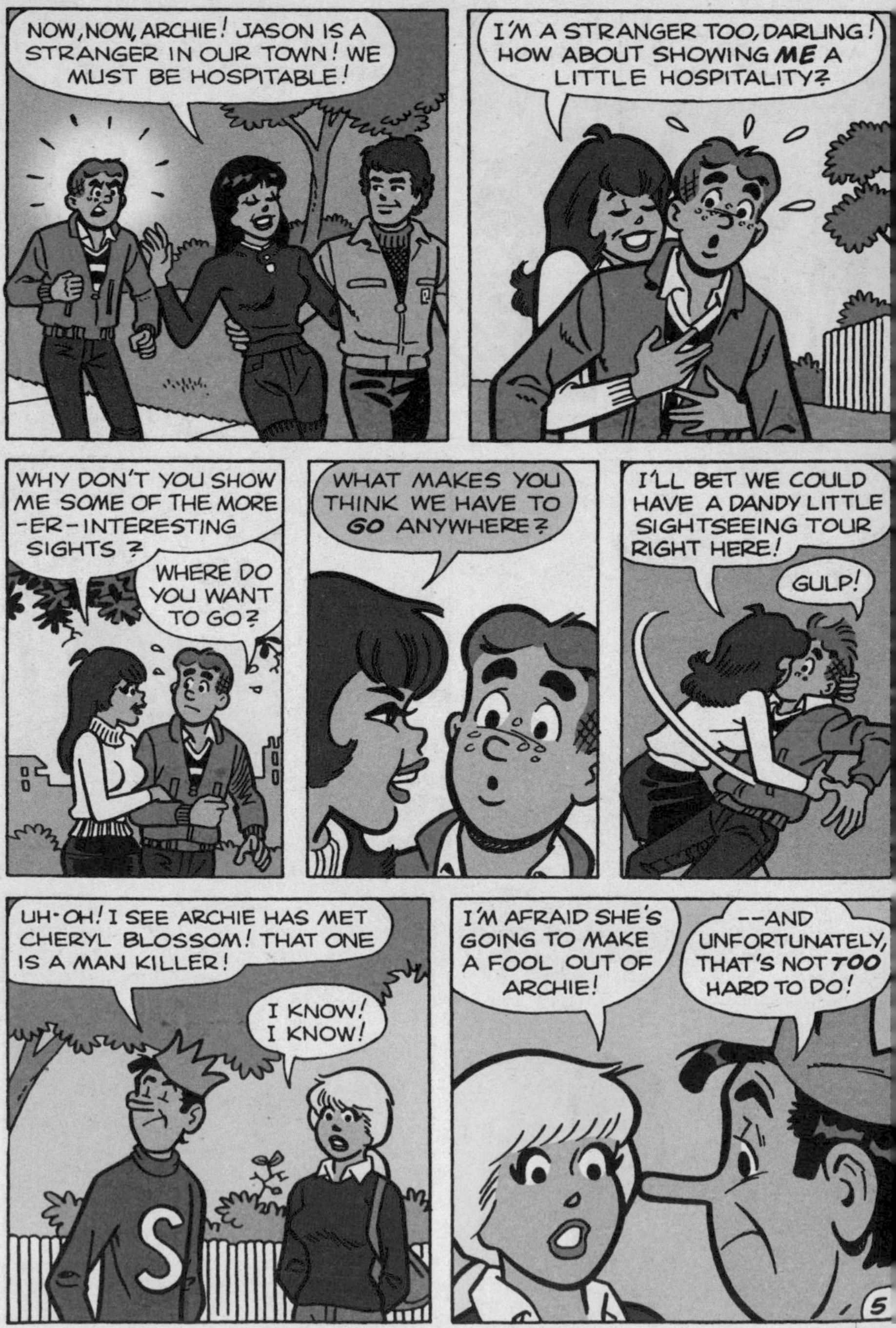
NOW, NOW, ARCHIE! JASON IS A STRANGER IN OUR TOWN! WE MUST BE HOSPITABLE!
I'M A STRANGER TOO, DARLING! HOW ABOUT SHOWING ME A LITTLE HOSPITALITY?
WHY DON'T YOU SHOW ME SOME OF THE MORE -ER- INTERESTING SIGHTS?
WHERE DO YOU WANT TO GO?
WHAT MAKES YOU THINK WE HAVE TO GO ANYWHERE?
I'LL BET WE COULD HAVE A DANDY LITTLE SIGHTSEEING TOUR RIGHT HERE!
GULP!
UH-OH! I SEE ARCHIE HAS MET CHERYL BLOSSOM! THAT ONE IS A MAN KILLER!
I KNOW! I KNOW!
I'M AFRAID SHE'S GOING TO MAKE A FOOL OUT OF ARCHIE!
--AND UNFORTUNATELY, THAT'S NOT TOO HARD TO DO!
5

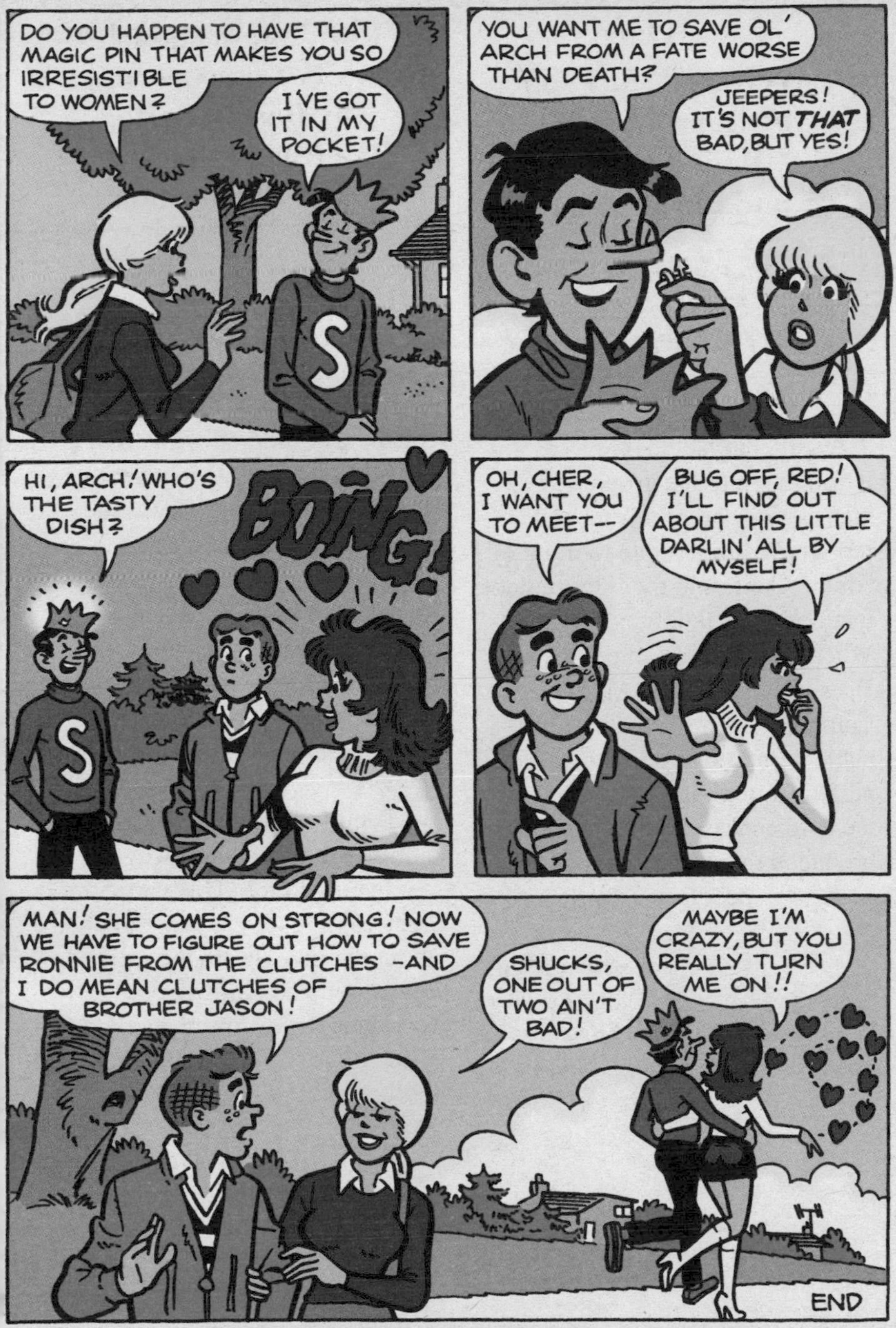
DO YOU HAPPEN TO HAVE THAT MAGIC PIN THAT MAKES YOU SO IRRESISTIBLE TO WOMEN?
I'VE GOT IT IN MY POCKET!
YOU WANT ME TO SAVE OL' ARCH FROM A FATE WORSE THAN DEATH?
JEEPERS! IT'S NOT *THAT* BAD, BUT YES!
HI, ARCH! WHO'S THE TASTY DISH?
BOING!
OH, CHER, I WANT YOU TO MEET--
BUG OFF, RED! I'LL FIND OUT ABOUT THIS LITTLE DARLIN' ALL BY MYSELF!
MAN! SHE COMES ON STRONG! NOW WE HAVE TO FIGURE OUT HOW TO SAVE RONNIE FROM THE CLUTCHES -AND I DO MEAN CLUTCHES OF BROTHER JASON!
SHUCKS, ONE OUT OF TWO AIN'T BAD!
MAYBE I'M CRAZY, BUT YOU REALLY TURN ME ON!!
END

Ace Place
Archie #325, 1983
by Dan DeCarlo,
Rudy Lapick
and Bill Yoshida

It looks like Pop Tate is closing up the Choklit Shoppe, but not if Archie and the Gang can help it!

Despite the fact that my introduction to the group came many years earlier, for me it's just simply impossible to think of Archie Comics in the '80s and not think of them fondly.

When I founded Diamond Comic Distributors in 1982, Archie Comics was one of the first big publishers to sign on with us. The perfect counterpart to my love of the comics was that the folks who produced them turned out to be such good people.

--Steve Geppi
*Founder,
Diamond Comic Distributors,
Excerpted from Archie Americana:
Best of the Eighties*

Roll 'em in the Isles
Archie's TV Laugh Out #101, 1985
by Dan DeCarlo,
Rudy Lapick
and Bill Yoshida

Growing up, nothing made me happier than going to the supermarket and picking up an Archie digest. My room was constantly cluttered with all of the titles, none of which went unread. I particularly loved the stories focused on the gals of the Archie universe, and Josie and the Pussycats especially appealed to me…these were girls who could make me laugh, solve mysteries and rock out! All while wearing some pretty awesome costumes!

As a child of the late '80s, the culture of the era has always been fascinating to me. This particular story captures everything notable about the time. From the girls' edgier, almost punk-ish cat costumes (leg warmers included!) to the issues of corporate greed and theft, it has it all!

--Jamie Rotante
Proofreader, Archie Comics

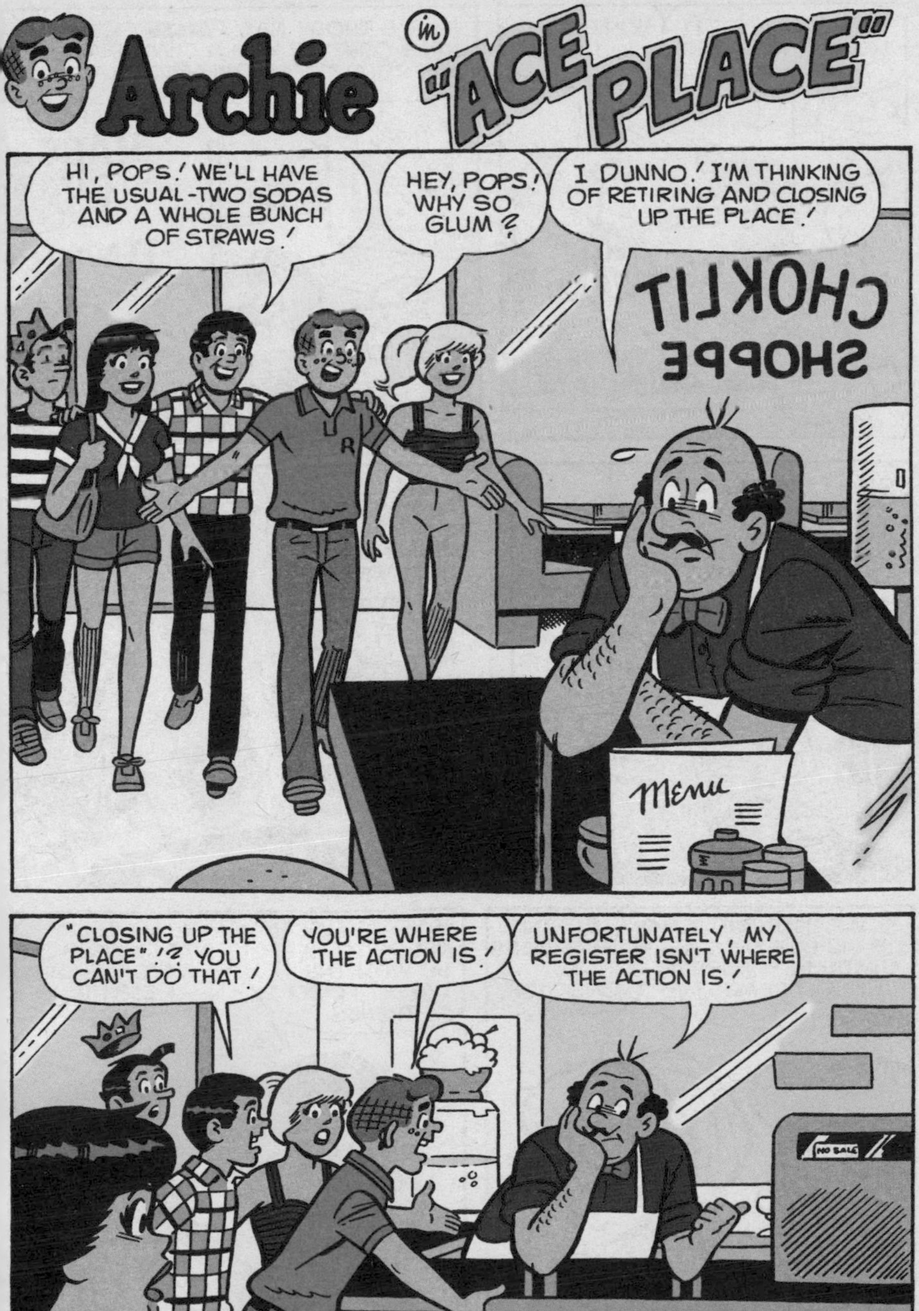
Archie in "ACE PLACE"
HI, POPS! WE'LL HAVE THE USUAL-TWO SODAS AND A WHOLE BUNCH OF STRAWS!
HEY, POPS! WHY SO GLUM?
I DUNNO! I'M THINKING OF RETIRING AND CLOSING UP THE PLACE!
CHOKLIT SHOPPE
MENU
"CLOSING UP THE PLACE"!? YOU CAN'T DO THAT!
YOU'RE WHERE THE ACTION IS!
UNFORTUNATELY, MY REGISTER ISN'T WHERE THE ACTION IS!
NO SALE

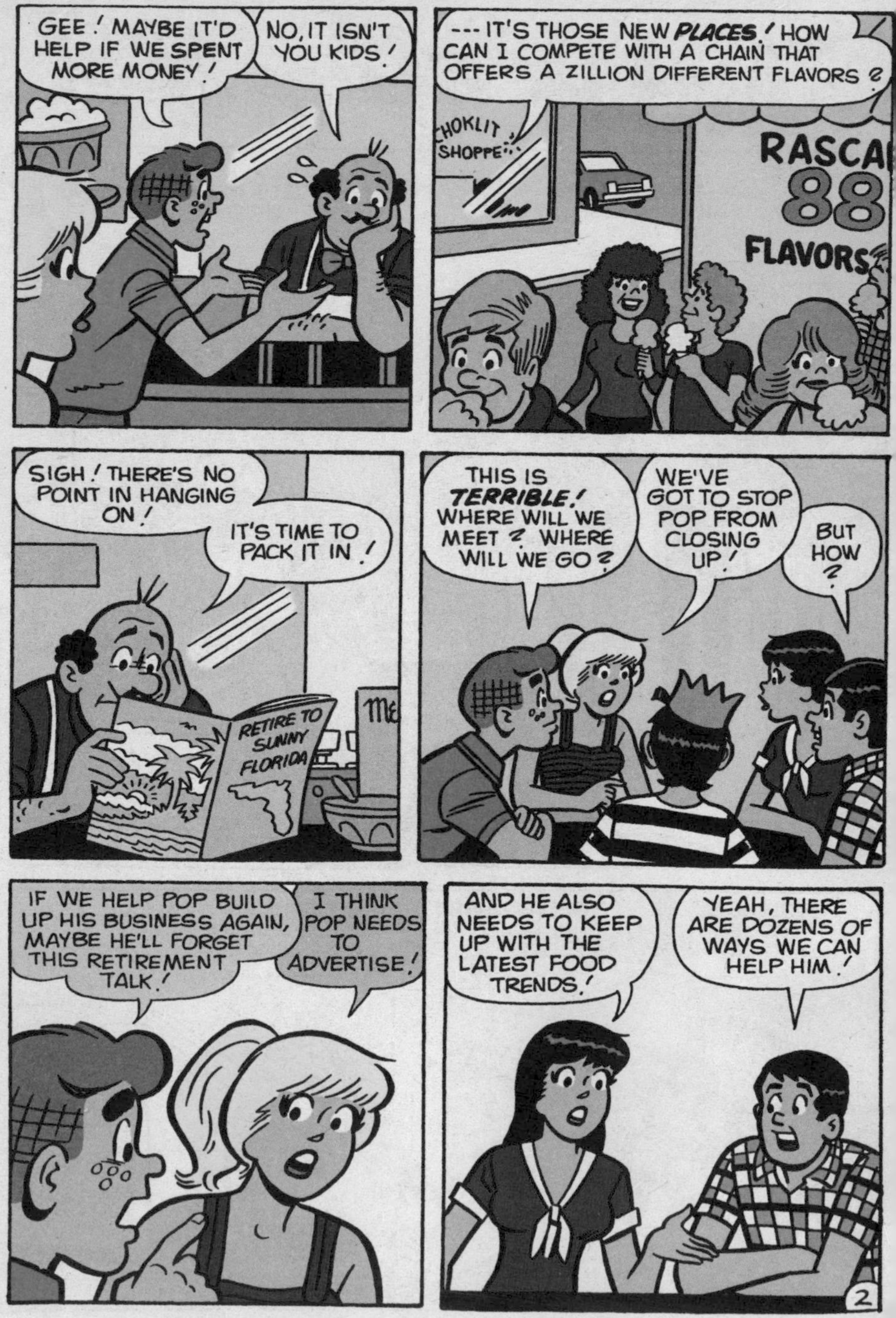
GEE! MAYBE IT'D HELP IF WE SPENT MORE MONEY!
NO, IT ISN'T YOU KIDS!
--- IT'S THOSE NEW PLACES! HOW CAN I COMPETE WITH A CHAIN THAT OFFERS A ZILLION DIFFERENT FLAVORS?
CHOKLIT SHOPPE
RASCA
88
FLAVORS
SIGH! THERE'S NO POINT IN HANGING ON!
IT'S TIME TO PACK IT IN!
RETIRE TO SUNNY FLORIDA
THIS IS TERRIBLE! WHERE WILL WE MEET? WHERE WILL WE GO?
WE'VE GOT TO STOP POP FROM CLOSING UP!
BUT HOW?
IF WE HELP POP BUILD UP HIS BUSINESS AGAIN, MAYBE HE'LL FORGET THIS RETIREMENT TALK!
I THINK POP NEEDS TO ADVERTISE!
AND HE ALSO NEEDS TO KEEP UP WITH THE LATEST FOOD TRENDS!
YEAH, THERE ARE DOZENS OF WAYS WE CAN HELP HIM!
2

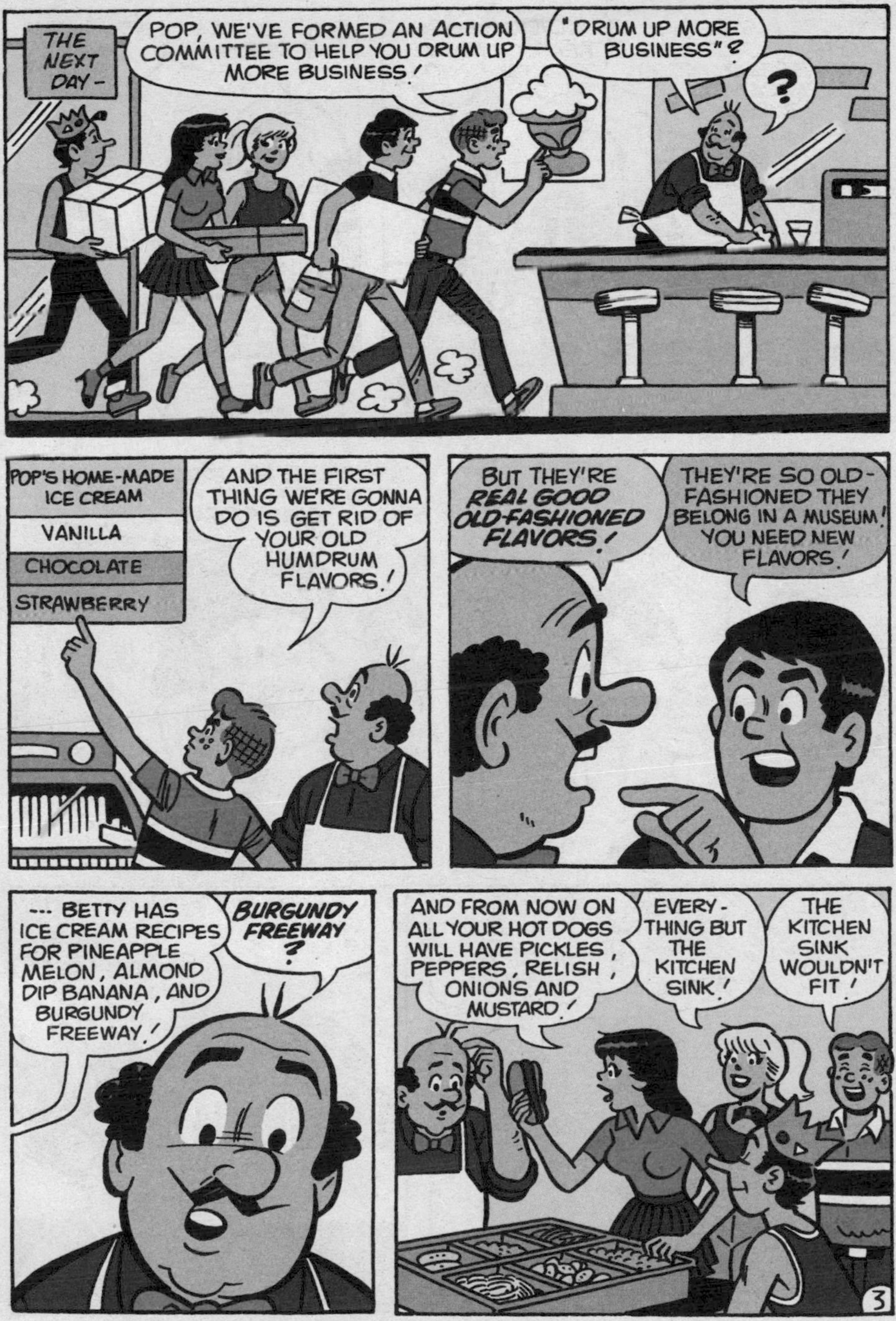
THE NEXT DAY -
POP, WE'VE FORMED AN ACTION COMMITTEE TO HELP YOU DRUM UP MORE BUSINESS!
"DRUM UP MORE BUSINESS"?
?
POP'S HOME-MADE ICE CREAM
VANILLA
CHOCOLATE
STRAWBERRY
AND THE FIRST THING WE'RE GONNA DO IS GET RID OF YOUR OLD HUMDRUM FLAVORS!
BUT THEY'RE REAL GOOD OLD-FASHIONED FLAVORS!
THEY'RE SO OLD-FASHIONED THEY BELONG IN A MUSEUM! YOU NEED NEW FLAVORS!
--- BETTY HAS ICE CREAM RECIPES FOR PINEAPPLE MELON, ALMOND DIP BANANA, AND BURGUNDY FREEWAY!
BURGUNDY FREEWAY?
AND FROM NOW ON ALL YOUR HOT DOGS WILL HAVE PICKLES, PEPPERS, RELISH, ONIONS AND MUSTARD!
EVERY-THING BUT THE KITCHEN SINK!
THE KITCHEN SINK WOULDN'T FIT!
3

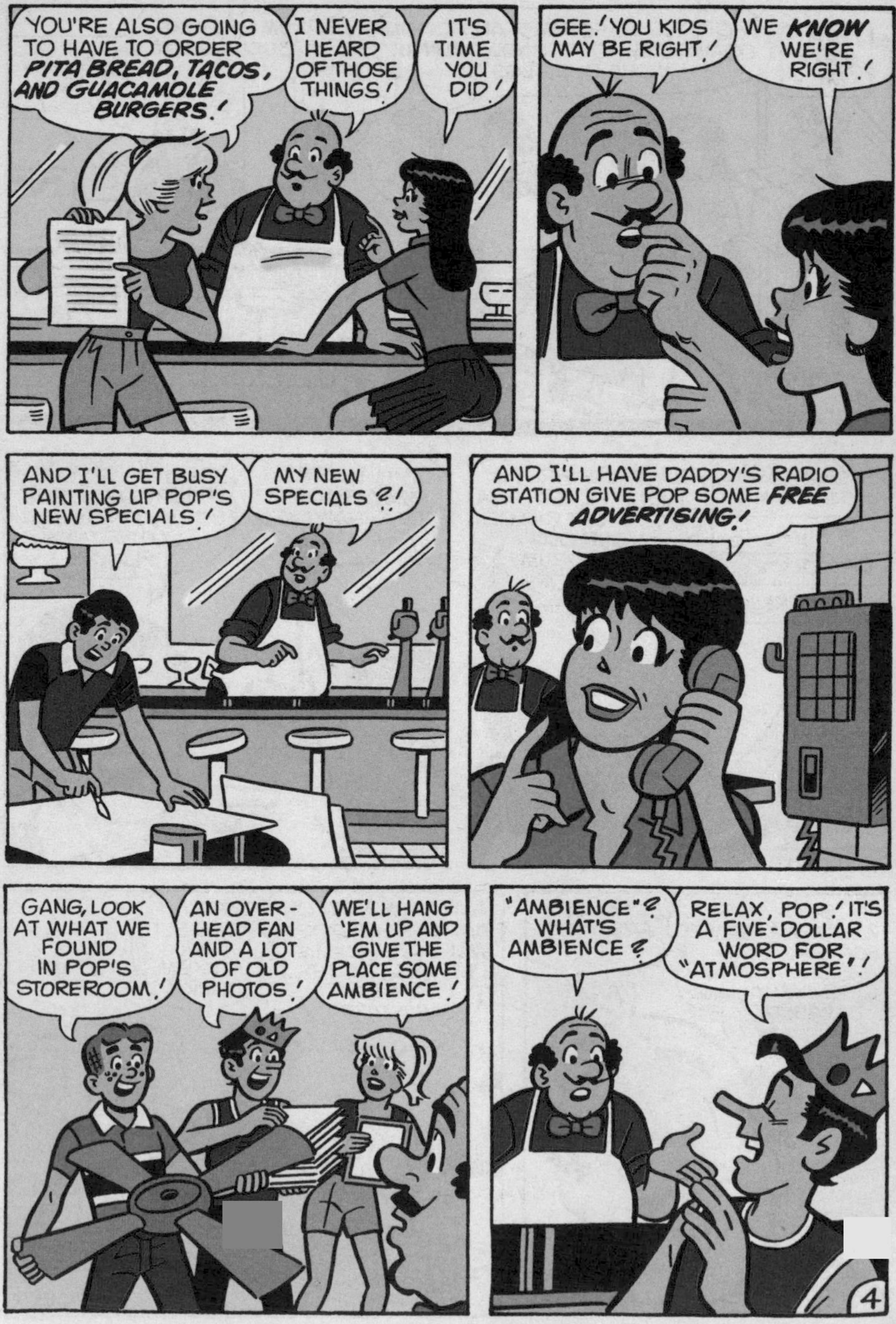
YOU'RE ALSO GOING TO HAVE TO ORDER PITA BREAD, TACOS, AND GUACAMOLE BURGERS!
I NEVER HEARD OF THOSE THINGS!
IT'S TIME YOU DID!
GEE! YOU KIDS MAY BE RIGHT!
WE KNOW WE'RE RIGHT!
AND I'LL GET BUSY PAINTING UP POP'S NEW SPECIALS!
MY NEW SPECIALS ?!
AND I'LL HAVE DADDY'S RADIO STATION GIVE POP SOME FREE ADVERTISING!
GANG, LOOK AT WHAT WE FOUND IN POP'S STOREROOM!
AN OVER-HEAD FAN AND A LOT OF OLD PHOTOS!
WE'LL HANG 'EM UP AND GIVE THE PLACE SOME AMBIENCE!
"AMBIENCE"? WHAT'S AMBIENCE?
RELAX, POP! IT'S A FIVE-DOLLAR WORD FOR "ATMOSPHERE"!
4

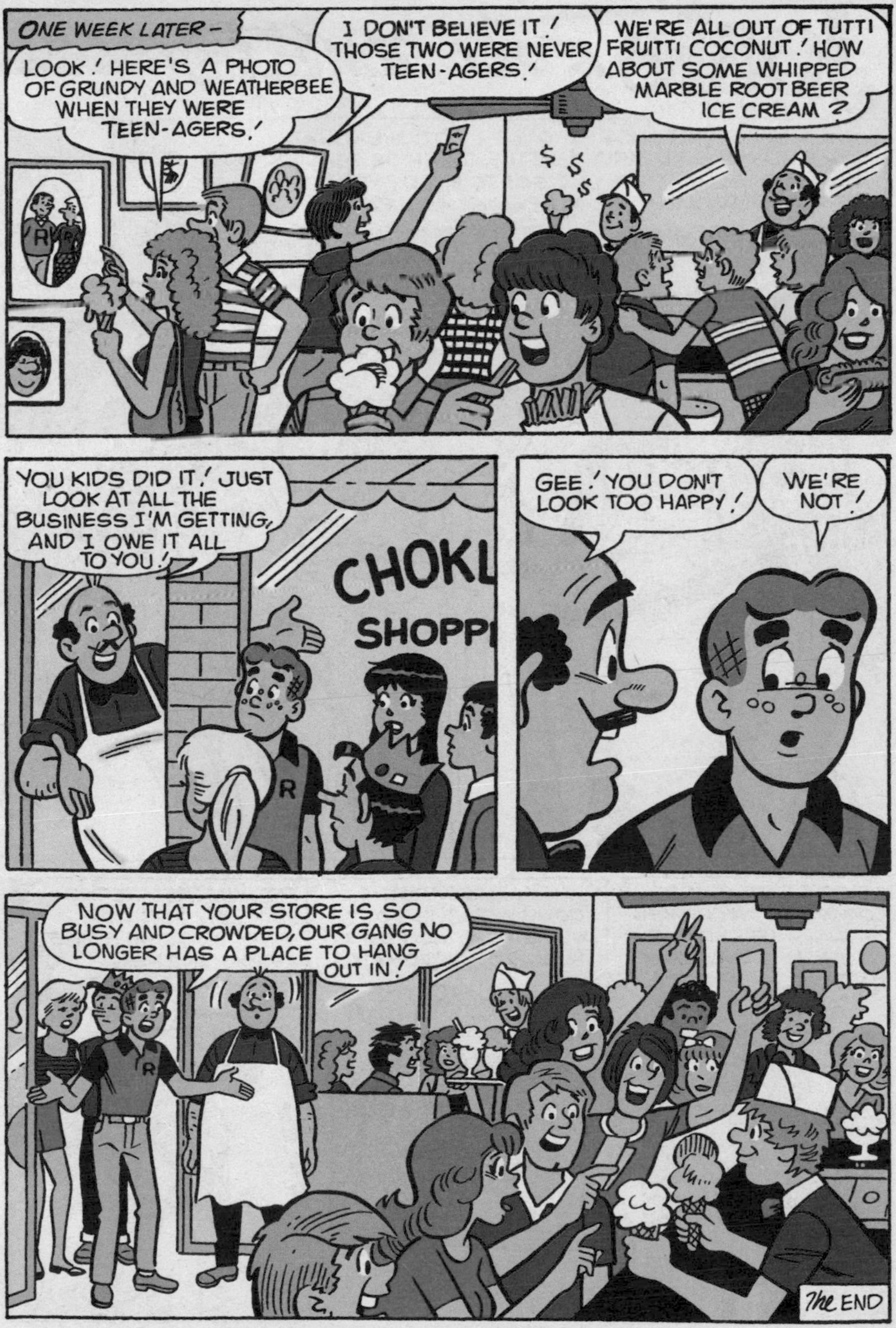
ONE WEEK LATER -
LOOK! HERE'S A PHOTO OF GRUNDY AND WEATHERBEE WHEN THEY WERE TEEN-AGERS!
I DON'T BELIEVE IT! THOSE TWO WERE NEVER TEEN-AGERS!
WE'RE ALL OUT OF TUTTI FRUITTI COCONUT! HOW ABOUT SOME WHIPPED MARBLE ROOT BEER ICE CREAM?
YOU KIDS DID IT! JUST LOOK AT ALL THE BUSINESS I'M GETTING, AND I OWE IT ALL TO YOU!
CHOKL
SHOPP
GEE! YOU DON'T LOOK TOO HAPPY!
WE'RE NOT!
NOW THAT YOUR STORE IS SO BUSY AND CROWDED, OUR GANG NO LONGER HAS A PLACE TO HANG OUT IN!
The END

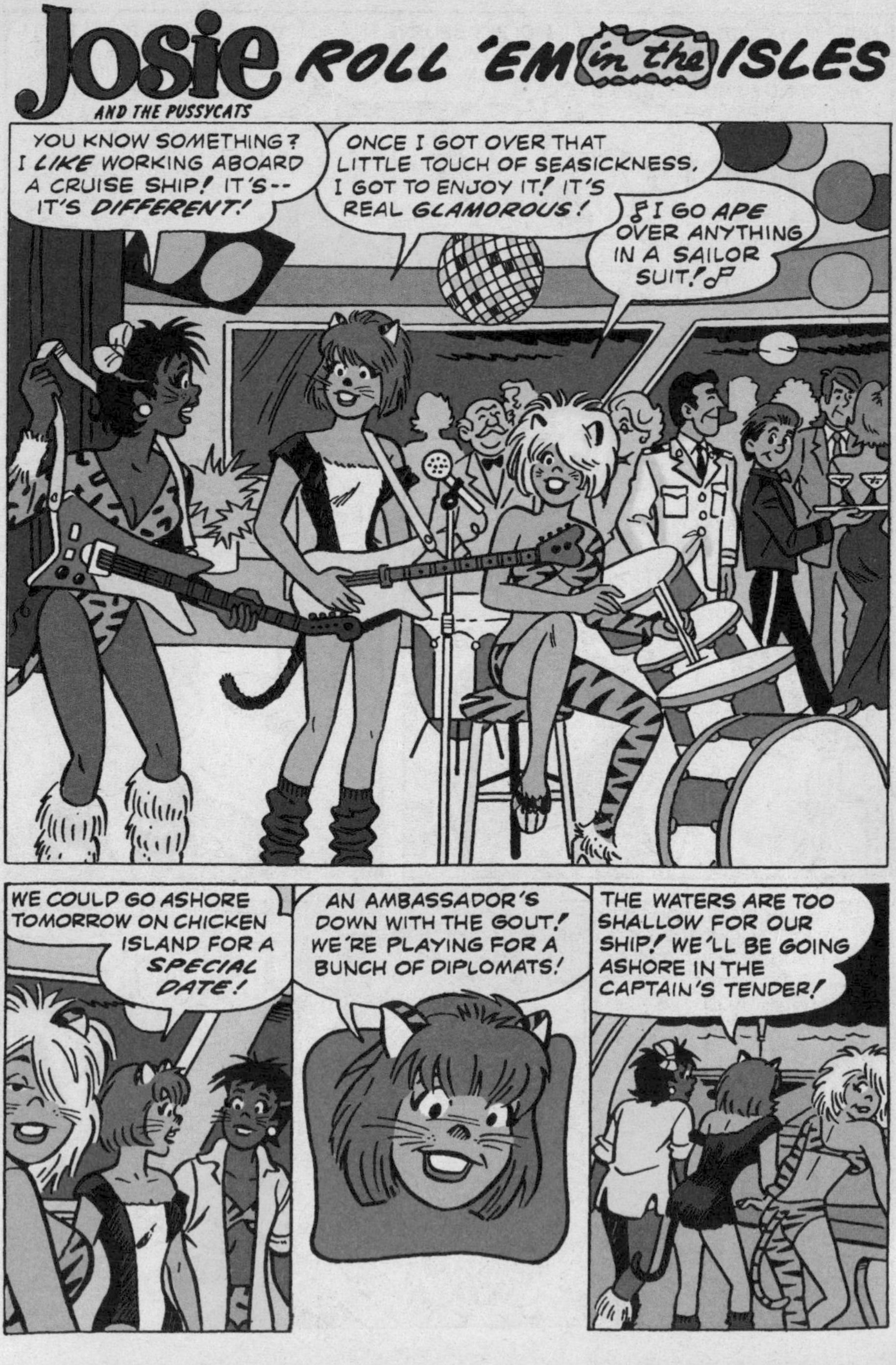
Josie
AND THE PUSSYCATS
ROLL 'EM in the ISLES
YOU KNOW SOMETHING? I LIKE WORKING ABOARD A CRUISE SHIP! IT'S-- IT'S DIFFERENT!
ONCE I GOT OVER THAT LITTLE TOUCH OF SEASICKNESS, I GOT TO ENJOY IT! IT'S REAL GLAMOROUS!
♪ I GO APE OVER ANYTHING IN A SAILOR SUIT! ♪
WE COULD GO ASHORE TOMORROW ON CHICKEN ISLAND FOR A SPECIAL DATE!
AN AMBASSADOR'S DOWN WITH THE GOUT! WE'RE PLAYING FOR A BUNCH OF DIPLOMATS!
THE WATERS ARE TOO SHALLOW FOR OUR SHIP! WE'LL BE GOING ASHORE IN THE CAPTAIN'S TENDER!

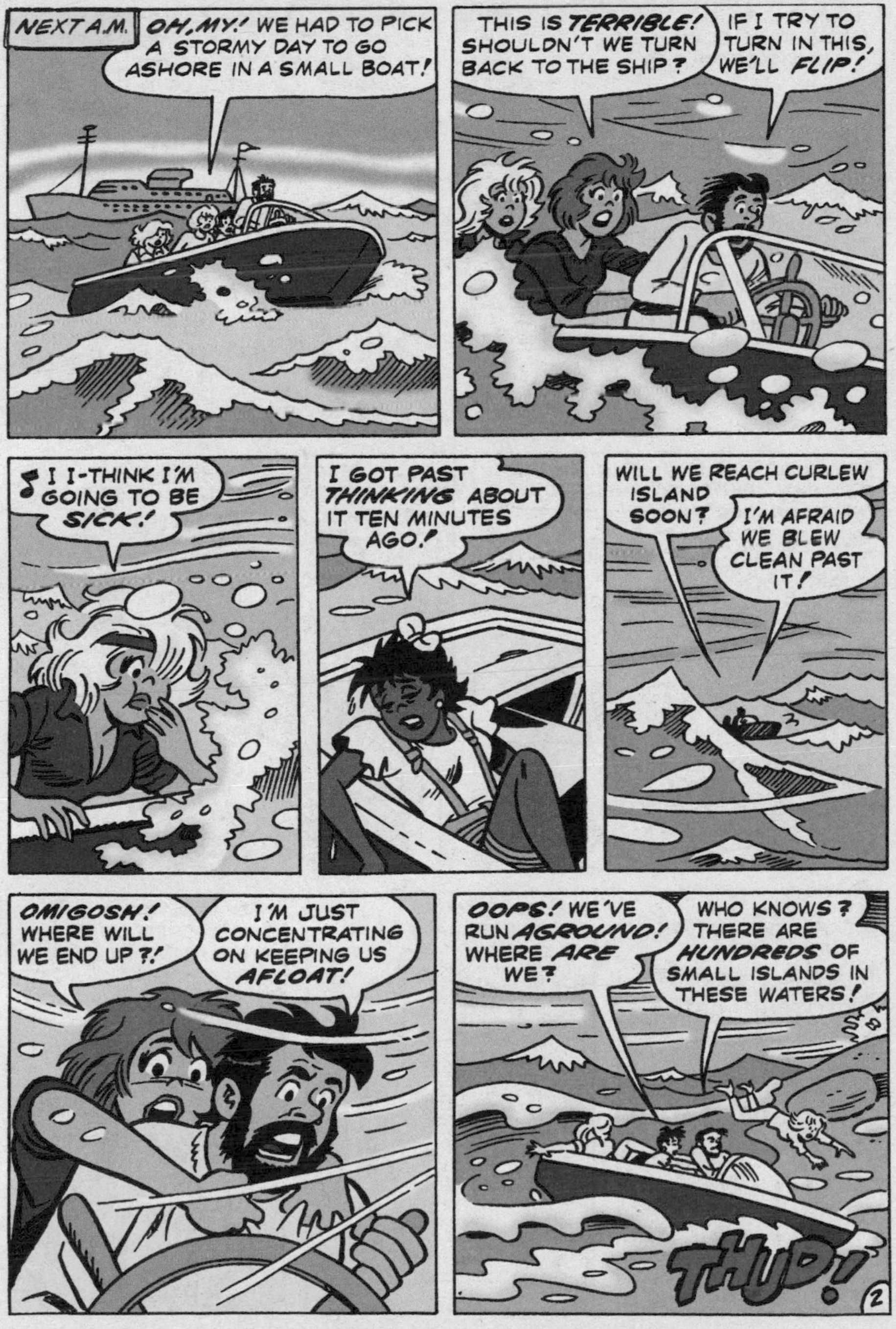
NEXT A.M.
OH, MY! WE HAD TO PICK A STORMY DAY TO GO ASHORE IN A SMALL BOAT!
THIS IS TERRIBLE! SHOULDN'T WE TURN BACK TO THE SHIP?
IF I TRY TO TURN IN THIS, WE'LL FLIP!
I I-THINK I'M GOING TO BE SICK!
I GOT PAST THINKING ABOUT IT TEN MINUTES AGO!
WILL WE REACH CURLEW ISLAND SOON?
I'M AFRAID WE BLEW CLEAN PAST IT!
OMIGOSH! WHERE WILL WE END UP?!
I'M JUST CONCENTRATING ON KEEPING US AFLOAT!
OOPS! WE'VE RUN AGROUND! WHERE ARE WE?
WHO KNOWS? THERE ARE HUNDREDS OF SMALL ISLANDS IN THESE WATERS!
THUD!
2

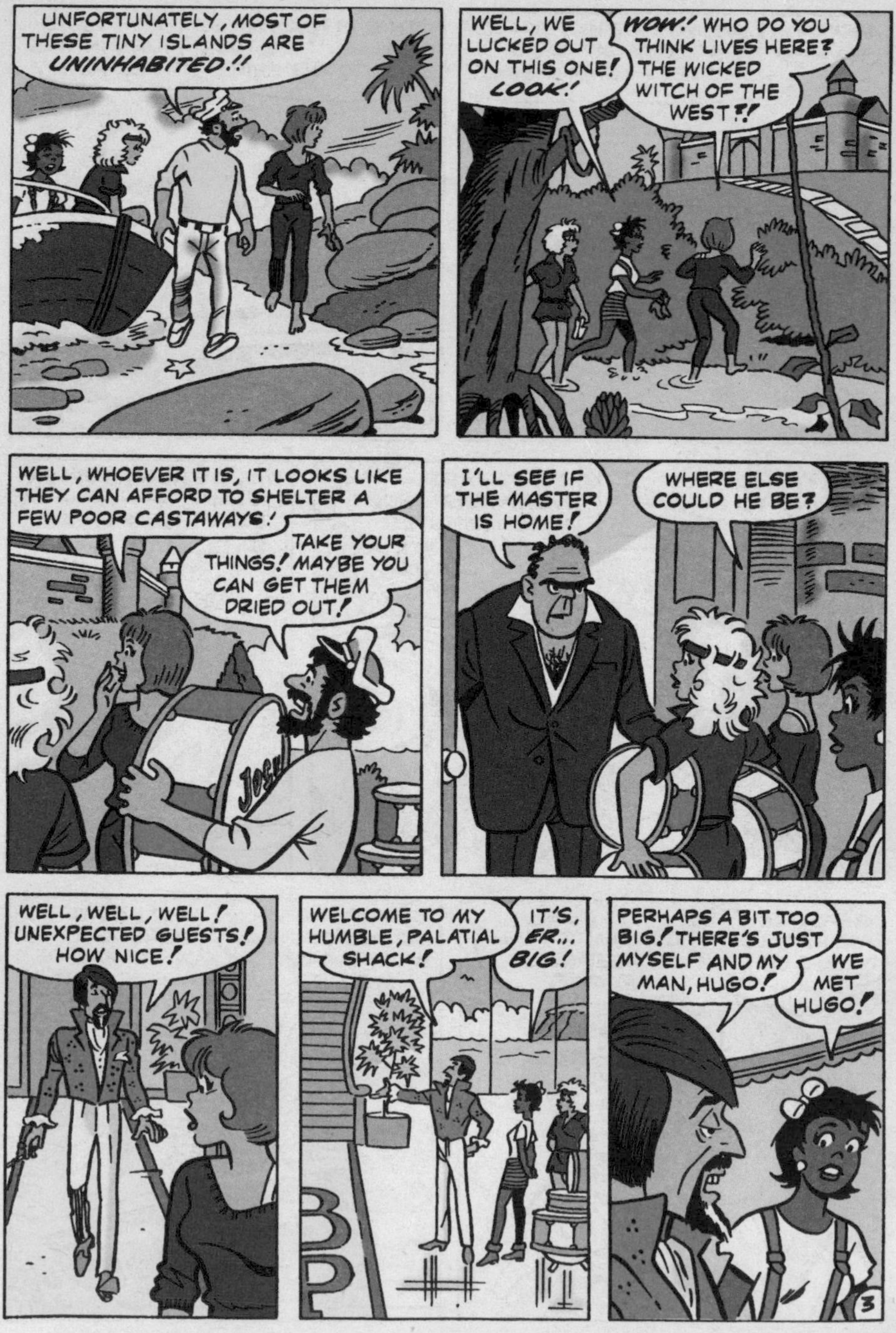
UNFORTUNATELY, MOST OF THESE TINY ISLANDS ARE UNINHABITED!!
WELL, WE LUCKED OUT ON THIS ONE! LOOK!
WOW! WHO DO YOU THINK LIVES HERE? THE WICKED WITCH OF THE WEST?!
WELL, WHOEVER IT IS, IT LOOKS LIKE THEY CAN AFFORD TO SHELTER A FEW POOR CASTAWAYS!
TAKE YOUR THINGS! MAYBE YOU CAN GET THEM DRIED OUT!
I'LL SEE IF THE MASTER IS HOME!
WHERE ELSE COULD HE BE?
WELL, WELL, WELL! UNEXPECTED GUESTS! HOW NICE!
WELCOME TO MY HUMBLE, PALATIAL SHACK!
IT'S, ER... BIG!
PERHAPS A BIT TOO BIG! THERE'S JUST MYSELF AND MY MAN, HUGO!
WE MET HUGO!
3

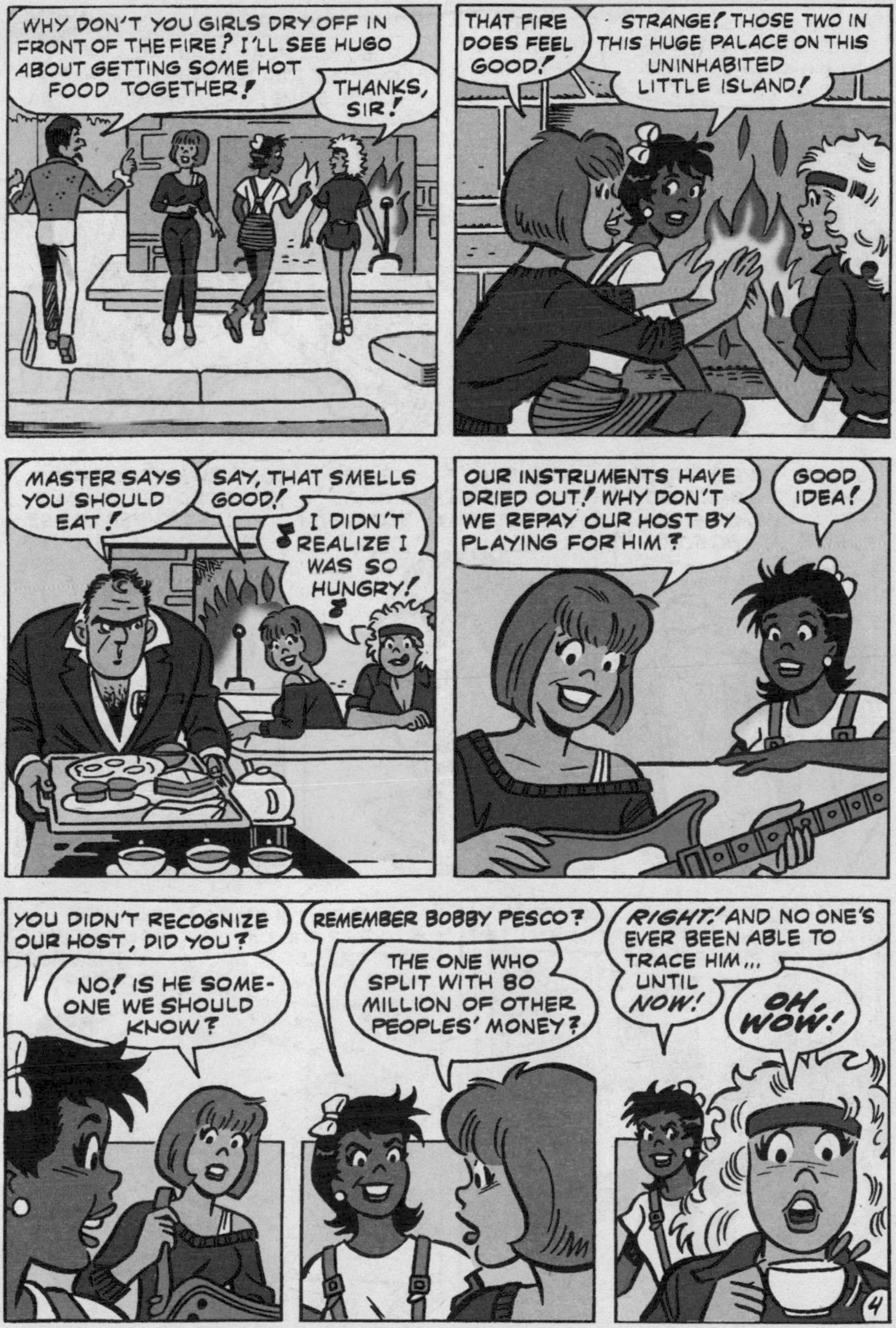
WHY DON'T YOU GIRLS DRY OFF IN FRONT OF THE FIRE? I'LL SEE HUGO ABOUT GETTING SOME HOT FOOD TOGETHER!
THANKS, SIR!
THAT FIRE DOES FEEL GOOD!
STRANGE! THOSE TWO IN THIS HUGE PALACE ON THIS UNINHABITED LITTLE ISLAND!
MASTER SAYS YOU SHOULD EAT!
SAY, THAT SMELLS GOOD!
I DIDN'T REALIZE I WAS SO HUNGRY!
OUR INSTRUMENTS HAVE DRIED OUT! WHY DON'T WE REPAY OUR HOST BY PLAYING FOR HIM?
GOOD IDEA!
YOU DIDN'T RECOGNIZE OUR HOST, DID YOU?
NO! IS HE SOMEONE WE SHOULD KNOW?
REMEMBER BOBBY PESCO?
THE ONE WHO SPLIT WITH 80 MILLION OF OTHER PEOPLES' MONEY?
RIGHT! AND NO ONE'S EVER BEEN ABLE TO TRACE HIM... UNTIL NOW!
OH, WOW!
4

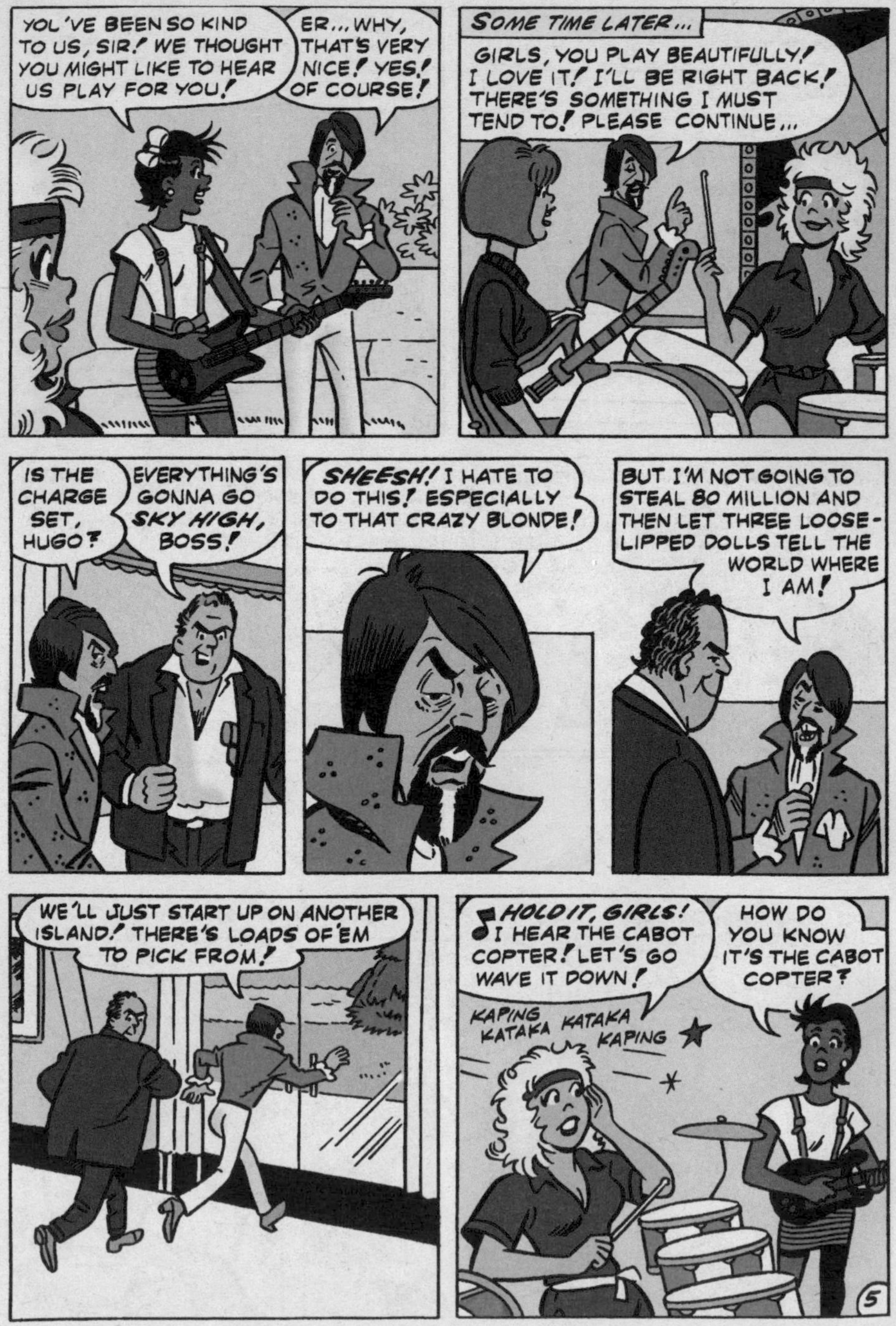
YOU'VE BEEN SO KIND TO US, SIR! WE THOUGHT YOU MIGHT LIKE TO HEAR US PLAY FOR YOU!
ER... WHY, THAT'S VERY NICE! YES! OF COURSE!
SOME TIME LATER...
GIRLS, YOU PLAY BEAUTIFULLY! I LOVE IT! I'LL BE RIGHT BACK! THERE'S SOMETHING I MUST TEND TO! PLEASE CONTINUE...
IS THE CHARGE SET, HUGO?
EVERYTHING'S GONNA GO SKY HIGH, BOSS!
SHEESH! I HATE TO DO THIS! ESPECIALLY TO THAT CRAZY BLONDE!
BUT I'M NOT GOING TO STEAL 80 MILLION AND THEN LET THREE LOOSE-LIPPED DOLLS TELL THE WORLD WHERE I AM!
WE'LL JUST START UP ON ANOTHER ISLAND! THERE'S LOADS OF 'EM TO PICK FROM!
HOLD IT, GIRLS! I HEAR THE CABOT COPTER! LET'S GO WAVE IT DOWN!
HOW DO YOU KNOW IT'S THE CABOT COPTER?
KAPING KATAKA KATAKA KAPING
5

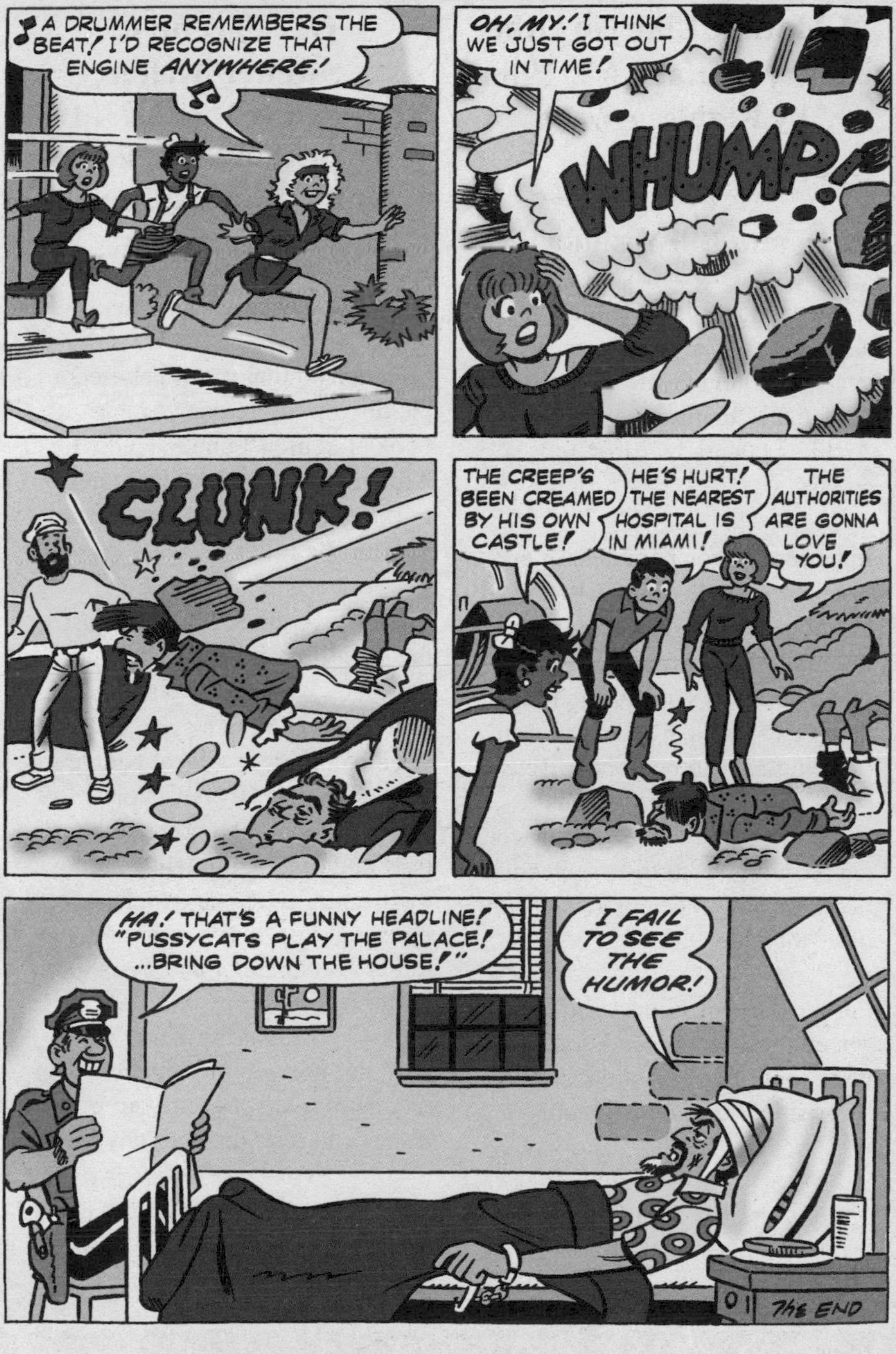
A DRUMMER REMEMBERS THE BEAT! I'D RECOGNIZE THAT ENGINE ANYWHERE!
OH, MY! I THINK WE JUST GOT OUT IN TIME!
WHUMP!
CLUNK!
THE CREEP'S BEEN CREAMED BY HIS OWN CASTLE!
HE'S HURT! THE NEAREST HOSPITAL IS IN MIAMI!
THE AUTHORITIES ARE GONNA LOVE YOU!
HA! THAT'S A FUNNY HEADLINE! "PUSSYCATS PLAY THE PALACE! ...BRING DOWN THE HOUSE!"
I FAIL TO SEE THE HUMOR!
THE END

A Mother Like No Other
Betty's Diary #2, 1986
by Kathleen Webb, Jeff Shultz, Rudy Lapick and Bill Yoshida

Betty Cooper has evolved as a character quite a bit over the years, and new facets of her are continually being revealed by Archie's talented writers and artists.

In fiction, good characters often just "are," while obviously flawed characters are made out to be more fascinating and attractive. What I love about this story is that it deftly examines the quiet yearning of a character to be good—Betty's small choices, the conscious perceptions she makes of her world to see things from the perspective of others and to celebrate someone other than herself.

For me, Betty's honest and sincere perspective and decisions throughout her day build subtly to a surprisingly affecting conclusion.

--Harold Buchholz
Executive Director of Publishing & Operations, Archie Comics

Old Faceful & Swelter Melter
New Archies Digest #3, 1988
by Joe Edwards, Rudy Lapick and Hy Eisman

The New Archies were my introduction to the Archie universe. So much so that when I started picking up the regular Archie books I couldn't understand why Archie had such short hair, and was missing his trademark (at least in my mind) mullet.

The New Archies arrived at just the right time for me. I was in 5th grade when the TV series first aired. I found a stash of New Archie comics at a local garage sale for only 5 and 10 cents a piece! I bought them all, and read them over and over again while eating my peanut butter sandwiches every morning. Some days I still get the urge to break out a jar of peanut butter (only Skippy will do!) cut the crust off, cut the sandwich in half, not horizontally but across in rectangular shapes, pull out my old issues and read them all day long!

--Stephen Oswald
Production Manager, Archie Comics

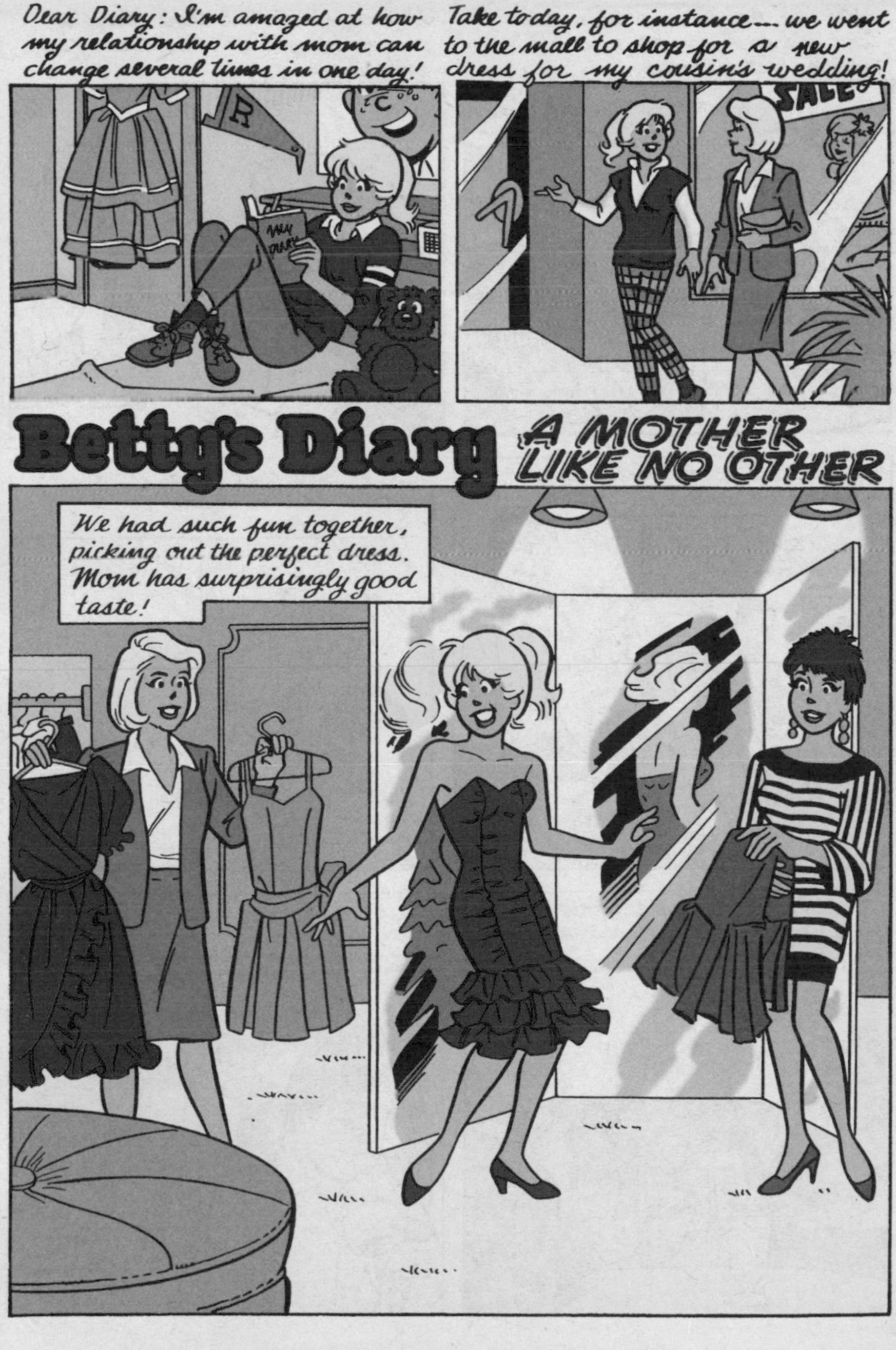
Dear Diary: I'm amazed at how my relationship with mom can change several times in one day!
Take today, for instance... we went to the mall to shop for a new dress for my cousin's wedding!
SALE
Betty's Diary
A MOTHER LIKE NO OTHER
We had such fun together, picking out the perfect dress. Mom has surprisingly good taste!

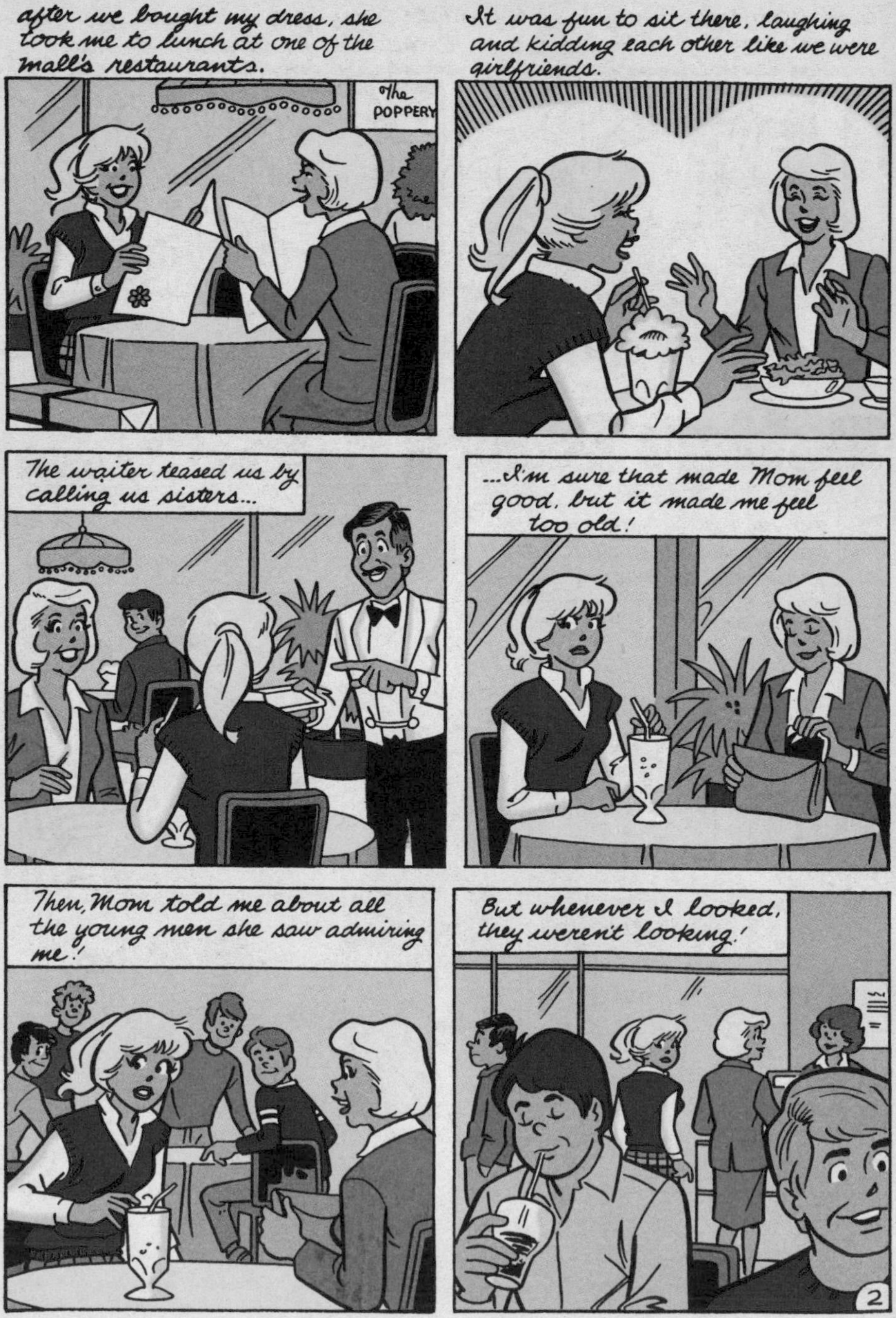

after we bought my dress, she took me to lunch at one of the mall's restaurants.
The POPPERY
It was fun to sit there, laughing and kidding each other like we were girlfriends.
The waiter teased us by calling us sisters...
...I'm sure that made Mom feel good, but it made me feel too old!
Then, Mom told me about all the young men she saw admiring me!
But whenever I looked, they weren't looking!
2

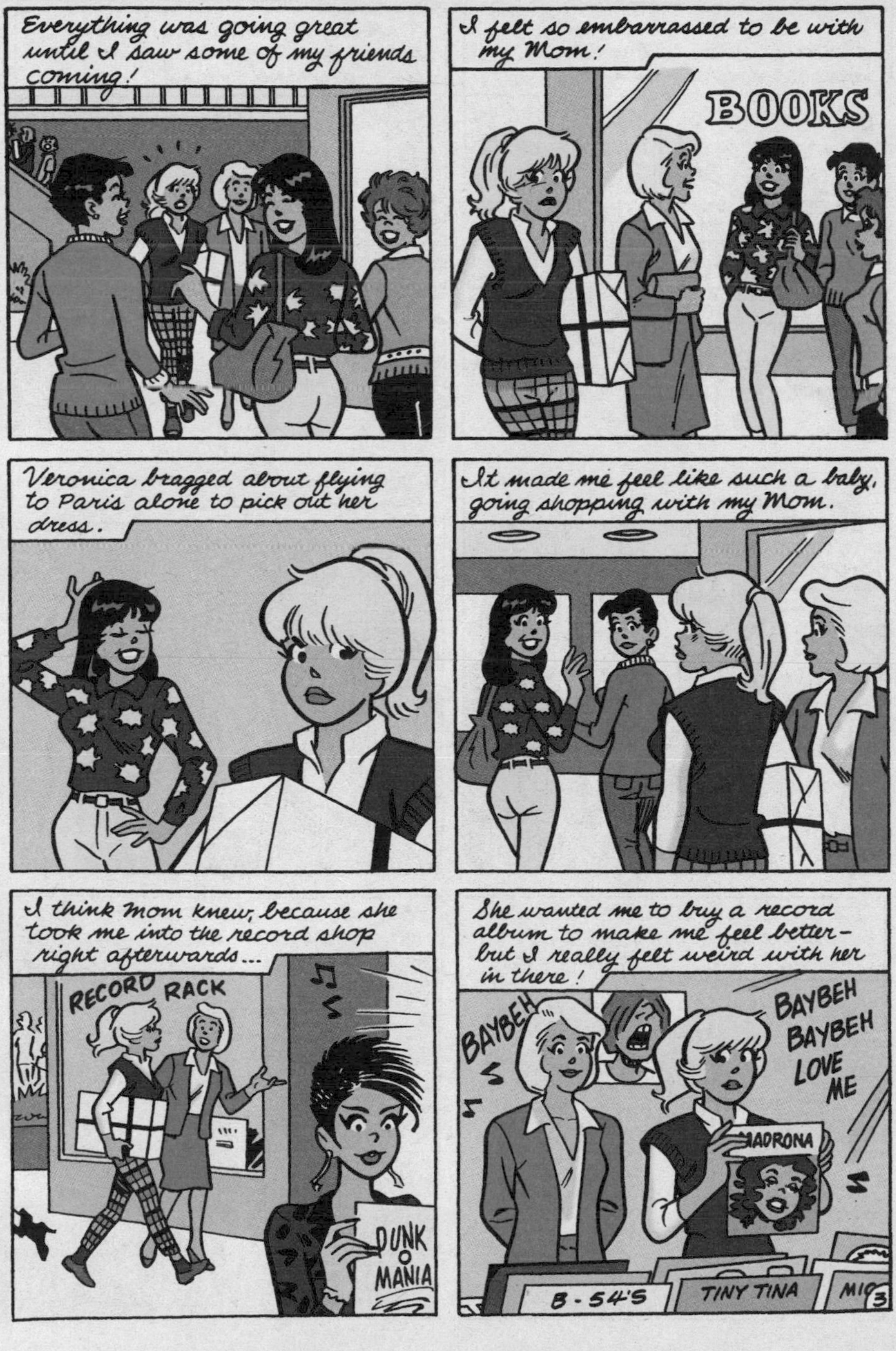
Everything was going great until I saw some of my friends coming!
I felt so embarrassed to be with my Mom!
BOOKS
Veronica bragged about flying to Paris alone to pick out her dress.
It made me feel like such a baby, going shopping with my Mom.
I think Mom knew, because she took me into the record shop right afterwards...
RECORD RACK
DUNK O MANIA
She wanted me to buy a record album to make me feel better—but I really felt weird with her in there!
BAYBEH
BAYBEH BAYBEH LOVE ME
MADRONA
B-54'S
TINY TINA
MIC
3

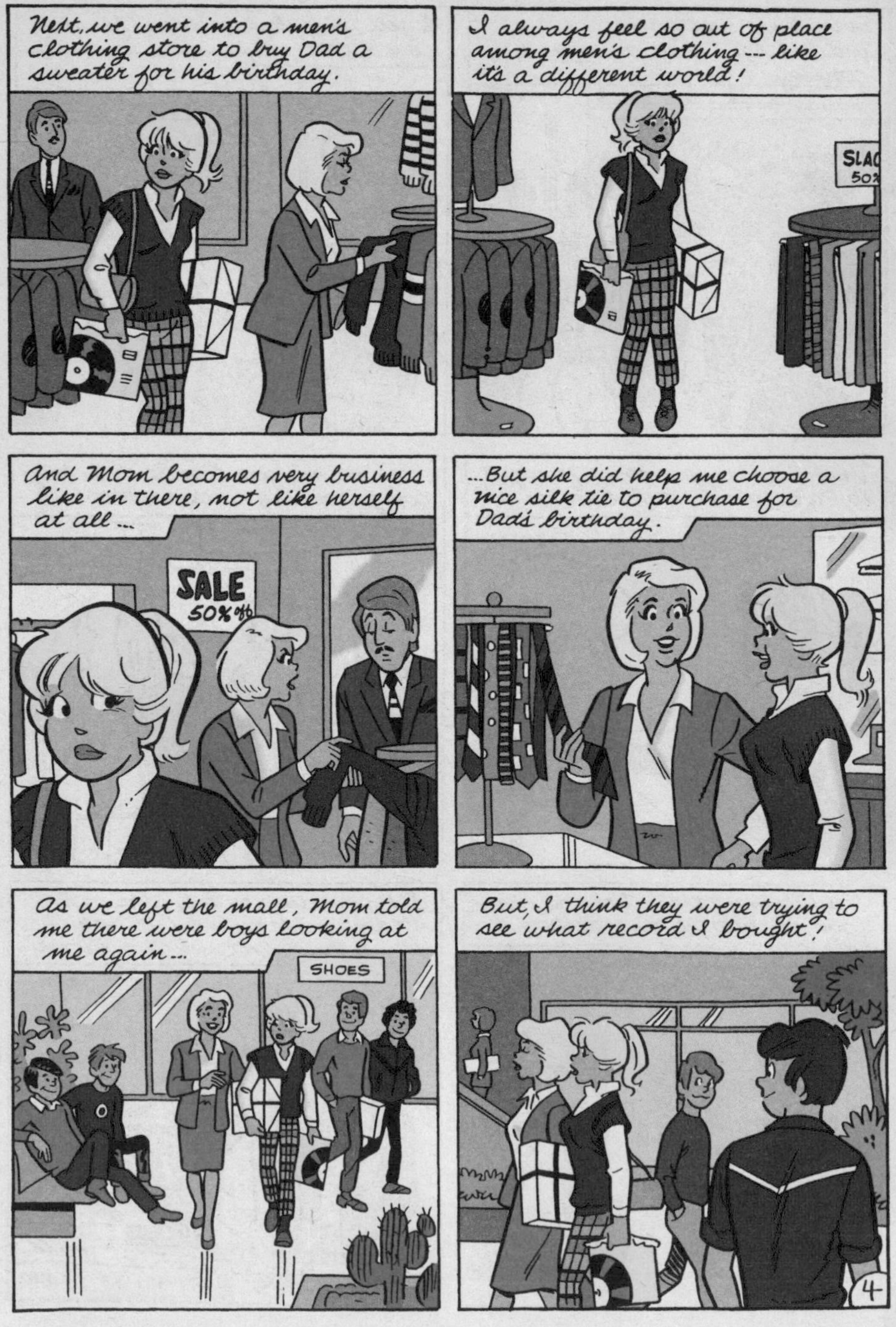
Next, we went into a men's clothing store to buy Dad a sweater for his birthday.
I always feel so out of place among men's clothing --- like it's a different world!
SLAC
50%
And Mom becomes very business like in there, not like herself at all ...
SALE
50% off
...But she did help me choose a nice silk tie to purchase for Dad's birthday.
As we left the mall, Mom told me there were boys looking at me again...
SHOES
But, I think they were trying to see what record I bought!
4

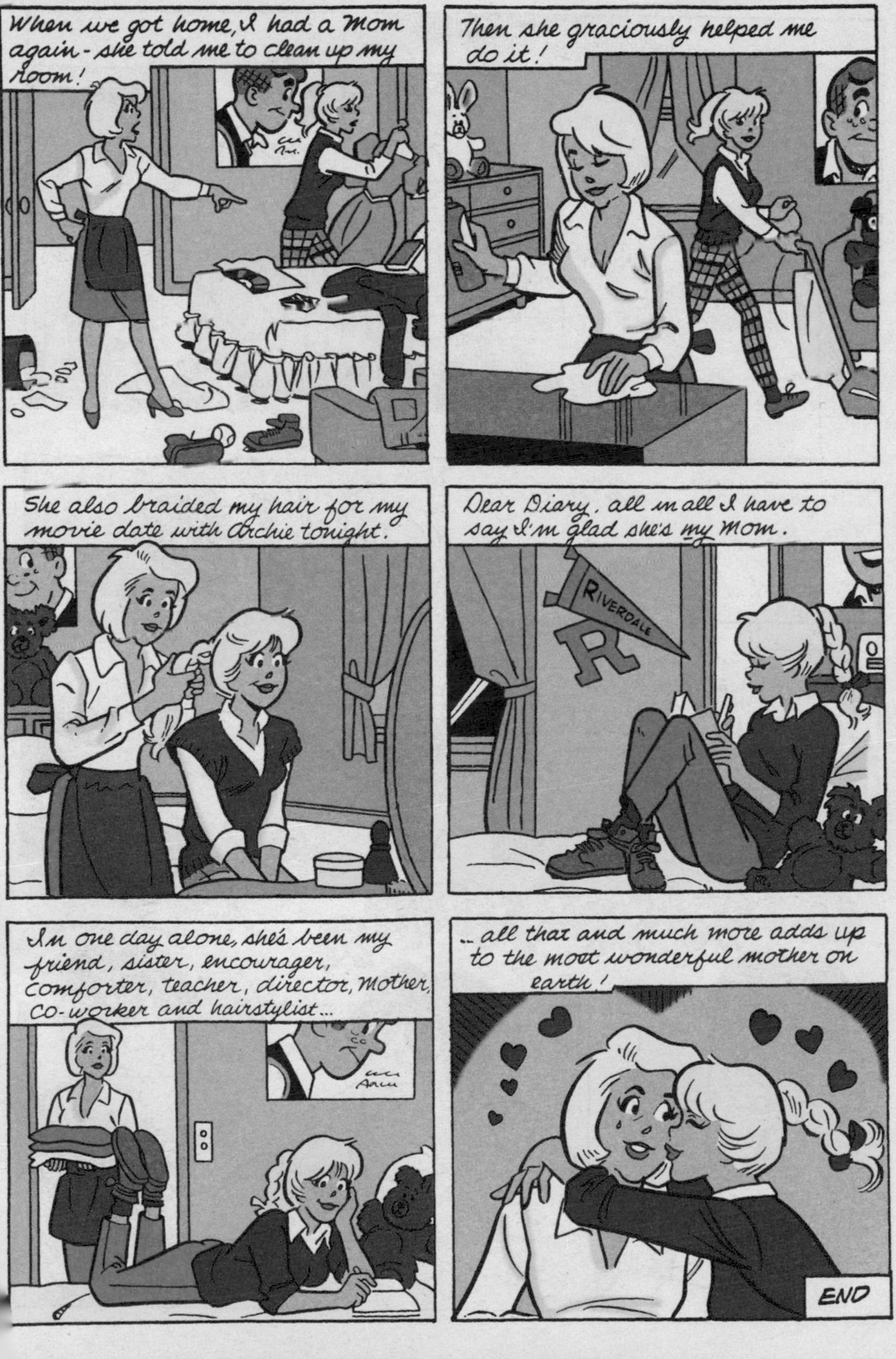
When we got home, I had a Mom again - she told me to clean up my room!
Then she graciously helped me do it!
She also braided my hair for my movie date with Archie tonight.
Dear Diary, all in all I have to say I'm glad she's my Mom.
RIVERDALE
R
In one day alone, she's been my friend, sister, encourager, comforter, teacher, director, Mother, co-worker and hairstylist...
... all that and much more adds up to the most wonderful mother on earth!
END

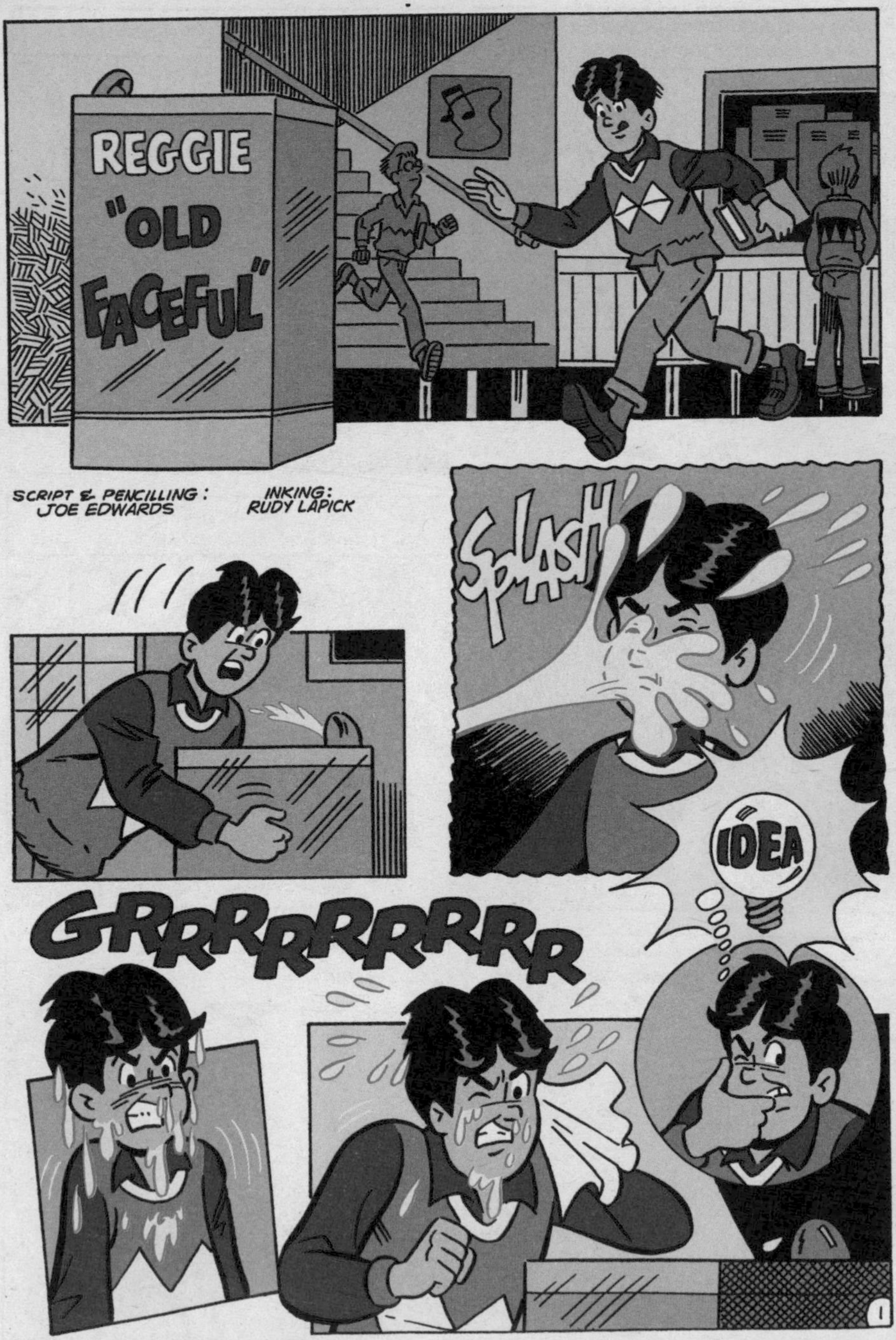
REGGIE
"OLD FACEFUL"
SCRIPT & PENCILLING : JOE EDWARDS
INKING: RUDY LAPICK
SPLASH
IDEA
GRRRRRRRRR
1

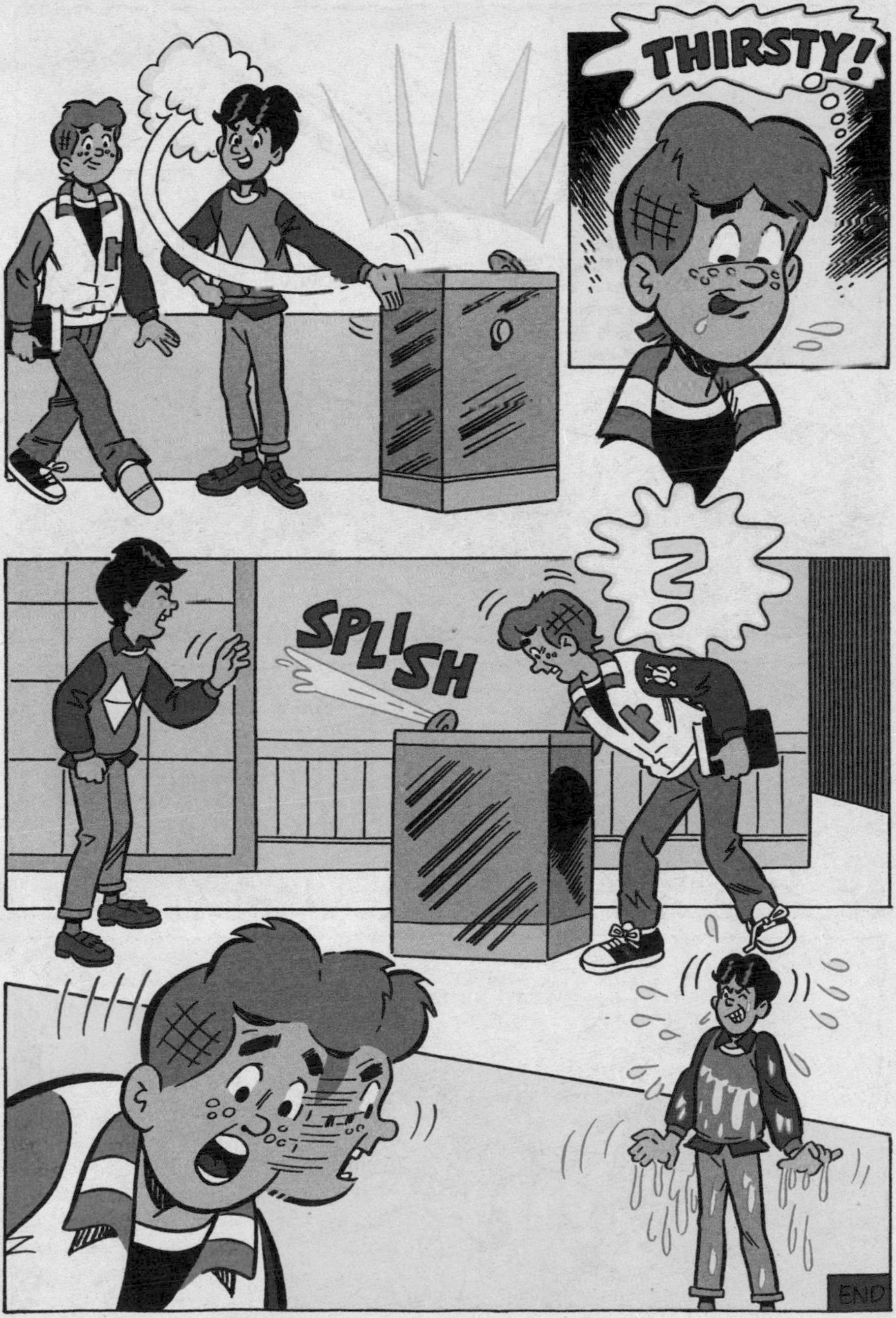
THIRSTY!
SPLISH
END

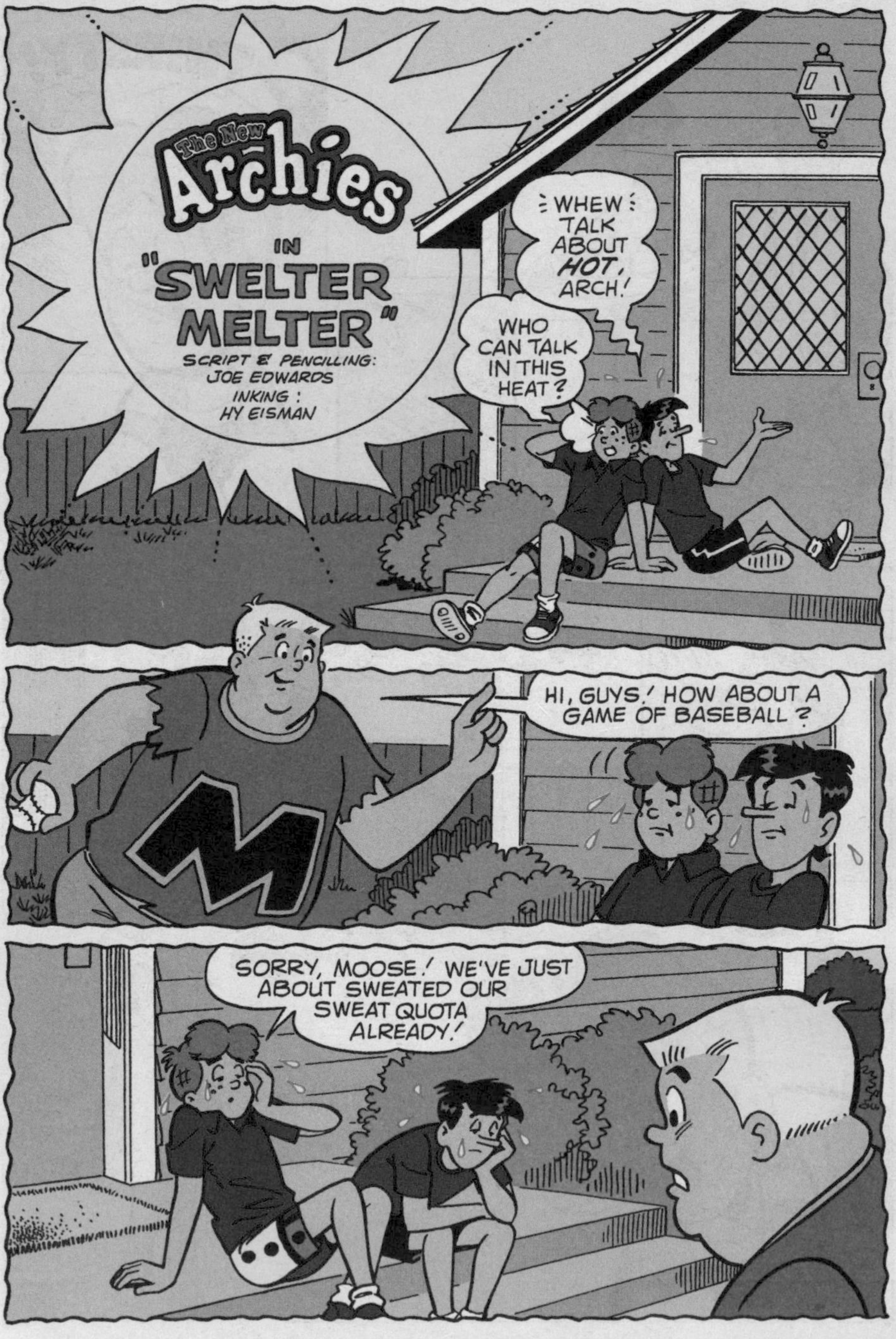
The New Archies
IN
"SWELTER MELTER"
SCRIPT & PENCILLING: JOE EDWARDS
INKING: HY EISMAN
WHEW TALK ABOUT HOT, ARCH!
WHO CAN TALK IN THIS HEAT?
HI, GUYS! HOW ABOUT A GAME OF BASEBALL?
SORRY, MOOSE! WE'VE JUST ABOUT SWEATED OUR SWEAT QUOTA ALREADY!

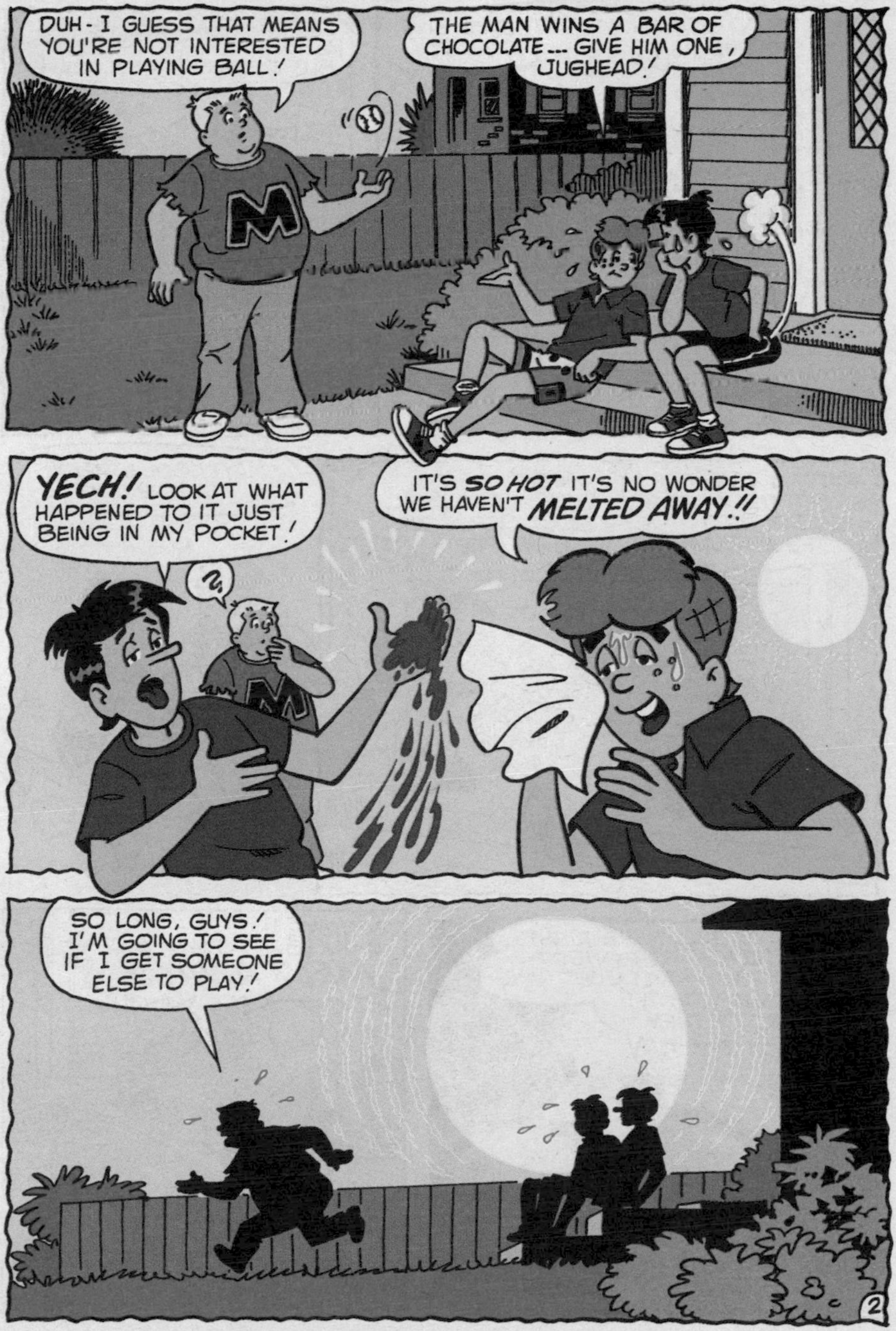
DUH - I GUESS THAT MEANS YOU'RE NOT INTERESTED IN PLAYING BALL!
THE MAN WINS A BAR OF CHOCOLATE ... GIVE HIM ONE, JUGHEAD!
YECH! LOOK AT WHAT HAPPENED TO IT JUST BEING IN MY POCKET!
IT'S SO HOT IT'S NO WONDER WE HAVEN'T MELTED AWAY!!
SO LONG, GUYS! I'M GOING TO SEE IF I GET SOMEONE ELSE TO PLAY!
2

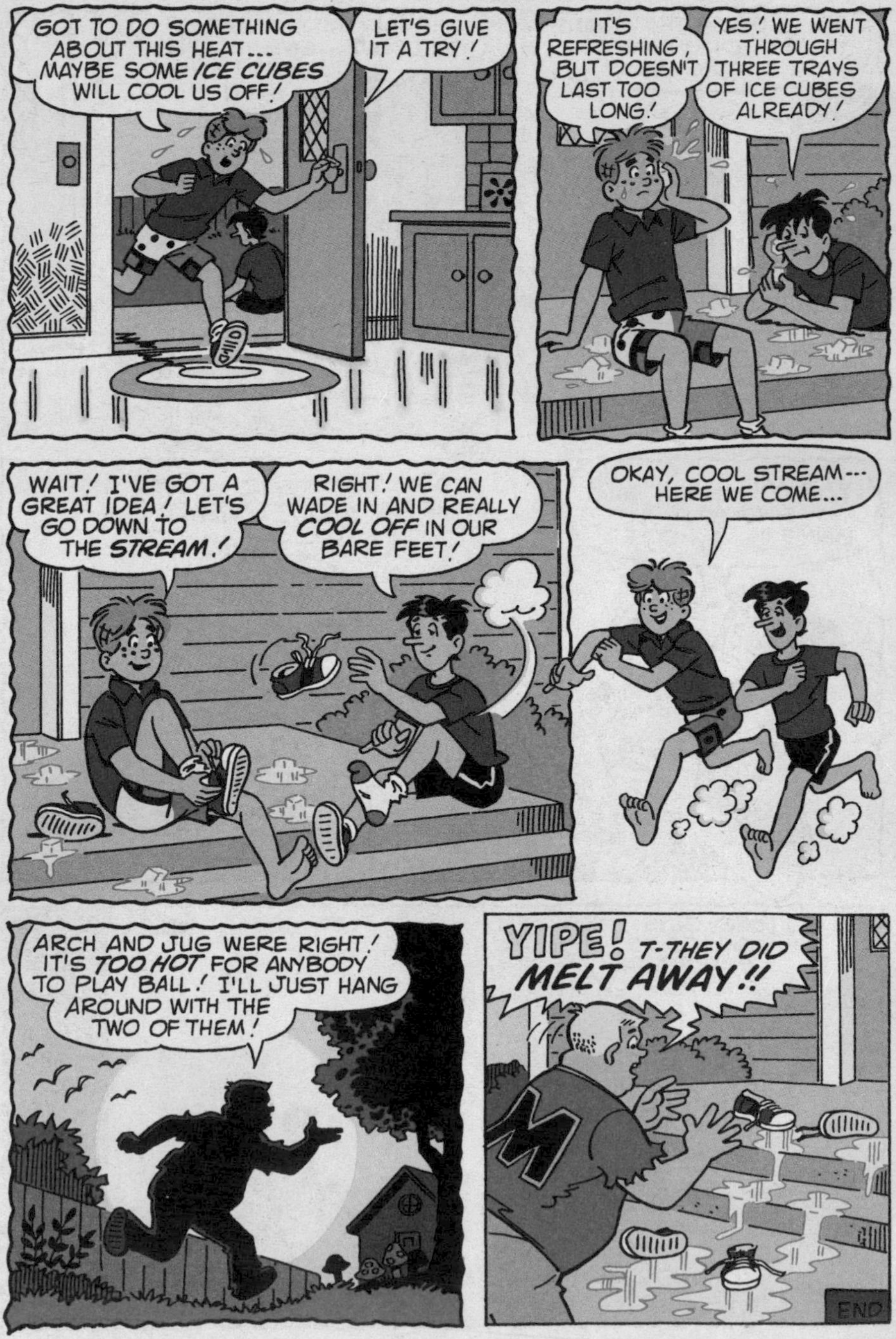
GOT TO DO SOMETHING ABOUT THIS HEAT... MAYBE SOME ICE CUBES WILL COOL US OFF!
LET'S GIVE IT A TRY!
IT'S REFRESHING, BUT DOESN'T LAST TOO LONG!
YES! WE WENT THROUGH THREE TRAYS OF ICE CUBES ALREADY!
WAIT! I'VE GOT A GREAT IDEA! LET'S GO DOWN TO THE STREAM!
RIGHT! WE CAN WADE IN AND REALLY COOL OFF IN OUR BARE FEET!
OKAY, COOL STREAM--- HERE WE COME...
ARCH AND JUG WERE RIGHT! IT'S TOO HOT FOR ANYBODY TO PLAY BALL! I'LL JUST HANG AROUND WITH THE TWO OF THEM!
YIPE! T-THEY DID MELT AWAY!!
END

Model Mania
Betty & Veronica #14, 1988
by George Gladir, Dan Decarlo, Rudy Lapick and Rod Ollerenshaw

Really, all of the stories in *Betty & Veronica #14* are gold to me. I must have memorized this book when I was 8 years old, but this lead story is the one that really stays with me. It epitomizes the challenges that teenagers have with cross-gender communication, but more importantly to the me of 1988, it featured lots of fun clothes and poses. Dan DeCarlo had an amazing way of making the girls fashionable and fun in a way that I envied, as I was limited to jeans and hand-me-downs. I rediscovered this book in my first few months at Archie Comics, when I was helping to assemble *Best of the Nineties Volume 1*. The fashion page from this book is also one of my favorite Archie things ever—it takes me right back to elementary school summers.

--Suzannah Rowntree
Features Editor,
Life with Archie Magazine

Robo-Teen
Laugh #13, 1989
by George Gladir, Rex Lindsey, Jon D'Agostino and Barry Grossman

When I was growing up, my mother would take me to the local comic shop and pick out some books. I would always get the latest issues of *Superman*, *Batman* and of course *Teenage Mutant Ninja Turtles*. It was during one of these trips to the comic shop that I can remember being given a stack of about four or five comics that the owner had in a box next to the register. It was a completely random stack and most of the titles I could honestly care less about, but hidden within was a beat up Archie book, specifically *Laugh #13*. I didn't know it at the time but "Robo-Teen" was just one of many Mighty Archie Art Players stories that parodied popular movies and television. Since working for Archie I've had the opportunity to enjoy most of them. I was also surprised to find out that Robo-Teen had never been reprinted; that is until I got involved and put it in *Archie Americana: Best of the Eighties Book 2!*

--Joe Morciglio
Project Coordinator,
Archie Comics

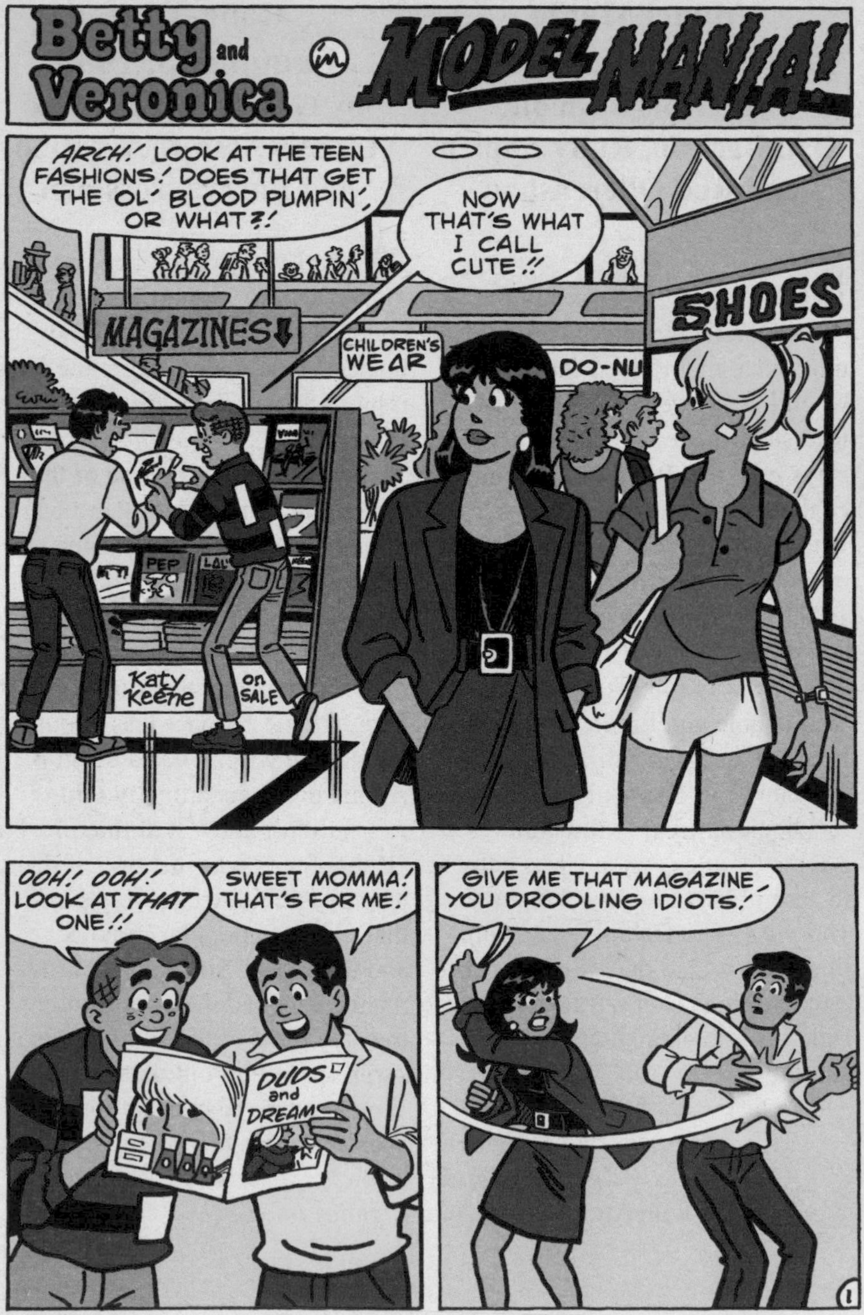
Betty and Veronica in MODEL MANIA!
ARCH! LOOK AT THE TEEN FASHIONS! DOES THAT GET THE OL' BLOOD PUMPIN', OR WHAT?!
NOW THAT'S WHAT I CALL CUTE!!
MAGAZINES
CHILDREN'S WEAR
DO-NU
SHOES
PEP
Katy Keene on SALE
OOH! OOH! LOOK AT THAT ONE!!
SWEET MOMMA! THAT'S FOR ME!
DUDS and DREAM
GIVE ME THAT MAGAZINE, YOU DROOLING IDIOTS!
1

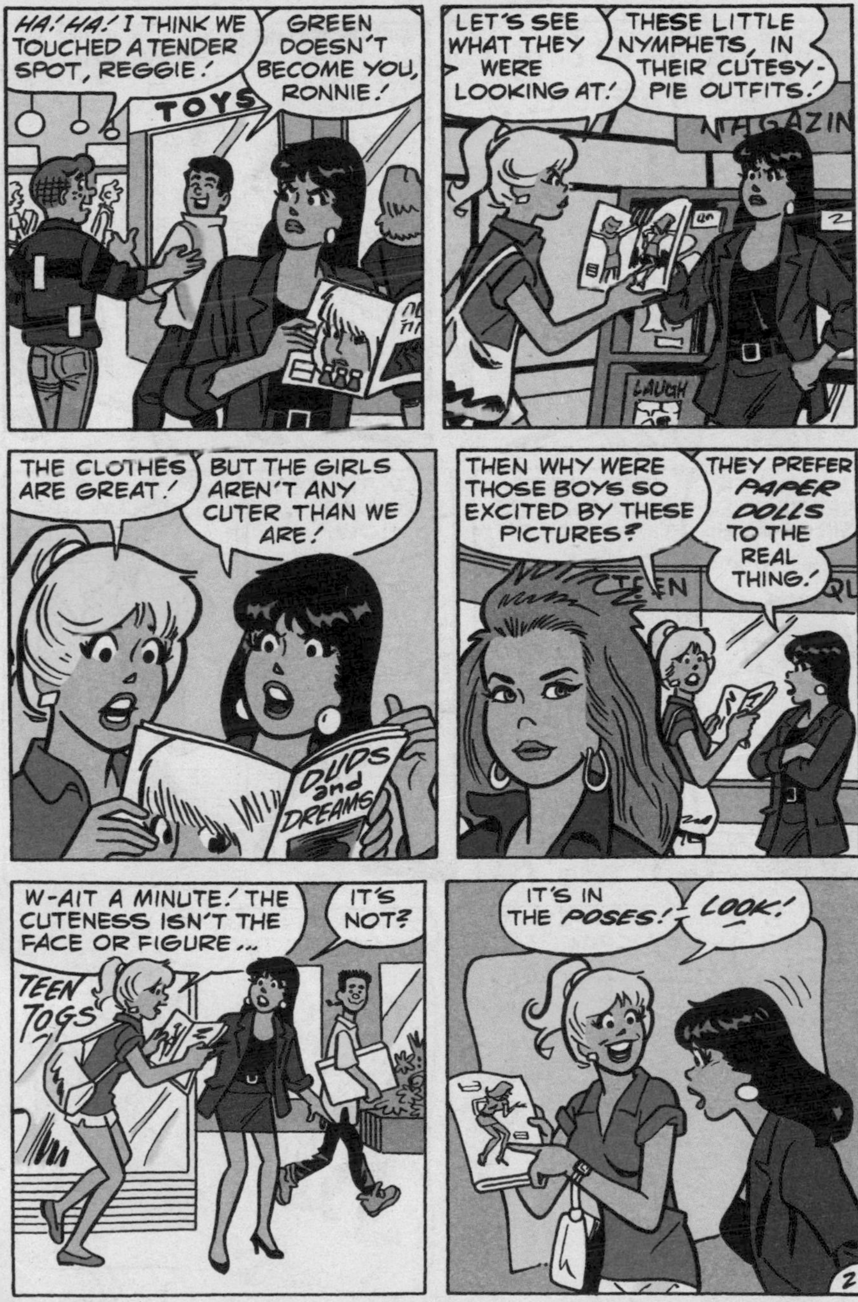
HA! HA! I THINK WE TOUCHED A TENDER SPOT, REGGIE!
GREEN DOESN'T BECOME YOU, RONNIE!
TOYS
LET'S SEE WHAT THEY WERE LOOKING AT!
THESE LITTLE NYMPHETS, IN THEIR CUTESY-PIE OUTFITS!
MAGAZIN
LAUGH
THE CLOTHES ARE GREAT!
BUT THE GIRLS AREN'T ANY CUTER THAN WE ARE!
DUDS and DREAMS
THEN WHY WERE THOSE BOYS SO EXCITED BY THESE PICTURES?
THEY PREFER PAPER DOLLS TO THE REAL THING!
TEEN
W-AIT A MINUTE! THE CUTENESS ISN'T THE FACE OR FIGURE...
IT'S NOT?
TEEN TOGS
IT'S IN THE POSES!
LOOK!
2

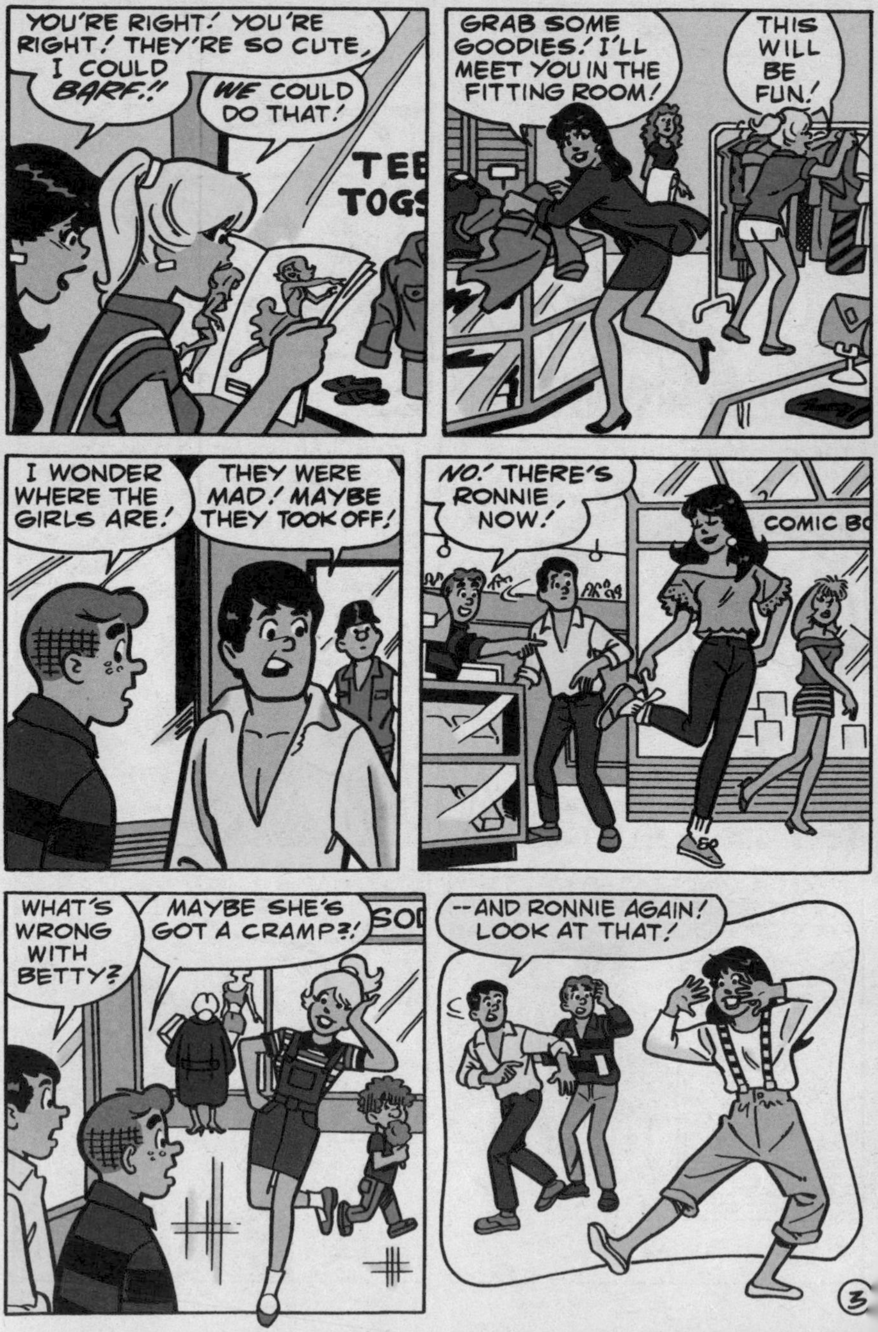
YOU'RE RIGHT! YOU'RE RIGHT! THEY'RE SO CUTE, I COULD BARF!!
WE COULD DO THAT!
TEE TOGS
GRAB SOME GOODIES! I'LL MEET YOU IN THE FITTING ROOM!
THIS WILL BE FUN!
I WONDER WHERE THE GIRLS ARE!
THEY WERE MAD! MAYBE THEY TOOK OFF!
NO! THERE'S RONNIE NOW!
COMIC BO
WHAT'S WRONG WITH BETTY?
MAYBE SHE'S GOT A CRAMP?!
SOD
--AND RONNIE AGAIN! LOOK AT THAT!
3

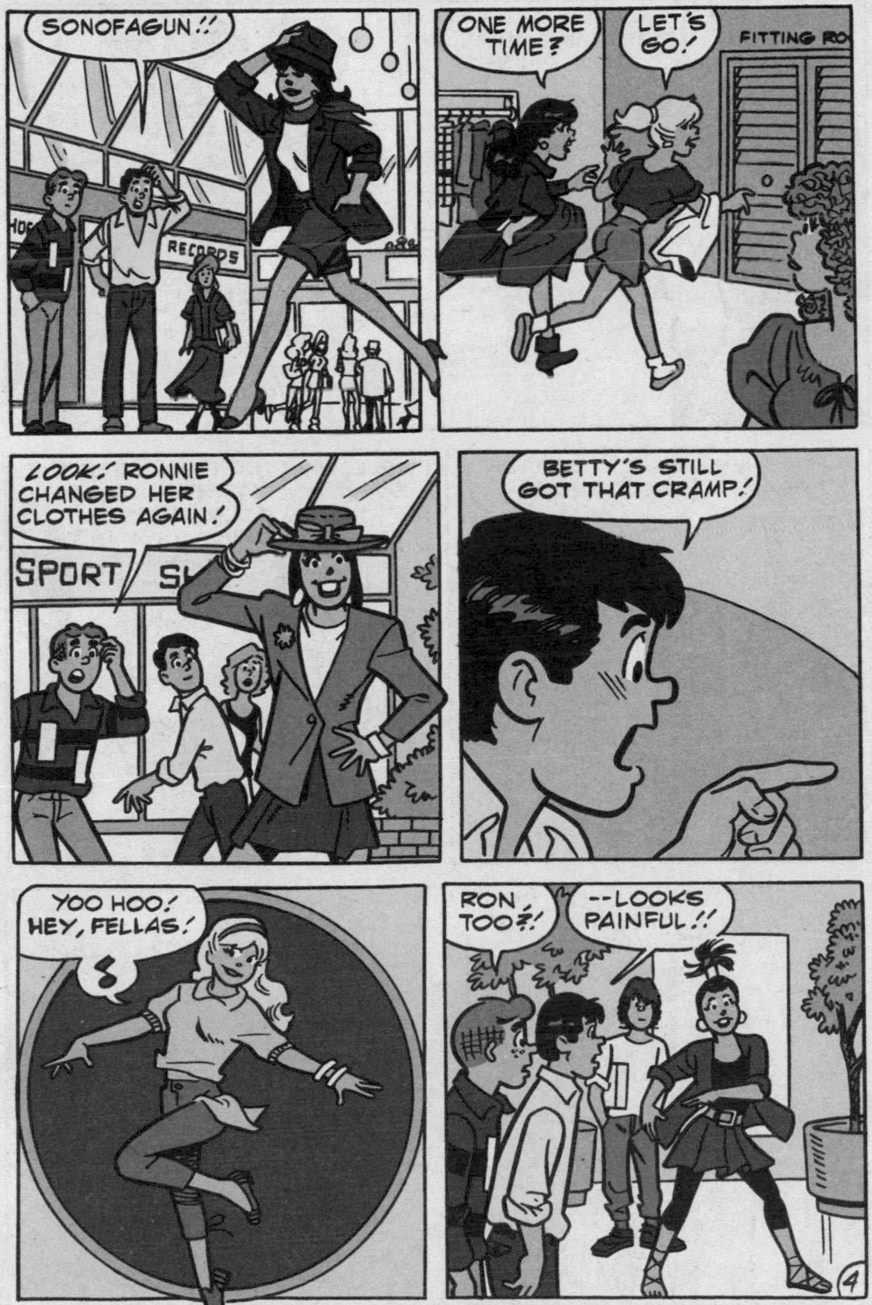
SONOFAGUN!!
RECORDS
ONE MORE TIME?
LET'S GO!
FITTING RO
LOOK! RONNIE CHANGED HER CLOTHES AGAIN!
SPORT
BETTY'S STILL GOT THAT CRAMP!
YOO HOO! HEY, FELLAS!
RON, TOO?!
--LOOKS PAINFUL!!
4

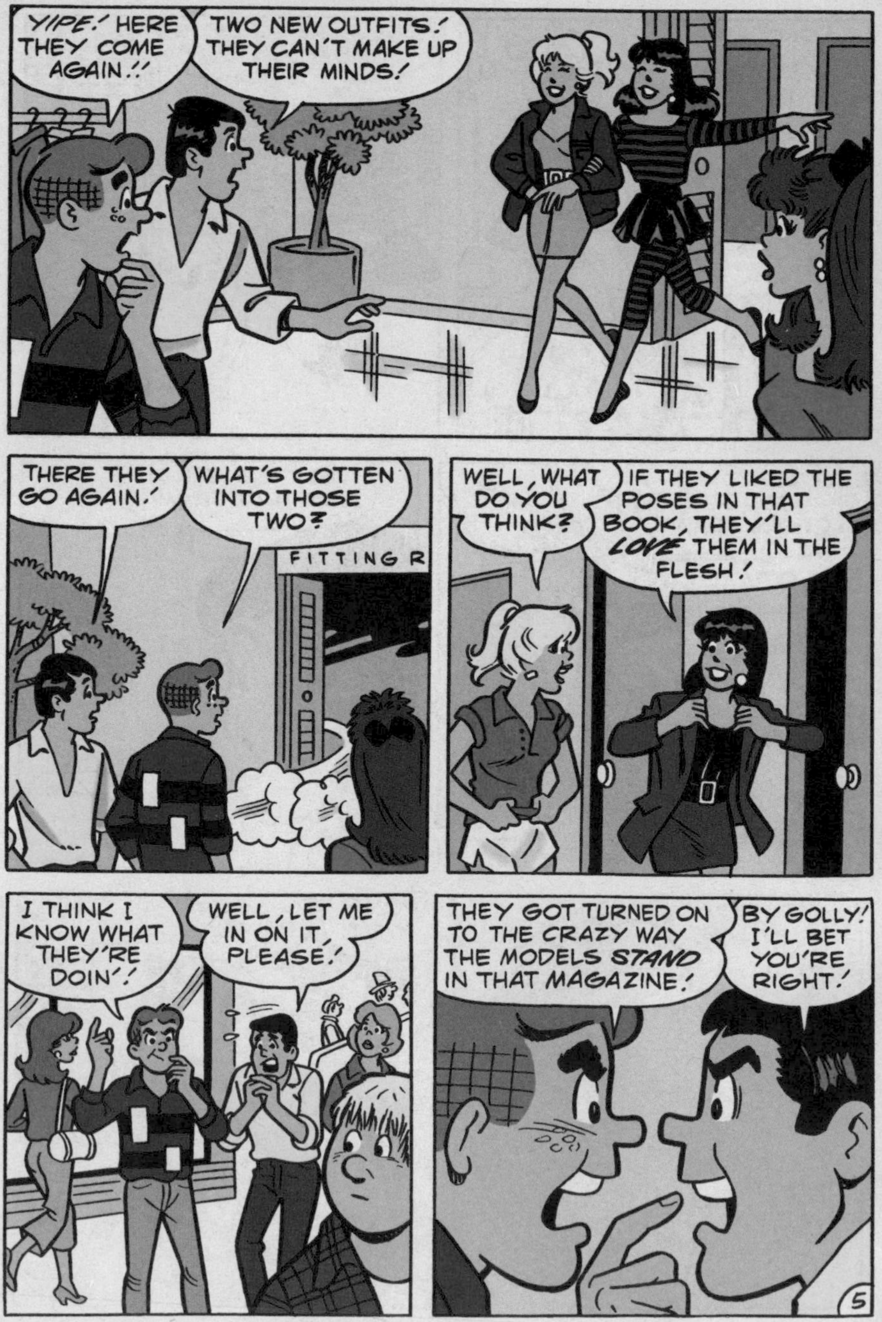
YIPE! HERE THEY COME AGAIN!!
TWO NEW OUTFITS! THEY CAN'T MAKE UP THEIR MINDS!
THERE THEY GO AGAIN!
WHAT'S GOTTEN INTO THOSE TWO?
FITTING R
WELL, WHAT DO YOU THINK?
IF THEY LIKED THE POSES IN THAT BOOK, THEY'LL LOVE THEM IN THE FLESH!
I THINK I KNOW WHAT THEY'RE DOIN'!
WELL, LET ME IN ON IT, PLEASE!
THEY GOT TURNED ON TO THE CRAZY WAY THE MODELS STAND IN THAT MAGAZINE!
BY GOLLY! I'LL BET YOU'RE RIGHT!
5

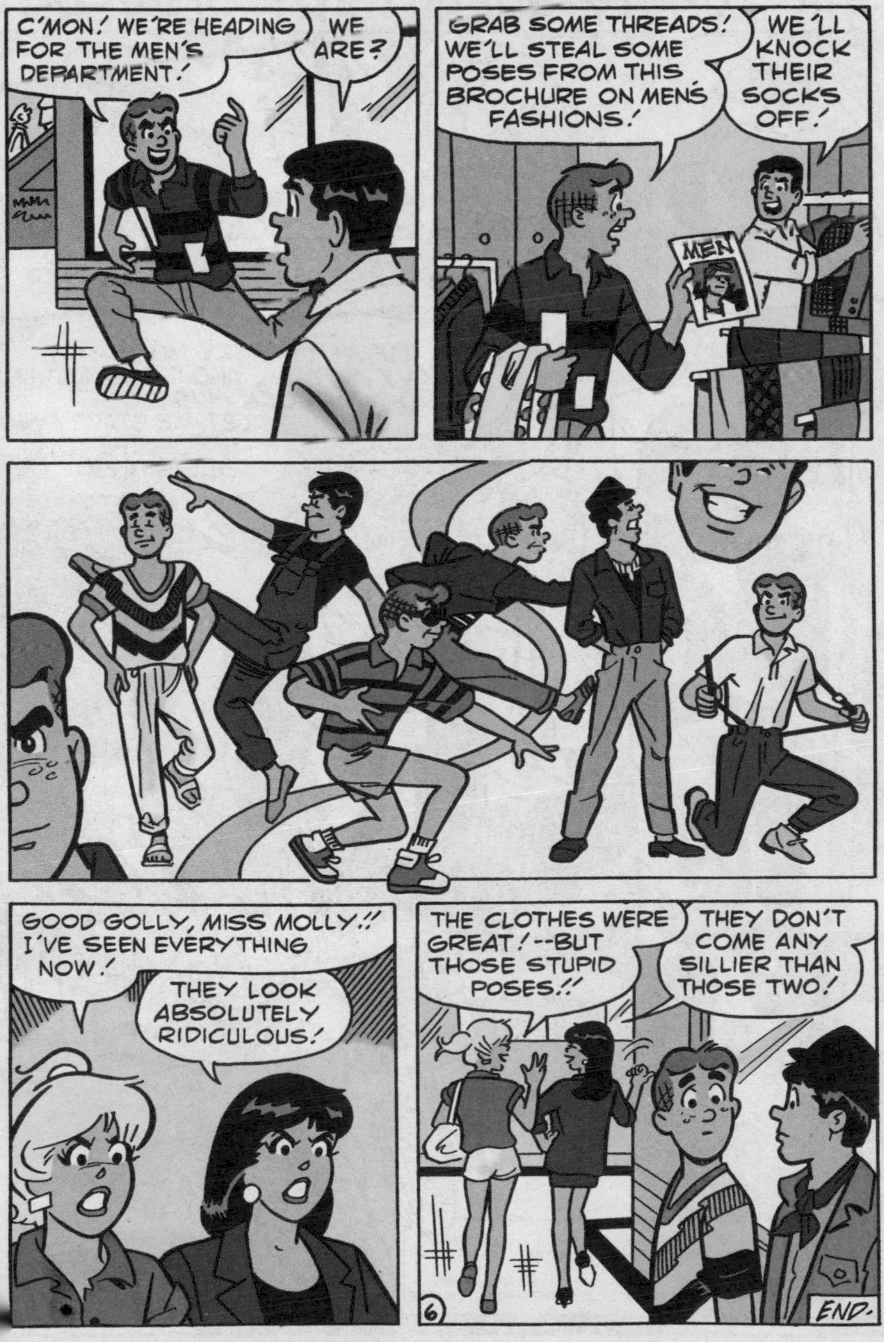
C'MON! WE'RE HEADING FOR THE MEN'S DEPARTMENT!
WE ARE?
GRAB SOME THREADS! WE'LL STEAL SOME POSES FROM THIS BROCHURE ON MEN'S FASHIONS!
WE'LL KNOCK THEIR SOCKS OFF!
MEN
GOOD GOLLY, MISS MOLLY!! I'VE SEEN EVERYTHING NOW!
THEY LOOK ABSOLUTELY RIDICULOUS!
THE CLOTHES WERE GREAT! --BUT THOSE STUPID POSES!!
THEY DON'T COME ANY SILLIER THAN THOSE TWO!
6
END.

THE MIGHTY ARCHIE ART PLAYERS

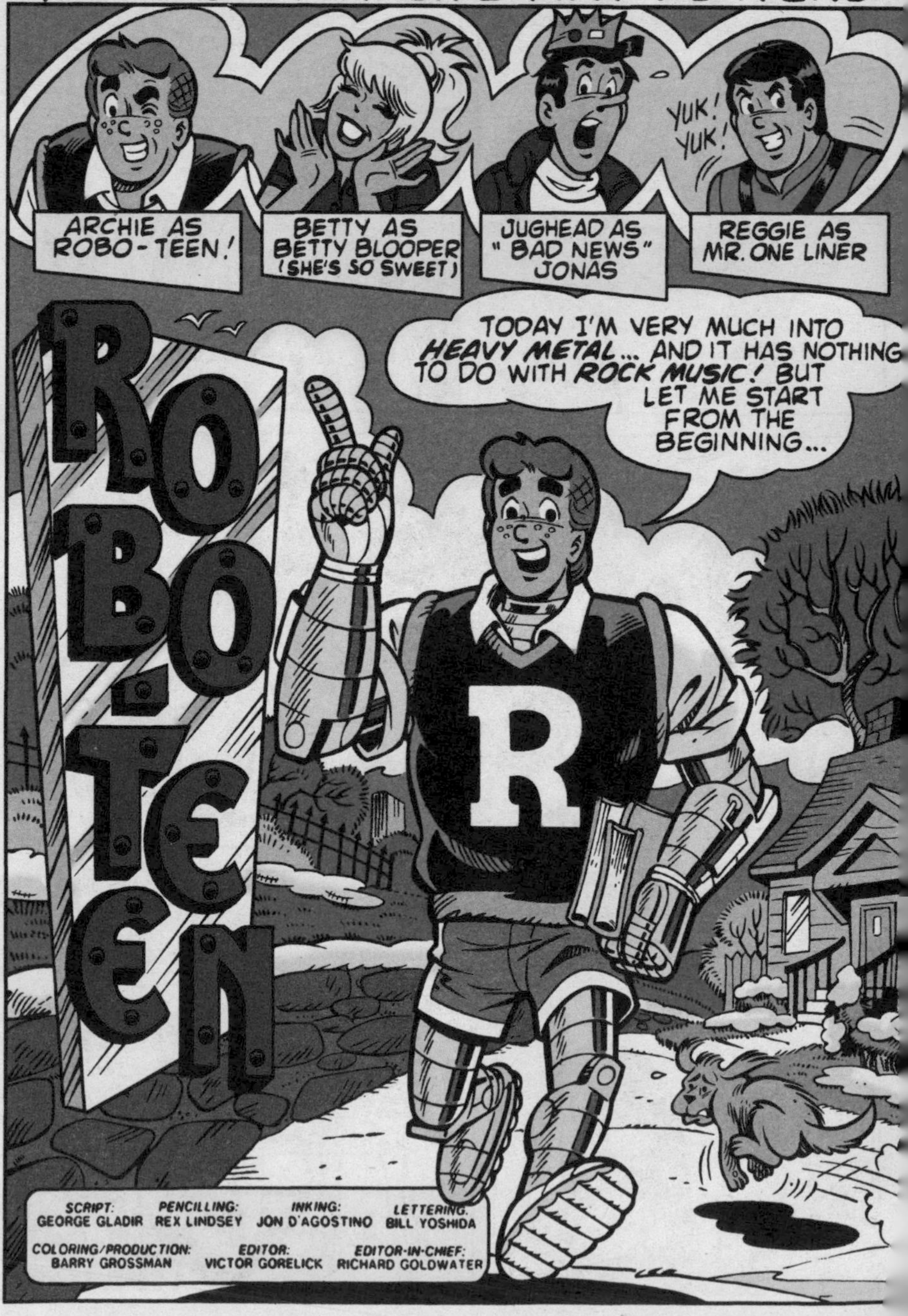
ARCHIE AS ROBO-TEEN!
BETTY AS BETTY BLOOPER (SHE'S SO SWEET)
JUGHEAD AS "BAD NEWS" JONAS
YUK! YUK!
REGGIE AS MR. ONE LINER
ROBO-TEEN
TODAY I'M VERY MUCH INTO HEAVY METAL... AND IT HAS NOTHING TO DO WITH ROCK MUSIC! BUT LET ME START FROM THE BEGINNING...
SCRIPT: GEORGE GLADIR PENCILLING: REX LINDSEY INKING: JON D'AGOSTINO LETTERING: BILL YOSHIDA
COLORING/PRODUCTION: BARRY GROSSMAN EDITOR: VICTOR GORELICK EDITOR-IN-CHIEF: RICHARD GOLDWATER

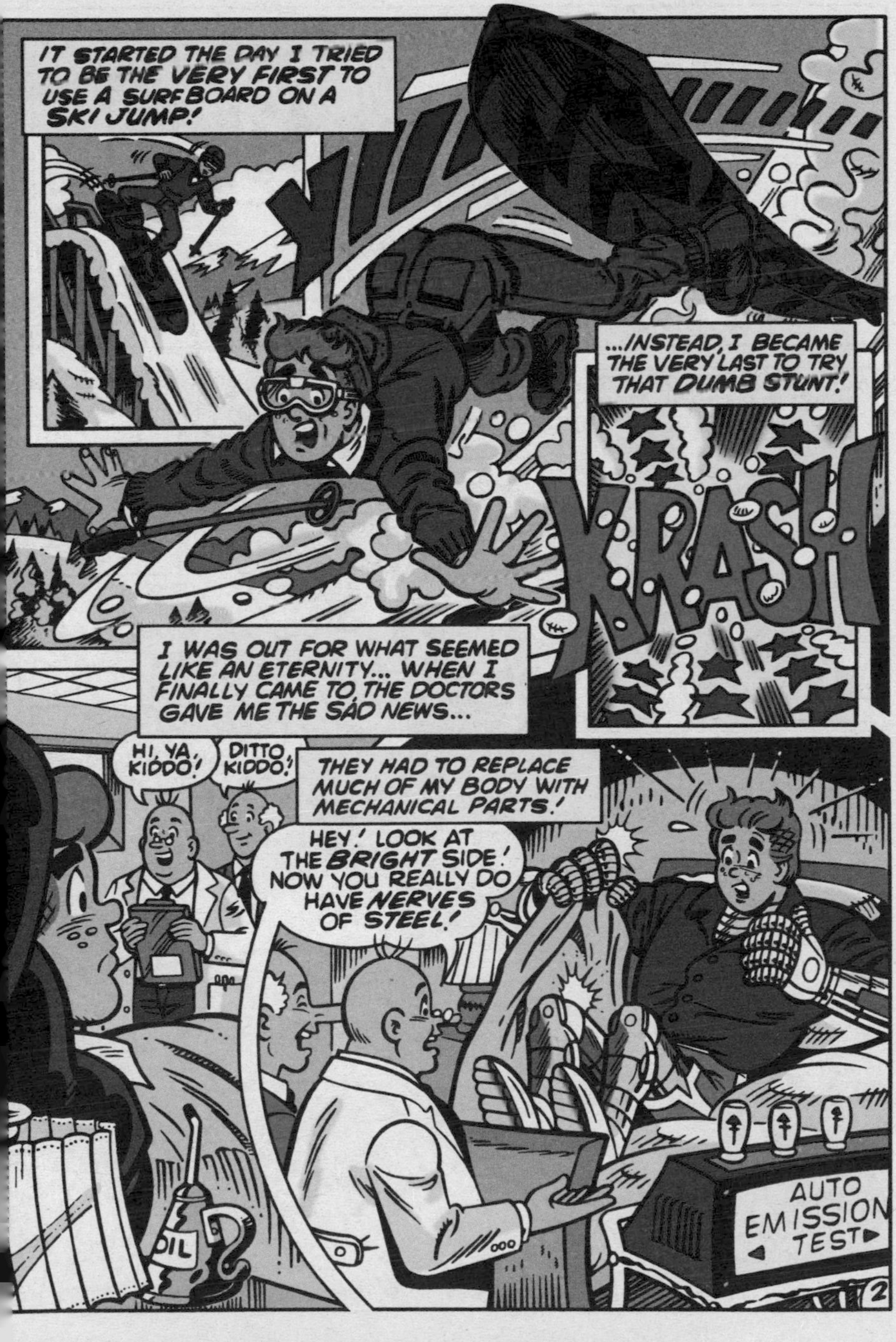
IT STARTED THE DAY I TRIED TO BE THE VERY FIRST TO USE A SURFBOARD ON A SKI JUMP!
...INSTEAD, I BECAME THE VERY LAST TO TRY THAT DUMB STUNT!
KRASH
I WAS OUT FOR WHAT SEEMED LIKE AN ETERNITY... WHEN I FINALLY CAME TO THE DOCTORS GAVE ME THE SAD NEWS...
HI, YA, KIDDO!
DITTO, KIDDO!
THEY HAD TO REPLACE MUCH OF MY BODY WITH MECHANICAL PARTS!
HEY! LOOK AT THE BRIGHT SIDE! NOW YOU REALLY DO HAVE NERVES OF STEEL!
OIL
AUTO EMISSION TEST
2

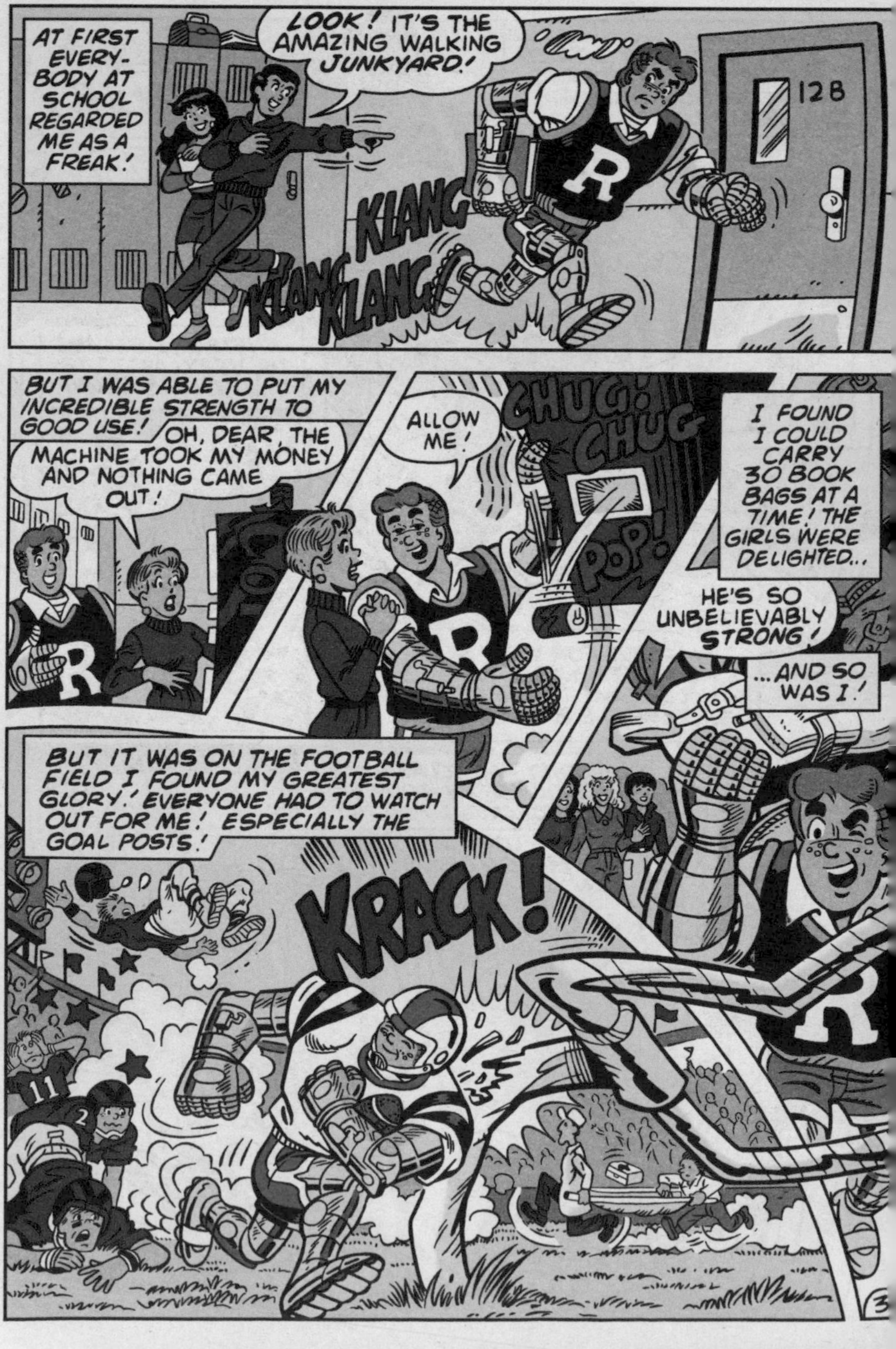
AT FIRST EVERYBODY AT SCHOOL REGARDED ME AS A FREAK!
LOOK! IT'S THE AMAZING WALKING JUNKYARD!
128
KLANG KLANG KLANG KLANG
BUT I WAS ABLE TO PUT MY INCREDIBLE STRENGTH TO GOOD USE!
OH, DEAR, THE MACHINE TOOK MY MONEY AND NOTHING CAME OUT!
ALLOW ME!
CHUG! CHUG
POP!
I FOUND I COULD CARRY 30 BOOK BAGS AT A TIME! THE GIRLS WERE DELIGHTED...
HE'S SO UNBELIEVABLY STRONG!
...AND SO WAS I!
BUT IT WAS ON THE FOOTBALL FIELD I FOUND MY GREATEST GLORY! EVERYONE HAD TO WATCH OUT FOR ME! ESPECIALLY THE GOAL POSTS!
KRACK!
11
2
3

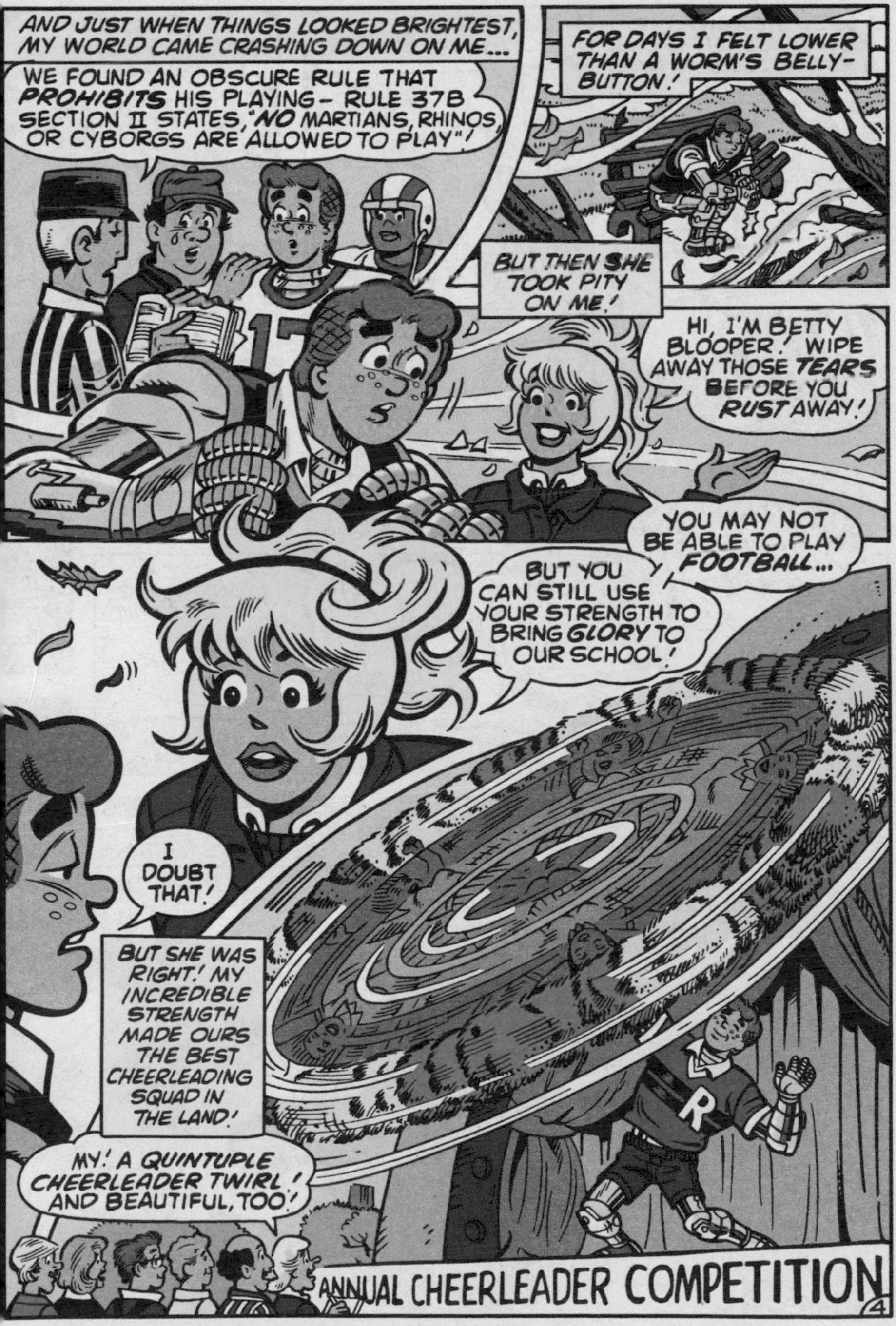
AND JUST WHEN THINGS LOOKED BRIGHTEST, MY WORLD CAME CRASHING DOWN ON ME...
WE FOUND AN OBSCURE RULE THAT PROHIBITS HIS PLAYING- RULE 37B SECTION II STATES, "NO MARTIANS, RHINOS OR CYBORGS ARE ALLOWED TO PLAY"!
FOR DAYS I FELT LOWER THAN A WORM'S BELLY-BUTTON!
BUT THEN SHE TOOK PITY ON ME!
HI, I'M BETTY BLOOPER! WIPE AWAY THOSE TEARS BEFORE YOU RUST AWAY!
YOU MAY NOT BE ABLE TO PLAY FOOTBALL...
BUT YOU CAN STILL USE YOUR STRENGTH TO BRING GLORY TO OUR SCHOOL!
I DOUBT THAT!
BUT SHE WAS RIGHT! MY INCREDIBLE STRENGTH MADE OURS THE BEST CHEERLEADING SQUAD IN THE LAND!
MY! A QUINTUPLE CHEERLEADER TWIRL! AND BEAUTIFUL, TOO!
ANNUAL CHEERLEADER COMPETITION
4

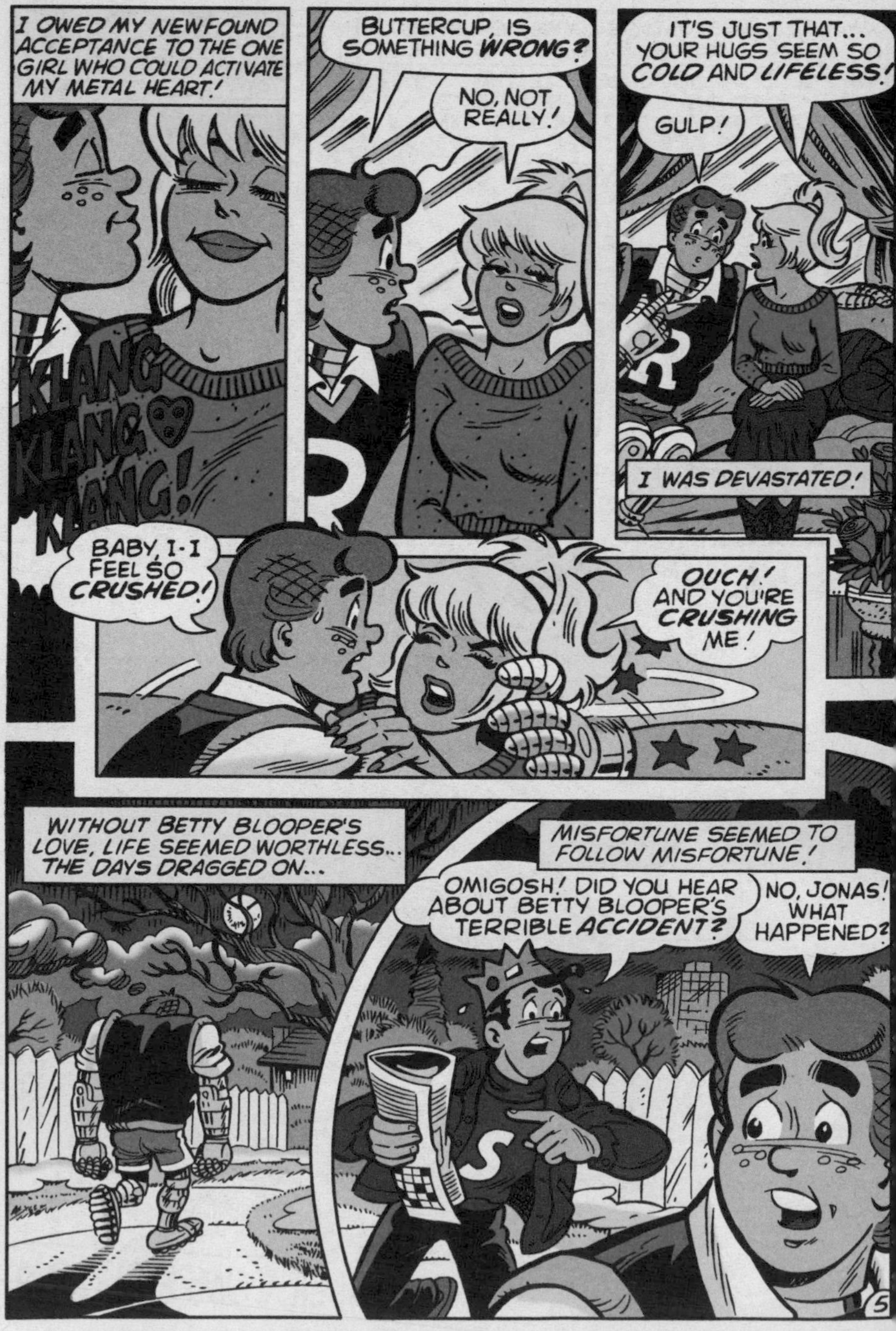
I OWED MY NEWFOUND ACCEPTANCE TO THE ONE GIRL WHO COULD ACTIVATE MY METAL HEART!
KLANG KLANG KLANG KLANG!
BUTTERCUP, IS SOMETHING WRONG?
NO, NOT REALLY!
IT'S JUST THAT... YOUR HUGS SEEM SO COLD AND LIFELESS!
GULP!
I WAS DEVASTATED!
BABY, I-I FEEL SO CRUSHED!
OUCH! AND YOU'RE CRUSHING ME!
WITHOUT BETTY BLOOPER'S LOVE, LIFE SEEMED WORTHLESS... THE DAYS DRAGGED ON...
MISFORTUNE SEEMED TO FOLLOW MISFORTUNE!
OMIGOSH! DID YOU HEAR ABOUT BETTY BLOOPER'S TERRIBLE ACCIDENT?
NO, JONAS! WHAT HAPPENED?
5

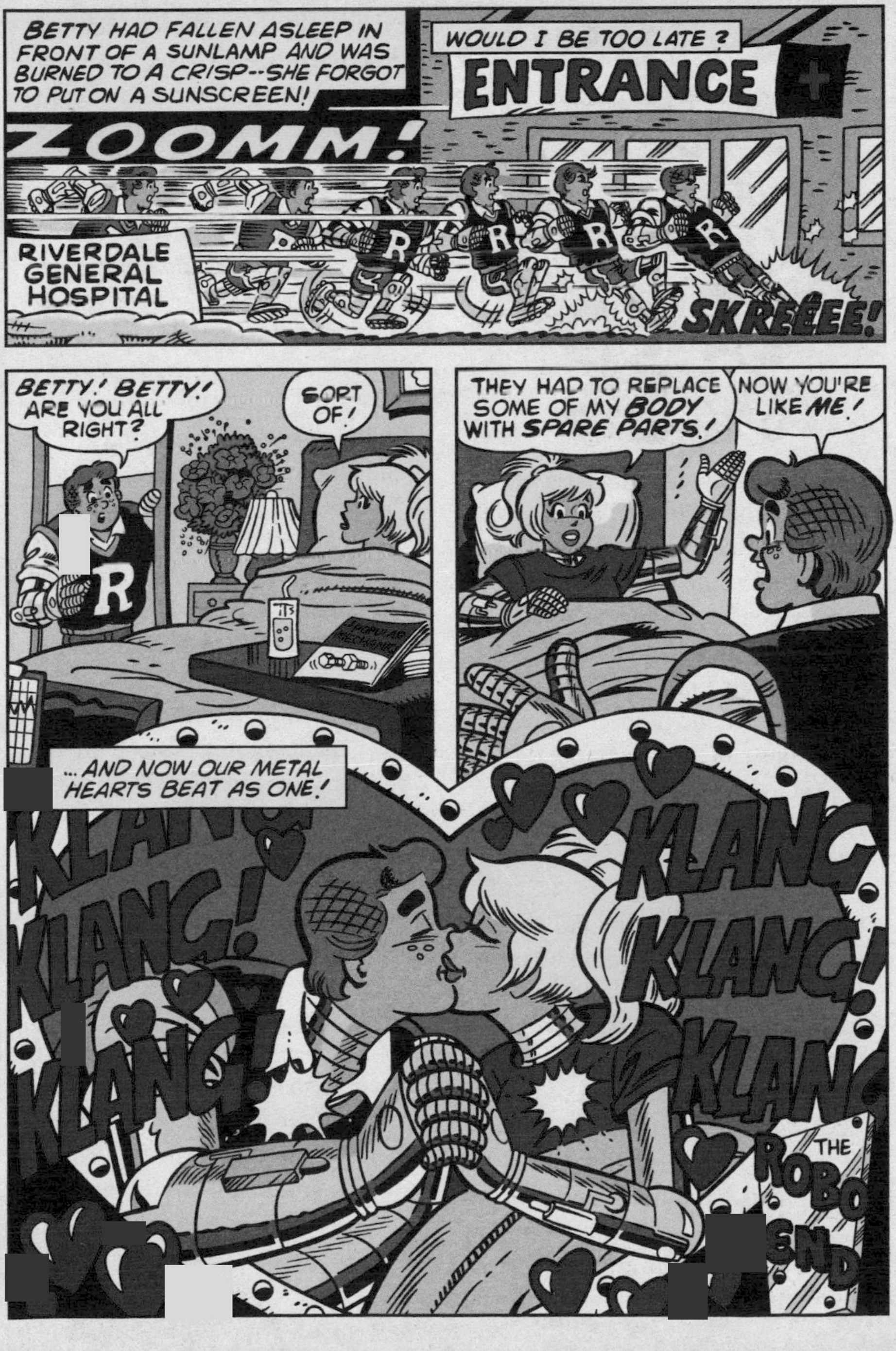
BETTY HAD FALLEN ASLEEP IN FRONT OF A SUNLAMP AND WAS BURNED TO A CRISP--SHE FORGOT TO PUT ON A SUNSCREEN!
WOULD I BE TOO LATE ?
ENTRANCE
ZOOMM!
RIVERDALE GENERAL HOSPITAL
SKREEEEE!
BETTY! BETTY! ARE YOU ALL RIGHT?
SORT OF!
THEY HAD TO REPLACE SOME OF MY BODY WITH SPARE PARTS!
NOW YOU'RE LIKE ME!
...AND NOW OUR METAL HEARTS BEAT AS ONE!
KLANG!
KLANG!
KLANG!
KLANG
KLANG!
KLANG
THE
ROBO
END

The 1990s

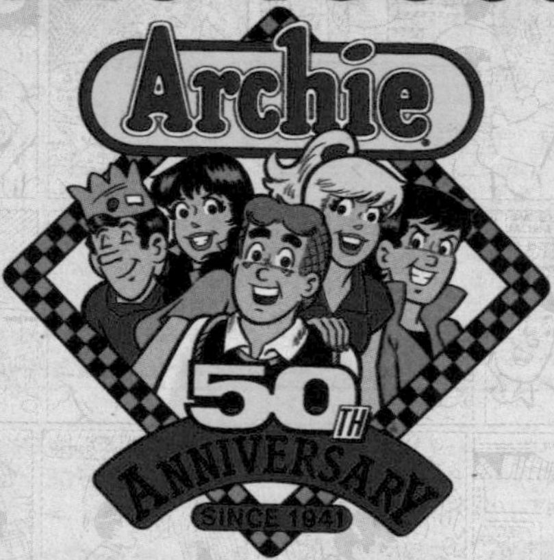
Archie
50TH
ANNIVERSARY
SINCE 1941

In reaction to the shallowness of the 1980s, the 1990s began with an effort to "keep it real." The decade started with some uncertainty due to a new conflict known as the Gulf War. Due to the rise in cable TV news channels like CNN, it was the first war in the modern era with around-the-clock TV coverage. If the '90s were about any one thing, it may be just that—"instant access" thanks to cable TV.

Aside from cable TV and talk radio, the 1990s were also a game-changer for one simple fact: the Internet, previously the domain of universities and government and military organizations, became available for everyone. While it really wouldn't find its feet until the 2000s, the internet made an impact early on and the "access" that cable and talk radio promoted would multiply in the ensuing decade.

Television also brought teen dramas, situational friend-based comedies that were a bit edgier than sitcoms past, and a wave of adult-targeted animated cartoon series that were even edgier. The music scene was reminiscent of the 1970s battle between classic rock and bubblegum pop, the grunge of the '90s rubbed elbows with boy bands and female teen sensations.

Perhaps the biggest splash was made, however, by video gaming, which became a dominant form of entertainment in the decade due to groundbreaking 3D graphics and consoles such as the Nintendo 64, Sony Playstation and Sega Saturn.

Meanwhile, Archie Comics too made another splash on TV. *Sabrina the Teenage Witch* was a hit as a live action cable-TV movie, leading to a prime-time sitcom series that spanned seven seasons and two networks. In the final two months of the decade, Archie and his friends would also return to TV in *Archie's Weird Mysteries*, a cartoon which cast the gang in sci-fi scenarios. Another hallmark of the era was inter-company crossovers. Characters from various "comic book universes" were routinely crossing over and in the 1990s Archie and his friends shared adventures with the Teenage Mutant Ninja Turtles, the Gen 13 characters from Image Comics and most famously, Marvel's vigilante known as The Punisher.

With the advent of instant access to society's ills and new, edgy TV shows, Archie provided a safe haven for families. By the '90s, the audience for Archie Comics was a little younger than before. Adults knew that Archie Comics were wholesome and safe for children. Perhaps because of this, the personalities of Archie and his friends began to be soften a bit—Jughead's over-indulgence in food and aversion to girls were lessened while Reggie's sarcastic barbs and tricks weren't always so mean-spirited. This was a "kinder and gentler" Archie, kid-friendly and still full of insights for those who were about to enter the often challenging high school experience.

Still, the writers and editors found some ways around the increasingly ordinary personalities. The first attempts included *Archie's Explorers of the Unknown, Jughead's Time Police* and *Jughead's Diner*. The next big departure came with *The New Little Archie Digest*, which introduced a radically different art style. Jughead underwent the biggest alteration—he became a Mohawk-sporting skate-punk with his own posse known as the "J-Head Brigade," a multi-ethnic crew that included females and the physically challenged. It was a brief change, but along with the introduction of Betty & Veronica's new plus-sized and popular friend Brigitte, these changes looked ahead to the diversity the company would embrace in the following decade.

To celebrate its 50th anniversary, the Archie Americana Series was launched. This was Archie's first paperback edition, collecting some of the greatest stories of the 1940s including milestone stories and first appearances. The series would be published over 20 years, cover seven decades and yield 12 volumes. Archie also published more licensed titles than ever, from the *Teenage Mutant Ninja Turtles* to classic Hanna-Barbera characters to video game favorite *Sonic the Hedgehog* and more. *Sonic* would, in fact, become not only Archie's most successful licensed title ever, but also the longest-running title based on a video game.

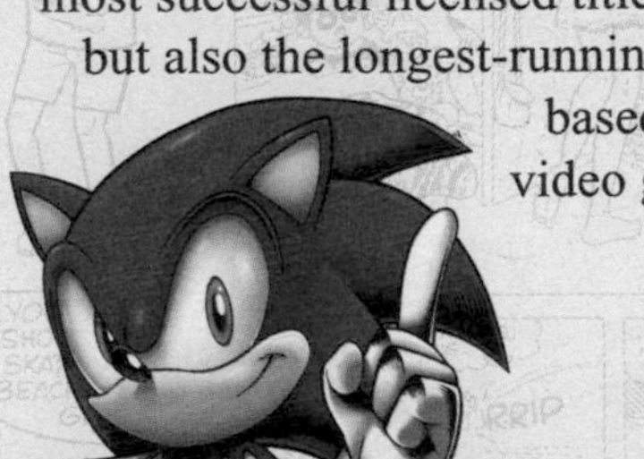

Cover Gallery
1990-1992

The '90s were filled with tons of new and revolutionary ideas. Some were fantastic, and even though they may not have been a hit at the time, have garnered a huge fan following. They say a picture is worth a thousand words, and for some of these titles, what more can you say?

--Joe Morciglio
Project Coordinator,
Archie Comics

A Sleigh in Time
Archie #397, 1992
by George Gladir
and Stan Goldberg

"A Sleigh in Time" is one of those unique stories that is both playful and extremely important, and I would think the impressive historic knowledge Archie demonstrates inspires students with the value and importance of such information. The element of time travel through American history teaches our two heroes, Archie and Jughead, a respect of where they came from and the American tragedy and milestones that have led us to the present. I love this story because of its innocence. An old man remarks in the beginning that he can't pay Archie and Jughead for shoveling snow because his "welfare checks didn't come." As adults, we know that this is a difficult issue that comes with an unpleasant history. Despite its tragedy, Archie and Jughead just innocently say, "It's OK," and they are on their way. As a teacher, I love this comic because it can be used to teach certain dates and events in American history.

--Nancy Silberkleit
Co-CEO, Archie Comics

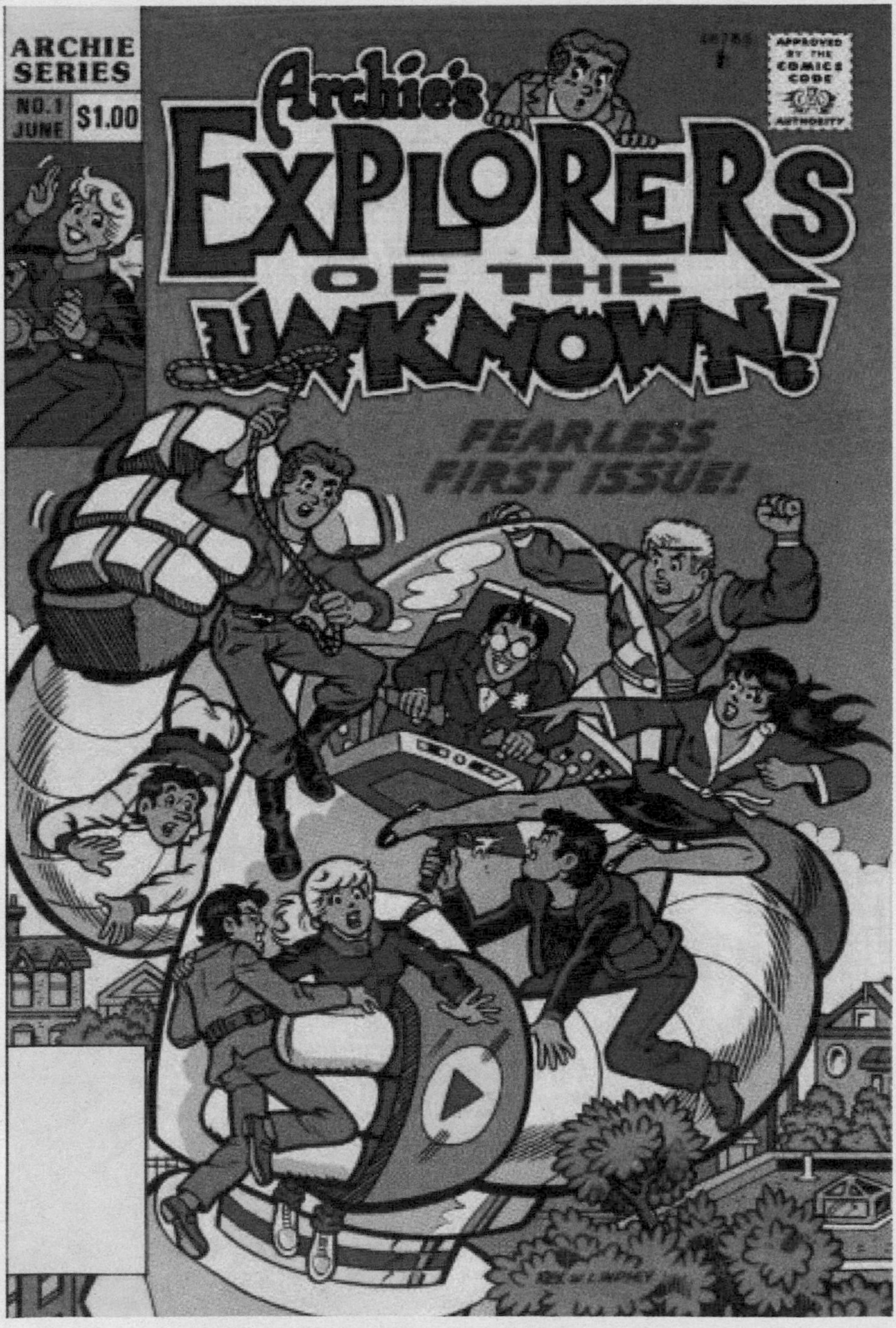
ARCHIE SERIES
NO. 1 JUNE
$1.00
APPROVED BY THE COMICS CODE AUTHORITY
Archie's
EXPLORERS
OF THE
UNKNOWN!
FEARLESS FIRST ISSUE!

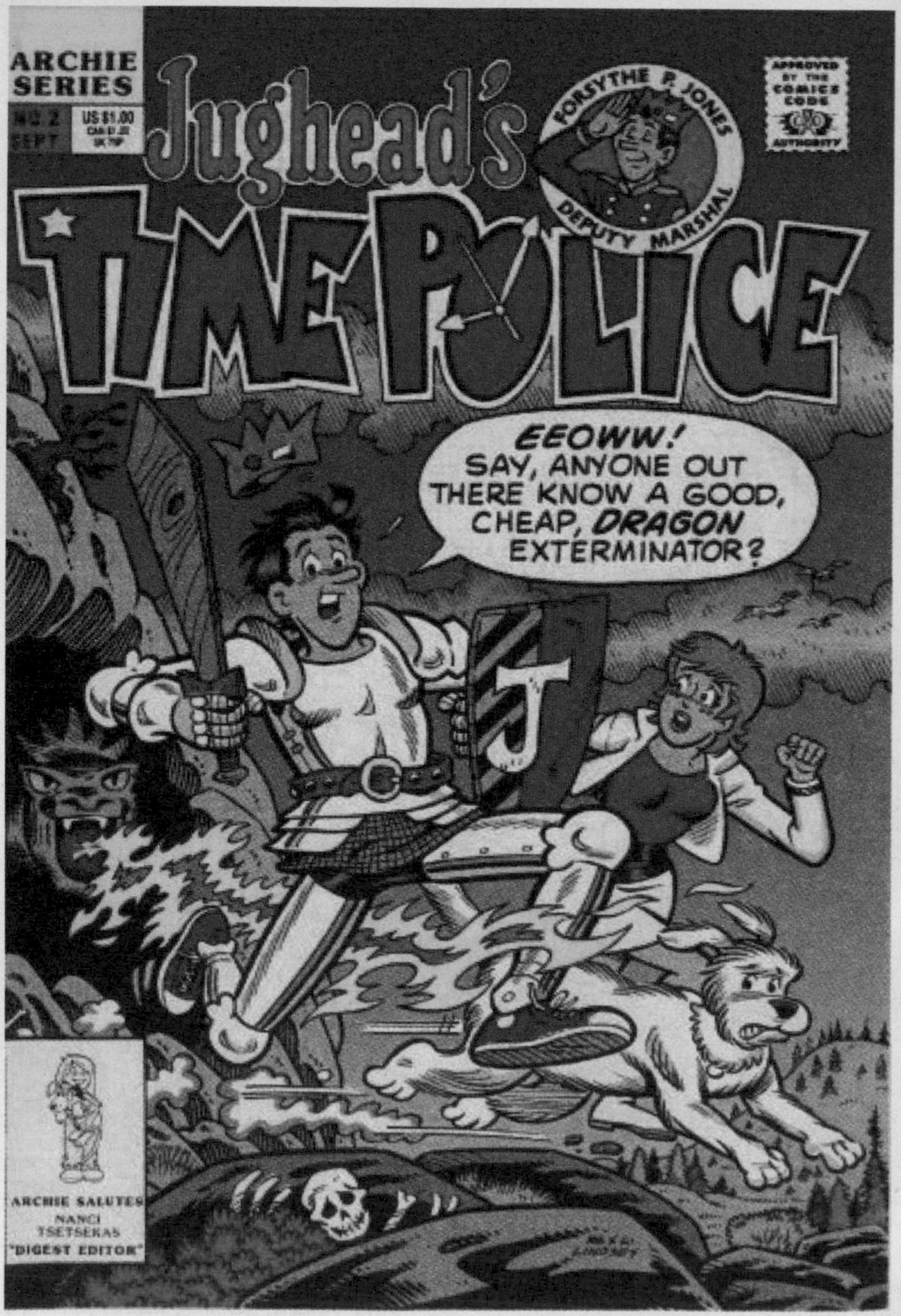
ARCHIE SERIES
US $1.00
Jughead's
FORSYTHE P. JONES
DEPUTY MARSHAL
APPROVED BY THE COMICS CODE AUTHORITY
TIME POLICE
EEOWW!
SAY, ANYONE OUT THERE KNOW A GOOD, CHEAP, DRAGON EXTERMINATOR?
J
ARCHIE SALUTES
NANCI
TSETSERAS
"DIGEST EDITOR"

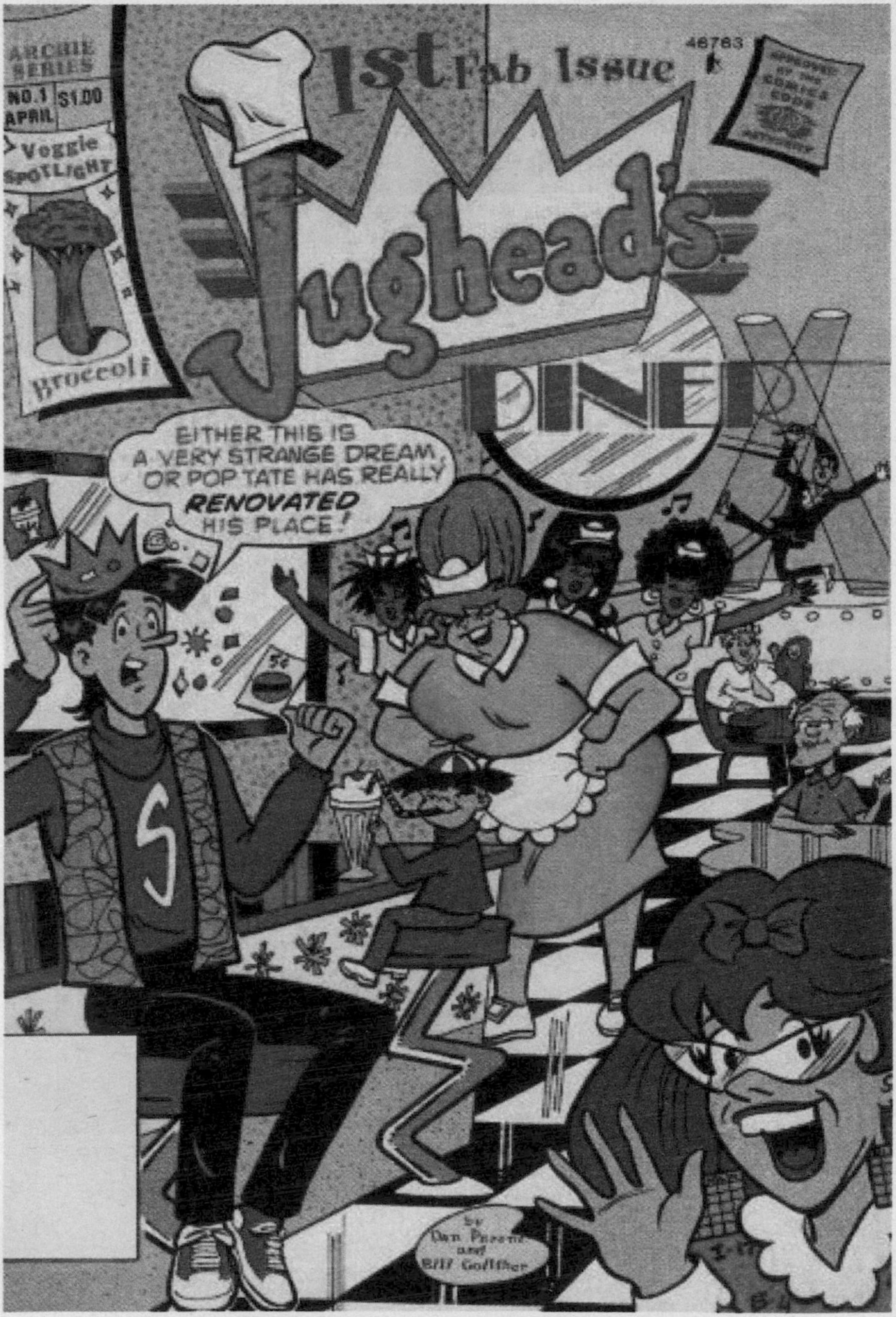
ARCHIE SERIES
NO.1 APRIL
$1.00
Veggie SPOTLIGHT
broccoli
1st Fab Issue
46783
Jughead's
DINER
EITHER THIS IS A VERY STRANGE DREAM, OR POP TATE HAS REALLY RENOVATED HIS PLACE!

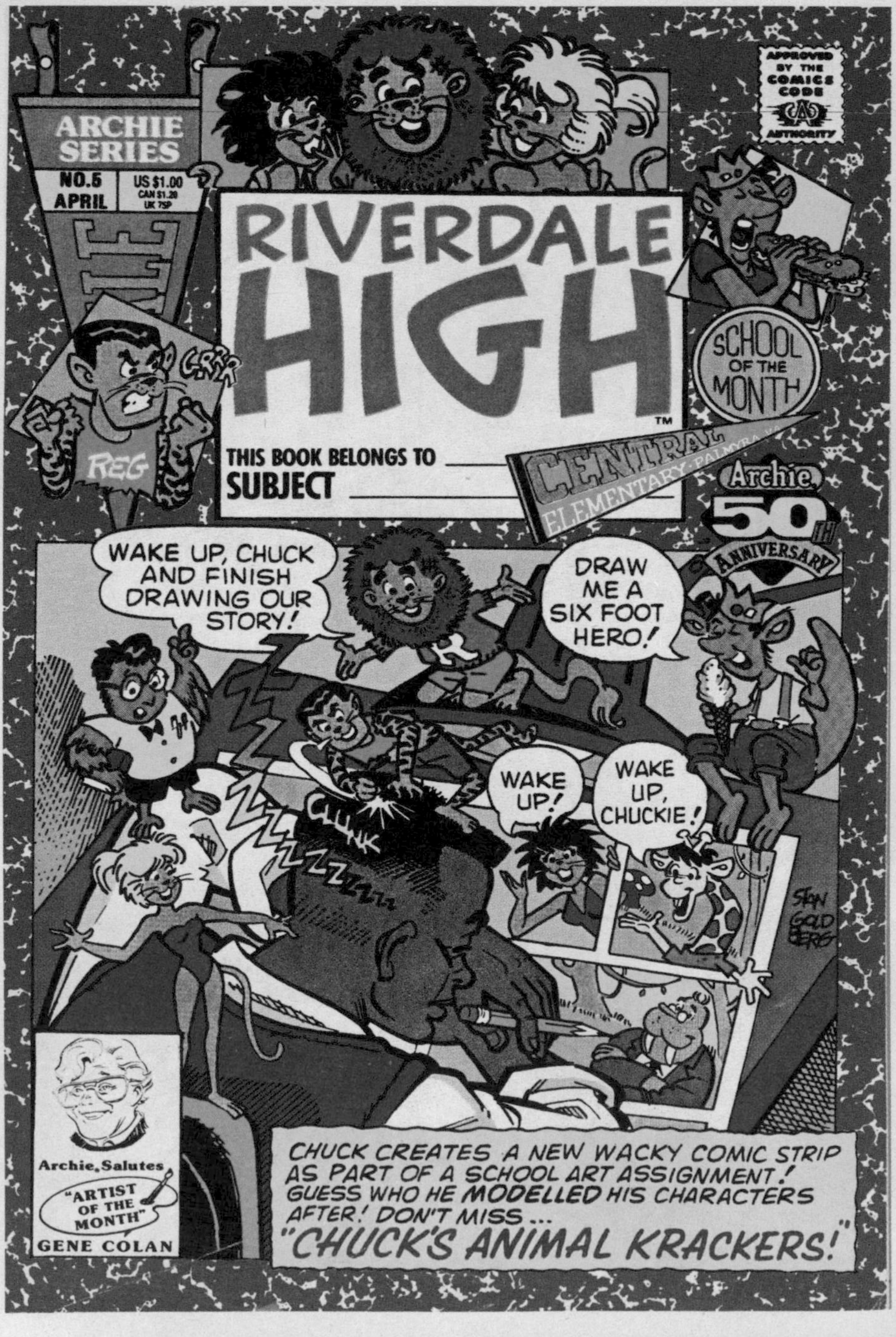
ARCHIE SERIES
NO.5 APRIL
US $1.00 CAN $1.20 UK 75P
APPROVED BY THE COMICS CODE AUTHORITY
RIVERDALE HIGH™
SCHOOL OF THE MONTH
THIS BOOK BELONGS TO
SUBJECT
CENTRAL ELEMENTARY PALMYRA VA
Archie 50TH ANNIVERSARY
REG
CRRR
WAKE UP, CHUCK AND FINISH DRAWING OUR STORY!
DRAW ME A SIX FOOT HERO!
WAKE UP!
WAKE UP, CHUCKIE!
CLUNK
ZZZZ
STAN GOLDBERG
Archie Salutes "ARTIST OF THE MONTH" GENE COLAN
CHUCK CREATES A NEW WACKY COMIC STRIP AS PART OF A SCHOOL ART ASSIGNMENT! GUESS WHO HE MODELLED HIS CHARACTERS AFTER! DON'T MISS ...
"CHUCK'S ANIMAL KRACKERS!"

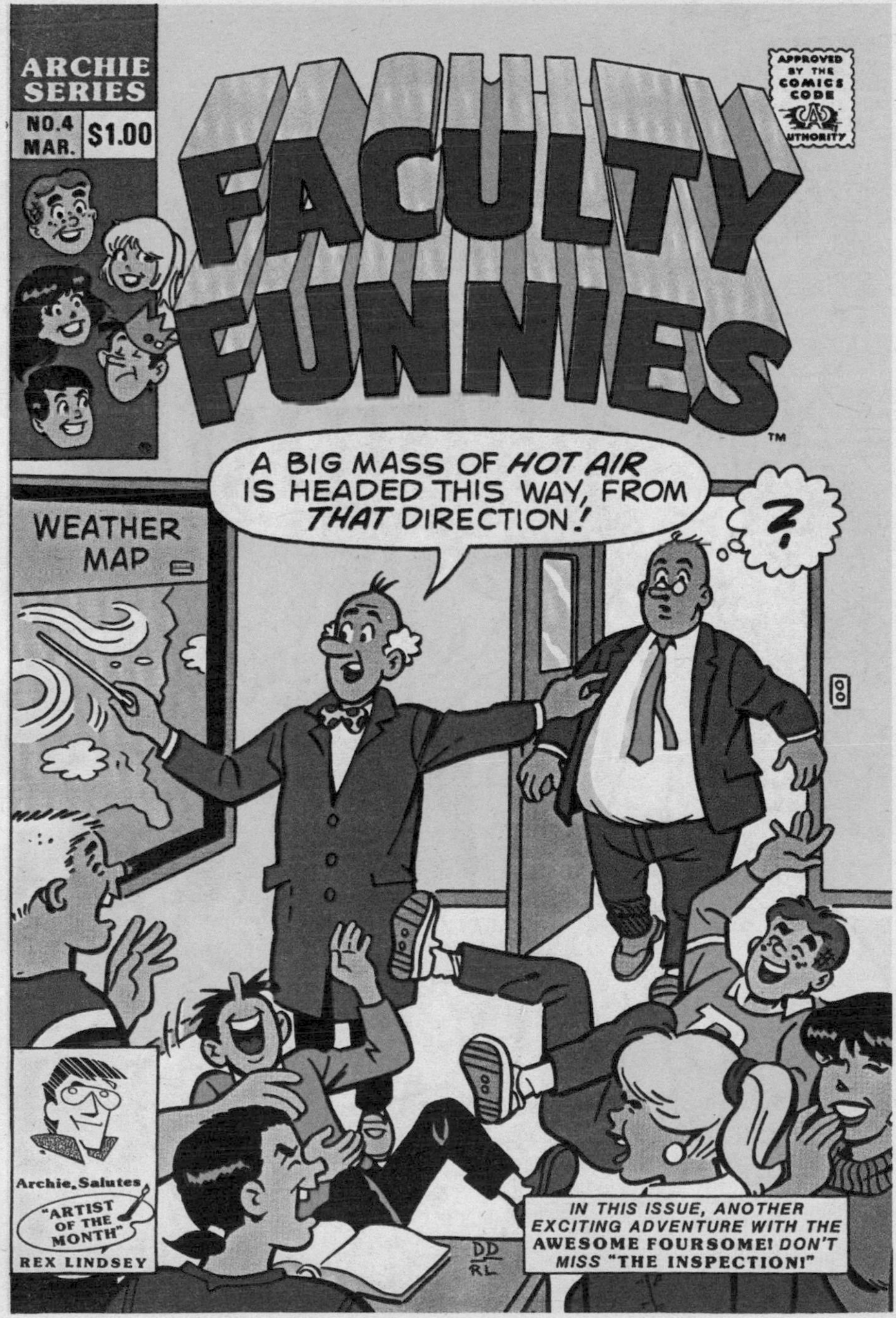
ARCHIE SERIES
NO.4 MAR.
$1.00
APPROVED BY THE COMICS CODE AUTHORITY
FACULTY FUNNIES
A BIG MASS OF HOT AIR IS HEADED THIS WAY, FROM THAT DIRECTION!
?
WEATHER MAP
Archie Salutes "ARTIST OF THE MONTH" REX LINDSEY
IN THIS ISSUE, ANOTHER EXCITING ADVENTURE WITH THE AWESOME FOURSOME! DON'T MISS "THE INSPECTION!"
DD RL

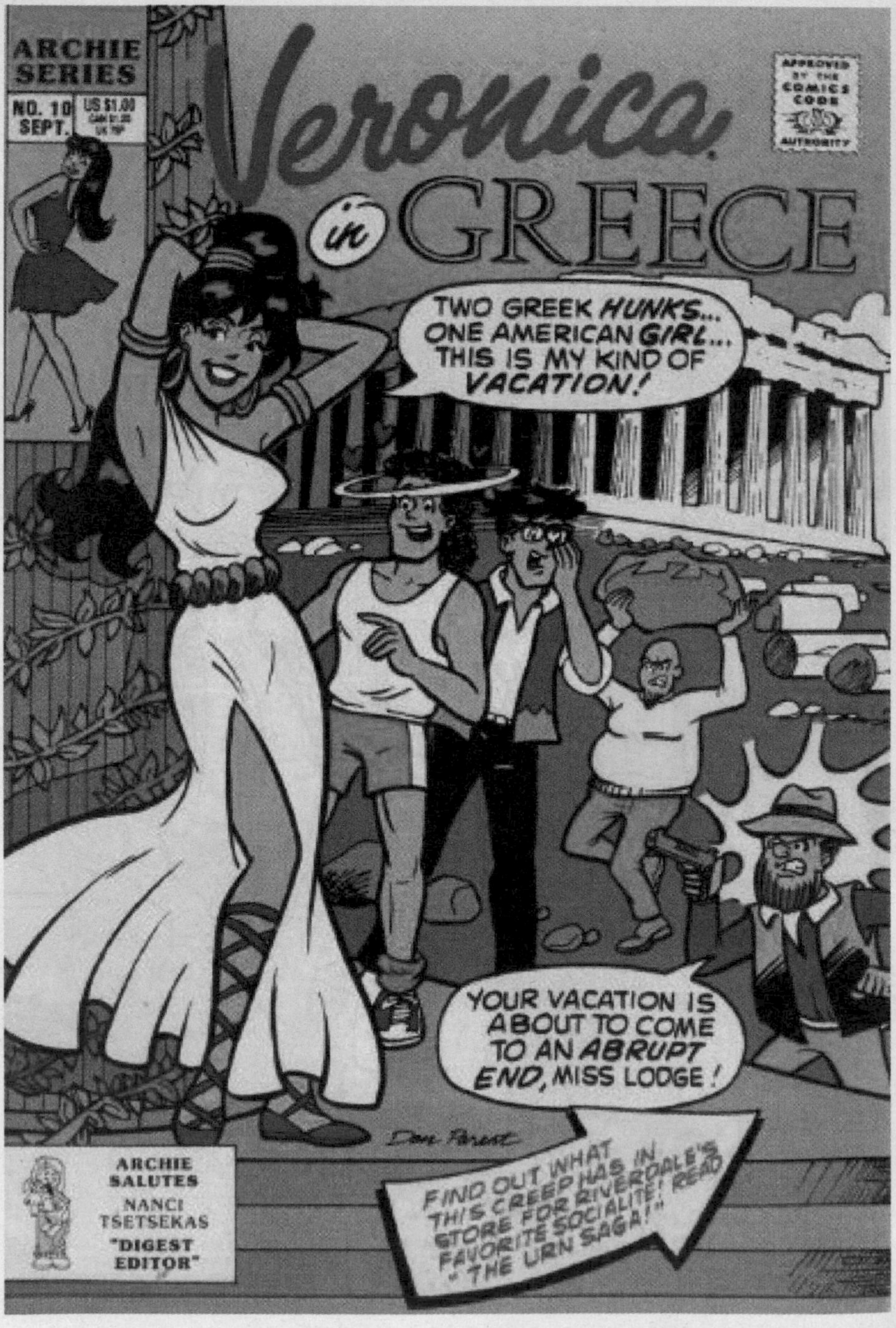
ARCHIE SERIES
NO. 10 SEPT.
US $1.00
APPROVED BY THE COMICS CODE AUTHORITY
Veronica in GREECE
TWO GREEK HUNKS... ONE AMERICAN GIRL... THIS IS MY KIND OF VACATION!
YOUR VACATION IS ABOUT TO COME TO AN ABRUPT END, MISS LODGE!
Dan Parent
ARCHIE SALUTES NANCI TSETSEKAS "DIGEST EDITOR"
FIND OUT WHAT THIS CREEP HAS IN STORE FOR RIVERDALE'S FAVORITE SOCIALITE! READ "THE URN SAGA!"

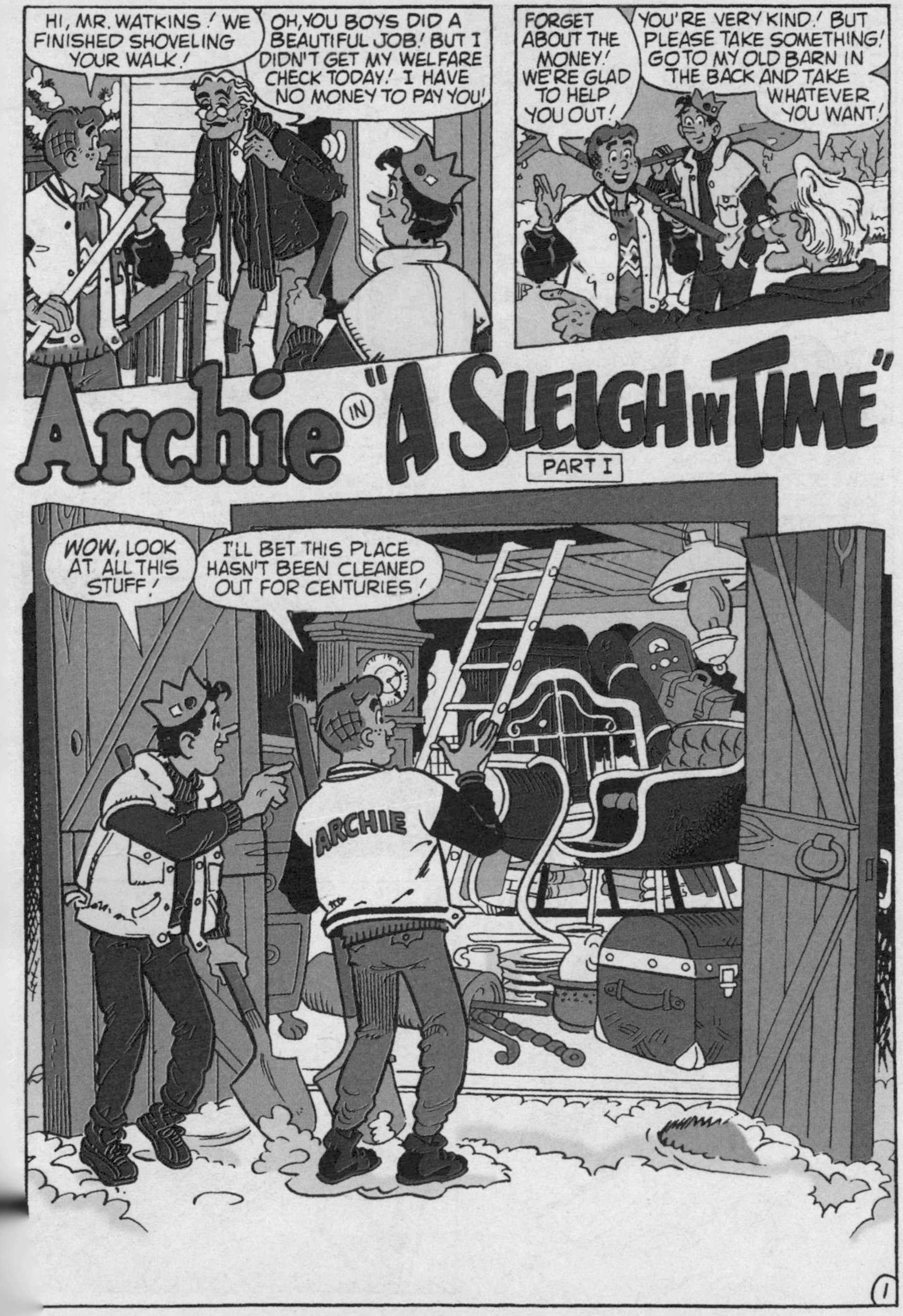
HI, MR. WATKINS! WE FINISHED SHOVELING YOUR WALK!
OH, YOU BOYS DID A BEAUTIFUL JOB! BUT I DIDN'T GET MY WELFARE CHECK TODAY! I HAVE NO MONEY TO PAY YOU!
FORGET ABOUT THE MONEY! WE'RE GLAD TO HELP YOU OUT!
YOU'RE VERY KIND! BUT PLEASE TAKE SOMETHING! GO TO MY OLD BARN IN THE BACK AND TAKE WHATEVER YOU WANT!
Archie IN "A SLEIGH IN TIME"
PART I
WOW, LOOK AT ALL THIS STUFF!
I'LL BET THIS PLACE HASN'T BEEN CLEANED OUT FOR CENTURIES!
ARCHIE
1

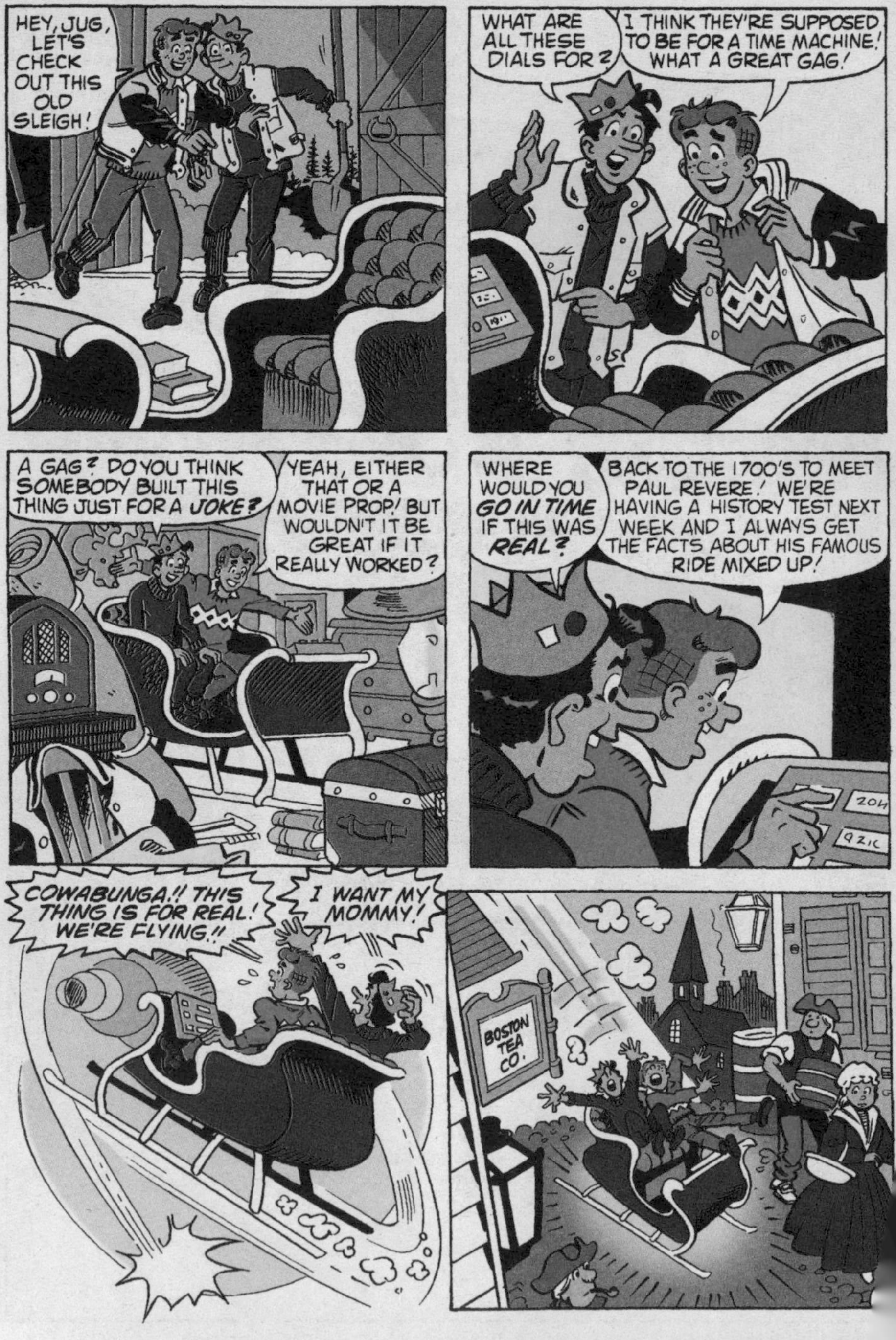
HEY, JUG, LET'S CHECK OUT THIS OLD SLEIGH!
WHAT ARE ALL THESE DIALS FOR?
I THINK THEY'RE SUPPOSED TO BE FOR A TIME MACHINE! WHAT A GREAT GAG!
A GAG? DO YOU THINK SOMEBODY BUILT THIS THING JUST FOR A JOKE?
YEAH, EITHER THAT OR A MOVIE PROP! BUT WOULDN'T IT BE GREAT IF IT REALLY WORKED?
WHERE WOULD YOU GO IN TIME IF THIS WAS REAL?
BACK TO THE 1700'S TO MEET PAUL REVERE! WE'RE HAVING A HISTORY TEST NEXT WEEK AND I ALWAYS GET THE FACTS ABOUT HIS FAMOUS RIDE MIXED UP!
COWABUNGA!! THIS THING IS FOR REAL! WE'RE FLYING!!
I WANT MY MOMMY!
BOSTON TEA CO.

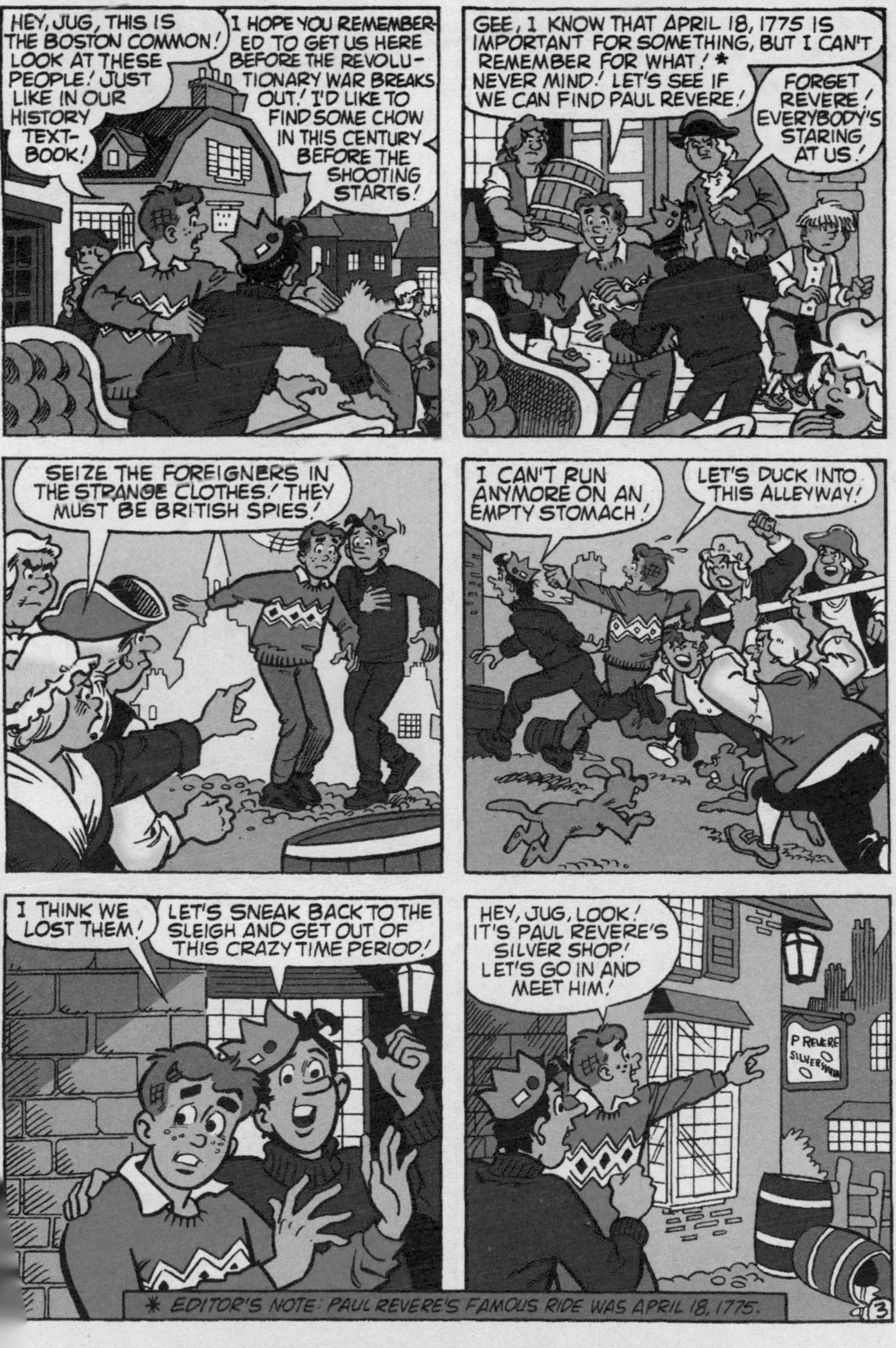
HEY, JUG, THIS IS THE BOSTON COMMON! LOOK AT THESE PEOPLE! JUST LIKE IN OUR HISTORY TEXT-BOOK!
I HOPE YOU REMEMBERED TO GET US HERE BEFORE THE REVOLUTIONARY WAR BREAKS OUT! I'D LIKE TO FIND SOME CHOW IN THIS CENTURY BEFORE THE SHOOTING STARTS!
GEE, I KNOW THAT APRIL 18, 1775 IS IMPORTANT FOR SOMETHING, BUT I CAN'T REMEMBER FOR WHAT! * NEVER MIND! LET'S SEE IF WE CAN FIND PAUL REVERE!
FORGET REVERE! EVERYBODY'S STARING AT US!
SEIZE THE FOREIGNERS IN THE STRANGE CLOTHES! THEY MUST BE BRITISH SPIES!
I CAN'T RUN ANYMORE ON AN EMPTY STOMACH!
LET'S DUCK INTO THIS ALLEYWAY!
I THINK WE LOST THEM!
LET'S SNEAK BACK TO THE SLEIGH AND GET OUT OF THIS CRAZY TIME PERIOD!
HEY, JUG, LOOK! IT'S PAUL REVERE'S SILVER SHOP! LET'S GO IN AND MEET HIM!
P REVERE
* EDITOR'S NOTE: PAUL REVERE'S FAMOUS RIDE WAS APRIL 18, 1775.
3

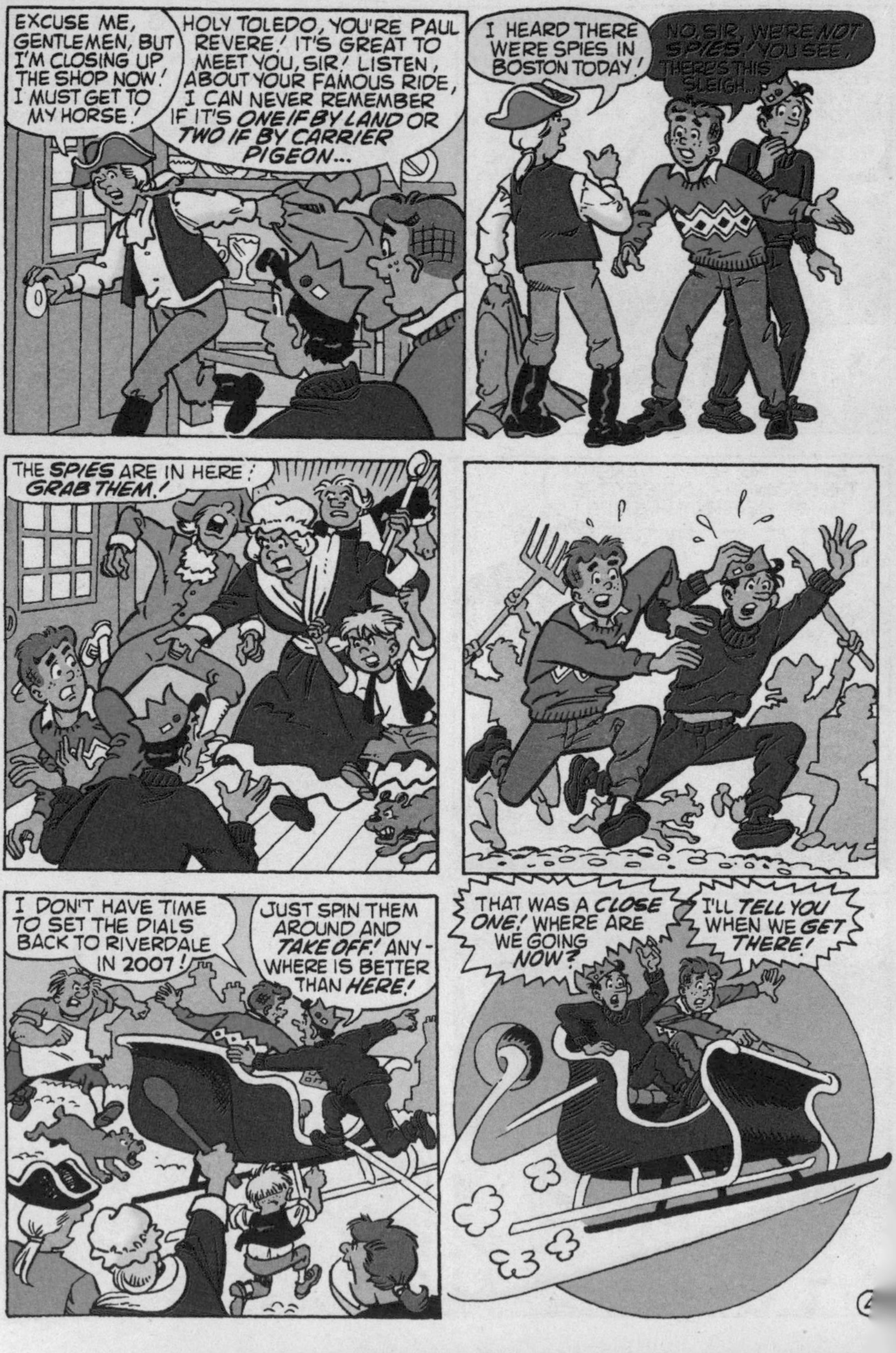
EXCUSE ME, GENTLEMEN, BUT I'M CLOSING UP THE SHOP NOW! I MUST GET TO MY HORSE!
HOLY TOLEDO, YOU'RE PAUL REVERE! IT'S GREAT TO MEET YOU, SIR! LISTEN, ABOUT YOUR FAMOUS RIDE, I CAN NEVER REMEMBER IF IT'S ONE IF BY LAND OR TWO IF BY CARRIER PIGEON...
I HEARD THERE WERE SPIES IN BOSTON TODAY!
NO, SIR, WE'RE NOT SPIES! YOU SEE, THERE'S THIS SLEIGH...
THE SPIES ARE IN HERE! GRAB THEM!
I DON'T HAVE TIME TO SET THE DIALS BACK TO RIVERDALE IN 2007!
JUST SPIN THEM AROUND AND TAKE OFF! ANYWHERE IS BETTER THAN HERE!
THAT WAS A CLOSE ONE! WHERE ARE WE GOING NOW?
I'LL TELL YOU WHEN WE GET THERE!

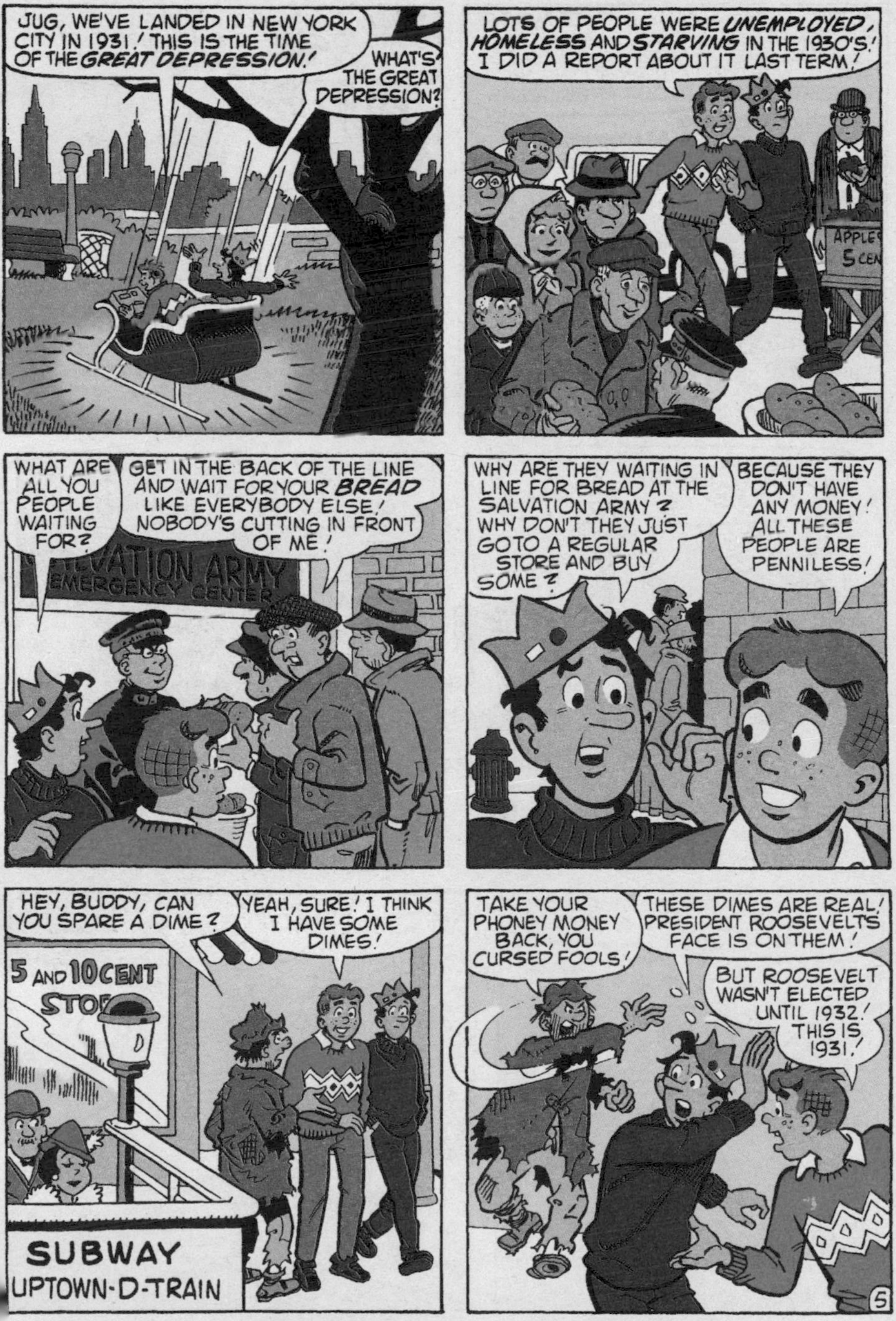
JUG, WE'VE LANDED IN NEW YORK CITY IN 1931! THIS IS THE TIME OF THE GREAT DEPRESSION!
WHAT'S THE GREAT DEPRESSION?
LOTS OF PEOPLE WERE UNEMPLOYED, HOMELESS AND STARVING IN THE 1930'S! I DID A REPORT ABOUT IT LAST TERM!
APPLES 5 CENTS
WHAT ARE ALL YOU PEOPLE WAITING FOR?
GET IN THE BACK OF THE LINE AND WAIT FOR YOUR BREAD LIKE EVERYBODY ELSE! NOBODY'S CUTTING IN FRONT OF ME!
SALVATION ARMY EMERGENCY CENTER
WHY ARE THEY WAITING IN LINE FOR BREAD AT THE SALVATION ARMY? WHY DON'T THEY JUST GO TO A REGULAR STORE AND BUY SOME?
BECAUSE THEY DON'T HAVE ANY MONEY! ALL THESE PEOPLE ARE PENNILESS!
HEY, BUDDY, CAN YOU SPARE A DIME?
YEAH, SURE! I THINK I HAVE SOME DIMES!
5 AND 10 CENT STORE
SUBWAY
UPTOWN-D-TRAIN
TAKE YOUR PHONEY MONEY BACK, YOU CURSED FOOLS!
THESE DIMES ARE REAL! PRESIDENT ROOSEVELT'S FACE IS ON THEM!
BUT ROOSEVELT WASN'T ELECTED UNTIL 1932! THIS IS 1931!
5

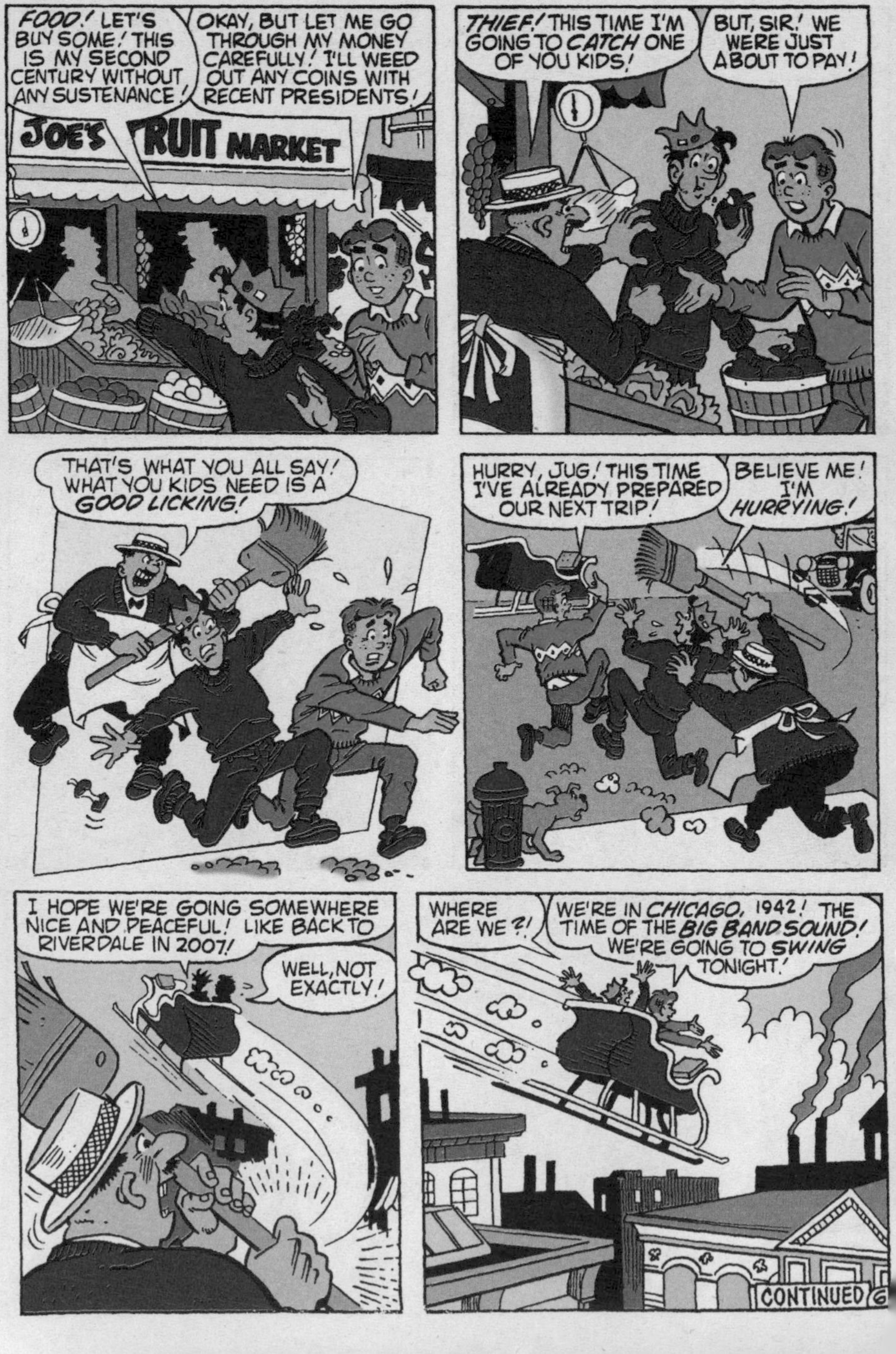
FOOD! LET'S BUY SOME! THIS IS MY SECOND CENTURY WITHOUT ANY SUSTENANCE!
OKAY, BUT LET ME GO THROUGH MY MONEY CAREFULLY! I'LL WEED OUT ANY COINS WITH RECENT PRESIDENTS!
JOE'S FRUIT MARKET
THIEF! THIS TIME I'M GOING TO CATCH ONE OF YOU KIDS!
BUT, SIR! WE WERE JUST ABOUT TO PAY!
THAT'S WHAT YOU ALL SAY! WHAT YOU KIDS NEED IS A GOOD LICKING!
HURRY, JUG! THIS TIME I'VE ALREADY PREPARED OUR NEXT TRIP!
BELIEVE ME! I'M HURRYING!
I HOPE WE'RE GOING SOMEWHERE NICE AND PEACEFUL! LIKE BACK TO RIVERDALE IN 2007!
WELL, NOT EXACTLY!
WHERE ARE WE ?!
WE'RE IN CHICAGO, 1942! THE TIME OF THE BIG BAND SOUND! WE'RE GOING TO SWING TONIGHT!
CONTINUED

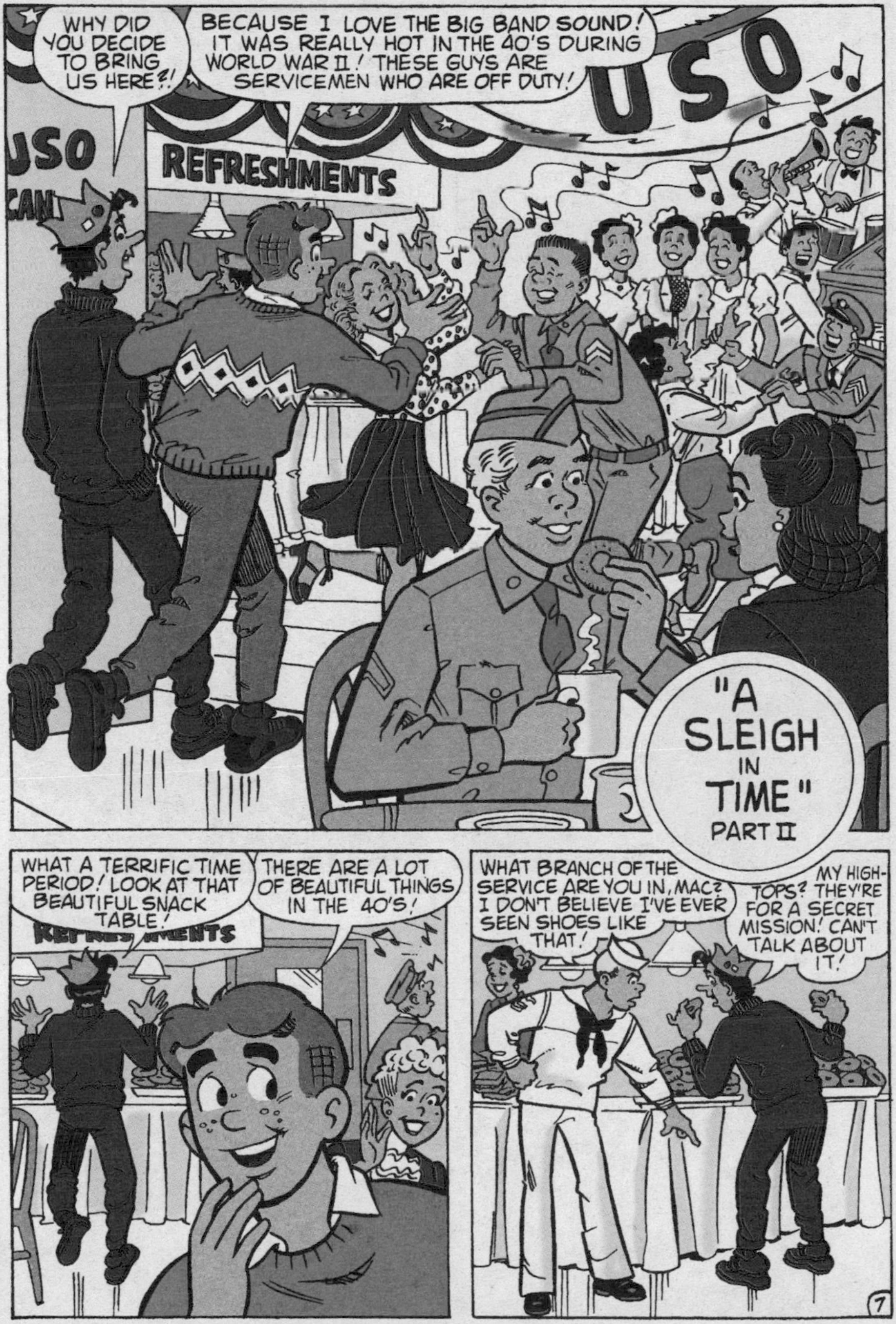
WHY DID YOU DECIDE TO BRING US HERE?!
BECAUSE I LOVE THE BIG BAND SOUND! IT WAS REALLY HOT IN THE 40'S DURING WORLD WAR II! THESE GUYS ARE SERVICEMEN WHO ARE OFF DUTY!
USO
USO
REFRESHMENTS
"A SLEIGH IN TIME" PART II
WHAT A TERRIFIC TIME PERIOD! LOOK AT THAT BEAUTIFUL SNACK TABLE!
THERE ARE A LOT OF BEAUTIFUL THINGS IN THE 40'S!
WHAT BRANCH OF THE SERVICE ARE YOU IN, MAC? I DON'T BELIEVE I'VE EVER SEEN SHOES LIKE THAT!
MY HIGH-TOPS? THEY'RE FOR A SECRET MISSION! CAN'T TALK ABOUT IT!
7

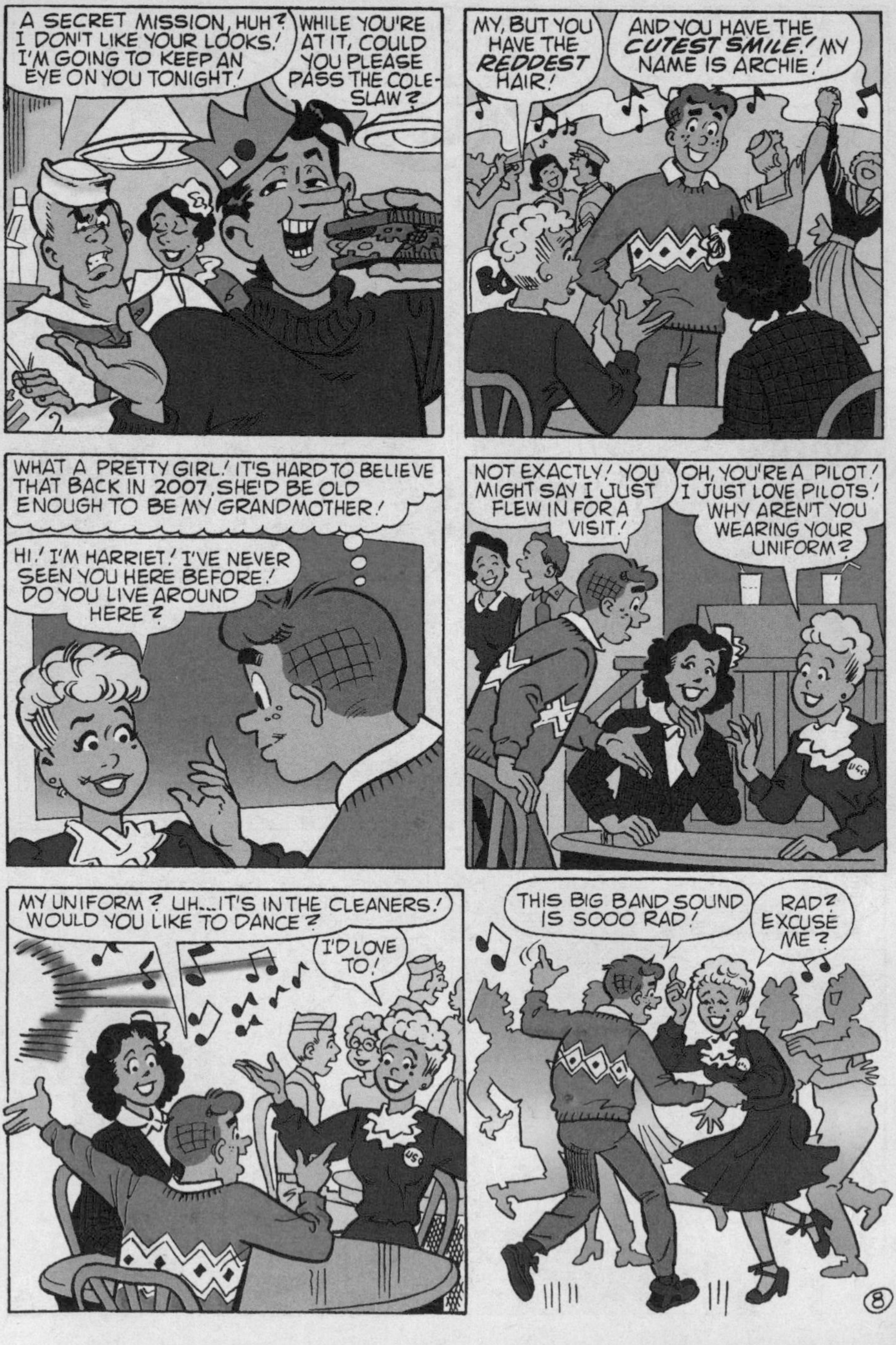
A SECRET MISSION, HUH? I DON'T LIKE YOUR LOOKS! I'M GOING TO KEEP AN EYE ON YOU TONIGHT!
WHILE YOU'RE AT IT, COULD YOU PLEASE PASS THE COLE-SLAW?
MY, BUT YOU HAVE THE REDDEST HAIR!
AND YOU HAVE THE CUTEST SMILE! MY NAME IS ARCHIE!
WHAT A PRETTY GIRL! IT'S HARD TO BELIEVE THAT BACK IN 2007, SHE'D BE OLD ENOUGH TO BE MY GRANDMOTHER!
HI! I'M HARRIET! I'VE NEVER SEEN YOU HERE BEFORE! DO YOU LIVE AROUND HERE?
NOT EXACTLY! YOU MIGHT SAY I JUST FLEW IN FOR A VISIT!
OH, YOU'RE A PILOT! I JUST LOVE PILOTS! WHY AREN'T YOU WEARING YOUR UNIFORM?
MY UNIFORM? UH...IT'S IN THE CLEANERS! WOULD YOU LIKE TO DANCE?
I'D LOVE TO!
THIS BIG BAND SOUND IS SOOO RAD!
RAD? EXCUSE ME?
8

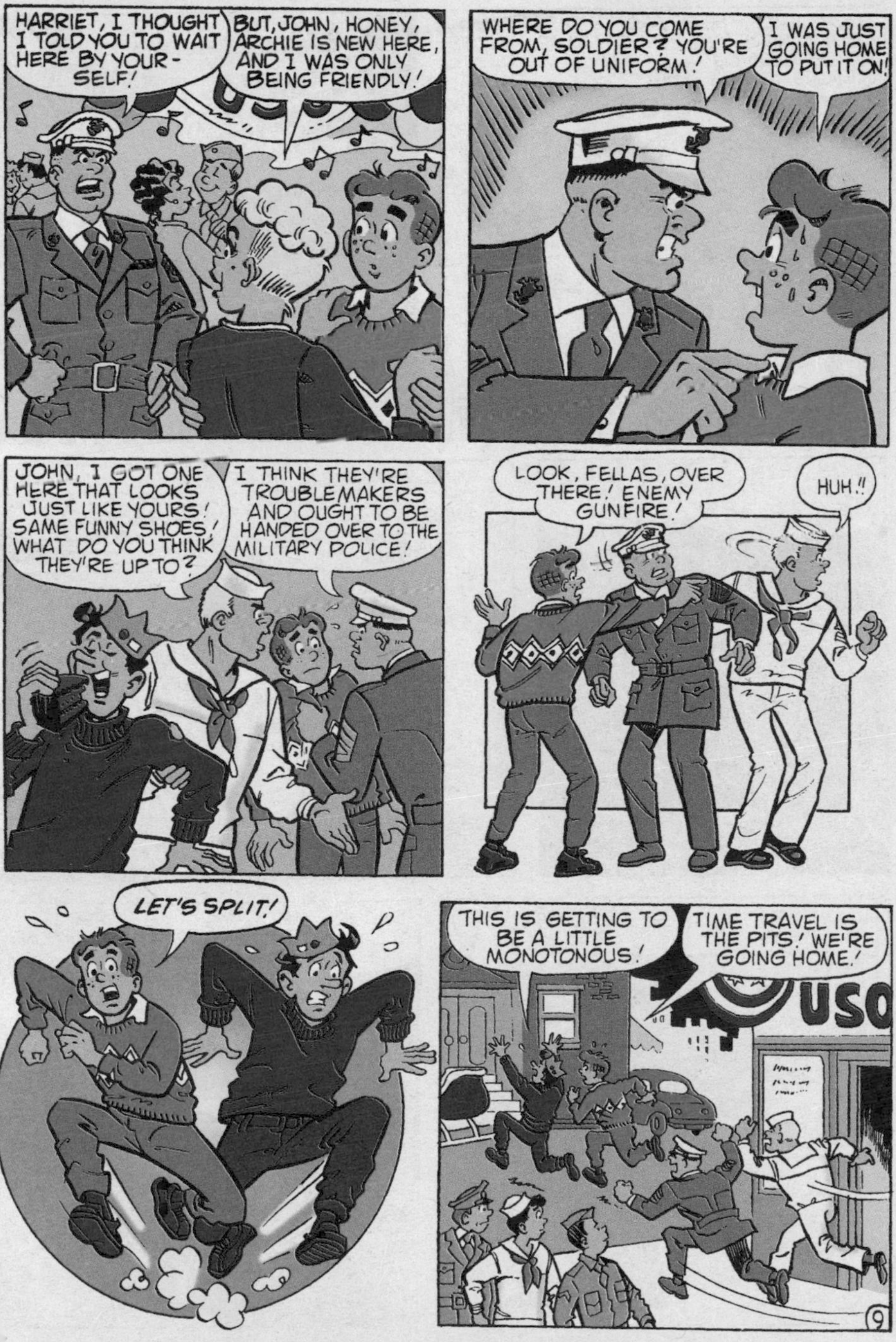
HARRIET, I THOUGHT I TOLD YOU TO WAIT HERE BY YOURSELF!
BUT, JOHN, HONEY, ARCHIE IS NEW HERE, AND I WAS ONLY BEING FRIENDLY!
WHERE DO YOU COME FROM, SOLDIER? YOU'RE OUT OF UNIFORM!
I WAS JUST GOING HOME TO PUT IT ON!
JOHN, I GOT ONE HERE THAT LOOKS JUST LIKE YOURS! SAME FUNNY SHOES! WHAT DO YOU THINK THEY'RE UP TO?
I THINK THEY'RE TROUBLEMAKERS AND OUGHT TO BE HANDED OVER TO THE MILITARY POLICE!
LOOK, FELLAS, OVER THERE! ENEMY GUNFIRE!
HUH!!
LET'S SPLIT!
THIS IS GETTING TO BE A LITTLE MONOTONOUS!
TIME TRAVEL IS THE PITS! WE'RE GOING HOME!
USO
9

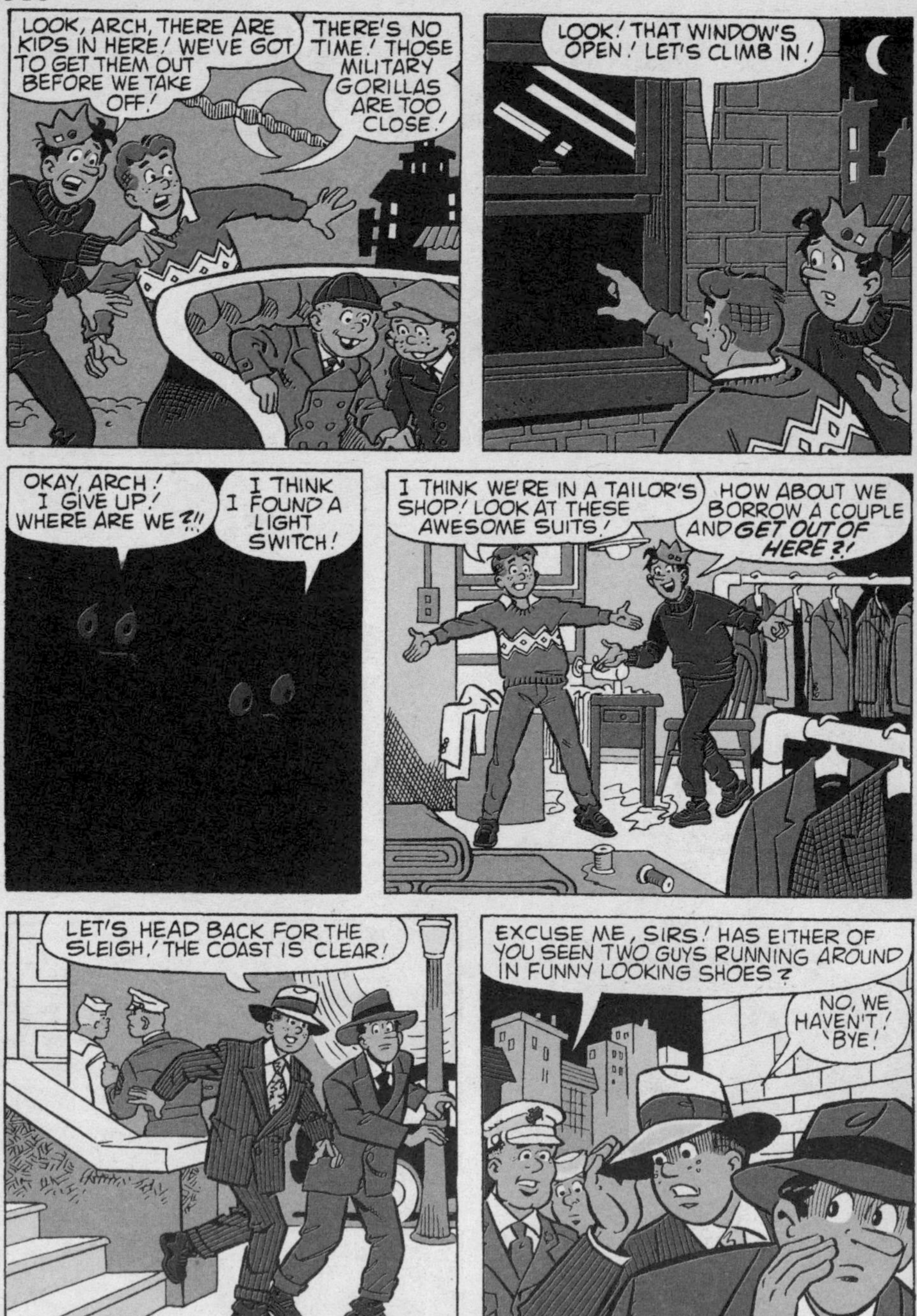
LOOK, ARCH, THERE ARE KIDS IN HERE! WE'VE GOT TO GET THEM OUT BEFORE WE TAKE OFF!
THERE'S NO TIME! THOSE MILITARY GORILLAS ARE TOO CLOSE!
LOOK! THAT WINDOW'S OPEN! LET'S CLIMB IN!
OKAY, ARCH! I GIVE UP! WHERE ARE WE ?!!
I THINK I FOUND A LIGHT SWITCH!
I THINK WE'RE IN A TAILOR'S SHOP! LOOK AT THESE AWESOME SUITS!
HOW ABOUT WE BORROW A COUPLE AND GET OUT OF HERE ?!
LET'S HEAD BACK FOR THE SLEIGH! THE COAST IS CLEAR!
EXCUSE ME, SIRS! HAS EITHER OF YOU SEEN TWO GUYS RUNNING AROUND IN FUNNY LOOKING SHOES ?
NO, WE HAVEN'T! 'BYE!
10

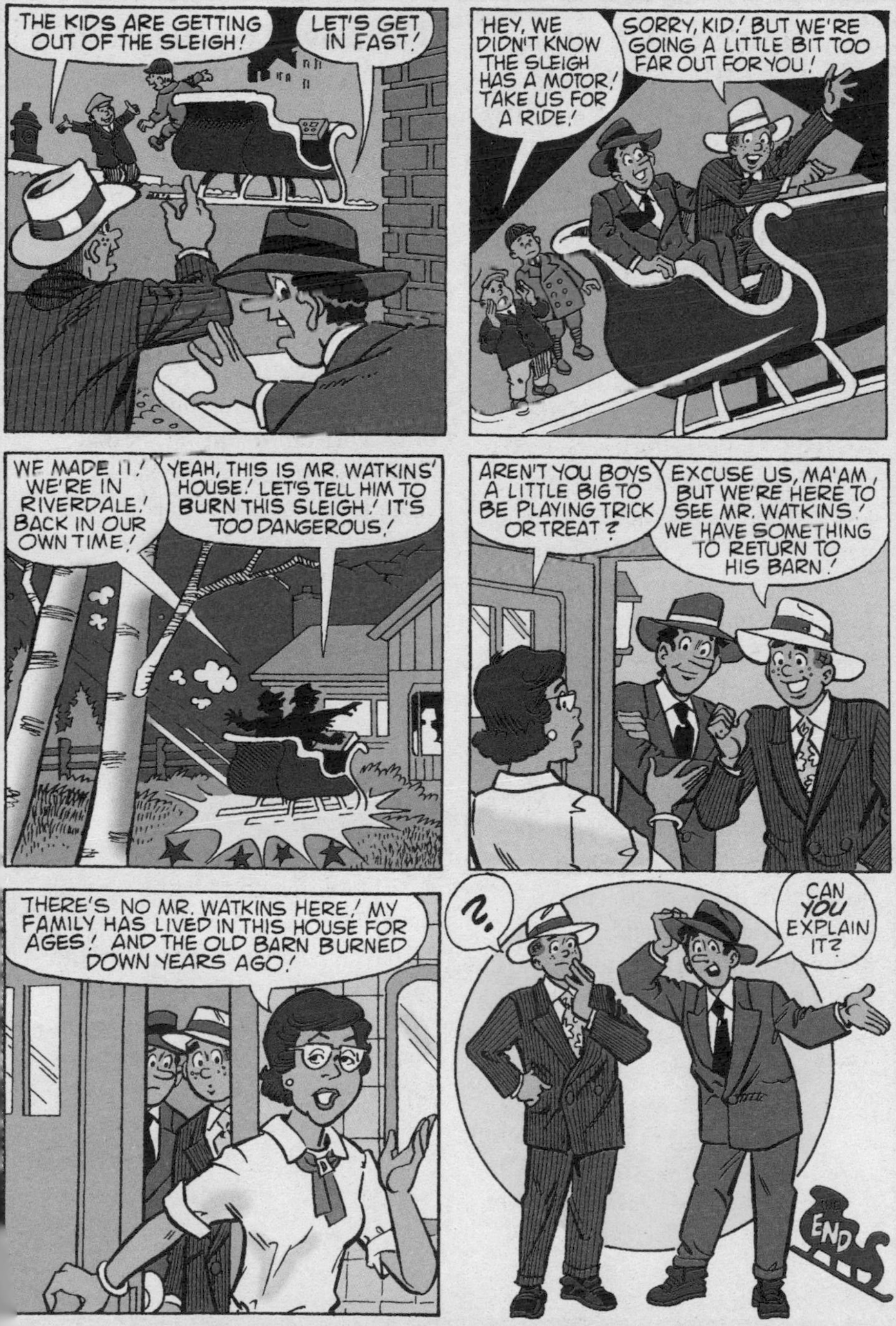
THE KIDS ARE GETTING OUT OF THE SLEIGH!
LET'S GET IN FAST!
HEY, WE DIDN'T KNOW THE SLEIGH HAS A MOTOR! TAKE US FOR A RIDE!
SORRY, KID! BUT WE'RE GOING A LITTLE BIT TOO FAR OUT FOR YOU!
WE MADE IT! WE'RE IN RIVERDALE! BACK IN OUR OWN TIME!
YEAH, THIS IS MR. WATKINS' HOUSE! LET'S TELL HIM TO BURN THIS SLEIGH! IT'S TOO DANGEROUS!
AREN'T YOU BOYS A LITTLE BIG TO BE PLAYING TRICK OR TREAT?
EXCUSE US, MA'AM, BUT WE'RE HERE TO SEE MR. WATKINS! WE HAVE SOMETHING TO RETURN TO HIS BARN!
THERE'S NO MR. WATKINS HERE! MY FAMILY HAS LIVED IN THIS HOUSE FOR AGES! AND THE OLD BARN BURNED DOWN YEARS AGO!
?
CAN YOU EXPLAIN IT?
END

Quivery Delivery/ Umbilical Miracle
Archie's Pal Jughead Comics #50 (Vol.2), 1993
by Al Hartley, Bill Golliher, Stan Goldberg and Mike Esposito

You're about to experience an event that was to go down in Archie Comics history. The next two stories, "Quivery Delivery" and "Umbilical Miracle," were parts 3 and 4 of a full-length issue of *Jughead* comics. The event: Jughead's mother is going to have a baby. The storyline began in issue #46 and worked its way to an unforgettable climax. Part 3 begins with Jughead's mom ready to give birth. With the clock ticking, Archie and Jughead are transporting Mrs. Jones to the hospital in the back of a pizza delivery van. An accident on the highway brings traffic to a halt. The clock keeps ticking. She's about to have the baby. What happens next?.... The clock keeps ticking.

--Victor Gorelick
Co-President & Editor-in-Chief,
Archie Comics

The Love Showdown Pt. 1
Archie #429, 1994
by Bill Golliher, Dan Parent and Stan Goldberg

It was one of those moments of spontaneous inspiration. I blurted out, "What if Betty & Veronica had a once-and-for-all competition for Archie's affections?" This was Archie Comics' first big media blitz, with an "event" story that held its own against the likes of "The Death of Superman." A personal triumph for me, as I came up with the concept and promoted the fine tale written by two of my faves, Dan Parent and Bill Golliher.

--Paul Castiglia
Writer and archivist,
Archie Comics

Bill Golliher and I came up with the "Love Showdown". It was a HUGE media event, probably the biggest thing UNTIL the Archie Wedding eclipsed it. But everybody wanted to know who Archie was throwing over B&V for.

--Dan Parent
Writer and illustrator,
Archie Comics

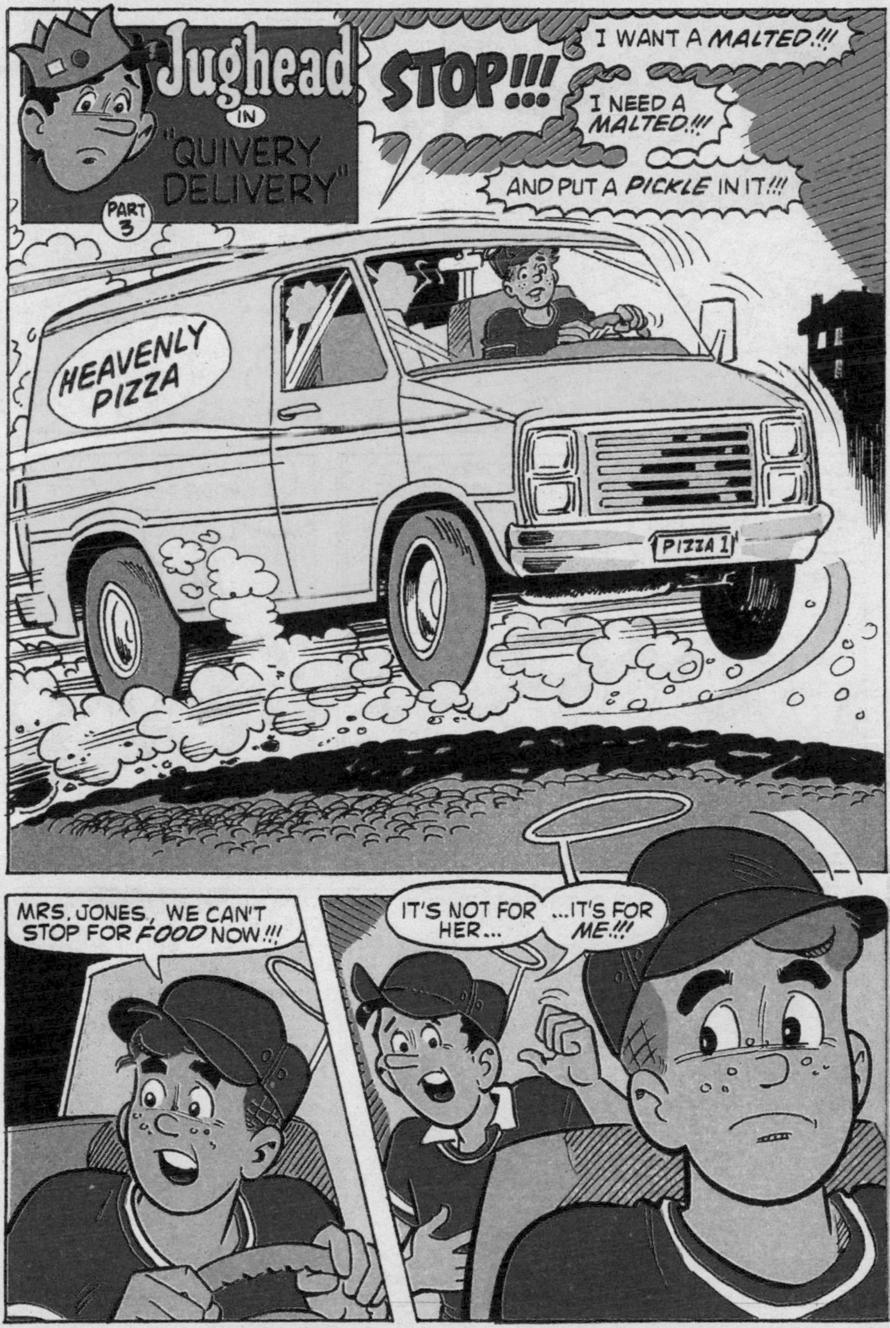
Jughead
IN
"QUIVERY DELIVERY"
PART 3
STOP!!!...
I WANT A MALTED!!!
I NEED A MALTED!!!
AND PUT A PICKLE IN IT!!!
HEAVENLY PIZZA
PIZZA 1
MRS. JONES, WE CAN'T STOP FOR FOOD NOW!!!
IT'S NOT FOR HER...
...IT'S FOR ME!!!

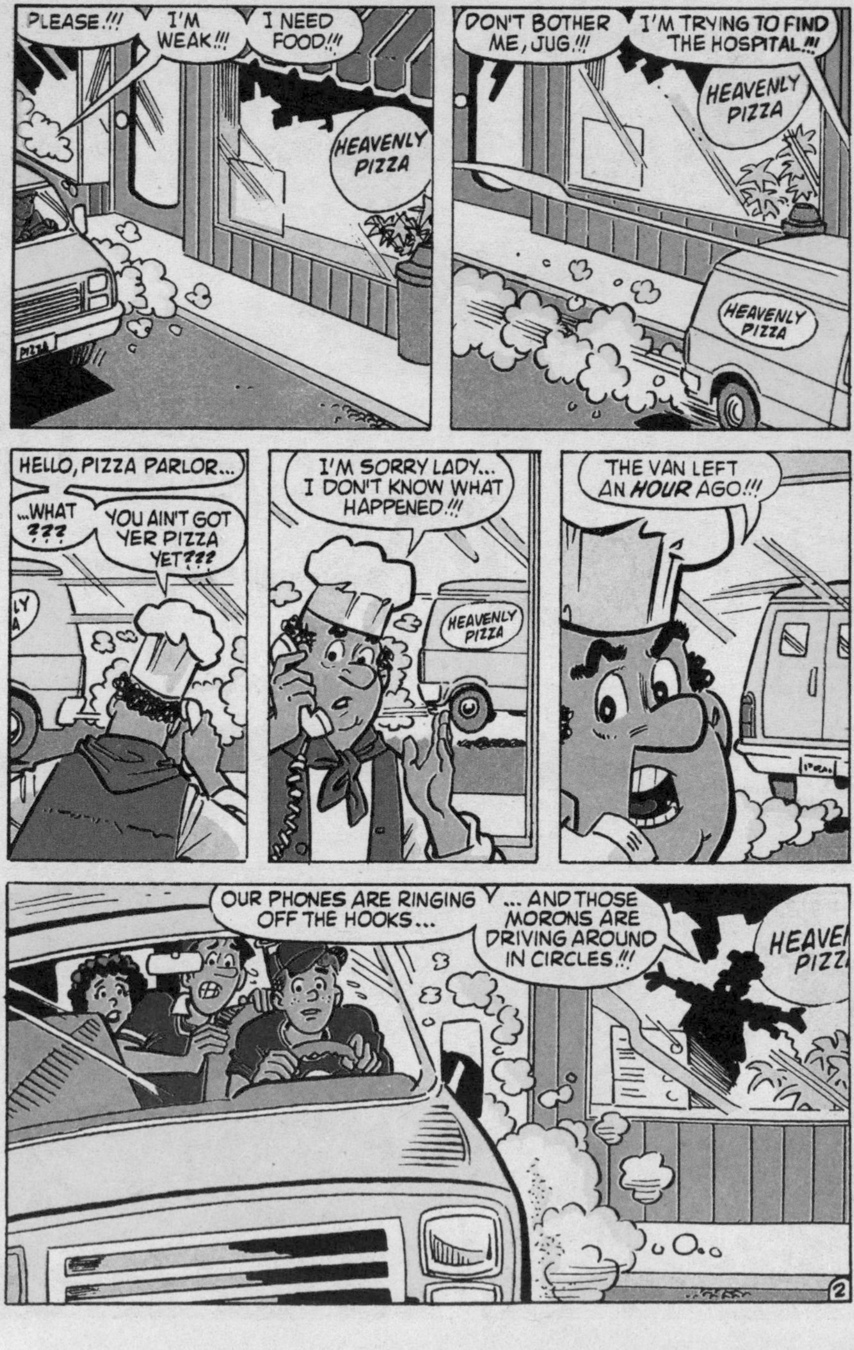
PLEASE!!!
I'M WEAK!!!
I NEED FOOD!!!
HEAVENLY PIZZA
DON'T BOTHER ME, JUG!!!
I'M TRYING TO FIND THE HOSPITAL!!!
HEAVENLY PIZZA
HEAVENLY PIZZA
HELLO, PIZZA PARLOR...
...WHAT ???
YOU AIN'T GOT YER PIZZA YET???
I'M SORRY LADY... I DON'T KNOW WHAT HAPPENED!!!
HEAVENLY PIZZA
THE VAN LEFT AN HOUR AGO!!!
OUR PHONES ARE RINGING OFF THE HOOKS...
... AND THOSE MORONS ARE DRIVING AROUND IN CIRCLES!!!
2

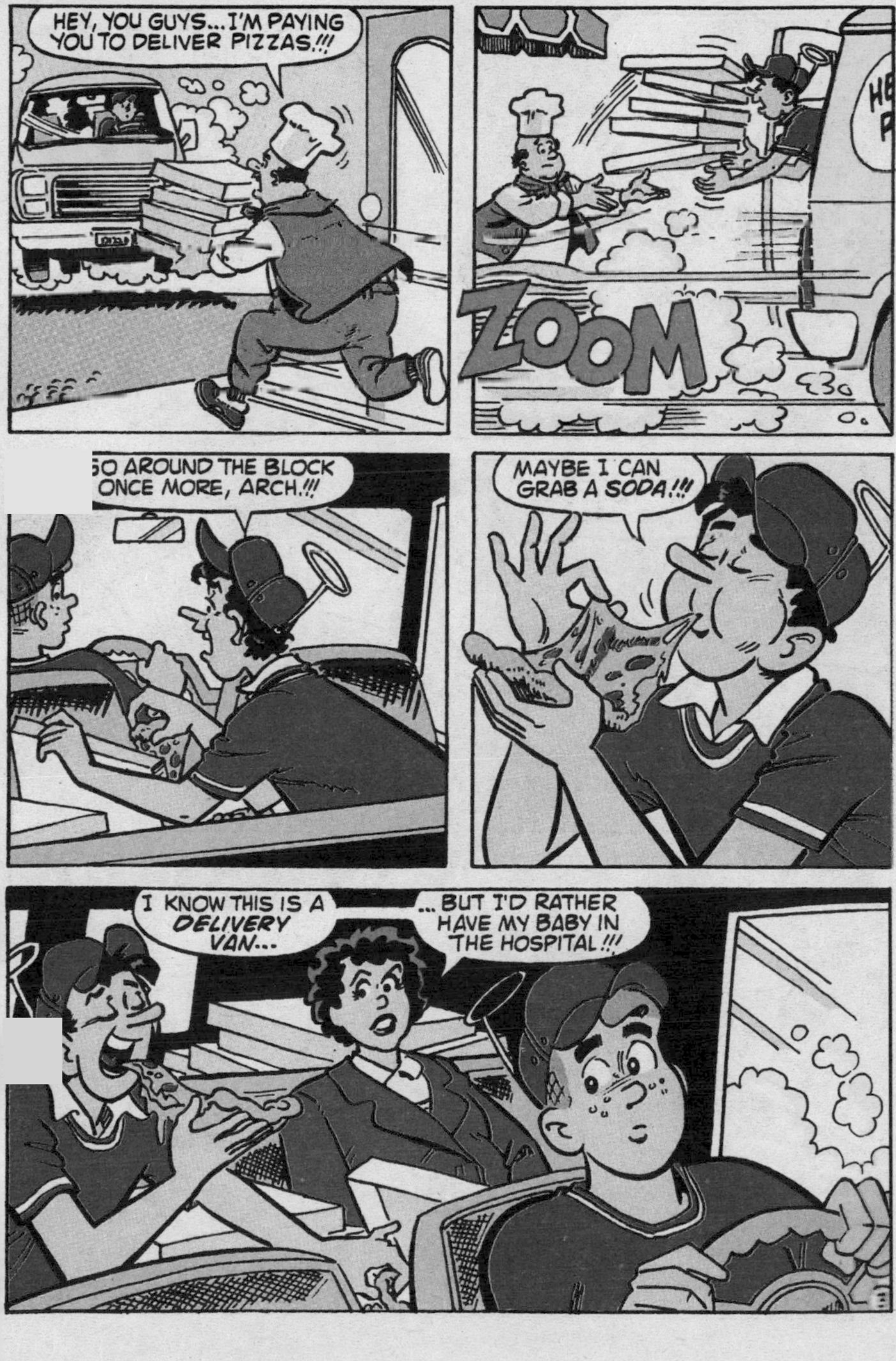
HEY, YOU GUYS...I'M PAYING YOU TO DELIVER PIZZAS!!!
ZOOM
GO AROUND THE BLOCK ONCE MORE, ARCH.!!!
MAYBE I CAN GRAB A SODA!!!
I KNOW THIS IS A DELIVERY VAN...
...BUT I'D RATHER HAVE MY BABY IN THE HOSPITAL!!!

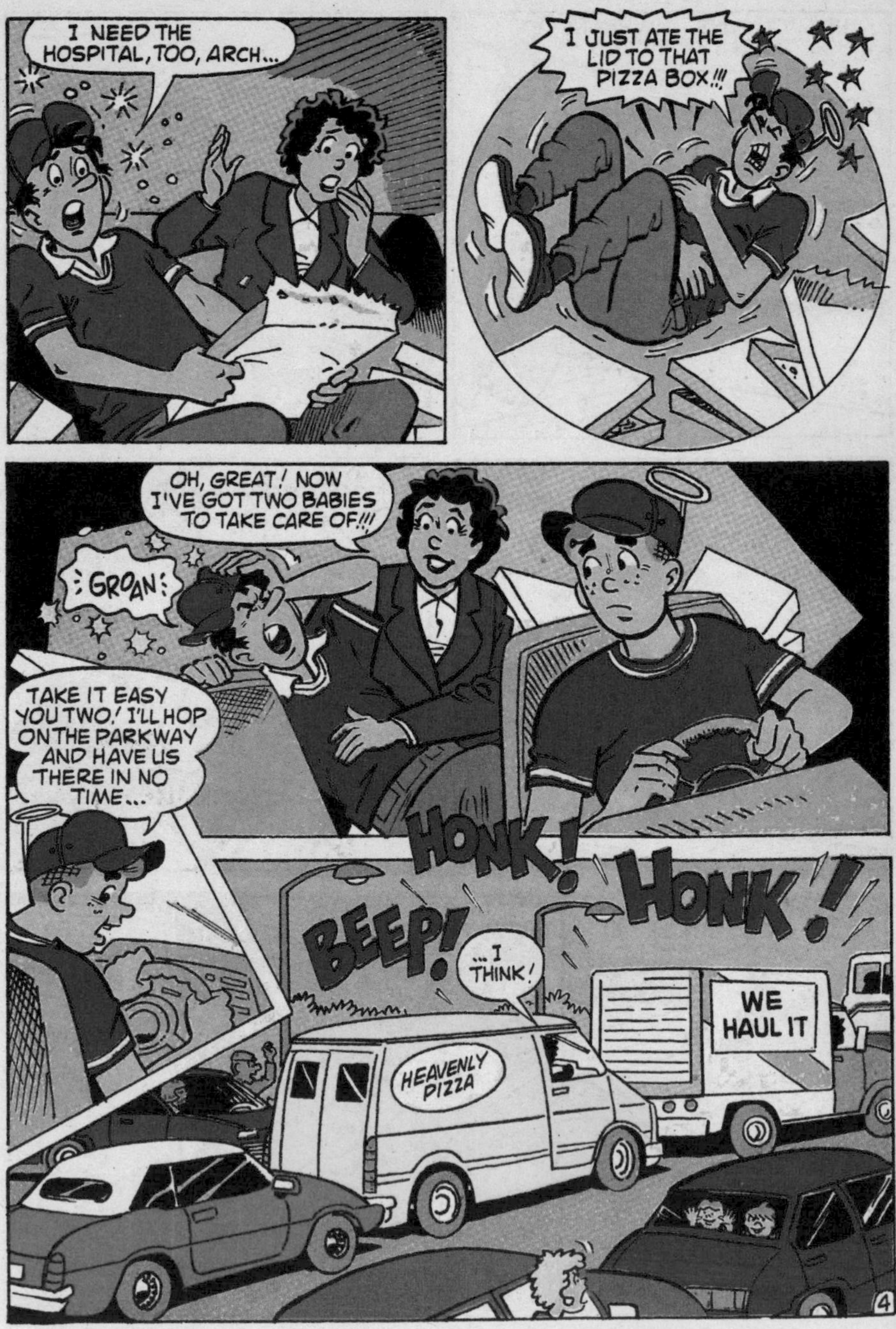
I NEED THE HOSPITAL, TOO, ARCH...
I JUST ATE THE LID TO THAT PIZZA BOX!!!
OH, GREAT! NOW I'VE GOT TWO BABIES TO TAKE CARE OF!!!
GROAN
TAKE IT EASY YOU TWO! I'LL HOP ON THE PARKWAY AND HAVE US THERE IN NO TIME...
HONK!
HONK!!
BEEP!
...I THINK!
WE HAUL IT
HEAVENLY PIZZA
4

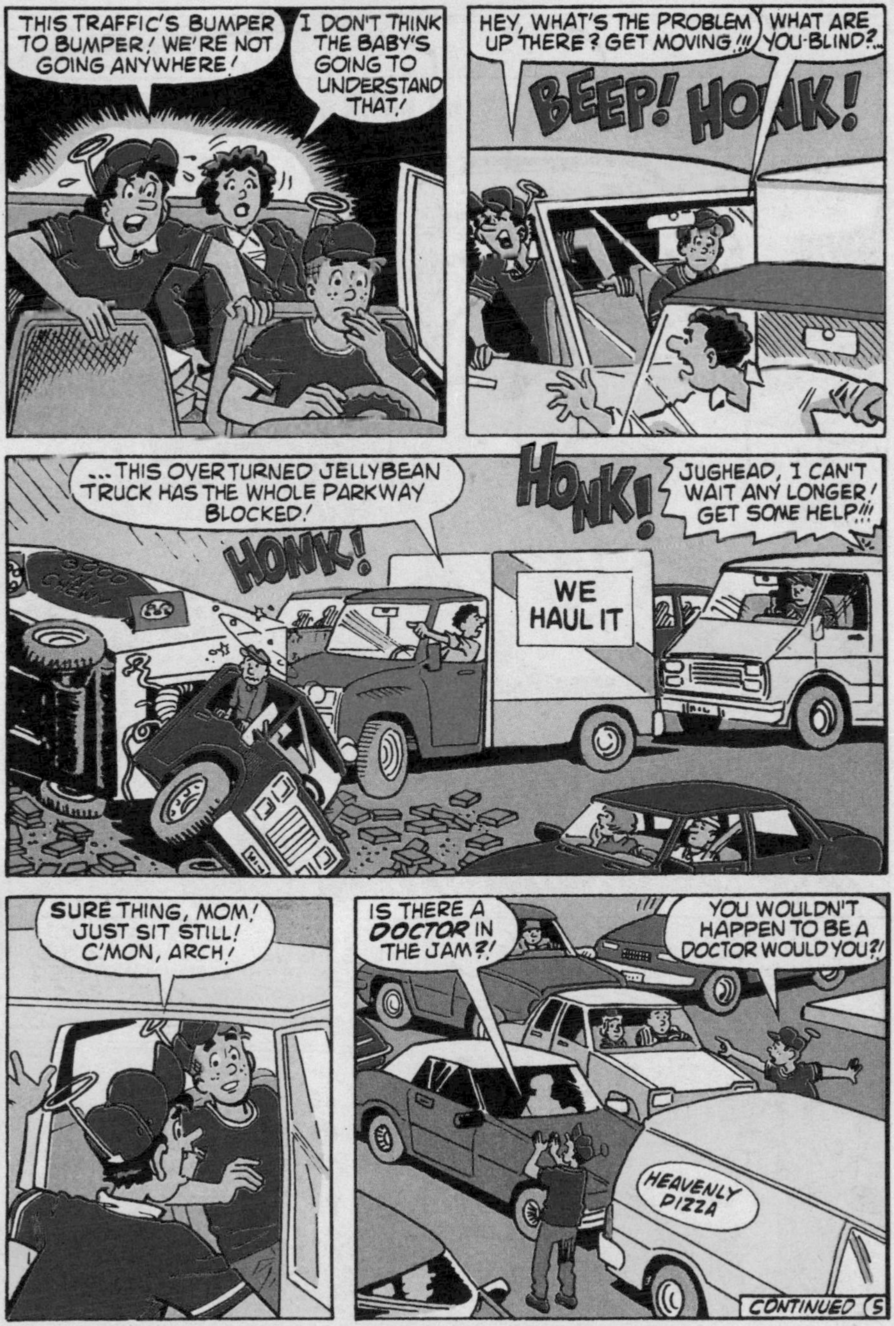
THIS TRAFFIC'S BUMPER TO BUMPER! WE'RE NOT GOING ANYWHERE!
I DON'T THINK THE BABY'S GOING TO UNDERSTAND THAT!
HEY, WHAT'S THE PROBLEM UP THERE? GET MOVING!!!
WHAT ARE YOU-BLIND?...
BEEP! HONK!
...THIS OVERTURNED JELLYBEAN TRUCK HAS THE WHOLE PARKWAY BLOCKED!
HONK!
JUGHEAD, I CAN'T WAIT ANY LONGER! GET SOME HELP!!!
HONK!
WE HAUL IT
SURE THING, MOM! JUST SIT STILL! C'MON, ARCH!
IS THERE A DOCTOR IN THE JAM?!
YOU WOULDN'T HAPPEN TO BE A DOCTOR WOULD YOU?!
HEAVENLY PIZZA
CONTINUED 5

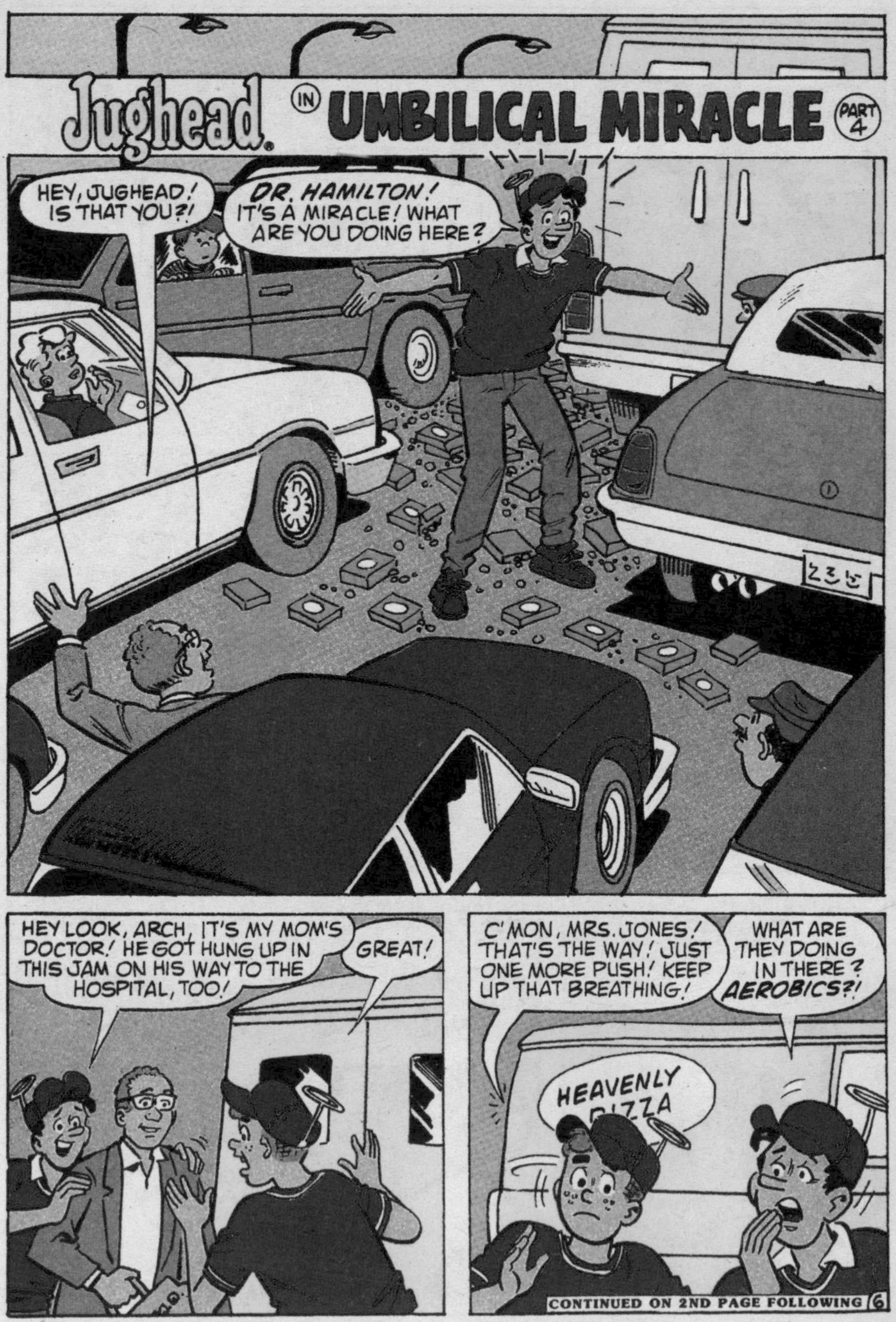
Jughead
IN
UMBILICAL MIRACLE
PART 4
HEY, JUGHEAD! IS THAT YOU?!
DR. HAMILTON! IT'S A MIRACLE! WHAT ARE YOU DOING HERE?
HEY LOOK, ARCH, IT'S MY MOM'S DOCTOR! HE GOT HUNG UP IN THIS JAM ON HIS WAY TO THE HOSPITAL, TOO!
GREAT!
C'MON, MRS. JONES! THAT'S THE WAY! JUST ONE MORE PUSH! KEEP UP THAT BREATHING!
WHAT ARE THEY DOING IN THERE? AEROBICS?!
HEAVENLY
CONTINUED ON 2ND PAGE FOLLOWING
6

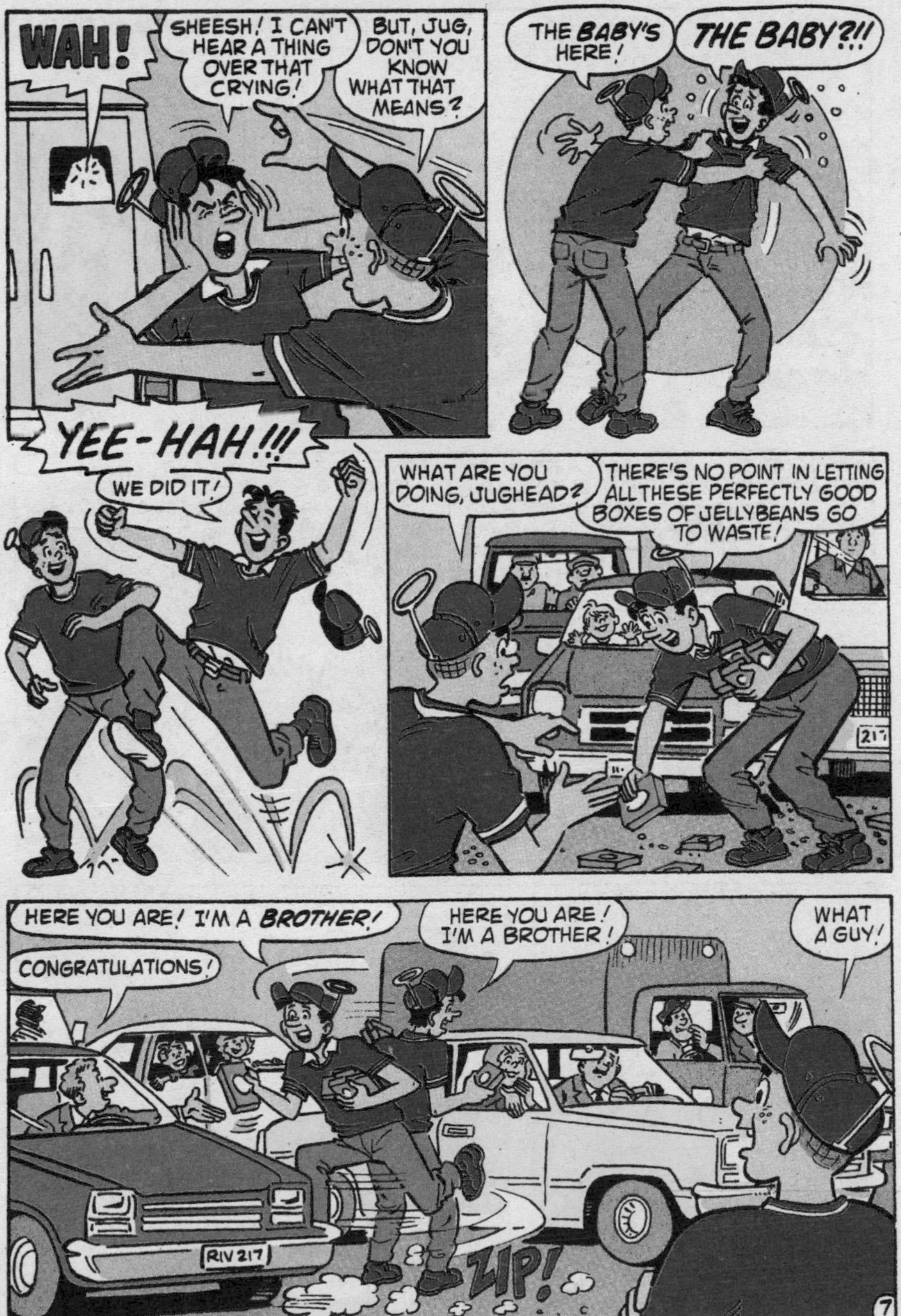
WAH!
SHEESH! I CAN'T HEAR A THING OVER THAT CRYING!
BUT, JUG, DON'T YOU KNOW WHAT THAT MEANS?
THE BABY'S HERE!
THE BABY?!!
YEE-HAH!!!
WE DID IT!
WHAT ARE YOU DOING, JUGHEAD?
THERE'S NO POINT IN LETTING ALL THESE PERFECTLY GOOD BOXES OF JELLYBEANS GO TO WASTE!
217
HERE YOU ARE! I'M A BROTHER!
CONGRATULATIONS!
HERE YOU ARE! I'M A BROTHER!
WHAT A GUY!
RIV 217
ZIP!
7

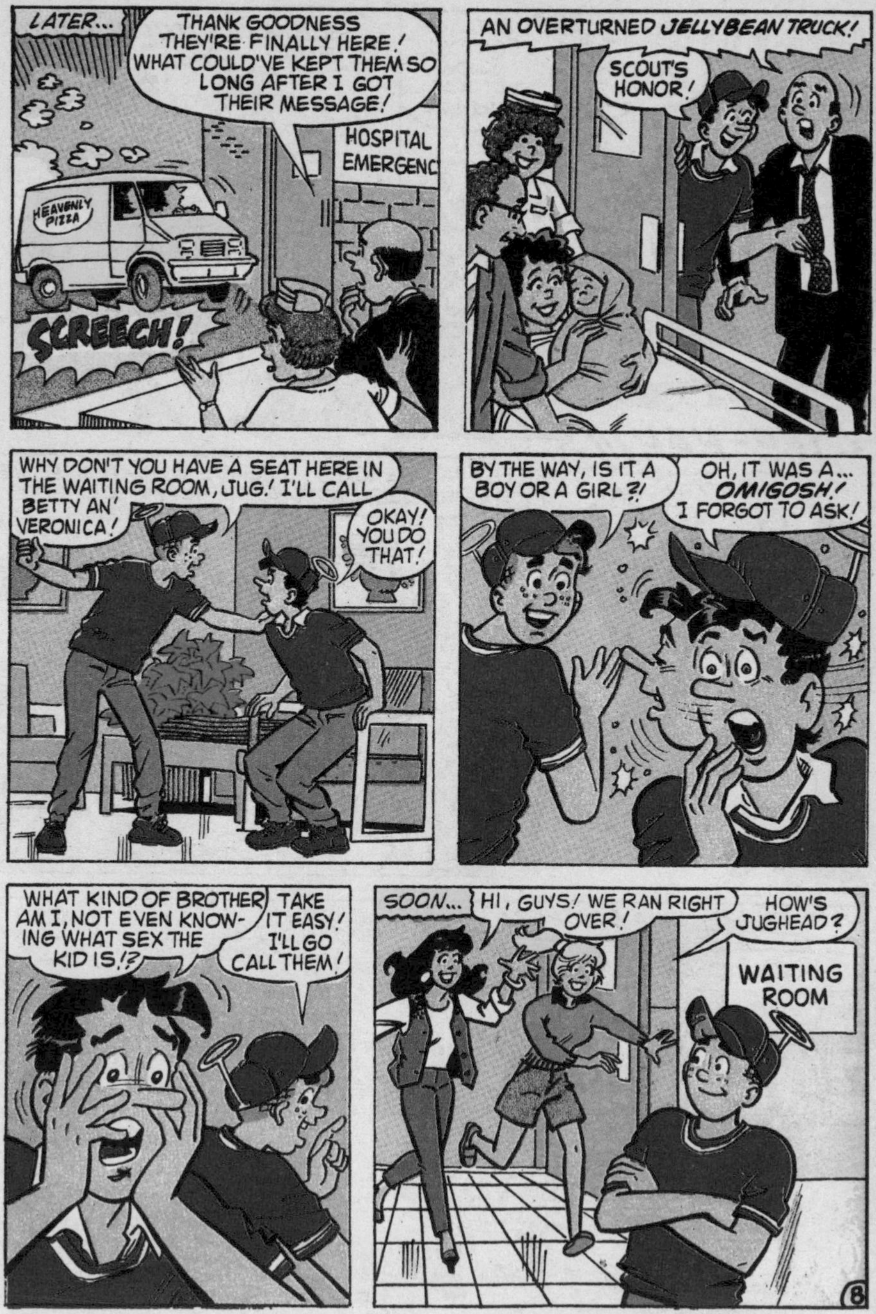
LATER...
THANK GOODNESS THEY'RE FINALLY HERE! WHAT COULD'VE KEPT THEM SO LONG AFTER I GOT THEIR MESSAGE!
HOSPITAL EMERGENC
HEAVENLY PIZZA
SCREECH!
AN OVERTURNED JELLYBEAN TRUCK!
SCOUT'S HONOR!
WHY DON'T YOU HAVE A SEAT HERE IN THE WAITING ROOM, JUG! I'LL CALL BETTY AN' VERONICA!
OKAY! YOU DO THAT!
BY THE WAY, IS IT A BOY OR A GIRL ?!
OH, IT WAS A... OMIGOSH! I FORGOT TO ASK!
WHAT KIND OF BROTHER AM I, NOT EVEN KNOWING WHAT SEX THE KID IS!?
TAKE IT EASY! I'LL GO CALL THEM!
SOON...
HI, GUYS! WE RAN RIGHT OVER!
HOW'S JUGHEAD?
WAITING ROOM
8

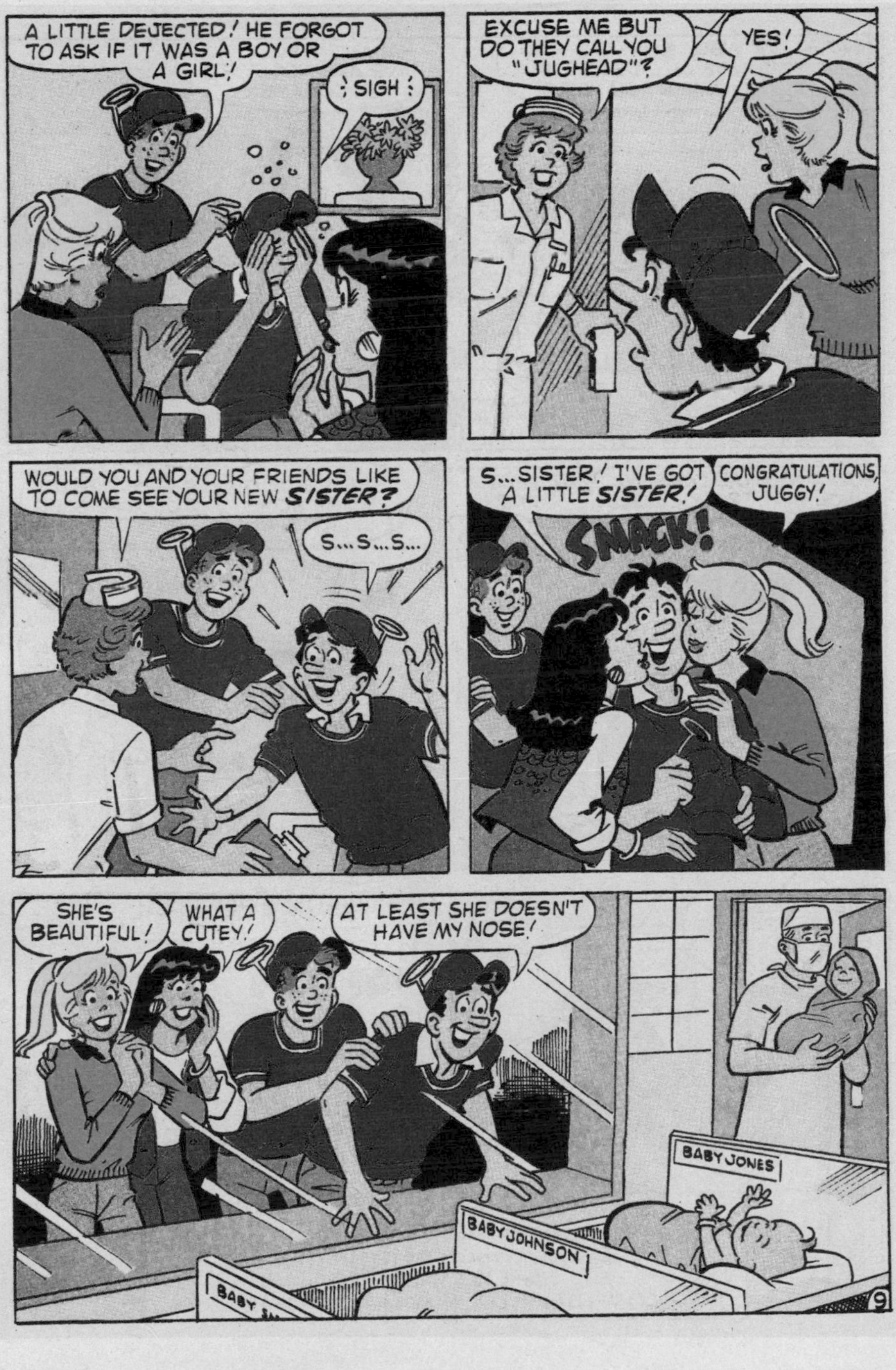
A LITTLE DEJECTED! HE FORGOT TO ASK IF IT WAS A BOY OR A GIRL!
SIGH
EXCUSE ME BUT DO THEY CALL YOU "JUGHEAD"?
YES!
WOULD YOU AND YOUR FRIENDS LIKE TO COME SEE YOUR NEW SISTER?
S...S...S...
S...SISTER! I'VE GOT A LITTLE SISTER!
CONGRATULATIONS, JUGGY!
SMACK!
SHE'S BEAUTIFUL!
WHAT A CUTEY!
AT LEAST SHE DOESN'T HAVE MY NOSE!
BABY JONES
BABY JOHNSON
9

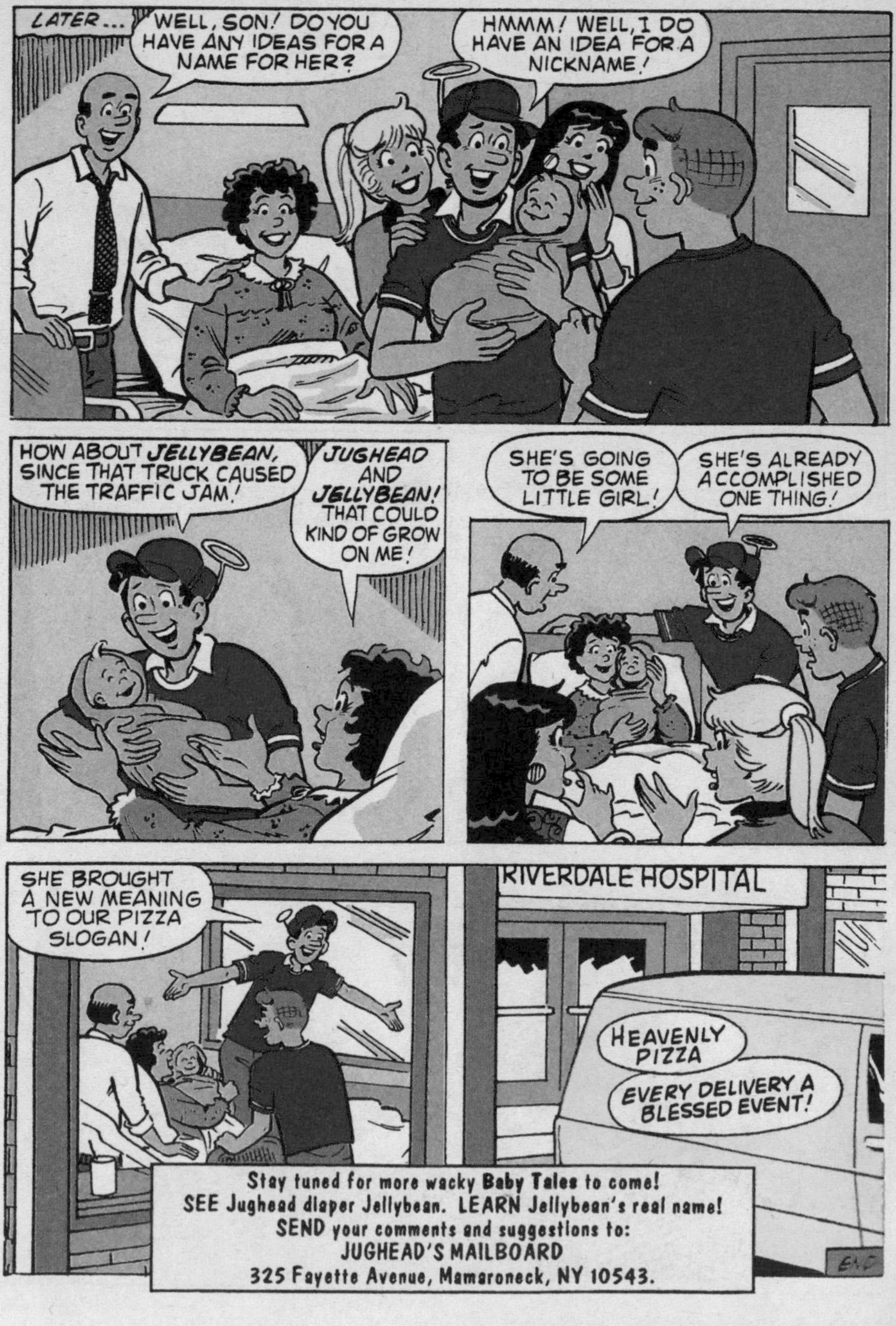
LATER...
WELL, SON! DO YOU HAVE ANY IDEAS FOR A NAME FOR HER?
HMMM! WELL, I DO HAVE AN IDEA FOR A NICKNAME!
HOW ABOUT JELLYBEAN, SINCE THAT TRUCK CAUSED THE TRAFFIC JAM!
JUGHEAD AND JELLYBEAN! THAT COULD KIND OF GROW ON ME!
SHE'S GOING TO BE SOME LITTLE GIRL!
SHE'S ALREADY ACCOMPLISHED ONE THING!
SHE BROUGHT A NEW MEANING TO OUR PIZZA SLOGAN!
RIVERDALE HOSPITAL
HEAVENLY PIZZA
EVERY DELIVERY A BLESSED EVENT!
Stay tuned for more wacky Baby Tales to come!
SEE Jughead diaper Jellybean. LEARN Jellybean's real name!
SEND your comments and suggestions to:
JUGHEAD'S MAILBOARD
325 Fayette Avenue, Mamaroneck, NY 10543.

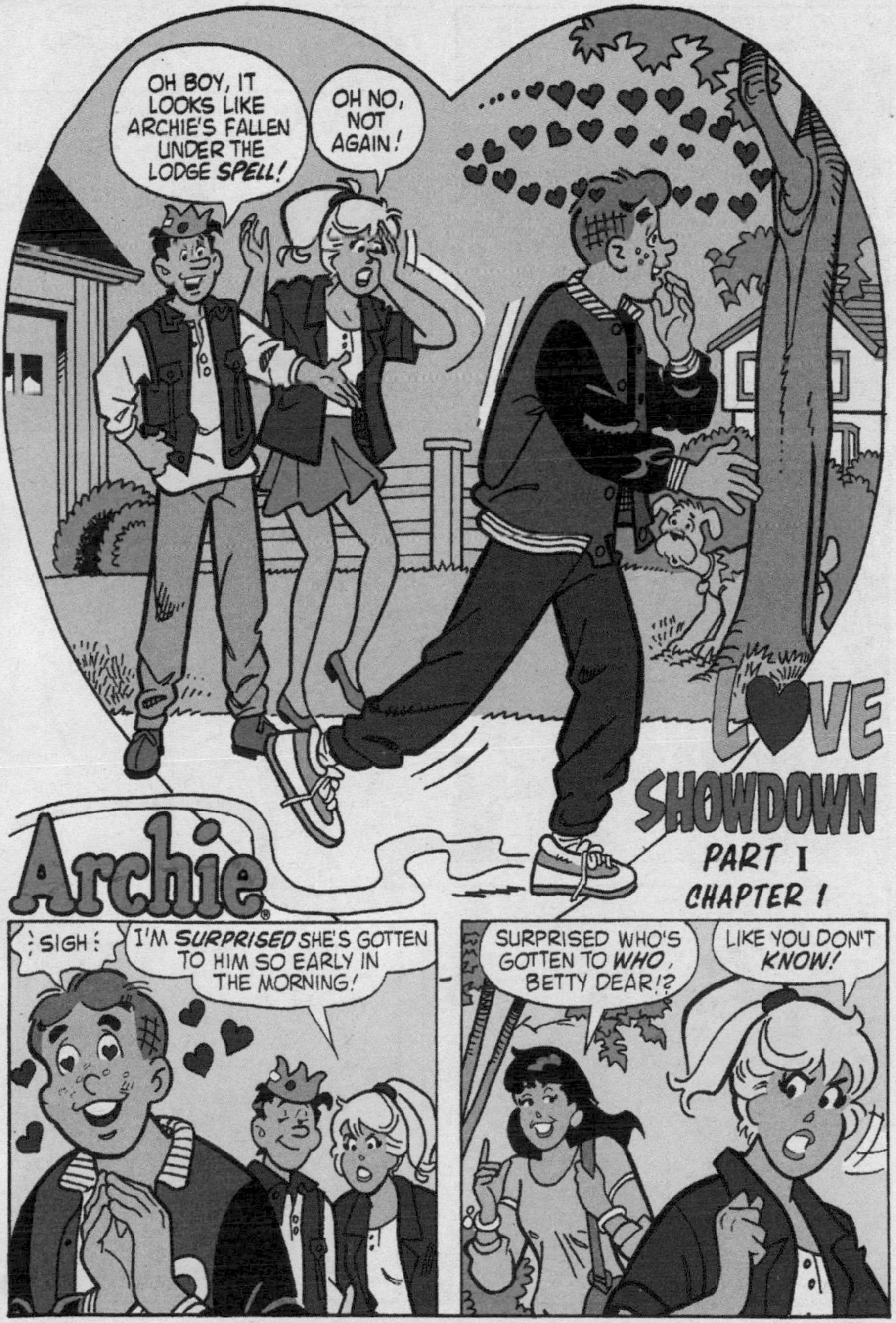
OH BOY, IT LOOKS LIKE ARCHIE'S FALLEN UNDER THE LODGE SPELL!
OH NO, NOT AGAIN!
Archie
LOVE SHOWDOWN
PART I
CHAPTER 1
SIGH
I'M SURPRISED SHE'S GOTTEN TO HIM SO EARLY IN THE MORNING!
SURPRISED WHO'S GOTTEN TO WHO, BETTY DEAR!?
LIKE YOU DON'T KNOW!

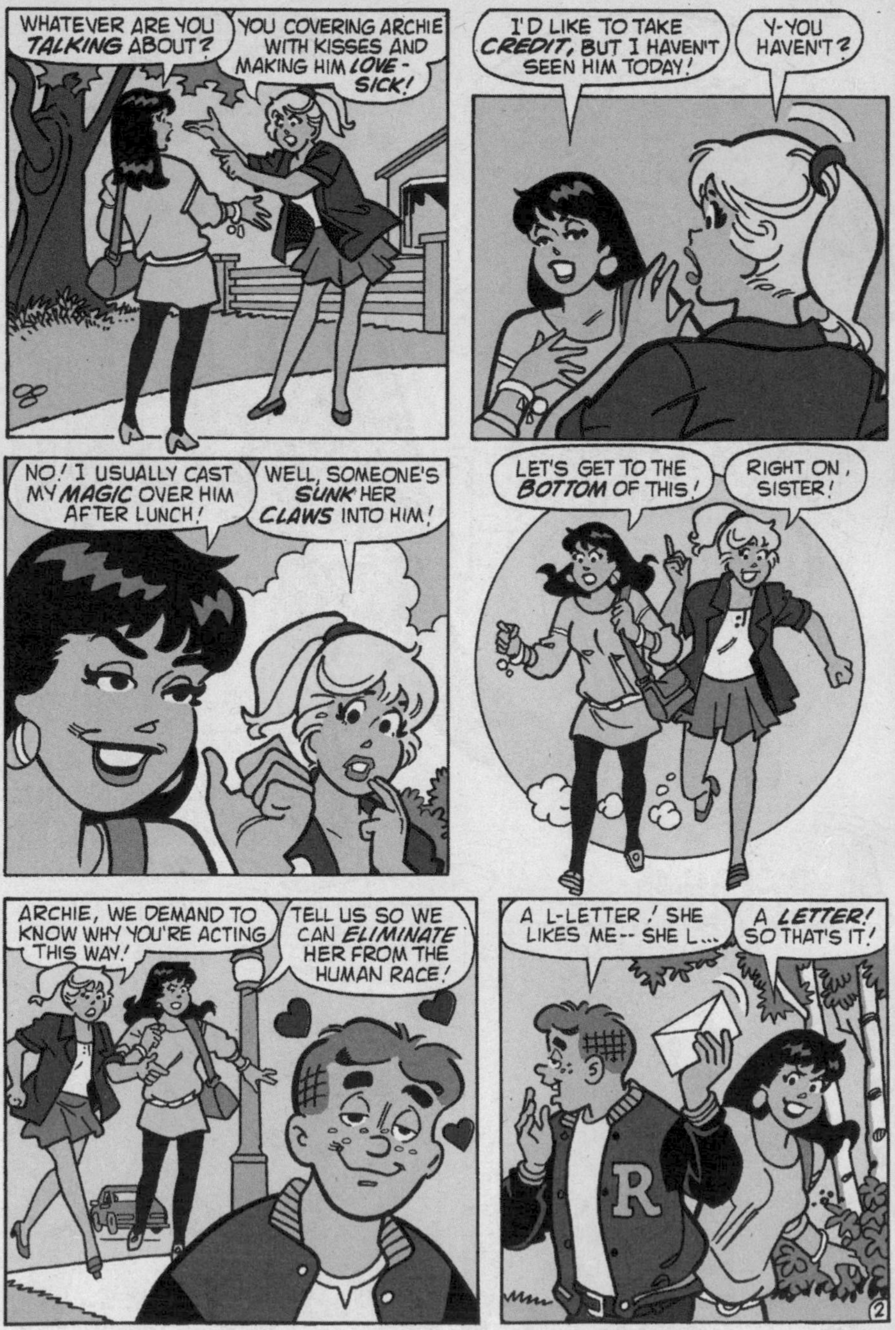
WHATEVER ARE YOU TALKING ABOUT?
YOU COVERING ARCHIE WITH KISSES AND MAKING HIM LOVE-SICK!
I'D LIKE TO TAKE CREDIT, BUT I HAVEN'T SEEN HIM TODAY!
Y-YOU HAVEN'T?
NO! I USUALLY CAST MY MAGIC OVER HIM AFTER LUNCH!
WELL, SOMEONE'S SUNK HER CLAWS INTO HIM!
LET'S GET TO THE BOTTOM OF THIS!
RIGHT ON, SISTER!
ARCHIE, WE DEMAND TO KNOW WHY YOU'RE ACTING THIS WAY!
TELL US SO WE CAN ELIMINATE HER FROM THE HUMAN RACE!
A L-LETTER! SHE LIKES ME-- SHE L...
A LETTER! SO THAT'S IT!
R
2

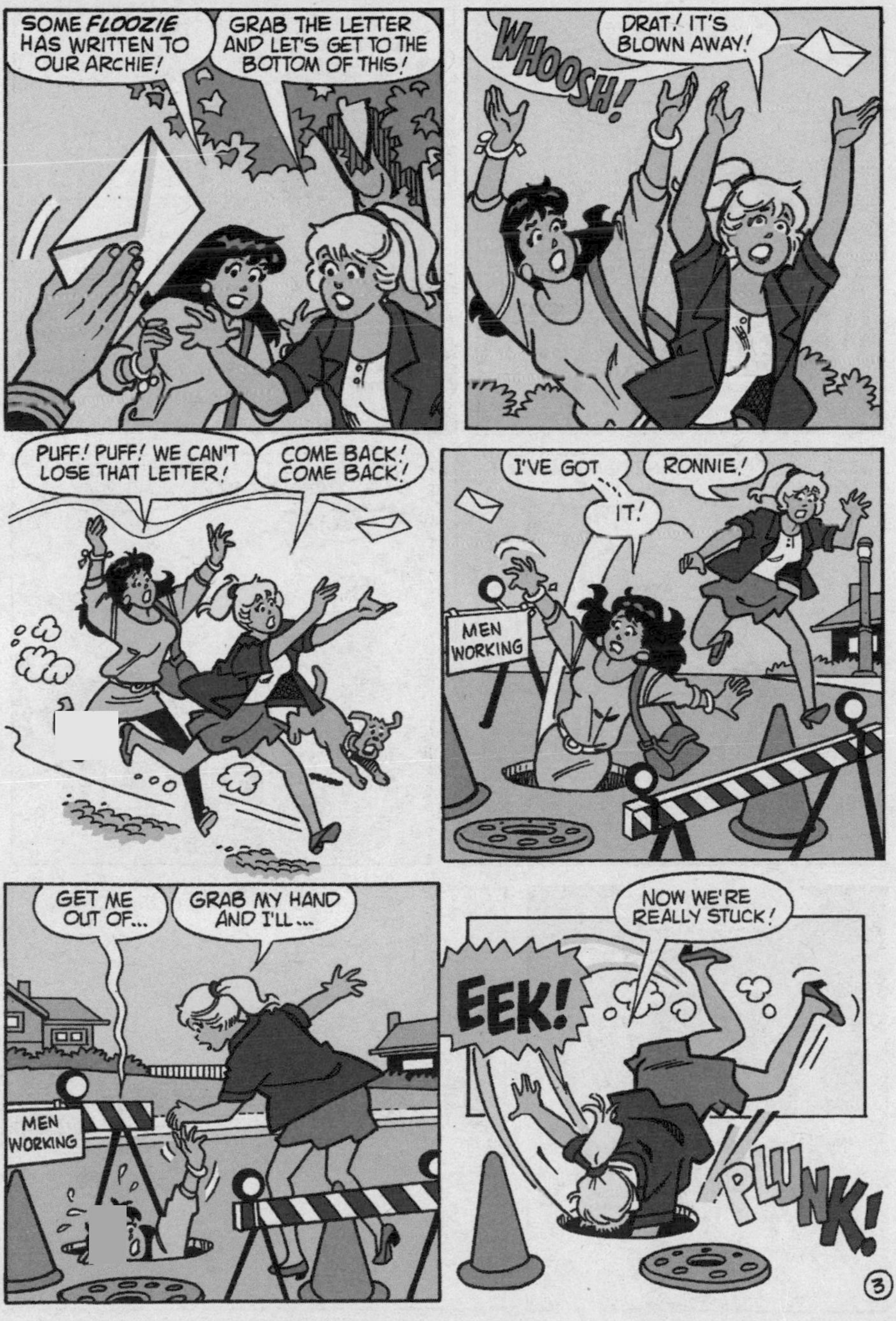
SOME FLOOZIE HAS WRITTEN TO OUR ARCHIE!
GRAB THE LETTER AND LET'S GET TO THE BOTTOM OF THIS!
WHOOSH!
DRAT! IT'S BLOWN AWAY!
PUFF! PUFF! WE CAN'T LOSE THAT LETTER!
COME BACK! COME BACK!
I'VE GOT
IT!
RONNIE!
MEN WORKING
GET ME OUT OF...
GRAB MY HAND AND I'LL...
MEN WORKING
EEK!
NOW WE'RE REALLY STUCK!
PLUNK!
3

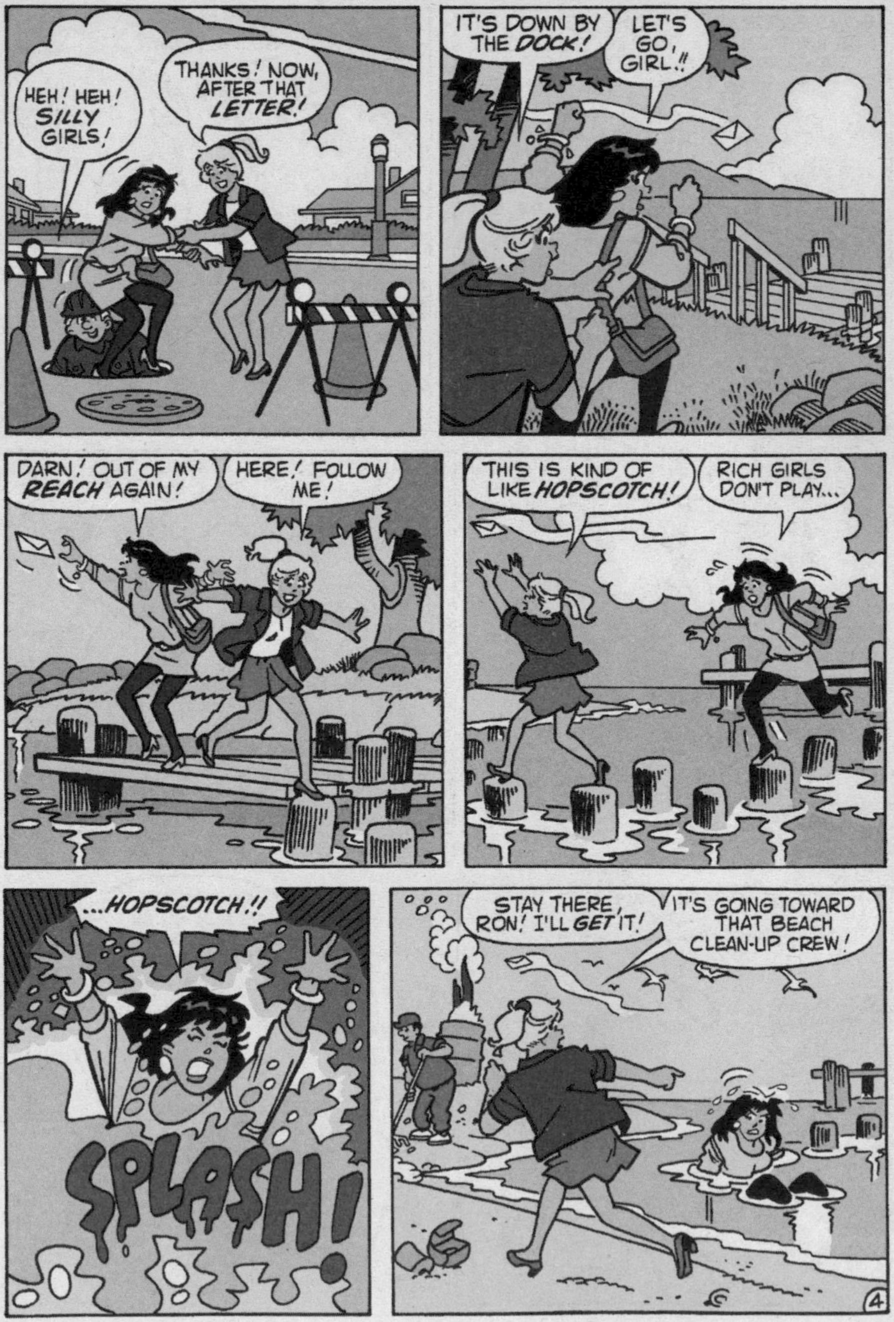
HEH! HEH! SILLY GIRLS!
THANKS! NOW, AFTER THAT LETTER!
IT'S DOWN BY THE DOCK!
LET'S GO, GIRL!!
DARN! OUT OF MY REACH AGAIN!
HERE! FOLLOW ME!
THIS IS KIND OF LIKE HOPSCOTCH!
RICH GIRLS DON'T PLAY...
...HOPSCOTCH!!
SPLASH!
STAY THERE, RON! I'LL GET IT!
IT'S GOING TOWARD THAT BEACH CLEAN-UP CREW!
4

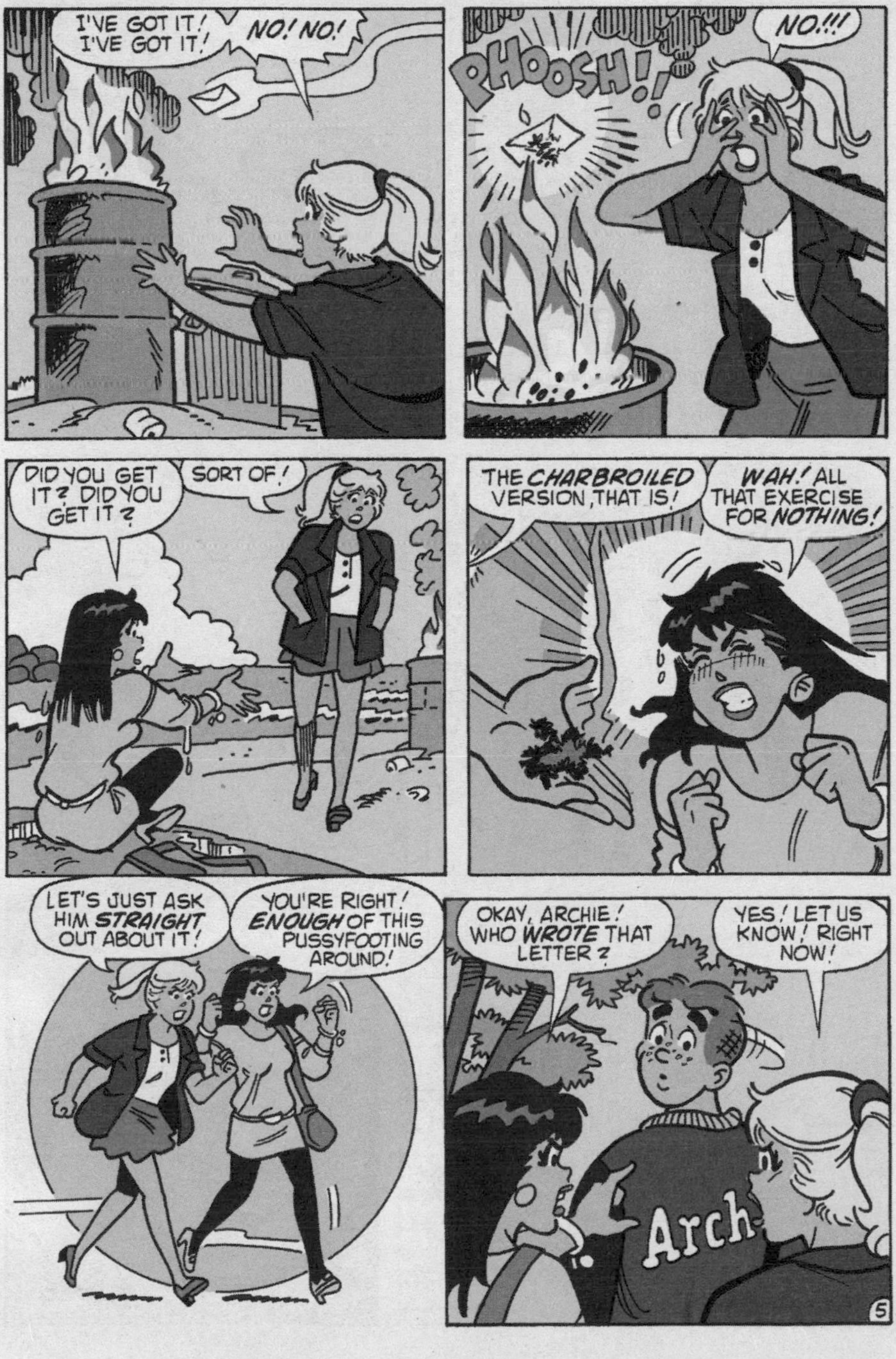
I'VE GOT IT! I'VE GOT IT!
NO! NO!
PHOOSH!!
NO!!!
DID YOU GET IT? DID YOU GET IT?
SORT OF!
THE CHARBROILED VERSION, THAT IS!
WAH! ALL THAT EXERCISE FOR NOTHING!
LET'S JUST ASK HIM STRAIGHT OUT ABOUT IT!
YOU'RE RIGHT! ENOUGH OF THIS PUSSYFOOTING AROUND!
OKAY, ARCHIE! WHO WROTE THAT LETTER?
YES! LET US KNOW! RIGHT NOW!
Arch
5

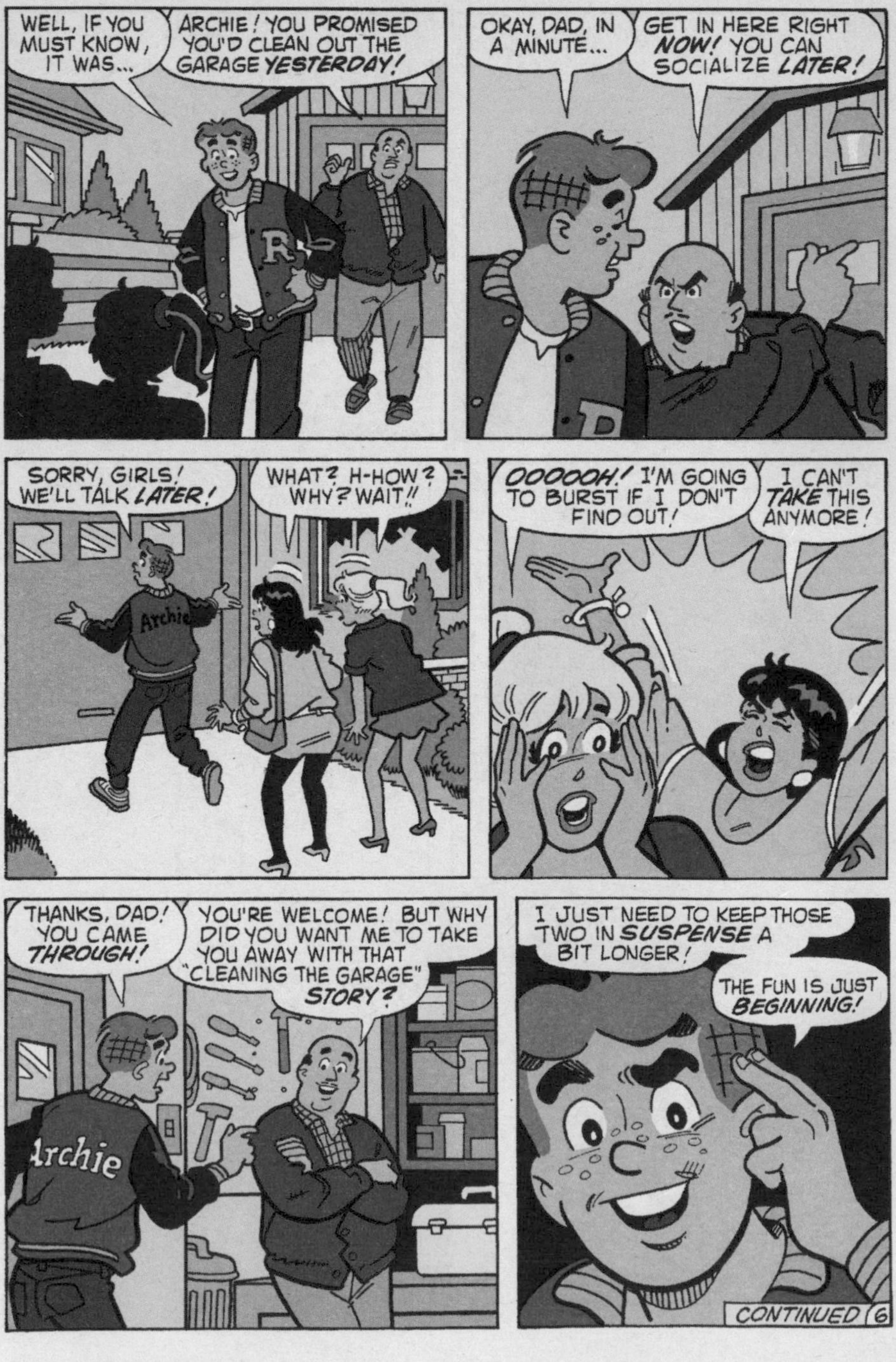
WELL, IF YOU MUST KNOW, IT WAS...
ARCHIE! YOU PROMISED YOU'D CLEAN OUT THE GARAGE YESTERDAY!
OKAY, DAD, IN A MINUTE...
GET IN HERE RIGHT NOW! YOU CAN SOCIALIZE LATER!
SORRY, GIRLS! WE'LL TALK LATER!
WHAT? H-HOW? WHY? WAIT!!
OOOOOOH! I'M GOING TO BURST IF I DON'T FIND OUT!
I CAN'T TAKE THIS ANYMORE!
THANKS, DAD! YOU CAME THROUGH!
YOU'RE WELCOME! BUT WHY DID YOU WANT ME TO TAKE YOU AWAY WITH THAT "CLEANING THE GARAGE" STORY?
I JUST NEED TO KEEP THOSE TWO IN SUSPENSE A BIT LONGER!
THE FUN IS JUST BEGINNING!
CONTINUED 6

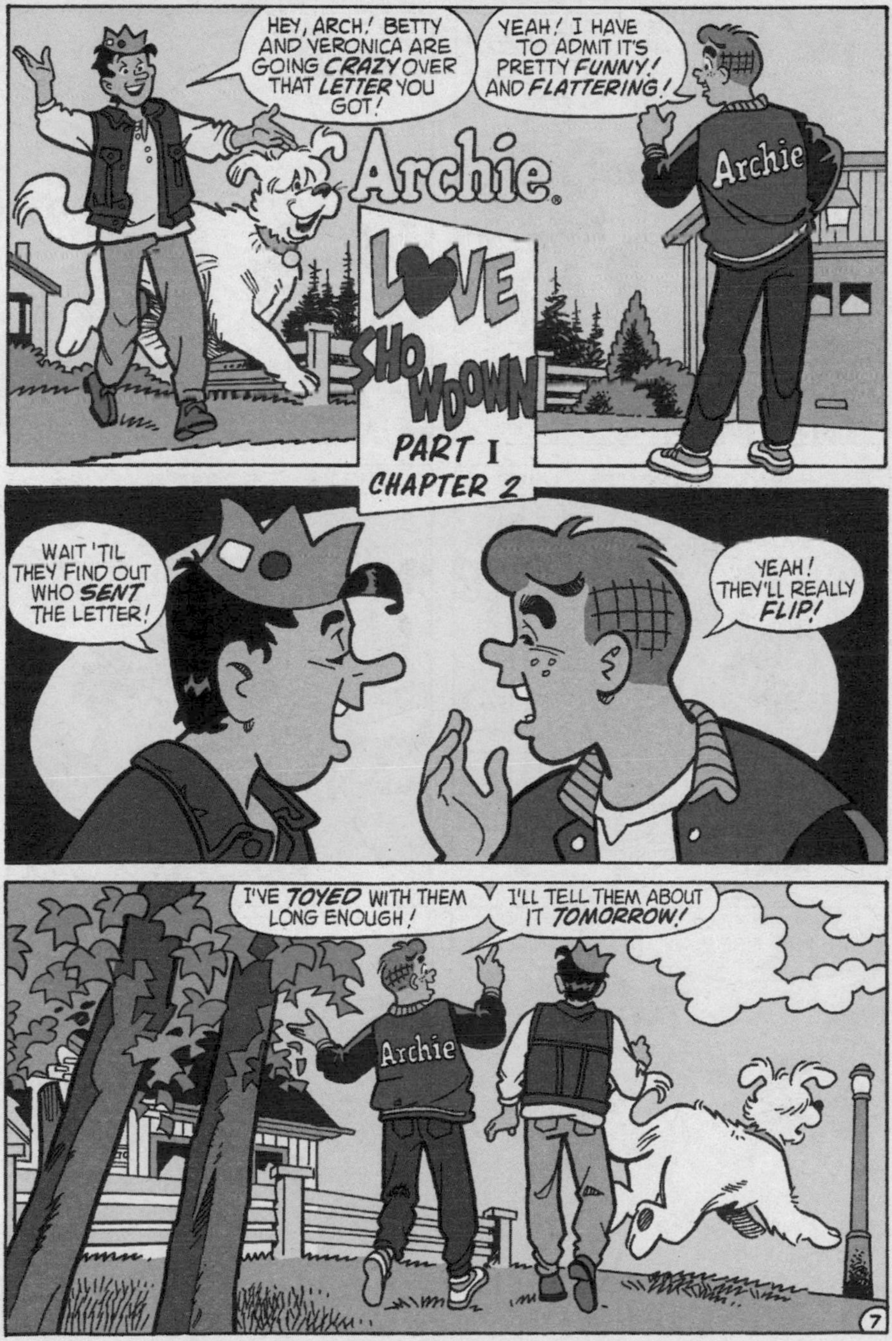
HEY, ARCH! BETTY AND VERONICA ARE GOING CRAZY OVER THAT LETTER YOU GOT!
YEAH! I HAVE TO ADMIT IT'S PRETTY FUNNY! AND FLATTERING!
Archie
Archie
LOVE SHOWDOWN
PART I
CHAPTER 2
WAIT 'TIL THEY FIND OUT WHO SENT THE LETTER!
YEAH! THEY'LL REALLY FLIP!
I'VE TOYED WITH THEM LONG ENOUGH!
I'LL TELL THEM ABOUT IT TOMORROW!
Archie
7

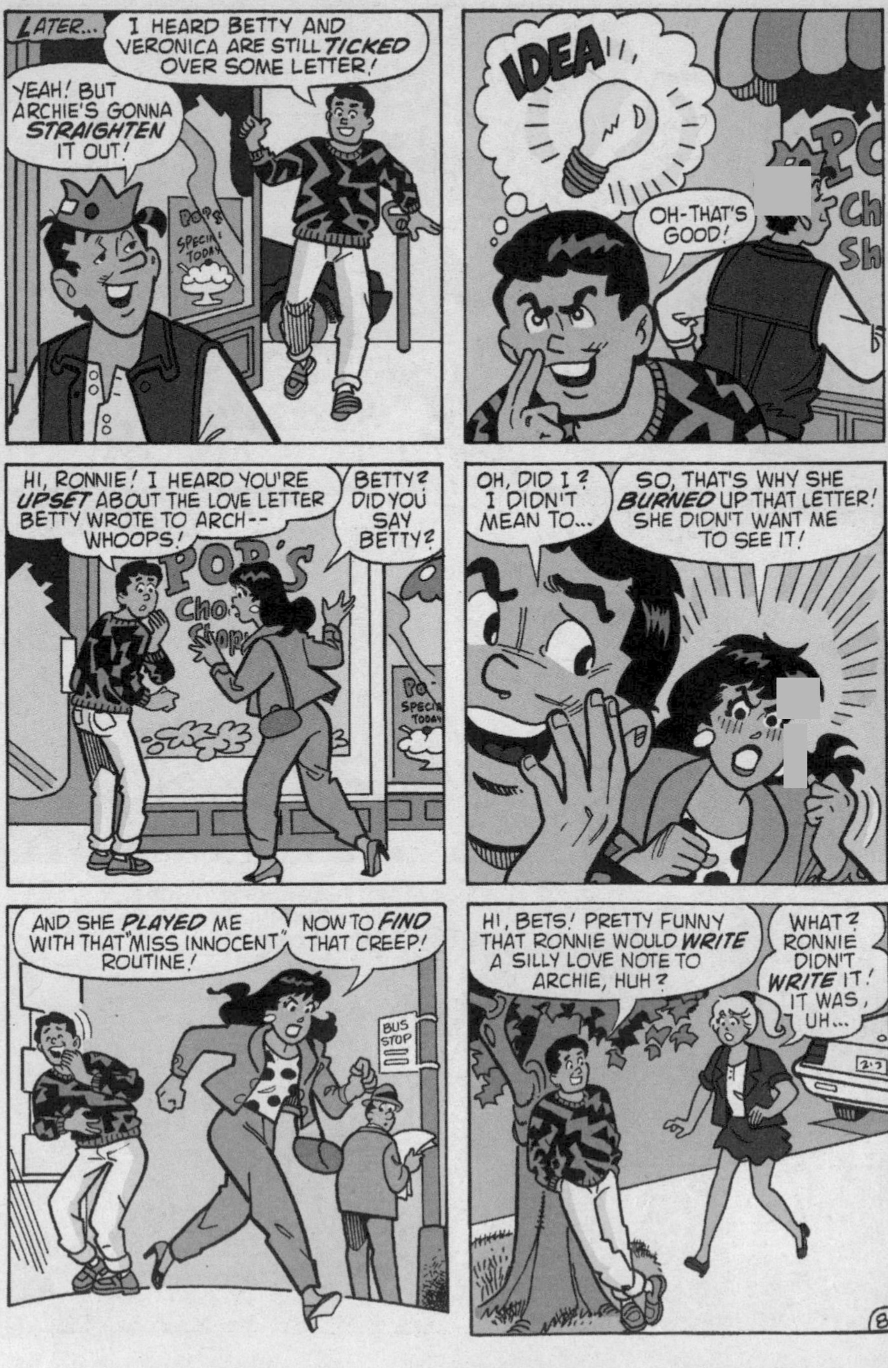
LATER...
I HEARD BETTY AND VERONICA ARE STILL TICKED OVER SOME LETTER!
YEAH! BUT ARCHIE'S GONNA STRAIGHTEN IT OUT!
POP'S SPECIAL TODAY
IDEA
OH-THAT'S GOOD!
HI, RONNIE! I HEARD YOU'RE UPSET ABOUT THE LOVE LETTER BETTY WROTE TO ARCH-- WHOOPS!
BETTY? DID YOU SAY BETTY?
OH, DID I? I DIDN'T MEAN TO...
SO, THAT'S WHY SHE BURNED UP THAT LETTER! SHE DIDN'T WANT ME TO SEE IT!
AND SHE PLAYED ME WITH THAT "MISS INNOCENT" ROUTINE!
NOW TO FIND THAT CREEP!
BUS STOP
HI, BETS! PRETTY FUNNY THAT RONNIE WOULD WRITE A SILLY LOVE NOTE TO ARCHIE, HUH?
WHAT? RONNIE DIDN'T WRITE IT! IT WAS, UH...
8

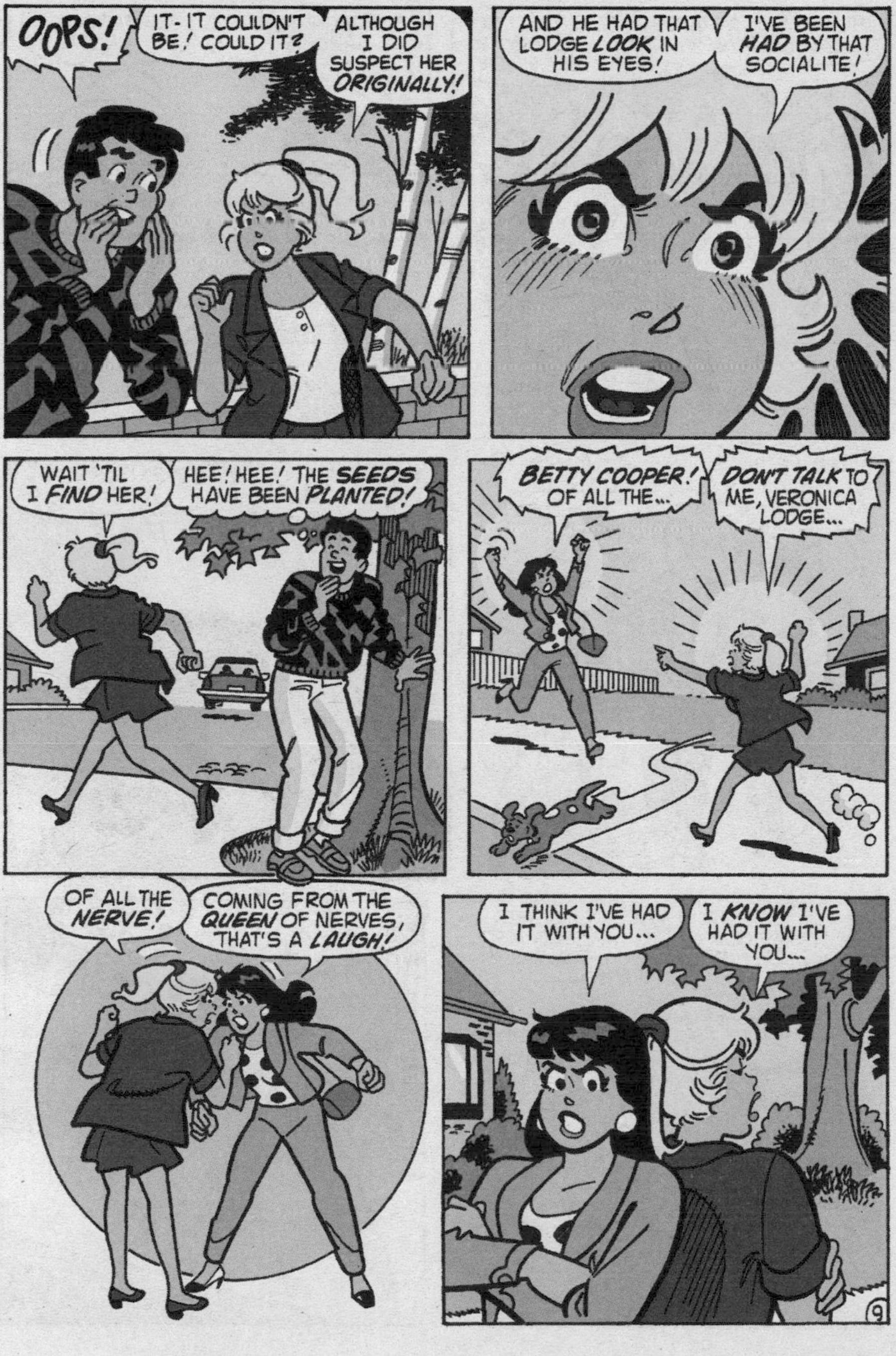
OOPS!
IT- IT COULDN'T BE! COULD IT?
ALTHOUGH I DID SUSPECT HER ORIGINALLY!
AND HE HAD THAT LODGE LOOK IN HIS EYES!
I'VE BEEN HAD BY THAT SOCIALITE!
WAIT 'TIL I FIND HER!
HEE! HEE! THE SEEDS HAVE BEEN PLANTED!
BETTY COOPER! OF ALL THE...
DON'T TALK TO ME, VERONICA LODGE...
OF ALL THE NERVE!
COMING FROM THE QUEEN OF NERVES, THAT'S A LAUGH!
I THINK I'VE HAD IT WITH YOU...
I KNOW I'VE HAD IT WITH YOU...
9

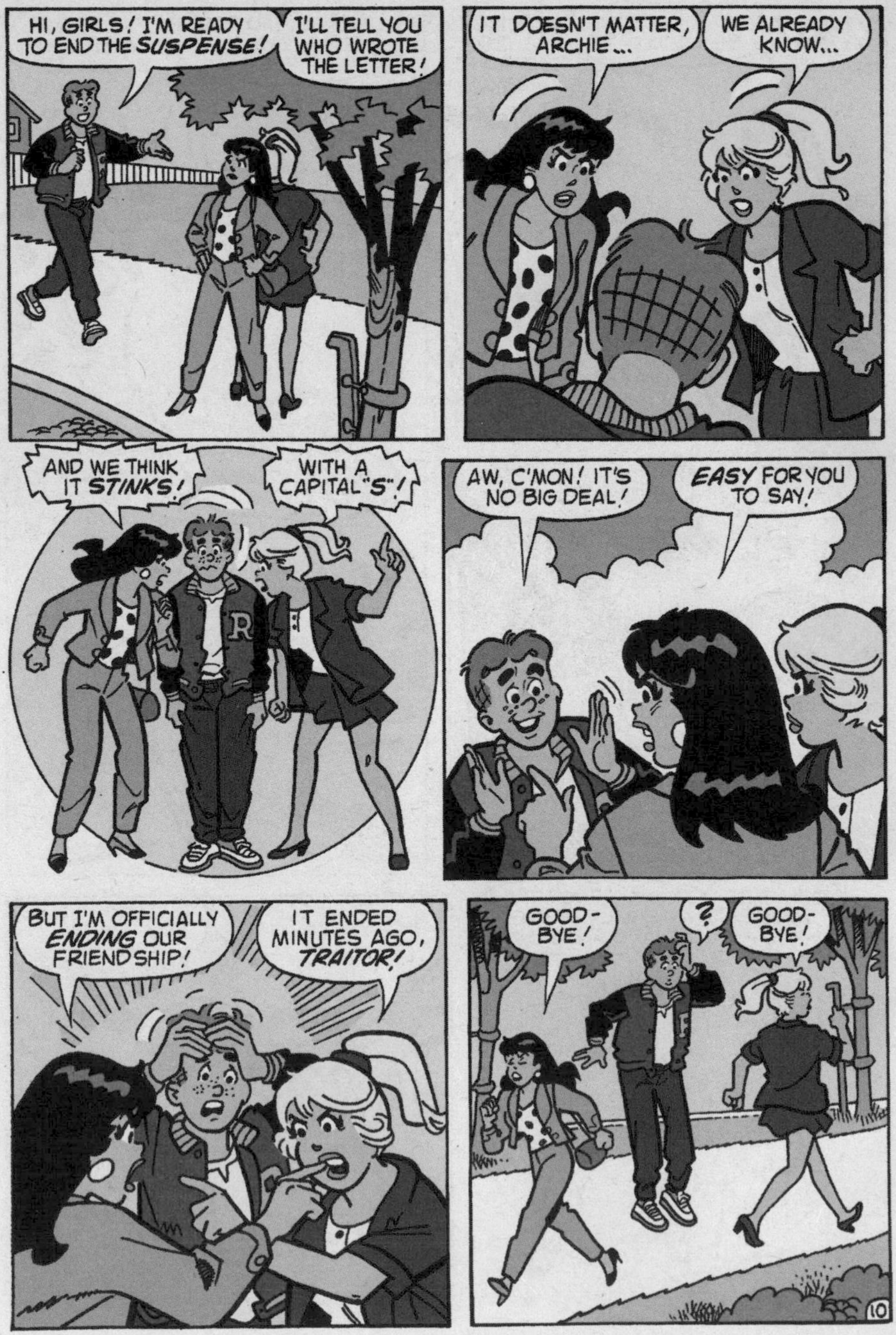
HI, GIRLS! I'M READY TO END THE SUSPENSE!
I'LL TELL YOU WHO WROTE THE LETTER!
IT DOESN'T MATTER, ARCHIE...
WE ALREADY KNOW...
AND WE THINK IT STINKS!
WITH A CAPITAL "S"!
AW, C'MON! IT'S NO BIG DEAL!
EASY FOR YOU TO SAY!
BUT I'M OFFICIALLY ENDING OUR FRIENDSHIP!
IT ENDED MINUTES AGO, TRAITOR!
GOOD-BYE!
?
GOOD-BYE!
10

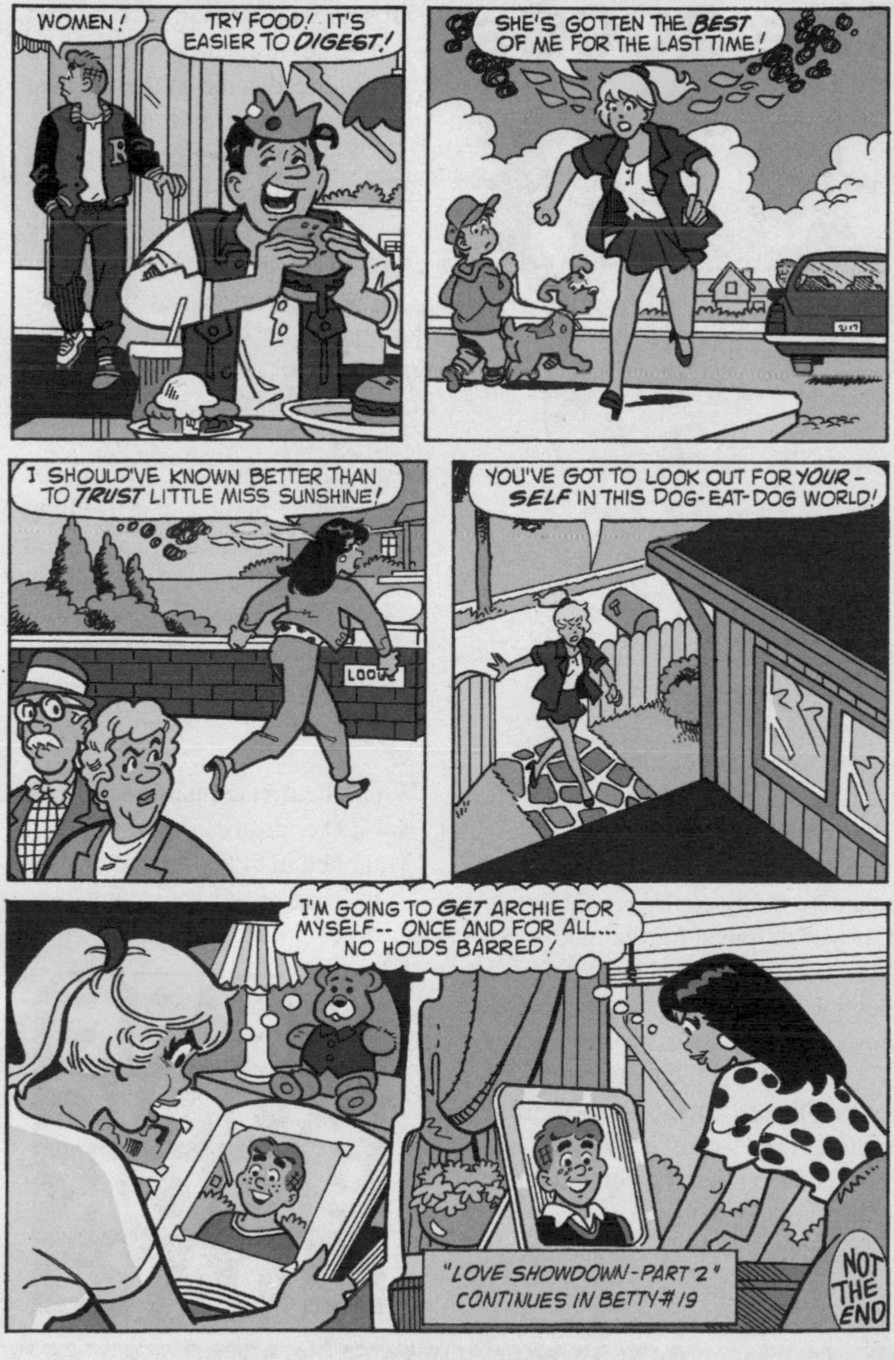
WOMEN!
TRY FOOD! IT'S EASIER TO DIGEST!
SHE'S GOTTEN THE BEST OF ME FOR THE LAST TIME!
I SHOULD'VE KNOWN BETTER THAN TO TRUST LITTLE MISS SUNSHINE!
YOU'VE GOT TO LOOK OUT FOR YOURSELF IN THIS DOG-EAT-DOG WORLD!
I'M GOING TO GET ARCHIE FOR MYSELF-- ONCE AND FOR ALL... NO HOLDS BARRED!
"LOVE SHOWDOWN-PART 2" CONTINUES IN BETTY #19
NOT THE END

The 2000s

It's no wonder then that the first decade of the new Millennium produced some of the greatest escapist entertainment ever. Computer-generated special effects advanced to the point that moviemakers could immerse viewers in fantasy worlds like never before. It was also the decade of dominance for computer-animated features with successful films from Pixar and other CGI-based studios.

Despite these changes, Archie was the primary publisher still selling most of its comics to a general audience through traditional mass-market retailers wherever magazines were sold in many different countries as well as in comic shops.

When historians look back upon the Millennium, they will note a decade filled with as much incident and change as the 1960s. The decade began on many controversial notes. The world braced for the unknown with the Y2K scare. The 2000 election of President George W. Bush over Clinton's Vice-President Al Gore led to a recount that lasted for months. In late 2001, the nation endured tragedy on its own soil as terrorists attacked the Pentagon and World Trade Center. The country then became involved in another long war with Iraq and faced further crises such as Hurricane Katrina.

When the first annual Free Comic Book Day promotional event was launched in 2002, Archie offered the first of several sought-after giveaway issues through the years.

New comic titles in this decade included *Archie's Weird Mysteries*, based on the animated series and launched in early 2000. The cartoon would go on to have a second wind in syndication a couple years after its initial run and grow more popular than ever. The other big entertainment news for Archie in the 2000s was the live-action *Josie & the Pussycats* movie.

Meanwhile, back in the comics, Archie's supporting cast continued to grow and become more diverse. Riverdale High welcomed such characters are Raj Patel, Kumi Tamura and Toño Diaz. Other notable arrivals included Adam Chisholm, a new boyfriend for Betty and rival for Archie; Nick St. Clair, a "bad boy" who appeared in the first of several highly publicized multi-part stories featuring the Archie gang rendered in a "realistic" art style dubbed the "New Look," and the real-life singing group The Veronicas.

Many major events happened in the world of Archie Comics toward the end of the decade.

Sabrina got a "manga makeover" and Katy Keene the fashion queen was revived. In an early attempt at a magazine format, the *Betty & Veronica Spectacular* comic added articles and other text features to each issue. In special digest editions, classic golden age issues like *Archie* and *Jughead* #1 were reprinted, framed by tales where the current Archie characters met their golden age counterparts.

The decade ended with the start of the "Archie Marries..." saga in October, 2009. Written by Michael Uslan, this multi-part storyline presented a glimpse into two possible futures for Archie.

In real life, the last few years of the decade were also poignant ones, as the Archie company was saddened by the loss of its two CEOs, Richard Goldwater and Michael Silberkleit.

Stepping into their shoes were founder John L. Goldwater's son Jon Goldwater and Michael's wife Nancy Silberkleit.

I Squid You Not
Sabrina #8, 2000
by Mike Gallagher
and Dave Manak

There's no need to *carp* over Sabrina the Teenage Witch. Fans have had a *whale* of a time *fishing* for more of her adventures!

That's exactly why it was no *fluke* that Mike Gallagher and Dave Manak were chosen to *tackle* Sabrina's animated adventures. As the new cartoon brought a younger Sabrina into the new Millennium, this dynamic duo came out of their *shells* to take this new approach and crank out story after spellbinding story!

So stop *trawling* around for the rest and read the best!

--Jon Gray
Illustrator,
Sonic the Hedgehog

Fall for It Classic!
Archie's Weird Mysteries #19, 2001
by Paul Castiglia
and Fernando Ruiz

Archie's Weird Mysteries was always a fun series for me just because I got to draw so many different and weird things. I especially loved it when I got to draw sci-fi stuff like robots and aliens. I had a lot of freedom in designing that kind of stuff. For example, the head of the robot announcer in this story is based on a blow dryer!

--Fernando Ruiz
Writer and illustrator,
Archie Comics

SALEM™ in "I SQUID YOU NOT"

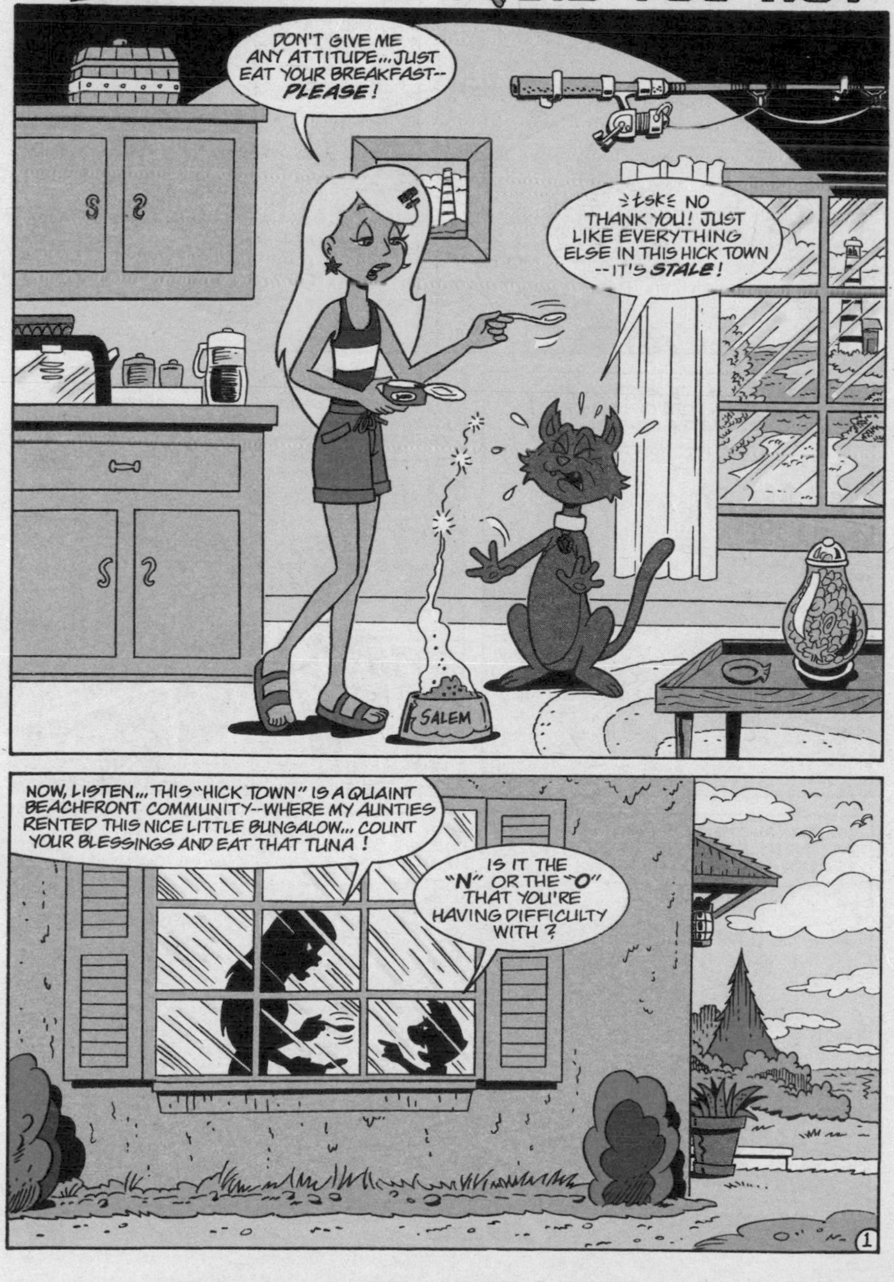
DON'T GIVE ME ANY ATTITUDE... JUST EAT YOUR BREAKFAST-- PLEASE!
TSK NO THANK YOU! JUST LIKE EVERYTHING ELSE IN THIS HICK TOWN --IT'S STALE!
SALEM
NOW, LISTEN... THIS "HICK TOWN" IS A QUAINT BEACHFRONT COMMUNITY--WHERE MY AUNTIES RENTED THIS NICE LITTLE BUNGALOW... COUNT YOUR BLESSINGS AND EAT THAT TUNA!
IS IT THE "N" OR THE "O" THAT YOU'RE HAVING DIFFICULTY WITH?
1

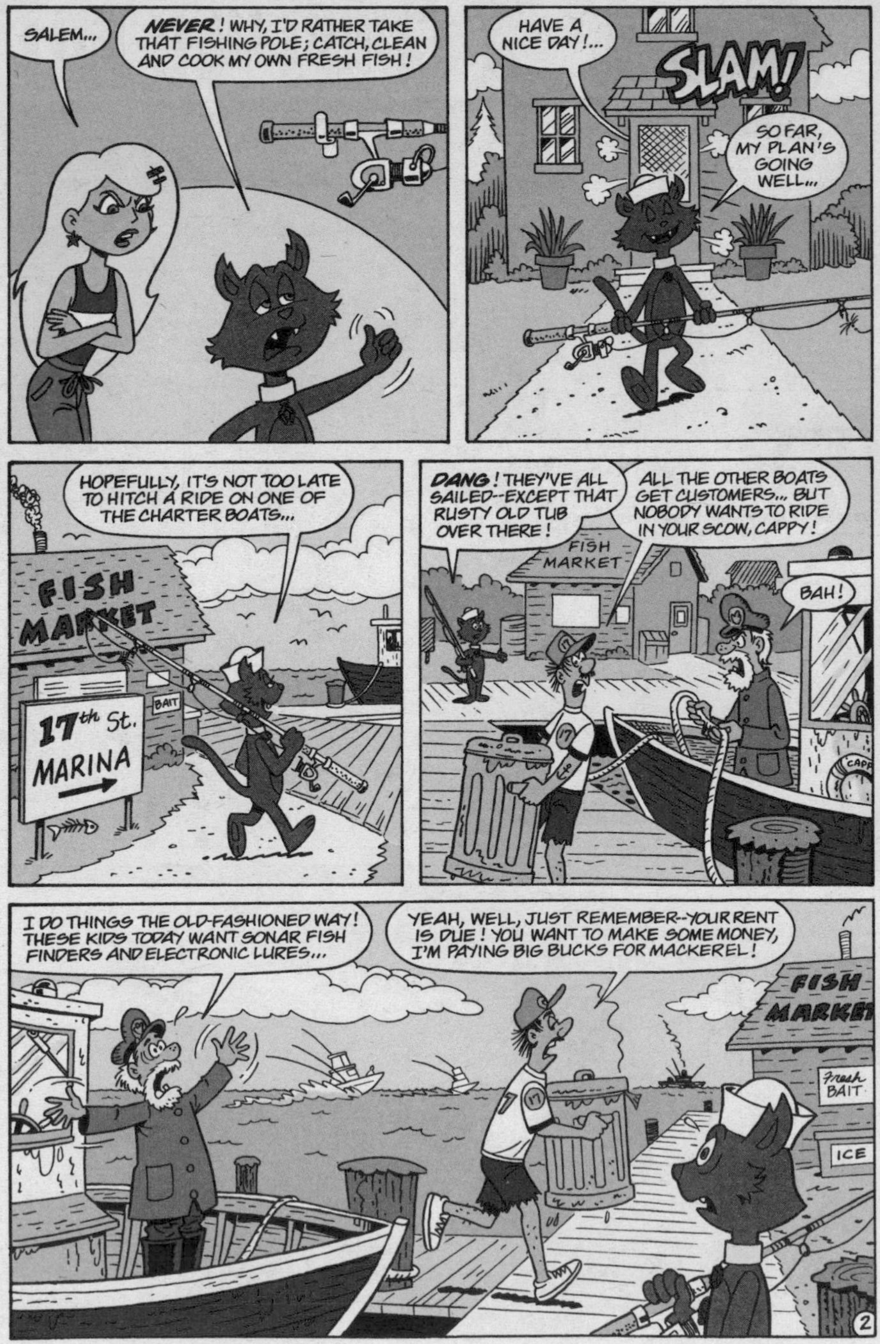
SALEM...
NEVER! WHY, I'D RATHER TAKE THAT FISHING POLE; CATCH, CLEAN AND COOK MY OWN FRESH FISH!
HAVE A NICE DAY!...
SLAM!
SO FAR, MY PLAN'S GOING WELL...
HOPEFULLY, IT'S NOT TOO LATE TO HITCH A RIDE ON ONE OF THE CHARTER BOATS...
FISH MARKET
BAIT
17th St. MARINA
DANG! THEY'VE ALL SAILED--EXCEPT THAT RUSTY OLD TUB OVER THERE!
ALL THE OTHER BOATS GET CUSTOMERS... BUT NOBODY WANTS TO RIDE IN YOUR SCOW, CAPPY!
FISH MARKET
BAH!
I DO THINGS THE OLD-FASHIONED WAY! THESE KIDS TODAY WANT SONAR FISH FINDERS AND ELECTRONIC LURES...
YEAH, WELL, JUST REMEMBER--YOUR RENT IS DUE! YOU WANT TO MAKE SOME MONEY, I'M PAYING BIG BUCKS FOR MACKEREL!
FISH MARKET
Fresh BAIT
ICE
2

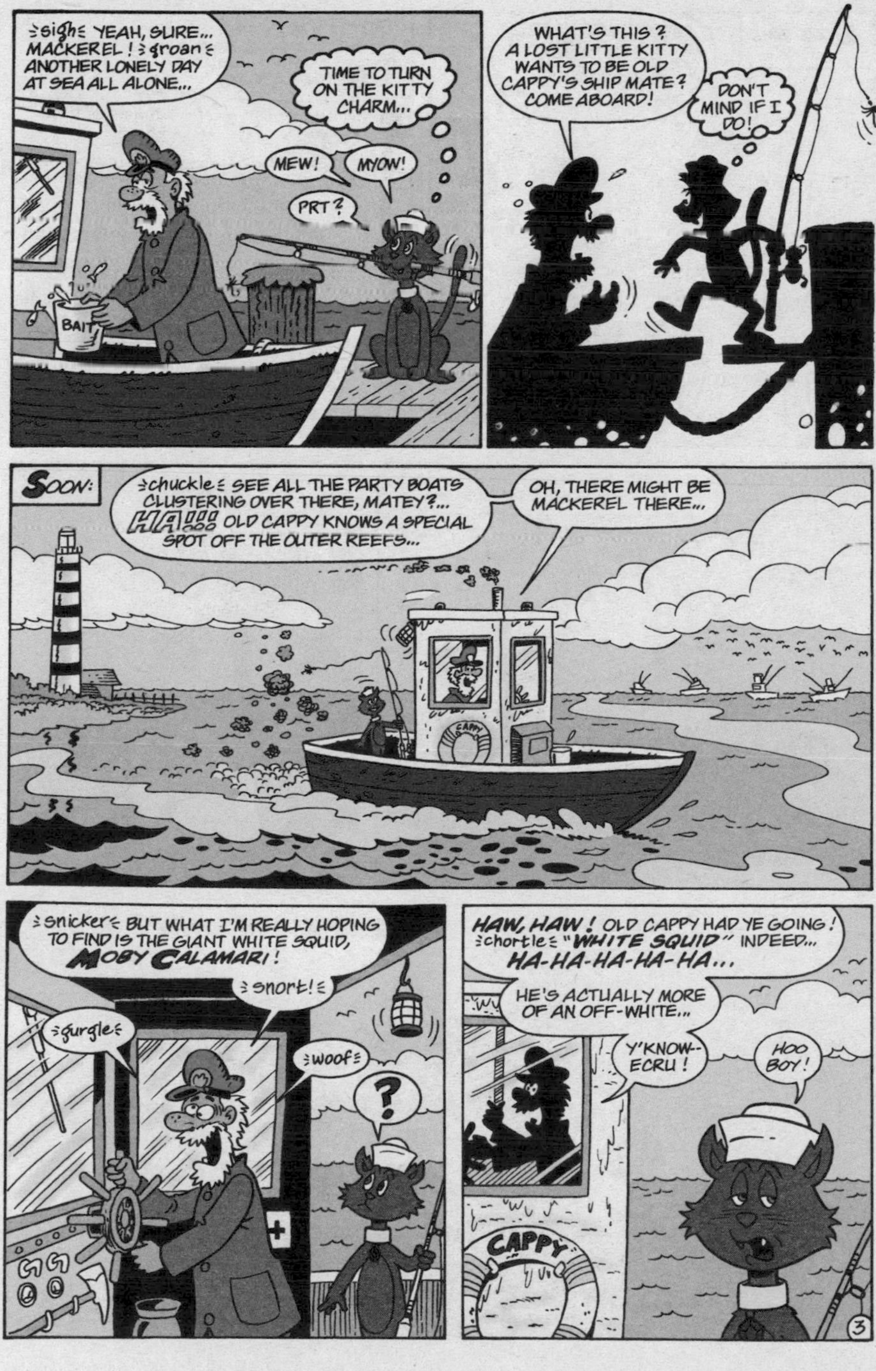
sigh YEAH, SURE... MACKEREL! groan ANOTHER LONELY DAY AT SEA ALL ALONE...
TIME TO TURN ON THE KITTY CHARM...
MEW!
MYOW!
PRT?
BAIT
WHAT'S THIS? A LOST LITTLE KITTY WANTS TO BE OLD CAPPY'S SHIP MATE? COME ABOARD!
DON'T MIND IF I DO!
SOON:
chuckle SEE ALL THE PARTY BOATS CLUSTERING OVER THERE, MATEY?... HA!!! OLD CAPPY KNOWS A SPECIAL SPOT OFF THE OUTER REEFS...
OH, THERE MIGHT BE MACKEREL THERE...
snicker BUT WHAT I'M REALLY HOPING TO FIND IS THE GIANT WHITE SQUID, MOBY CALAMARI!
snort!
gurgle
woof
?
HAW, HAW! OLD CAPPY HAD YE GOING! chortle "WHITE SQUID" INDEED... HA-HA-HA-HA-HA...
HE'S ACTUALLY MORE OF AN OFF-WHITE...
Y'KNOW--ECRU!
HOO BOY!
CAPPY
3

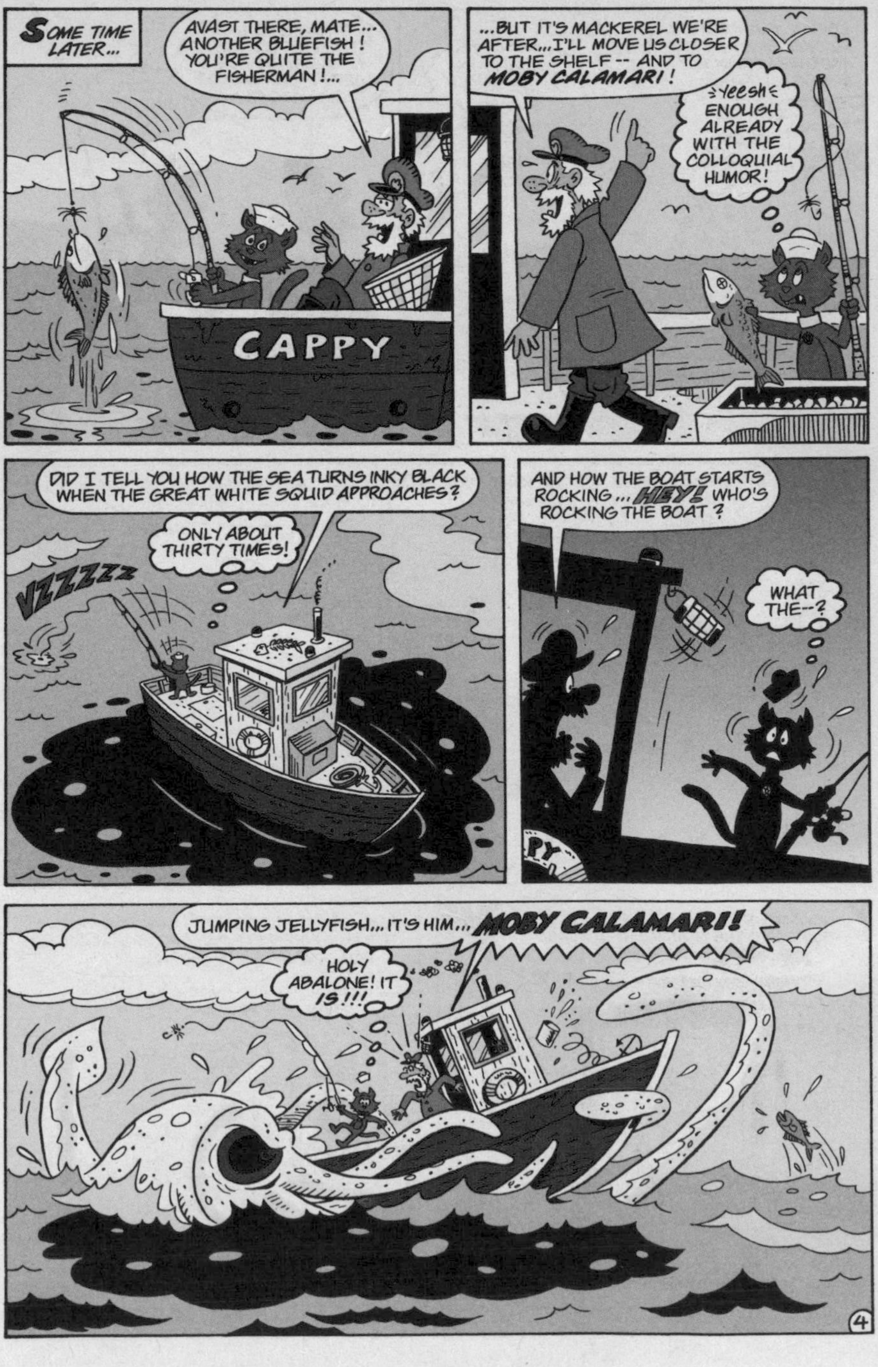
SOME TIME LATER...
AVAST THERE, MATE... ANOTHER BLUEFISH! YOU'RE QUITE THE FISHERMAN!...
CAPPY
...BUT IT'S MACKEREL WE'RE AFTER... I'LL MOVE US CLOSER TO THE SHELF -- AND TO MOBY CALAMARI!
Yeesh ENOUGH ALREADY WITH THE COLLOQUIAL HUMOR!
DID I TELL YOU HOW THE SEA TURNS INKY BLACK WHEN THE GREAT WHITE SQUID APPROACHES?
ONLY ABOUT THIRTY TIMES!
VZZZZZ
AND HOW THE BOAT STARTS ROCKING... HEY! WHO'S ROCKING THE BOAT?
WHAT THE--?
JUMPING JELLYFISH... IT'S HIM... MOBY CALAMARI!
HOLY ABALONE! IT IS!!!
4

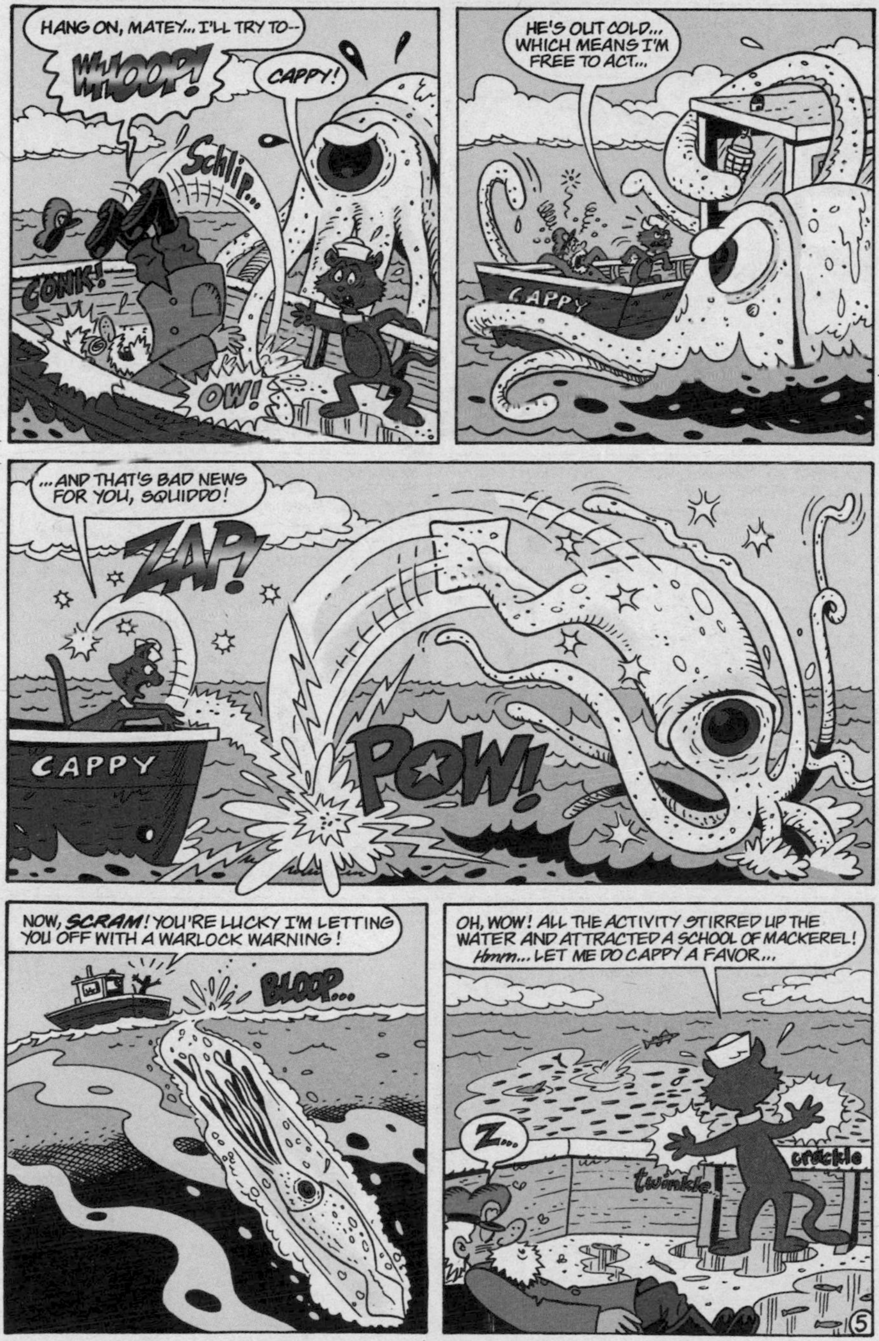
HANG ON, MATEY... I'LL TRY TO--
WHOOP!
CAPPY!
Schlip...
CONK!
OW!
HE'S OUT COLD... WHICH MEANS I'M FREE TO ACT...
CAPPY
...AND THAT'S BAD NEWS FOR YOU, SQUIDDO!
ZAP!
CAPPY
POW!
NOW, SCRAM! YOU'RE LUCKY I'M LETTING YOU OFF WITH A WARLOCK WARNING!
BLOOP...
OH, WOW! ALL THE ACTIVITY STIRRED UP THE WATER AND ATTRACTED A SCHOOL OF MACKEREL! Hmm... LET ME DO CAPPY A FAVOR...
Z...
crackle
twinkle
5

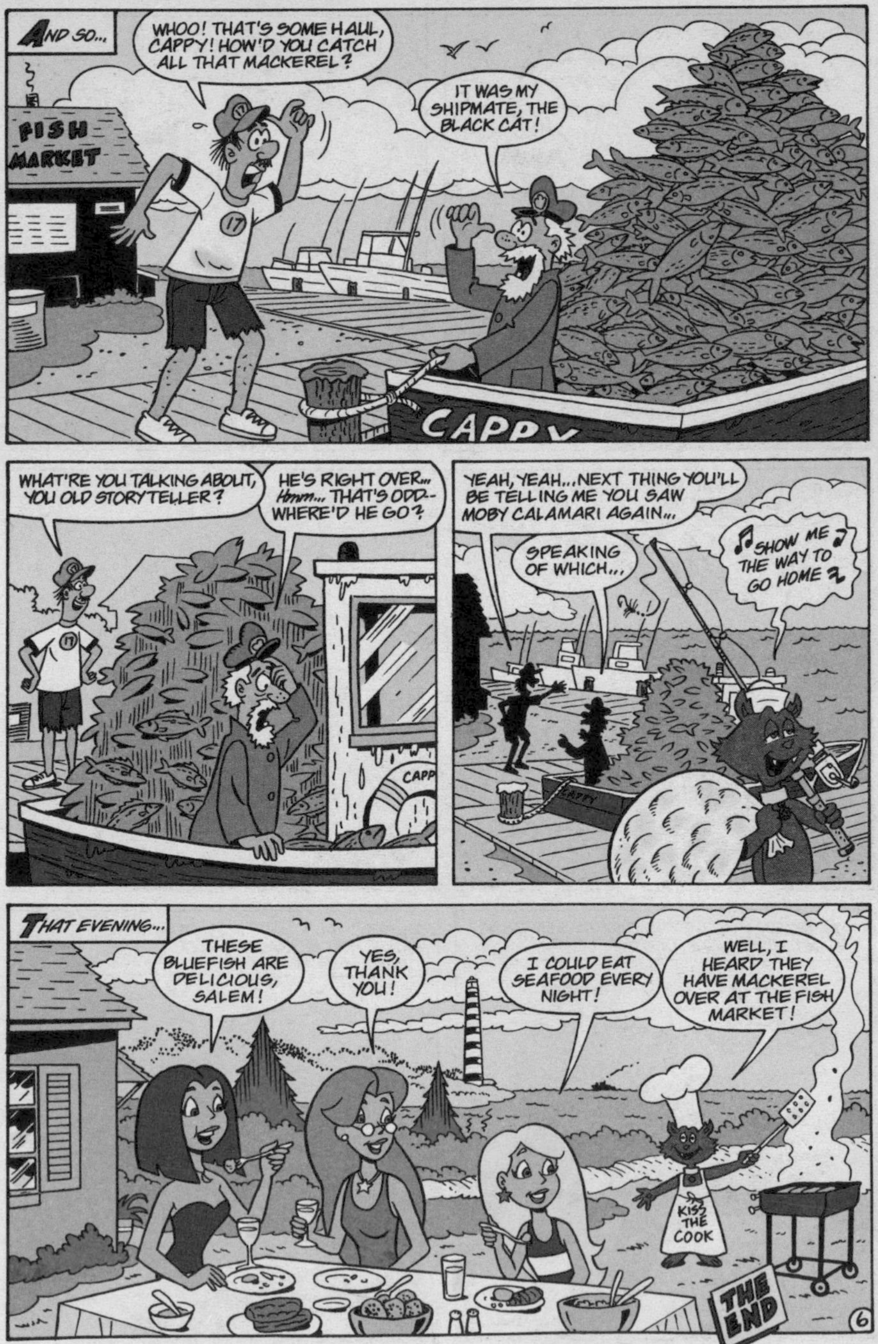
AND SO...
WHOO! THAT'S SOME HAUL, CAPPY! HOW'D YOU CATCH ALL THAT MACKEREL?
IT WAS MY SHIPMATE, THE BLACK CAT!
FISH MARKET
CAPPY
WHAT'RE YOU TALKING ABOUT, YOU OLD STORYTELLER?
HE'S RIGHT OVER... Hmm... THAT'S ODD-- WHERE'D HE GO?
CAPP
YEAH, YEAH... NEXT THING YOU'LL BE TELLING ME YOU SAW MOBY CALAMARI AGAIN...
SPEAKING OF WHICH...
SHOW ME THE WAY TO GO HOME
CAPPY
THAT EVENING...
THESE BLUEFISH ARE DELICIOUS, SALEM!
YES, THANK YOU!
I COULD EAT SEAFOOD EVERY NIGHT!
WELL, I HEARD THEY HAVE MACKEREL OVER AT THE FISH MARKET!
KISS THE COOK
THE END
6

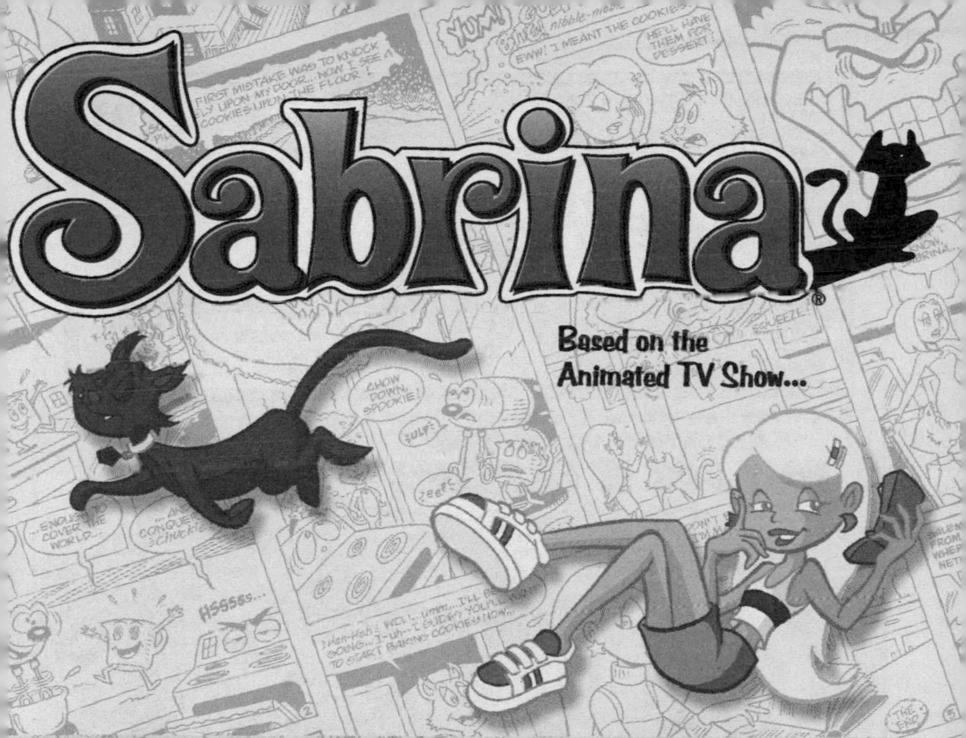
Sabrina®
Based on the Animated TV Show...

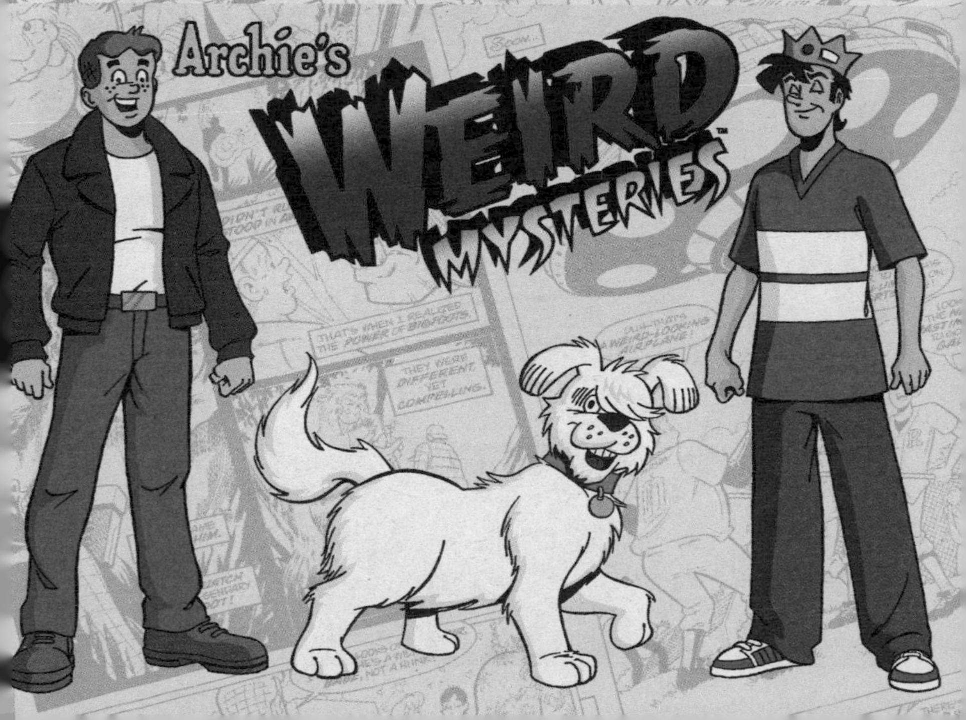
Archie's
WEIRD™
MYSTERIES

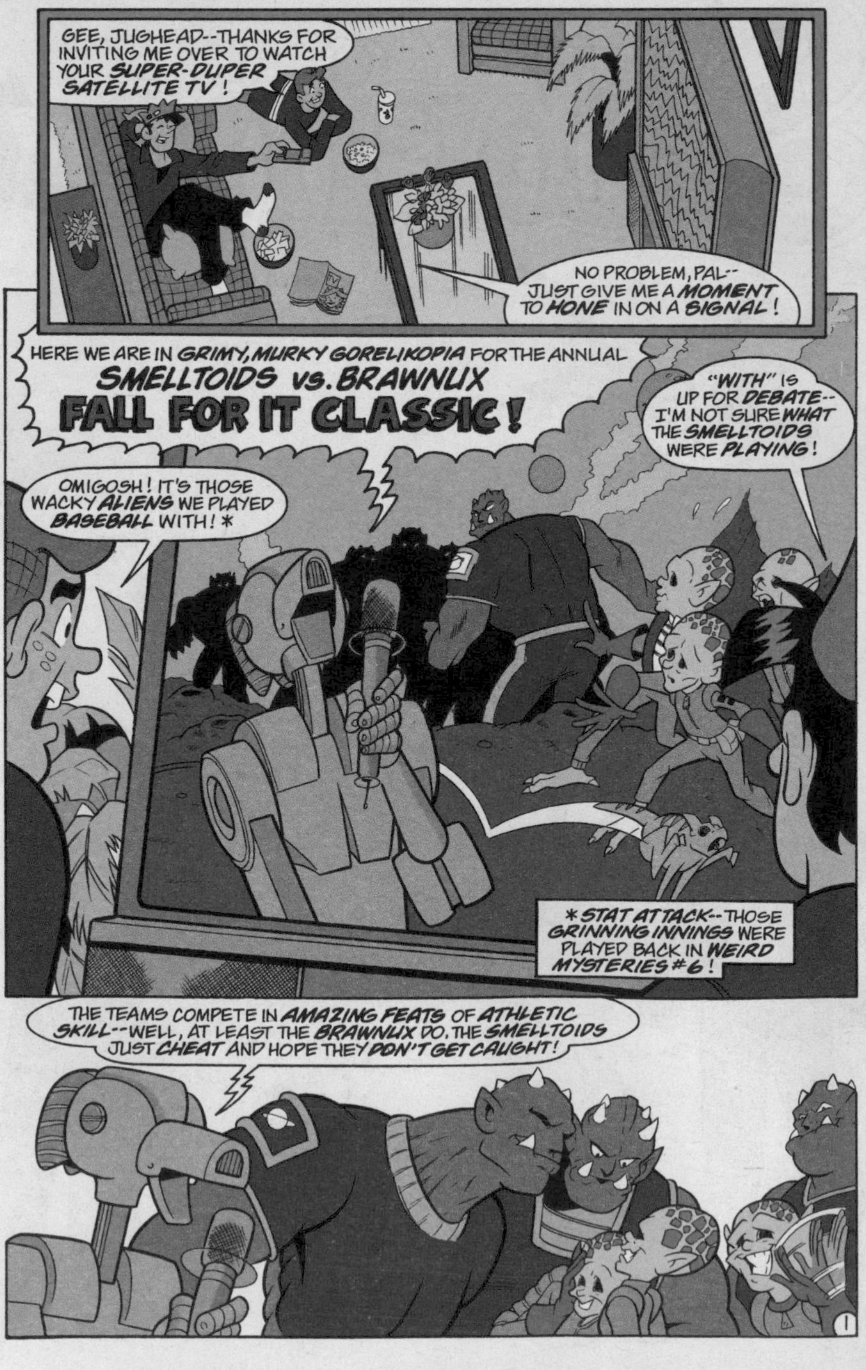
GEE, JUGHEAD--THANKS FOR INVITING ME OVER TO WATCH YOUR SUPER-DUPER SATELLITE TV!
NO PROBLEM, PAL-- JUST GIVE ME A MOMENT TO HONE IN ON A SIGNAL!
HERE WE ARE IN GRIMY, MURKY GORELIKOPIA FOR THE ANNUAL SMELLTOIDS vs. BRAWNUX FALL FOR IT CLASSIC!
"WITH" IS UP FOR DEBATE-- I'M NOT SURE WHAT THE SMELLTOIDS WERE PLAYING!
OMIGOSH! IT'S THOSE WACKY ALIENS WE PLAYED BASEBALL WITH! *
* STAT ATTACK--THOSE GRINNING INNINGS WERE PLAYED BACK IN WEIRD MYSTERIES #6!
THE TEAMS COMPETE IN AMAZING FEATS OF ATHLETIC SKILL--WELL, AT LEAST THE BRAWNUX DO. THE SMELLTOIDS JUST CHEAT AND HOPE THEY DON'T GET CAUGHT!
1

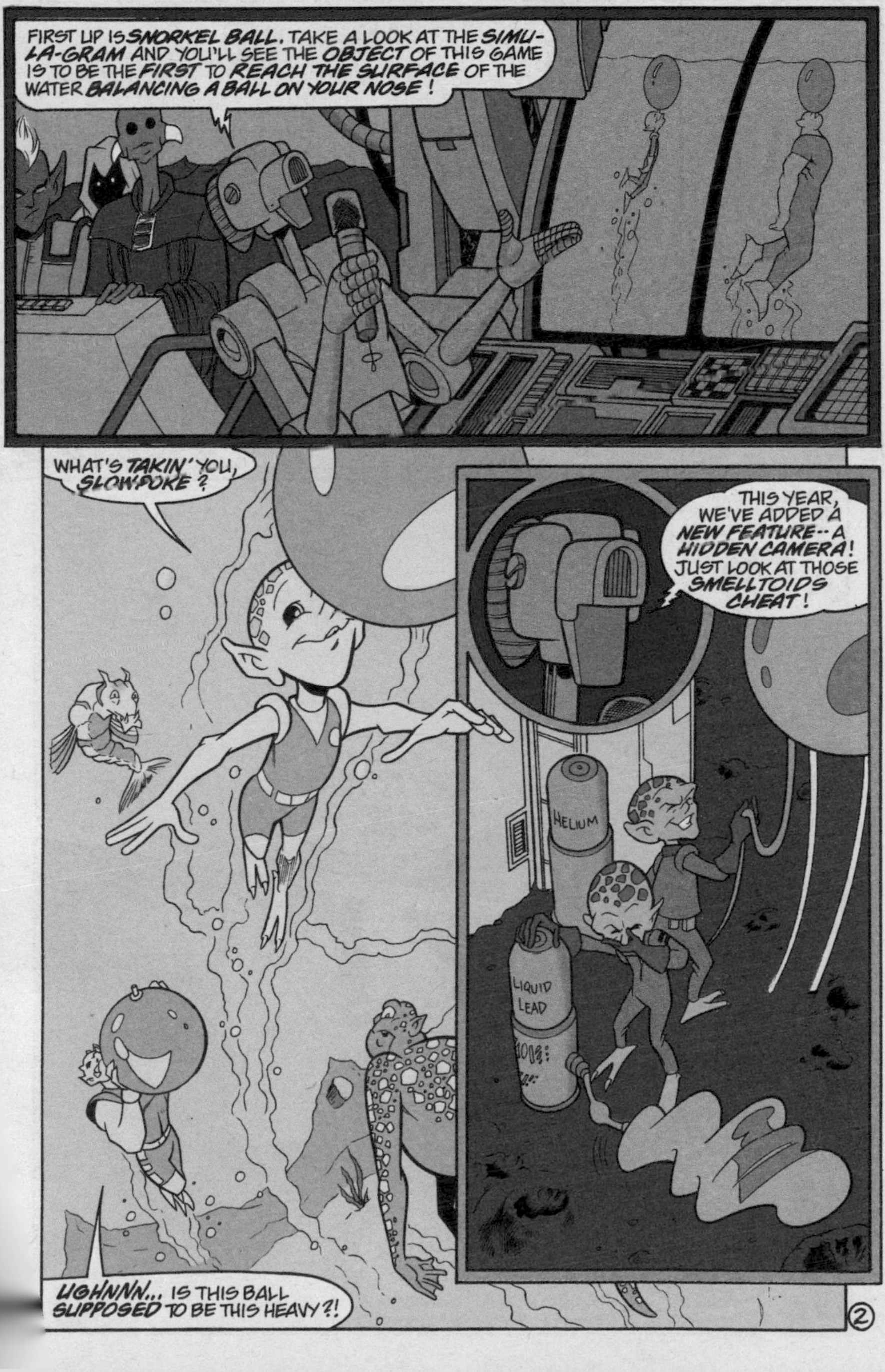
FIRST UP IS SNORKEL BALL. TAKE A LOOK AT THE SIMU-LA-GRAM AND YOU'LL SEE THE OBJECT OF THIS GAME IS TO BE THE FIRST TO REACH THE SURFACE OF THE WATER BALANCING A BALL ON YOUR NOSE!
WHAT'S TAKIN' YOU, SLOWPOKE?
THIS YEAR, WE'VE ADDED A NEW FEATURE-- A HIDDEN CAMERA! JUST LOOK AT THOSE SMELLTOIDS CHEAT!
HELIUM
LIQUID LEAD
UGHNNN... IS THIS BALL SUPPOSED TO BE THIS HEAVY?!
2

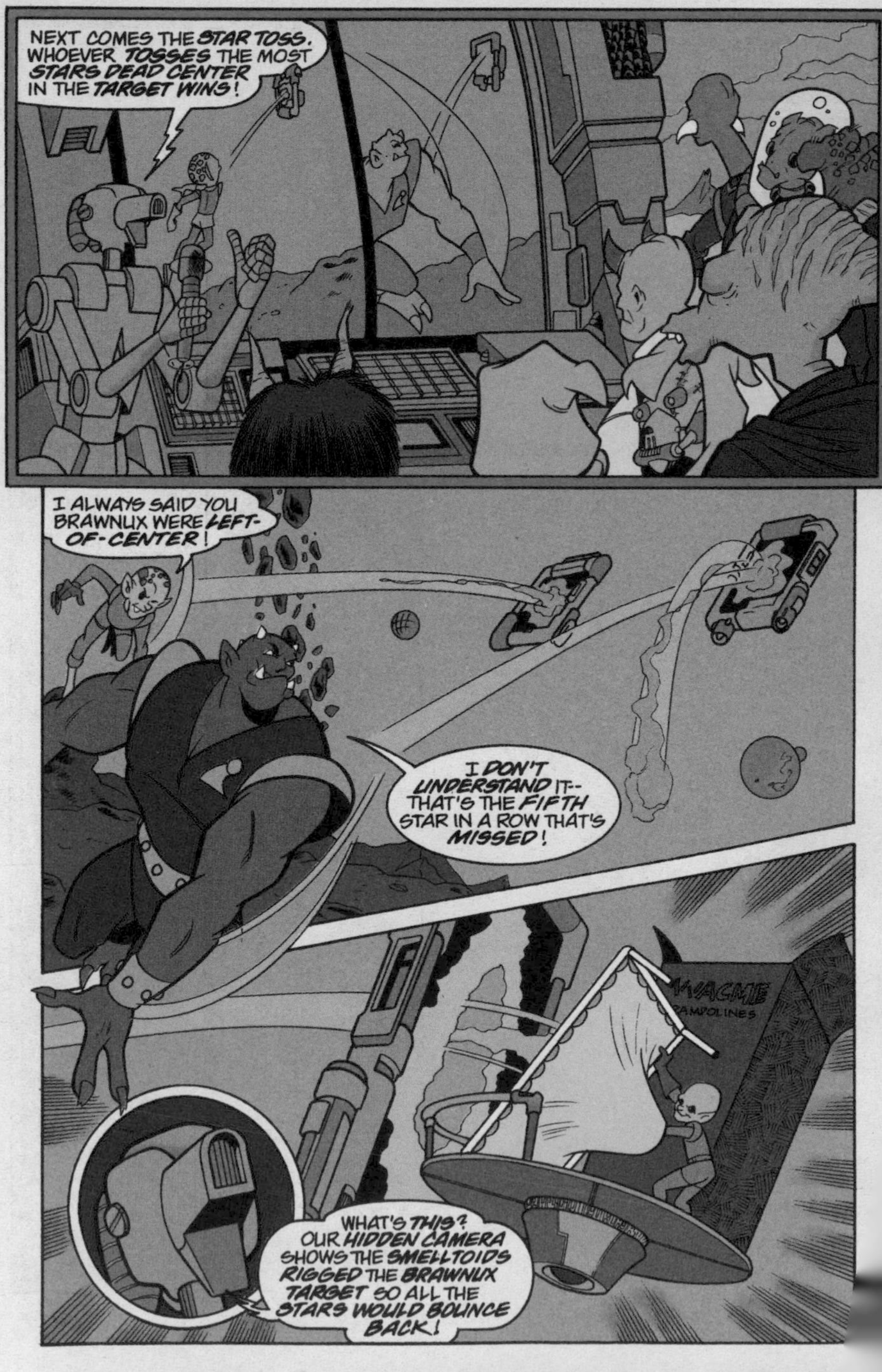
NEXT COMES THE STAR TOSS. WHOEVER TOSSES THE MOST STARS DEAD CENTER IN THE TARGET WINS!
I ALWAYS SAID YOU BRAWNUX WERE LEFT-OF-CENTER!
I DON'T UNDERSTAND IT--THAT'S THE FIFTH STAR IN A ROW THAT'S MISSED!
ACME
WHAT'S THIS? OUR HIDDEN CAMERA SHOWS THE SMELLTOIDS RIGGED THE BRAWNUX TARGET SO ALL THE STARS WOULD BOUNCE BACK!

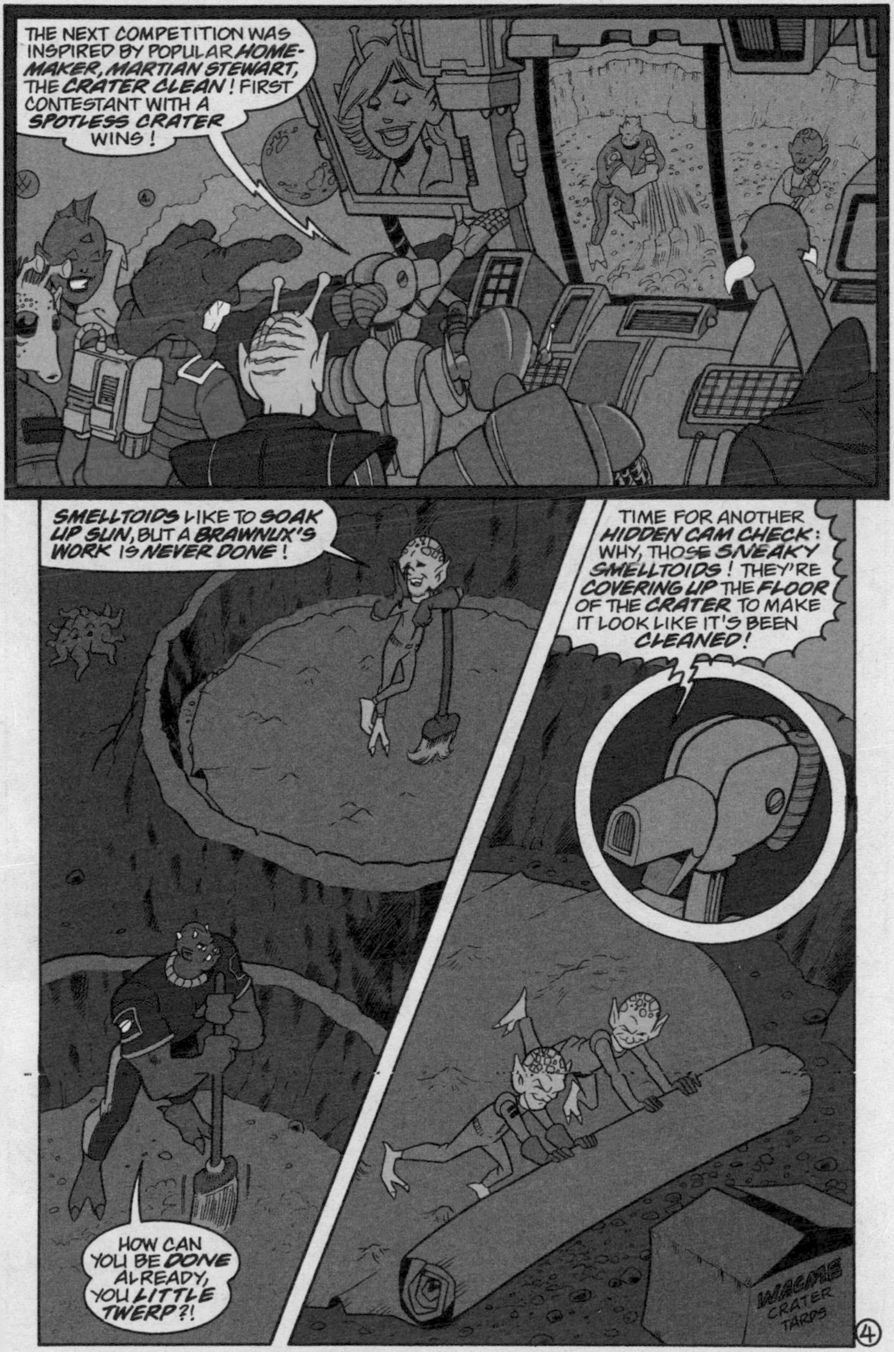
THE NEXT COMPETITION WAS INSPIRED BY POPULAR HOME-MAKER, MARTIAN STEWART, THE CRATER CLEAN! FIRST CONTESTANT WITH A SPOTLESS CRATER WINS!
SMELLTOIDS LIKE TO SOAK UP SUN, BUT A BRAWNUX'S WORK IS NEVER DONE!
HOW CAN YOU BE DONE ALREADY, YOU LITTLE TWERP?!
TIME FOR ANOTHER HIDDEN CAM CHECK: WHY, THOSE SNEAKY SMELLTOIDS! THEY'RE COVERING UP THE FLOOR OF THE CRATER TO MAKE IT LOOK LIKE IT'S BEEN CLEANED!
CRATER TARPS
4

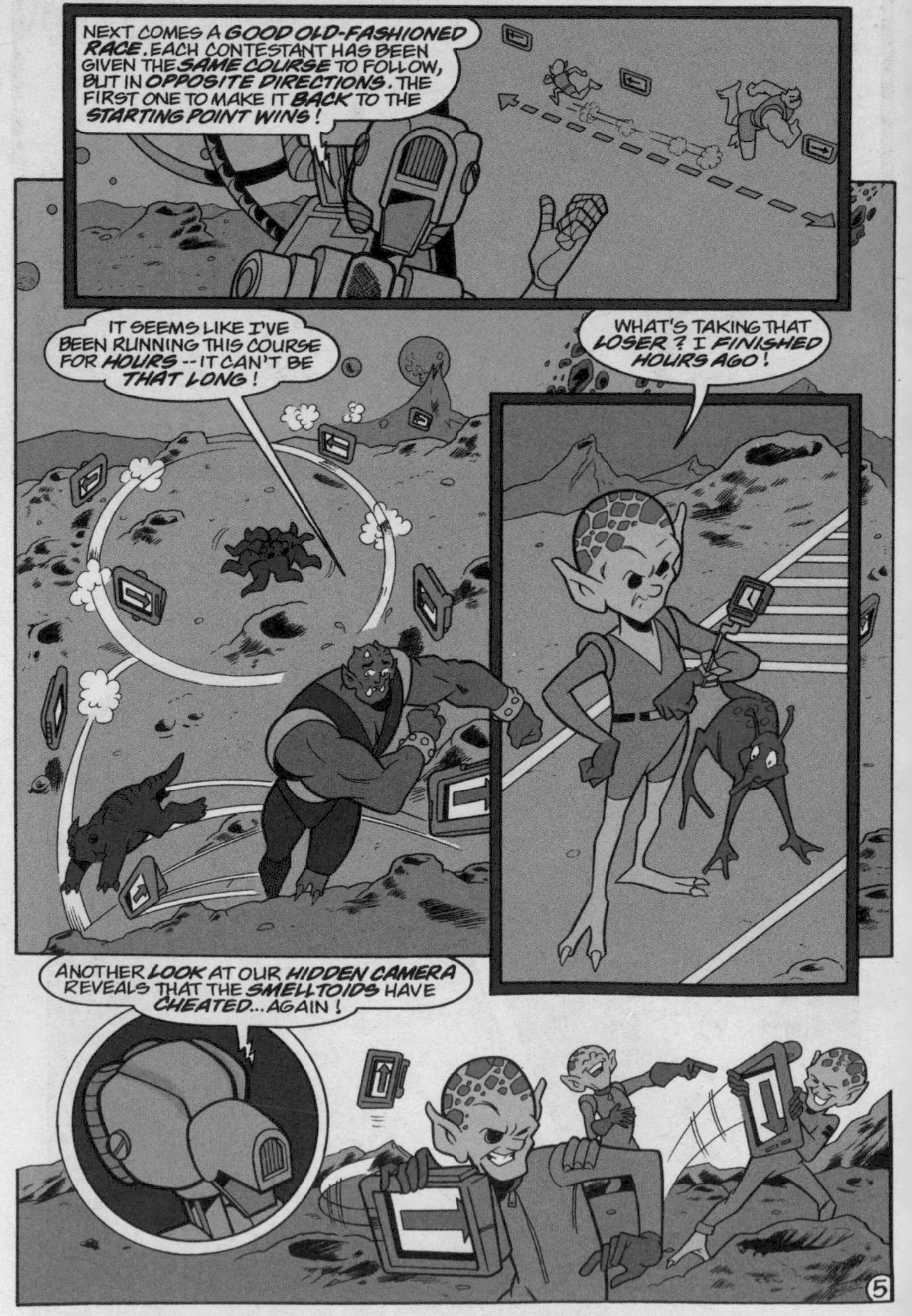
NEXT COMES A GOOD OLD-FASHIONED RACE. EACH CONTESTANT HAS BEEN GIVEN THE SAME COURSE TO FOLLOW, BUT IN OPPOSITE DIRECTIONS. THE FIRST ONE TO MAKE IT BACK TO THE STARTING POINT WINS!
IT SEEMS LIKE I'VE BEEN RUNNING THIS COURSE FOR HOURS -- IT CAN'T BE THAT LONG!
WHAT'S TAKING THAT LOSER? I FINISHED HOURS AGO!
ANOTHER LOOK AT OUR HIDDEN CAMERA REVEALS THAT THE SMELLTOIDS HAVE CHEATED... AGAIN!
5

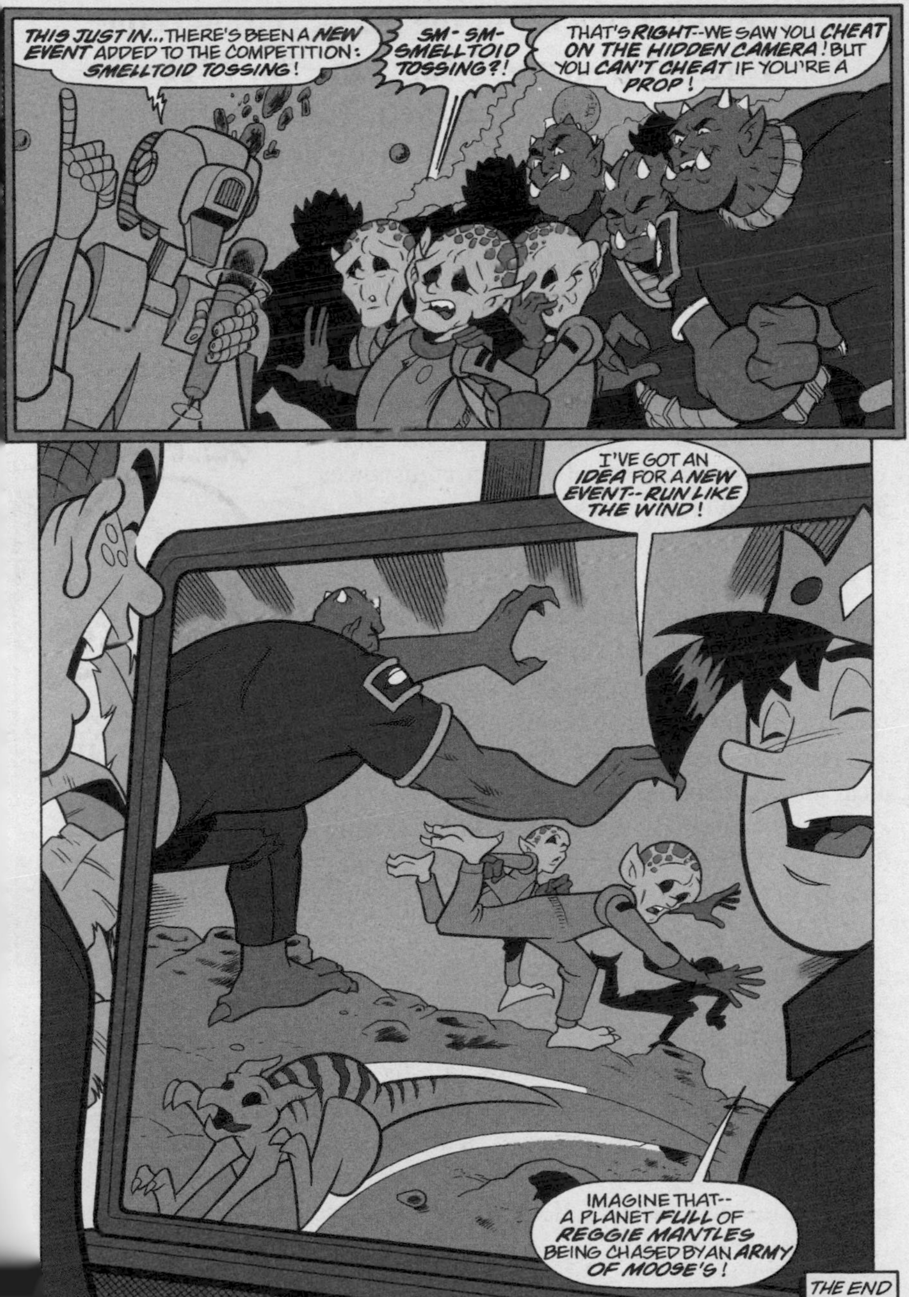
THIS JUST IN... THERE'S BEEN A NEW EVENT ADDED TO THE COMPETITION: SMELLTOID TOSSING!
SM-SM-SMELLTOID TOSSING?!
THAT'S RIGHT--WE SAW YOU CHEAT ON THE HIDDEN CAMERA! BUT YOU CAN'T CHEAT IF YOU'RE A PROP!
I'VE GOT AN IDEA FOR A NEW EVENT--RUN LIKE THE WIND!
IMAGINE THAT-- A PLANET FULL OF REGGIE MANTLES BEING CHASED BY AN ARMY OF MOOSE'S!
THE END

Chat Fight, Frenemy of the State, Dating Game
Life With Archie Magazine #6, 2011
by J. Torres, Rick Burchett, Terry Austin, John Workman and Jason Jensen

Almost two years ago, I was pouring coffee in the Archie Comics kitchen when Co-CEO Jon Goldwater stuck his head in through the door and asked me how much time it would take me to put together a formal pitch centered around the idea of a teen Jinx. About a year later, Jon would show me a beautiful, formally framed picture of Jinx that Joe Edwards had drawn and dedicated to him when he was a child. I've been lucky enough to work on this project in the best of circumstances: under a boss who loves what he does.

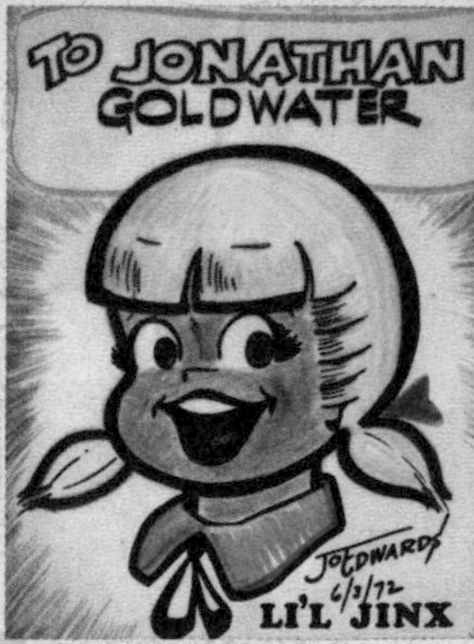
TO JONATHAN GOLDWATER
LI'L JINX

I knew from the start that I wanted to create a teenage world that would be different from that of Riverdale. Betty and Veronica have perfection covered, but what about all the girls in the world who aren't millionaire heiresses, and can't cook a seven course meal in between overhauling a car and maintaining ideal grades? How many high school girls do you know who can go for years without looking anything less than flawless? Well, there was the one in my school … but I swear I'm not jealous of her anymore.

So I designed Jinx to have a personality that a teenager could relate to: a flawed one. The great thing about this is that I didn't have to shove the characters into roles that didn't make sense in order for this to work. Jinx's impulsive, keep-up-with-the-boys attitude, her father Hap's inability to understand her, Charley's cruelty, Gigi's background as a child star, Mort's insecurity… it all adapted neatly to an age where the emotion is dialed up to 11. The Jinx comic, thanks to the efforts of the entire creative team, does what I envisioned: it's entertaining, realistic and comforting.

--Suzannah Rowntree
Features Editor, Life with Archie Magazine

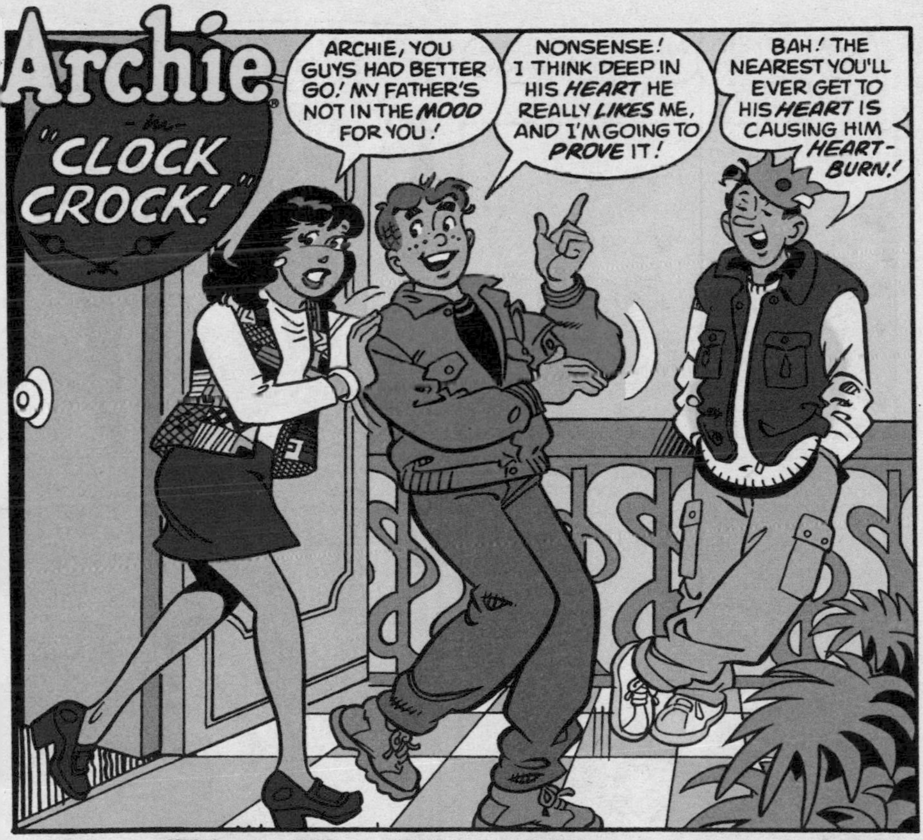
Archie
in
"CLOCK CROCK!"
ARCHIE, YOU GUYS HAD BETTER GO! MY FATHER'S NOT IN THE MOOD FOR YOU!
NONSENSE! I THINK DEEP IN HIS HEART HE REALLY LIKES ME, AND I'M GOING TO PROVE IT!
BAH! THE NEAREST YOU'LL EVER GET TO HIS HEART IS CAUSING HIM HEART-BURN!

SCRIPT: BILL GOLLIHER | PENCILS: STAN GOLDBERG | INKING: BOB SMITH | LETTERING: BILL YOSHIDA | COLORING: BARRY GROSSMAN | EDITOR: VICTOR GORELICK | EDITOR-IN-CHIEF: RICHARD GOLDWATER

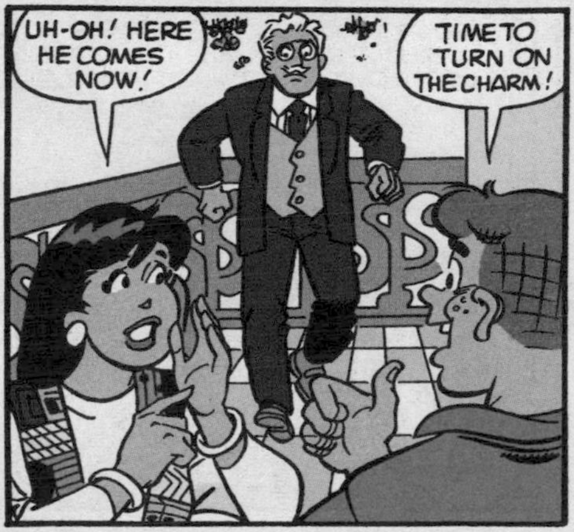
UH-OH! HERE HE COMES NOW!
TIME TO TURN ON THE CHARM!

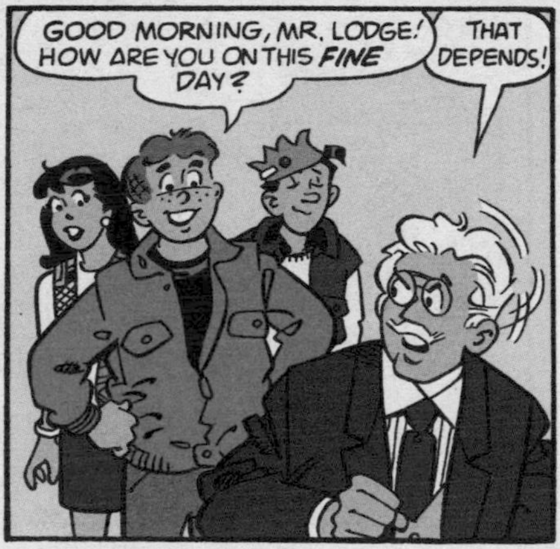
GOOD MORNING, MR. LODGE! HOW ARE YOU ON THIS FINE DAY?
THAT DEPENDS!

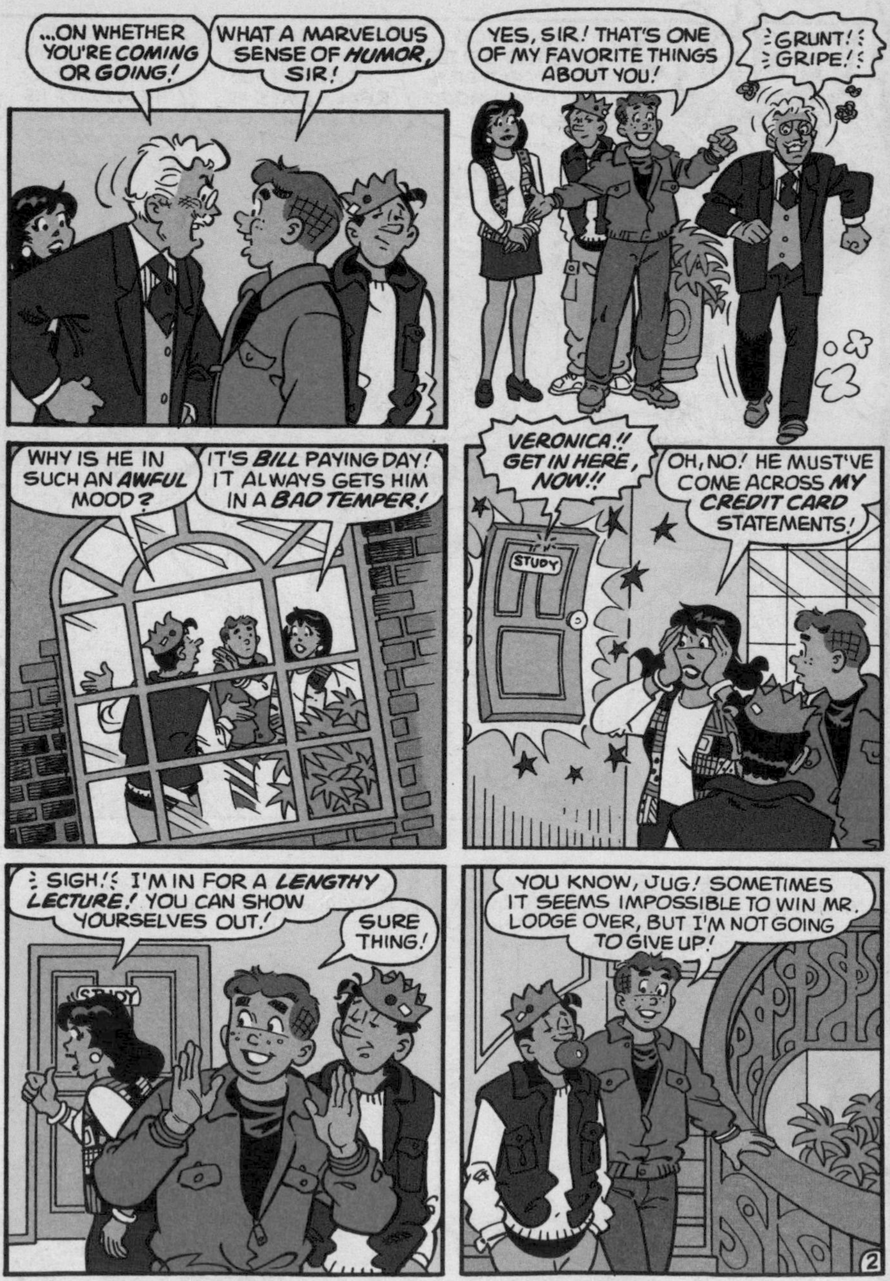
...ON WHETHER YOU'RE COMING OR GOING!
WHAT A MARVELOUS SENSE OF HUMOR, SIR!
YES, SIR! THAT'S ONE OF MY FAVORITE THINGS ABOUT YOU!
GRUNT! GRIPE!
WHY IS HE IN SUCH AN AWFUL MOOD?
IT'S BILL PAYING DAY! IT ALWAYS GETS HIM IN A BAD TEMPER!
VERONICA!! GET IN HERE, NOW!!
STUDY
OH, NO! HE MUST'VE COME ACROSS MY CREDIT CARD STATEMENTS!
SIGH! I'M IN FOR A LENGTHY LECTURE! YOU CAN SHOW YOURSELVES OUT!
SURE THING!
STUDY
YOU KNOW, JUG! SOMETIMES IT SEEMS IMPOSSIBLE TO WIN MR. LODGE OVER, BUT I'M NOT GOING TO GIVE UP!
2

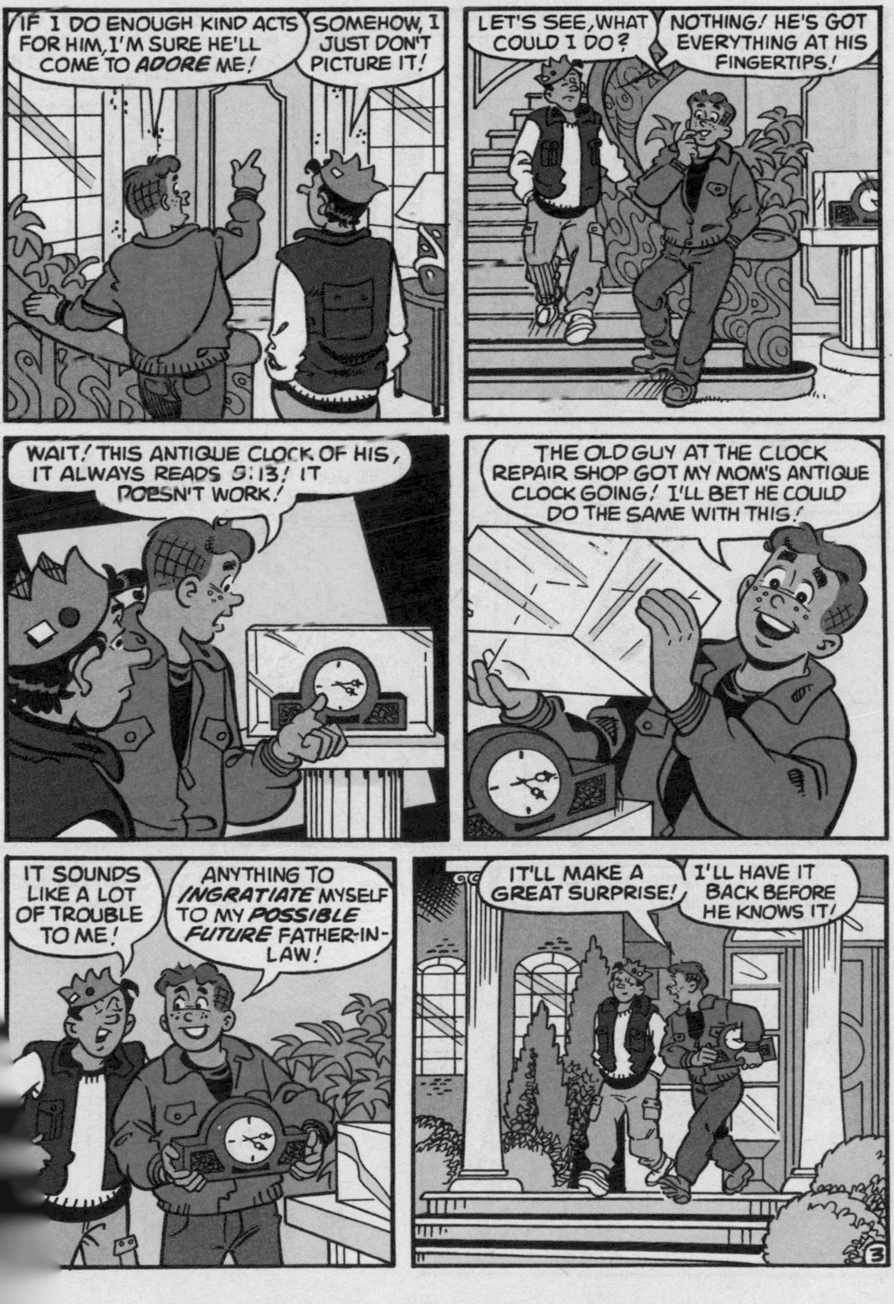
IF I DO ENOUGH KIND ACTS FOR HIM, I'M SURE HE'LL COME TO ADORE ME!
SOMEHOW, I JUST DON'T PICTURE IT!
LET'S SEE, WHAT COULD I DO?
NOTHING! HE'S GOT EVERYTHING AT HIS FINGERTIPS!
WAIT! THIS ANTIQUE CLOCK OF HIS, IT ALWAYS READS 3:13! IT DOESN'T WORK!
THE OLD GUY AT THE CLOCK REPAIR SHOP GOT MY MOM'S ANTIQUE CLOCK GOING! I'LL BET HE COULD DO THE SAME WITH THIS!
IT SOUNDS LIKE A LOT OF TROUBLE TO ME!
ANYTHING TO INGRATIATE MYSELF TO MY POSSIBLE FUTURE FATHER-IN-LAW!
IT'LL MAKE A GREAT SURPRISE!
I'LL HAVE IT BACK BEFORE HE KNOWS IT!
3

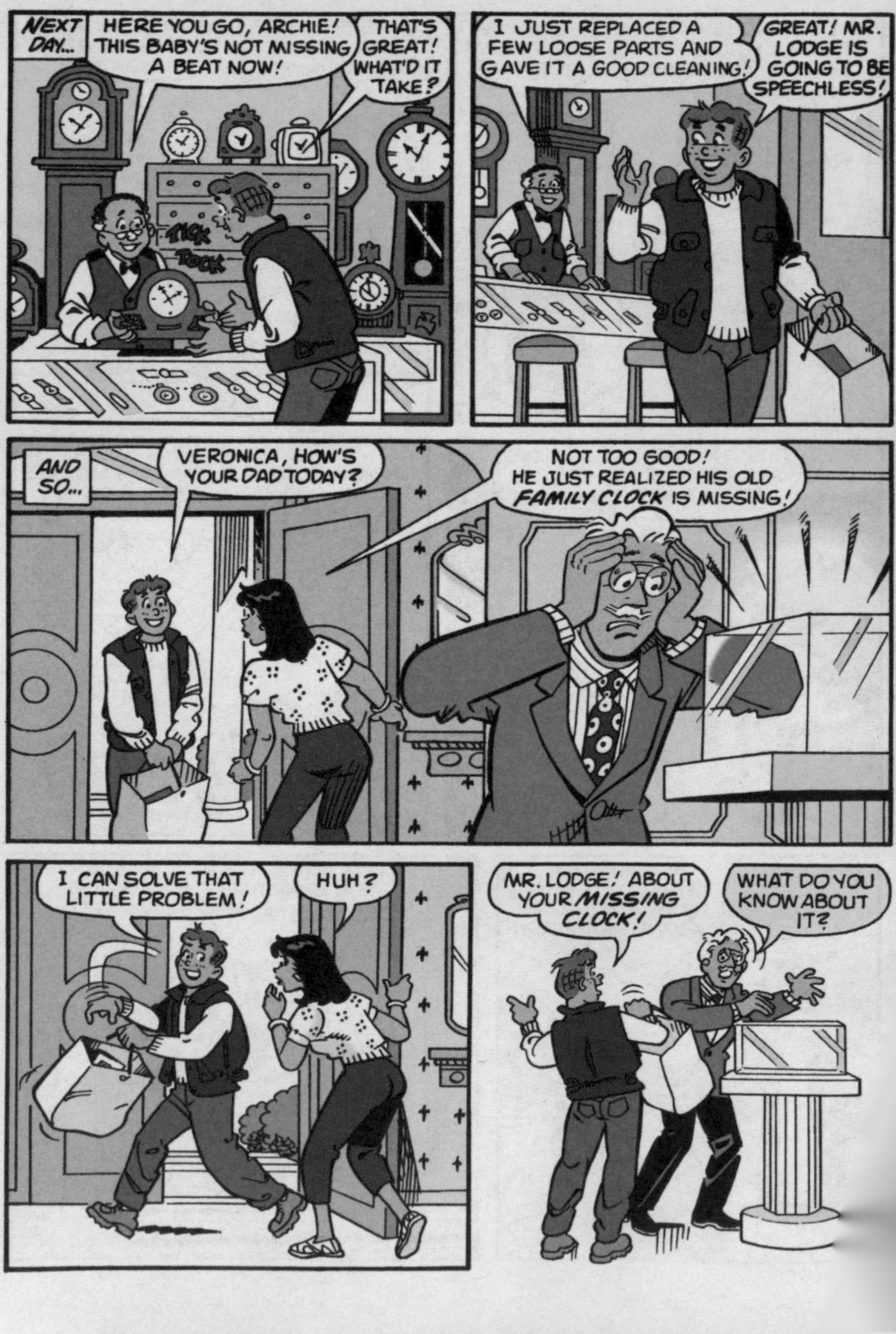
NEXT DAY...
HERE YOU GO, ARCHIE! THIS BABY'S NOT MISSING A BEAT NOW!
THAT'S GREAT! WHAT'D IT TAKE?
TICK
TOCK
I JUST REPLACED A FEW LOOSE PARTS AND GAVE IT A GOOD CLEANING!
GREAT! MR. LODGE IS GOING TO BE SPEECHLESS!
AND SO...
VERONICA, HOW'S YOUR DAD TODAY?
NOT TOO GOOD! HE JUST REALIZED HIS OLD FAMILY CLOCK IS MISSING!
I CAN SOLVE THAT LITTLE PROBLEM!
HUH?
MR. LODGE! ABOUT YOUR MISSING CLOCK!
WHAT DO YOU KNOW ABOUT IT?

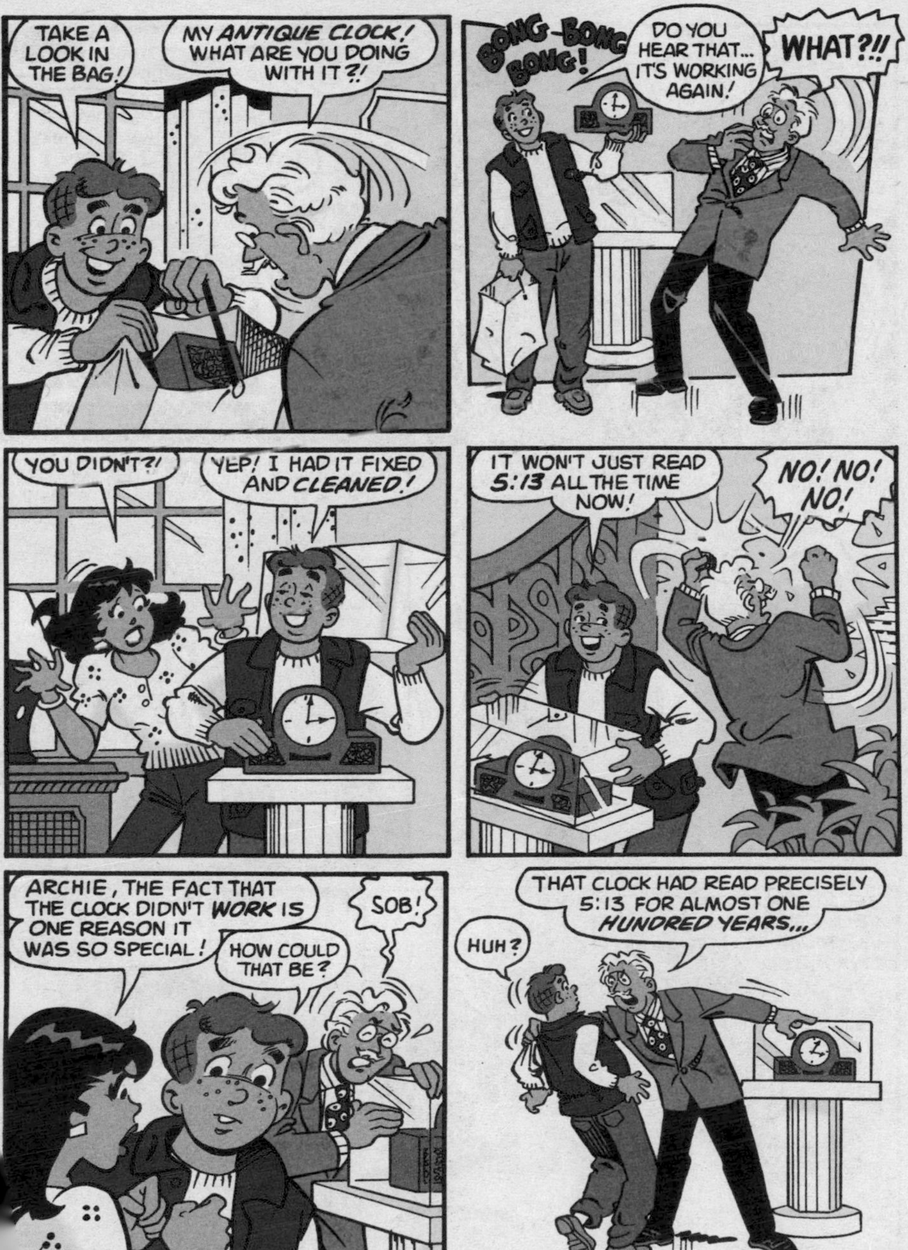
TAKE A LOOK IN THE BAG!
MY ANTIQUE CLOCK! WHAT ARE YOU DOING WITH IT?!
BONG-BONG BONG!
DO YOU HEAR THAT... IT'S WORKING AGAIN!
WHAT?!!
YOU DIDN'T?!
YEP! I HAD IT FIXED AND CLEANED!
IT WON'T JUST READ 5:13 ALL THE TIME NOW!
NO! NO! NO!
ARCHIE, THE FACT THAT THE CLOCK DIDN'T WORK IS ONE REASON IT WAS SO SPECIAL!
SOB!
HOW COULD THAT BE?
THAT CLOCK HAD READ PRECISELY 5:13 FOR ALMOST ONE HUNDRED YEARS...
HUH?
5

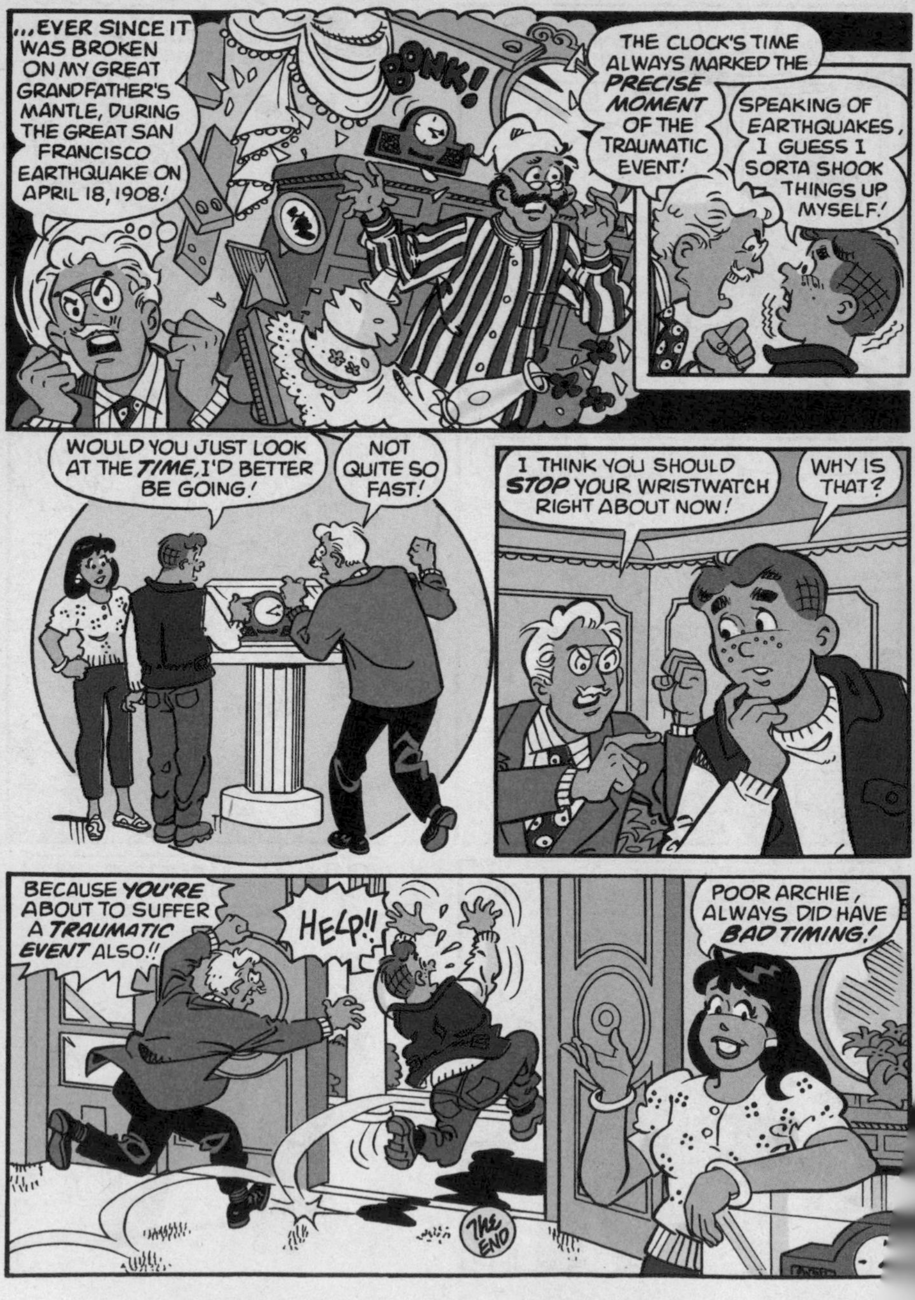
...EVER SINCE IT WAS BROKEN ON MY GREAT GRANDFATHER'S MANTLE, DURING THE GREAT SAN FRANCISCO EARTHQUAKE ON APRIL 18, 1908!
BONK!
THE CLOCK'S TIME ALWAYS MARKED THE PRECISE MOMENT OF THE TRAUMATIC EVENT!
SPEAKING OF EARTHQUAKES, I GUESS I SORTA SHOOK THINGS UP MYSELF!
WOULD YOU JUST LOOK AT THE TIME, I'D BETTER BE GOING!
NOT QUITE SO FAST!
I THINK YOU SHOULD STOP YOUR WRISTWATCH RIGHT ABOUT NOW!
WHY IS THAT?
BECAUSE YOU'RE ABOUT TO SUFFER A TRAUMATIC EVENT ALSO!!
HELP!!
POOR ARCHIE, ALWAYS DID HAVE BAD TIMING!
THE END

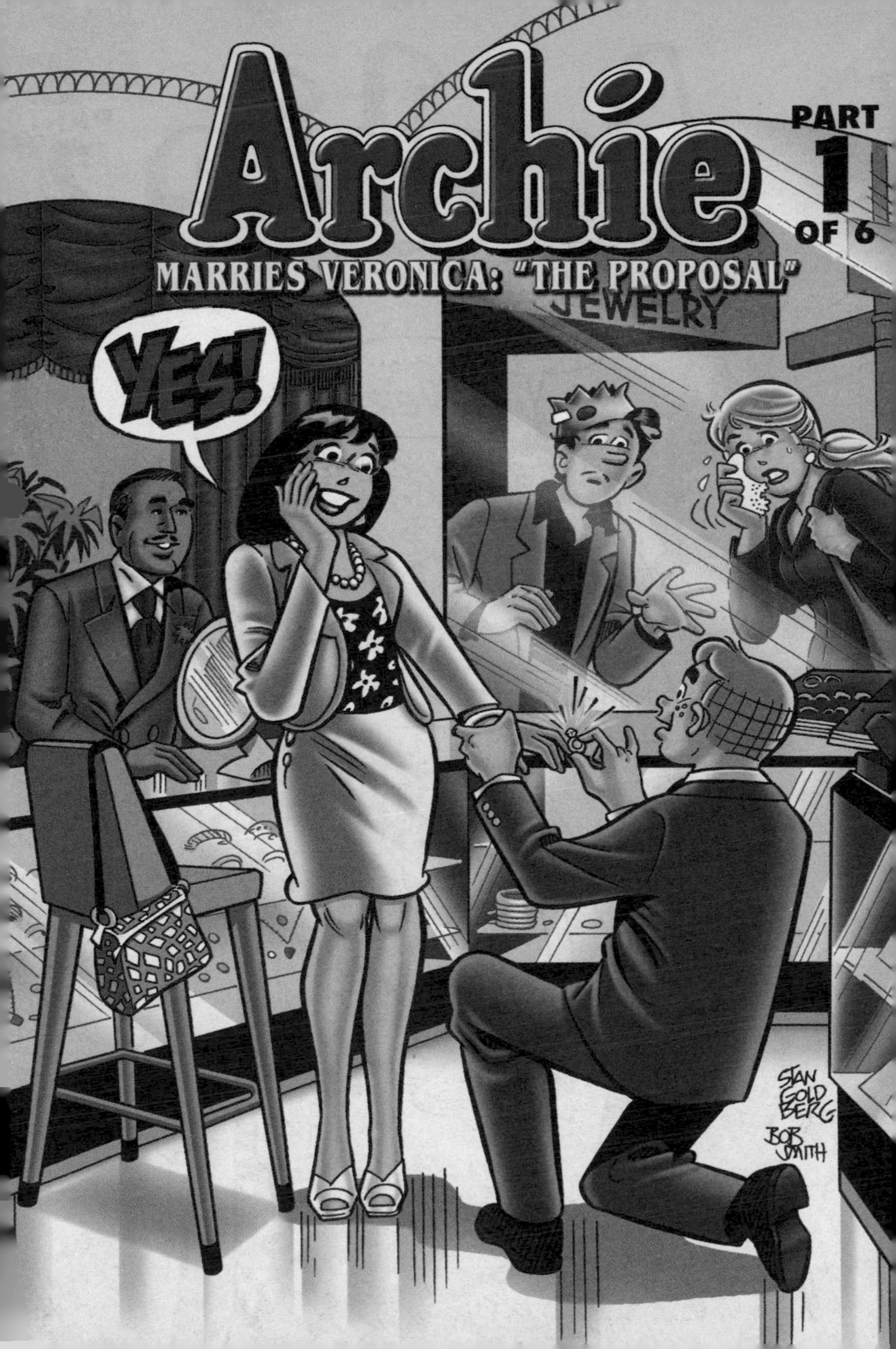
Archie
PART 1 OF 6
MARRIES VERONICA: "THE PROPOSAL"
JEWELRY
YES!
STAN GOLDBERG
BOB SMITH

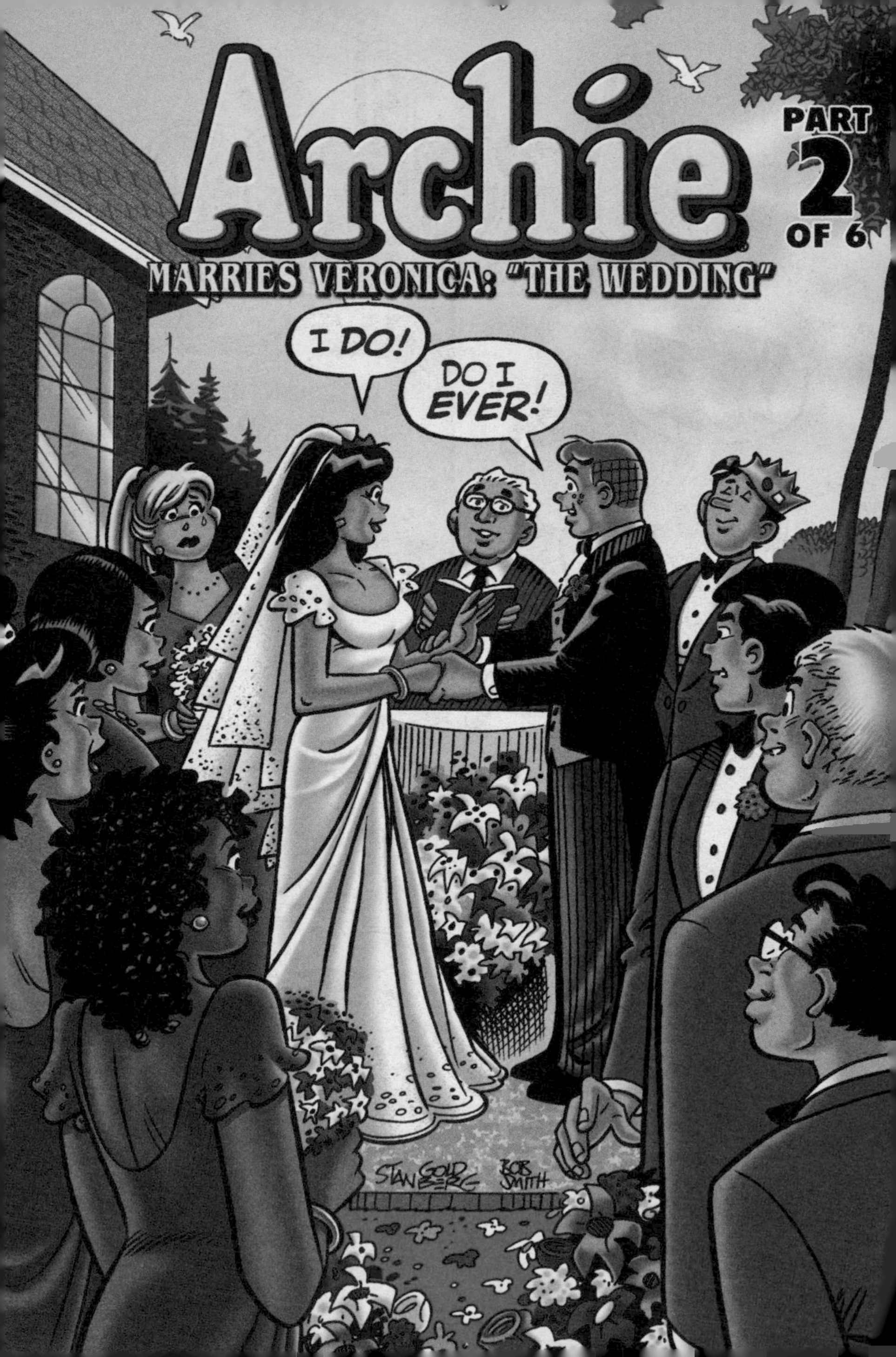
Archie
PART 2 OF 6
MARRIES VERONICA: "THE WEDDING"
I DO!
DO I EVER!
STAN GOLDBERG
BOB SMITH

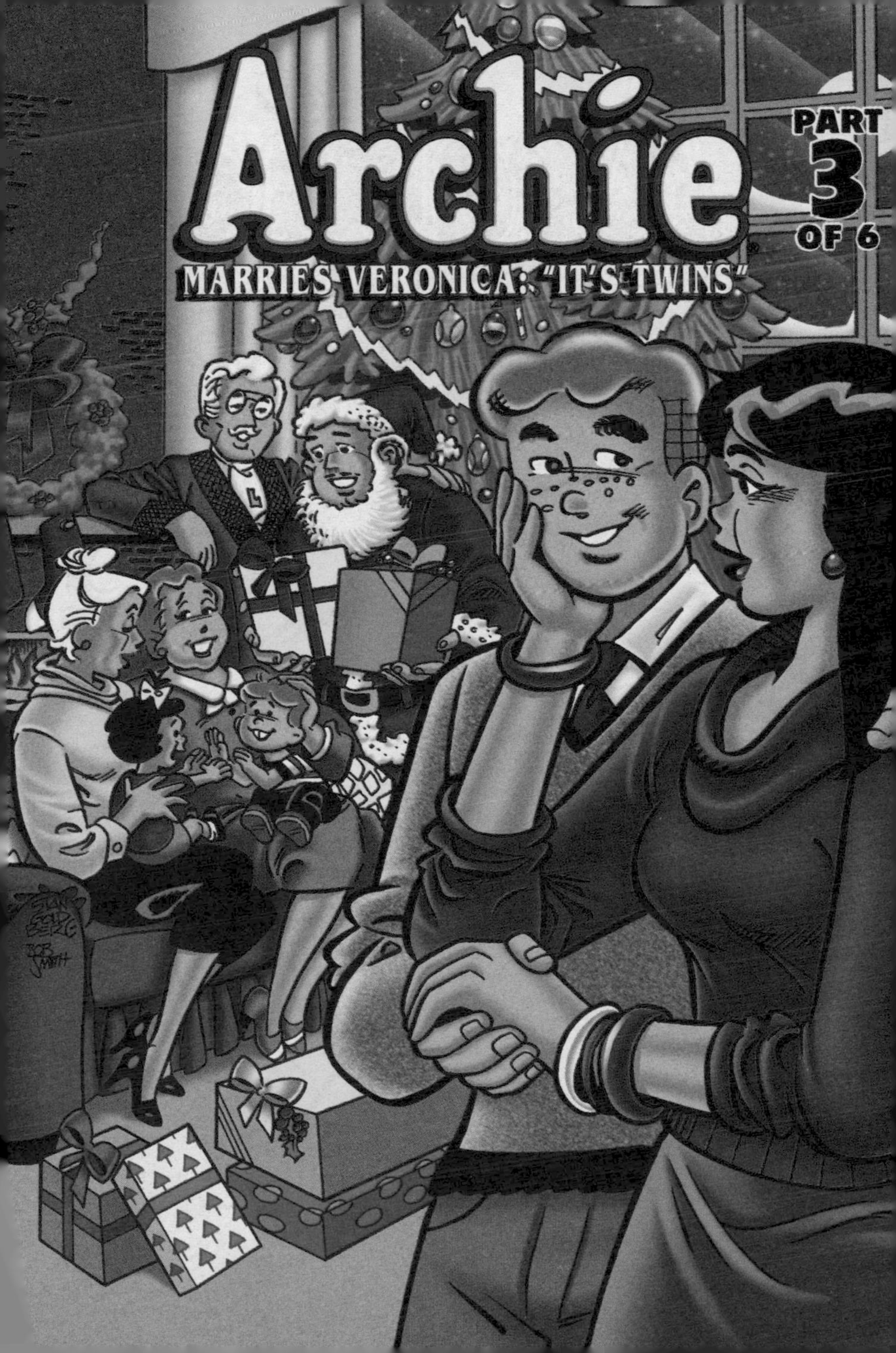
Archie
MARRIES VERONICA: "IT'S TWINS"
PART 3 OF 6
STAN GOLDBERG
BOB SMITH

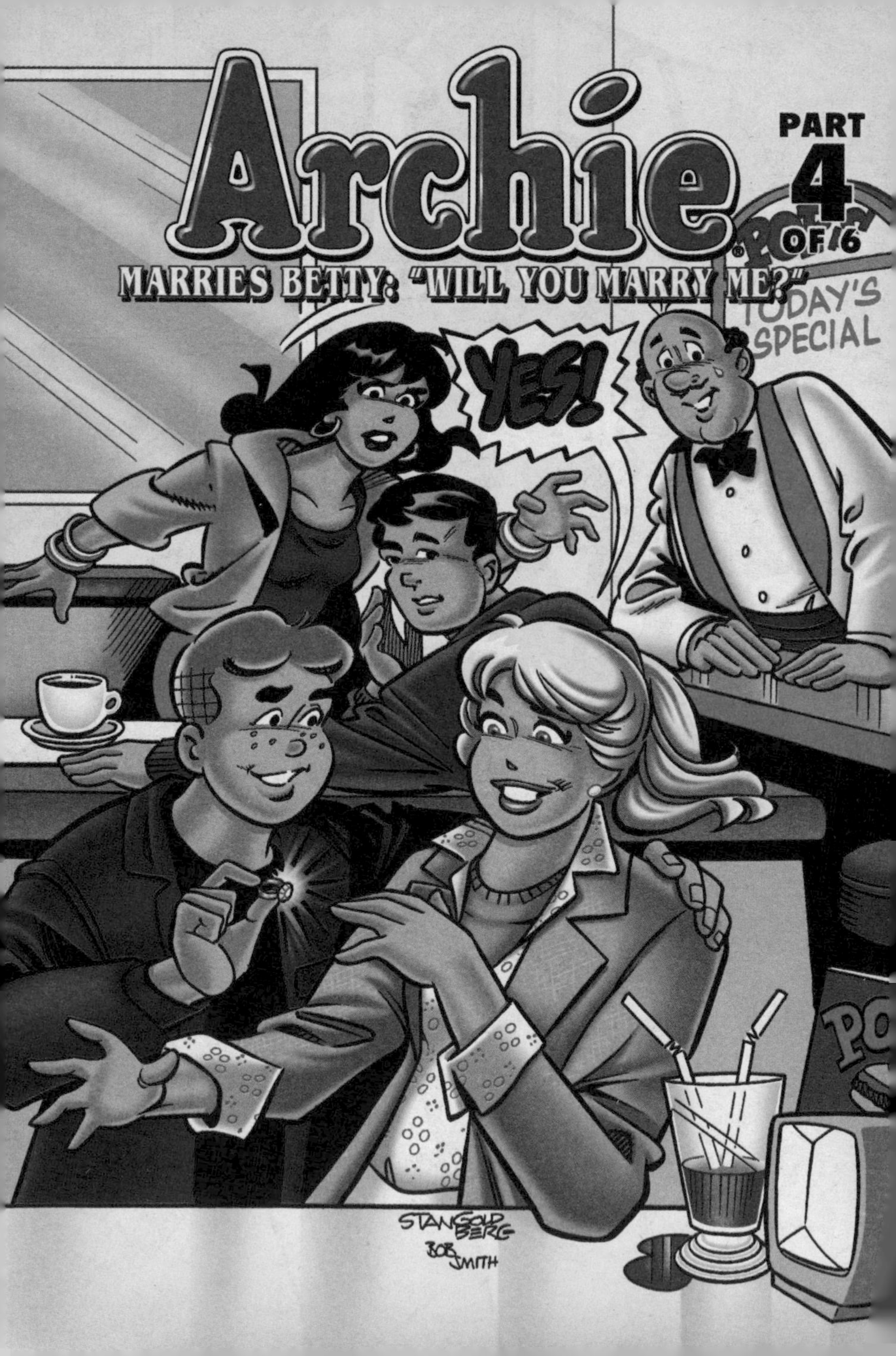
Archie
PART 4 OF 6
MARRIES BETTY: "WILL YOU MARRY ME?"
TODAY'S SPECIAL
YES!
STAN GOLDBERG
BOB SMITH

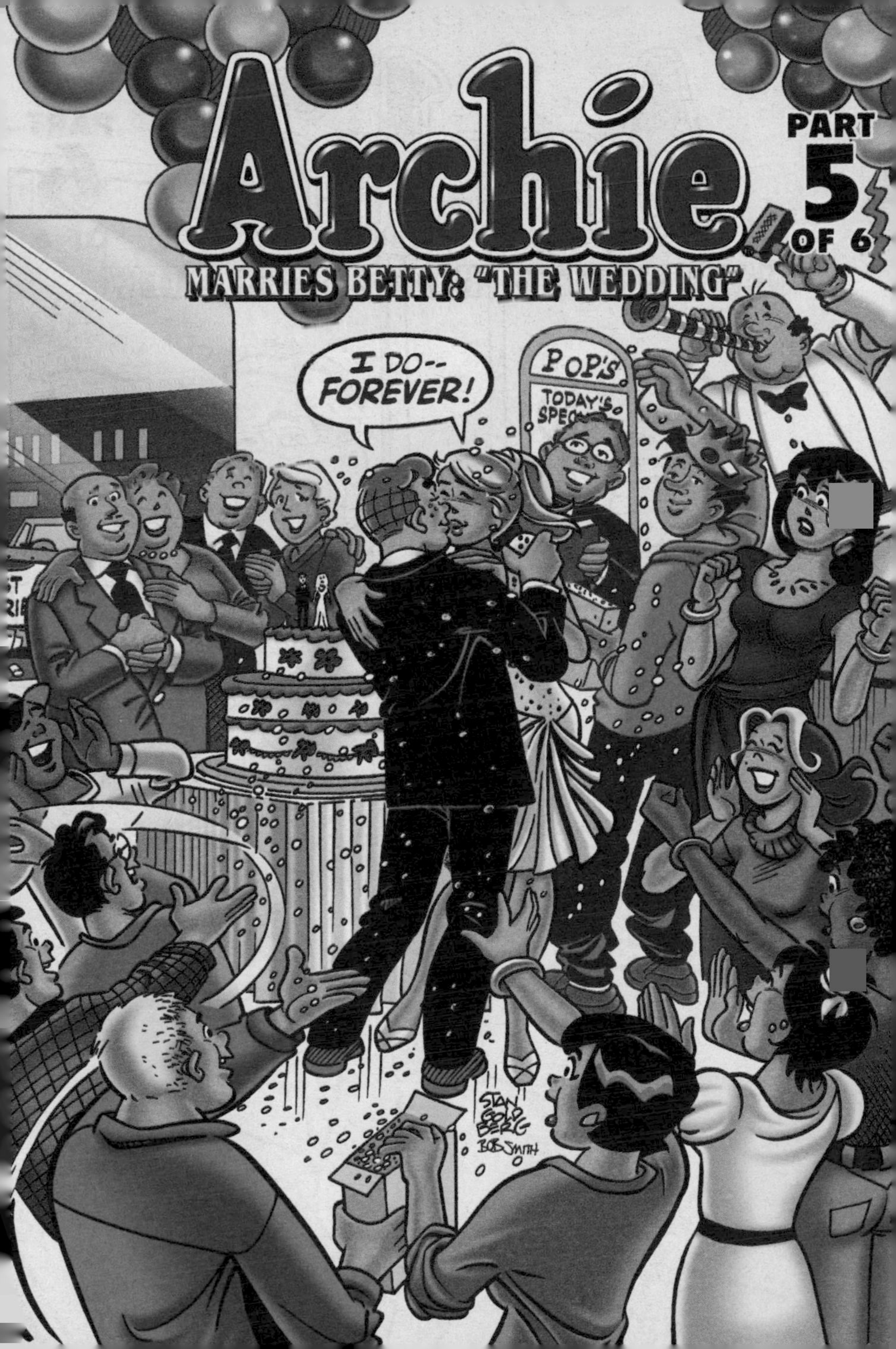
Archie
MARRIES BETTY: "THE WEDDING"
PART 5 OF 6
I DO-- FOREVER!
POP'S
TODAY'S
STAN GOLDBERG
BOB SMITH

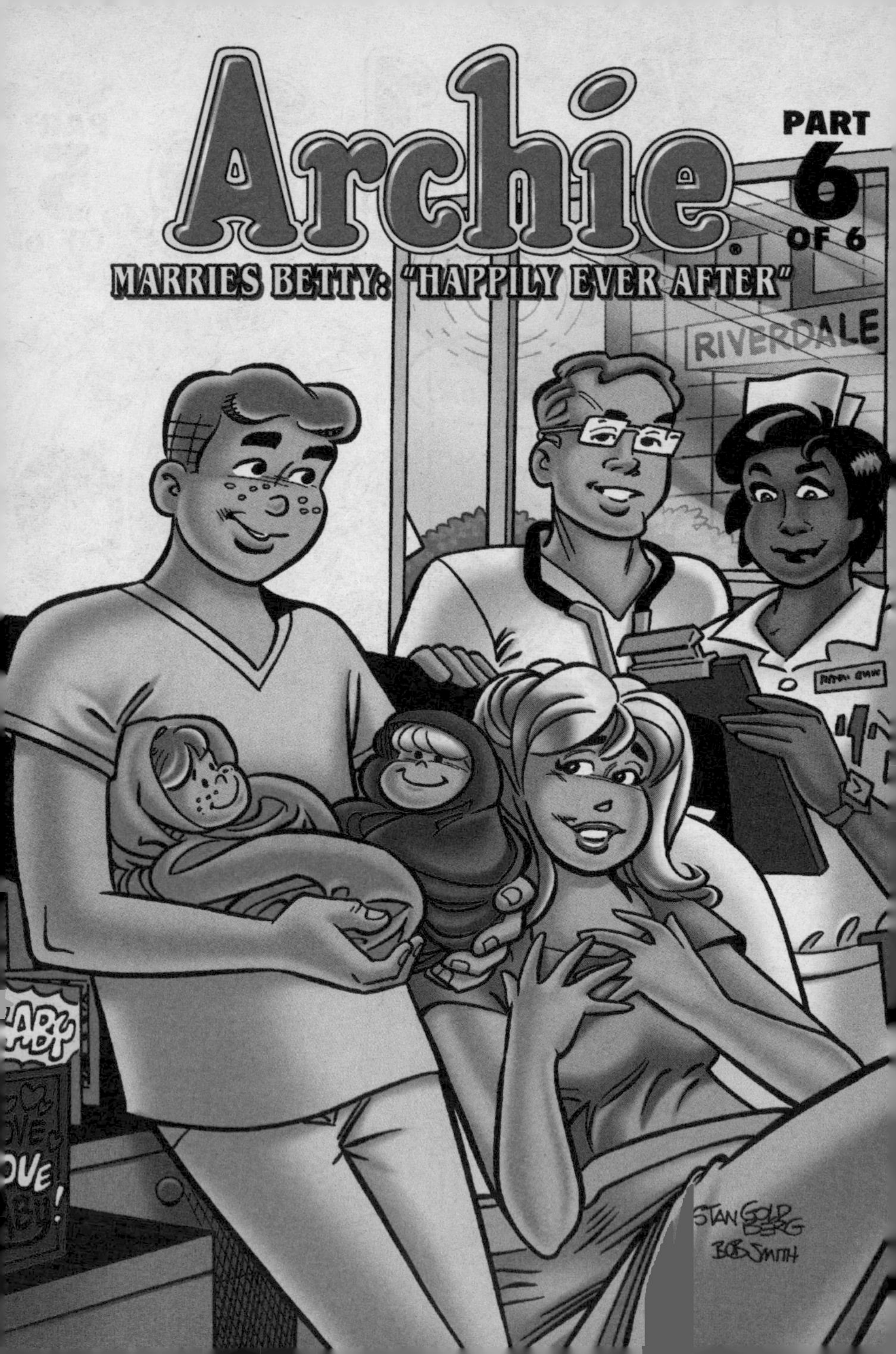
Archie®
MARRIES BETTY: "HAPPILY EVER AFTER"
PART 6 OF 6
RIVERDALE
STAN GOLDBERG
BOB SMITH

THE ARCHIE WEDDING

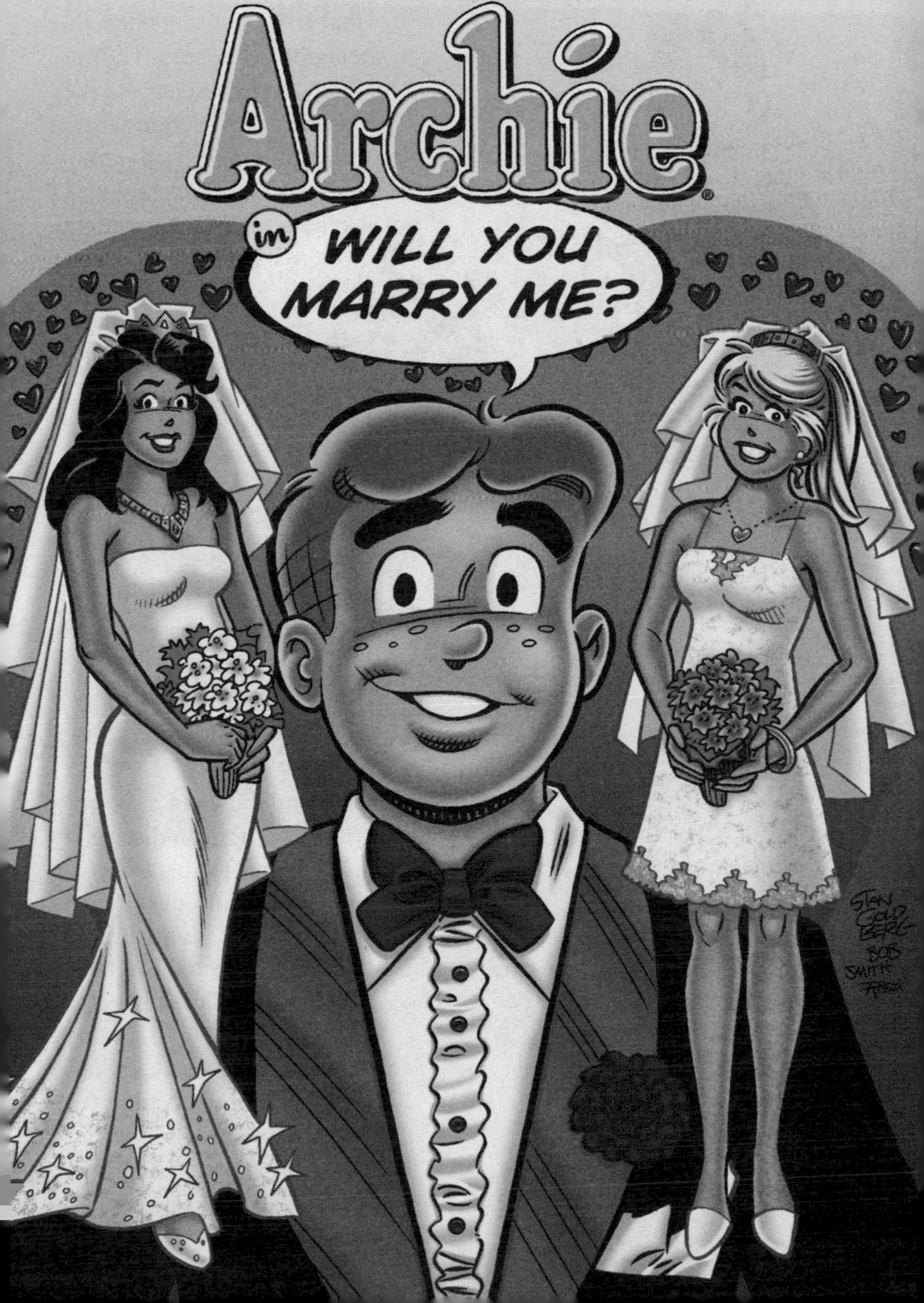
Archie
in
WILL YOU MARRY ME?

2010 and Beyond

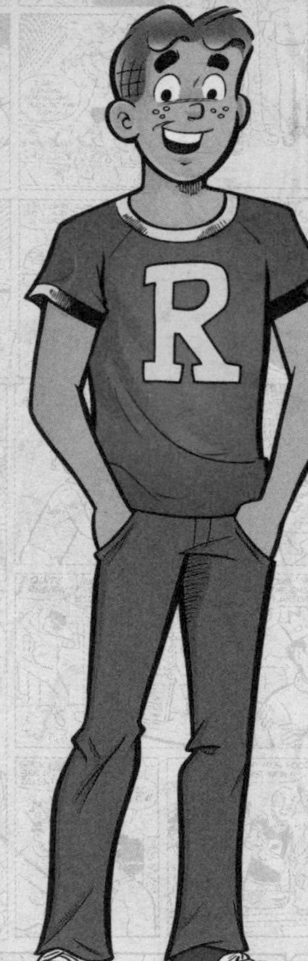

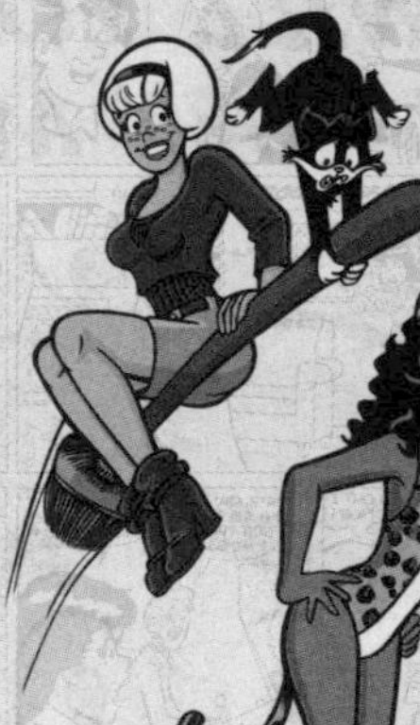

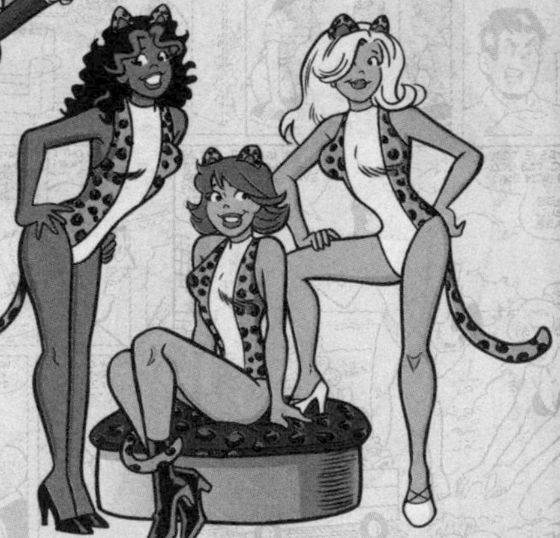

Timeless. That is a word that describes things that have achieved a certain level of excellence, that resonate no matter when they were created. In film, *The Wizard of Oz* or *It's A Wonderful Life*. In music, The Beatles or Bruce Springsteen. In comic books, of course you have Batman, Superman, and Spiderman. They are the timeless "superheroes." Archie, Betty, Veronica, Jughead, Reggie and Riverdale have achieved that level of excellence, that special timelessness. They are not "superheroes" but they represent everything that is special about America: family, friendship, inclusiveness and the unshakeable feeling that with the support of your family or friends, no problem is insurmountable.

Archie and the gang have been part of the American discussion for 70 years. That is fabulous. Archie has also introduced many other friends along the way, including Sabrina the Teenage Witch, Josie and the Pussycats, and Katy Keene to name but a few. In 2010, the United States Post Office honored Archie with a stamp—cementing his place in the fabric of America. However, our first 70 years are only the beginning.

In the past two years, we have launched many exciting new initiatives. Our Archie App has been wildly successful. We have broken ground with our brand new critically acclaimed comic magazine *Life With Archie,* which has the best art and writing of any comic book released today. We have introduced a new character in Riverdale, Kevin Keller. His appearance was met with tremendous support and the first issue in which he appeared, *Veronica #202*, sold out. We are putting a great deal of resources into the book market, and we are releasing more and more graphic novels on a monthly basis. Archie, in year 70, is increasing its production!

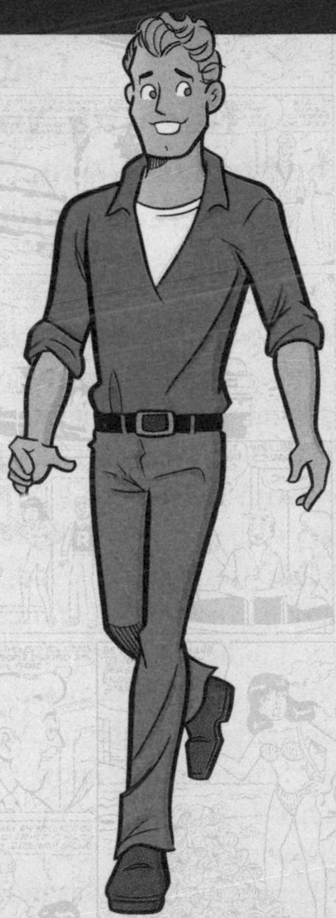

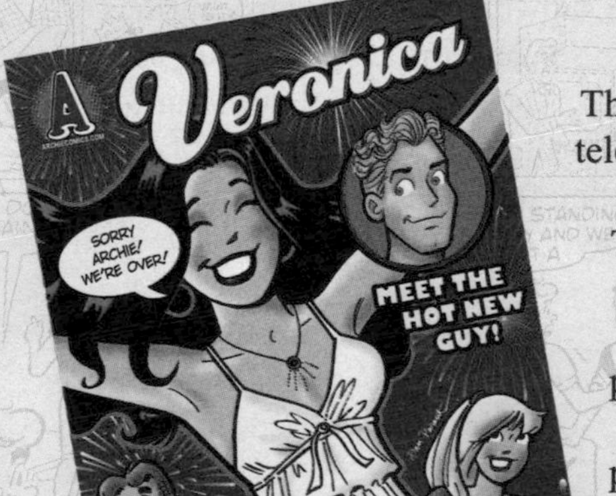
Veronica
SORRY ARCHIE! WE'RE OVER!
MEET THE HOT NEW GUY!

This is just the beginning. Animation, television, feature film and digital and virtual worlds are all in our future. This is all just beginning to happen. Most importantly, we could not do any of this without our fans—the people who read our stories. We are forever grateful and thrilled to be part of your lives. The first 70 years took Archie and the gang on a wild adventure.The next 70 promise to be even more exciting.

--Jon Goldwater

Co-CEO, Archie Comics

Lodge a Complaint
Life with Archie Magazine #1, 2010
by Michael Uslan, Norm Breyfogle, Joe Rubenstein,
Jack Morelli and Glenn Whitmore

What would happen if Archie chose Veronica? Betty? Choose Veronica and you'll marry into a family of wealth and influence; pick Betty and you're just another middle-class newlywed couple working for a living. Michael [Uslan]… left me with a wealth of material to work with and about a ton of questions and "what ifs" to explore. I've been given new ways of looking at the Riverdale gang, especially the two ladies in question. And, I'll admit, when I first started working on *Life With Archie: The Married Life*, I kind of, sort of leaned towards Betty. I didn't know any Lodges where I grew up in East Flatbush, Brooklyn, but I knew plenty of families like the Coopers. I even had a crush on the pretty blonde girl who lived next door to us on East 89th Street. Then I got to know Veronica, not only in the context of the Married Life storyline, but in the pages of the regular Archie titles as well. After writing a few stories that showcased both her insecurities and her strengths, it was tough not to see past the superficial spoiled rich girl facade to the woman beneath. Add to that the flawed-but-tough lady she's showing herself to be in the alternate worlds of the Married Life, and it's difficult not to start falling for her. Even if I do feel a little guilty every time I have to write Betty.

--**Paul Kupperberg**
Writer, excerpted from an afterword in
Archie: The Married Life Book 1

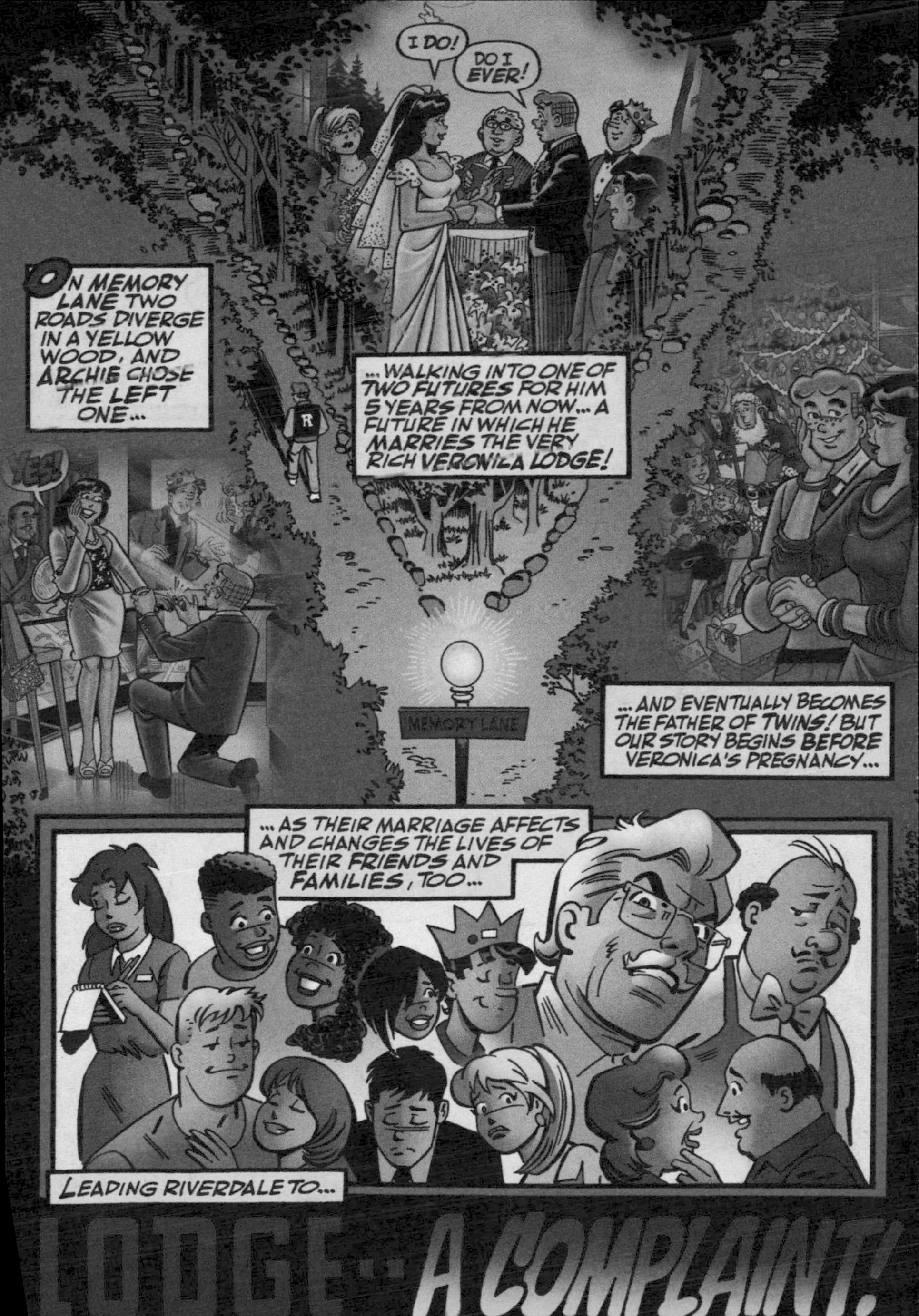
I DO!
DO I EVER!
ON MEMORY LANE TWO ROADS DIVERGE IN A YELLOW WOOD, AND ARCHIE CHOSE THE LEFT ONE...
...WALKING INTO ONE OF TWO FUTURES FOR HIM 5 YEARS FROM NOW... A FUTURE IN WHICH HE MARRIES THE VERY RICH VERONICA LODGE!
MEMORY LANE
...AND EVENTUALLY BECOMES THE FATHER OF TWINS! BUT OUR STORY BEGINS BEFORE VERONICA'S PREGNANCY...
...AS THEIR MARRIAGE AFFECTS AND CHANGES THE LIVES OF THEIR FRIENDS AND FAMILIES, TOO...
LEADING RIVERDALE TO...
LODGE-- A COMPLAINT!

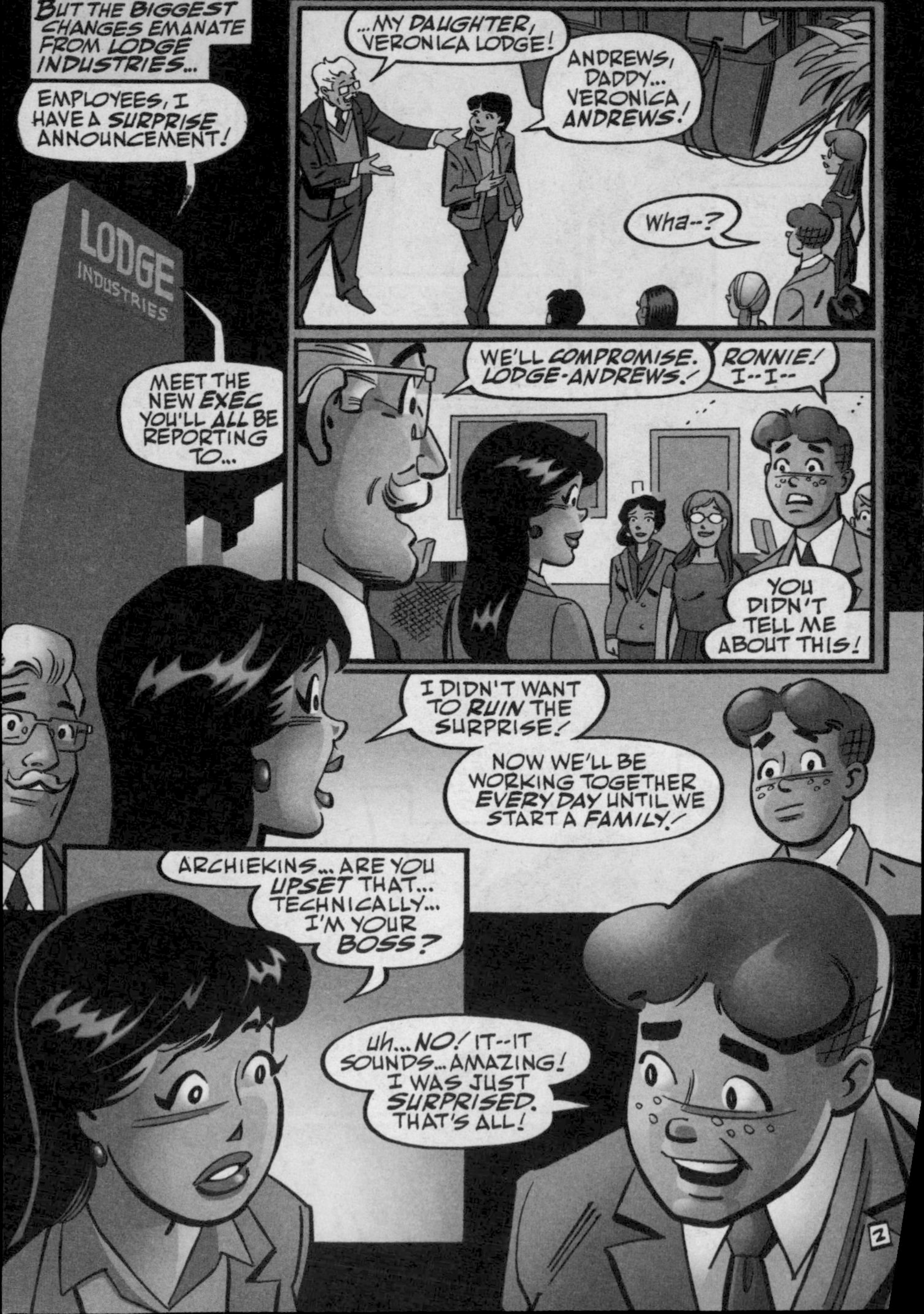

BUT THE BIGGEST CHANGES EMANATE FROM LODGE INDUSTRIES...
EMPLOYEES, I HAVE A SURPRISE ANNOUNCEMENT!
LODGE INDUSTRIES
MEET THE NEW EXEC YOU'LL ALL BE REPORTING TO...
...MY DAUGHTER, VERONICA LODGE!
ANDREWS, DADDY... VERONICA ANDREWS!
Wha--?
WE'LL COMPROMISE. LODGE-ANDREWS!
RONNIE! I--I--
YOU DIDN'T TELL ME ABOUT THIS!
I DIDN'T WANT TO RUIN THE SURPRISE!
NOW WE'LL BE WORKING TOGETHER EVERY DAY UNTIL WE START A FAMILY!
ARCHIEKINS... ARE YOU UPSET THAT... TECHNICALLY... I'M YOUR BOSS?
uh... NO! IT--IT SOUNDS... AMAZING! I WAS JUST SURPRISED. THAT'S ALL!
2

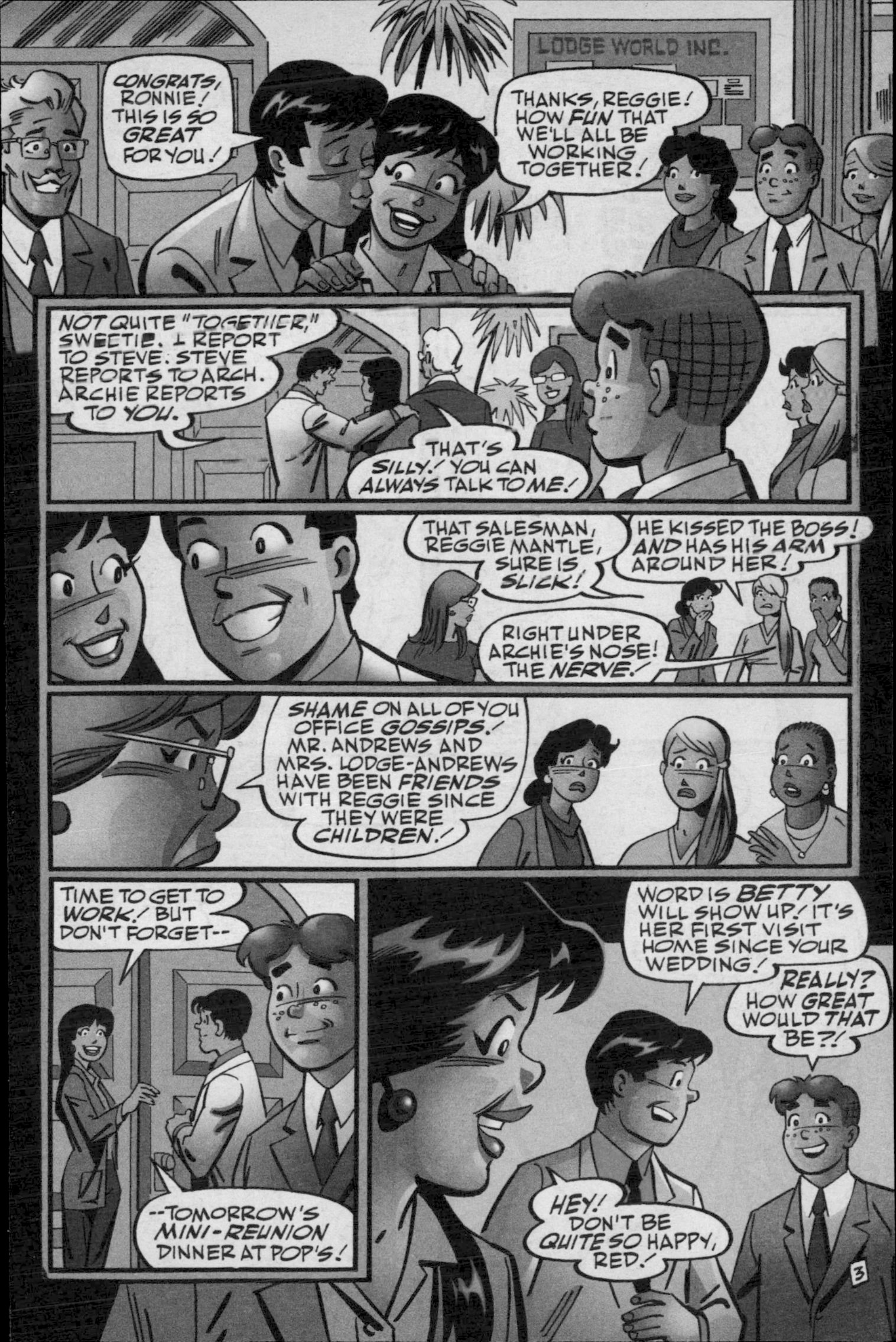

LODGE WORLD INC.
CONGRATS, RONNIE! THIS IS SO GREAT FOR YOU!
THANKS, REGGIE! HOW FUN THAT WE'LL ALL BE WORKING TOGETHER!
NOT QUITE "TOGETHER," SWEETIE. I REPORT TO STEVE. STEVE REPORTS TO ARCH. ARCHIE REPORTS TO YOU.
THAT'S SILLY! YOU CAN ALWAYS TALK TO ME!
THAT SALESMAN, REGGIE MANTLE, SURE IS SLICK!
HE KISSED THE BOSS! AND HAS HIS ARM AROUND HER!
RIGHT UNDER ARCHIE'S NOSE! THE NERVE!
SHAME ON ALL OF YOU OFFICE GOSSIPS! MR. ANDREWS AND MRS. LODGE-ANDREWS HAVE BEEN FRIENDS WITH REGGIE SINCE THEY WERE CHILDREN!
TIME TO GET TO WORK! BUT DON'T FORGET--
--TOMORROW'S MINI-REUNION DINNER AT POP'S!
WORD IS BETTY WILL SHOW UP! IT'S HER FIRST VISIT HOME SINCE YOUR WEDDING!
REALLY? HOW GREAT WOULD THAT BE?!
HEY! DON'T BE QUITE SO HAPPY, RED!
3

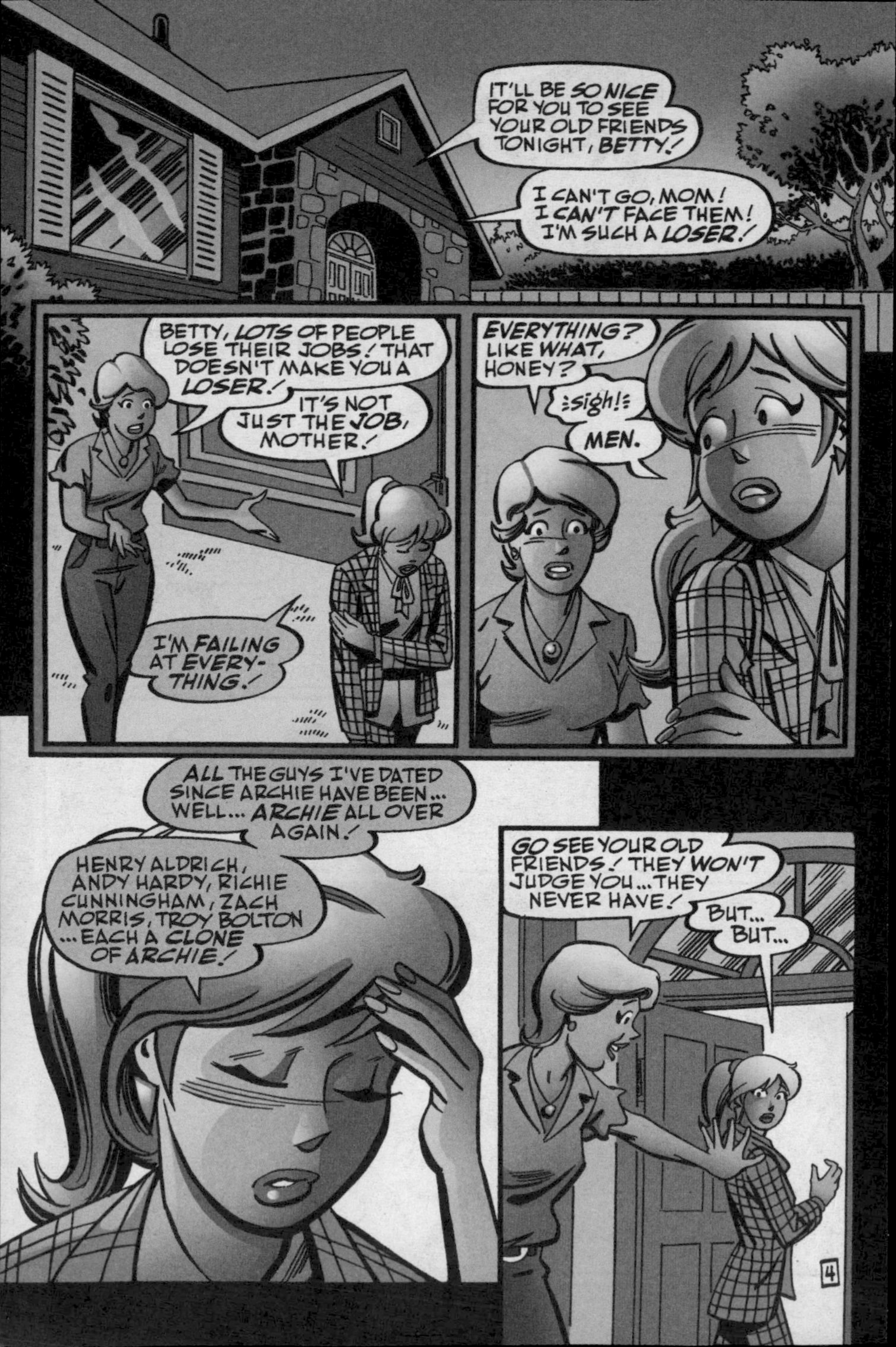
IT'LL BE SO NICE FOR YOU TO SEE YOUR OLD FRIENDS TONIGHT, BETTY!
I CAN'T GO, MOM! I CAN'T FACE THEM! I'M SUCH A LOSER!
BETTY, LOTS OF PEOPLE LOSE THEIR JOBS! THAT DOESN'T MAKE YOU A LOSER!
IT'S NOT JUST THE JOB, MOTHER!
I'M FAILING AT EVERY-THING!
EVERYTHING? LIKE WHAT, HONEY?
sigh!
MEN.
ALL THE GUYS I'VE DATED SINCE ARCHIE HAVE BEEN... WELL... ARCHIE ALL OVER AGAIN!
HENRY ALDRICH, ANDY HARDY, RICHIE CUNNINGHAM, ZACH MORRIS, TROY BOLTON ...EACH A CLONE OF ARCHIE!
GO SEE YOUR OLD FRIENDS! THEY WON'T JUDGE YOU...THEY NEVER HAVE!
BUT... BUT...
4

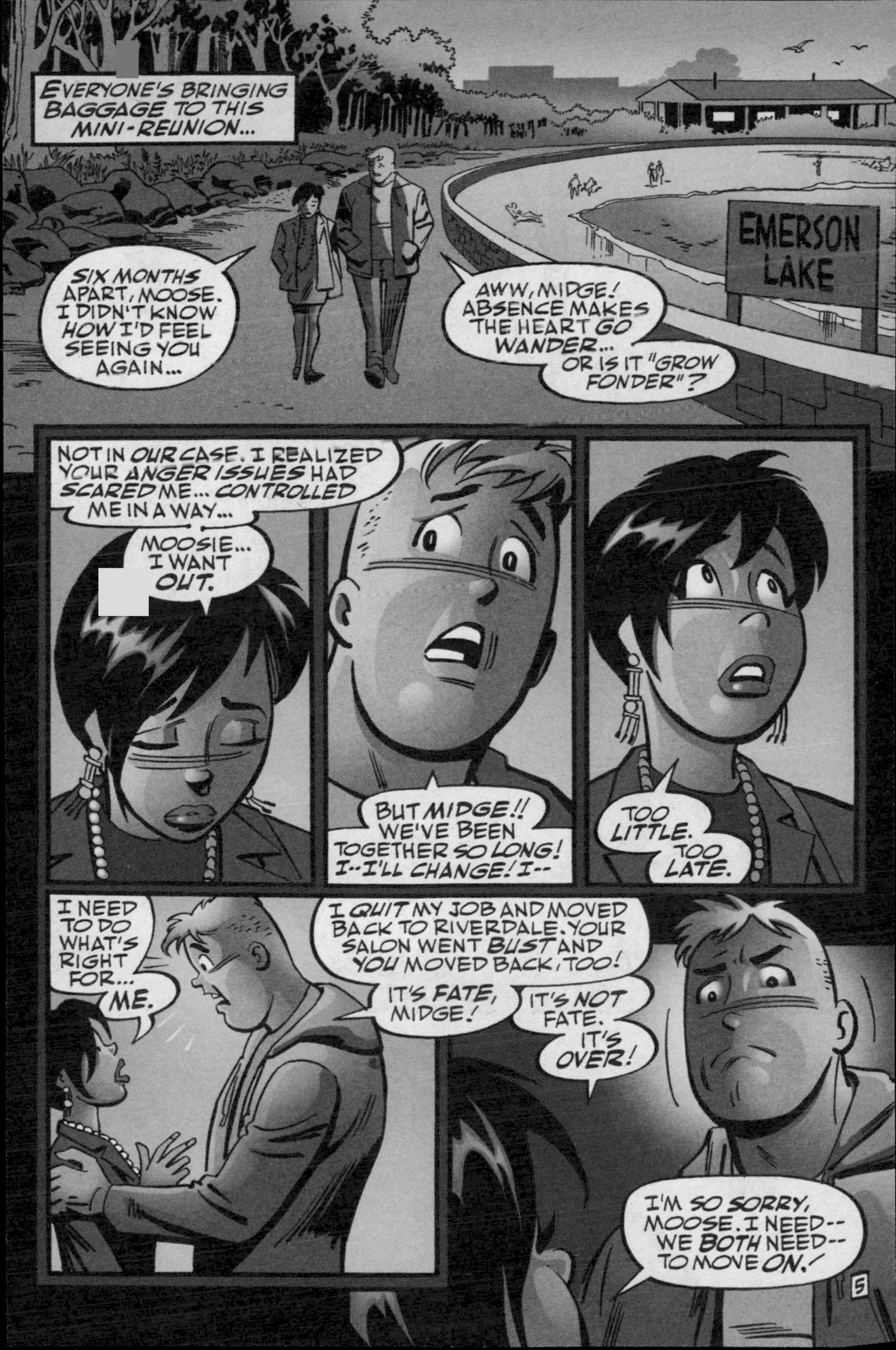
EVERYONE'S BRINGING BAGGAGE TO THIS MINI-REUNION...
SIX MONTHS APART, MOOSE. I DIDN'T KNOW HOW I'D FEEL SEEING YOU AGAIN...
AWW, MIDGE! ABSENCE MAKES THE HEART GO WANDER... OR IS IT "GROW FONDER"?
EMERSON LAKE
NOT IN OUR CASE. I REALIZED YOUR ANGER ISSUES HAD SCARED ME... CONTROLLED ME IN A WAY...
MOOSIE... I WANT OUT.
BUT MIDGE!! WE'VE BEEN TOGETHER SO LONG! I--I'LL CHANGE! I--
TOO LITTLE. TOO LATE.
I NEED TO DO WHAT'S RIGHT FOR... ME.
I QUIT MY JOB AND MOVED BACK TO RIVERDALE. YOUR SALON WENT BUST AND YOU MOVED BACK, TOO!
IT'S FATE, MIDGE!
IT'S NOT FATE. IT'S OVER!
I'M SO SORRY, MOOSE. I NEED-- WE BOTH NEED-- TO MOVE ON.
5

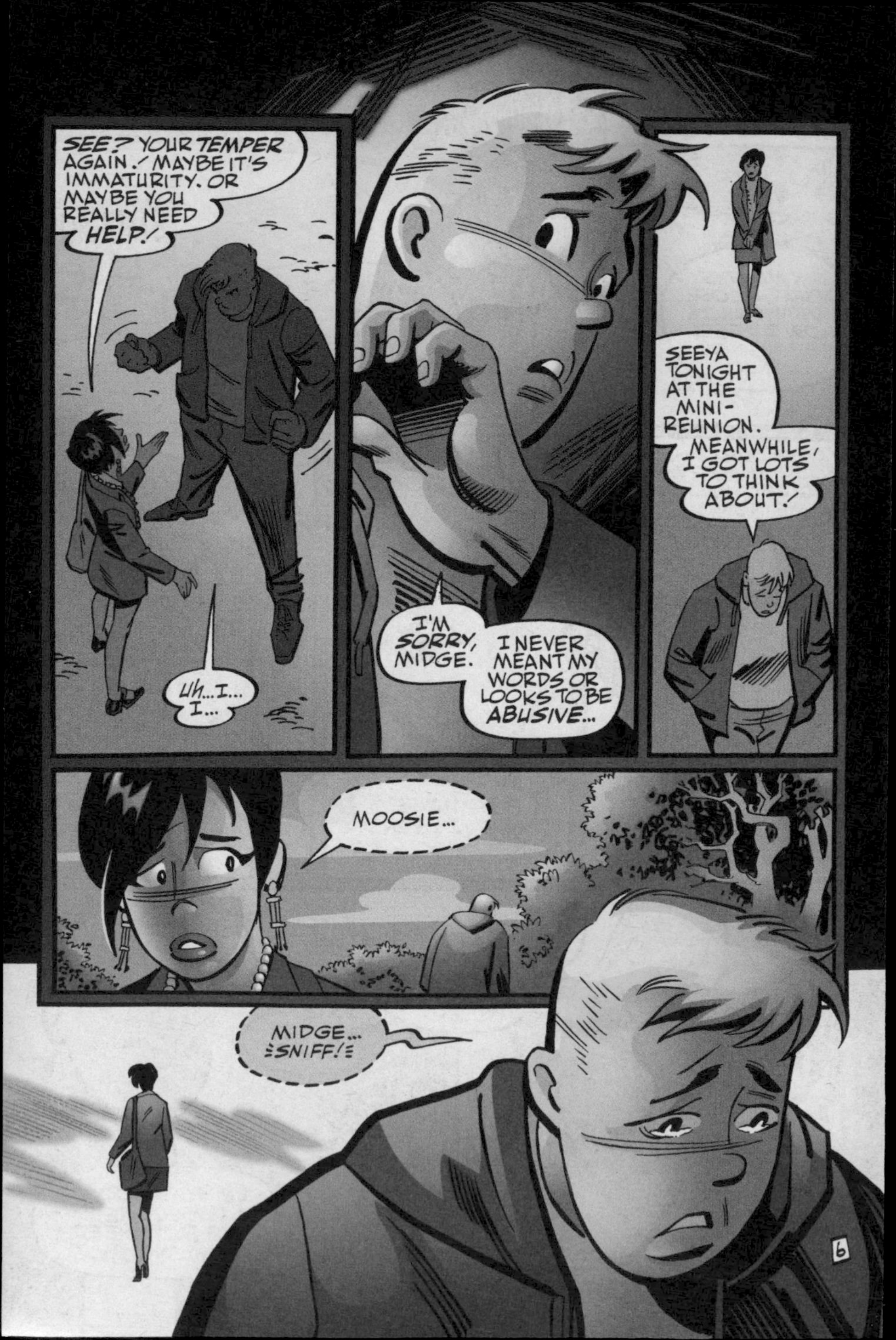
SEE? YOUR TEMPER AGAIN.! MAYBE IT'S IMMATURITY. OR MAYBE YOU REALLY NEED HELP!
UH...I... I...
I'M SORRY, MIDGE.
I NEVER MEANT MY WORDS OR LOOKS TO BE ABUSIVE...
SEEYA TONIGHT AT THE MINI-REUNION.
MEANWHILE, I GOT LOTS TO THINK ABOUT!
MOOSIE...
MIDGE... SNIFF!

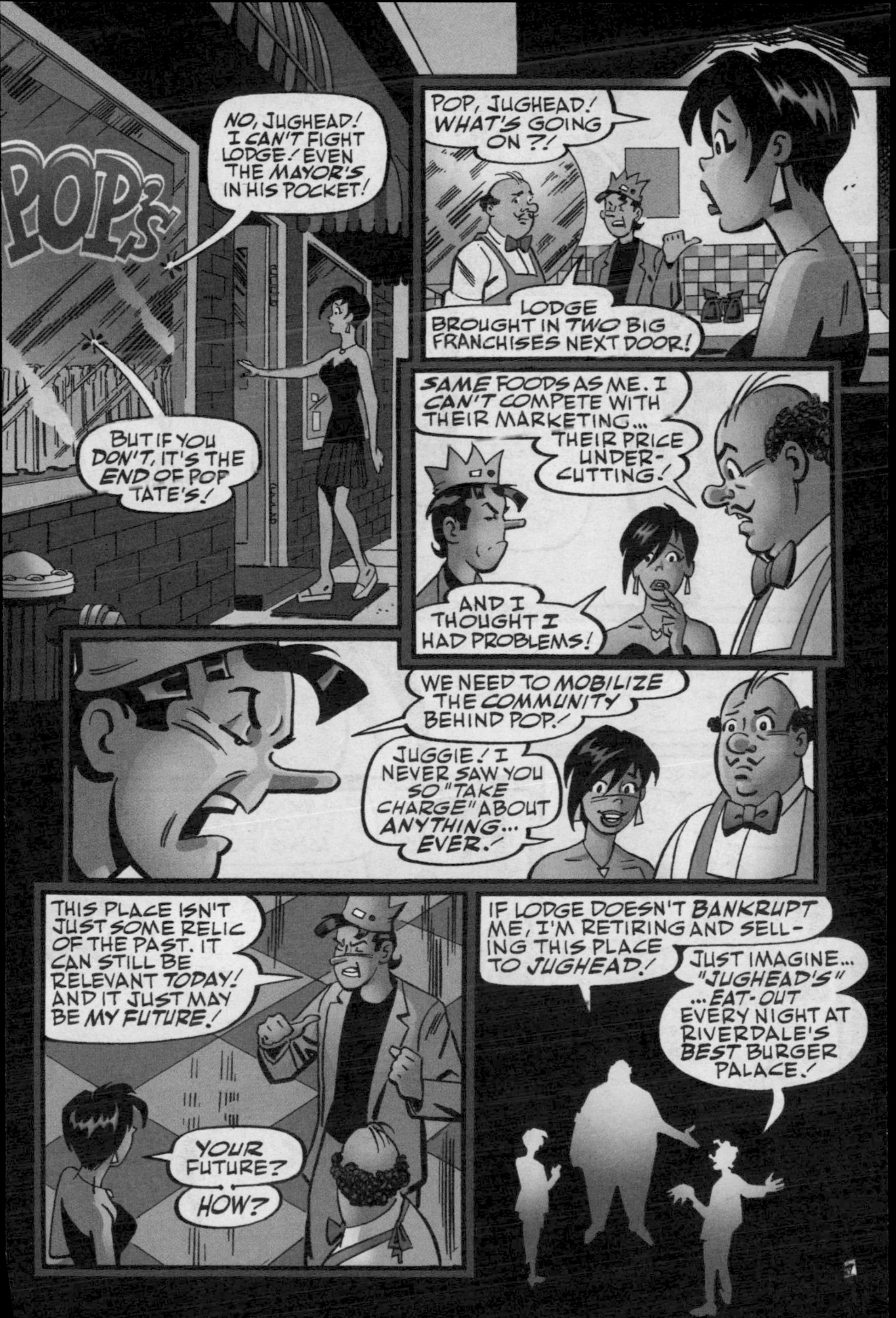
POP'S
NO, JUGHEAD! I CAN'T FIGHT LODGE! EVEN THE MAYOR'S IN HIS POCKET!
BUT IF YOU DON'T, IT'S THE END OF POP TATE'S!
POP, JUGHEAD! WHAT'S GOING ON?!
LODGE BROUGHT IN TWO BIG FRANCHISES NEXT DOOR!
SAME FOODS AS ME. I CAN'T COMPETE WITH THEIR MARKETING...
THEIR PRICE UNDER-CUTTING!
AND I THOUGHT I HAD PROBLEMS!
WE NEED TO MOBILIZE THE COMMUNITY BEHIND POP!
JUGGIE! I NEVER SAW YOU SO "TAKE CHARGE" ABOUT ANYTHING... EVER!
THIS PLACE ISN'T JUST SOME RELIC OF THE PAST. IT CAN STILL BE RELEVANT TODAY! AND IT JUST MAY BE MY FUTURE!
YOUR FUTURE?
HOW?
IF LODGE DOESN'T BANKRUPT ME, I'M RETIRING AND SELL-ING THIS PLACE TO JUGHEAD!
JUST IMAGINE... "JUGHEAD'S" ...EAT-OUT EVERY NIGHT AT RIVERDALE'S BEST BURGER PALACE!

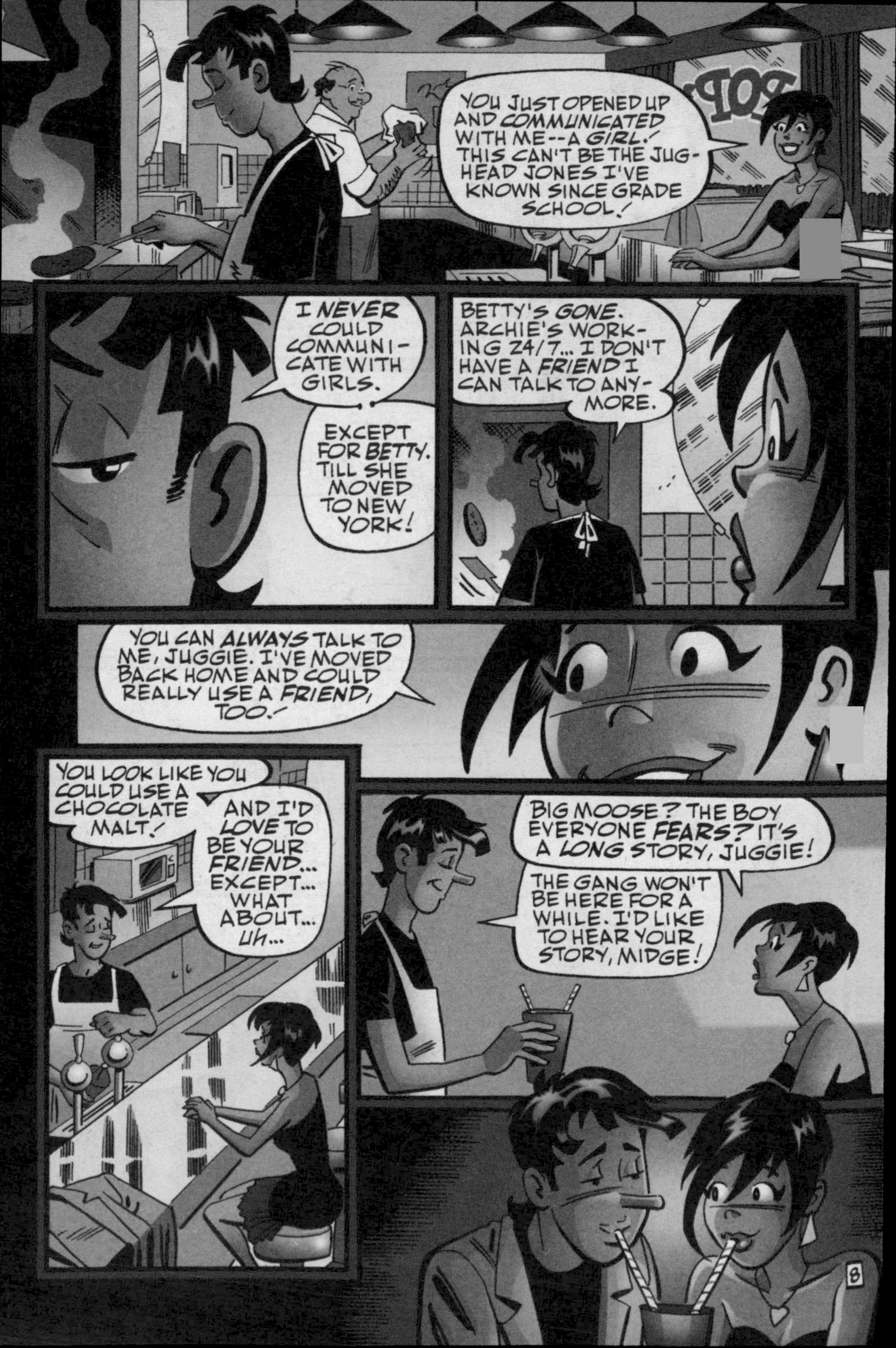

YOU JUST OPENED UP AND COMMUNICATED WITH ME--A GIRL! THIS CAN'T BE THE JUGHEAD JONES I'VE KNOWN SINCE GRADE SCHOOL!
I NEVER COULD COMMUNICATE WITH GIRLS.
EXCEPT FOR BETTY. TILL SHE MOVED TO NEW YORK!
BETTY'S GONE. ARCHIE'S WORKING 24/7... I DON'T HAVE A FRIEND I CAN TALK TO ANYMORE.
YOU CAN ALWAYS TALK TO ME, JUGGIE. I'VE MOVED BACK HOME AND COULD REALLY USE A FRIEND, TOO!
YOU LOOK LIKE YOU COULD USE A CHOCOLATE MALT!
AND I'D LOVE TO BE YOUR FRIEND... EXCEPT... WHAT ABOUT... UH...
BIG MOOSE? THE BOY EVERYONE FEARS? IT'S A LONG STORY, JUGGIE!
THE GANG WON'T BE HERE FOR A WHILE. I'D LIKE TO HEAR YOUR STORY, MIDGE!
8

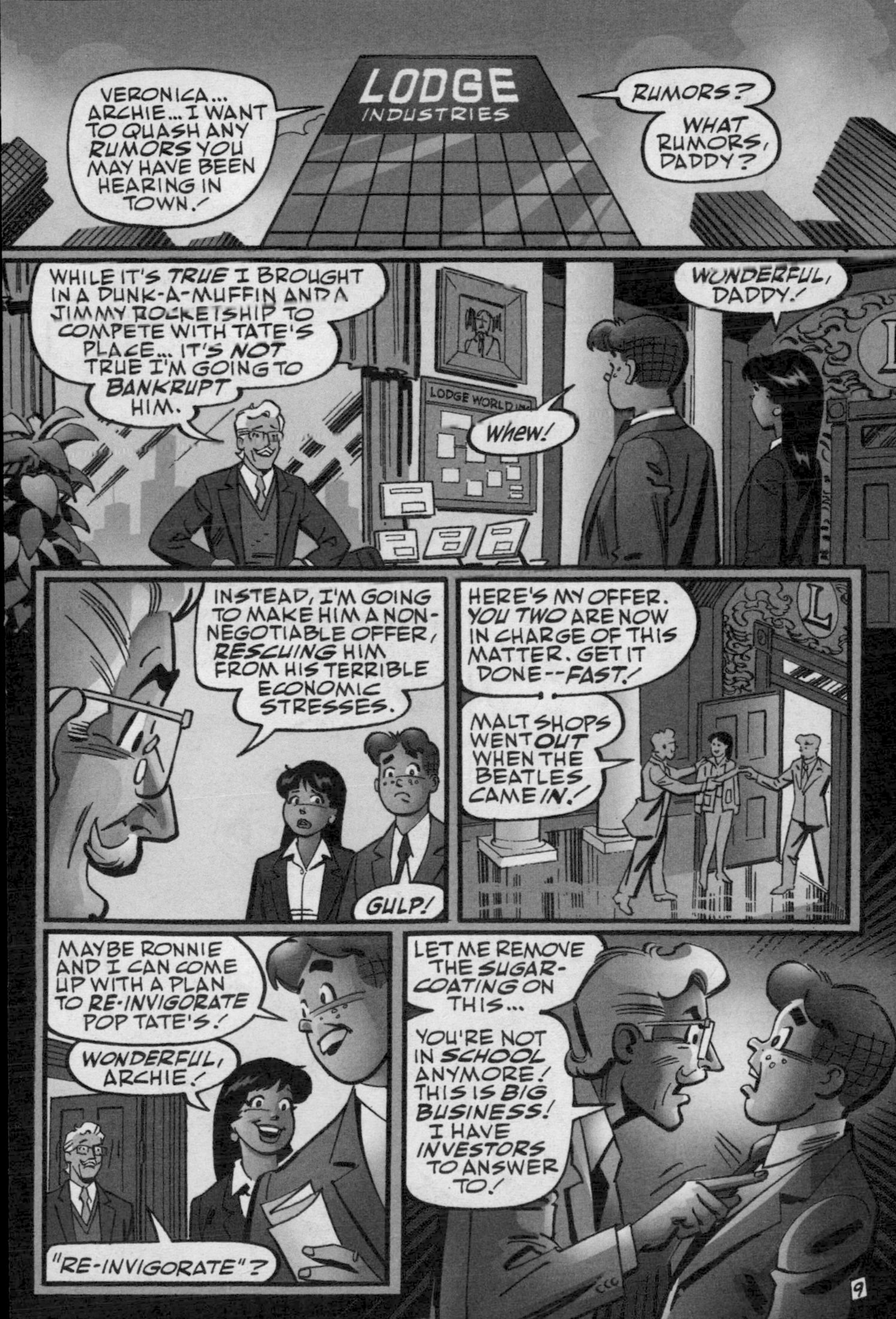
LODGE
INDUSTRIES
VERONICA... ARCHIE... I WANT TO QUASH ANY RUMORS YOU MAY HAVE BEEN HEARING IN TOWN.!
RUMORS?
WHAT RUMORS, DADDY?
WHILE IT'S TRUE I BROUGHT IN A DUNK-A-MUFFIN AND A JIMMY ROCKETSHIP TO COMPETE WITH TATE'S PLACE... IT'S NOT TRUE I'M GOING TO BANKRUPT HIM.
WONDERFUL, DADDY!
LODGE WORLD INC.
Whew!
INSTEAD, I'M GOING TO MAKE HIM A NON-NEGOTIABLE OFFER, RESCUING HIM FROM HIS TERRIBLE ECONOMIC STRESSES.
GULP!
HERE'S MY OFFER. YOU TWO ARE NOW IN CHARGE OF THIS MATTER. GET IT DONE--FAST!
MALT SHOPS WENT OUT WHEN THE BEATLES CAME IN.!
MAYBE RONNIE AND I CAN COME UP WITH A PLAN TO RE-INVIGORATE POP TATE'S!
WONDERFUL, ARCHIE!
"RE-INVIGORATE"?
LET ME REMOVE THE SUGAR-COATING ON THIS...
YOU'RE NOT IN SCHOOL ANYMORE! THIS IS BIG BUSINESS! I HAVE INVESTORS TO ANSWER TO!

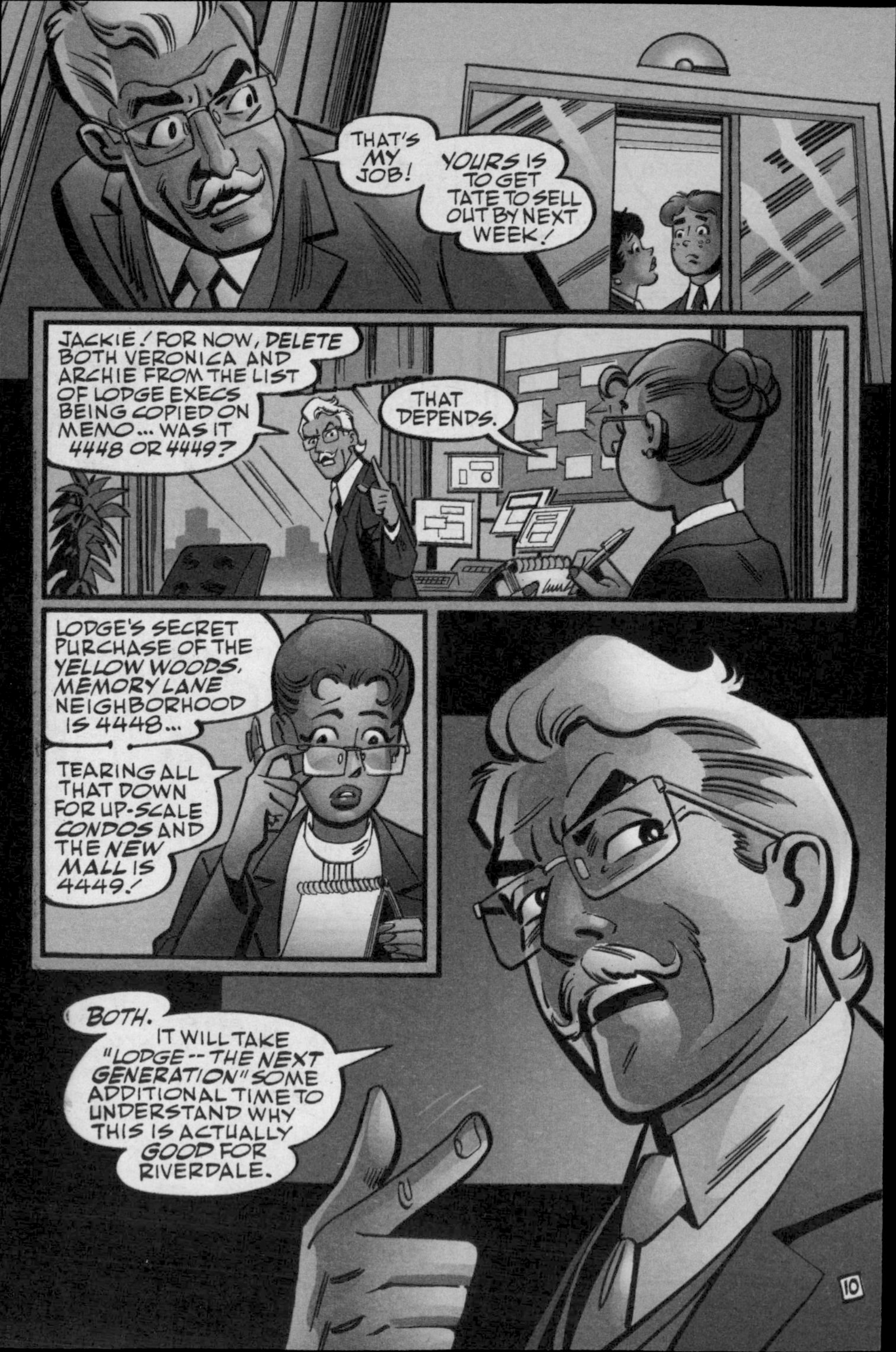
THAT'S MY JOB!
YOURS IS TO GET TATE TO SELL OUT BY NEXT WEEK!
JACKIE! FOR NOW, DELETE BOTH VERONICA AND ARCHIE FROM THE LIST OF LODGE EXECS BEING COPIED ON MEMO... WAS IT 4448 OR 4449?
THAT DEPENDS.
LODGE'S SECRET PURCHASE OF THE YELLOW WOODS, MEMORY LANE NEIGHBORHOOD IS 4448...
TEARING ALL THAT DOWN FOR UP-SCALE CONDOS AND THE NEW MALL IS 4449!
BOTH.
IT WILL TAKE "LODGE -- THE NEXT GENERATION" SOME ADDITIONAL TIME TO UNDERSTAND WHY THIS IS ACTUALLY GOOD FOR RIVERDALE.
10

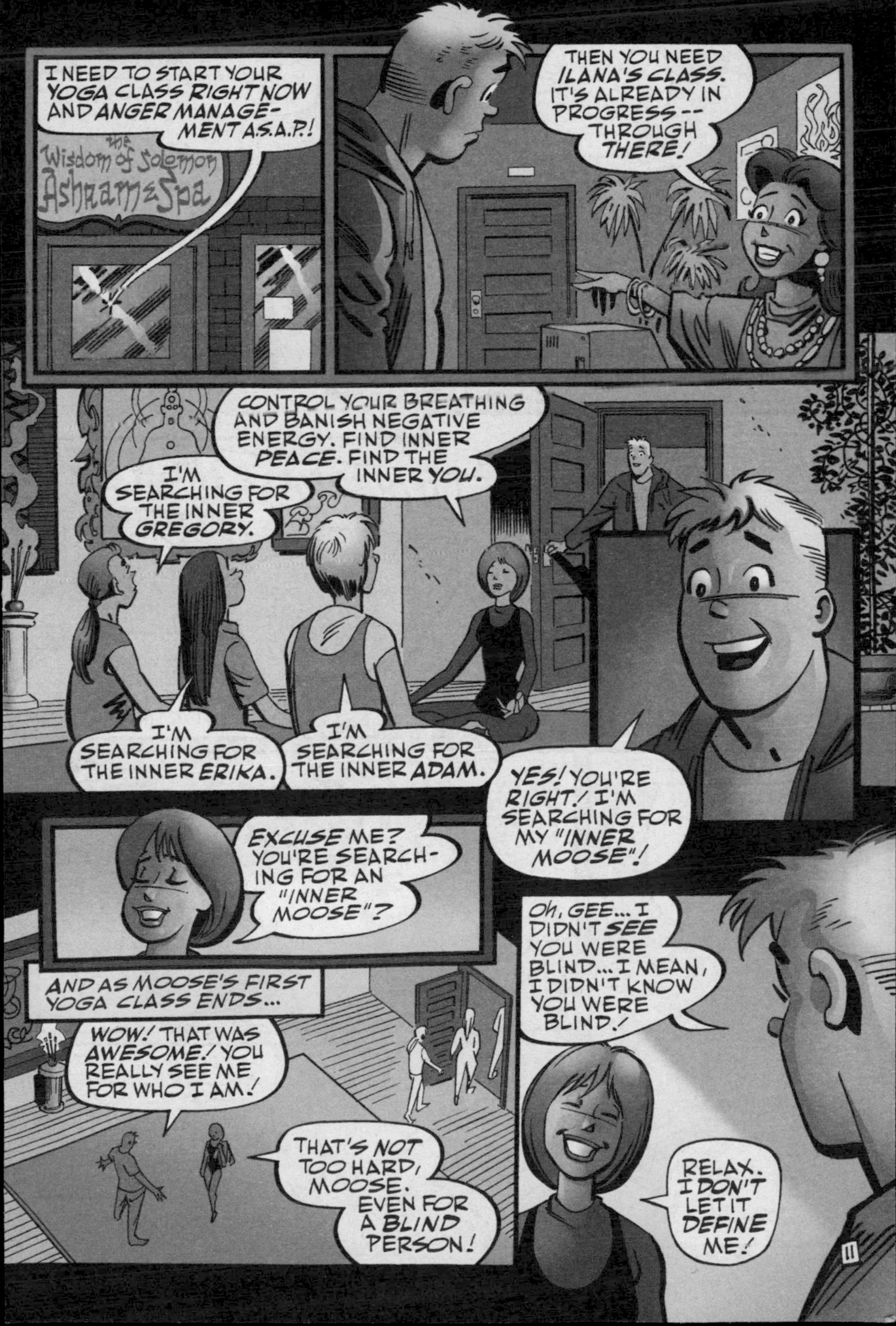
I NEED TO START YOUR YOGA CLASS RIGHT NOW AND ANGER MANAGEMENT A.S.A.P.!
the Wisdom of Solomon Ashram & Spa
THEN YOU NEED ILANA'S CLASS. IT'S ALREADY IN PROGRESS -- THROUGH THERE!
CONTROL YOUR BREATHING AND BANISH NEGATIVE ENERGY. FIND INNER PEACE. FIND THE INNER YOU.
I'M SEARCHING FOR THE INNER GREGORY.
I'M SEARCHING FOR THE INNER ERIKA.
I'M SEARCHING FOR THE INNER ADAM.
YES! YOU'RE RIGHT! I'M SEARCHING FOR MY "INNER MOOSE"!
EXCUSE ME? YOU'RE SEARCHING FOR AN "INNER MOOSE"?
AND AS MOOSE'S FIRST YOGA CLASS ENDS...
WOW! THAT WAS AWESOME! YOU REALLY SEE ME FOR WHO I AM!
THAT'S NOT TOO HARD, MOOSE. EVEN FOR A BLIND PERSON!
OH, GEE... I DIDN'T SEE YOU WERE BLIND... I MEAN, I DIDN'T KNOW YOU WERE BLIND!
RELAX. I DON'T LET IT DEFINE ME!
11

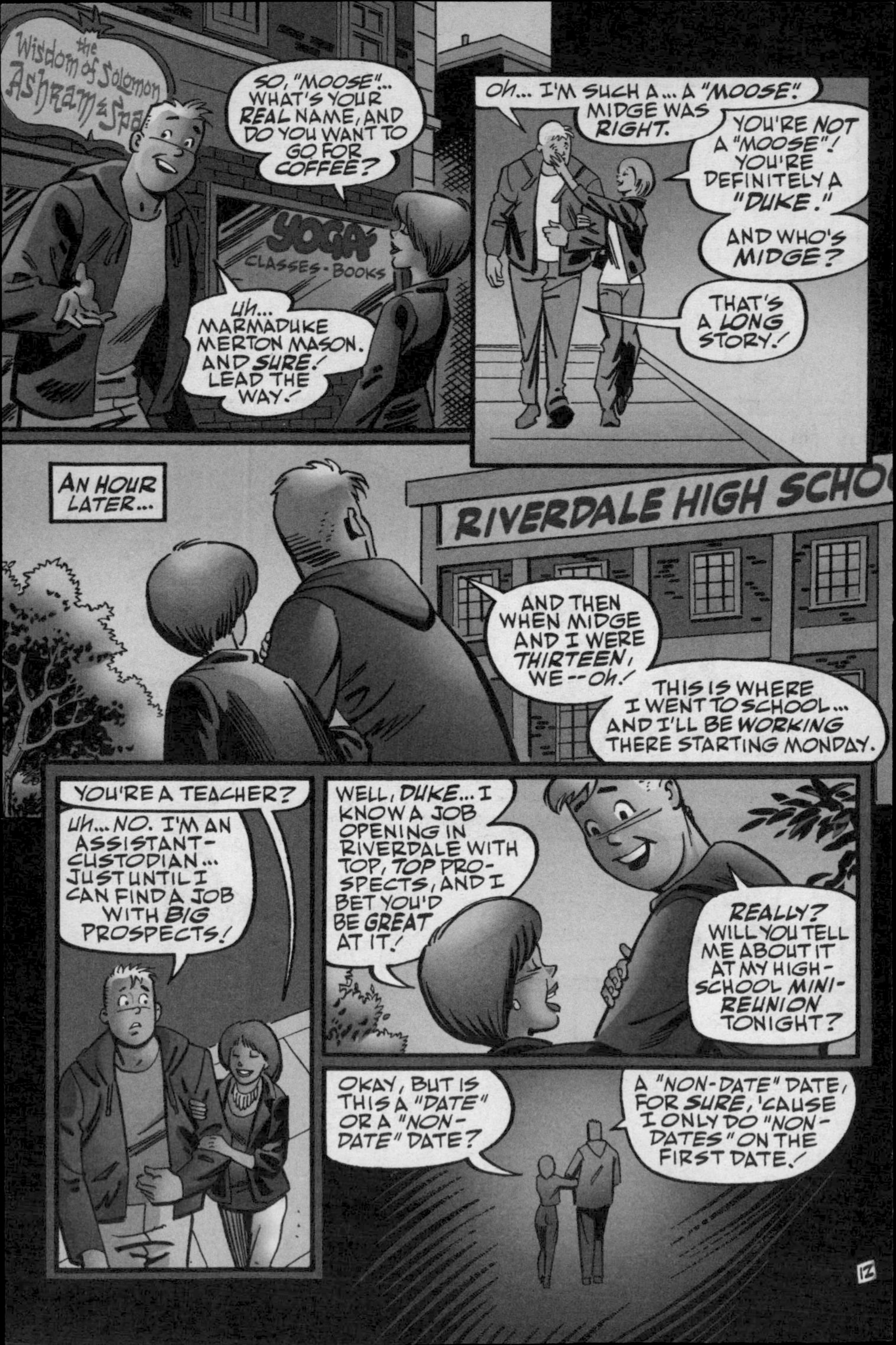
the Wisdom of Solomon Ashram & Spa
SO, "MOOSE"... WHAT'S YOUR REAL NAME, AND DO YOU WANT TO GO FOR COFFEE?
YOGA CLASSES - BOOKS
UH... MARMADUKE MERTON MASON. AND SURE! LEAD THE WAY!
OH... I'M SUCH A... A "MOOSE"! MIDGE WAS RIGHT.
YOU'RE NOT A "MOOSE"! YOU'RE DEFINITELY A "DUKE."
AND WHO'S MIDGE?
THAT'S A LONG STORY!
AN HOUR LATER...
RIVERDALE HIGH SCHO
AND THEN WHEN MIDGE AND I WERE THIRTEEN, WE--OH!
THIS IS WHERE I WENT TO SCHOOL... AND I'LL BE WORKING THERE STARTING MONDAY.
YOU'RE A TEACHER?
UH... NO. I'M AN ASSISTANT-CUSTODIAN... JUST UNTIL I CAN FIND A JOB WITH BIG PROSPECTS!
WELL, DUKE... I KNOW A JOB OPENING IN RIVERDALE WITH TOP, TOP PROSPECTS, AND I BET YOU'D BE GREAT AT IT!
REALLY? WILL YOU TELL ME ABOUT IT AT MY HIGH-SCHOOL MINI-REUNION TONIGHT?
OKAY, BUT IS THIS A "DATE" OR A "NON-DATE" DATE?
A "NON-DATE" DATE, FOR SURE, 'CAUSE I ONLY DO "NON-DATES" ON THE FIRST DATE!
12

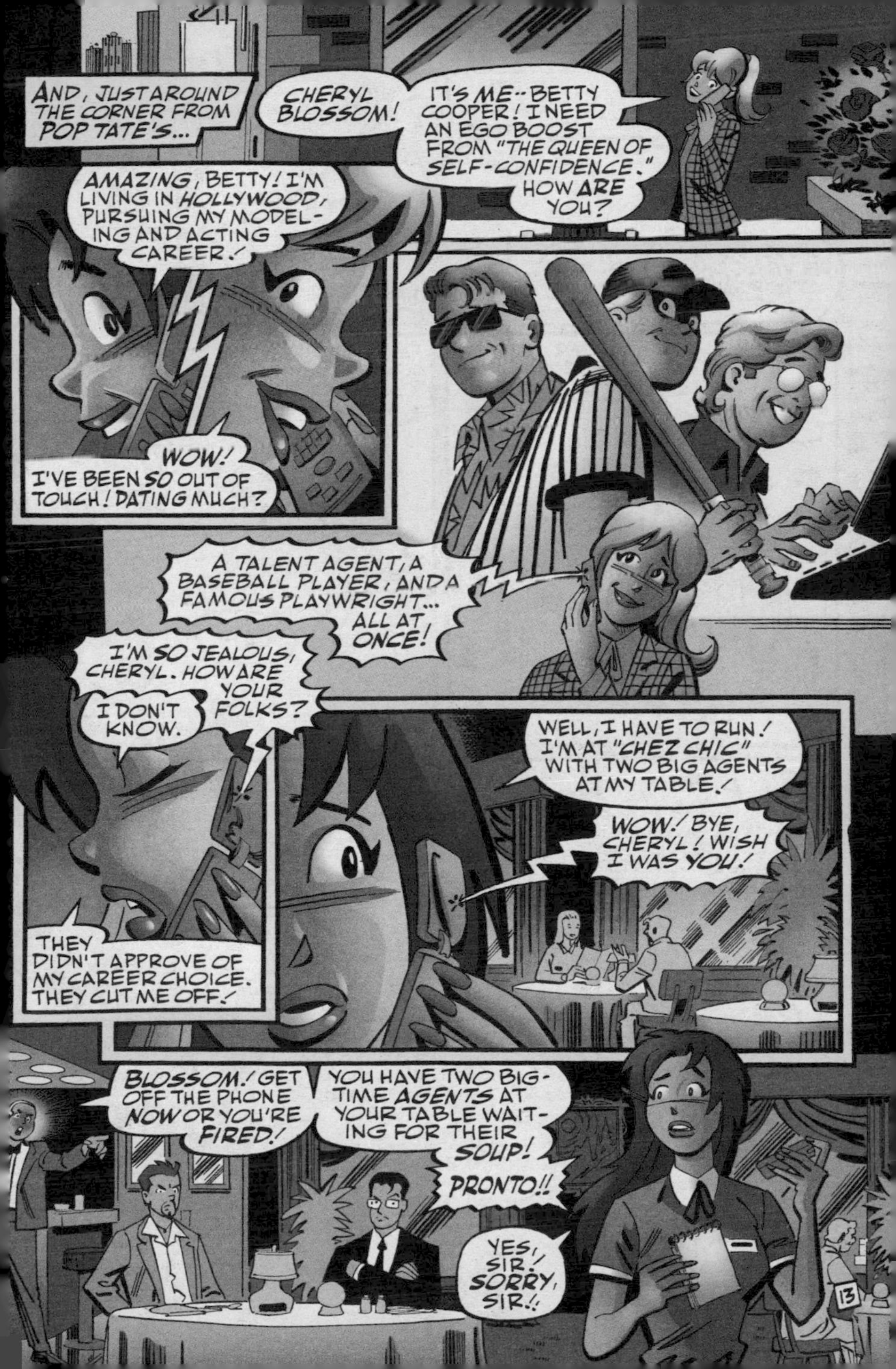

AND, JUST AROUND THE CORNER FROM POP TATE'S...
CHERYL BLOSSOM!
IT'S ME-- BETTY COOPER! I NEED AN EGO BOOST FROM "THE QUEEN OF SELF-CONFIDENCE." HOW ARE YOU?
AMAZING, BETTY! I'M LIVING IN HOLLYWOOD, PURSUING MY MODELING AND ACTING CAREER!
WOW! I'VE BEEN SO OUT OF TOUCH! DATING MUCH?
A TALENT AGENT, A BASEBALL PLAYER, AND A FAMOUS PLAYWRIGHT... ALL AT ONCE!
I'M SO JEALOUS, CHERYL. HOW ARE YOUR FOLKS?
I DON'T KNOW.
THEY DIDN'T APPROVE OF MY CAREER CHOICE. THEY CUT ME OFF!
WELL, I HAVE TO RUN! I'M AT "CHEZ CHIC" WITH TWO BIG AGENTS AT MY TABLE!
WOW! BYE, CHERYL! WISH I WAS YOU!
BLOSSOM! GET OFF THE PHONE NOW OR YOU'RE FIRED!
YOU HAVE TWO BIG-TIME AGENTS AT YOUR TABLE WAITING FOR THEIR SOUP!
PRONTO!!
YES, SIR! SORRY, SIR!
13

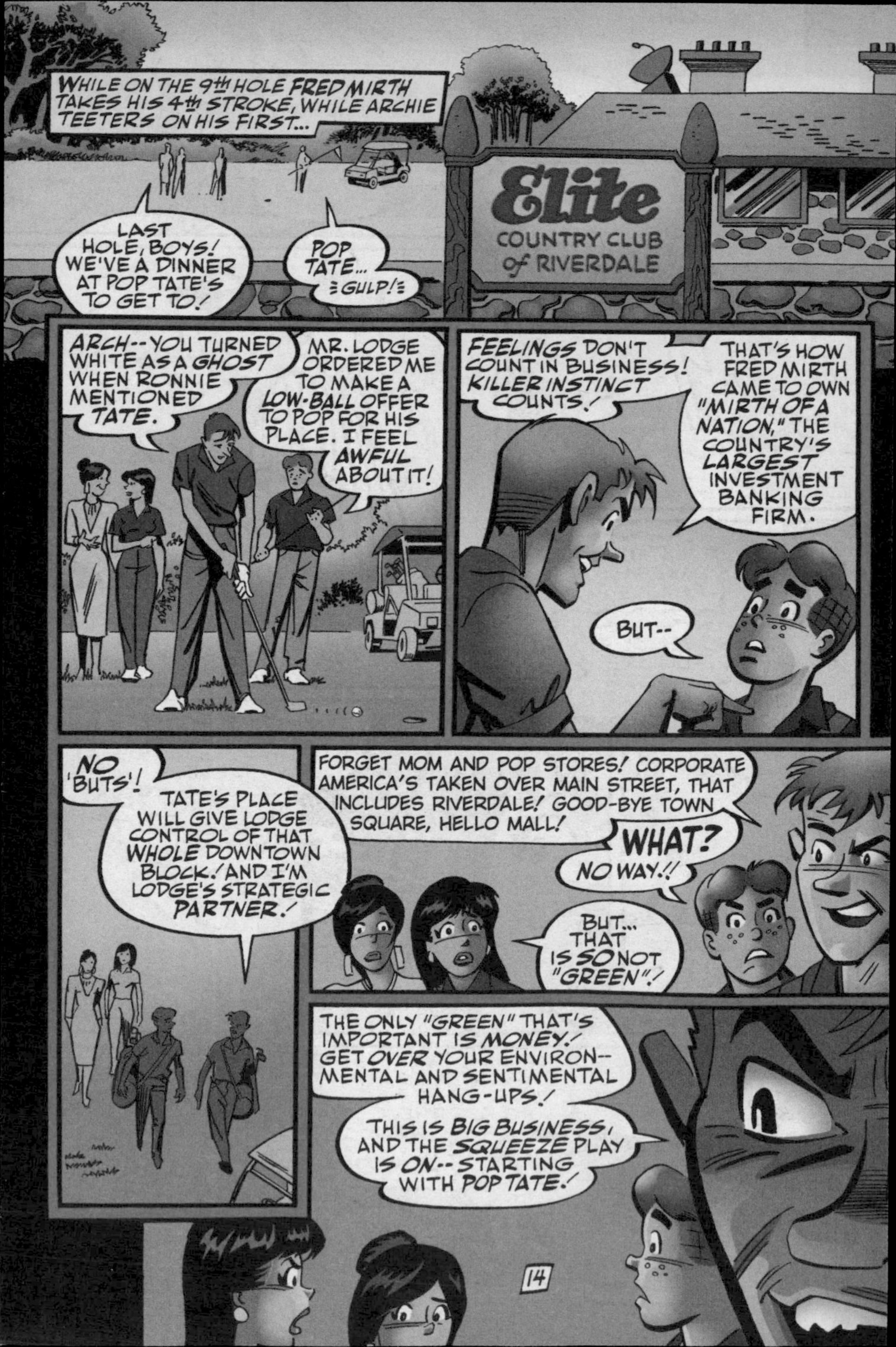
WHILE ON THE 9th HOLE FRED MIRTH TAKES HIS 4th STROKE, WHILE ARCHIE TEETERS ON HIS FIRST...
Elite COUNTRY CLUB of RIVERDALE
LAST HOLE, BOYS! WE'VE A DINNER AT POP TATE'S TO GET TO!
POP TATE... GULP!
ARCH--YOU TURNED WHITE AS A GHOST WHEN RONNIE MENTIONED TATE.
MR. LODGE ORDERED ME TO MAKE A LOW-BALL OFFER TO POP FOR HIS PLACE. I FEEL AWFUL ABOUT IT!
FEELINGS DON'T COUNT IN BUSINESS! KILLER INSTINCT COUNTS!
THAT'S HOW FRED MIRTH CAME TO OWN "MIRTH OF A NATION," THE COUNTRY'S LARGEST INVESTMENT BANKING FIRM.
BUT--
NO 'BUTS'!
TATE'S PLACE WILL GIVE LODGE CONTROL OF THAT WHOLE DOWNTOWN BLOCK! AND I'M LODGE'S STRATEGIC PARTNER!
FORGET MOM AND POP STORES! CORPORATE AMERICA'S TAKEN OVER MAIN STREET, THAT INCLUDES RIVERDALE! GOOD-BYE TOWN SQUARE, HELLO MALL!
WHAT? NO WAY!!
BUT... THAT IS SO NOT "GREEN"!
THE ONLY "GREEN" THAT'S IMPORTANT IS MONEY! GET OVER YOUR ENVIRON-MENTAL AND SENTIMENTAL HANG-UPS!
THIS IS BIG BUSINESS, AND THE SQUEEZE PLAY IS ON--STARTING WITH POP TATE!
14

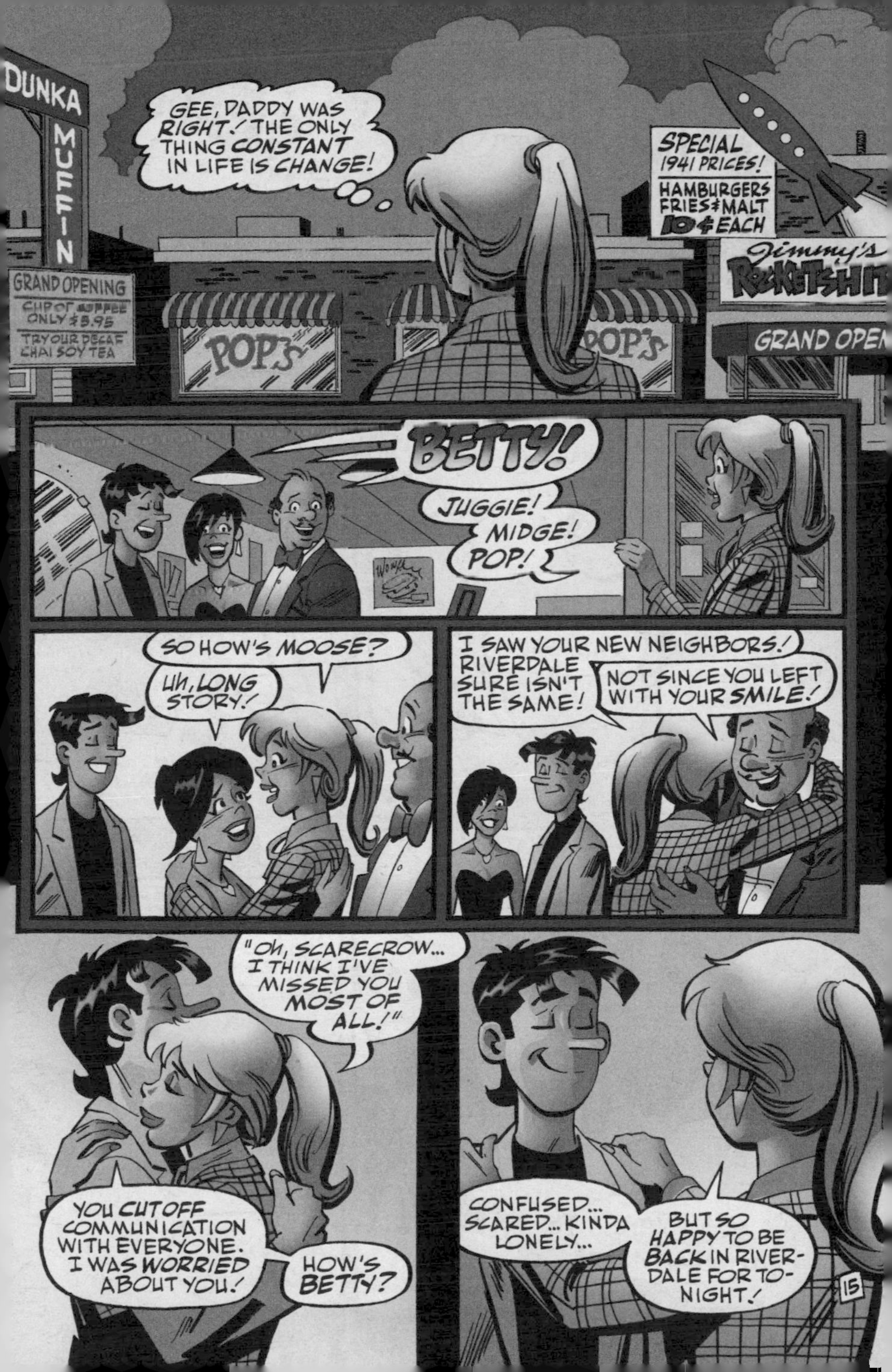
DUNKA MUFFIN
GRAND OPENING
CUP OF COFFEE ONLY $5.95
TRY OUR DECAF CHAI SOY TEA
GEE, DADDY WAS RIGHT! THE ONLY THING CONSTANT IN LIFE IS CHANGE!
SPECIAL 1941 PRICES!
HAMBURGERS FRIES & MALT 10¢ EACH
POP'S
POP'S
GRAND OPEN
BETTY!
JUGGIE! MIDGE! POP!
SO HOW'S MOOSE?
UH, LONG STORY!
I SAW YOUR NEW NEIGHBORS! RIVERDALE SURE ISN'T THE SAME!
NOT SINCE YOU LEFT WITH YOUR SMILE!
"OH, SCARECROW... I THINK I'VE MISSED YOU MOST OF ALL!"
YOU CUT OFF COMMUNICATION WITH EVERYONE. I WAS WORRIED ABOUT YOU!
HOW'S BETTY?
CONFUSED... SCARED... KINDA LONELY...
BUT SO HAPPY TO BE BACK IN RIVERDALE FOR TONIGHT!
15

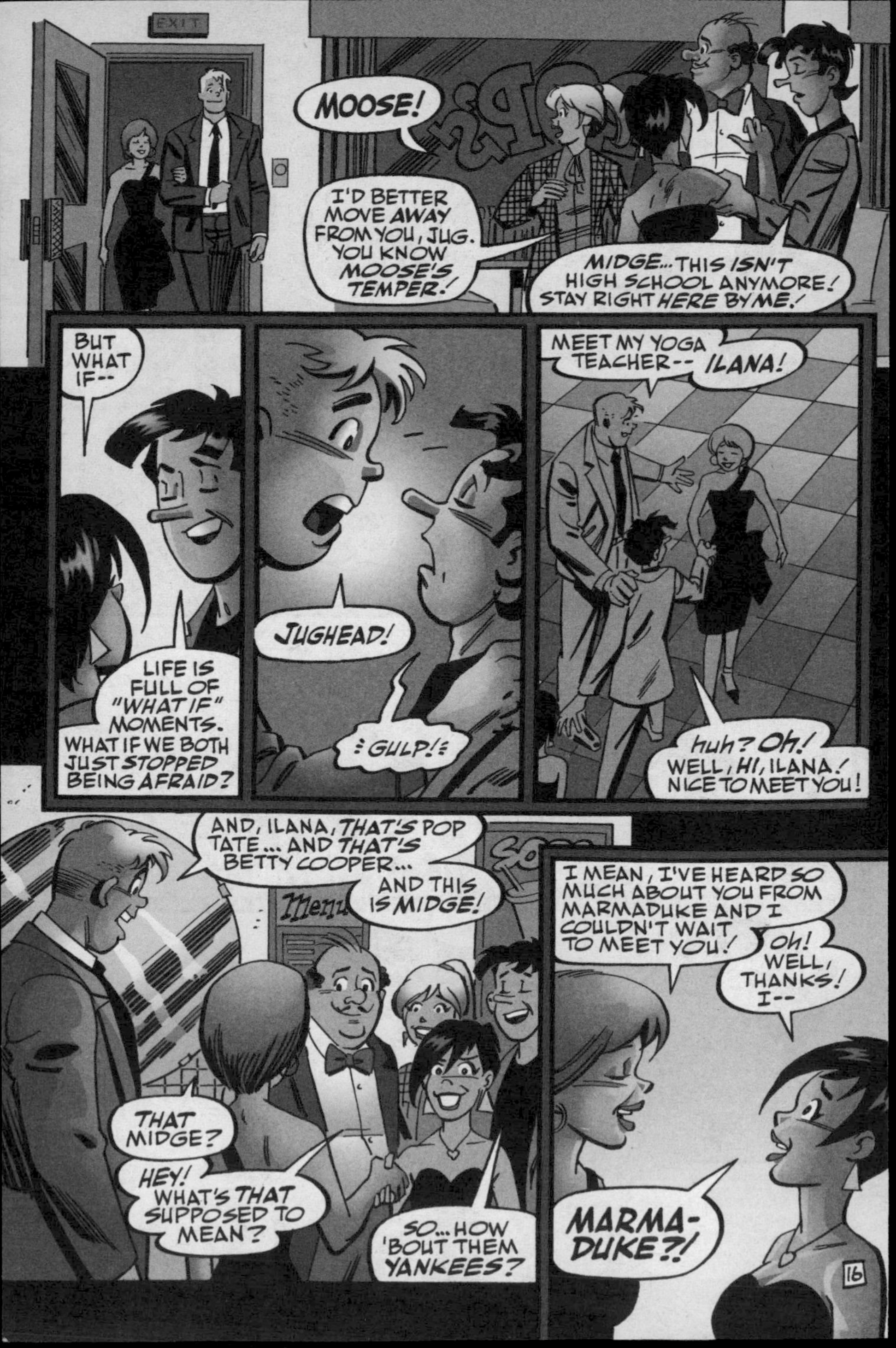
EXIT
MOOSE!
I'D BETTER MOVE AWAY FROM YOU, JUG. YOU KNOW MOOSE'S TEMPER!
MIDGE... THIS ISN'T HIGH SCHOOL ANYMORE! STAY RIGHT HERE BY ME!
BUT WHAT IF--
LIFE IS FULL OF "WHAT IF" MOMENTS. WHAT IF WE BOTH JUST STOPPED BEING AFRAID?
JUGHEAD!
GULP!
MEET MY YOGA TEACHER-- ILANA!
huh? Oh! WELL, HI, ILANA! NICE TO MEET YOU!
AND, ILANA, THAT'S POP TATE ... AND THAT'S BETTY COOPER...
AND THIS IS MIDGE!
Menu
THAT MIDGE?
HEY! WHAT'S THAT SUPPOSED TO MEAN?
SO... HOW 'BOUT THEM YANKEES?
I MEAN, I'VE HEARD SO MUCH ABOUT YOU FROM MARMADUKE AND I COULDN'T WAIT TO MEET YOU!
Oh! WELL, THANKS! I--
MARMA-DUKE?!
16

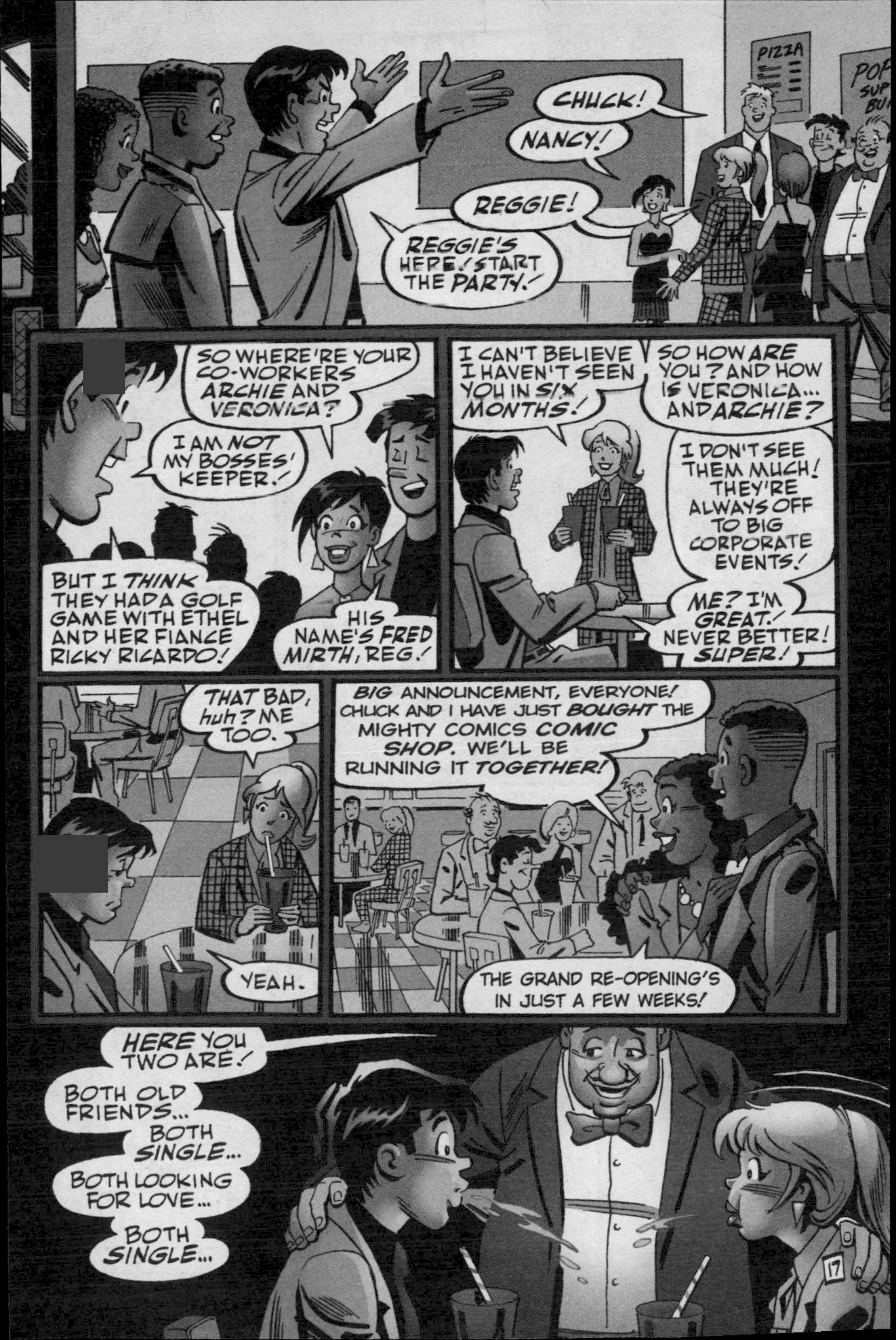
PIZZA
CHUCK!
NANCY!
REGGIE!
REGGIE'S HERE! START THE PARTY!
SO WHERE'RE YOUR CO-WORKERS ARCHIE AND VERONICA?
I AM NOT MY BOSSES' KEEPER!
BUT I THINK THEY HAD A GOLF GAME WITH ETHEL AND HER FIANCE RICKY RICARDO!
HIS NAME'S FRED MIRTH, REG!
I CAN'T BELIEVE I HAVEN'T SEEN YOU IN SIX MONTHS!
SO HOW ARE YOU? AND HOW IS VERONICA... AND ARCHIE?
I DON'T SEE THEM MUCH! THEY'RE ALWAYS OFF TO BIG CORPORATE EVENTS!
ME? I'M GREAT! NEVER BETTER! SUPER!
THAT BAD, huh? ME TOO.
YEAH.
BIG ANNOUNCEMENT, EVERYONE! CHUCK AND I HAVE JUST BOUGHT THE MIGHTY COMICS COMIC SHOP. WE'LL BE RUNNING IT TOGETHER!
THE GRAND RE-OPENING'S IN JUST A FEW WEEKS!
HERE YOU TWO ARE!
BOTH OLD FRIENDS...
BOTH SINGLE...
BOTH LOOKING FOR LOVE...
BOTH SINGLE...

HIYA GANG!

BETTY! THE GANG'S ALL HERE!

'CEPT DILTON! WONDER WHATEVER HAPPENED TO HIM?

HEY, POP... CAN I TALK TO YOU FOR A MINUTE...IN PRIVATE?

SOUNDS OMINOUSLY LIKE BUSINESS, M'BOY! CERTAINLY ...BUT I INCLUDE JUGHEAD NOW ON ALL BUSINESS MATTERS.

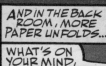

AND IN THE BACK ROOM, MORE PAPER UNFOLDS...

WHAT'S ON YOUR MIND, SON?

WELL, POP... MR. LODGE WANTS ME TO GIVE YOU THIS OFFER TO BUY YOUR CHOKLIT SHOPPE.

OH. I SEE.

IT'S A GOOD OFFER, ARCH?

IT'S THE BEST MR. LODGE IS GOING TO MAKE, JUG... IN LIGHT OF THE NEW COMPETITION.

COMPETITION LODGE HIMSELF CREATED... SO HE COULD LOW-BALL POP OUT OF BUSINESS!

I HAD DREAMS OF BEING ABLE TO FINALLY RETIRE.

ARCH, POP'S WILLING TO TURN THIS PLACE OVER TO ME! I HAVE GREAT IDEAS! I KNOW I CAN MAKE THIS WORK!

BUT, JUG! YOU DON'T STAND A CHANCE WITH ALL THE COMPETITION

18

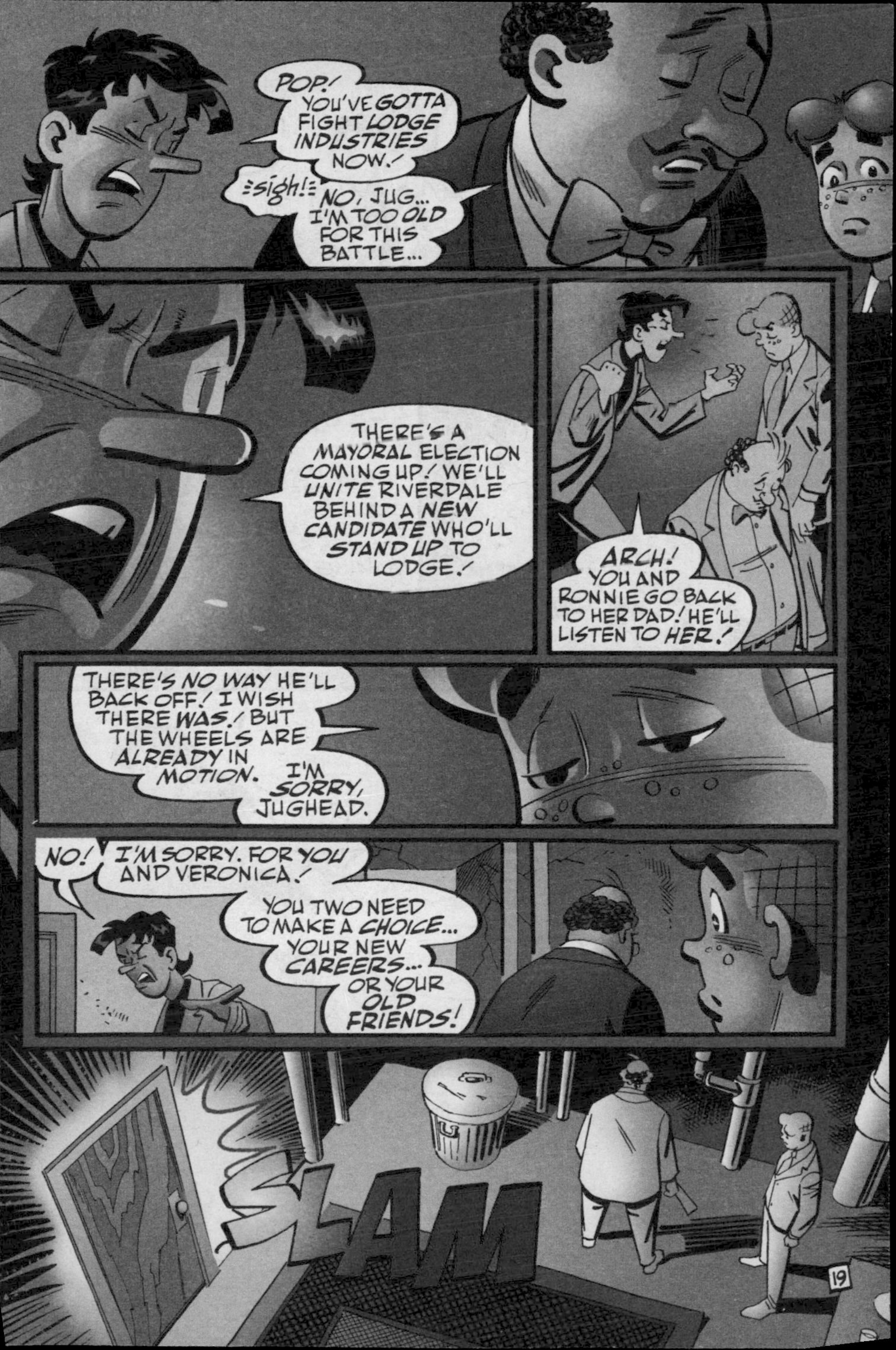
POP! YOU'VE GOTTA FIGHT LODGE INDUSTRIES NOW.!
sigh! NO, JUG... I'M TOO OLD FOR THIS BATTLE...
THERE'S A MAYORAL ELECTION COMING UP! WE'LL UNITE RIVERDALE BEHIND A NEW CANDIDATE WHO'LL STAND UP TO LODGE.!
ARCH! YOU AND RONNIE GO BACK TO HER DAD! HE'LL LISTEN TO HER.!
THERE'S NO WAY HE'LL BACK OFF! I WISH THERE WAS.! BUT THE WHEELS ARE ALREADY IN MOTION. I'M SORRY, JUGHEAD.
NO! I'M SORRY. FOR YOU AND VERONICA.!
YOU TWO NEED TO MAKE A CHOICE... YOUR NEW CAREERS... OR YOUR OLD FRIENDS!
SLAM
19

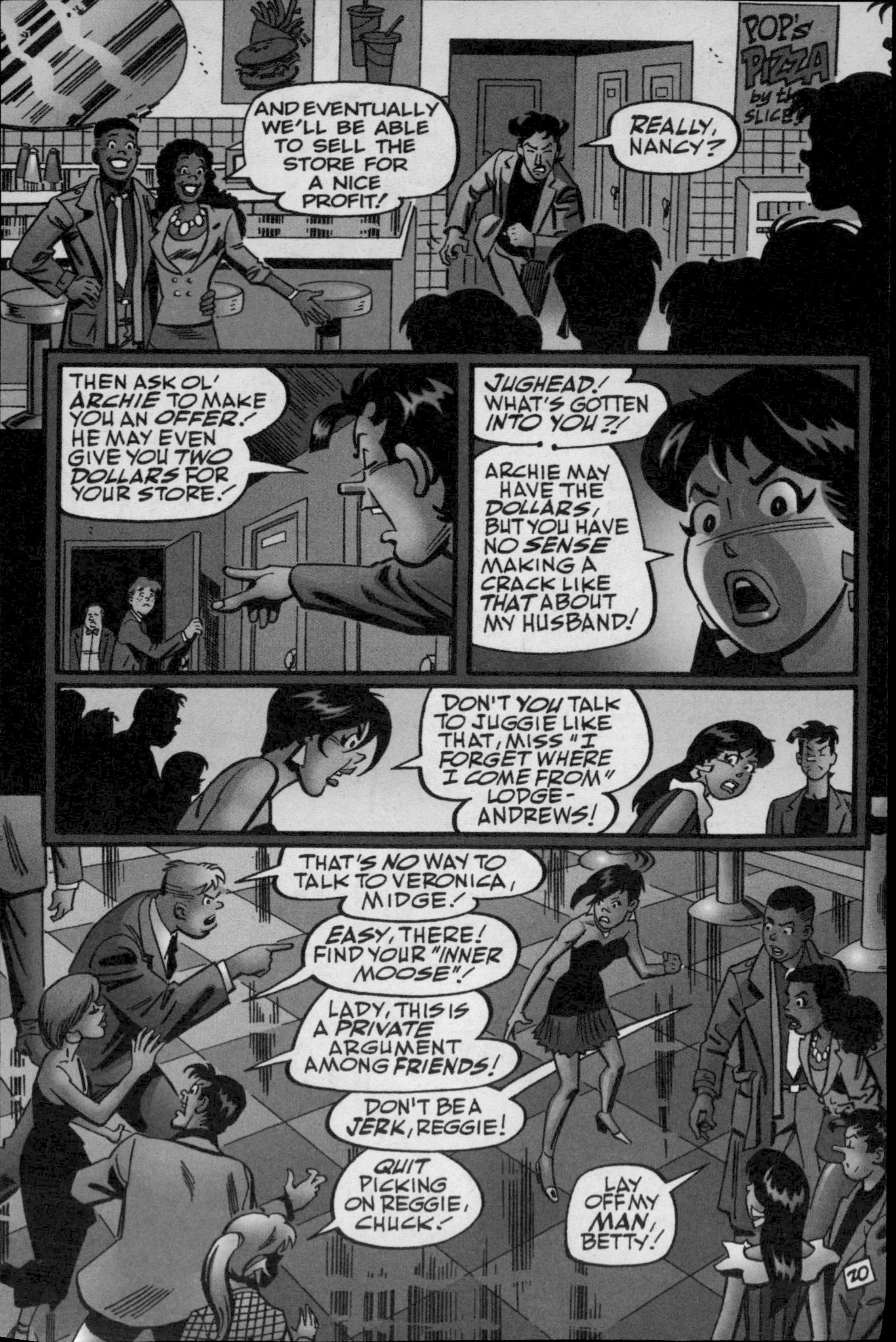
POP's PIZZA by th SLICE
AND EVENTUALLY WE'LL BE ABLE TO SELL THE STORE FOR A NICE PROFIT!
REALLY, NANCY?
THEN ASK OL' ARCHIE TO MAKE YOU AN OFFER! HE MAY EVEN GIVE YOU TWO DOLLARS FOR YOUR STORE!
JUGHEAD! WHAT'S GOTTEN INTO YOU?!
ARCHIE MAY HAVE THE DOLLARS, BUT YOU HAVE NO SENSE MAKING A CRACK LIKE THAT ABOUT MY HUSBAND!
DON'T YOU TALK TO JUGGIE LIKE THAT, MISS "I FORGET WHERE I COME FROM" LODGE-ANDREWS!
THAT'S NO WAY TO TALK TO VERONICA, MIDGE!
EASY, THERE! FIND YOUR "INNER MOOSE"!
LADY, THIS IS A PRIVATE ARGUMENT AMONG FRIENDS!
DON'T BE A JERK, REGGIE!
QUIT PICKING ON REGGIE, CHUCK!
LAY OFF MY MAN, BETTY!
20

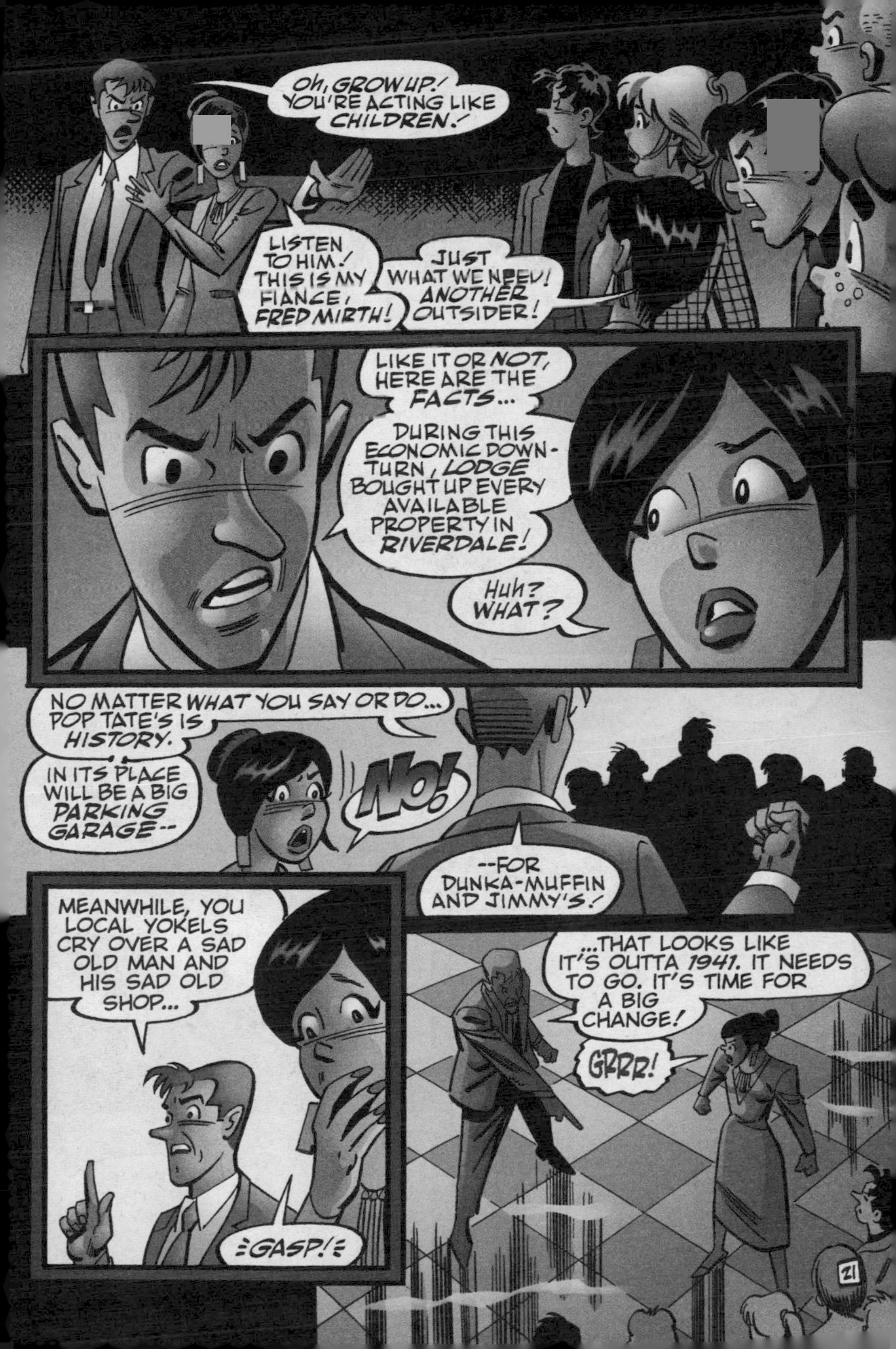
Oh, GROW UP! YOU'RE ACTING LIKE CHILDREN.!
LISTEN TO HIM! THIS IS MY FIANCE, FRED MIRTH!
JUST WHAT WE NEED! ANOTHER OUTSIDER!
LIKE IT OR NOT, HERE ARE THE FACTS...
DURING THIS ECONOMIC DOWN-TURN, LODGE BOUGHT UP EVERY AVAILABLE PROPERTY IN RIVERDALE!
Huh? WHAT?
NO MATTER WHAT YOU SAY OR DO... POP TATE'S IS HISTORY.
IN ITS PLACE WILL BE A BIG PARKING GARAGE--
NO!
--FOR DUNKA-MUFFIN AND JIMMY'S!
MEANWHILE, YOU LOCAL YOKELS CRY OVER A SAD OLD MAN AND HIS SAD OLD SHOP...
GASP!
...THAT LOOKS LIKE IT'S OUTTA 1941. IT NEEDS TO GO. IT'S TIME FOR A BIG CHANGE!
GRRR!
21

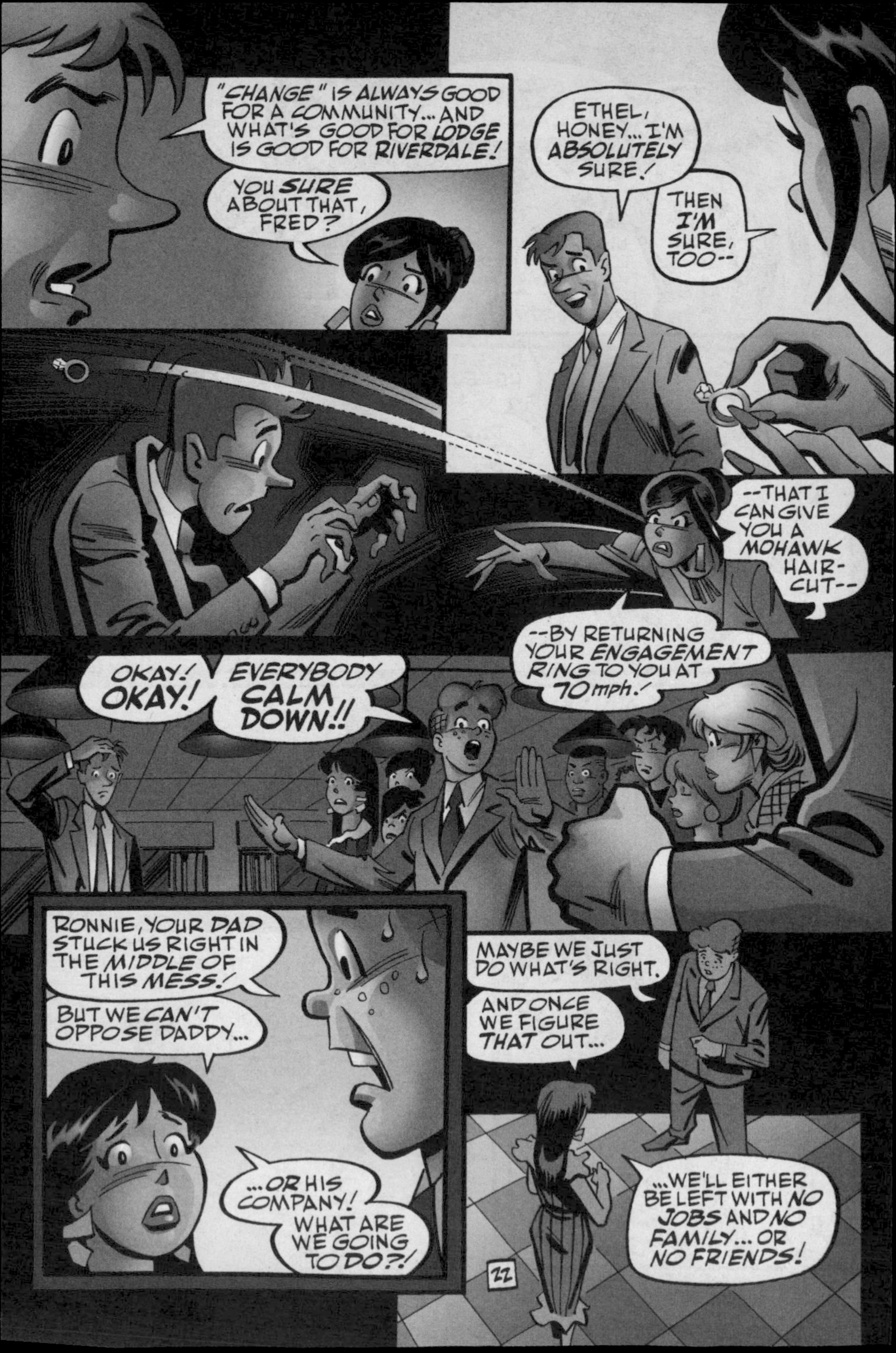
"CHANGE" IS ALWAYS GOOD FOR A COMMUNITY... AND WHAT'S GOOD FOR LODGE IS GOOD FOR RIVERDALE!
YOU SURE ABOUT THAT, FRED?
ETHEL, HONEY... I'M ABSOLUTELY SURE!
THEN I'M SURE, TOO--
--THAT I CAN GIVE YOU A MOHAWK HAIR-CUT--
--BY RETURNING YOUR ENGAGEMENT RING TO YOU AT 70 mph.!
OKAY! OKAY!
EVERYBODY CALM DOWN!!
RONNIE, YOUR DAD STUCK US RIGHT IN THE MIDDLE OF THIS MESS!
BUT WE CAN'T OPPOSE DADDY...
...OR HIS COMPANY!
WHAT ARE WE GOING TO DO?!
MAYBE WE JUST DO WHAT'S RIGHT.
AND ONCE WE FIGURE THAT OUT...
...WE'LL EITHER BE LEFT WITH NO JOBS AND NO FAMILY... OR NO FRIENDS!
22

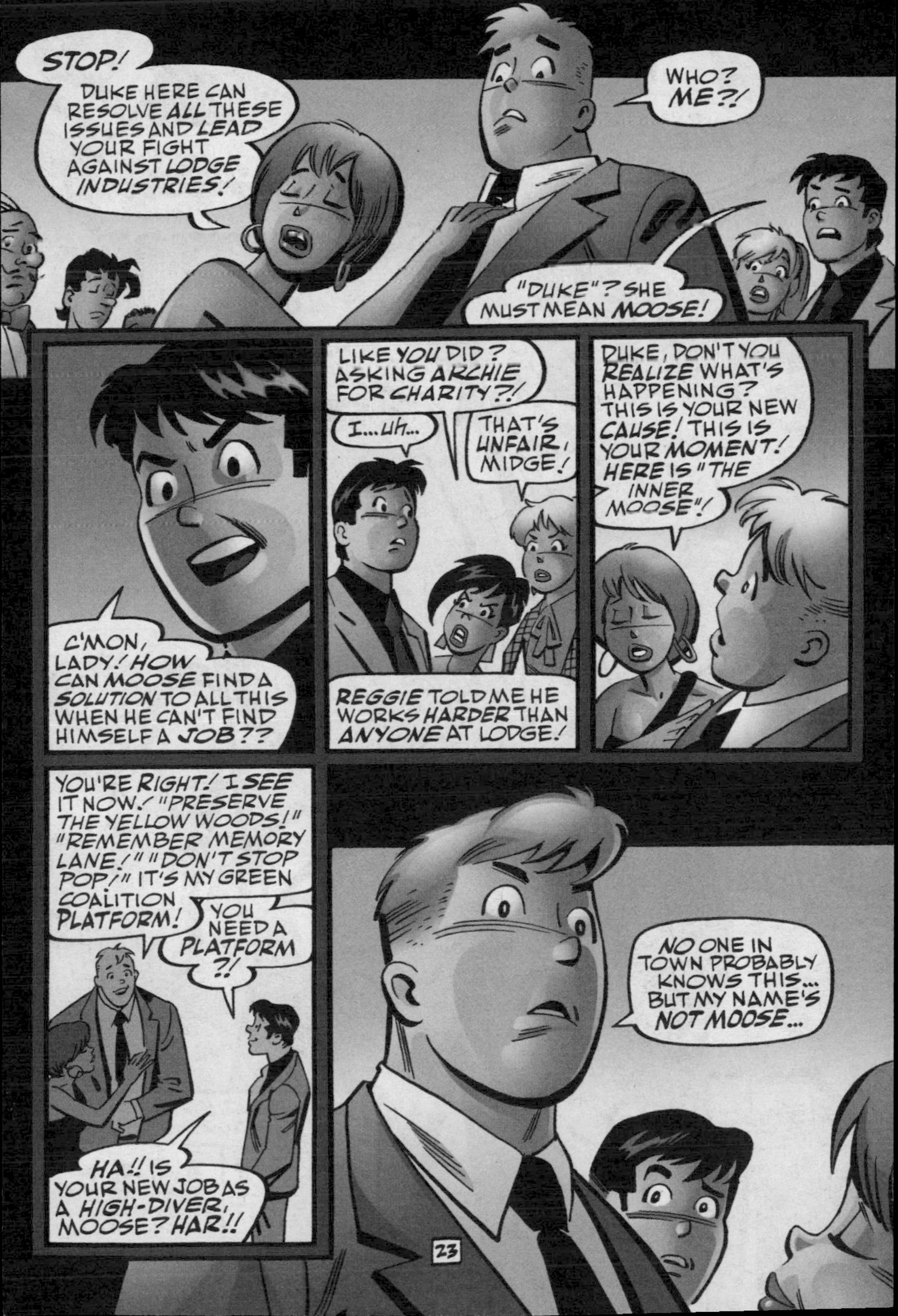

STOP!
DUKE HERE CAN RESOLVE ALL THESE ISSUES AND LEAD YOUR FIGHT AGAINST LODGE INDUSTRIES!
WHO? ME?!
"DUKE"? SHE MUST MEAN MOOSE!
C'MON, LADY! HOW CAN MOOSE FIND A SOLUTION TO ALL THIS WHEN HE CAN'T FIND HIMSELF A JOB??
LIKE YOU DID? ASKING ARCHIE FOR CHARITY?!
I...uh...
THAT'S UNFAIR, MIDGE!
REGGIE TOLD ME HE WORKS HARDER THAN ANYONE AT LODGE!
DUKE, DON'T YOU REALIZE WHAT'S HAPPENING? THIS IS YOUR NEW CAUSE! THIS IS YOUR MOMENT! HERE IS "THE INNER MOOSE"!
YOU'RE RIGHT! I SEE IT NOW! "PRESERVE THE YELLOW WOODS!" "REMEMBER MEMORY LANE!" "DON'T STOP POP!" IT'S MY GREEN COALITION PLATFORM!
YOU NEED A PLATFORM?!
HA!! IS YOUR NEW JOB AS A HIGH-DIVER, MOOSE? HAR!!
NO ONE IN TOWN PROBABLY KNOWS THIS... BUT MY NAME'S NOT MOOSE...

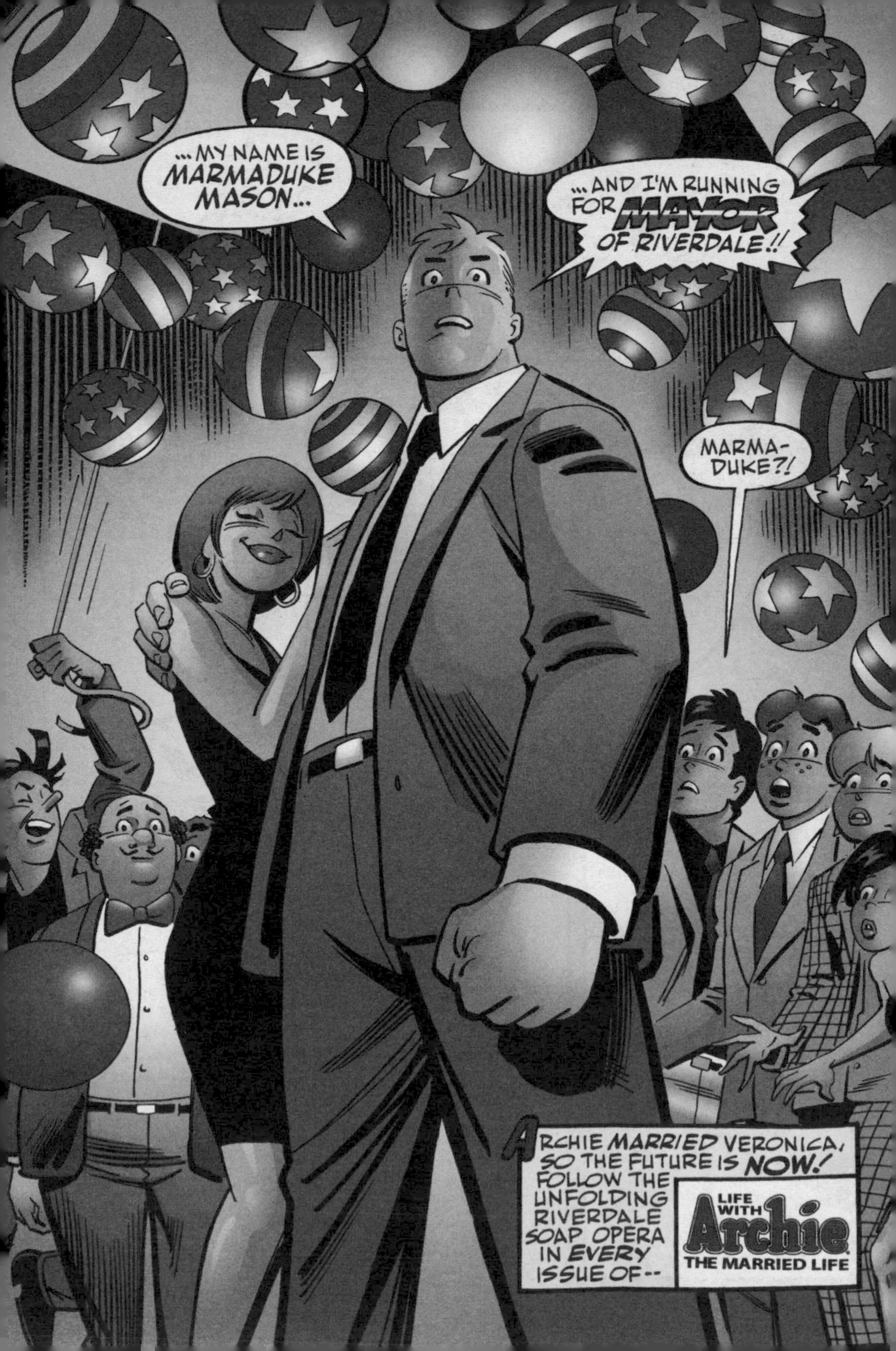
...MY NAME IS MARMADUKE MASON...
...AND I'M RUNNING FOR MAYOR OF RIVERDALE!!
MARMA-DUKE?!
ARCHIE MARRIED VERONICA, SO THE FUTURE IS NOW! FOLLOW THE UNFOLDING RIVERDALE SOAP OPERA IN EVERY ISSUE OF--
LIFE WITH Archie
THE MARRIED LIFE

Egology
Tales from Riverdale Digest #37, 2010
by Craig Boldman, Fernando Ruiz, Jon D'Agostlno and Joe Morciglio

This story marked a milestone for me. When I started working at Archie in 2008 the company was in a much different place than it is now. We had time to mess around and would play "Which Archie character are you?" I got Reggie, due to a penchant for pranks (sorry, Paul!) and an ego to boot. Early in 2009, I was given the opportunity to color stories to be used in the digests. They were mostly non-credited reprint stories. Then one day I was offered the chance to color new stories that had never been done before! This was great! My time to shine! Finally I could color a story and get my name in the book! After coloring it I soon found out that the story wasn't going to be a lead story, it was a back-up story which only listed writer, penciler and inker credits. Talk about a shot to the ego. I guess it was fate that my own ego be humbled by a story about Reggie's!

--Joe Morciglio
Project Coordinator, Archie Comics

Snug as a Jug in a Rug
Jughead #206, 2011
by Craig Boldman, Rex Lindsey

Fear not! Silly slapstick humor is alive and well at Archie Comics in the form of *Jughead* comics.

I picked this story because Craig Boldman's script is a modern example of what Archie has done so well over the years. It's character-based, lean, fast-paced, and highly imaginative. It has one of Archie's signature punny titles. And with artist Rex Lindsey's own visual take on the characters and their surroundings, it adds up to a fresh Archie experience: a little bit classic, a little bit modern, and a lot of fun.

--Harold Buchholz
Executive Director of Publishing & Operations, Archie Comics

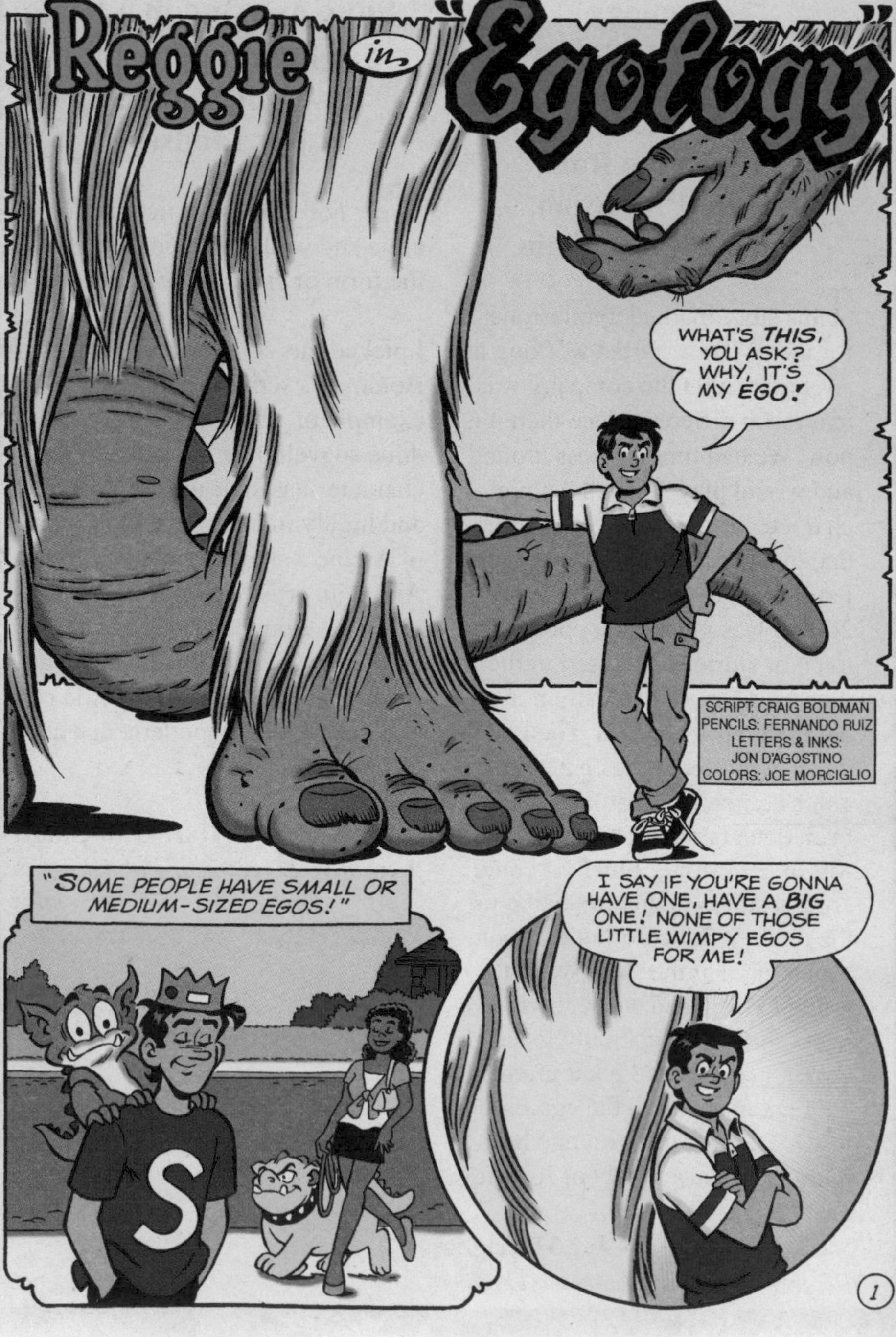
Reggie in "Egology"
WHAT'S THIS, YOU ASK? WHY, IT'S MY EGO!
SCRIPT: CRAIG BOLDMAN
PENCILS: FERNANDO RUIZ
LETTERS & INKS: JON D'AGOSTINO
COLORS: JOE MORCIGLIO
"SOME PEOPLE HAVE SMALL OR MEDIUM-SIZED EGOS!"
I SAY IF YOU'RE GONNA HAVE ONE, HAVE A BIG ONE! NONE OF THOSE LITTLE WIMPY EGOS FOR ME!
1

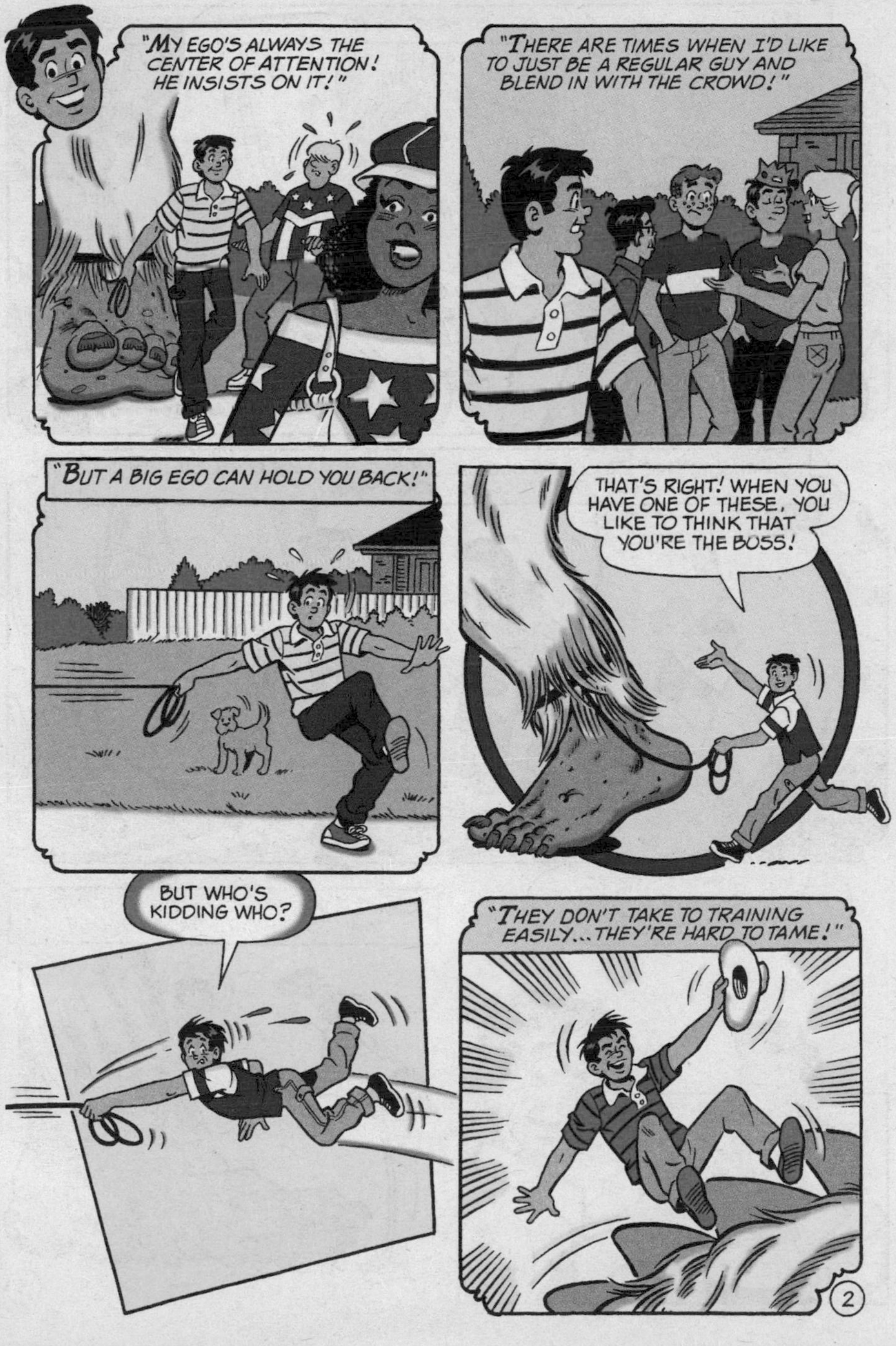
"MY EGO'S ALWAYS THE CENTER OF ATTENTION! HE INSISTS ON IT!"
"THERE ARE TIMES WHEN I'D LIKE TO JUST BE A REGULAR GUY AND BLEND IN WITH THE CROWD!"
"BUT A BIG EGO CAN HOLD YOU BACK!"
THAT'S RIGHT! WHEN YOU HAVE ONE OF THESE, YOU LIKE TO THINK THAT YOU'RE THE BOSS!
BUT WHO'S KIDDING WHO?
"THEY DON'T TAKE TO TRAINING EASILY...THEY'RE HARD TO TAME!"
2

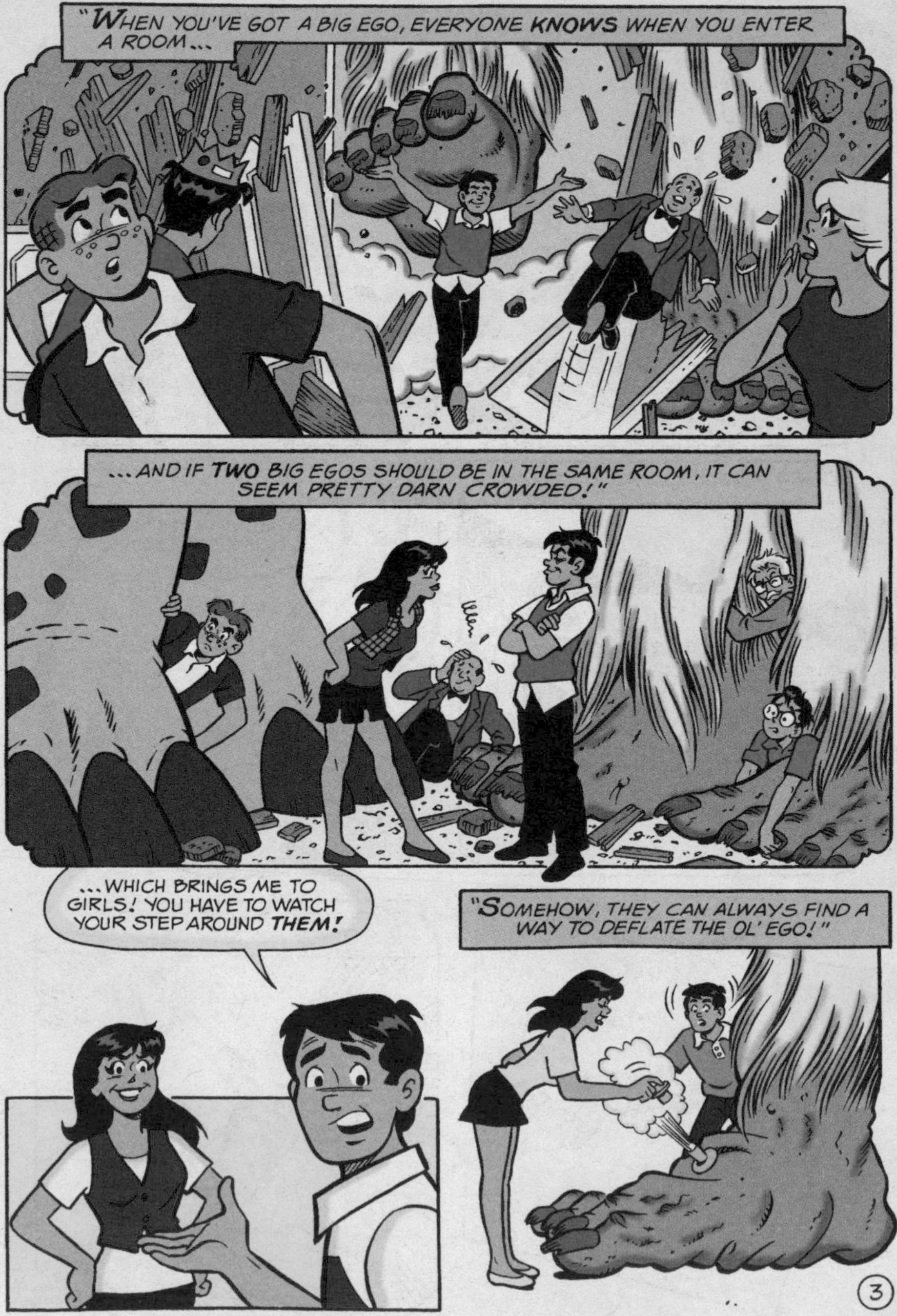
"WHEN YOU'VE GOT A BIG EGO, EVERYONE KNOWS WHEN YOU ENTER A ROOM...
...AND IF TWO BIG EGOS SHOULD BE IN THE SAME ROOM, IT CAN SEEM PRETTY DARN CROWDED!"
...WHICH BRINGS ME TO GIRLS! YOU HAVE TO WATCH YOUR STEP AROUND THEM!
"SOMEHOW, THEY CAN ALWAYS FIND A WAY TO DEFLATE THE OL' EGO!"
3

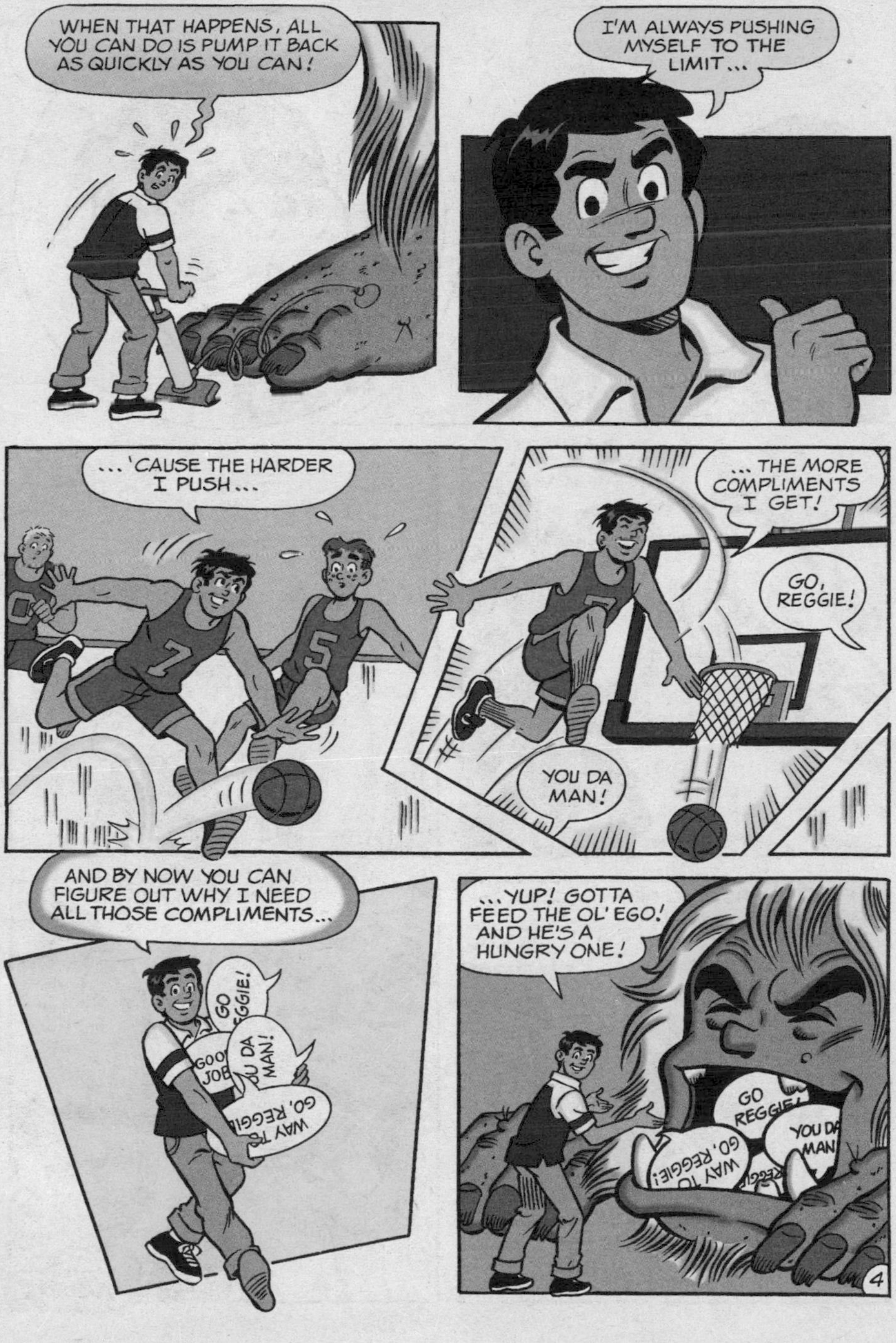
WHEN THAT HAPPENS, ALL YOU CAN DO IS PUMP IT BACK AS QUICKLY AS YOU CAN!
I'M ALWAYS PUSHING MYSELF TO THE LIMIT...
...'CAUSE THE HARDER I PUSH...
...THE MORE COMPLIMENTS I GET!
GO, REGGIE!
YOU DA MAN!
AND BY NOW YOU CAN FIGURE OUT WHY I NEED ALL THOSE COMPLIMENTS...
GO REGGIE!
...YUP! GOTTA FEED THE OL' EGO! AND HE'S A HUNGRY ONE!
4

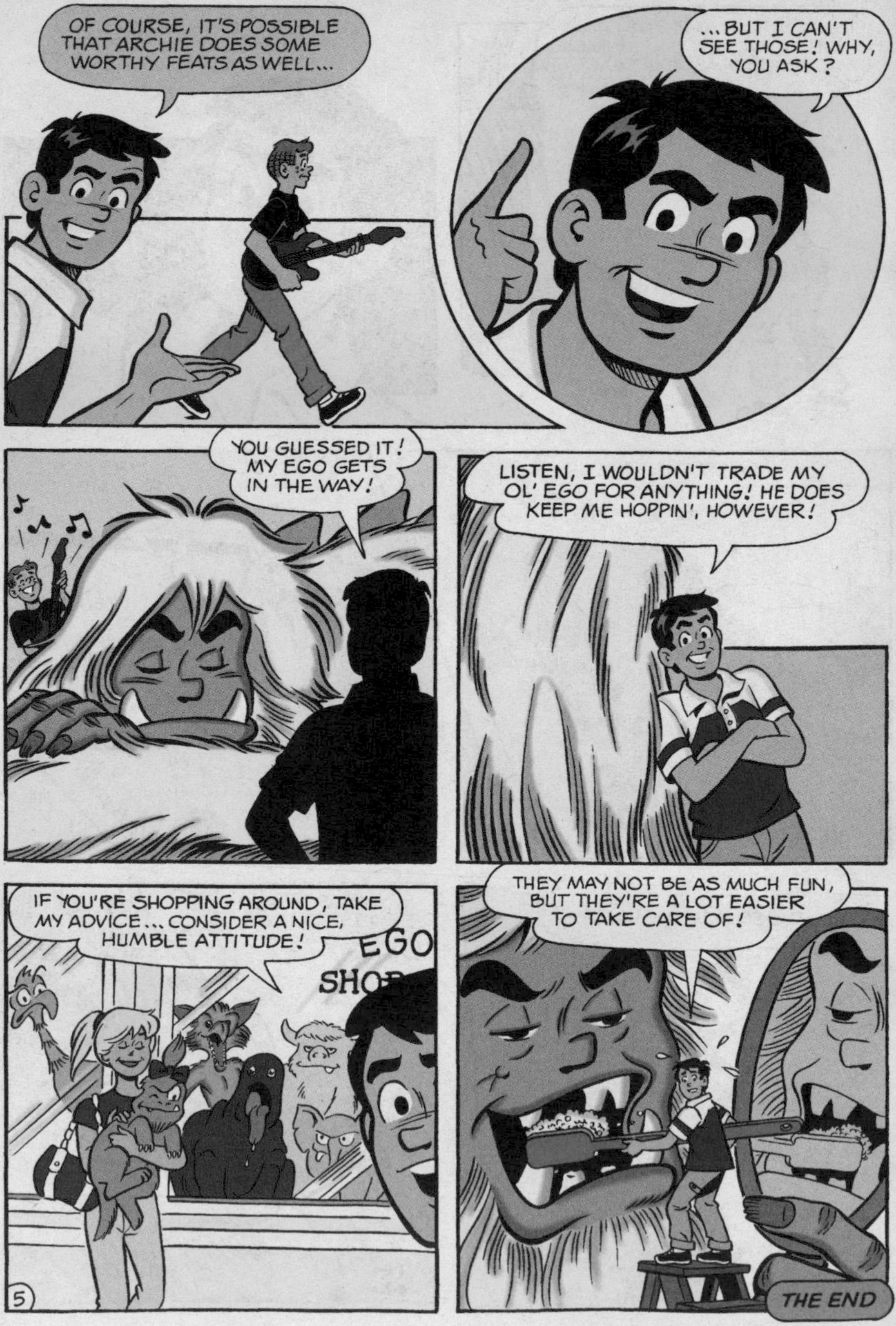
OF COURSE, IT'S POSSIBLE THAT ARCHIE DOES SOME WORTHY FEATS AS WELL...
...BUT I CAN'T SEE THOSE! WHY, YOU ASK?
YOU GUESSED IT! MY EGO GETS IN THE WAY!
LISTEN, I WOULDN'T TRADE MY OL' EGO FOR ANYTHING! HE DOES KEEP ME HOPPIN', HOWEVER!
IF YOU'RE SHOPPING AROUND, TAKE MY ADVICE... CONSIDER A NICE, HUMBLE ATTITUDE!
EGO
THEY MAY NOT BE AS MUCH FUN, BUT THEY'RE A LOT EASIER TO TAKE CARE OF!
5
THE END

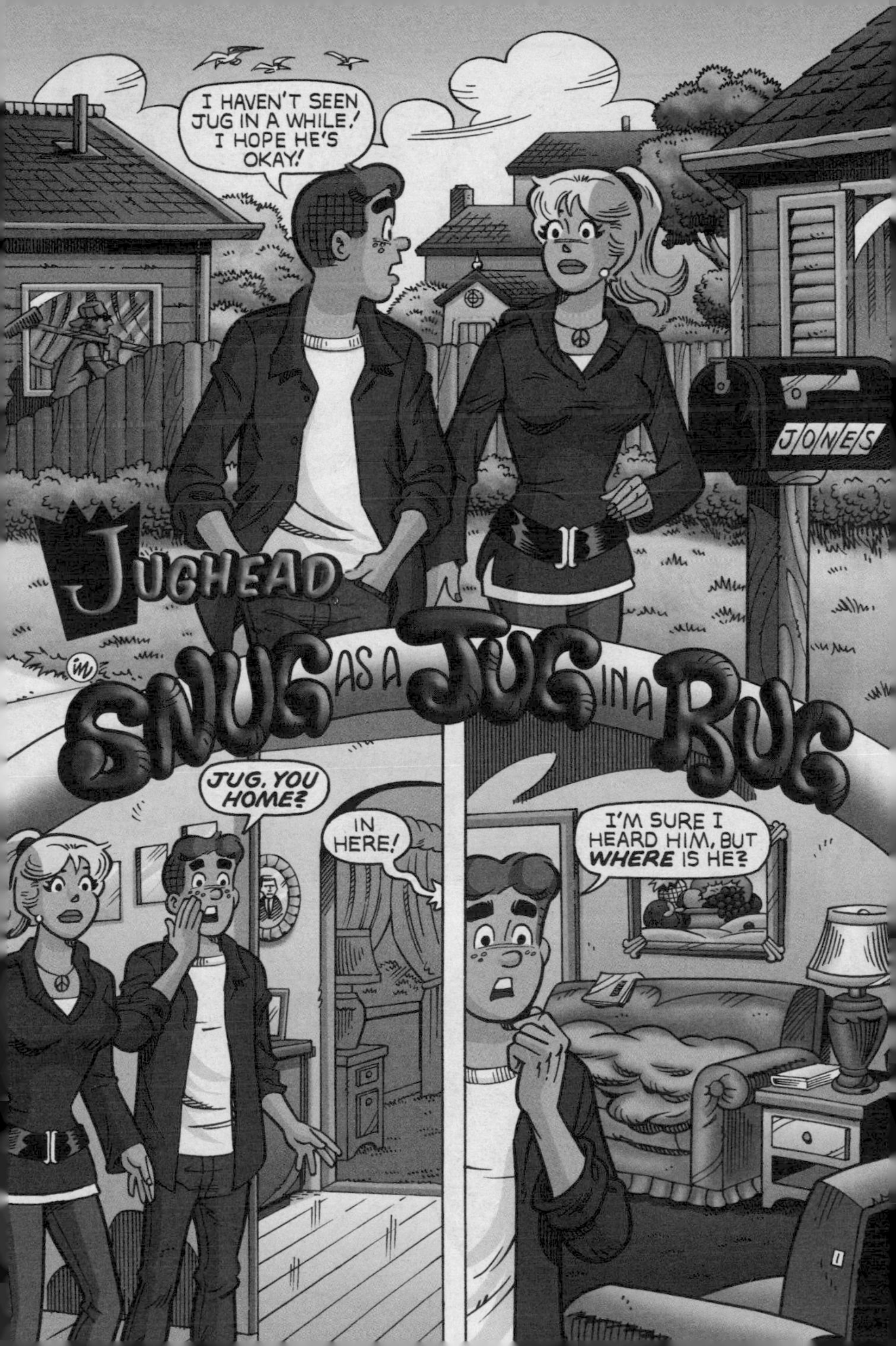
I HAVEN'T SEEN JUG IN A WHILE! I HOPE HE'S OKAY!
JONES
JUGHEAD
in SNUG AS A JUG IN A RUG
JUG, YOU HOME?
IN HERE!
I'M SURE I HEARD HIM, BUT WHERE IS HE?

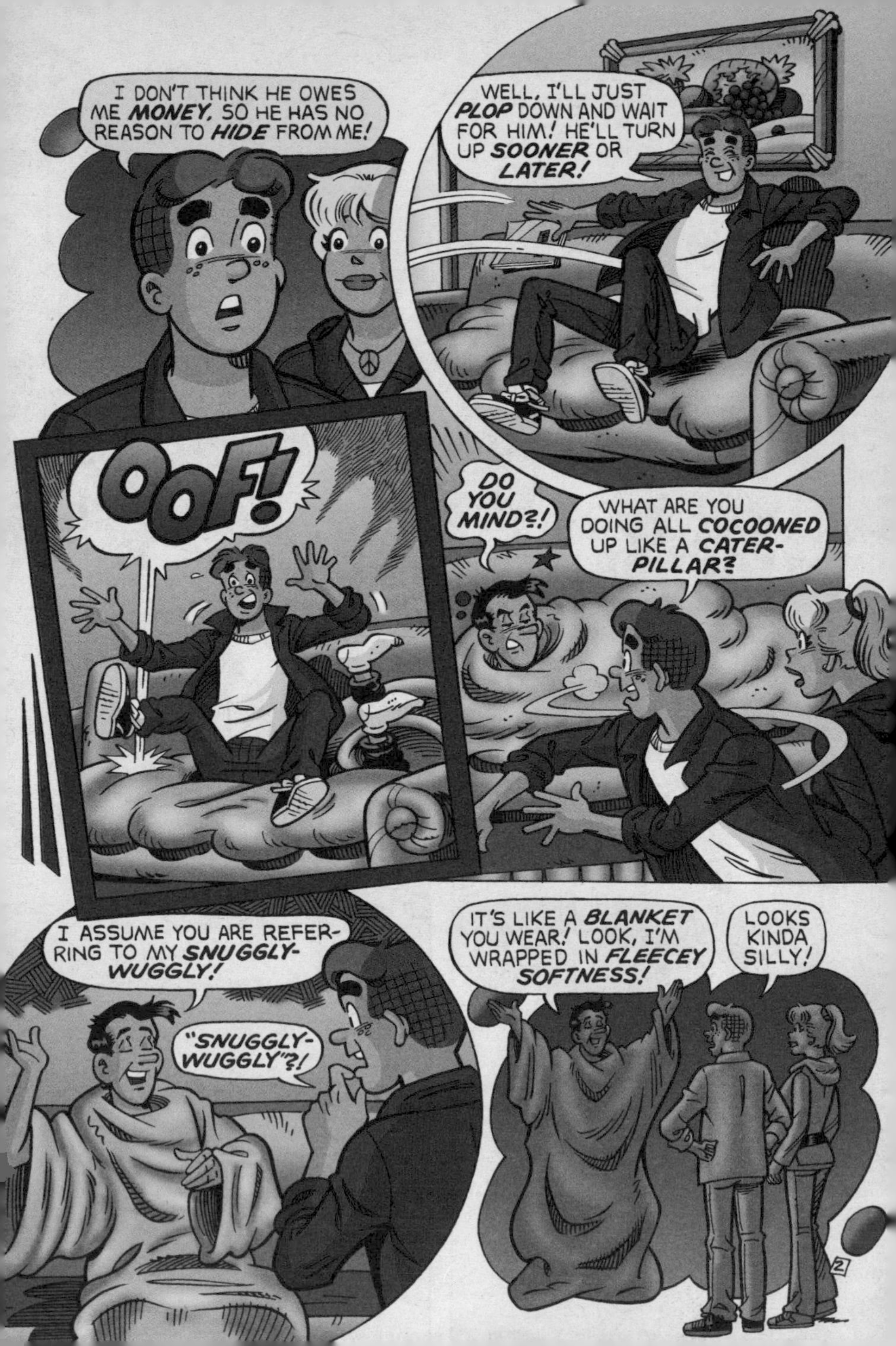
I DON'T THINK HE OWES ME MONEY, SO HE HAS NO REASON TO HIDE FROM ME!
WELL, I'LL JUST PLOP DOWN AND WAIT FOR HIM! HE'LL TURN UP SOONER OR LATER!
OOF!
DO YOU MIND?!
WHAT ARE YOU DOING ALL COCOONED UP LIKE A CATER-PILLAR?
I ASSUME YOU ARE REFER-RING TO MY SNUGGLY-WUGGLY!
"SNUGGLY-WUGGLY"?!
IT'S LIKE A BLANKET YOU WEAR! LOOK, I'M WRAPPED IN FLEECEY SOFTNESS!
LOOKS KINDA SILLY!
2

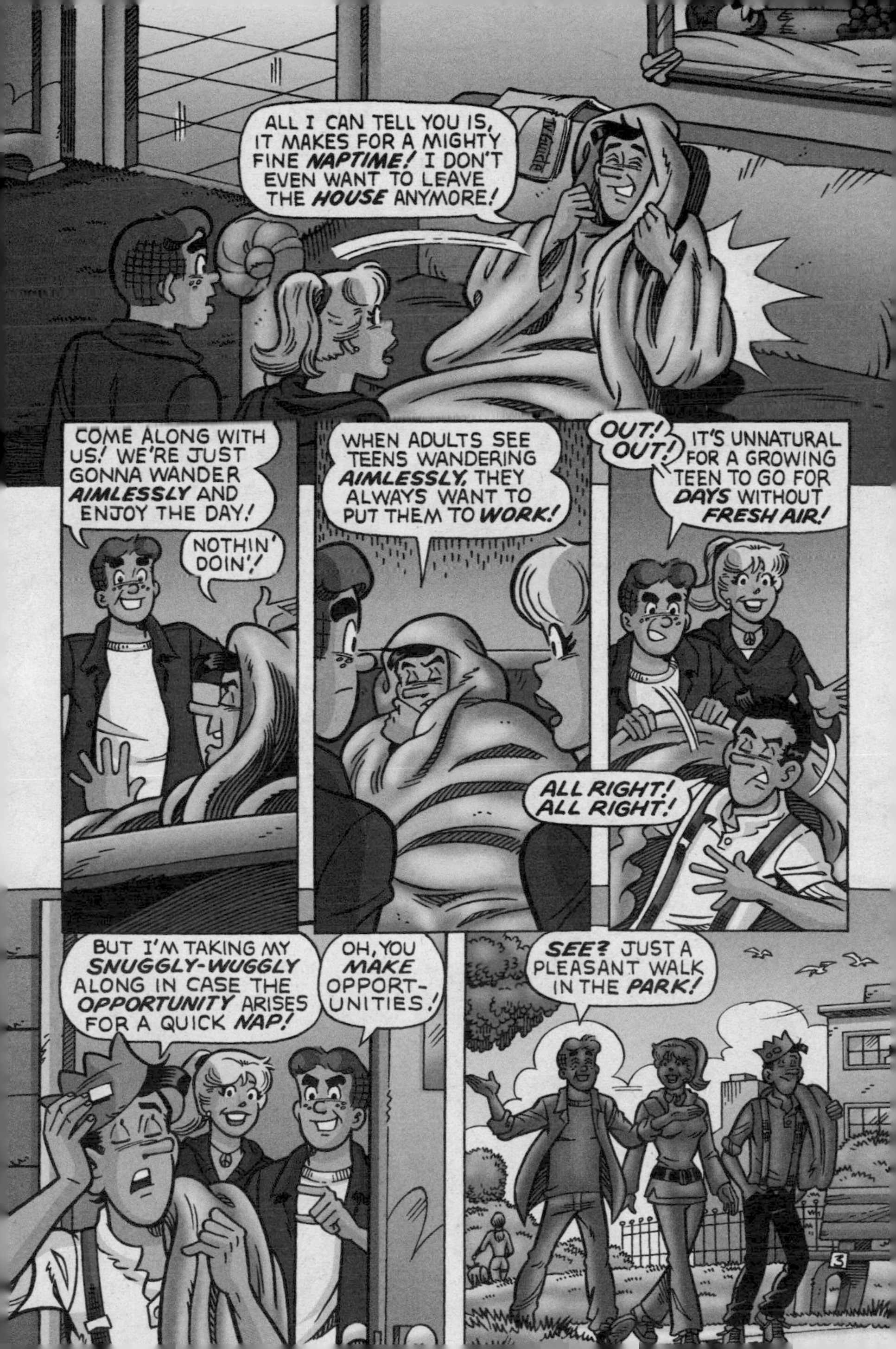
ALL I CAN TELL YOU IS, IT MAKES FOR A MIGHTY FINE NAPTIME! I DON'T EVEN WANT TO LEAVE THE HOUSE ANYMORE!
COME ALONG WITH US! WE'RE JUST GONNA WANDER AIMLESSLY AND ENJOY THE DAY!
NOTHIN' DOIN'!
WHEN ADULTS SEE TEENS WANDERING AIMLESSLY, THEY ALWAYS WANT TO PUT THEM TO WORK!
OUT! OUT!
IT'S UNNATURAL FOR A GROWING TEEN TO GO FOR DAYS WITHOUT FRESH AIR!
ALL RIGHT! ALL RIGHT!
BUT I'M TAKING MY SNUGGLY-WUGGLY ALONG IN CASE THE OPPORTUNITY ARISES FOR A QUICK NAP!
OH, YOU MAKE OPPORT-UNITIES!
SEE? JUST A PLEASANT WALK IN THE PARK!
3

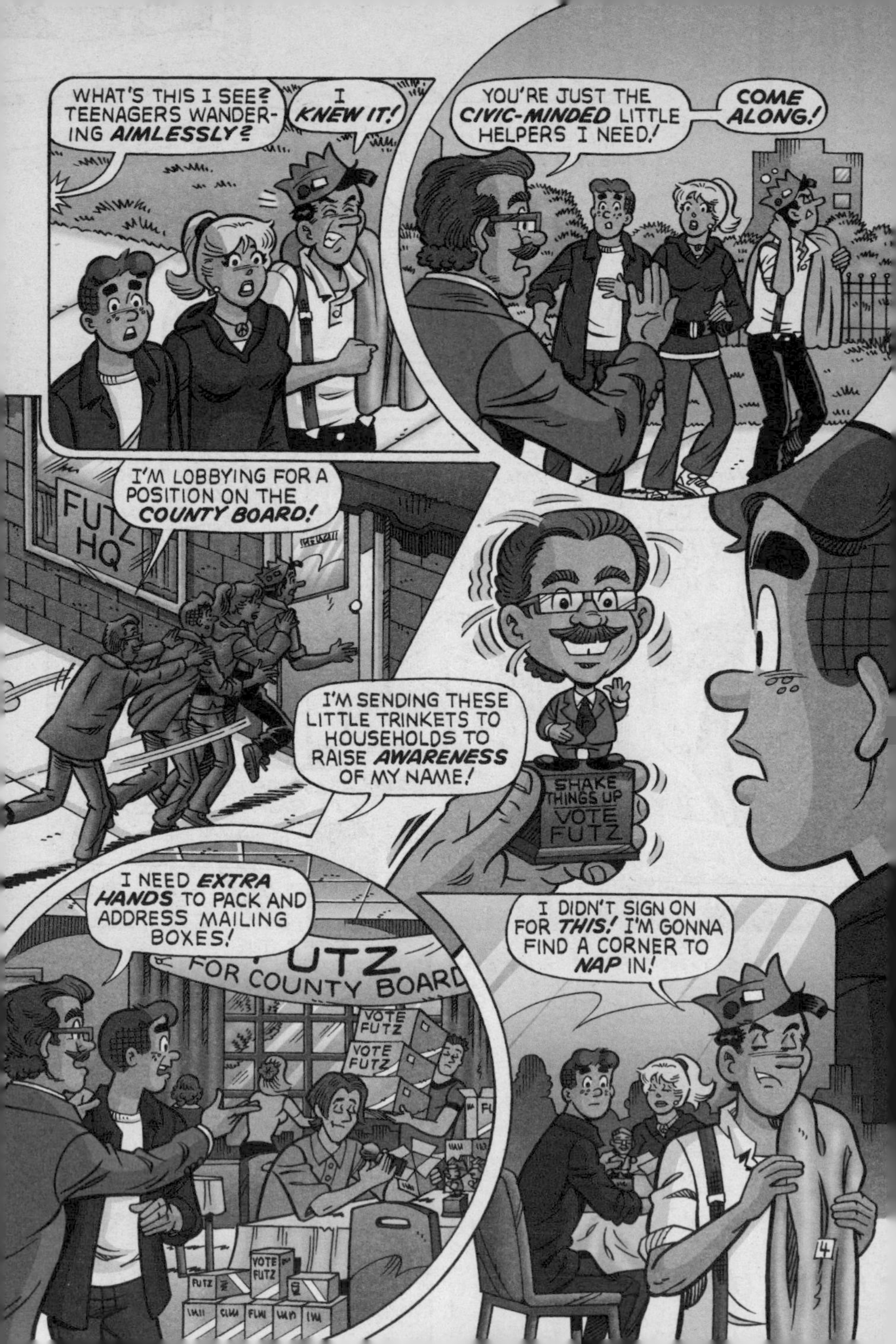
WHAT'S THIS I SEE? TEENAGERS WANDERING AIMLESSLY?
I KNEW IT!
YOU'RE JUST THE CIVIC-MINDED LITTLE HELPERS I NEED!
COME ALONG!
FUTZ HQ
I'M LOBBYING FOR A POSITION ON THE COUNTY BOARD!
I'M SENDING THESE LITTLE TRINKETS TO HOUSEHOLDS TO RAISE AWARENESS OF MY NAME!
SHAKE THINGS UP VOTE FUTZ
I NEED EXTRA HANDS TO PACK AND ADDRESS MAILING BOXES!
FUTZ FOR COUNTY BOARD
VOTE FUTZ
VOTE FUTZ
VOTE FUTZ
FUTZ
I DIDN'T SIGN ON FOR THIS! I'M GONNA FIND A CORNER TO NAP IN!
4

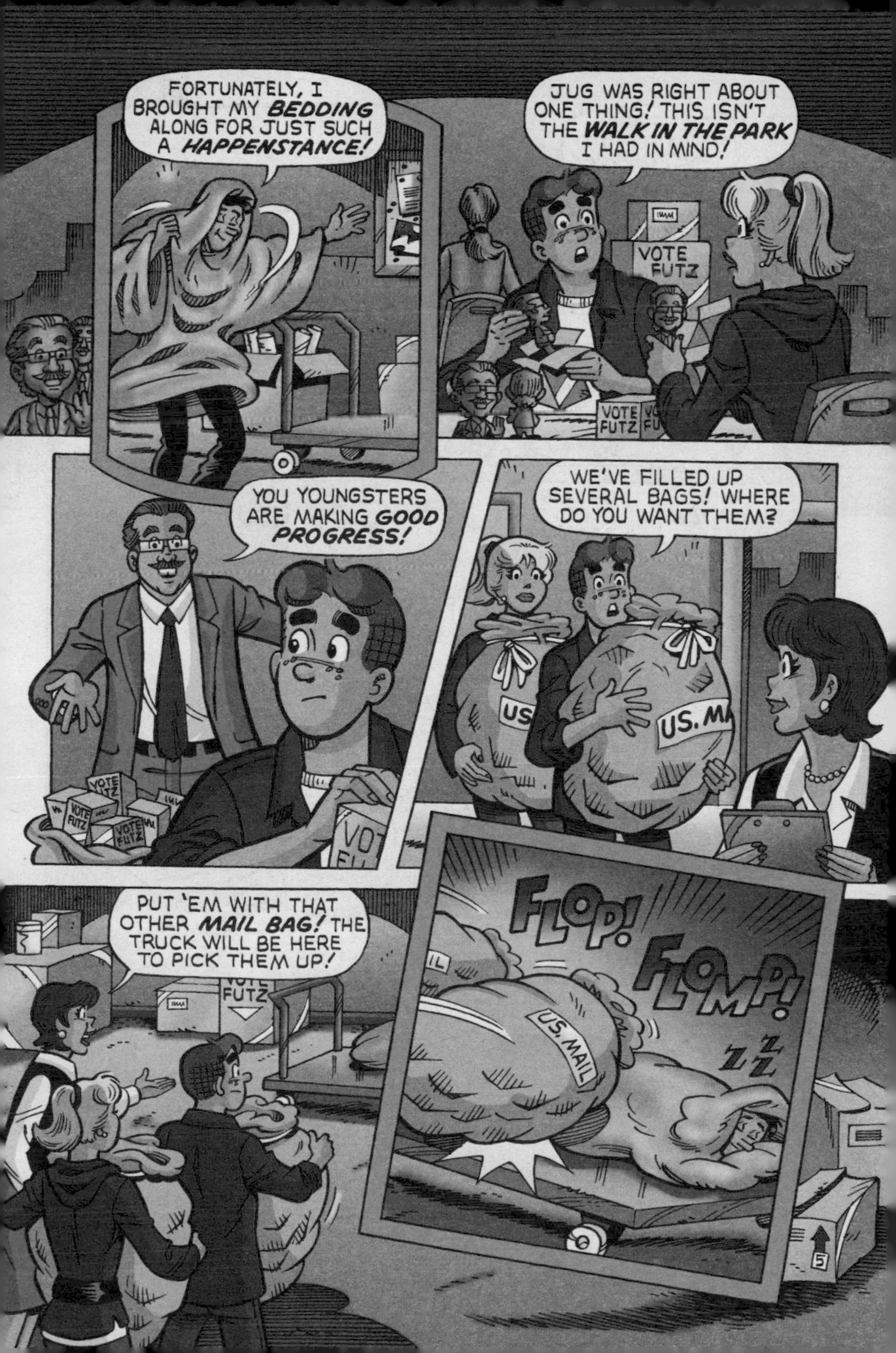
FORTUNATELY, I BROUGHT MY BEDDING ALONG FOR JUST SUCH A HAPPENSTANCE!
JUG WAS RIGHT ABOUT ONE THING! THIS ISN'T THE WALK IN THE PARK I HAD IN MIND!
VOTE FUTZ
YOU YOUNGSTERS ARE MAKING GOOD PROGRESS!
WE'VE FILLED UP SEVERAL BAGS! WHERE DO YOU WANT THEM?
PUT 'EM WITH THAT OTHER MAIL BAG! THE TRUCK WILL BE HERE TO PICK THEM UP!
FLOP! FLOMP!
US. MAIL
ZZZ
5

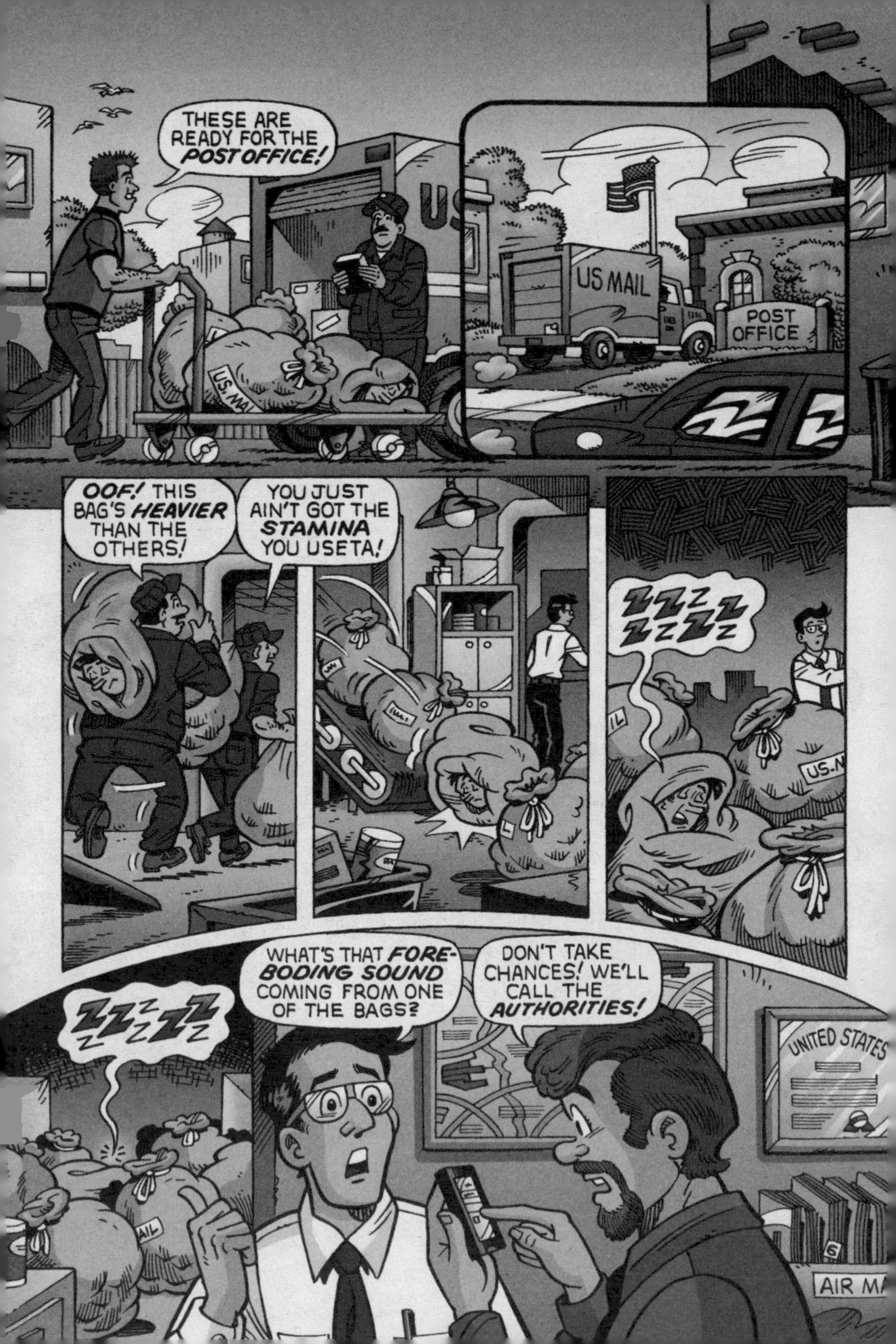
THESE ARE READY FOR THE POST OFFICE!
US
US.MAIL
US MAIL
POST OFFICE
OOF! THIS BAG'S HEAVIER THAN THE OTHERS!
YOU JUST AIN'T GOT THE STAMINA YOU USETA!
ZZZZZZZZ
US.M
WHAT'S THAT FORE-BODING SOUND COMING FROM ONE OF THE BAGS?
DON'T TAKE CHANCES! WE'LL CALL THE AUTHORITIES!
ZZZZZZZZ
UNITED STATES
AIL
AIR MA

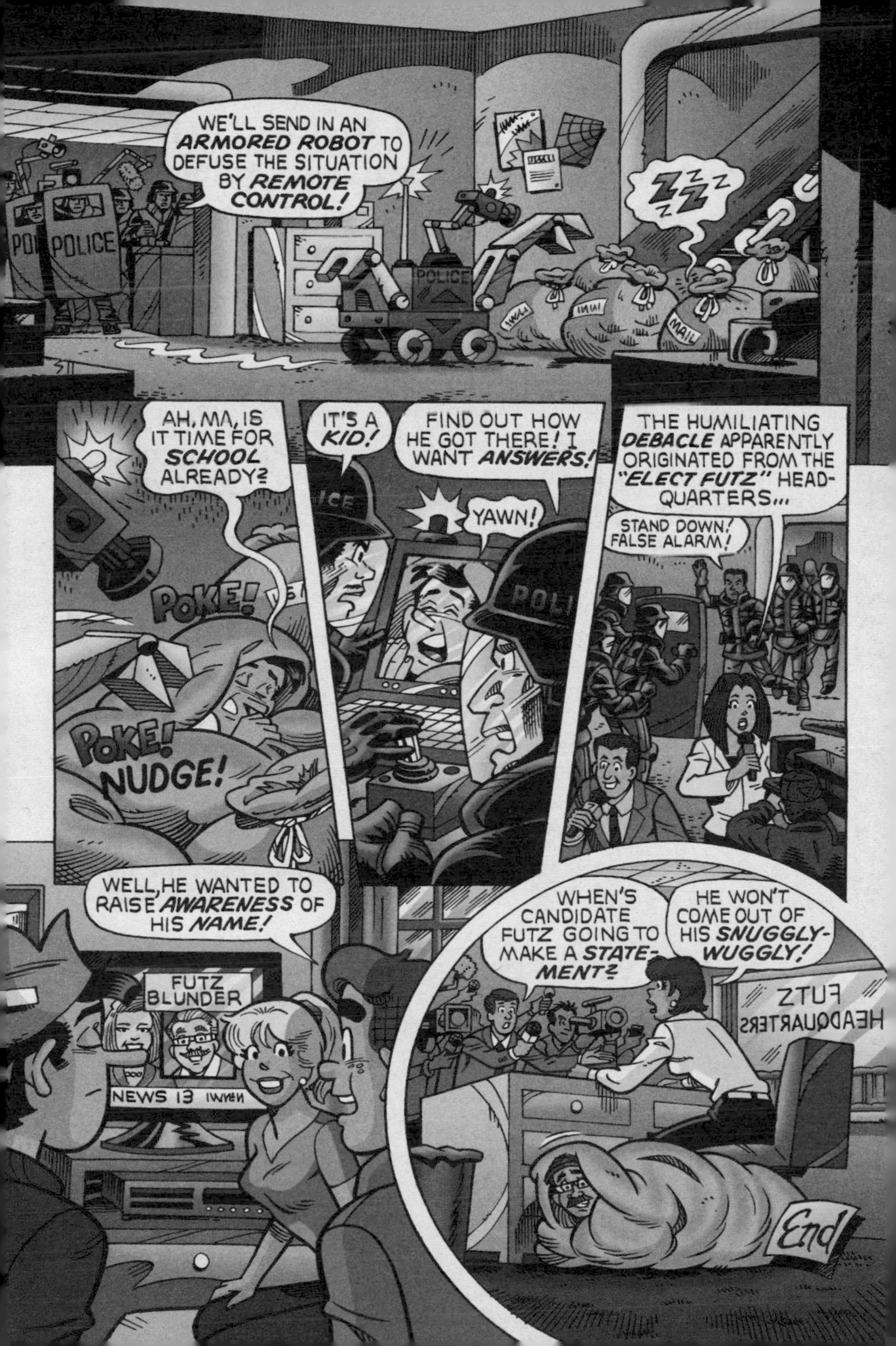

WE'LL SEND IN AN ARMORED ROBOT TO DEFUSE THE SITUATION BY REMOTE CONTROL!
POLICE
ZZZZ
MAIL
AH, MA, IS IT TIME FOR SCHOOL ALREADY?
POKE!
POKE!
NUDGE!
IT'S A KID!
FIND OUT HOW HE GOT THERE! I WANT ANSWERS!
YAWN!
THE HUMILIATING DEBACLE APPARENTLY ORIGINATED FROM THE "ELECT FUTZ" HEADQUARTERS...
STAND DOWN! FALSE ALARM!
WELL, HE WANTED TO RAISE AWARENESS OF HIS NAME!
FUTZ BLUNDER
NEWS 13
WHEN'S CANDIDATE FUTZ GOING TO MAKE A STATEMENT?
HE WON'T COME OUT OF HIS SNUGGLY-WUGGLY!
End

Chat Fight, Frenemy of the State, Dating Game
Life With Archie Magazine #6, 2011
by J. Torres, Rick Burchett, Terry Austin, John Workman and Jason Jensen

Almost two years ago, I was pouring coffee in the Archie Comics kitchen when Co-CEO Jon Goldwater stuck his head in through the door and asked me how much time it would take me to put together a formal pitch centered around the idea of a teen Jinx. About a year later, Jon would show me a beautiful, formally framed picture of Jinx that Joe Edwards had drawn and dedicated to him when he was a child. I've been lucky enough to work on this project in the best of circumstances: under a boss who loves what he does.

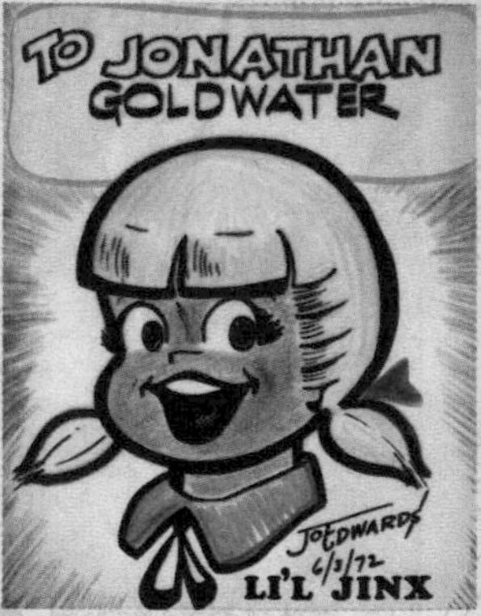
TO JONATHAN
GOLDWATER
JOE EDWARDS 6/3/72
LI'L JINX

I knew from the start that I wanted to create a teenage world that would be different from that of Riverdale. Betty and Veronica have perfection covered, but what about all the girls in the world who aren't millionaire heiresses, and can't cook a seven course meal in between overhauling a car and maintaining ideal grades? How many high school girls do you know who can go for years without looking anything less than flawless? Well, there was the one in my school … but I swear I'm not jealous of her anymore.

So I designed Jinx to have a personality that a teenager could relate to: a flawed one. The great thing about this is that I didn't have to shove the characters into roles that didn't make sense in order for this to work. Jinx's impulsive, keep-up-with-the-boys attitude, her father Hap's inability to understand her, Charley's cruelty, Gigi's background as a child star, Mort's insecurity… it all adapted neatly to an age where the emotion is dialed up to 11. The Jinx comic, thanks to the efforts of the entire creative team, does what I envisioned: it's entertaining, realistic and comforting.

--Suzannah Rowntree
Features Editor, Life with Archie Magazine

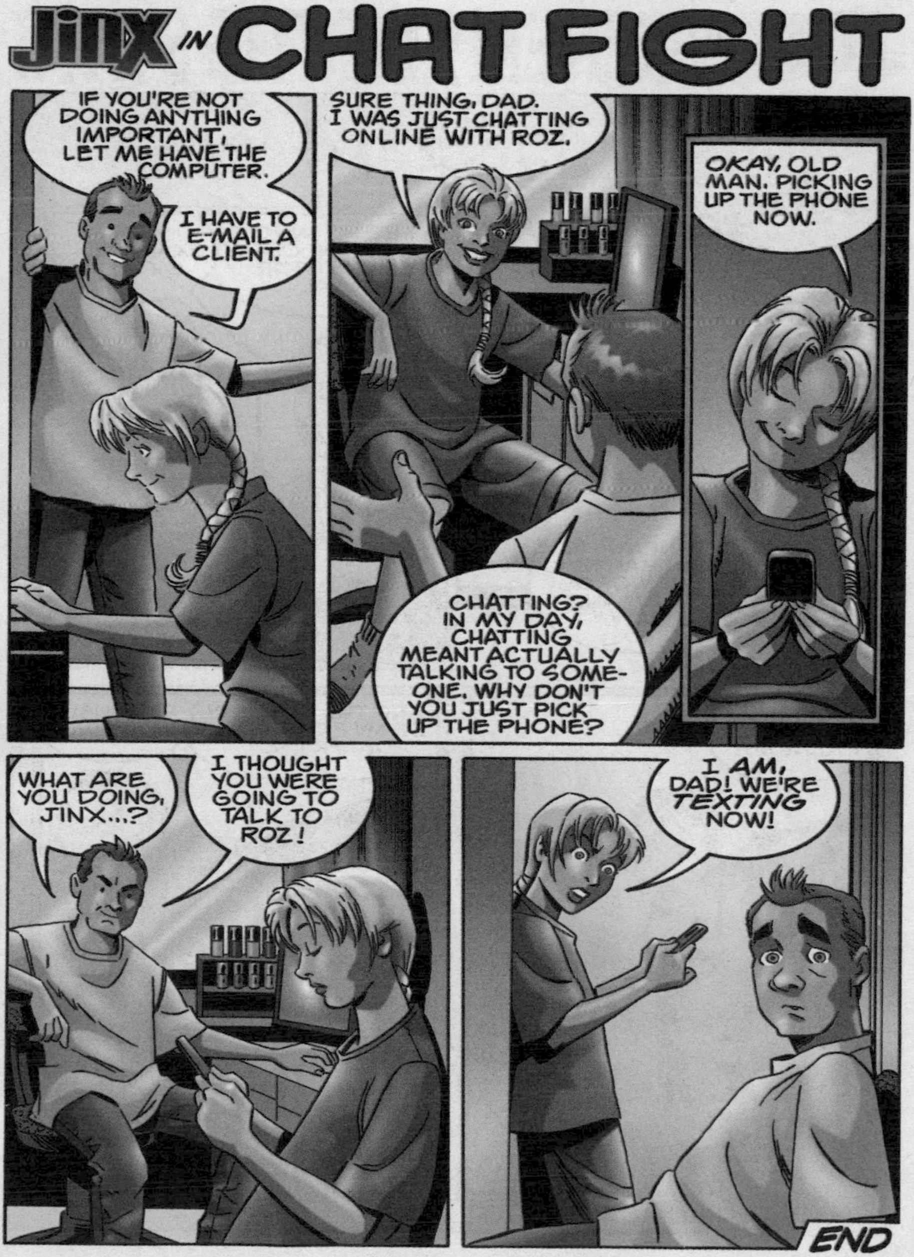
JINX IN CHAT FIGHT
IF YOU'RE NOT DOING ANYTHING IMPORTANT, LET ME HAVE THE COMPUTER.
I HAVE TO E-MAIL A CLIENT.
SURE THING, DAD. I WAS JUST CHATTING ONLINE WITH ROZ.
CHATTING? IN MY DAY, CHATTING MEANT ACTUALLY TALKING TO SOME-ONE. WHY DON'T YOU JUST PICK UP THE PHONE?
OKAY, OLD MAN. PICKING UP THE PHONE NOW.
WHAT ARE YOU DOING, JINX...?
I THOUGHT YOU WERE GOING TO TALK TO ROZ!
I AM, DAD! WE'RE TEXTING NOW!
END

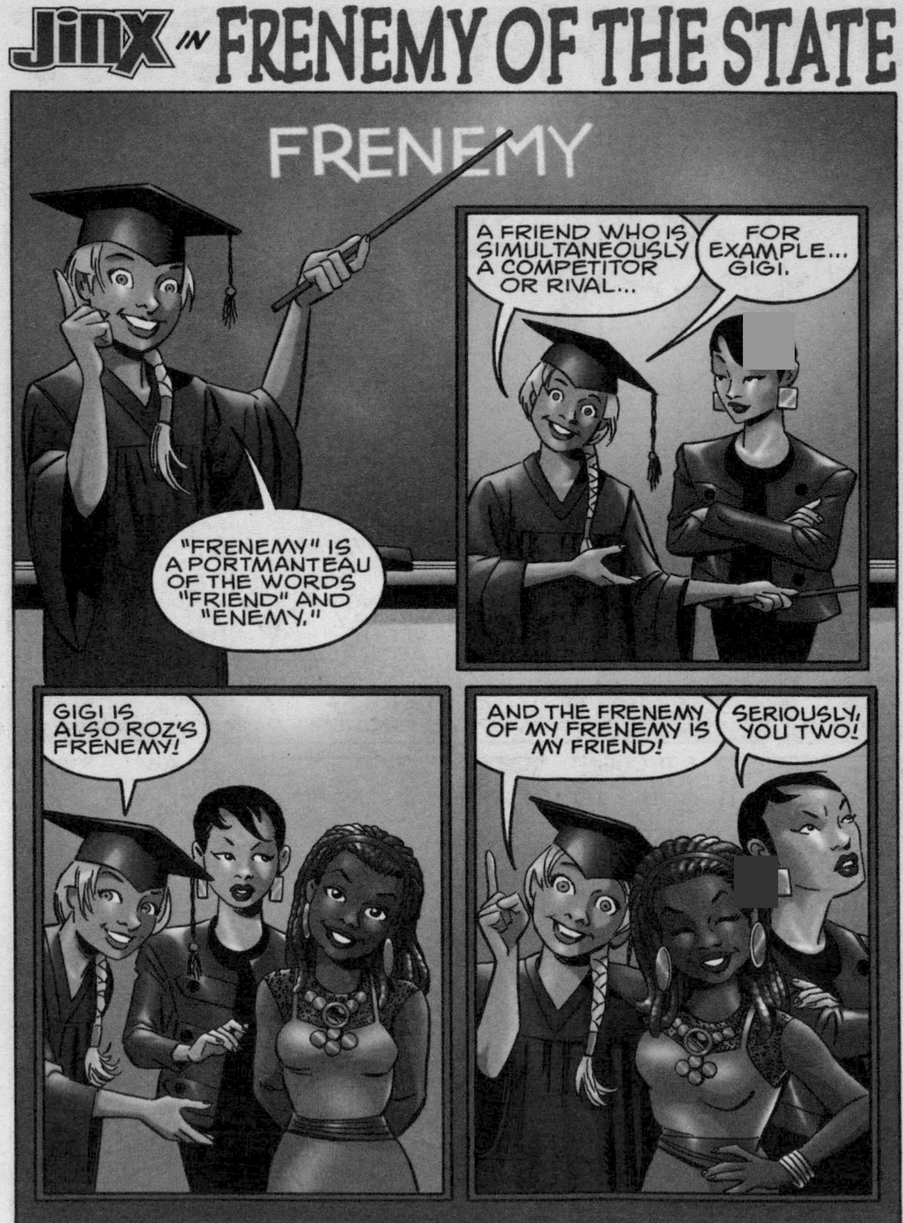
JINX IN FRENEMY OF THE STATE
FRENEMY
"FRENEMY" IS A PORTMANTEAU OF THE WORDS "FRIEND" AND "ENEMY."
A FRIEND WHO IS SIMULTANEOUSLY A COMPETITOR OR RIVAL...
FOR EXAMPLE... GIGI.
GIGI IS ALSO ROZ'S FRENEMY!
AND THE FRENEMY OF MY FRENEMY IS MY FRIEND!
SERIOUSLY, YOU TWO!

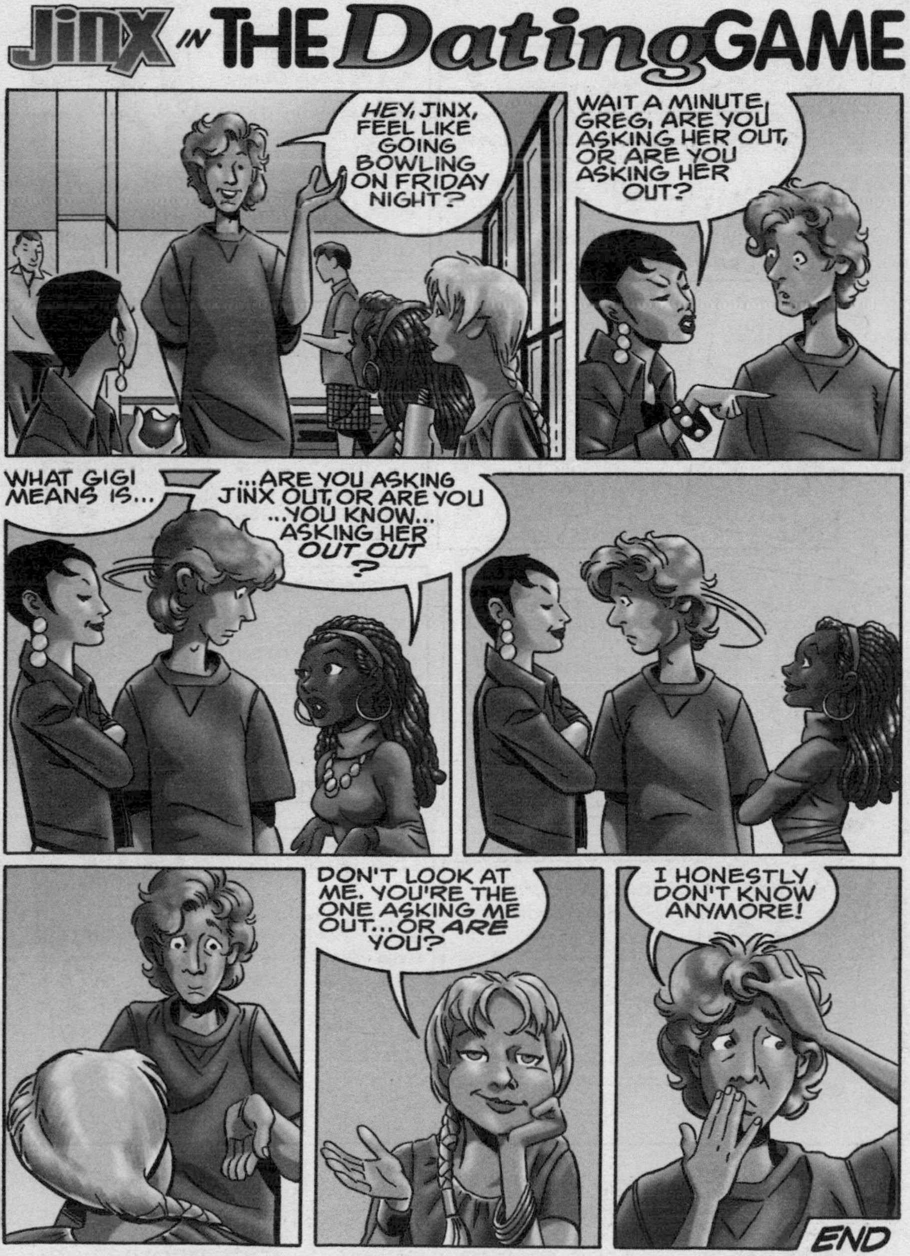
JINX IN THE Dating GAME
HEY, JINX, FEEL LIKE GOING BOWLING ON FRIDAY NIGHT?
WAIT A MINUTE, GREG, ARE YOU ASKING HER OUT, OR ARE YOU ASKING HER OUT?
WHAT GIGI MEANS IS...
...ARE YOU ASKING JINX OUT, OR ARE YOU ...YOU KNOW... ASKING HER OUT OUT?
DON'T LOOK AT ME. YOU'RE THE ONE ASKING ME OUT... OR ARE YOU?
I HONESTLY DON'T KNOW ANYMORE!
END